JACK ZERO
and the
Missing Man

Kyle A. Lince

DEDICATION

To all those holding this book in your hands (or on your digital device). My
deepest gratitude

ACKNOWLEDGMENTS

Thanks to Chelsea, for all her patients and understanding.

Thanks to Michael T. Lince for his amazing artwork, that dons the cover of this book.

Thanks to all those that read this book! Your support is what keeps all creators dreaming and filling our lives with wonder!

CHAPTER 1
THE MISSING MAN

Electricity surged signaling the constant connection and disconnection of live energy pulsing across the complex design of circuitry. The power groaned wildly and then reduced to a mild thrumming when the connection was fully active. The sparking pulsated harder as it rose and dipped, adding a strobe of flashing light that repeatedly tore through the darkness. Lightening arced upward, scraping the ceiling, leaving a blackened scratch and the smell of singed paint and ceiling tile. The owners of the facility would not be happy. At least until they saw the results of their experiment. The I-ZAN Corporation was a very generous benefactor, and its Chief Operation Officer, Helga Breithaupt, ignored all the complaints and damages in order to let the experiments continue. I-ZAN wanted results. They demanded it.

"Is it ready this time?" Doctor Heinrick Strommel yelled over the sounds. He felt the same energy as the electricity generated.

"Yes," Doctor Janus Steinwick screamed in response. "I recalibrated the device to register energy spikes which should disable the kickback we've been getting from the transfer."

Strommel didn't hear a word that Steinwick screamed. He simply smiled and nodded his thick, balding head in compliance. Steinwick saw part of the nod. The glare of the energy bolts reflected strongly from Strommel's protective eyewear making it difficult to see anything. He figured Strommel had the same problem. Steinwick stood in front of a control board complete with several buttons, keyboards, and levers that all blinked and blipped cyclically. He typed in several lines of code from the keyboard, watching the syntax grow on the monitor nearby. Once finished he slid a series of levers and flipped several switches that raised the low thrumming back to an unwieldy whining. He grasped a long lever with his right hand, looked up at Strommel, and began nodding. Strommel saw the nod beyond the glare and proceeded to reach down to his feet. On the floor was an animal cage in which was a small, orange-haired spider monkey.

Strommel unlatched the gate and picked up the cowering creature from the corner of the cage. The monkey quickly scaled Strommel's arm and clutched him around the neck tightly. It was obvious the poor beast was terrified. Strommel stroked her head gently, whispering gently into the creature's ear. "Shhhh," Strommel's voice was not the most reassuring. "It's alright, Madeline. You'll be alright, girl."

Strommel held Madeline up on his shoulder, cradling her tightened body with one arm while his other reached to a small case on a nearby equipment table. His fingers unfastened the two latches that secured the top of the case. He flipped the lid of the case open and withdrew a syringe gun, which he gripped, wrapping his hand around the handle and forefinger on the trigger. A clear liquid sloshed in the vile attached to the back, jutting out the back at a forty-five degree angle. Inside the liquid, a small, black, electronic device floated precariously. Strommel gently raised the syringe up to the base of Madeline's skull and inserted the needle into the soft muscle where it met the neck. The long needle reached deeply into her head, the tip penetrating the edge of her brain. Madeline howled loudly as Strommel pulled the trigger. The syringe hissed as the liquid injected into Madeline's head.

Strommel pried Madeline's interlocked fingers apart and drew her away from his torso. He stepped over to a clear Plexiglas container and placed her quickly inside before snapping the latch closed. Madeline banged her fists erratically against the walls of the container, her screeches muffled by the surging of electricity. Strommel watched Madeline claw the seams of the container, consumed completely by fear. The container was long, roughly six feet in length and around four feet high. It sat atop a narrow conveyer belt that led into the direction of the energy.

Steinwick saw Madeline was contained and pressed the buttons on his console. He pressed a settings control labeled distance and turned the corresponding dial clockwise two clicks. He then pressed in a physical destination of four feet. Once he completed the settings, he poised his hand over the large green, plunger-styled button marked 'start.' He looked over at Strommel and nodded. Strommel returned his nod and wrapped his hands around the lever to activate the conveyer belt. The gears whined as they began to move. Madeline stopped scratching the seams and looked around in confusion as she began to move along the belt. She began to scream and scramble as the belt moved her towards the crackling electrical field.

Despite all of Madeline's attempt to stop, the speed of the belt was too much for her to overcome. Madeline became less occupied by escaping the container and more by the pain that consumed her head. She wrapped her large hands around her head, squeezing her temples tightly, as if she was about to caver in her skull. Strommel watched her struggle; he saw her reaction to the pain as he felt remorse deeply in the pit of his stomach. He could stop it; stop her pain. All he had to do was signal Steinwick and he could stop the machine. He regretted the use of implants. Injecting such a powerful device into Madeline's brain was a risk, there was no telling what could happen, but it was the most effective way to initialize the creation of a wormhole. The brain is the most powerful computer in the world, and unlike any other computer, it can reason. Strommel stared blankly as Madeline slid along the belt and soon passed into the cool blue sphere of electricity that swallowed her into its awaiting maw, all the while she screamed in vain.

Both Strommel and Steinwick turned their eyes from the bright flash that washed over the entire room. As quickly as the flash came, it dissipated as the electrical surge began to die down. Strommel looked into the container to see what had become of Madeline. As he had hoped, she was gone. Steinwick pulled the handle to shut down the machine. The electric crackle and hum of the machine mixed with the grinding gears and Madeline's howl were all gone. The lab fell silent. Strommel's ears rang with a low tinny noise; he stuck his finger deep into his ear and wriggled it around, trying to clear the noise somehow. No luck.

Under the silence, Steinwick grew uncomfortable. He finally spoke, "Well? Did it work?"

Strommel could barely hear, but got the gist of Steinwick's question. Unfortunately, he had no answer. He simply shrugged. At that moment, the lights dimmed repeatedly, slowly at first and then more erratically before it ultimately ceased. Both Steinwick and Strommel looked at one another, unsure of the cause and even unsure as to what may happen next.

Strommel stepped from behind the conveyer belt and cautiously walked forward. It was densely quiet; the sound of Strommel's shoes clomping against the metallic floor of the lab seemed overbearing. Steinwick wrinkled his nose in reaction to the noise. Strommel walked around the conveyer belt, inspecting it carefully for any trace of Madeline, but she was gone. It had been some time since she disappeared and Strommel was growing concerned. Had they miscalculated? Had they actually obliterated her instead?

"Anything?" Steinwick's voice trembled, a layer of concern lacing his voice.

"Nothing," Strommel replied with reluctance. Guilt and

disappointment tinged his heart. He stopped and dropped his hands to his side in defeat. He felt a stirring in the pit of his stomach. Poor Madeline, he thought. Maybe it wasn't such a good idea to test the device on a live subject. As Strommel hung his head, his nostrils flared, detecting an odor. It was a heavy stench, like something burning. Strommel looked around, curiously at first. He followed the scent, a few feet from the conveyer belt. He reached his hand before himself, his fingers outstretched. He could feel energy, electricity, as if it were suspended, hanging in midair. His fingertips could feel the electricity in the air; it tingled down through his hand and up his arm. It was invigorating. Just before his fingers, a small ball of blue lightening began to grow, crackling and pulsating, as it grew larger by the second. Within moments, it was the size of a basketball, bolts of electricity dancing around the blue, pulsating light in the center. Strommel stepped further away, not knowing what might happen as the ball got larger and closer to him. In just a matter of seconds, the ball was the nearly three feet in diameter. The edges of the field began to distort, changing from spherical to more organic, taking the shape of an animal. The intensity of the pulsating light began to wane, quickly disappearing, leaving the form of Madeline in its place.

Strommel was elated that Madeline was alive! She was no longer in the container, but now sitting, calmly, in the center of the room, four feet from where she last was. It worked. The machine actually worked. Years of hypothesizing and theorizing, believing that his seemingly insane idea would actually work, years of trying and failing. Now he stood there in a moment of speechlessness, amidst his success. It worked.

"You did it!" Steinwick shouted with glee, he threw his arms high above his head and stifled a scream.

"Yes," Strommel smiled. "*WE* did."

"It was your research and tireless work that made this happen. I was merely an assistant." Steinwick worked as a Professor of physics at the New Utica University, a position he held for a number of years. However, teaching was never enough. Steinwick needed to pursue his love for science and discovery. When his university classmate, Strommel, contacted him two years ago to 'revolutionize the way we travel the world,' he couldn't refuse. After several failures, he achieved success.

"You sell yourself short, my friend," Strommel said as he knelt on the floor next to Madeline. She was cooing softly. He could smell the stench of singed hair. It must be a side effect of the transportation, he thought. He reached his hand and stroked the hair on Madeline's head. A mild charge of electricity snapped at his fingertips. He could feel the energy that surrounded her; it was warm and soft. Curiously, Madeline seemed less vibrant than usual; in fact, she was extremely lethargic.

A cluster of clouds scratched across the night sky as the reached like outstretched tendrils, covering the swollen moon that tried to light the blackened sky.

A pair of headlights cut through the thick darkness as they came to a stop in front of the research institute. The vehicle was a small, black sedan, with white walled tires. The car had a classic bullet nose design on its grill. The polished chrome glinted from the glow of the headlamps. The car was filled with four large men, all dressed in three-piece, dark blue, pinstriped suits. Three of the four men wore wide-brimmed fedoras; the fourth man was a hulking brute who spilled over the sides of his seat, simply kept his shaven head exposed.

The driver held a cigarette tightly between his pursed lips; his cheeks sank in as he took a drag deeply into his lungs. "We make this quick. Our orders are clear. In and out. General Zimm doesn't want a mess in there," he turned to look at the man with shaven head. "Are we clear?"
The man with the shaven head slowly turned his head to face the driver, his eyes narrowed and piercing, "You are only in charge of acquiring the device, not of the mission, lieutenant."

The driver hesitated, stammering as he spoke, "Y-yes sir, I was simply stating—"

The man with the shaven head cut him off, "'Yes sir, Colonel Huun,' is all you need to say. Am I clear," he hissed.

"Yes, sir."

Huun opened his door and slowly got out, leaving Lieutenant Crust to absorb Huun's words. He waited until the two grunts in the back got out before he finally opened his own door and exited the vehicle. He stood for a moment, looking at the moon as it occasionally ducked behind the clouds, took one last puff from his cigarette, dropped it to the ground and crushed it under his foot. He clasped his jacket and turned to Huun, who was watching the front of the research institute quietly.

"On your order sir," he finally managed.

Huun silently moved toward the door, signaling their advance.

Crust turned to the two grunts, "Move out gentlemen."

"I think there may be something wrong with Madeline," Strommel said with concern, his voice dropping in tone, taking a more serious repose.

"How do you mean?" Steinwick set down his pad. He never liked it when Strommel's voice dropped to that pitch. It never lead to anything good. "Is she alright?"

"I'm not entirely sure," Strommel reached over to the table nearby. There was a red rubber ball about the size of a grapefruit. It squeaked when he wrapped his fingers around it and picked it up. It was Madeline's toy, one of her favorites. He grabbed it in an attempt to ignite her excitement, as it often did. Whenever Madeline had a rough day, they would bring out her rubber ball to which she would excitedly interact. A simple toy brought her mounds of endless joy.

Strommel turned and called to her, "Madeline."

Madeline sat still, her head lowered to the ground.

"Madeline," he called louder this time. "I have your toy."

Still no reaction.

Strommel's heart sank. Had the transfer affected Madeline in a much greater way than they anticipated? She sat in profile, slowly swaying, rocking gently back and forth. Strommel called her name one last time before he tossed the rubber ball underhand at the melancholy ape. The ball sailed through the air and bounced off Madeline's head. The ball bounced off the wall and several times across the floor before coming to a stop at Steinwick's feet. Steinwick bent over and picked up the ball. Strommel looked over at Madeline. He noticed her expression changed, her brow furrowed quickly, her lips curled into a sinister snarl. Her eyes flashed at Strommel who now palmed the ball in his hand. She quickly stood upright and raised her arms into the air, letting out an ear-splitting roar that shook the glass in the windows of the room. Strommel froze, his eyes bulging in fear. Madeline's face had changed. The clear plastic of the container had conformed to her body. Her left half was completely emaciated; her flesh clear and her internal organs charred and appeared melted. Strommel gasped, his fingers snapped opened and the ball fell from his grasp to the floor, he quickly clasped his hand over his mouth. The red ball rolled across the floor, the color contrasted in the stark white room, its bright red reflected into the enraged eyes of Madeline.

The malformed creature once known as Madeline turned her sights onto Strommel, ground her front palms firmly onto the floor, pumped her rear limbs, and launched into the air. Her half-exposed face contorted as she opened what had once been her mouth to bare her teeth and howl as she charged at Strommel. Strommel stepped backward, his hands in front of his face in a pathetic attempt to defend himself. He knew it would do him no good, he reflexively bent his knees while stepping backward causing him to fall onto his back. He hit the ground hard; his lungs expunged all the air they held. Madeline was in full bore as she prepared to launch herself into the air for the kill. She sprang from her haunches, her long arms reaching out far in front of her small torso. Strommel watched as Madeline's disfigured face came into view. His heart sank and his hopes dashed. It was almost over. It was as if it was happening in slow motion, her sailing form, a pop, and Madeline's body suddenly jerked in midair, falling with a hard, wet thud at Strommel's side. Strommel sat up quickly, his heart pounding hard against his ribs. He clutched his chest and looked over at the crumpled corpse of Madeline. She was almost unrecognizable. Strommel looked in the direction of the pop to see Steinwick holding a gun. Steinwick's expression was vacant. The gun, Strommel thought, he never approved, but Steinwick insisted. He said it was a necessity. He was right. Strommel looked down at Madeline. Despite what she had become, he felt terrible. After all, it was his fault. Tears began to fill Strommel's eyes. How could he have been so stupid? How could he have let it get this far?

He turned to Steinwick, both to look away from the abomination he created, and to look at his friend. "Thank you, my friend," Strommel choked back his sorrow.

"This was not supposed to happen," Steinwick said.

"I know," Strommel's mind was working overtime, trying to comprehend what had happened. "The container."

"What?" Steinwick looked at Strommel awkwardly.

"Don't you see? Madeline's transformation. The transparent flesh and compromised organs. Sending her through the Interportal with the container must have amalgamated the molecules."

Steinwick was confused, "But we have sent multiple objects through before, why is this any different?"

Strommel picked himself up and ran to the control console. He typed feverishly at the keyboard, reading the data that rapidly flashed across the monitor. When he saw what he was looking for he struck the escape key, freezing the screen.

"Carbon," Strommel said mechanically.

"What?" Steinwick said confusion and fear equally gripping his brain.

Strommel forgot for a moment about that tragedy that befell Madeline mere moments ago, the excitement of discovery surged up his spine and electrified his brain. The answer to Madeline's madness was before him. Carbon.

"Madeline, like all life, is made up mostly of carbon. The vibrations created by the machine, that induce the ability to pass through from one point to another is based on the genetic make-up of only living creatures."

"But most things contain carbon, what difference does that make?"

"Of course, Carbon 12 makes up all life on earth. It is the most stable and can bond with almost anything to create chains of sticky amino acids that can eventually create forms of life. The Intraportal device generates a harmonic frequency that communicates with the carbon-12 make-up of all species allowing for the crystal-like changes to take place in the body and enable the ability to pass through the portal and transport the life form to another designated location. When Madeline passed through our harmonic waves it also vibrated the container and forced the carbon-12 to break apart and bond with the container, creating the malformations and mutations to her personality and form. The device is only able to transport carbon-12 based forms at its current settings; I should have seen this before. We simply focused the harmonics on the Gaussian bell curve, as would anyone manipulating elements, but several renditions and modifications need to be made to that curve in order to communicate with multiple objects."

"So we failed," Steinwick, lamented as he glanced at his wristwatch.

"No," Strommel said enthusiastically, his energy returning. "But maybe, just maybe, if we could connect a device that generates multiple waves in order to allow other objects to pass we could revolutionize the way the world transports itself."

"Prototype," Strommel whispered lowly.

"What?" Steinwick asked Strommel to repeat himself.

"The Prototype," Strommel repeated, this time at the top of his lungs. He skipped excitedly across the white room to a filing cabinet that housed four drawers and stood slightly skewed from the corner. He flipped open the second drawer and thumbed quickly through the manila folders that laced the tray, multicolored tabs representing the different categories contained in each. Strommel's thick fingers stopped on a blue tab, which he immediately spread, opening the folder and removing its contents. It was a large, quartered blueprint. Strommel laid it out flat on the workbench near the machine's controls. The blueprints were a complex array of cubes and integrated circuitry all representing one multilayered device. The top was labeled 'multi-composite inducer.'

"This is it, our chance at redemption," Strommel cheered. "Our chance to ensure that poor Madeline's fate was not all for nothing." Strommel pulled a large black device from his workstation and rolled it over in his hands, studying it closely, excitedly. "I had one at my home office. This is the second prototype. It just needs a few slight modifications. Based on today's results I could have a functioning device in under an hour."

Steinwick looked down at his watch again, his brow furrowed with anticipation, "I'm sorry."

"There's no need for apologies, my friend," Strommel placed a friendly hand on Steinwick's shoulder. He noticed Steinwick's expression and wanted to reassure his colleague. "The shortcomings were a result of my own oversight."

"No," Steinwick's voice dropped to a more somber tone. He broke Strommel's hand from his shoulder as he stepped away.

"Let me get some supplies and we can get to work," Strommel made his way out of the testing area and into the supply room. Steinwick watched his colleague leave, his skin growing hot and uncomfortable. Steinwick's brain was on fire as he second-guessed the decisions he recently made.

The door to the lab interrupted Steinwick's thoughts as it suddenly burst open. Four large men poured into the room, each wearing ill-fitted pinstriped suits. The man in the front was tall, thick with broad shoulders and swollen muscles. He held a tommy gun in his massive hands, making it look like a small pistol, the round bullet chamber rested on his forearm. Steinwick recognized the brute as Colonel Huun. The man frightened Steinwick immensely. Huun stepped aside as a shorter, thinner man, made his way up beside him. The other two subordinates fanned out across the lab to position themselves defensively in opposite corners, their guns at the ready.

"Greetings, Doctor," the shorter man said with a sinister grin.

"Lt. Crust," Steinwick swallowed hard. "But…but you're early."

"Good to see you remember us."

"Wait, you're early," Steinwick whispered nervously. "I was told you wouldn't be here until I alerted your leader."

"That WAS the arrangement, but our Master was growing impatient," Crust walked slowly around Steinwick as he spoke, sizing the man up. "The time has come for us to acquire the machine."

"W-wait, can't we wait until next week, the device isn't ready yet."

"No more time to wait, now is the time to move," Huun interjected, his massive form more threatening than his tone.

"Janus, who are these men?" Strommel asked, surprise lacing his voice, as he reentered the lab, his arms loaded with scrap parts in a container that was too small to hold them.

"We represent your benefactor, Dr. Strommel," Crust hissed.

"I'm sorry, I wasn't aware of any benefactor," Strommel was even more confused. He turned to Steinwick, "What is he talking about Janus?"

"We should do what he says," Steinwick whispered.

Huun crept forward, the seams of his suit whining, preparing to split, with each step he took. "Bring the device," Huun growled, motioning to the device with the muzzle of the gun.

Steinwick began to pull the controls apart, packing them into an attaché case. "What are you doing?" Strommel growled through gritted teeth.

"Surviving," Steinwick replied. "If you want to live, I would do the same. These men are armed and they look serious. I don't want to die."

"We can't let them take this, it's our work!"

"Life is more important."

Crust cocked his revolver, "Time to go, gentlemen."

Strommel paused for a moment, his heart pounding, his mind racing. He couldn't let these strange men take his work. He had to do something, but what? Strommel had never been one to act irrationally. His entire life had been a series of planned events, from his conception to where he attended boarding school and private university, to what he wore to work every morning. He always wore a simple selection of a white dress shirt and black, pleated, pressed slacks. Just like Albert Einstein, a choice hero, not by chance. This was the first time in his entire life that Strommel made a move, a decision, without the benefit of plan. No thought of consequences, the pros or cons of the choice he made as he threw the box of spare parts that stretched across his arms, threw it at Huun and Crust who stood with surprise as the parts rained down upon them. The impact of the box didn't hurt, but the shock of the moment and Strommel running away certainly stung their pride. The parts knocked the pistol that Crust held and skewed the direction of Huun's rifle. Huun squeezed the trigger and fired of a series of rounds into the floor. The two men positioned in the corners of the room moved as if they were covered in heavy weights, their reactions sluggish. They became more consumed with watching the reactions of their superiors than to notice Strommel making his move. The distraction was enough for Strommel to grab his machine and run from the lab.

Crust recovered quickly to see Strommel run from the room. He screamed at the two guards who were now rushing to his aid, "What are you doing you idiots! He's getting away! After him!"

The two men opened fire on the doorway, but Strommel had already disappeared around the corner. They quickly ran after Strommel.

What was I thinking?' Strommel thought to himself. He tried to control his erratic breathing. Strommel cut the lights in the research room, making it too dark too see. He hoped it would be enough. He dodged behind a long workbench, concealed by the solid front that wrapped around all side of the table. He quickly pulled the component he swiped from the belt they had sent Madeline through earlier. He began pressing buttons, more at random, as he wasn't sure where to go. Another unplanned moment. Each depression of the button resulted in a quick chirp. He tried to muffle the sound by placing it under his lab coat. He heard the sound of feet scuffling into the room, just beyond the workbench from where he was hiding. He could hear the sliding of steel and the click of the chamber locking a round into place. He didn't have much time.

"Come out, Doctor," the first man chided. "There's nowhere to go." The goon walked slowly, heel to toe, making his footsteps quieter in the open storage room, the click of his boots echoing slightly. He slowed his pace, listening for movement of any kind. There were only six workbenches set side by side in three rows, an opening that stretched up through the middle of them. The first goon turned and signaled for his partner to stay positioned at the door, in case Strommel attempted to outfox them and make a break for it. If there was one thing he knew, it was never to underestimate your enemy, no matter how old, overweight, lazy, or out-of-shape they seemed. If you keep your guard up, you will be prepared. Better to kill than be killed as his trainer always told him. He was a soldier and he was prepared for anything.

Strommel tried to finish typing the coordinates into the device, but stifled a gasp when he realized he only had the directional component and not the tracer. The directional component only punched a hole into space, but didn't allow for a means of controlling the location the device would take its traveler. It didn't matter now. It was too late to go back and get the tracer. He had to take his chances, unplanned chances. The thought of it made Strommel queasy. He shook the feeling and continued pressing the buttons. He could only muffle the sound so much, and in between steps, the goons heard it loud and clear. He had little time left before they found him. Strommel began to disrobe quickly, remembering his research and what happened to non-carbon elements when pushed together through a wormhole. It was uncomfortable, but necessary. He reached into his pocket and pulled out the injection gun. He placed it at his temple and pulled. He yelped loudly as the piercing of the needle lit up his nerve ending throughout his body. He was now equipped to travel.

"He's in the back!" The first goon shouted as he broke into a sprint toward the workbench in the last row. He prepared his gun as he made the final bench, he turned and aimed but instead of seeing Strommel crouched behind he was greeted with a bright flash of light that threw him backward.

The second goon that was positioned at the door jumped at the abruptness of the light and the thrumming sound it produced. "Hey!" He shouted as he watched his partner get thrown backward, his spine bending awkwardly as he hit a bench hard. It made a loud snap that could be heard over the thrumming sound. "No!"

He ran to the back workbench just as the air surrounding Strommel began to vibrate violently, sending ripples of light that spread outward like still water disrupted by a stone. "Stop!" The second soldier yelled at the small naked, elderly man, his voiced barely heard over the building noise. The soldier didn't hesitate as he raised his pistol and began firing at Strommel. The bullets exited the muzzle of the gun in slow motion, bending in every different direction imaginable as they hit the waves. The bullets changed trajectory in midair, some going straight upward, other down or sideways as if Strommel was protected by a shield. The soldier watched in amazement, his mouth agape, as the bullets whizzed and winged in complete disorder instead of at their target. How was this possible? He thought. The ripples began to retract back toward Strommel, converging into a central location, around the device on Strommel's hand. A tear split open from nowhere, as if a knife cut through the air and separated the molecules. Strommel looked up at his assailant and let go a slight, half-cocked smile, and then moved into the tear.

"I said stop!" The soldier called one last time as he reached his arm to stop Strommel's escape. It was a bold, but foolish move as he met a fate much worse than his partner did. He screamed in agony as the arm he grabbed the fleeing Strommel with tore loose from his torso, as if it were made of paper mache, popping as it came loose from the ball joint where it rested. The tearing didn't end there, the waves continue into the soldier's torso, eating away at his ribs and side, carving out his organs and leaving a hollow, burnt slab in place. Strommel disappeared and the soldier's smoldering form slumped onto the ground, the flayed skin cracking and crumbling like the ash end of a cigarette.

By the time Huun and Crust entered the workroom, it was far too late. The young soldier that ambitiously volunteered for what was supposed to be a simple snatch and grab fell to the floor, his body singed and burned as the hole that hung in the air quickly vanished. "Damn!" Huun roared, realizing the hole was Strommel escaping. His compassion for fallen comrades had always been nonexistent. He was never one to become attached to anyone or anything. Only the mission mattered. A true mercenary.

"Where did he go?" Crust grabbed Steinwick roughly, shaking him as he pressed his pistol under Steinwick's chin.

"I-I don't know," Steinwick said, he winced from the pain the muzzle caused under his chin as Crust twisted it hard.

"Find him!"

"I can't," Steinwick's voice trembled. "He only took the transporter, not the tracer. I can't tell where he went, not unless he activates the device again, and I know he's too smart for that."

"We had a deal. You get us the device; we give you sanctuary complete with wealth and power. Now you're useless to us," Crust cocked his revolver with his thumb, still holding it under Steinwick's chin.

"W-wait. W-wait," Steinwick said, placing his hands on the revolver and pulling it out from under his chin. He rubbed the skin that was now red and raw. "I can still get you the device."

Crust lowered his gun, "How?"

"Strommel took the device, but it's not the only one. There's a second prototype. It's not perfect, but can work."

"Where?" Crust growled.

Steinwick looked at the gun in Crusts' hand, "S-Strommel's. It's at Strommel's. H-he keeps it in his office in his house."

Crust stood motionless before he relaxed his face, his expression of anger and frustration now calm and placid. "Thank you Dr. Steinwick. Your services have been greatly appreciated."

"I live to serve the Master," Steinwick bowed his head slightly.

"Yes you did," Crust stuffed his gun into his breast holster.

"Forever Destiny!" Steinwick saluted.

Crust turned away from Steinwick who sighed quietly.

Steinwick perked, "Wait, what if the police come around asking questions, what do I tell them?"

"Don't worry, we'll handle that," Crust looked to Lyntz and nodded slightly. Over his shoulder, Crust spoke in a low tone to Steinwick, "Forever Destiny."

Lyntz raised his pistol and fired two shots into Steinwick's head. The look of surprise was froze on Steinwick's face; his jaw slacked, as his lifeless body slumped to the floor.

"Clean him up!" Huun stepped forward and growled, "I want this place wiped and torched in twenty!"

Crust turned to Lyntz, "And get a replacement."

CHAPTER 2
ENTER: JACK ZERO

"Stop!" Jack Zero called out, his gun drawn from its holster and aimed in the air. He wanted to fire; a warning shot at least, but opted to hold off. Sure, he was near a public place, but also, bullets cost money. Despite what he was being paid, he had to pinch every penny.

The man Jack pursued kept a good chase, constantly one-step ahead. Jack had tracked the man to a nearby warehouse, where he knew the suspect was usually at to pick up a shipment of arms; after all, he was a convicted arms dealer or at the very least worked for one. However, Jack wasn't interested in arms, it was the stolen goods that the suspect had in his possession, goods he tried to pawn or use to quell a bet, either reason the goods were the sole reason he was hired to follow this man.

This was not where Jack hoped he would be; he never liked to have full on foot chases. They hardly ever ended well, and most of the time you were too exhausted to bring in the collar. When the elderly woman and her husband came into his office, he thought their case was going to be a simple surveillance and acquisition. Jack Zero was a Private Investigator, a man in his mid-thirties. He was fit, as it came with the territory, especially from his previous job as a homicide detective for the city police force for nearly six years, at least until his discharge, a fact he never liked to talk about. He kept pace, each step pushing him further. It was hard to keep pace, especially when you had to hold your fedora in place with one of your hands. His trench coat tails flapped behind him, restricting his ability to fully extend his legs. Right now, a desk job wasn't sounding too bad as opposed to chasing thugs for little old ladies.

The elderly woman, a Mrs. Graves, came to Jack's office three days ago; her husband, a tall, gaunt man that hardly spoke, accompanied her. He wore a sullen expression on his long face. A face that traced up to a pointed head encircled by short cropped white hair. He sat expressionless while his wife, a short, stout woman with tight curls of blue, who wore a flower dress and a flashy pearl necklace, spoke.

"I was recommended to you Mr. Zero, by a mutual friend. They spoke highly of you, a Mrs. Beasley."

"Oh, yes, Beasley, long-lost sister, I remember," Jack felt more confident. "So what is it that I can do for you, Mrs. Graves?"

"Well, what I tell you may seem odd, but I think my gardener has stolen my unmentionables."

Jack sat silent for a moment. It certainly did sound silly, a gardener stealing an elderly woman's underwear. "I'm sorry, Mrs. Graves, but I don't think I'm the right person for your case. It's not really worth my time, or any person's time for that matter, to track yours or anyone's underwear."

Mr. Graves let out a low guffaw that sounded more like a cough.

Mrs. Graves was giggling lightly, her hand over her mouth, "Oh, Mr. Zero, you misunderstand, he didn't steal my underwear, he stole my unmentionables, my jewels."

Jack stared, confused, "I'm not following you."

"Mr. Zero, my family name is Barbie. My great, great grandfather was Klaus Barbie, head of the Nazi Gestapo in Lyons, also known as the '*Butcher or Lyons.*' The jewels were stolen from the men and women he tortured during his time there, mementos he kept of each prisoner he killed. These were an embarrassment, a mistake. Our family wished to return them to the families of those he murdered, but there was never an accurate record of which belonged to whom. Therefore, they have been hidden and unmentioned for over a century. I'm sure this may sound strange, but I had wished to be rid of these cursed things since I inherited them four decades ago."

"If you want them gone, then they're gone, problem solved. So why do you need me?"

"You don't seem to understand, Mr. Zero, I can never allow these jewels to find their way into the world."

"I still don't understand."

"These jewels represent the blood and tears of many murdered innocents. I would be shamed if they were released into the world as if they were some meaningless commodity. I know what my family did was wrong and nothing I do can make it right, but I have enough trouble living with this that I can't bear to see anyone gaining from their worth."

Jack thought for a moment about the elderly woman's words, about her concern. It seemed strange to him, maybe this wasn't the case for him, "Mrs. Graves, I understand your concern," Jack lied. "Maybe you could look to the police."

"I'll pay you five thousand with a fifteen hundred dollar retainer."

Jack's face lit up, "Like I said, I'll get started right away."

It didn't take long for this odd case to take several odd turns, leading Jack on this, what he felt was an unnecessary foot chase. "Stop!" He found himself calling out again. Like it worked the first couple of times. The man he pursued, a sleazy man by the name of Neal Andrew Thall, also known by the moniker "the Caveman," an appropriately given name as his facial features appeared to be concaved into his face, leaving his forehead protruding. Not to mention the fact that his arms were longer than his torso and hung past his knees, that and his hunched over posture gave him the appearance of his hands dragging behind him.

This simple physical anomaly did allow Jack to keep track of his quarry with some ease, but it also gave "the Caveman" the advantage when he needed to thrust his body into the air. Jack and Thall had a long history together, not just in the way of cat and mouse, but also as brothers in arms. Jack had first met Thall when he had completed his basic training in North Carolina. Ten weeks at Fort Bragg had been gratuitous at best, physically preparing him for his future endeavor. It was during that time that a General by the name of Varcar Zimm, one of the most celebrated and decorated men in the military had scouted Jack at that time. Zimm had been selected to head the elite group of soldiers known as the Skytroopers, a division Jack had enlisted in, along with Thall. Jack and Thall became bunkmates, but never really got along well. Years after their time together, Jack followed the course of law enforcement and Thall went in an opposite direction, occasionally placing them at odds with one another. Jack had always thought Thall would find a direction along the right path, especially with the guidance of the military and fellowship of Skytroopers, but it seemed to push him to be more apprehensive toward authority. It was a shame that he slipped through the cracks and fell so deeply into the criminal life that his underworld roots were now too ingrained to break free.

Caveman pressed himself to move faster, attempting to lose Jack. Jack rolled his eyes in disbelief as he began to pump his legs harder, extending his stride. His arm was beginning to tingle, which commonly happened when he exerted himself. Ever since he was 'fused,' a slang word for anyone with technology implanted within their body, in particular, his arm. His arm had always tingled during strenuous times, and curiously, whenever the weather changed. If not for the nanites, his arm wouldn't even function or worse yet, may have had to be amputated. Fortunately, he had opted for the infusion. This particular operation was the first of its kind. Jack had lost the ability to use his arm during a mission, resulting in possible amputation. However, a very influential and intelligent doctor had offered to operate, promising the opportunity for his arm to be repaired, not replaced or removed, but the same arm as good as new. The injection of the nanites animated his dead tissue and repaired his once useless arm, which sometimes had a glitch. He still managed as best he could despite no understanding what it was capable of doing. He flexed his arm up and held it steady for a moment as he continued to run. Caveman kept his pace as he ran up a ramp toward an open fire escape.

'*Oh great*,' Jack thought, knowing Caveman's capabilities. He watched as Caveman easily reached his long arm up over his head and snapped his fingers around the bottom rung of the ladder. He just as quickly kicked his feet out from under his body and swung himself up to a higher rung, planting his feet firmly and then pivoting his body upward until he was able to step onto the lower platform. Once Caveman was full upright on the platform, he turned and shot Jack a coy smile and flicked a two-fingered salute from his forehead before he scaled the remainder of the fire escape like an ape climbing a tree.

"Son of a bitch," Jack murmured as he looked up at the ladder that Caveman grabbed. It was nearly ten feet in the air, way out of his reach. He made an ill-fated attempt to jump and missed the rung by several feet. He was going to have to find another way.

Caveman looked across the open rooftop; it was wide-open save for the seven or eight bulky air conditioning units that took up large chunks of the roof. They weren't even a concern; he had a good lead ahead of Jack. Caveman glanced quickly over the edge. He saw Jack attempting to reach the fire escape, fortunately with no luck. He smiled to himself, grabbed the brim of his hat and pulled it down tight over his head before he launched into a full sprint across the roof of the building. Caveman had the ability to reach speeds much more quickly than most people, thanks to the help of nanites injected into his legs. He had himself illegally fused in order to increase his endurance, despite his own physical limitations. Many people had explored the world of illegal operations for physical enhancements and he was no stranger to any illegal activity.

Caveman ran swiftly, his long arms pumping at his sides, his knuckles nearly scraping against the rooftop. He could see the separation of this rooftop and the next just ahead. Just one leap from his short legs and he was free and clear of that pesky private dick. Caveman quickly reached the lip of the roof, placed his dominant foot down and pushed off hurling his disproportioned body into the air, his limbs flailing like a wind sox in a heavy breeze at his side. He looked below to see the smallness of the alley beneath him, the dumpster the size of his thumb; seconds later, he slammed his wide feet onto the concrete of the adjacent building's roof. His hands outstretched as they caught him from hitting his hooked nose against the gravelly rooftop. Through gritted teeth, Caveman hoisted his hulking mass up, stood erect and dusted himself clean. He was slightly shaken from his near facial collision, but he wasn't about to let it slow him down. Caveman was soon back into his sprint, trying to maintain his pace, needing to keep a step ahead of his pursuer, whom he was certain had given up by now. Cops took time to learn not to mess with the Caveman. He laughed to himself as he began to run across the rooftop, the sound of crunching and grinding of gravel under his feet. He needed to get to the next rooftop. He could see the seam that separated the next roof from the one he ran across. He began to pick up his speed, the surge of energy that the nanites provided him coursed through his legs, invigorating them. He could feel the breeze brush coolly across his skin, the sound of his arms whirred like a turbine powering up as they churned back and forth. He closed in on the roof's ledge, quickly stepping onto the lip and repeating his earlier performance, leaping high into the air and curling his knees up under his chest. As he sailed closer to the edge of the other roof, he saw he was more in control of this approach. He quickly shot his arm from his side, pointing them outward like a sail in order to steady his drop. He extended his feet toward the roof below, anticipating the impact. His feet clopped as they struck the flat roof. The roof cracked slightly from the impact, a result of its weakened abandoned condition. As he landed, his knees buckling only slightly, he laughed aloud, proud of his accomplishment. He looked back at the roof behind him and was amazed at the gap he crossed. It was far wider than the first, but he had more control of his tech. He turned to continue his escape when he was stopped by the impact of a cold metallic object that connected with a resounding clang against his forehead before everything went black.

Caveman lay motionless on the roof, but he was not unconscious. He craned his neck awkwardly up as he watched Jack approach, his gun poised at Caveman's head, ready to use.

"Wha--" Caveman stammered in surprise and pain. His head throbbed from whatever it was that hit him. "How the Hell did you get up here 'fore me?"

"You just gotta be smarter than your quarry, which in your case, would be everyone," Jack smirked.

"Well, looks like ya finally got me, Zero," bemoaned Caveman as he rubbed his head with his large hand.

"You always have to make things harder than they have to be, don't you," Jack replied.

"Just like ol' times, eh, Jack?"

"Being as fused with tech as you are, I'm surprised you remember anything."

"What? You don' like the new me? I'm state-of-the-art."

"I hardly recognize you."

"Oh, gimme a break, man. You act all high n' mighty, like you ain' ever been 'fused." Caveman grinned, his teeth dark and stained. "How's that arm a' yers doin'?"

Jack rubbed his right arm gently, remembering the injury he obtained and how the military promised they would fix it. Infusion. It was the buzzword of the past decade, but had been around for several. It was the process of injecting a host body with nanotechnology in order to assist the host physically, allowing a paraplegic to walk with the use of their own legs, or a blind person to see with their own eyes. It all seemed well and good, science being used to benefit humankind. Unfortunately, it didn't work out that well. Many of those who took the infusion were subject to dissolution of their other functions. Suddenly the paraplegic who could now walk, lost control of their arms, or diminished brain activity; the blind could no longer smell or taste. Science could never correct the problem, despite their constant advances. Even Jack's own arm lost sensation every now and again.

Jack focused on Caveman, a man that took full advantage of infusion. He no longer resembled the same man that Jack once served beside. "From what I remember, you didn't follow direction too well," Jack smirked. "Maybe that's why the General had you do so much prison time."

"It's 'cause he liked me better n' you."

"You would think that, Thall," Jack chided.

With the mention of his real name, Caveman grew agitated, his face contorting into a menacing rage. "Don't call me that, flatfoot, my name is Caveman," he snarled, his teeth gnashed tightly.

"Alright, enough pleasantries, let's cut to the chase; where're the jewels you stole," Jack kept his gun trained as he spoke.

"I don't know whatchyer talkin' about."

"Oh, c'mon, Caveman, you don't remember a clutch of jewelry you somehow happened upon from a poor, defenseless old woman whose home you were working as a gardener?"

Caveman smiled, "I 'member her. Crazy ol' bat thought she was talkin' to Jesus all the time, husband never said squat."

"You know what is rather odd about this story, the fact that you were working as gardener, let alone working," Jack said. "Who would've thought you'd gone legit?"

"Legit? Me? Not ev'rythin' is what it seems, Zero."

Jack grimaced. '*What did he mean by that?*' He thought to himself. It didn't matter; he just needed to finish the case. "Where are the jewels?"

"I ain't got 'em."

"That's not what I asked."

"It don't matter, they's already gone. I pawned 'em to a guy over a week ago."

"Who?"

"I ain't tellin' you."

Jack fired the gun just over Caveman's shoulder, the bullet cracking the roof. He fired twice more, both bullets chewing into the rooftop. Caveman did not move, he only smiled, a wide-mouthed, toothy grin, although he had very few teeth to really call it "toothy."

"I know you Zero, you won't shoot me," Caveman challenged.

Jack's body tightened, starting at his toes, up his legs, through his torso, across his arms, and down to his finger, namely his finger poised over the trigger of his revolver. He squeezed the trigger again; firing a shot over Caveman's other shoulder. Caveman was right.

"You're right, Caveman, I won't kill you," Jack walked away, listening to Caveman scramble clumsily to his feet.

"You shoulda' killed me, Zero," Caveman roared.

Jack didn't turn around as he heard Caveman bellow and prepare to charge. Instead he smiled to himself as he heard the weakened floor crack and crumble from where he had fired the bullets into the roof. It gave way underneath Caveman's feet, sending him flailing into the abandoned building below.

"You should've stayed still," Jack quipped. He holstered his revolver as he walked to the edge of the collapsed roof. He pressed his foot gently, testing its stability before venturing too close. When he determined it was safe, he cautiously leaned over to peer into the gaping hole. He saw Caveman, crumpled on the floor that was nearly three stories down. He watched closely as Caveman twitched slightly, indicating he was still alive. That was a relief, not much good for information if he's dead. The sun shone through the hole in the decimated roof, a bright glint sparkled against the content that had fallen from Caveman's breast pocket, which became exposed from the top of a small black, velvet bag, the top had opened, displaying the dazzling objects that were hidden inside. *The jewels!* Jack realized. So the thief did have them after all.

For once things were going his way. He could get the jewels for his client and would finally get paid. He still needed to bring Caveman in, after all there might be a reward attached to him. First, Jack had to find his way down, which from the condition of the roof, was not going to be easy. It seems that Caveman had ripped the ladder that lead to the roof from its bolted casing when he fell, most likely grasping for anything to hold on to. No such luck. Now he was stranded. He could use a transport right now. Jack stood near the crater that Caveman fell through, looking down at the rooftop and wondering whether or not it would hold for now. As he looked down at his feet a line zipped by him and a metallic spear buried itself into the brittle rooftop. Jack raised an eyebrow as he studied the object. It looked like a cross between the tip of an arrow and sinker for a fishing pole. The tiny object was no larger than his thumb and it was attached to a thick metal cable. Before his eyes could trace where the cable had originated, another arrowhead sank near his other foot, and within seconds, two more affixed themselves a few feet away, each making a swishing noise as they cut rapidly through the air, the attached cables spiraled upward until they were completely taut. The sky above Jack lit up, brighter than the sun that already beat down on him, as if a second sun had suddenly appeared. Jack looked up, shielding his eyes with his hand from the blinding light. He could see the air rippling around the light, a result of the heat that was being emitted. By looking up, he realized it wasn't the sun, but the exhaust ports and thrusters of a Guard Seven – Model Twelve Law Enforcement Hover Vehicle, LEHV, something he hadn't seen in sometime. Not since his departure from the force.

"Halt right where you are!" A voice belted from above, reverberating through an amplified megaphone.

Jack reluctantly raised his hands in the air, his palms exposed, more as a sign of trust than surrender. He remembered when he was an Enforcement Officer; exposed palms were a sign of not needing to use extreme prejudice. He hoped that still was the case. He watched as the vehicle lowered slowly, the pilot obviously looking for a secure place to latch. The Law Enforcement Hover Cruiser, or LEHV, was a standard issue vehicle given to all military and law enforcement agencies across the globe. It was initially developed more than a decade ago by the military, and understanding the benefits, they eventually handed it down to national agencies and local governments to be used as a better means of defending cities and fighting crime. It definitely gave them the upper hand; crime had dropped nearly 40% globally. It was truly a marvel, but also a dangerous weapon if in the wrong hands. Jack remembered the safe guards that had been put in place. Retinal ID scans, hand print and thumb print matches, and a DNA swab, it got even more complicated once you opened the door.

None of that mattered now. The more important questions were 'Who was this?' and 'Who was interrupting his collar?'

The spiked anchors that embedded at his feet jostled for a moment, tilting slightly as the winches that held the cables began to whir drawing the LEHV in closer to the rooftop. The LEHV drifted to the building's ledge forcing Jack to move quickly aside. As quickly as the winches stopped, the passenger door flipped open. A long, sculpted pair of legs slipped from inside. Jack's eyes traced their smooth skin up to the tight skirt that hugged every curve up to her waist. He was transfixed, her form tantalizing as she emerged completely from the vehicle. She was beautiful, her skin smooth and fair, like porcelain. Her ebony hair spilled across her shoulders, tasseled mildly from the breeze the LEHV stirred up. He looked to her eyes. They were hidden behind the dark lenses of a pair of sunglasses. She walked confidently toward him.

"Thank you, Mr. Zero, we appreciate your assistance," The woman said sternly. "But we will take it from here."

"How do you know me?"

The woman's expression remained like granite, "It's my business to know."

Two other men exited the LEHV and began repelling through the hole in the roof to the unconscious Caveman below. Jack didn't like this at all. Another LEHV roared from up high and was brought down close to the building roof. It hovered along the center of the roof until it was over the opening. The doors of the second LEHV opened and three more men repelled from inside, disappearing into the hole. Jack became more annoyed. This was not going as planned.

"Wait a second," Jack said "What's going on here? This is my collar!"

"Not anymore," The woman replied.

"Who are you?"

She didn't answer. Instead she ignored Jack and threw a glance down into the hole where Caveman still lay unconscious. "That man down there is wanted for questioning."

"Questioning?" Jack was nervous she was stepping onto his case. This was his, he had to make sure it wasn't taken from him; he had a woman relying on him. Plus, he wanted to get paid. "That's my collar down there, no way are you taking him in before me."

"I don't care if he's your long lost brother that man is coming in with me."

"Who do you think you are, lady?"

"Everything you are not!" She shot back acidly.

"Hold on! There is no way I'm letting you get away with this." Jack marched up to the agent and gripped her shoulder.

The woman snapped her head around, her lips curled up in a snarl. She wrapped her fingers around Jack's forearm and quickly readjusted her weight. With a quick twist of her waist the woman yanked Jack's arm forward. The force was so quick that Jack didn't realize what was happening until he was halfway through the air, his feet off the ground and going over his head. In a second Jack was flat on his back, sharp pain shooting up and down his spine. Jack let out a cough as the remaining air in his lungs was forced out from the impact of his back striking the roof. Even more quickly than he had been taken down, she threaded her finger through a belt loop on Jack's pants to which she heaved toward her, flipping Jack onto his stomach. She then grabbed both of Jack's wrists and she straddled him, clasping her laser-fastened restraints tightly around. They clicked in place as they secured with a beep, the blinking red light indicating the locking as they tightened together.

Jack tried to gain his bearings, "What the hell are you doing?"

"Arresting you," she snarled.

The larger of the two agents, returned from below and silently followed orders, grabbing Jack roughly by his collar, hoisting him up onto his feet. The man then proceeded to frisk Jack, removing his revolver and COMM device.

"Hey, Tarzan, be careful with those," Jack shouted over his shoulder.

The stone-faced man placed Jack's possession in a small plastic bag. He then shoved Jack roughly as he guided him to the hovering vehicle.

Jack was loaded into the back of the LEHV, his forehead bruised almost as badly as his ego. He watched out the window angrily as three more men repelled into the opening of the roof and encircled Caveman's unconscious form. One of the men noticed the small clutch of jewels that had spilled near where Caveman fell. He stuffed it into a plastic bag with Caveman's other effects before they lifted him up from the shoulders, sat him upright, and then wrapped a series of belts around his torso. Then, each of the men unclasped an extra cable from their harnesses and connected them to Caveman. They then signaled upward at the LEHV with a thumbs-up. Caveman was hoisted into the air, his body swaying precariously from his weight and size. The Vehicle roiled the cable up, allowing for Caveman to ascend vertically without hitting the edges of the hole. The LEHV then shifted its position to lower Caveman down near the other LEHV anchored to the building. The woman had barked a few orders that Jack couldn't hear over the LEHV's engine, but within a matter of minutes, Caveman was loaded inside and the LEHV's engine screamed as it climbed into the sky.

The woman looked back at Jack as she climbed in the hovering LEHV, the two men who had arrested him were now climbing in as well. She offered a sarcastic smile.

"Thanks for the assist," she shouted to Jack over the engine as she slid the door closed. Soon the LEHV disappeared into the sky.

"Son of a bitch," Jack mumbled to himself. He rested his head against the window of the LEHV, looking out at the view. He watched as the city shrank quickly below.

CHAPTER 3
UNDER ARREST

The New Utica Law Enforcement Headquarters towered over the city, a large spire that housed an observation platform at the top. The platform was surrounded by glass and had several openings with wide berths that had room enough for the constant take off and landings of the LEHV's.

It wasn't long before Jack had been ushered, rather roughly he might add, to his own personal prison cell. His neighbor was the still unconscious form of Neal Andrew Thall, also known as the Caveman. Jack let out a quiet chuckle as he rolled over on his thin mattress that rested on a thick piece of metal that could slide in and out from the wall. This was ridiculous, he didn't belong here. This was all some big misunderstanding. Jack put his hands behind his head as he looked up at the dull gray ceiling. The lithium light wedged into the seam of the center of the ceiling flickered lightly. Jack determined it occurred every two minutes and thirteen seconds. He had officially been in their too long. What had it been? Two, three hours max. It felt more like three weeks. How long could they keep him in here? And under what charges?

Jack listened to the sounds around him, it was mostly quiet except for some minor metal hinges squealing. Jack found it odd that with all the advancements in technology over the past decades, standard prison cells still used metal barred doors. Not that metal bars were the only security used on a cell. Laser fortification that surged through the bars and ran through the walls, floor, and ceiling was a major deterrent for anyone contemplating escape. That agent! If he ever saw her again, it would be too soon, and if he did he would truly give her a piece of his mind. What was taking so long?

As thoughts flopped around in Jack's head, his concentration of self-pity was quickly interrupted by a guffaw of laughter, deep and penetrating. Caveman.

"This is really rich," Caveman laughed heartily. "The mighty crusader, Jack Zero, my cell neighbor."

"Get stuffed, Thall," Jack retorted.

Caveman's demeanor changed from a smile to a snarl, "Don't call me that! That's my sub-name. You call me Caveman, Zero."

Sub-name, a common term that fusers referred to as their 'subhuman' name. It always irritated Jack to hear when anyone used this term, it didn't mean anything, it was just a way of referring to their nanotech advancements.

"Jus' like ol' times, though, eh?"

"It's not like any times," Jack returned Caveman's previous snarl. "There were no old times and these aren't new times and there never will be."

"So that wasn't me an' you sharin' a prison cell way back when?" Caveman pressed his face between the bars that separated their two cells. "If my mem'ry serves me correctly and, despite my outward appearance, it does, you were arrested for commitin' a pretty serious crime."

"You don't know what you're talking about."

"Oh no? You mean it wasn't you that was arrested, tried, and court marshaled?"

Jack turned away from Caveman.

"For a guy whose mouth wouldn't stop runnin' for as long as I known him, he now has nothin' to say. Why not, Zero? This charge that got you with isn't good enough for you?"

"Shut up," Zero managed, his voice low and quiet.

Caveman could see he hit a nerve; it was only his nature to dig further, "You only chatty when the charge is murder?"

"SHUT UP!" Jack snapped, he sat up and leered hard at Caveman. He wanted to punch him in his smiling face.

"Uh-oh." Caveman smirked, "Seems big, bad hero Jack Zero isn't so good after all, is he?"

"Listen, THALL," Jack was sure to stress Caveman's true name. "There was never any murder! I was not court marshaled. General Zimm's death was an accident, for which I was exonerated."

"Right, yeah, and dishonorably discharged, I heard it all before," Caveman chided. "But the truth of it is you murdered him, lied about it, and got away with it. No matter how you look at it, you are no better'n me. In fact, I's say you was worse'n me even. Jack Zero, nothin' but a cold blooded killer."

Jack balled his hands into fists.

"How's that make you feel?"

Jack stood and approached Caveman who still hung his face between the bars. They stared intently at one another, their eyes bore into the other.

Caveman spoke first, "Whaddya gonna do, Zero, hit me?"

"No," Jack pushed on Caveman's chest, causing him to stumble backward. Unfortunately, Caveman's feet were locked in place, as Jack stood on his loosened shoelaces, not allowing him to gain his footing. Caveman grunted as he fell hard on his back, his head hitting the cement floor with a loud '*thwap,*' he had been knocked out. "I won't have to. Sweet dreams, Thall."

The sound of Caveman's lungs letting out air was cut short by the sound of whistling and wolf calls from outside his cell. Jack moved to the front of his cell to see the slender form of a young, attractive woman scurrying quickly past the row of convicts that lined the hallway. Trying not to make eye contact, the woman was escorted by an armed officer, but it didn't concern the prisoners all that much as they continued their hooting and hollering.

As the woman came closer, Jack realized she was on her way to see him, and there was only one woman who would come to see him, Ceinwen Sagorsky.

"Mr. Zero," her sweet voice was refreshing after the gruff, scratching sound that was Caveman's own voice, which resembled two pieces of granite being rubbed together. But not Ceinwen, her voice was mellifluous in tone. "Oh, Mr. Zero, I'm sorry it took so long to get here, the traffic on the way over was murder."

Jack cut her off, "Thanks for coming, Winnie."

Ceinwen winced as the sound of the name Winnie, she didn't like when anyone called her that. However, she didn't mind if he called her Winnie. At least she put up with it. After all, she worked for Jack as his assistant, his girl Friday. She always happened to be the first person he called whenever he was in trouble. She was perky and petite. Her brown hair wrapped around her shoulders neatly, loose curls that hung freely and bounced as she walked. No one else ever called her Winnie. Ceinwen was such a proper name her family felt it should be maintained as such. No other pronunciation was ever aloud. "I'm sorry, Mr. Zero, I tried but they wouldn't let me talk to anyone upstairs."

The scent of her sweet perfume was alluringly intoxicating; he took it in with a deep breath. It was so much better than the musty, sweaty stench that drifted from both his beaten mattress and Caveman's body. "Hey it's okay, you did your best."

"I talked to the District Attorney directly--"

Jack interrupted Ceinwen, "Winnie, no! You can't talk to the DA," Jack threw his head back. "He hates my guts. I wanted you to talk to Arnie Qualtry, the lawyer that helped us out on that Burmaster case."

"I couldn't find his number," Ceinwen looked apologetically at Jack. "I did the best I could, sorry."

Jack looked at Ceinwen; he couldn't stay mad at her. She was the most loyal employee, and friend that he had. "It's alright, I appreciate your help."

Jack wrapped his hands around the bars as he leaned in toward Ceinwen.

She smiled meekly. "No, I'm the one who should be sorry," she said sweetly. She placed her hands near Jack's, hoping he would place his hand reassuringly on top of hers, maybe even interlace their fingers, a gesture that could meld them together. She could feel her heart flutter as Jack loosened his fingers and slid them down the bars. The feeling quelled as quickly as it came when she watched his hands droop to his sides.

"Look, Mr. Zero," Ceinwen swallowed hard. "I was thinking."

"About what?"

"I was thinking, um," she stammered, searching for the words she wanted to say at the risk of looking foolish. "I thought maybe we could, y'know, you and me, could, I dunno. Look, you know how sometimes people that are together all the time get close? And that when they get close and they get to know one another, they get, I dunno, feelings about—I mean…I'd do anything for you…"

Jack stood up and approached Ceinwen again. She felt her face grow flush and her palms sweat. Could this be the chance, could he finally be listening to what she had to say? Could he feel what she was feeling?

"Ceinwen," Jack's voice was low, tender, "I know what you're saying."

"You do?"

"Of course," Jack smiled widely. "Lartanner."

Ceinwen stared at Jack, confused, "Lartanner?"

"Commissioner Lartanner," Jack finished. Once again, Ceinwen's hopes were dashed of having a moment, one that she had longed for, hoped for, but never had. What would it take to get him to notice her? What more could she do? Then on the other hand, why did she still bother? Jack reached his hand through the bars and touched her face with his fingertips. That was why. The contact of his fingers against her cheek was electric. Her body shook beneath her clothes; she could feel the hair on her skin stand up straight.

Jack whispered to her, "I need you to get in touch with Lartanner for me. Tell him what happened."

Ceinwen tried to speak, still taken aback by Jack's touch. "S-sure," was all she managed. How could she say no to him? She felt like she never could. Her mother was right; she always fell for the wrong kind of guys. Ever since high school she seemed to get involved with either men who lead less than favorable lives, or those that just didn't seem to notice her at all. From what she remembered, it was mostly the latter.

"I'll, um, I'll see what I can do."

"You're a doll, Winnie," Jack smiled his warm, charming smile. The one that made her heart melt every time he flashed it to her. "If I could reach through these bars, I'd kiss you."

"I might just let you," Ceinwen smiled coyly. She leaned in closer, her eyes closed. She could feel Jack's breath on her chin. She could feel her extremities tingle. Could *this* be that moment?

"Ceinwen," Jack said, his voice laden with confusion. "What are you doing?

Ceinwen snapped out of her romanticized trance, "Nothing. Nothing. I mean, I'm going to speak with Commissioner Lartanner."

"Good, and could you hurry, I'd like to get out of here as soon as possible."

Her heart broken, she simply replied with a gravely, "Sure." Ceinwen did her best to choke back her tears as she walked away from Jack, just as she had so many times before, disappointed.

CHAPTER 4
MEET THE SAVIOR OF THE CITY

'You would think with all the technological advances, they would improve the speed of the elevator,' Jack thought. It certainly moved slowly enough. And what was with the music?

Ceinwen smiled at him, happy she had succeeded in getting Jack out of his cell. He still hadn't thanked her, but his beaming smile was thanks enough. They rode up the elevator in silence, Ceinwen waiting for Jack to speak first. He never did.

The elevator doors slid open, a faint hissing sound accompanying the movement. Jack made a motion to step through the doors, but was stopped by a young woman wearing horned-rimmed pink glasses, her hair pulled up high and tight on her head, resembling a bright red beehive. She pushed herself in front of him. Jack clenched his teeth, "Hello Tatyana".

"What are you doing here? Weren't you banned from the premises?" She spoke in a nasally, high pitched tone that could crack glass.

"I wasn't banned," Jack affirmed, trying not to look her directly in the eye. Once Tatyana locked her gaze on you, she was relentless in not allowing you to speak over her. It was a strange power she possessed. "I was…relieved of my duty."

"Which translates to a ban."

Jack gripped Tatyana by her shoulders and pushed her aside, still not making eye contact. He slid passed her as he spoke, "It's good to see you again, Tatyana. We'll have to speak again when you have more time."

"Hey!" She called out as he walked quickly away. The doors to the elevator slid shut before Ceinwen could join Jack, cutting her off as it returned to the lower levels.

Commissioner Lartanner was in no mood for any of this; one of his best former investigators, Jack Zero, yelling in his ear. He couldn't make any sense of any of it, it was just a barrage of noise. After only a few moments he yelled, "Alright! Enough!"

Jack quickly fell quiet. To Lartanner, it was welcoming. "Thank you," Lartanner breathed a sigh of relief. "Now what is going on here?"

"Maybe I should ask you why you're sending your people to intercept my collar?" Jack lashed.

"What are you talking about?"

"I was just about to place Neil Thall into my custody when one of your LEHV's swooped down and muscled me out of my fare."

"You know how it goes down, Zero," Lartanner turned his back from Jack to look out the sixth story window that overlooked the cityscape behind him. "The NULE has jurisdiction over all criminal activity in the city. If we're investigating a case that you happen to be investigating, I'm sorry, but my people get first crack."

"I still want my pay," Zero argued.

Lartanner sat at his desk and reached his hand out before him. As if calling it from nowhere, a screen lit up before him, projected onto thin air as if it were a transparent piece of glass suspended in the air. He waved his hand at the base of the screen and a virtual keyboard slid down. Lartanner began typing feverishly, both to get the information he sought and to get Jack out of his office faster. Jack watched from behind, seeing Lartanner type his information in reverse. He could see Lartanner accessed the recent arrest records database. In the search box he typed Neil Thall's name and pressed the space before him that represented the "Search" button. The screen came alive, several records scrolled up the screen, all alphabetical, as Jack remembered. The endless list continuously scanned, not showing any sign of stopping. The erratic display finally froze as all the entries disappeared from view.

"Sorry, Zero, but none of my officers nabbed your man. You must be mistaken."

"What are you saying, I'm crazy?" Jack became infuriated. "I was there; I saw one of your officers swoop in and shove me aside. And to top it off, she arrests me," Jack turned around, frustrated by what felt like a pointless argument. Fortunately for him it was at an opportune moment as he watched the same woman that he confronted earlier walk into the precinct. "As a matter of fact, that's her!" Jack pointed to the tall, slender woman who walked confidently toward Lartanner's office.

"Her?" Lartanner said. "She's not one of mine."

"Then who the hell is she?" Jack asked, watching her as she walked, her legs moving at a hypnotic rhythm. Her feet passed one in front of the other, like a runway model she was sleek and sheer, beautiful. All the while Jack stared at the mysterious stranger, he never heard Commissioner Lartanner speaking to him.

"Zero!" Lartanner shouted. "Are you listening to me?"

Jack shook his head, breaking her siren spell on him. "Huh?" Jack snapped back to reality. "Yeah sure, whatever you say."

Jack watched as Tatyana walked up to block the woman's path. '*Good luck,*' he thought. The mysterious woman pushed past Tatyana without saying a word. Who is she? She opened Lartanner's office door and marched straight inside, she was followed by two other men in dark suits and ties, their hair slicked back tightly against their heads. They wore frozen expressions that sent chills down Jack's spine.

"I need six rooms, one window office, a large conference room, three adjoining rooms and records room. I'll also need to requisition five computers, three installed with access to federal database records and two with standard form files included. There isn't much time so I would assume your slack-jawed expressions mean you aren't aware what is happening or you were expecting a man in charge," she stopped for a short breath. "I'm Agent Nicolina Frisco, Federal Bureau of Investigation." She waved her badge in front of their faces. It was a picture with her and the letters 'FBI' in a bold blue Helvetica font. She folded the badge wallet closed and stuffed it back in the breast pocket of her blazer. "My team is going to be taking over a large part of this department."

Lartanner stood, waving his hands, "Hold on one second. On who's authority, I was never notified."

"On his," Frisco pointed her thumb over her shoulder, gesturing to a flock of men wearing high-end three-piece suits, all clustered in a diamond formation, protecting the one figure in the center.

As the flock approached the Commissioner's office, they parted, allowing the central figure to move freely and enter through the door. Before the Commissioner stood one of the most prominent men in the state, and currently the country. Senator Jansen Glorm. Glorm was the challenger in the biggest and most heated presidential election in decades.

"S-Senator Glorm," Lartanner stammered, surprised that such an important and influential person would pay such a personal visit to his precinct, his office. Glorm. The name commanded respect, and if the recent polls were any indication, the next president. "I heard about the recent threats made to your office. I want to assure you my men are prepared to help in any way possible."

"The Bureau is handling the investigation, Commissioner," Frisco interjected boldly.

"Did my agent place our needs?" His voice was smooth and even, filled with confidence.

"Yes, of course, I got a memo that agents from your office would be coming to our precinct, but I wasn't aware you would be with them. Are you sure it's wise to be openly accessible?"

Glorm smiled confidently, "Don't think some threats, idle or serious, are going to prevent me from continuing my campaign. Being President is difficult and important, especially when lobbying against terrorists and their organizations. The minute I show them my weakness, that's when they win."

Lartanner nodded, "Don't worry about your requests, we'll get you whatever you need, sir. I don't mean to pry, but what brings you here into my precinct?"

"I apologize for such short notice, Lantern is it?"

"Lartanner."

"Lartanner, yes. Let me ask you, how much do you know about the terrorist movement sprung by Humankind Against Robo-Technology, a.k.a. the HART?" Glorm smiled precariously.

"The HART?" Lartanner started.

"A vicious terrorist network," Frisco interjected.

"You think they're here in New Utica?" Jack forced himself into the conversation. Frisco threw him a nasty look while Glorm ignored him.

"Since I began rallying for a militaristic response to the ever-growing threat that they pose, not only to our nation, but to several nations across the globe. This group initially comes across as a sympathetic ally to a financially destitute nation, offering them empty promises of salvation from impoverish conditions with wealth and prosperity, only to exploit their susceptibility. What we've learned is if they don't join willingly, the HART threatens them by cutting off their imports of food and resources, forcing the country to no other alternative but to bend to their whim until they are no longer able to resist, allowing the HART to invade and take control of the national government. Currently, these tactics have forced several countries in both Europe and Asia to reluctantly join. Once elected, I plan to put together a task force that will infiltrate and disseminate the group quickly and cleanly before any of this threat of World War goes any further.

"Our Government fears the HART's purpose is to recruit these susceptible countries into an army. The President feels that the army they have amassed thus far is a considerable threat to the United States. We've received word from our intelligence overseas that there are rumblings of a planned invasion of our shores in the coming weeks. The HART has been sending its agents to cities all over the country assessing our vulnerabilities."

Lartanner looked confused. He was a good cop, but his

understanding didn't often stretch much beyond his own microcosm of the city. "What's the purpose of their movement? What is it they really want?'

"To purge all dependence on technology in humankind," Jack stepped forward, interrupting again.

"Who the hell is this jerk?" Frisco asked rudely.

"THIS jerk," Jack scowled, "Is the guy whose collar you swooped up and stole out from under."

"Oh, yes, I recall your…disheveled appearance," Frisco matched Jack's scowl, "So you're of no consequence."

"Listen, lady," Jack was no longer going to play nice, "You are a lady, right?" Jack tingled at the sight of Frisco's agitation to his intentional insult. "I was hired to retrieve certain stolen items for a client of mine and I intend to get them back. They were on Caveman, I mean Thall. You know the other guy you brought in with me."

"You mean you were able to arrest Neal Thall?" Glorm sounded surprised.

"He's detained downstairs right now, my men are bringing him up," Frisco explained.

"Good," Jack snorted. "I want my collar, and my lost wages."

Frisco stifled a laugh, as she looked Jack up and down, "Yeah, I bet you haven't been paid yet, and by the looks of you, I bet you haven't had a payday in quite some time."

"Well it's the only way I can afford to take you out to dinner," Jack sounded complimentary. "You'll just have to shave first."

"Enough!" Glorm grew tired of the childish bickering. "I fight less with my wife and we're divorced."

Lartanner ignored the banter between Jack and Frisco. He felt his chest tighten at the thought of a monster ship attacking his city. "Do you think New Utica is one of the planned targets?"

"It's most likely," replied Glorm. "We intercepted a communiqué between a HART Agent known as Low Master Felton Crust with a source here in New Utica," explained Agent Frisco.

Shivers ran up Jack's spine. The name Felton Crust was one he hadn't heard in a long time, it was a name he just as soon forget. Like Thall, It didn't take long for Jack to put the pieces of the puzzle together. He was a very thorough investigator and relied on his skills of deduction to understand why things happen. "Thall," Jack realized. "There using known felons that have underworld attachments to supply them with intel in order to make a more discreet assault. It makes perfect sense."

Glorm smiled, "I'm impressed. Your officers are quite impressive Commissioner Lartanner."

"He is not one of my men," Lartanner was quick to correct Glorm.

"Not anymore."

"Oh?"

"Zero was relieved of his duty over two years ago."

"Relieved?" Jack snorted. "More like forced out of duty."

Lartanner let out a breath he had been holding in, then said through gritted teeth, "Zero, now is not the time."

"Of course not," Jack retorted. "Now is never the time especially when discussing my reinstatement."

"Zero? Jack Zero, is it?" Glorm shook Jack's hand firmly. "I've heard of you."

Jack cocked an eyebrow as he looked curiously at Glorm, "Me?"

"Jack Demetrius Zero, Lieutenant First-Class, a decorated member of the 1138-HJ Skytroopers under the command of General Varcar Zimm, ran several successful missions into Eastern Asia, Northern and Central Africa, among other places, which remain classified; who was ultimately dishonorably discharged from service," Glorm's teeth shone brightly between his upturned lips. "How's that for memory?"

Jack was taken aback. Glorm eerily prattled off an immense amount of facts about Jack's past, which he didn't know everything, and tried to keep as private as possible; even Lartanner didn't know much of his service time, "Creepy," Jack quipped. "And spot on, except for the dishonorably part."

"Of course," Glorm replied mockingly. "I saw how you reacted when Agent Frisco mentioned Felton Crust. You know that name, don't you? Let me also ask you, do the names Neal Thall, Gregg Darr, Markyn Firth, Graham Borton, Phineas Wald, Caspar Huun, or Palmer Rey have any meaning to you?"

Jack swallowed hard, "They sound familiar."

"I thought they might," Glorm smiled. "Why don't you enlighten us?"

"They were all part of my outfit, Skytroopers. A good group of men, the best. We were a tight unit, knew each other's strengths and weaknesses. We could anticipate any one of the others moves, which made it a benefit when we were in the field. The problem was they were all too good. Loyal all, especially to Zimm."

"They'd follow him to Hell wouldn't they?"

Jack nodded.

Glorm continued, "Except you."

Jack was somber as he spoke, "Zimm and me never saw eye to eye. I always questioned his orders. The end wasn't, shall we say, a clean break. Everyone took Zimm's death hard, blamed me for it."

"Not everyone."

Jack didn't like where this questioning was going. Despite his internally infuriating knowledge, Jack couldn't help but perk his curiosity, "I'm sure you don't keep such detailed tabs on all of your constituents, so how is it you know so much about me?"

"Do you remember a Colonel Frederick Dowbromski?" Glorm asked.

Jack's stomach knotted at the sound of the name, "Rings a bell."

"I was a member of the Military Internal Investigation Service under the charge of Colonel Dowbromski when General Zimm was under surveillance for his questionable activities. My friction with Zimm was why Dowbromski approached me to be a mole. I was more than happy to help. I haven't seen any of those men since Zimm's funeral."

Agent Frisco slipped a photograph from an envelope and handed it to Jack, "Recognize any of them?"

Jack studied the picture carefully, it was grainy and some images were slightly blurred, but the body types were recognizable. There were two men in the image, a tall man no older than he wearing a dark jumpsuit, his hair cropped tight to his head in traditional military fashion. The other man was rather large in stature, tall and muscular, in fact more muscular than any average person was, even more than an average weightlifter. Jack had only seen one man with a build like this once before.

"Yeah, I recognize them. That short guy on the right, I'm fairly certain that's Crust. The other one he's unmistakably Huun."

Agent Frisco snatched the picture back and stuffed it away in its envelope, "Just as we suspected."

Glorm raised an eyebrow, "Mr. Zero, Did you know that those men in your unit, have all recently been involved in illegal activities related to the HART terrorist movement."

"I'm not surprised," Jack scoffed. "They were always involved in something illegal. Although, I'm surprised they would be recruited into the HART if the HART values its stance on anti-infusion. All of Zimm's men had some form of infusion."

"Including yourself."

Jack turned away, embarrassed at the truth, "Not voluntarily."

"But you did, along with all of Zimm's men. It's like they say about tight units, they all follow the same paths," Glorm's tone was accusation.

"I'm not like them!" Jack became defensive.

Glorm smiled a greasy grin, he relished in his grilling, "I find it fascinating that all those other men under his command unanimously went AWOL, their lives left behind, only to reemerge as agents of a global terrorist collective, don't you?"

"Like I said, I'm not like them."

"What I find confusing is that only two of Zimm's men didn't join them," Glorm glared. "One of those two someone's is you, Mr.

Zero. Why is that?"

"With all the facts you have on me, I'm surprised you don't already know the answer to that."

Agent Frisco pushed forward, "Just answer the question."

Jack stared for a long moment at Frisco, trying to figure her out as best he could. She was hard to read. "I was never one to follow Zimm's orders."

Lartanner added, "Or anyone else's."

Frisco stifled a laugh. Jack shot her a dirty look.

"Do you remember a Phineas Wald?" Glorm inquired.

Jack was silent for a moment, he didn't need to think, he knew the answer, but was nervous to hear the name spoken after so long, "Yeah, I know him."

"He never followed Zimm either."

"Wald had his own set of problems, he was never one to follow anything; we were all surprised he lasted as long as he did in the military."

"Do you know of his whereabouts now?" Agent Frisco asked.

"Haven't seen him in years," Jack complied. "Last I heard he was in a mental hospital outside of Philadelphia."

Frisco added, "He checked himself out of there over a year ago and disappeared, no one, not even his family, know where he went or if he's even alive."

"I don't know where he is," Jack felt himself getting defensive again.

"We're suspicious he joined his other expatriates as a terrorist," Glorm added.

"What does that have to do with me?"

"I want you to inform me if he tries to make contact with you."

"Why should I?" Jack retorted, "Besides, why would he contact me? I don't owe him anything."

Agent Frisco intervened, "If he does, you will inform us, or I will make your life miserable if you don't."

"I find that hard to believe," Jack smiled coyly.

"Mr. Zero, I don't think you realize the gravity of what we're dealing with here. A team of trained killers all of which know more about this country than we would like to admit, working for a known terrorist organization. Them being here is not only a threat to our safety and security, but to our way of life," Glorm sneered. "If you're hiding something, we will find it. Maybe you're someone we need to keep an eye on?"

"Just try getting close to me, see how well it's worked for everyone else."

Glorm stood back a moment, "Is that a threat, Mr. Zero?"

"Not at all, I'm well aware of the consequences of threatening any superior," he threw a look at Lartanner.

"After your debacle with Zimm, I'm not surprised." Glorm continued, "Then you'll also recall what can happen to someone who impedes an investigation."

"I do." Jack stewed, he hated that Zimm's name was brought up again, a name he would wish to forget.

"Then I recommend you keep your nose out of this case. Do we have a clear understanding, Mr. Zero?" Glorm's tone turned more threatening.

"Crystal," Jack replied cynically, trying to keep his attitude up, despite his desire to punch Glorm in the face. Unfortunately, he also knew the consequences of striking a superior, or even worse, as a civilian striking a member of government.

"Quite astute, Detective. You may leave at any time," Glorm sneered. "But don't go too far, we may still need to ask you questions."

Jack looked from Glorm's glare to Frisco's stern expression and then to Lartanner's. Lartanner looked up at Jack like the one a disappointed father would his shamed son. His eyes signaled for Jack to exit. Jack swallowed his pride and slowly, reluctantly, left Lartanner's office.

Satisfied, Glorm then turned to Frisco, "You may continue, Agent."

Outside Lartanner's office, Jack clenched his fists in frustration. Tatyana swiveled in her seat to see Jack standing there.

"Kicked you out, didn't they?" She said snidely.

"I've got to get back in there."

"Not gonna happen."

C'mon, Tatyana," Jack pleaded. "You've gotta let me back in or let me hear what they're saying."

"You know I can't"

Jack cocked his head playfully, "Tatyana."

She rolled her eyes and pointed to the elevators. Jack wasn't going anywhere. He folded his arms and slumped into a chair.

Jack paced back and forth outside Lartanner's office. Tatyana glared angrily at him, shooting daggers from her eyes as she grew more and more annoyed at the appearance of the disheveled detective. She wished he would just leave, but he was always persistent.

"You can sit down, you know," she said disdainfully.

Jack ignored her, continuing his pacing until he heard the door of Lartanner's office click open.

Glorm stepped from within, followed by Agent Frisco, "As

fascinating as this all is, I'm afraid we need to begin to get to work." Glorm gestured for Agent Frisco to walk before him; he then turned to Lartanner, "I expect the rooms and equipment to be available within the next two hours." Glorm passed through the door leaving Lartanner to rub his forehead with his thumb and forefinger. "If you'll excuse us, we have a suspect to interrogate."

"Hold up a second," Jack chased after Glorm and Frisco. "May I have a word with you for a moment, Senator?"

"What can I do for you, Mr. Zero?" Glorm turned to Jack, folding his arms.

"Sir, I understand your purpose here, but I need to speak to Cavema-," Jack caught himself using Caveman's sub name. "Mr. Thall, your suspect."

"Mr. Zero here is a civilian," Frisco made a note to point out.

"Agent Frisco is right, you are a civilian."

Jack felt his skin begin to heat up; he threw a burning stare at Frisco, "I was once an officer in the U.S. Military and of the NULE. I may work in the public sector, but I still practice law enforcement. In regards to Mr. Thall, I don't need to even speak to him directly; I simply need to retrieve an item that was in Thall's possession that one of your agents picked up during their apprehension."

Glorm looked at Frisco, his eyebrow raised curiously, "Tell me, Mr. Zero, what item?"

"I was hired by a woman who Thall had stolen the item from, some jewels. It would be jake if I could get them back to return to my client, you understand, don't you?"

Glorm stared for a long moment at Jack. He looked over at Frisco who was shaking her head. He then turned back to Jack, Glorm let out a lungful of breath he had sucked in before finally speaking. "Alright, Mr. Zero," He finally spoke. "We'll let you get back your item, but only through the evidence locker and no speaking with Mr. Thall, understood?"

Jack beamed, "Understood."

"Agent Frisco will assist you," Glorm instructed.

"Sir?"

"Agent, you can take a moment to assist Mr. Zero, here. After all, I can handle Thall myself."

Frisco frowned, looking as if she was ready to explode. She closed her eyes and spoke calmly, "I would be happy to help you, Mr. Zero."

Glorm smiled broadly, "Good." He began to walk away, "I'll catch you up when you get back, Agent." Glorm caught up with several other well-dressed agents and headed toward the interrogation room.

Frisco looked over at Jack who smiled brightly at her. It was annoying. "Let's go."

Caveman sat hunched in the small metal chair that adorned the scantily dressed interrogation room. He rested his hands on the large wooden table, the only other piece of furniture in the room, his fingers laced together. He chewed incessantly on the inside of his cheek, a nervous habit he practiced when boxed into uncomfortable situations. He looked at the mirror that was on the wall opposite where he sat. Caveman knew it was a two-way mirror and that he was certain there were officers watching him on the other side. He reached up and scratched his eye with his middle finger, making certain that anyone watching saw which finger he was using.

The door on the side of the room clicked opened and two men dressed in black, well-pressed suits walked in silently and stood on either side of the door. Caveman watched the two men curiously. They seemed like G-men to him. The sight of them made him suddenly feel important. The thought of the federal government interested in him made him sit up straight in the undersized chair. Caveman watched the door intently as Senator Glorm walked in behind them. Caveman took mental notes of this man, he looked important. His suit was much nicer than the others were and he was equally well groomed looking like he took extra good care of himself. He was definitely important.

"Well, looky you. I mus' be real special to have someone as important as you to come all the way down here ta' see me."

Glorm threw on his best smile as he sat across from Caveman, "What makes you think I'm someone of importance?"

Caveman snorted, "Are ya kiddin'? Look at ya', the way yer dressed, the way ya' smell." Caveman sniffed the air.

"Mr. Thall, my name is Jansen Glorm."

"Senator Glorm?" Caveman sounded surprised. "A senator all the way down here ta' see l'il ol' me? Oh, man I knew I shoulda' played my lucky numbers."

Glorm continued his charm, "Mr. Thall, I represent the Unites States Government, as senator of the fifth largest district in the nation, I want you to understand that you are in the custody of--"

"Blah, blah, blah," Caveman interrupted sarcastically. "Skip the bullshit, I know my rights."

"Well, good, that will make this go more quickly then."

"I wanna lawyer," Caveman turned away from Glorm's stare.

"Trust me, Mr. Thall," Glorm became serious. "A lawyer won't be necessary."

Caveman looked back at Glorm suspiciously, "What's all this about?"

"I want you to tell me about a lost shipment of guns, Mr. Thall"

"I don' know nuthin' 'bout no guns, and don' call me Thall, my name is Caveman."

Glorm could see Caveman squirm uncomfortably in his seat. It gave him slight joy. "Of course, Caveman. But I need you to remember your contract with a man named Crust."

The evidence locker room was large, but felt small when moving between the overstuffed, narrow hallways formed by the storage cabinets. There were hundreds, maybe thousands of storage cabinets. Had it not been for the alphanumeric classification system, items would be easily misplaced and lost. Jack greeted the archive coordinator, Grudge, a greasy, mole-like man who spoke little. He simply glared with beady eyes over his horned-rim glasses. Jack never knew why they called him Grudge, probably held one pretty intensely, he assumed. Once he saw Frisco's badge, he wordlessly handed her a map containing the location and the container number that housed Caveman's possessions, the ones he had on him at the time of his arrest.

Grudge opened the gate to the evidence room. He motioned for Frisco and Jack to walk inside. He then handed Frisco a slip of paper, "Last aisle all the way at the end. Left side, top shelf."

They entered swiftly. Jack walked alongside Frisco, trying to maintain her obviously hastening stride. "Where's the fire, Agent?" Jack teased, matching her pace.

"No fire, just hurrying," Frisco said coldly, clearly annoyed to have to talk to him.

"Any particular reason, Nikki?"

Frisco stopped. She turned and faced Jack. Her eyes were narrow slits, her pupils smoldered, burning so that he had to avert his gaze at moments. "I don't like being called Nikki. I don't like this. I don't like you. I'm here because I was ordered. I was not directed to speak to you or interact in any way. You may have the Senator buying into your bullshit, but I am not, nor will I ever. You want to lay on the charm, save it for the local strip club. While we are down here, don't look at me, don't talk to me, don't even think about me, because, if you do, I will do things to you that will haunt your dreams for the rest of your life. You won't be able to take a piss without looking fearfully over your shoulder, you get me?"

Jack stared blankly at Frisco for a long moment, "You have really pretty eyes."

"You're an asshole," Frisco sneered coldly before she turned and continued deeper into the archives.

'She has buttons and they're easy to push,' Jack thought.

The remainder of their walk was silent. Frisco made her way down a narrow aisle, Jack followed closely. Their shoulders scraped either side as they maneuvered through, each twisting their body, sidling through cautiously. Frisco stopped and looked at the piece of paper that Grudge had handed her; it read 'Thall, N /7658-4.'

"Here it is," Frisco reached up, trying to grab the drawer. It was above her reach. She tried to increase her height by standing on her tiptoes. It was still difficult to reach. Jack squeezed up behind her, "Let me give you a hand," the space was confined, tight, almost intimate, his body pressed firmly against hers. He reached above her and grabbed the metal drawer. His face was nearly buried into her hair; it smelled incredible, like some kind of melon, perhaps. It was intoxicating, so much so that he nearly forgot to bring the drawer down. He pulled and slid it forward, trying to set it on any available ledge.

"You could move," Frisco sounded more annoyed than usual.

"Sorry," Jack snapped back to reality. He quickly stepped aside, steadying the tray over his head as he did his best not to stumble while saving face. Despite his best efforts, Jack clumsily tripped over his own feet as he tried to squeeze from behind Frisco, nearly spilling the drawer's contents across the floor. "Excuse me."

Jack tried not to look at Frisco, missing the small smirk that adorned the corner of her mouth. He set the metal drawer on a nearby ledge. He flipped the top open and began to rummage through the contents, searching for the missing item belonging to the kindly Mrs. Graves. There seemed to be quite a few items in the tray for one person. His fingers raked along the various items, sifting out bullets of varying sizes, a small handgun that only fit a few of the bullets he felt, a collection of knives and other unidentifiable tools. He rummaged a few times over before he finally found what matched the description of the item Mrs. Graves lost. He pulled the small clutch out, which knocked a COMM device that fell from out of the shadows. Jack looked more intently, at the device. He focused on the comm. device; that was rectangular with glass screens. He quickly snatched it up and stuffed it into his pocket, hoping not to be noticed. '*This could prove useful*,' he thought

"Well?" Frisco finally spoke behind him, causing Jack to be startled by her appearance.

"Jeez," Jack said, clutching his chest.

"Is it in there?"

Fortunately, she hadn't noticed his taking the device, Jack realized. "Yep, got it," he said holding up the clutch of jewels.

"Fine, just put back the tray, will you?"

"Sure."

"You know the way out," Frisco walked past him and was out of view. Jack replaced the drawer and made his way through the series of narrow aisles and up to the front of the evidence archival room.

"Where ya goin', friend?" Grudge was tinkering with a robotic device at his desk, not looking up a Jack.

"I was in here with Agent Frisco, one of Senator Glorm's lackeys, Lartanner knows I'm here," Jack explained. "You just saw me."

"Where's your authorization?"

Jack reached into his pocket and retrieved a visitor's pass, which he handed to Grudge. Grudge swiped the card, still not looking up at Jack. "You're clean," Grudge grumbled.

"Thanks," Jack said accepting the returned pass from Grudge. "Have a good one." Jack left, barely hearing the inaudible grunt Grudge let out.

The main headquarters of the New Utica Police Department sat in the northern section of the city, a good thirty blocks from Jack's office. He was short on funds so there was no point in hailing a cab. He was walking the streets were teaming with traffic, the sounds of squealing brakes and honking horns filled the thick, muggy air. Jack stood for a moment and collected his thoughts. It seemed strange to watch several federal agents and a U.S. Senator appear and order Lartanner around so easily, especially since Lartanner always deemed himself a no-nonsense, take-no-crap kind of cop. Yet, he seemed to buckle so quickly. Something didn't seem right. Jack knew what to expect, heavier police shifts and a regiment of military troops would be patrolling the city. This could make anyone uptight.

Jack watched the people that filled the sidewalks, walking quickly and taking long strides to make it to their destinations. They had no idea what was happening, what could be happening under their noses. Jack tried to shake his uneasy feeling. He reached his hands deep into his coat pockets. He felt the velvet bag that held the jewelry he retrieved from the evidence room. He also felt the COMM device. He pulled it out discreetly and rolled it over in his hand. He needed to check to see if it had any stored recorded data that could give him clues to what Thall was truly doing. However, he couldn't look at it here; he would wait until he got back to his office. He shoved it back in pocket and walked nonchalantly over to the hotdog cart that was parked outside the precinct. The smell of the dogs filled his nostrils and he realized how hungry he was, he hadn't eaten all day.

"Afternoon, Hank," Jack spoke fondly to the cart attendant Hank, a small round man who always wore a wide grin. His thick glasses slid down his small nose, which he had to constantly push up with his chubby fingers. His greasy black hair was thinning and receded to the middle of his head. Jack remembered stopping here when he worked at the precinct; Hank had a comforting way about him that was welcoming to him. "How's things?"

"Jack Zero!" Hank returned with an enthusiastic greeting, "It's been a long time."

"Yeah, well, I haven't had much reason to come around here lately."

"Sure, you're a self-made man now, like me," Hank smiled and poked his chest with his thumb.

Jack let out a snort on Hank's comment.

"What'll it be?" Hank beamed. "The usual?"

"How about a veggie dog with the works, no relish."

"Coming right up!"

"Business' about to pick up for you, huh?"

"Already has, noticing a lot of G-Men activity in and out of this place," Hank gestured to the precinct with the hotdog he held with tongs, dripping the excess water off before he dropped it into a bun.

"Really?" Jack played naïve. "How long has that been going on?"

"For a few hours now, but I've seen 'em around here for the past couple a' weeks, seems to be very hush, hush. I see them come in but I never see them leave."

"Whaddya think it means?" Jack handed Hank cash.

"Word on the street is that there's a big arms movement happening," Hank handed Jack his hotdog, condiments dripped on his fingers. "Rumor has it that the G-Men are sneakin' all around the city looking for anyone with connections and ties to arms dealings. They're scoopin' 'em up and draggin' 'em all in for questioning. If you ask me none of it sounds jake."

Jack took a bite of his hotdog as he looked back at the precinct, thinking about Agent Frisco and her apprehension of Thall, "No, it doesn't sound jake at all."

"Who knows what's jake with all the happenings in the underbelly of this city," Hank handed Jack his change. "At least we can count of the Blue Sox winning the pennant this year."

"Yeah," Jack was distant, his mind racing about everything, his past, the present. It all seemed too coincidental to be resurfacing now.

Hank smiled, "You have yourself a nice day, Mr. Zero. Don't be stranger."

"You too," Jack returned his smile and tipped the brim of his fedora. "And I won't." He held up his hotdog, "Still the best in town."

Jack continued to consume his hotdog while walking across the busy intersection, not noticing the man in the thick black coat and matching fedora that followed him stealthily from a distance.

Jack hurried through the door to his office flat at a rapid pace, the tail of his trench coat billowing behind him. He quickly slammed the smoked glass door with the words: '*Jack Zero: Private Investigator*' stenciled in a black arch, which shook the glass violently, shifting loose from its own mooring. The office was quite modest, small yet roomy. There was a desk directly across from the door where Jack's assistant Ceinwen Sagorsky greeted everyone who entered. The round room had a couch and two plush chairs along the walls next to a door that was Jack's personal office. As Jack walked in, he didn't look up at Ceinwen, whose light brown hair glowed warmly under the desk lamp. Her black-framed glasses, which she only wore at the office, seemed a bit large for her narrow face. She kept her attention completely on him. Her jaw throbbed as it gyrated from the constant chewing she did on the wad of bubble gum in her mouth. The gum popped and cracked randomly each time her jaw moved.

"Mr. Zero," Ceinwen nearly jumped out from behind her desk. "I'm so glad you're back."

"Hey, Winnie," Jack said, exhaustion in his voice. "Jack, alright, just call me Jack." He quickly walked past her not even looking at her.

"Jack, sir, wait," Ceinwen pleaded, more loudly this time.

Jack stopped; he could feel the grip of annoyance build up in his stomach as he paused to collect himself before he undeservedly blew up at the poor girl. Jack then pasted a smile onto his face and spun around on his heel to face her. "What," Jack snapped, but soon caught himself and changed his tone. "Can I do for you," he finished with a smile.

"Mr. Zero, um, Jack, sir," she reached out with a stack of papers that she handed over to Jack. "These are your phone messages, Mrs. Graves called, she said she remembered a few other details since she last spoke to you, although she couldn't remember what they were over the phone, but…"

Jack's face lit up as he reached into his inner breast pocket of his coat, "That reminds me." Jack pulled out a small clutch that clinked and clattered as he shook it.

"You got the jewels?" Ceinwen asked with anticipation.

"I got the jewels," Jack said confidently. "Now we can get paid past the retainer."

"That's good news," she replied, blowing a bubble and popping it before speaking again. "Because, as for the messages, one is from the electric company, your payment is late, another from the COMM company, an invoice of payment reminder, it was a recorded message."

"Oh, right, I forgot about those."

"Also, there's a call from someone named Nick Frisco, but he sounded a bit feminine if you ask me."

Jack cut Ceinwen off, "Nikki called?"

"Yeah, so it's a girl then?" Ceinwen responded thickly, although Jack couldn't notice her subtle hint at jealousy.

"What did she say?" Jack asked impatiently.

"Y'know, it's funny," Ceinwen laughed sarcastically. Now she was the one feeling annoyed. "I had the toughest time getting your attention when you walked in that door, but I mention the name Nick Frisco and suddenly I have you undivided attention."

"Nikki," Jack corrected.

"Of course, Nikki, my mistake," Ceinwen moved silkily past Jack, half trying to get him to notice her and half trying to prove she was sexy. "Sounds like some two-bit floosy if you ask me."

"I didn't" Jack said wryly, her attempts going unnoticed.

"I see; the great detective stands strong for the common man, fighting injustices and wronging the rights as he continues on his crusade to better the world, but gets all weak in the knees for some dame with great gams and a smile."

"I never said she smiled, but you are right about the gams," a devilish grin crept slowly across Jack's face.

Ceinwen watched the sly grin broaden and her blood boiled in anger at his chauvinistic response. "There is more to a woman than great gams," she began to shout. "Maybe if men looked deeper into a woman's heart and mind they would see that there was more to like than a cheap skirt that whisks by, but maybe they could see there was something meaningful that could grow into something real and true, not just some cheap fling for kicks. I always expected more from you especially, *MISTER Zero*," Ceinwen collected her handbag and shawl, draping the latter over her arm as she made her way around her desk toward the door. She pulled open the front door and spoke over her shoulder before leaving, "I'm going to lunch. I'll be back in an hour."

Jack smiled meekly. "Hey Winnie, I'm sorry." he said apologetically. "I had a rough morning. Look, I'll be in my office, just program my calls to VoiceMate and lock the door so no one comes in. Oh and can you call Mrs. Graves? Let her know I have our payday."

Ceinwen hesitated for a short moment. Jack wasn't a bad guy, he usually treated her pretty well, and he paid well, at least when he could. She cared for him, more deeply than she cared to think but would never admit to it. It didn't matter; he didn't notice her like that. "Sure thing, Mister Zero." Ceinwen said defeated as she stepped back to her desk and pressed a series of buttons on her desk COMM that chirped in response.

"Thanks," Jack smiled as Ceinwen made her way out the door, securing the latch as she crossed through, closing the door gently as she left. Ceinwen smiled to herself, more at how Jack's smile made her feel than at her gratification of his apology. It wasn't until halfway through her lunch that she forgot about the client waiting patiently in Jack's office.

CHAPTER 5
A NEW CLIENT

The door to Jack's office pushed inward, sticking on the frame, which it detached from, vibrating like a plucked guitar string. It continued, creaking slowly as it swung open. It was a traditional oak door with a smoked, pocked glass window that had his name stenciled in thick black letters on the outside. Jack entered his office, closing the door quietly behind him as he flicked on the lights. He smiled at the stencil, seeing his name like that was gratifying, despite no longer seeing the same view on the other side as he did when he worked for the NULE. He never should have been relieved of duty. Unfortunately, one's past can certainly return to haunt you, he could attest to that. Jack's office was small, compact, nearly the size of a closet. Well, maybe not that small. It did fit his large desk, multiple filing cabinets, and a couch, not to mention all the papers and files stacked around, cluttering the room. He planned to organize it…someday.

The room was sultry; the evening air had a habit of sneaking in through the worn windows making it feel as if there were no walls to begin with. Fortunately, the ceiling fan was working, cooling his sweaty skin as it rotated irregularly. The hum of the fan whirring and whining was the only sound that filled the quiet of the room.

Jack pulled the COMM device he had taken from NULE Headquarters and turned it over in his hand repeatedly. It was unusual. He flipped it over to see the other side revealing a very solid design with grated ridges covering the interior electronics, meaning it was one that was designed to withstand heavier communications and larger distances more efficiently. It was military issued, much like the kind Jack carried when he was in the service. He ran his thumbs along the edge of the screen, pressing it in slightly. It snapped. The sound jolted him as it gave the impression of breaking. It didn't, it just loosened from whatever the makeshift frame that was holding it in place. He scratched at the screen, prying it loose. He popped it out and peeled it free. Jack flipped on his lamp desk to get a better view of the concealed device. Underneath was a smaller, thinner screen, one Jack recognized as completely military. There was a scratched out serial number, all of which started with U-S. There was also a faded U.S. Flag logo that appeared under the small screen. Not just any military, but United States military. Why would Thall have this? He, or whoever gave it to him, was going to lengths to ensure it wasn't identified as a military device. As he spun the device over again in his hands, the desk lamp caught a glint of dis-colorization along the bottom of the device. He held it flat under the light to get a better look at what appeared to be an inverted triangle with five long, thin rectangles jutting outward from the flat base. Jack dropped the device on the desk as he realized he was looking at the symbol for the dark HART.

Thall wasn't just moving weapons potentially for the HART; he was in regular contact with them. That means he has already met with them. That means they are already here in the U.S. Everything that Glorm and his group had speculated and feared seems to already have happened, or soon will. Maybe there were stored messages on the COMM, he was certain Thall didn't know how to erase them, let alone access the lower memory of the device that stored them; fortunately, he did. However, it wasn't as easy as a button push, instead it required a bit of ingenuity. He was going to have to pay a visit to Helix. He tossed the COMM in the air and caught it on his open palm. He then slid open the top right hand drawer of his desk and dropped the object inside. It clanked as it bounced into place before Jack slammed the drawer shut. It wasn't important now. He leaned back in his chair, swiveled around, pushed aside the thick curtains and looked out of his office window behind him. Sun spilled into the dark room. It was a gorgeous afternoon, the sun was at its apex, shining warm and bright. A few fluffy white clouds drifted lazily across the bright blue backdrop. It was a placid sight that left Jack feeling calm and warm. It distracted Jack from the cold, bitter coffee he sipped from his mug. He gagged at the acrid flavor not realizing it had been sitting out for some time. He went to the coffee maker on the other side of the room and dumped the remaining liquid from his mug into the glass pot. He then looked for a place to dispose of the remnants in the pot, ultimately dumping it in the potted plant by the door. He turned the warmer on and began to prepare another pot, flipping on the radio transceiver while he worked. He hadn't listened to the news for some time. It seemed important to him, especially with the state of the world as it were. The transmitter pod was a small round base about the size of the coffee mug he held. Resting upon the small base was a white sphere about the size of a baseball. The sphere was hollow and smooth in spots, but cracked in others. It resembled finished marble in appearance, but plastic in touch. Jack pressed the largest of three buttons on the pod, activating the transmitter. It erupted with energy and life; the base glowed brightly, pushing the sphere into the air where it levitated gently, floating about two inches above the base. The sphere emitted a neon blue glow that crackled, as it grew brighter.

Almost instantly, a male information reporter's voice emitted from the transmitter device, "With the financial crisis of deepening recession in Eastern Europe, many nations fall to the lure of the Humankind Against Robotic Techno-Infusion united organization, also known as the HART. With its influence already in control of several countries in most of Asia and Southern Africa, the HART seems to be reaching further North. Many analysts in Washington are watching the HART closely and have theorized that the world could be edging closer to another global conflict.

We received an anonymous message from a man claiming to be the head military strategist of the HART, known as the High Master. He made a statement regarding their tactile advancements, claiming they are not in any way maneuvering to militaristically place themselves, but are only interested in assisting countries that are struggling financially and economically."

The reporter's voice was replaced by the gruff accent that sounded vaguely familiar, but the voice was digitally altered to be completely recognizable. "We hope to unify the human race as a global economy and eliminate the idea of lesser beings and instead making the world a cleaner, purer place." The words made Jack's skin crawl and blood curdle. He knew the words of the man speaking were not genuine. Military actions taken to unify people always ended poorly. He was certain the HART had an underlying sinister agenda, especially if it had recruited people like Huun and Crust from Zimm's old unit. They never held the interest of any humans except themselves. Jack often though of the time he spent in the service. Jack had served in the US Military for nearly eight years before becoming a public servant. He had enlisted fresh out of high school, becoming involved in the aerial branch. His ability to handle a weapon and adapt to any style of hand-to-hand combat resulted in him being recruited by the Skytroopers. At the time it was exciting, an exceptional fit for him. In his youth, he always felt he had an axe to grind against the world. His expression came in the form of missions of no mercy, assassinations and overthrowing any unruly leader his commanding officer ordered to be "removed from office." His team had gone on nearly thirty missions before he began to feel what he could only describe as guilt. It was that final mission that caused him to leave the military, all thanks to Varcar Zimm.

A voice in the room snapped Jack's head up. He twisted his body to follow his head, his hands swinging wildly. One hand caught the transmitter and knocked it free from the base. It rolled off the table and onto the floor where it rolled along the hardwood until it touched the slender foot in a silky red high-heel pump. As if from out of nowhere a beautiful, slender woman was seated on the couch across from his desk. Jack nearly jumped out of his chair, startled by the sight of her. He hadn't heard her come in and Ceinwen didn't mention anything about someone waiting for him. So where did she come from? It was as if she had appeared from thin air.

At that moment, a modest chime was heard, like a signal from an oven that had been fully preheated. It made Jack raise an eyebrow, curiously admiring its timing. It was signaling that the coffee had finished, despite the machine being nearly ten-years-old; it could still brew in under six minutes.

The mysterious woman on the other side of his office was a tall, lean, and lovely. She wore a bright red dress that hugged her curves tightly, accentuating her sleek body. The top of the dress seemed tighter than the bottom, pushing her breasts together and upward, creating two large crescents bobbing above the neckline. Her face was soft, her skin fair. She had lovely features, defined cheekbones, a blossom nose, deep blue eyes all framed by her dark, ebony hair.

"Mr. Zero?" the woman's voice was smooth, silky.
Not only her unexplained entrance took Jack, but also her poise matched to her beauty. She sat tall, her shoulders back, one foot in front of the other in a straight line, her appearance almost angelic.

"Where did you come from?" Jack's voice nearly cracked like a prepubescent boy.

"I have been watching you for some time," she smiled playfully.

Jack looked confused. He was sure there was no one in this room when he entered. He may not be the world's greatest detective, but he was sure he would notice a person sitting in this tiny office. He held back questioning her as of now. "Pretty neat trick, you must be some kind of magician, or a really good player at hide and seek."

"I don't play games," she replied.

"Neither do I," Jack matched her flirtatious manner. "But I'm sure you give a great chase."

"I have my moments," her crimson lips turned upward in a salacious grin.

"I'll bet you do," Jack returned an even more devilish grin.

"My name is Mrs. Evelyn Strommel."

'Mrs.? Damn.' The grin fell from Jack's face. He returned to his desk with his mug and slumped backward in his chair, a sense of defeat in his eyes. Although the name sounded familiar to Jack, "Strommel, huh?"

"Henrich."

"Huh?" Jack asked at the odd word she spewed.

"That's my husband. Dr. Heinrich Strommel."

The response threw Jack for a loop. The name Heinrich Strommel sounded familiar, but he couldn't remember exactly from where. Then it struck him like a ton of bricks. He remembered Strommel was the doctor who repaired his injured arm all those years ago. Jack remembered being a candidate for nanite infusion therapy, one of the early guinea pigs. Jack had endured nearly three months of daily physical therapy before even getting a consult with Strommel. He never met with Strommel while preparing for the surgery, but was certain he was the man who did the procedure. He couldn't complain much as his arm did work, despite a few tinges of pain that accompanied it. "Dr. Heinrich Strommel? How could I forget, his research fixed my arm, changed my life," Jack smiled as he rotated his shoulder. He figured for that, he could give her a listen, "What can I do for you, Mrs. Strommel?"

"I need your help," her voice became more expressive. Her movements were mesmerizing, her complexion, flawless. Her features were so striking to Jack that he couldn't take his eyes off her. She was, dare he say, perfect. Everything about her was the ideal description a man would give to describe the perfect woman. However, what was more striking about her than her features was her reason for being there.

Her beautifully breathy voice began, "He's missing."

"Missing?" He asked, more as a means of distracting his infatuation.

"For nearly two days now," she wrung her hands tensely, gripping and tightening her grasp of her shoulder bag straps. "He called me on Tuesday, he said he was working late, but he never came home. It's not like my husband to not come home."

Jack could understand why as his gaze drifted to the top of her blouse where the crescents of her ample breasts danced with each breath she took. She was absolutely stunning. Jack tried to focus. "Are you sure he's missing and not just, I don't know, out?"

"He is out somewhere, I just don't know where."

An odd response, Jack thought. "No, what I mean is, perhaps he went somewhere without telling you. Is there any place that he would normally go, a bar? Nightclub? Gentleman's club? Bowling alley?"

"No, none of those."

"Do you have suspicions that your husband was having--" Jack hesitated. He didn't want to say anything too offensive. He had a feeling she was a bit naïve. He sucked in his breath before releasing the remainder of his sentence, "--an affair?"

Evelyn's face contorted in disgust. "How dare you, Mr. Zero," her tone was appalled at his insinuation. "My husband is a kind and loyal man. He would never engage in such carnal activities when he is quite satisfied at home."

She was some woman. "Of course, I just want to be sure I cover any type of motive."

"Of course."

"What about enemies? Did your husband have any known enemies that may have wanted to hurt him out of revenge?"

"No," a growing look of concern crossed Evelyn's face. "No one I know of, like I said, my husband is a kind man, there is no logical reason anyone would want to kill him."

"What does your husband do now, Mrs. Strommel?"

"Please, call me Evelyn," she was more relaxed now.

Jack swallowed the last drops of coffee from his mug. He then stood and walked to the coffee pot to pour himself another cup, "Would you care for a cup of coffee, Mrs. Strommel?"

"Evelyn," she corrected.

"Right," Jack smiled. "Evelyn."

"No thank you," she replied with a smile. "To answer your question, my husband is currently the chief medical research analyst at a scientific research center called 'I-ZAN Research Institute and Application.'"

Jack raised an eyebrow. Her being married to a scientist didn't seem likely, unless maybe he had a lot of money. "You married a scientist, huh?" Jack snorted.

"You find that odd, Mr. Zero?"

"No, of course not," he tried to recover delicately. "Well, maybe, with you, yeah, I guess I do." So much for delicate.

"You think it strange that a woman like me would find an older egghead, like Heinrich, attractive?" Evelyn came on seductively, rising from her seat and slinking toward Jack elegantly. She walked with one foot in front of the other, as if floating above the ground, agile, much like a cat walking a high fence. '*She was incredible*,' Jack thought.

She leaned in closely to Jack, "Maybe I only married him for his money; after all he is one of the country's leading Nano physicist, and worth quite a bit of money. His research is sought the world over, even by our own government," Evelyn lips were close to Jack's; he could feel her breath warm his chin. She continued, "But let me ask you this, Mr. Zero. If my husband were gone, and I received his money, why would I need to come to you?"

"Perhaps you need me to find his body," Jack spoke nervously. "Most insurance providers won't disperse money without proof of death."

"Perhaps," she pulled away, stepping away from Jack's desk. "Or perhaps I want my husband returned to me safely."

"Why not go to the police?"

"You know better than I how the police function," she snorted. "They won't start a search until he's been missing for at least 72 hours. Besides, I need someone who can devote their complete attention and resources in finding my husband. And they will be compensated quite well."

Evelyn slipped her hand slowly inside her handbag and pulled out a small, thick padded manila envelope. She handed it across the desk to Jack. He immediately tore it open and dumped its contents on his desk. A tightly bound stack of money thumped as it struck the oak desktop. Jack picked it up and thumbed the wad, noting quickly with his eyes as to whether or not the bills were legitimate. They certainly were. One couldn't be too cautious. It was rare to see paper money these days. Most people paid with thumbprint transfers or magnetic readers. You were looking for discretion when you paid in cash. Jack wanted to squeal with delight, but held his cool as he set the bills back onto the desk. He calmly folded his hands while interlocking his fingers. He leaned forward, "Well then," he smiled boyishly. "What can you tell me about your husband?"

"Please, I don't wish to speak of this anymore here," Evelyn stood, her shoulders back, accentuating every curve of her perfect body. "I fear I can't trust anyone. You never know who may be listening."

A conspiracy nut to boot. Jack tried not to let out too loud of a laugh. "Where would you like to meet then?"

"Come by my house this evening," She handed Jack a slip of paper that contained her address. "I'll have my chef prepare a lovely dinner."

"Sure," Jack immediately replied. "Sounds great."

"Be there by six-o'clock," Evelyn winked as she slinked out of his office door, Jack couldn't help but feel a bit flustered and somewhat aroused. She was truly beautiful and alluring. He felt slightly guilty for accepting the invitation when deep in his mind he had ulterior motives. Jack's heart beat steadily in his chest, thumping rhythmically and not skipping until Jack snapped alert from the closing of his office door. Even though Evelyn had left, her sweet aroma hung lightly in the air.

CHAPTER 6
ENTER HELIX

Huun sat motionless for going on nearly four hours. His legs were crossed, his feet tucked under the upper thigh of the opposite leg. His hands rested, palm up, on his knees, his thumb and forefingers creating circles, as he breathed steadily. He was deeply entranced, not noticing the pacing that Crust was doing across the floor in front of him. Crust was upset, frustrated, and tired. He occasionally shot glances over at Huun, wondering how he could be so calm. Was he not concerned about the failure they experienced? Was he not concerned as to how their leader would react? Apparently not. Of course, it wasn't their leader whom was in charge of obtaining the item. It was him. He failed. It was his charge and failure was his responsibility and as any member of the HART was aware, their leader was not very forgiving.

There was a crack in the air as Huun's COMM device hummed to life, a blue beam shone up into the room. The beam fanned out to reveal the shape of a tall man wearing a cloak that covered his face.

"Forever Destiny," Huun said as he lowered his head respectfully.

"Forever Destiny," the cloaked figure responded. "Report?"

Huun raised his head, "We are ahead of schedule, sir. We have begun to implement the process for dispersal."

"Excellent," the cloaked figure hissed. "But I sense there is a problem?"

Huun nodded, "We arrived at the I-ZAN Institute as per the designated time set by Dr. Steinwick. However, when we entered to obtain the device…well…we lost Dr. Strommel."

The cloaked figure stood still and silent for a long moment. His silence was the only time Huun felt fear. He never wanted to upset the Master of the HART.

"Rest assured," Huun quickly added. "We are searching for him now."

"Does he have what Steinwick promised?"

"Yes."

"Good," the cloaked Master said. "Then I expect you and your men to double your efforts and acquire the device. The window is closing. If you have not located Strommel or the device by the time of the President's arrival, then your failure will be your execution."

Huun swallowed hard. Fear slowly crept up his stomach and into his throat. He was a large, powerful man, but even he recognized the higher power before him. "Y-yes, my Master."

"Forever Destiny," the cloaked man raised his hand above his head in salute.

Huun duplicated the salute, "I will not fail you. Forever Destiny."

The image of the cloak figure faded before him. Huun was left alone with his thoughts and fear. He would not fail again.

The bell chime that sound with the opening of the door had a nostalgic feel to the corner shops of long before. The difference is with this shop, the chime was to run a sweep of any customer upon entering, a laser scan immediately sent a detailed report of the person's criminal history, an unusual practice even in today's paranoid times, but Jack knew Helix was an unusual person.

"Well, well, well, Jack Zero." Helix, his face hidden behind a welding mask, but his thick, burly beard visible along each side, lifted it up to greet his visitor. He ran a very tight business; there was nothing that happened in his self-contained world that he didn't know everything about. He didn't even need to look up from the pile of exposed circuitry that was spread out before him to which he devoted his undivided attention. "What, pray tell, has rolled you into my place?"

Jack watched as sparks sprayed from the soldering torch Helix poised strategically over one of the boards. Helix was a young man in his later twenties, smart beyond any realm Jack knew. Helix had attended the Massachusetts Institute of Technology, earning a Master's Degree in both robotics and Bioengineering. He was on a promising fast track to a high profile career with a government contract in the Psi-Optics Research and Development division before he developed his acute paranoia. It was during his time working for the government that Helix began to think that they were tracking every person through their nanotech implants. He had tried to sabotage one of their production plants that got him arrested and brought up on charges of treason. During his arraignment, Helix opted to represent himself and somehow convinced a jury that he was justified in his actions. He was acquitted and released, but still lives in fear of being under constant surveillance. After years of running, he shook his fear of being followed and watched, ultimately settling in New Utica. Helix was the best electronics seller and repair, but Jack knew his underground dealings in black market electronics and new technologies. No one knew more about machines than Helix. He wore his clothing loose and dark, his explanation was that it muted the frequencies "they" bombarded us with regularly. His hair was black, messy, and unkempt and was a striking contrast to his pale white skin. Jack flinched at each shriek of sparks that flowered.

"I'm sorry to say it's not a social call," Jack chided.

"When is it ever?" Helix responded. "What do you need from me?"

Jack stepped forward, "Well, I—"

"WAIT!" Helix quickly looked up at Jack through his soldering lenses, which were dark, polarized circles that were embedded in a frame that wrapped around his head. "Don't bring your poison in here, you know the drill."

Helix pointed his finger to a large metallic device that hung from the ceiling just inside the breezeway. There was an arm that came from a central pivot and bent down with a series of red lights lining the inside. Jack rolled his eyes and let out an exasperated sigh as he stood under the arm. Helix picked up a large remote and clicked a button that immediately charged the machine. It whined slowly until it thrummed regularly, charging. The arm then began to swing in full circles around Jack, the red bulbs emitting low-level beams that ran across Jack's body. Within a few seconds, the machine slowed and the lights dimmed. Once the machine stopped, Jack stepped past its reach.

Helix looked at a portable screen attached to the remote, studied it briefly and set it down to the side, "You're clean."

"I showered especially for you," Jack continued joking, knowing how it annoyed Helix.

"It's not checking your hygiene, moron, it's checking your Nano-enhancement transmissions and receptions," Helix responded immaturely. "I don't want your tainted cooties coming into my place, bouncing signals every which way, causing problems." Jack snorted loudly. He was amazed that at the size of Helix's intelligence, he had a low level of social interactivity. It was as if he had the intelligence of Einstein and the maturity of a prepubescent boy.

"Yeah, I get it. Too bad it can't detect that stick in your ass."

Helix took off his goggles and cocked his head as he stood, "Did you come for a reason or to annoy me? If it's the latter you know where the door is."

"Alright, alright, relax will ya'. You think with all your smarts, someone would've programmed you a sense of humor," Jack pulled the COMM device he took from NULE Headquarters out of his coat pocket. He held it out to Helix, "I need you to crack this."

Helix snatched the device from Jack's hand. He looked at it closely, analyzing its casing and then weighted it carefully in his palm, "This isn't a commercial grade COMM device."

He unclasped the outer shell that was being used as a disguise to make it look more commercial. He looked at the device contained underneath; it had a much thicker metal casing. He noticed the dark blue insignia along the underside. He felt a wave of heat flash across his face, "Is this what I think it is?"

"Yep," Jack confirmed. "The mark of the HART."

Helix felt his throat close, fear gripped him suddenly, "H-how did you get this?" Helix continuously flipped the device repeatedly in his hands. He was half-curious to study the device and half paranoid as to what the device may contain.

"I found it, thought maybe you could tell me what was on it."

"Not likely. This is heavily fortified, state of the art high-impact casing. This is heavy duty security attached," Helix grabbed a nearby screwdriver and stabbed it into the screw in the upper left corner. He yelped as a small surge of electricity shot up the screwdriver and into his arm. "Just as I thought, built in tamper-resistant guard. I'm willing to bet there's a serious encryption used to prevent hacking the memory databanks." Helix looked up at Jack, "This isn't going to be easy."

Jack scowled mockingly, "When has that ever stopped the great Helix before? Are you telling me you're backing down from a challenge?"

Helix looked back at the device for a long moment, as if disassembling it mentally. He then pulled a pair of insulated gloves from under his counter. He slid them over his hands and snapped them tight, "I'm going to need some time with this."

"You've got as much time as you need."

"Don't over extend me; I may never get through this."

"I have the utmost confidence in your hacking abilities. Remember the time you hacked the NULE headquarters security system?"

"How could I forget, you arrested me for it," Helix smirked.

"And I also got you lose, don't forget that."

"How can I when you constantly remind me."

"I'll get you a nice retainer for your services."

Helix scoffed, "Just like last time, huh?"

"Oh c'mon, those tickets to the Blue Sox were completely jake," Jack winked. "Box seats."

"Tickets don't pay the bills, besides, I hate baseball."

Jack pushed the door open, "Cash, got it."

Jack slipped through the door as Helix called behind him, "UNMARKED!"

CHAPTER 7
THE STROMMEL ESTATE

The Strommel mansion was massive; it reached high into the cloudy sky in the outskirts of the city. The property opened from a large iron gate to a rolling, well-manicured front yard with a string of trees that lined both sides of the lengthy driveway. The cobblestone driveway stretched for nearly a quarter of a mile before it reached the large, redbrick structure of the main house. The pointed spires surrounding the roof seemed to scratch the clouds that drifted overhead. The front steps were twenty high under a covered archway that lead to two immense, solid oak doors. Jack ran his hands along his wrinkled clothes. Suddenly, the attire that was adequate any other day felt dirty and wrong. Jack was breathless as he craned his neck to look up at the doors. It was quite an intimidating sight. Jack almost felt like a vagrant, not comfortable with the idea of being a guest inside. He shook the feeling and quickly ran up the steps to ring the bell.

The bell was loud, echoing like a church bell as it chimed his arrival. He waited for a long moment, looking around at the surrounding property, noting how it was so well secluded from the noise of the city. The rich sure knew how to live. The lock of the door clicked behind him. Jack spun around on his heel. As the hinges creaked open from the weight of the doors, Jack expected to come face-to-face with a housekeeper, but instead was greeted by the warm, lovely face of Evelyn Strommel.

"Good evening, Mr. Zero." She said, her voice smooth and silky. "I'm so glad you made it."

"Certainly," Jack smiled in return. "Anything for a client."

Evelyn stepped aside and gestured for Jack to enter, "Won't you come in?" Jack walked through the doorway, past Evelyn; her sweet scent filled his nostrils with her intoxicating fragrance. She looked incredible, flawless. He watched her raven hair flow magnificently across her shoulders as she pushed the heavy doors closed. This was going to be quite a challenge, trying to restrain his libido. She was a client. She was married. He couldn't see her as anything more. Could he?

She strode past him, her head high, her poise magnificent. She threw a look over her shoulder to Jack, "Please follow me."

Jack didn't need to be asked twice, he immediately followed, like an eager puppy, which he soon slowed down as he felt he was appearing over eager. He followed Evelyn down a long hallway with an enormous vaulted, arched ceiling. Every five feet there was a thick carved wooden beam with elaborate markings that ran from the floor to the apex of the ceiling on both sides. Several large paintings with gold carved frames aligned on either side of the passageway. Each was a similar style of older men standing regally next to their wives. He read the nameplates at the base of each frame as he walked past. 'Fagan Strommel,' 'Ustys Strommel,' 'Fagan Strommel II,' 'Ustys Strommel II,' 'Ustys Strommel III.' Geniuses all, except when naming their children. At the end of the line of same names came a unique name for the group, 'Dr. Heinrich Strommel.' Jack stopped to look at the painting of Dr. Strommel, a stout, balding man with his hands grasping his lapel. Jack instantly recognized the face of the man who repaired his arm. He had the same features as all the other paintings, except he was young, probably in his twenties. He was painted with his wife, Evelyn, who looked exactly as she did before him. '*She certainly aged well*,' he thought.

"This is your husband?" Jack asked Evelyn.

"Yes," Evelyn replied, slinking beside Jack.

"How come you're not in there with him like all the others?" Jack inquired.

"This was painted right after we were married," she replied matter-of-factly.

Jack looked her up and down, "He doesn't seem like your type."

"You know what they say, love is blind," she smiled.

"Blind, or wealthy?" Jack challenged.

"I know what many people think of me, Mr. Zero," Evelyn took a defensive stance, folding her arms confidently. "A gold digger, money hungry, I've heard them all. But attraction is not always based on physical traits. Sometimes it's cerebral."

"I'm sorry, I wasn't insinuating—"

"I understand, it's your nature to be curious," she dropped her arms and stepped closer to Jack.

"I like to know everything about my clients," Jack swallowed nervously. He could feel the heat from her skin as she drew closer.

"Everything?" She whispered.

"E-Everything," he stammered.

"I respect that," Evelyn moved past Jack, her eyes locked on his. She sauntered past him, her ruby lips spread in a playful grin.

'*This was definitely a challenge*,' Jack thought. He followed Evelyn into the room that lay at the end of the hall. It was a large, open room with another high vaulted ceiling. The only furniture in the long room was a matching length cherry wood dining table complimented with surrounding chairs, sixteen in total. On the table was a spread of several platters filled with food including finger sandwiches, fruit, cookies, and tea. It looked and smelled appetizing, making Jack realize how famished he really was. Evelyn sat at the chair on the far end of the table from the door. Jack walked around the table, slowing, not quite sure what to do. He wasn't used to such extravagant, and luxurious, décor.

"Uh...where, um, should I--" Jack said uncomfortably.

"Right next to me is quite fine," Evelyn smiled, patting the empty chair to her left.

Jack hesitantly pulled the chair back and sat down.

"I had my staff make up a little lunch, I hope you're hungry."

He was. "This is quite an impressive spread," Jack was complimentary. "But what I need from you is fairly simple and we could've handled it back at my office."

"I told you, I don't trust anyplace else. Besides, that's not very hospitable on my part," Evelyn's comment seemed a bit off-putting. "This is much more comfortable, yes?"

"Sure," Jack lied. "This house is great, but it's a bit quiet. I'm surprised you don't mind staying here all alone."

"Normally there are many people bustling around the house, but I decided to give my staff the afternoon off, everything has been out of control since my husband disappeared. I have been feeling overwhelmed and was needing some peace of mind."

Jack cocked an eyebrow, "First let me ask, why me?"

"I don't understand."

"Why come to me, a private investigator, when you could go to the police?"

"I already told you, the police are useless," she said bitterly.

"I don't buy it," Jack said skeptically. "The only people who use a P.I. are those that don't want their business known."

Evelyn hesitated, her eyes lowered, as if debating that now was the time to tell the truth or continue a lie, an expression Jack was all too familiar seeing. "I contacted them initially when he first didn't come home, but they said he needed to be gone for at least 72 hours, even then they told me he was probably just out and forgot to tell me. But I know my husband; he always calls when he leaves work. He always lets me know where he is going and what he is doing. I know something is wrong, time is short and I can't wait much longer. I heard from a girlfriend of mine that she contacted a P.I. when the police were little help. I saw your ad in the COMM listings and called your assistant."

"I just want to be sure we're all jake here. Although, I'm fairly certain the police are looking into your husband's disappearance," Jack reassured.

"I'm not looking for fairly, Mr. Zero. I need results. Can you deliver results?"

"I'll devote my time to solving your case."

"You don't know how good that is to hear. My husband has been missing for nearly five days now. I fear for his life and feel time is of the essence."

Jack sat back; she was truly concerned, he noted. "You said you didn't think he had any enemies, why all of a sudden are you concerned for his life?"

"Perhaps I haven't been entirely truthful with you, Mr. Zero," she admitted.

"Please, call me Jack." Jack wanted to sound reassuring; he wanted her to trust him. "Why don't you tell me about those concerns in a bit, first, let's start at the beginning, where was your husband when you last saw him?"

Evelyn placed her face in her hands before taking in a deep breath, "It was here, just before he left for work at the I-Zan Research Institute. We had breakfast, waffles, his favorite. He finished his meal and then kissed me goodbye as he always does, told me he loved me, and then he left."

"And that's all?"

"I remember he said to me before he left that he was going to work late, so when he wasn't home by midnight or two in the morning, I thought nothing of it. Even by six o'clock, I was not surprised he hadn't come home yet. It wasn't the first time he was gone all night, but it was when it reached dinner time the next evening and he hadn't called," Evelyn choked back tears. "So, I called his office, no answer. I called his personal COMM device. Nothing. That's when I grew concerned. He never missed a contact session with me. I called Janus, hoping he would know where Heinrich was, but he said he hadn't seen him since he left for the day the night before. It was as I feared."

Jack interrupted, "Who's Janus?"

"Janus Steinwick is Heinrich's partner. They had been developing a new device together, revolutionary he boasted about it."

"What type of device was it?" Jack asked.

Evelyn continued, "It's technical, I'm not too sure. I believe he said it was some kind of a transportation device. It was supposed to revolutionize how we moved. Some sort of transmodifier, or whatever. Heinrich said it allowed matter to be moved from one part of the world to another instantaneously by creating a, what did he call it…wormhole?"

Jack thought about what she had been telling him. "What can you tell me about this…Janus?"

Evelyn squirmed in her chair a bit. She grabbed the teapot on the table between them. She offered some to Jack who smiled with a nod, accepting the hot drink. Evelyn spoke as she poured both their cups, "Janus is also Heinrich's best friend. He trusts him completely."

Evelyn dropped a teabag in each cup and slid one over to Jack. Jack slid his finger through the handle and pulled the cup closer. He bobbed the bag in his cup, the water turning brown, "You don't sound as if you trust him."

"Well, it's hard to trust someone who betrays your husband," Evelyn's eyes narrowed as she spoke. She then picked up the creamer and offered some to Jack.

Jack shook his head as he prodded further, "Betrayed?"

"Yes, this was not the first project Heinrich worked on with Janus. A few years back they had developed a means of manipulating atomic energy, but eliminating the effects of nuclear fallout. An impressive feat. He had hoped to channel the technology for a cleaner source of energy for fueling electricity or even vehicle propulsion. However, Janus took the technology and sold it to the government much to Heinrich's protests.

"You mean like hover conversion?" Jack inquired.

"No, more like mass transportation."

"So like large airships?"

"Again, no. I'm talking more along the lines of instantaneous travel. Let me ask you, Detective Zero, have you ever heard of trans-dimensional displacement?"

Jack shook his head.

"I'm not surprised," Evelyn smirked. "Imagine being able to instantaneously moving from one side of the Earth to another. Live in Los Angeles and want breakfast in Paris. You could be there in the blink of an eye, thanks to my husband's invention."

"That sounds incredible. No wonder so many people are after it."

"It destroyed my husband, threw him into a deep depression to a point where he had nearly given up on everything," she paused. "Even life."

"He tried to kill himself?"

Evelyn laughed loudly, it echoed across the large room, resonating with a metallic tinge. It sent chills down Jack's spine, "Of course not," she replied. Jack was relieved at the response fearing it could have been more disturbing. "Heinrich felt mankind was untrustworthy. He spent much of his time in his home office, tinkering and developing. Before you knew it he developed a solution to the human problem, an artificial intelligence inside a microcomputer that when combined with similar machines could create sensibility and reasoning."

Jack let out a snort, "Yeah right, rational machines. How'd that work out for him?"

Evelyn's expression grew cold as she stared hard at Jack, "Actually, very well. My husband's genius is never appreciated. He developed some of the most incredible creations this world has ever seen."

"I'm sorry, I didn't mean to--"

"I'm sorry, Mr. Zero," Evelyn composed herself. "Sometimes I get defensive when my husband's integrity is of question."

"Look, I'll do everything I can to find your husband," Jack placed his hand reassuringly over hers. She reciprocated with her other hand before she broke down and cried, she released her hands and buried her face in them. She wept softly. Jack hesitated before he put his hand on her shoulder, comforting her.

"Please, Jack," Evelyn looked up, her eyes wet, black mascara streaking her soft, warm cheeks. "Please find my husband."

CHAPTER 8
SCENE OF THE CRIME

The thickening clouds blanketed the moonlight making the night dark as the lights surrounding I-ZAN Research Institute were all turned off giving the appearance of a heavy black shroud covering the entire landscape. Jack crept cautiously toward the front of the building. The door had been kicked in and the glass shattered, cluttering the foyer floor. Yellow beams crisscrossed in front of the doorway, while black, bold letters reading 'Police Line: Do Not Cross' scrolled across each beam. This was both a warning and a deterrent. Unfortunately, it worked; if anything crossed the path of the beam, it would send an alarm to the local precinct, alerting them of a potential intruder, resulting in a series of squad rovers and LEHVs that would descend in a matter of minutes. Fortunately, Jack was aware of this and knew the tricks and techniques to bypass the security. It was quite simple actually, a flaw in the design of the light beam used to detect movement in breaking the signal across. Most people try a mirror, but law enforcement was prepared for that, the mirror simply reflects, those savvy enough know you need to refract the light signal. Jack reached into his trench coat pocket and pulled out a small round lollipop. He peeled off the cellophane wrapper popped it into his mouth, rolling the stick in his fingers for a moment. He then pulled the sucker free and slowly moved it into the range of the directional beam blocking a wide berth. The moistened lollipop bent the beam upward, arcing it high, near the doorway's upper arch. The beams arc was high enough for Jack to slip under and through into the darkness of the building's foyer. Once he had made it all the way through he pulled the lollipop from the beams path and watched the light bounce back into shape, not obstructing its simple programmed task. He smiled to himself as he popped the sucker back into his mouth. However, something wasn't right. He began to heave and choke repeatedly. His gags echoed throughout the dark and empty building. He pulled the lollipop free of his mouth and looked at it sourly. The drawback of using the lollipop was that the beam absorbed the sweet flavor, leaving it tasting burnt and salty.

He discarded the flavorless treat into the nearby wastebasket and made his way through the labyrinth-like hallways that made up the office and facilities. His shoes echoed as they clicked against the tiled floor. He didn't take the precaution of muffling his footsteps and watching where he was going, he knew that the building was sectioned off and closed until further notice of the New Utica Law Enforcement. He was walking somewhat aimlessly. He wasn't sure where he was going or what he was looking for. All he had to go on was what Evelyn told him, that the last time she had spoken to her husband was five days ago and that he would be "working late." This wasn't the first time a man may have lied to his wife, he worked those types of cases all the time; they paid the bills, quickly. However, some of the details in Evelyn's description of the type of work Dr. Strommel did made Jack think he didn't have the time to pursue a carnal appetite. Coming to his place of work was as good a start as any, not to mention again it was the only lead he had.

The hallway before him was creepy and gave Jack an eerie feeling as he slowed his pace. He produced a small palm light from his effects kit that he carried in a small messenger's bag he wore across his shoulder to his hip. It was the most convenient way to carry the items he needed, plus having them slung on your side made them more accessible. Jack crept slowly along the wall, peering into each room he passed, looking for any sign of evidence. As he worked his way deeper into the building he came to a set of double glass doors, they marked the entrance to the research area. He approached the door slowly. Since the power was off, the automatic doors were not functioning. He gripped the handle and pulled, but the door didn't respond. He tried to push, but nothing happened. Even though the electricity was off, the digital locks still held. *'That means the auxiliary power is still running,'* Jack surmised to himself. Unfortunately, Jack didn't have any special tricks to get past this.

He quickly scanned his surroundings. His eyes latched onto a small ventilation grate that undoubtedly concealed a crawlspace. Jack scraped his hand deep into his messenger bag and pulled out a small finger length metal wand. He slid his thumb along the shaft of the wand, which activated a thin layer of metal that transformed into the shape of a flat-headed screwdriver. He inserted the head into the screw slot, slid his thumb again, and the screw twisted and fell to the floor. He repeated the steps until he finished each screw, making sure to collect them as they fell free. Once the screws were all removed, he slid his fingers along the seam of the grate and the wall it was pressed against. It took some coaxing, but he managed to loosen the grate and pull it free. He set it off to the side, grabbed his palm light, and clicked it on. He shone the beam into the ventilation shaft. It was clean, looking brand new as if it had been installed yesterday. Jack wasn't shy of getting dirty, but this certainly made the idea of stuffing oneself into a narrow passageway more appealing. Jack squeezed into the vent and shimmied himself along using his elbows and toes. He inched along slowly, keeping the light on, now clamped firmly between his teeth. It wasn't long before he made it to another vent, looking into the room on the opposite side. He pushed the grate that sealed him from within, but it didn't budge; obviously secured in the same way as the other grate had been. It posed a slight dilemma to which Jack relied on his own ingenuity and bag of tricks. He painstakingly slid his hand down to his side and fumbled through his bag until his fingers touched a cylinder that had a very distinct pattern along its grip. He managed to bring the device up to his face and into the light that still held within his mouth. The device was a bronze cylindrical object with a black rubber grip. The grip had several raised designs that encircled the body of the device. The rubber not only helped keep the object firmly within ones grasp, but it also acted as a ground. The tip of the device rose up into a soft point. Within the point was a small, hollow opening with a clear, dome protruding slightly above the opening. Jack wrapped his hand firmly around the grip, his thumb reached up and rested on a small red activator plate. He aimed the tip of the device at the lower right hand corner of the grate and pressed the plate. A narrow red beam emitted from the opening and reached the grate. Jack held it steady, concentrating it on the spot until the metal of the grate began to glow red. Within moments, the metal burst into a white-hot flame and melted. Jack continued to move the beam along the edge of the grate until there was enough give for him to push open the grate. The metal was still quite hot. He wrapped his hand in his sleeve as he pushed the grate free of the wall. He then slid out of the vent and entered the room.

The research lab was devastated. Overturned tables, shattered glass scattered across the floor, bullet holes dotting the sterile, white wall. Jack walked carefully around the debris, trying not to disturb anything, a basic law enforcement trait. There was a conveyer belt in the center of the room, which seemed a bit odd as it didn't seem to go anywhere or serve a purpose of any kind. There was an excessive amount of orange-colored hair strewn across the room, leaving a thin layer on many of the computer controls and the conveyer belt. He plucked a few strands and stuck them in a clear plastic bag. He was curious as to whom, or what, the hair belonged. There was undoubtedly a struggle, but the outcome was unclear. He walked to the bullet holes that ran along the length of the wall, trailing in a downward pattern. He looked at them closely, tracing them with a pencil he removed from his bag; he ran the tip of the pencil along the holes, judging their size and width. He'd seen marks from weapons like this before, definitely a heavy assault rifle, perhaps an AK-52 or 55, much like its long out-of-production predecessor, the AK-47, it was a rapid-fire weapon. Despite laws, anyone could get one of these easily, but whoever was wielding this rifle held it with confidence and fired each shot with precision. A professional. Most likely military. Jack had seen enough militaristic gunplay to feel confident in his surmise. There was no trace of blood along the wall or floor, which was a good sign. That meant the intended victim was able to avoid the deadly fire.

Jack followed the trail of holes. They lead to an open doorway into a room filled with tables. At first glance, the room seemed only to have been involved in a minor skirmish. It wasn't until Jack looked to the back of the room that the real damage became visible. Jack gasped as he saw what was left of the room. The back wall appeared as if it had been ripped from its joints, tables were sliced at rounded angles, and the floor seemed to have been scooped out of the ground. It was an awesome and shocking sight all at once, like nothing Jack had ever seen before. How could this have happened? What could have caused such inexplicable damage? Jack couldn't wrap his mind around this.

"Pretty impressive, huh?" A familiar voice sounded from behind Jack.

He spun around on his heel quickly; his hand instinctively flipped back the tail of his coat and gripped the handle of his revolver, ready to draw. To his own surprise, he was face-to-face with Agent Frisco, who looked stunning in the low light even more than he remembered.

"Agent Frisco," Jack released a tense grip from his revolver, then drew his coat closed. "What a pleasant surprise."

"Can it, Zero," Frisco chided, her tone layered with frustration and annoyance. "You were instructed to stay away from this case further."

"What are you talking about? I am staying away from that case," Jack smirked. "This is a brand new case."

"Yeah, I know. We spoke with Mrs. Strommel a couple of hours ago for questioning, and she kindly stated that she no longer needed our help, explaining that she hired outside help. Oddly enough, a P.I.," Frisco walked slowly around Jack, circling him like a predator circles its prey. "Naturally, I thought of you."

"I'm flattered."

"Don't be," Frisco deflated Jack's ego. "I knew you would stop here first, you know why?"

"Because I'm smart?"

"Because you're predictable. I know how you think and what you will do."

"So?"

"So, I'm here to give you a friendly warning; stay off this case. If the senator catches you following this case, he'll prosecute you and your former superior won't stop him."

"You really know how to charm a guy."

Frisco took on a more serious tone than before, "This is no joke, the HART is an extremely dangerous organization. They may not seem so on the surface, but there is something much more sinister about what they are doing. Senator Glorm is not taking any chances at letting the HART get away. He won't let anything, or anyone, stand in his way."

"Well, he doesn't have to get all worked up about me," Jack snorted. "I'll be sure to keep my distance."

Jack began to walk away; Frisco could see she wasn't reaching him on any level. She inhaled deeply and quickly exhaled a lungful of air. "Jack," she implored.

Jack stopped. She called him 'Jack.' She hadn't done that before. He was beginning to get to her. He liked that. She continued, "I know we didn't get off on the right foot, but despite what you may think, I don't want to see you get hurt."

"Why Agent Frisco, is that concern I hear in your voice?"

"This isn't a joke, Zero," Frisco grew angry. "When things begin to conspire, and you're in the crossfire, I can't help you anymore. I'm warning you now, please step back from this."

"I'll take that into consideration," Jack stepped in closer to Frisco; close enough to feel her breath on his chin. "Now if you'll excuse me, I have work to do." Jack turned away and walked into the darkness of the room, toward the gaping hole that stared into the emptiness of the world around.

Frisco made her way for the door, looking back one last time at Jack on the other side of the room. The weight between them was heavy, the air thick. She spoke quietly before she left, "I hope when next we meet Zero, it's on the same side."

Jack didn't respond. He stood motionless, waiting for Frisco to leave. When he finally knew she was gone, he lowered his head remorsefully. He didn't wish to be cold, but he couldn't afford to be weak. If there was one thing he took away from his military experience, it was never show your weakness. Zimm's training, he fought so hard to please him, now he tried hard to forget it, but you can't forget something that becomes so ingrained in your brain, your life. He shook the thoughts from his head. He didn't come to dwell in the past, he had work to do.

Jack immediately began to search for any sign of Strommel's most recent presence. He started from the mysterious hole that consumed the room. He walked slowly around the deep concave that was once the floor. He tapped his foot along the edge, attempting to determine if it was safe. When he felt comfortable with its structure, he stepped inside. He felt the edge of the hole. It was smooth at the base, but tapered upward into a series of grooves that looked like sand on a beach that had conformed to the constant rhythm of the waves. With careful study, he could tell the concrete floor had been eroded by an extreme amount of heat. What could have possibly caused such damage?

Jack continued looking around the room from the vantage point in the center of the hole. It was then that Jack noticed an out of place item on the floor just out of reach. The unusual item he came across was rumpled under one of the overturned tables in the room. He climbed from the hole and, using a pencil, scooped the item from the floor. He held it up to his eyes, studying the object. It was a sock.

"A sock?" Jack asked himself. "What is one sock doing here?"

It was a man's sock, and it didn't rule out that Strommel was having an affair. In fact, this made him think it was even more a possibility, had it not been for the damage to the room. Jack bagged the sock and moved from this room to another smaller, adjacent room.

As he stepped through the door, he noticed it was an office. Like his own, cluttered with many items. The difference is that this room looked as if the clutter was more organized. There was a beautiful cherry wood desk against one wall. Two of the walls were overtaken by bookcases that each ran from floor to ceiling. There was no space on any of the shelves. The wall next to the desk was a large, picture window framed by luscious, thick curtains. Around the side edges of the window were several framed pictures and certificates of achievements.

Jack looked at the framed images on the wall. Several were of Strommel and his wife; vacationing on the French Riviera, sailing on the ocean in a yacht, and dressed to the nines for what appeared to be a fund raiser. Each image they were smiling brightly.

'They must really be in love,' Jack thought. He looked across the wall at the other images. There was another of their wedding day; Strommel was thinner with a thicker head of dark hair. His wife still looked as beautiful then as she did now; her hair still long, full and raven-black, her skin smooth and soft, not a wrinkle in sight. Incredible how some peoples genes were.

Jack made his way to the filing cabinet that was stuffed in the far corner of the office; it was four drawers high with a lock at the top corner that secured everything inside. Jack reached into his messenger's bag, pulled out a small leather case that, when rolled open, revealed a small tool set, each piece was a different length and width, and nestled in their own pouch. He sized up the opening of the lock, ran his fingers across each tool until he found what appeared to be the right size. He slid it from its pouch and quickly loosened the lock, popping the drawer open. He pulled the drawer's handle toward himself and it rolled open freely.

"Jake," Jack whispered to himself as he began thumbing through the label tabs. They each read like a chapter from a bizarre science-fiction novel, 'Robotics,' 'Anthropocentric Development,' 'Wormhole Teleportation.' Each drawer seemed to house a particular theme of projects. It was in the third drawer that Jack came across the medical theories and research. The one marked 'Nanotechnology' caught his attention. He pulled out the folder that was stuffed with papers and brought it over to the desk, trying to find a clear space. He moved aside some loose, unfilled forms and hand-written notes. Jack rifled through the stack of papers. Despite being such a large amount of information, it was only filled with useless data. It was strange, what was apparently clear was that this Dr. Strommel was one of the most brilliant minds in the world; a child prodigy, graduating high school at fourteen, attending Harvard and graduating by seventeen with a medical degree, taking a residency at eighteen where he began to explore ways to assist patients in repairing damaged tissue. He was then given an enormous grant that aided his research from the government, opening his access to technology and his research with nanotechnology.

An incredible life, one only lived by someone with incredible gifts and drive like Strommel. Jack thumbed over another large stack of orange folders. Each was labeled with the word "Patient" accompanied by a letter and number combination. As he waded through the list:

Patient 3F12
Patient 15D
Patient 677S

The list read on and on. It stated strange terms, such as *Rational Machines*. '*What the hell was a Rational Machine?*' He thought. However, Jack stopped at the sight of a familiar name: *RATIONAL MACHINE: EXPERIMENT ONE*. His heart dropped, falling from his chest and into his stomach. Before him were two words that he never thought he would see together: Experiment One. Jack didn't realize he had been holding his breath. He shook his head snapping himself back to reality. He was still sitting at the desk in Strommel's office, the lighting surrounding him was dim. Darkness not only surrounded him physically, but now surrounded him mentally. His brain was struck with memories that stirred him, haunted him and regenerated thoughts he'd just soon forget.

He ran his hand across the outside of the folder's jacket, his fingertips feeling the smooth coating that embossed the exterior. He couldn't believe what he was looking at. Strommel, the same physician that had experimented on him, still kept his records on file. Jack had always wondered what had happened, what exactly they had done to him when

71

they were simply 'repairing his arm.' Things were never the same since. Knowing that within this folder contained secrets about the next level of experimentation, a fully automated and rational robotic technology. He moved his fingers to the edge of the folder, burrowing them under the cover and running it down slowly. He hesitated. Should he open it? What secrets could it hold? Was it wise to dredge up the past? On the other hand, it could help solve the reason for Strommel's disappearance. As Jack's finger began to lift the cover up, a sound startled him, he dropped the flap. He looked out into the hallway through the open glass office where a shadow grew ominously across the wall. Perhaps Frisco was still here. '*But if it isn't--,*' Jack moved his hand and unfastened his revolver from its holster. He pulled it up slowly, preparing for anything. He watched the shadow intently as it grew larger. Whoever, or whatever, it was, was coming up fast. Jack brought his revolver up to his chest, pointing it in the direction of the door. As if alerted to him, the shadow stopped and quickly withdrew, merging with the darkness from where it came.

'*Never a good sign,*' Jack thought. Jack slowly rose from the chair and edged himself against the wall. He slinked slowly around the doorway and into the hallway. If the shadow disappeared because it knew he was here, then there was no point in being subtle. He still didn't want to be an obvious target. He could hear voices in the distance, muffled but audible. Jack moved closer toward the sounds.

"Hurry, make it quick," a booming voice said.

Another voice cut in, "Did you finish your sweep?"

"Yes," a meeker voice replied.

The booming voice returned, "Sweep again."

"What?"

"Sweep again," The booming voice growled more deeply, menacingly.

"Why?"

"Are you questioning me?"

"N-no," the meek voice stammered nervously.

"Then. Sweep. Again."

Jack could hear the man leave what he assumed were his superiors. The footsteps grew louder as they quickened in pace. In fact, they sounded like they were coming closer to him. Jack suddenly felt panic overwhelm him, he had to move and hide fast. Jack turned and ran back toward the office, but he couldn't hide in there. The room was too open and obvious. He needed something better, more secluded. Unfortunately, the office was at the end of the hallway. There was no place to go but back.

The meek-voiced soldier, named Klotz, walked up the dimly lit hallway. He pulled out a cigarette and slid it between his lips. He lit it with an outdated lighter, flicking open the metal lid and striking the flint to ignite the flame, the only true way to enjoy a well-crafted, flavorful smoke. Since strict laws had been put into place to ban traditional smoking using tobacco, synthetics were the only means of enjoying a smoke. '*Fortunately,*' Klotz smiled to himself. '*The High Master had connections in Southeast Asia, where they still manufactured the real deal.*' He inhaled a lungful of smoke, his body tingling from the nicotine. It was true bliss. He felt sorry for the rest of the world that had to endure the synthetics. Klotz walked up the hallway further, past the glass-encased office. He peeked his head inside and looked around slowly. It was quiet. He walked in and made his way to the window on the far side. With his finger and thumb, he separated the venetian blinds and peered outside. The view was impressive. The entire cityscape of New Utica was breathtaking. The night had set in and the lights burned the sky, leaving a sharp glowing orb curved above the buildings. The twinkling lights marked a prime target ready for the taking. The HART was nearly ready to unleash their master plan. It was about time too, Klotz thought. After years of planning, it was near perfect only a few obstacles left to eliminate and their leader could ascend and take his place where he belonged.

Klotz took another drag as he stepped backward and sat on the edge of the desk. He rested the cigarette between his lips as he looked down at the contents of the desk. Strewn across were several folders all labeled with strange letter/number combinations. Klotz picked one up and held it open. He flipped through the papers inside. They all contained scribbles and what appeared to be recommendations of some kind. Klotz couldn't make sense of any of it, it was gibberish. He threw the folder back on the table. It slid across the other folders and over the edge of the desk, spewing papers behind. Klotz walked around to see the mess that he created. He blew out a puff of smoke before he bent over to pick it up, not instantly noticing a man tucked uncomfortably under the desk. Jack held his breath, holding still, trying not to make a sound. He could swear the pounding of his heart, that filled his ears, could be heard in the room as well. He watched as the man that had been loitering in the room leaned down, his arm and shoulder in view. The glow of his cigarette lighting up Jack's face. He was about to be given away.

Jack gripped his revolver tightly, drawing it up higher, preparing for the worst. If he had to fire, he could eliminate this guy, but maybe not all the men that lurked in the front of the building. Jack prepared and took aim.

"What the hell are you doing?" Jack recognized the voice from the front room speaking to the man with the booming voice.

Klotz looked up surprised, "Oh, uh, nothing, Sgt. Lyntz." Klotz stood and saluted. The cigarette dangled from his lower lip before falling to the floor. Still lit, it bounced once and then rolled under the desk, under

Jack's shoes and resting on the loose papers that fell from the desk.

"Did you finish your sweep?" Lyntz asked again.

"Just finishing up now," Klotz made his way to the doorway.

The paper that covered the cigarette smoldered, smoke began to billow, slowly rising up from behind the desk. Lyntz reviewed Klotz intently, pressing his superiority, "You are walking a thin line, Klotz. The Colonel is not the kind of man you want to make angry."

"No sir," Klotz responded heavy-heartedly.

"Return to your duties and we'll forget about your disrespect."

Klotz nodded eagerly as he walked past Lyntz.

Jack felt his chest loosen, relieved by his stroke of luck. He lowered his revolver, his eyes following. They fell to the floor where they caught the sight of a piece of paper that was slowly disappearing, being devoured by a red-orange cinder. Jack's eyes grew large at the sight of the smoldering sheet. He reached over to grab it before it burst into flame.

WOOSH!

Too late.

As Lyntz exited the office to follow Klotz a sound and smell alerted his senses. Lyntz turned to look beyond the sole desk at the end of the room where a small flickering glow danced against the wall. Lyntz reached into his pinstriped jacket and drew his pistol.

"Klotz!" Lyntz called behind.

Klotz saw the ember light and ran back into the office, "Sir, allow me, I'll handle it."

Klotz ran to where the fire had spread to several more of the scattered papers he had dropped along the floor. He began to stomp on them. The fire had crept so closely to Jack, he had no choice but to pat out the papers near him. Soon the fire appeared under control, Klotz and Jack both sighed relief.

Klotz looked under the desk to see Jack offer an innocent smile back. "Thanks," Klotz said catching his breath.

"No problem," Jack replied with false confidence.

Klotz prepared to move toward the door, but stopped just in front of the desk as realization sank in. The realization that the man under the desk was not one of his. As he turned, he reached into his jacket and gripped his pistol. Jack was prepared. He could hear the movements of the man and quickly thrust his shoulder, the shoulder of the arm that had been fused and modified, upward into the desk, lifting it off the floor. He felt his arm tingle as he surged with adrenaline. Before Klotz could fully draw his weapon, Jack had brought the desk erect and shoved it roughly in Klotz's direction. The massive desk took him by surprise as it fell directly onto him, papers sliding from the desk, floating in the air and drifting listlessly to the ground. Klotz lost his grip on his pistol, dropping it to the floor as he stumbled backward from the weight of the desk. The fulcrum motion of the desk forced its weight to shift onto Klotz, pushing his body backward causing him to smash through the window behind him. Klotz fell with the desk following until it caught the lip of the window and flipped onto Klotz's unconscious form, leaving him pinned on the ground. Lyntz returned to check on the noises that Klotz was making, despite orders to the contrary. He watched in shock at the man who appeared from out of nowhere, reacting slowly with his drawn pistol. Jack saw his advantage and charged the stunned man, connecting his head and shoulders in Lyntz's midsection, his arms wrapped around his body. Lifting the man from his feet, Jack carried Lyntz across the open hallways and slammed his spine into the wall on the other side. Lyntz's back crunched against the wallboard, denting it inward. The pain seared fast and sharply, filling his head with agony. He dropped open his jaw to scream, but Jack threw a right hook and slacked Lyntz's jaw, knocking him silent to the floor.

Jack took a moment to catch his breath, but did not notice the flames reignite in the waste paper basket.

In the front foyer, Commander Caspar Huun watched as Crust and his men hoisted the transporter device onto a hovercart that drifted near the exit. The four men lifting were struggling with the awkward size and mass the device offered. Huun chuckled to himself at the sight of the men grunting to hoist the device onto the cart. He knew he could easily lift it himself but preferred to let the others fend for themselves. Each man grunted loudly as they lifted the device, resting it slowly on the hovercart's flatbed, which sagged considerably as the new weight was introduced. The sound of the men and the grinding metal of the transporter sliding across the flatbed into place, echoed across the high ceiling in the foyer, but underneath the noise, what Huun could swear sounded like the tinkling sound of glass, filled his ears. Huun cocked his head in the direction of the noise. It was where he last ordered Klotz to search and Lyntz to follow. The sound was followed by a series of low thuds.

"Crust, Fulst," Huun bellowed at the chattering men. "Grab your pieces and follow me."
The two men didn't hesitate as they grabbed their weapons and followed Huun.

Jack stood defensively, his chest heaving as he fought to catch his breath quietly. He knew he didn't have much time before the other men arrived. He needed to get out and fast. The crack of gunfire filled the darkened and empty hallway outside. Bullets whizzed through the air, burying themselves in the wall behind Jack. So much for a fast, discreet getaway.

"WAIT!" Huun screamed.

Huun's men lowered their arms as Jack emerged slowly from the shadow of the hallway. His jaw nearly hit the floor as he looked upon a ghost of his past. "Sgt. Casper Huun," Jack said as he stepped into the light. He felt his chest tighten as his eyes locked on the face of a man he revered as a deadly adversary. It had been a long time since their last confrontation, one that didn't end on good terms as Jack remembered.

Huun smirked, "Well, well, well. If it isn't Lt. Zero. Gentlemen, you are in the presence of the great Jack Zero." Huun walked forward slowly as Jack took a defensive stance. Huun relished in this. "Apparently, you don't remember the etiquette to salute your superior."

"Last I checked, scum wasn't too superior," Jack growled.

Huun threw his head back and laughed loudly, "You were always good for a laugh." Huun looked through the office door, seeing the shattered glass of the window he looked back at Jack. "I take it my man went through there."

"Still room for one more," Jack gritted his teeth and raised his fists.

"That's cute, Zero." Huun scowled.

"What can I say; I like to piss people off."

"You and I always had our differences."

"Yeah, good thing I smeared that difference all over the pavement, Zimm deserved everything he got and I'm glad I delivered it to him."

Huun stepped forward, his gait wide from his long legs. He stomped his foot in front of Jack's, making them face-to-face Jack, his face darker, fiercer than Jack remembered. "How dare you defile the memory of General Zimm."

Jack struck a nerve, he liked that. "He did that on his own."

"You don't know what you're dealing with." Huun composed himself, shelving his rage within. "I do hope you are only here by coincidence and not snooping around. As I recall, you had a tendency to stick your nose wherever it didn't belong."

"I'm looking for someone," Jack quickly spoke. "Dr. Heinrich Strommel. You know of him?"

Huun turned away from Jack, he raised his eyebrow at Crust, signaling him to be prepared to fire, "Never heard of him."

Jack furrowed his brow, "Call it a hunch, but I somehow don't believe you."

"Too bad."

The fire in the office had expanded; the flames had erupted and began devouring the carpet that stretched across the floor. Jack looked over quickly to see the books were beginning to incinerate. His escape was becoming less and less likely as both options for an exit were now blocked.

Huun saw Jack's distraction. He acknowledged with a nod to Crust, "Kill him." Crust quickly raised his rifle and began to fire. Jack didn't give himself time to think, he unwittingly ran into the flames and dove through the office doorway, bullets now bouncing all around him, shattering the glass that separated the office from the hall and burning into the other connected halls. Glass rained down onto Jack as bullets shattered what remained; he shielded his head with his arms while running toward the window he previously hurled Klotz through.

"Stop him!" Huun roared.

Crust and Fulst trained their pistols and fired repeatedly at Jack. Jack didn't waste time as he threw himself out the window.

Huun screamed to the remaining men in the hallway, "Get that fire under control!"

The men nodded and began to work at putting out the fire. Huun then grabbed a fourth soldier and pulled him by his lapel until he was close enough for him to whisper, "Get those explosives set, NOW!"

The man saluted and ran back to the front of the facility. Huun marched into the office, not fazed by the fire licking at his sides.

Jack tucked his head into his chest as his body plummeted to the ground; he landed on his right shoulder and rolled himself over onto his feet. Bullets continued to tear through the wall, sailing above Jack's head. He had to get as far away as possible. He pressed his body close to the ground and began slinking away. Huun had stepped into the window's frame to see Jack slithering along the ground. He took careful aim and fired. Fortunately, Jack had made it to the remains of the desk he had heaved through the window, finding shelter from the next barrage of bullets. The heavy rain of gunfire chewed through the thick desk rapidly. Jack could see his makeshift shield disappearing quickly. The gunfire continued. Jack looked for any place he could grab a break, find another hiding spot that was more bulletproof, but the nearest tree was at least twenty feet away. Any move he made away from the desk would get him killed quicker than if he stayed here. But what option did he have? Splinters filled the air around him and covered his hat and shoulders. He was running out of time. And desk. Maybe if he ran in a serpentine pattern, he could avoid a fatal shot. The night wind blew past his exposed ear. The desk was almost gone. Jack closed his eyes and prepared for what could very well be his last run. He raised himself on his haunches and prepared to spring up and run for the trees, but before he launched, the night air became suddenly silent, the gunfire dissipated.

'*What a stroke of luck*,' he thought. Maybe they assumed he was dead and left, or maybe they simply thought they had scared him enough and he wasn't worth anymore of their concern. Not likely. Jack felt the desk behind him begin to shake. It caused him to jump back. To his surprise, the desk began to rise slowly into the air. The man he thought he had rendered unconscious was now awake, alert, and angry. Klotz stood, his arms raised over his head, bracing the desk effortlessly. Jack watched in awe as Klotz brought his hands together and snapped the desk in two as if it were a twig. The sound of the wood cracking and splintering echoed across the open courtyard of the facilities, supplies that were once housed in the desk drawers were scattered across the grass and whatever remained now trickled down onto Jack's head. How was this man able to foster up such strength after having a nearly 300-pound desk dropped on his head. Klotz roared like a lion ready to pounce. Jack realized it wasn't the right time to investigate what was driving this maniac, but instead, it was time to run.

Jack bolted from where he was crouched just as the two halves of the desk slammed into the ground, nearly striking him. The impact of the desk against the solid ground split the desk further, burying some pieces into the ground and sending other in Jack's direction. One heavy piece spiraled into the air and hit Jack along his right shoulder, forcing him to stumble slightly before he was able to recover and continuing his dash for the trees.

The strength this man had mustered was unlike any he had ever encountered. Just like Caveman, he must be fused. This definitely gave Jack's adversary the advantage. Klotz began to pump his legs, running after Jack. Jack was running at full speed, fortunate to find a slight decline, which made his ability to pick up speed easier. Jack had run a distance before he started to feel winded. He was afraid to look over his shoulder, afraid at what he might see. The thought of hulking form of Klotz barreling down on him was terrifying enough to not need to see the real thing. His pursuer was no longer a man; he was something else, a beast, a monster even. He could see the dark etched outline of the tree line ahead, striking against the dark night sky. If he could only reach that, he might be able to be in the clear. However, Jack's hopes were dashed when he reached a gently decline. He stumbled as his foot bent forward. He quickly regained his balance and used the slope to attempt to outwit his pursuer. Unfortunately, Klotz took the same approach. He could hear Klotz picking up speed, his feet slamming against the earth letting out a grunt at each foots impact. Klotz was gaining ground on Jack even faster. The trees were close but seemed so far away. Klotz was right behind Jack. He stretched his thick arm forward, reaching for Jack. His fingertips brushing the nape of Jack's neck. Within seconds, Klotz would be able to wrap his fingers around his neck and squeeze until his eyes bulged and his head exploded. Klotz now reached forward a second time. The touch of calloused fingers pressed the flesh of his neck. Death seemed a certainty. Jack instinctively closed his eyes and heard a pop. He was glad it wasn't painful, the feeling of his throat being crushed or blood vessels erupting. The pop was followed by a loud wail that echoed across the courtyard, the cry of pain, of death. Not only didn't he feel pain, but he hadn't even cried out.

Jack felt his legs stop running. He opened his eyes slowly and turned to see the corpse of Klotz lying face down. Jack's thoughts were reeling around his head. What the hell happened? The river of crimson that flowed from under and the exit wound through his back proved he was shot. But by whom?

"What the hell are you waiting for?" Agent Frisco's voice called from the tree line. "RUN!"

He smiled at the sight of her. It was good to see her, even more so under the circumstances.

"He's down there!" Jack heard shouts from up the hill at the facility. It was Huun and his men and they were heading toward him.

"C'mon Zero! Move your ass!"

There was no time to waste as Jack ran toward Frisco. She grabbed his hand and pulled him along with her. "Let's go!" She ordered. They ran together into the darkness, bullets sang through the air and past their heads, burrowing into trees, shredding bark all around them. One bullet tore across Jack's shoulder, flaying the skin. He winced, but ignored the pain. He just wanted to focus on the escape. And Frisco.

Huun ran down the decline, heading in the fleeing Zero's direction, only to find that Jack was nowhere in sight. He had escaped.

"NO!" Huun's scream echoed across the treetops and courtyard. He heaved as he looked into the darkness, his thoughts only on killing Jack Zero.

Crust caught up to Huun, stopping at his side, "What happened?"

Huun, still heaving angrily, gestured to the body of Klotz.

"Zero?" Crust asked.

Huun shook his head, "No, he had help."

"Should we go after him?"

"Take Falst with you," Huun sneered. "But be quick." He snapped his fingers, "We've got a job to finish."

The branches snapped back in his face as Jack ran through the thickening forest. He followed closely behind Frisco who continued pushing the foliage from their path. Jack was breathing laboriously. Not only had he fended off a large, mammoth of a man, but he had been following Frisco for nearly half-an-hour. They seemed to be directionless, not really heading any particular way. His legs were burning, exhaustion taking control. He slowed his pace until he stopped running altogether.

Frisco felt Jack's hand slide from her grasp. She quickly stopped and turned to see Jack hunched over, his hands on his knees as he panted heavily.

"What are you doing?" Frisco said frantically. "We need to keep going."

"I'm tired," Jack panted. "I need to rest."

"We don't have time!"

Jack began to steady his breathing as he stood up, "Oh, c'mon, we've put enough distance between us and them to afford taking a rest."

"You don't get it, Zero," Frisco's voice sounded desperate. "These men, they're not like regular men. Did you not see what they were capable of?"

"I think I got a pretty good view first hand," Jack said wryly.

"You have no idea what you're dealing with do you?"

"Sure I do, you came back for me because you care about me," Jack flashed his smile at Frisco whose expression looked far less than enthused.

"Fine, stay here and let them find you," Frisco scowled. "But there will be no protection if they do."

"You know, the first time I met you, I didn't get you, but now I do," Jack looked at Frisco, cocking an eyebrow.

"Oh yeah, and how's that?"

"You like me."

"What?"

"You like me."

"Are you insane?"

Jack smiled playfully, "Not in the least. In fact, I see clearly. You. Like. Me."

"Oh please," Frisco rolled her eyes, obviously annoyed.

"Don't deny it."

"What are you, twelve?"

"You like me," Jack chided in a singsong voice.

"You really are an immature idiot," Frisco grimaced.

"You can't ignore there's some sort of attraction between us," Jack sidled up to Frisco.

Frisco put her hand around Jack's throat as he got closer, "How about if you touch me I end your miserable existence quickly."

Jack stepped away from Frisco, his arms raised in the air in the same fashion as when he first encountered her on the rooftop. She released her grip on his neck. He tried to hide the physical pain that she had caused him, stifling a cough. "Alright, alright," Jack managed, his voice a bit raspy from her tight clasp. "I just…I appreciate you coming to help me out."

Frisco's usually stoic expression faltered as she cracked a smile. Jack couldn't help but notice the standout expression, "Is that a smile I see?"

Frisco turned away, partially embarrassed and partially to break away from Jack's longing stare. "Don't look at me like that."

"Like what?" Jack asked.

A massive explosion shattered the silence that was hanging precariously between them. Jack nearly stumbled over Frisco, but caught himself as he turned to see the remains of a mushroom cloud climbing into the dark night sky before dissipating into a darker black smoke.

Frisco, whose mouth was agape at the sight of the flames, suddenly clamped her jaw shut before growling at Jack, "I won't even ask what you did!"

Jack smirked slightly, awkwardly, as he shrugged his shoulders as innocently as he could. He knew he was there for the fire, but didn't realize it was that bad. This moment was cut short as well. The sound of a tree branch snapping broke the growing tension that Frisco was beginning to feel weigh on her. She gripped her pistol in her holster, drew it, and pulled it up to her chest, "What was that?"

"You were right. We need to go now," Jack said as he looked into the darkness for any sign of movement.

The pop of gunfire shattered the heavy silence around them. They found them. Jack ran and grabbed Frisco's hand, pulling her behind him as he ran. Within moments, their pursuers had caught up to them. "THERE THEY ARE!" and "AFTER THEM!" were shouts that came from behind them, which was followed shortly by more snaps of gunfire. Bullets tore through the branches around Jack and Frisco's heads. Leaves rained down upon them as they loosened from their nesting spots. Frisco felt a bullet pass between her and Jack. Cracks of gunfire echoed around the trees surrounding them, as bullets seemed to shower around them, amazingly missing them at every serpentine pass they made weaving around the trees. Jack began to pull Frisco to the left, but she was pulling to the right.

"What are you doing?" Jack screamed.

Frisco looked deeply into Jack's eyes, "Can you trust me?"

Jack hesitated for a moment, the shouts and stampede of footsteps were coming closer. There wasn't much time for thought to which Jack was left with no alternative. Jack relinquished control and followed Frisco as they went to the right. Branches continued to slap their faces and scratched their exposed skin as the forest became more and more dense. Frisco pulled on Jack's arm as they ran deeper into the trees. The sound of their pursuers began to fade slightly, giving Jack the reassurance that they were widening the gap between them.

"Don't slow down," Frisco called behind her.

Jack huffed along, "Wouldn't dream of it."

They ran for what felt like hours, reaching the edge of the tree line. Once they broke free of the tendril-like branches that scratched at their skin and clothes, Frisco stopped and released her grip of Jack's hand. Jack could feel the cool night air slide over his warmed hand. He almost missed her touch. Frisco, on the other hand, reached her now freed hand into her coat pocket and produced a COMM device that she instantly tapped the small row of buttons that lined its base. Her thumb danced in what appeared to be a Prouxm pattern, but sent a signal that received an instant response. No sooner had she finished tapping the keys that a LEHV dropped quietly out of the sky. It ended its descent just above the ground where it bobbed lightly. She stepped to the door and typed the code that snapped the door open.

"C'mon," she screamed over the whine of the engine.

"Thanks," Jack said loudly. "I owe you one."

"Don't thank me just yet."

Jack stepped forward and grabbed the handrail that ran along the top of each door. Just as he sidled his weight into the vehicle he felt a cold snap clamp across his wrist. Frisco had placed a shackle on him. The expression on her face said it all, enraging Jack, "What the hell do you think you're doing?"

"I'm arresting you," she grinned. "Again."

CHAPTER 9
UNDER ARREST...AGAIN

Jack soon found himself in the familiar surroundings of Commissioner Lartanner's office. It was a case of extreme déjà vu as the events of the morning repeated themselves in the late hours of the night, from the shaky ride over in the LEHV to being shoved in a holding cell before being yanked out and then thrown here. Once again sitting opposite Lartanner, only now his former boss was even less than thrilled to see him, especially since he looked as if he was awoken from an especially lucid sleep to come and sort out another mess.

Jack offered a smile, "I'm sure you're wondering why I'm here."
"No. I'm wondering WHAT THE HELL *I'M* DOING HERE?!" Lartanner was furious, his face pink, his eyes narrow slits. "I am absolutely speechless. I don't understand how we can be sitting in the exact same place, for the exact same reason on the exact same day?"

"I didn't want you to miss me."

"DAMMIT ZERO, SHUT UP!" Lartanner screamed, a vein protruded from his forehead and throbbed with each syllable he spat. "You have no idea how badly I want to throw you into the cell for the rest of your washed up life, but for some inexplicable reason, that I cannot even fathom, I somehow find myself sticking my neck out for you again."

"And no one appreciates it more than me, sir," Jack tried to sound sincere, but it came off as snarky.

"Are you trying to give me an ulcer?" Lartanner swallowed a handful of antacid tablets followed by a mouthful of liquid from his coffee mug. "What was it for this time?"

"Well, the short list is entering a sealed crime scene, tampering with evidence, willful destruction of property, malicious mischief--"

"ENOUGH! I don't want to hear anymore," Lartanner rubbed his forehead roughly, massaging the pain that still lingered from the morning. "My hands are tied on this, you know. Senator Glorm is on his way down here as we speak and I understand he's livid with what happened. If he throws the book at you, I have no choice but to oblige."

"Can I at least explain what I found there?"

"No, I'm not listening to some bullshit story about HART agents running amok. How you had nothing to do with destroying a million dollar facility. I don't want to hear it."

"Of course not, you're more interested in burying the truth," Jack snapped back.

"You have no idea what's going on here, Zero!" Lartanner's face was changing from pink to red. "This city isn't your playground to come and go anywhere you please. The problem is you don't think about the consequences, you never did."

"I only want answers."

"At what cost? Don't you see what your reckless attitude gets you? Had Agent Frisco not been there the damage you caused could've been worse. Had the explosion not been contained as it had, you might have cratered half the neighborhood. Have you any idea how many innocent families live there?"

"That explosion was timed and set to only evaporate the facility, nothing more than a cover up now wiped clean," Zero said in his defense.

The conversation began to ebb toward civil when it was cut short by the door to Lartanner's office being forcefully pushed open. Glorm barged through the office door and stormed across the room, his feet clomping hard against the tiled floor. His face was twisted into a foul grimace, his brow furrowed and creased deeply. "I cannot believe what I am hearing about here, I cannot!"

Jack stood up and waved his hands reassuringly, "Senator, listen, I can explain everything."

Glorm raised a single hand toward Zero, not making any eye contact with him. He looked only at Frisco, "Let me hear it."

"Sir," Frisco swallowed as she spoke. "I happened upon Mr. Zero at the research facility, even after he was instructed not to interfere, but I had suspicions that he would. When I found him there, I confronted him and warned him to leave the premises, but just as his jacket explains, Zero has no respect for authority and took it upon himself to continue interfering within a crime scene."

"And you didn't arrest him at that time, why?" Glorm was curt.

"Well sir, I...I..." Frisco stammered, searching her mind for the best, most plausible answer. "I thought that maybe Mr. Zero could be trustworthy."

"Trustworthy?" Glorm said, surprised and repulsed by her answer.

"Yes sir," she replied.

"Trustworthy?" Jack, too, sounded surprised.

Frisco threw him a dirty look in return and then refocused her most serious face for Glorm.

Glorm turned his attention to Jack, "Is this funny? Blowing up a major research facility is a joke? Give me one good reason why I shouldn't throw you in jail for the rest of your failed life?"

"Casper Huun," Jack said flatly.

"What?" Glorm's tone softened.

Lartanner looked perplexed, "Who?"

"When I was in the facility, I saw a group of men. They were being ordered by that man from your surveillance photo, Casper Huun," Jack explained slowly. "I'm pretty sure you can rattle off all the facts about him, can't you Senator."

Glorm took in a deep, both cleansing and calming, breath. He then obliged Zero's request, "I'm quite familiar as are you, I'm sure; Sgt. Huun, second in command to Gen. Zimm. Shortly after Zimm's death and the subsequent court martial of you and the members of your squad. Huun had taken the dishonorable treatment of Zimm to heart. He attacked his own legal defense team, killing one and injuring the other two. Shortly after his arraignment, he disappeared during transport to a secured military facility. Confirmation of his appearance in Southeast Asia by our field men created speculation he had joined the HART."

"Well, just as you suspected, he's back, he's not too happy with me I might add."

"Tell him to get in line," Lartanner growled.

Jack ignored Lartanner's snide comment, "Seems to still be holding a grudge over the whole Zimm thing." Jack offered a smile, "If it's any consolation, you were right; if Huun's joined the HART, then they're here and we've just seen the beginning of what they're capable of."

Glorm was silent. Being speechless was not something Glorm was known for; he was a man who always spoke his mind even at the adversity of congress. Glorm would easily state his opinions on unemployment and education without a regard as to offending his colleagues. However, here he stood before Jack, his brain overwhelmed, trying to make sense of this shocking information. It gave Jack a charge of pleasure to know he had been able to shut him up.

Lartanner squirmed in his seat, feeling uncomfortable from the expression of fear that colored Glorm's face. "If this Huun character is wanted, why not just arrest him."

"It won't be that easy," Jack scoffed.

"Why not?" Frisco inquired.

Glorm finally broke his pensive silence, "No, he's right. Huun is a survivor. His military training isn't just about survival, though. It goes deeper. It's more like eradication of the unfit."

"Huun always believed in kill or be killed," Jack interjected. "He practiced what he preached. I personally witnessed him leveling an entire village just to flush out a handful of men. He has no regard for life or innocence."

"All I need is a face-to-face and he's mine," Frisco made a gun with her fingers and took aim, lining her sights on Jack.

"You don't get it, Nikki," Jack said. Frisco threw him an even more sinister look than she had earlier, to which Jack corrected, "I mean Agent Frisco. Huun is not a regular man, he's a monster. And if he's like any of his men, he's been fused."

"There's something I didn't tell you, Agent," Glorm addressed Frisco. "According to intelligence reports, when Huun was discharged from his service to the United States, we feel he defected to several sovereign nations, looking to sell American secrets to the highest bidder. Most countries alerted our intelligence to this, but not before he defected to the HART"

"So you weren't kidding," Lartanner looked shocked, "You mean there are HART agents here?"

Jack looked at Lartanner and mouthed, "Told you." Lartanner shook it off, looking for an answer from Glorm.

"As we feared," Glorm replied looking to Agent Frisco. She nodded slightly in return.

Jack noticed the silent exchange between them, "I want in."

"Excuse me?" Glorm responded to Jack.

"Whatever the two of you have planned, I want in."

"You're still a loose cannon, Zero, who has several charges to answer for," Lartanner cried.

Glorm stepped forward, standing over Jack who still sat, shackled to the chair, "I appreciate your resolve, Mr. Zero, but you are too much of a liability. We're dealing with sensitive matters in harrowing times, the last thing we need is you screwing things up."

"Wait a second, you need me," Jack argued, "I know Huun, I know how he thinks, I can help you."

"Yes, you can, by staying out of the way," Glorm walked to the door, "Because of your information, I'll see to it that all charges will be dropped save you keep your nose out of this. If you so much as cough anywhere near this case I will slap you back in a cell faster than you can say sorry. And this time you won't be let out."

Glorm threw a look at Lartanner and optically gestured to Jack's restraints. Lartanner understood and prepared to release Jack once Glorm and Frisco were out of range. "Once again, Zero, you are one lucky sonuva bitch."

"What can I say, the man loves me."

"Can it, Zero. Just because he got you off doesn't get you off scot-free. You so much as cross paths with the Senator or his agents, I'll have you back in here so fast you'll beg me for mercy."

"I'm sensing a pattern between you two."

Lartanner placed the control for the restraints on Jack's wrists on the edge of his desk. He then got up and walked to the door. Jack squirmed in his seat, trying to look back at Lartanner who was smiling. "Wait, where are you going?" Jack sounded confused, desperate.

"I'm tired; I'm going home and going to bed."

"No, no, no, no, no," Jack repeated. "You can't just leave me here."

"Have a good night, Zero," Lartanner left the room, leaving Jack alone, still restrained.

"DAMMIT!" Jack screamed as the door closed behind him and left him in the dark.

It took Jack nearly an hour to finagle his way out of the restraints. He had fallen over in the chair nearly a dozen times before he had been able to get himself situated and was able to twist himself around and grasp the keypad to release the magnetic lock on his restraints. Unfortunately, by the time he freed himself the Senator and his agents were long gone, along with Lartanner. Jack then caught a cab back to his office. Jack needed sleep. It was late and he hadn't slept well in days. He would have gone back to his apartment, but he owed his landlady the rent for the past two months. Invariably, she would see him attempting to sneak into his apartment, whether through the front door or the fire escape, and brow beat the rent out of him. Moreover, he knew, you couldn't squeeze blood from a stone, so he would be better off sleeping in his office then trying to explain why he doesn't have any money.

His office was dark and empty, a metaphor that stretched into his daily life as of late. No matter how hard he tried, things were not working out as he had hoped; first getting his collar taken from him, then being chased by a ghost from his past, and then being arrested…twice. And worst of all, he still hasn't been paid. He shoved his body against the door to his office, pushing it apart from the door jam. He still had to deliver the jewels to Mrs. Graves. He would do it tomorrow. Tonight, he would sleep. It took him all of eight minutes to fall asleep. Jack reached up to the top drawer of a file cabinet that ran the height of the wall to ceiling and pulled it down.

Hidden within was a pre-made bed, complete with blankets and pillows. It was a convenient place to keep a bed whenever he was working late on a case and needed to crash. Unfortunately, he had resorted to sleeping here more often since he was close to losing his apartment. It wasn't by choice but he had been without a case for nearly six weeks and was only able to afford paying his office rent and Ceinwen. Instead, he opted to not pay on his lease and just sleep in his office. It was cozy enough, since he didn't have anyone, a family or significant other, not even a pet, it was an easy decision. Besides, he spent enough time here, as it was, why not just move in.

Jack plopped himself onto the bed, kicking off his shoes before swinging his legs around. He was exhausted, his eyes heavy, like lead, closing once his head sank into the pillow. His joints locked and his muscles ached. He was asleep in less than a minute. Sleep felt good. Better than it had in a long time. Jack felt himself slip into the dreamscape.

Jack never remembered his dreams. He was sure he dreamed, but whenever he woke, he never remembered them from the night before. Perhaps it was that he always awoke with his mind racing, starving to finalize a thought from the previous day; or perhaps it was that he simply liked waking with a clear mind, free of worry, doubt, or confusion. On the other hand, maybe it was simply that he never really had a good night sleep. Just like tonight.

When he felt the hand clamp over his mouth, Jack felt his heart stop. It was a moment of terror. Someone was in his office. Someone was in his place, in his room, the room where he slept, felt safe. Jack nearly screamed before he realized it was stifled by the tight clamp the hand held over his mouth. He instinctively grabbed the hand and began to pull at it, but it was as if it was welded tightly to his mouth.

Was this a dream?

No.

It couldn't be.

He was remembering this.

Jack switched into his survival instinct, he blindly reached his arms behind him until his hands found something he could grip and hold tightly. With all his strength that he had left, Jack pulled forward, yanking his assailant off their own feet and flipping them over his head. The thick body flew through the air effortlessly, crashing hard onto the top of his desk. All the semi-neat and tidy items skittered about. The assailant slid across to the other side, crashing to the floor.

Jack wasted no time, leaping after the assailant, not wanting to allow any opportunity to counter attack. He landed onto the thick form, which he knew was that of a man. He threw a series of hard punches, connecting with the man's shoulder, stomach and chest. He pulled the man up by his collar and prepared for another barrage. The man shoved him away, but Jack held on. He quickly grabbed the lamp that dangled off the edge of his desk and raised it high, preparing to strike. The assailant reached up and grabbed the lamp, but not to wrest it free of Jack's grip, but instead to turn it on.

The light clicked. The brightness of the incandescent bulb illuminated the room, despite its low wattage. Jack squinted, diminishing the amount of harsh light that rushed at his eyes. Jack drew back his fist, ready to punch. But before he threw his fist, his eyes focused on the man cringing before him, his hands raised in attempts to shield the forthcoming blows.

Jack recognized the meek face that coward before him, "Phineas?" The man lowered his hands; they were covered in gloves with the finger tips removed. His hair was uneven, unclean, and unkempt. His face was decorated by a large amount of growth from not having shaved in several days. He also carried a pungent odor that stopped Jack from getting any closer to the man. Even though it had been years, Jack recognized the man before him.

"Phineas Wald," Jack wanted to smile, but he felt more annoyed than relieved it was a friend. "What the hell are you doing here?"

"Hi Jack," Phineas Wald offered a smile.

"You sonuva bitch," Jack sighed, but panting hard to catch his breath. "I can't believe you're here."

"I came to see you."

"You could've called first. C'mon out of there," Jack guided Phineas from behind his desk and lead him over to the couch against the wall on the other side. Phineas didn't stay seated on the couch. He stood, pacing slightly and looking antsy while Jack sat across from him on the foot of his foldout bed. "It's good to see you. It's been, I don't know, at least nine years."

"Ten."

"It's funny I should bump into you, though," Jack snorted. "I seem to be bumping into a lot of our old buddies from the Unit tonight."

Phineas spoke, "I'm sorry I sneaked up on you like this, I didn't know how else to come see you."

"I know that look, Phineas. You looked spooked. You had that look on that mission in Egypt. What's going on?"

"I just got into town three days ago, been laying low, getting a feel for the security measure this city takes. I must admit state-of-the-art. ID scanners at every third street corner, roving cameras that travel just above cloud cover, difficult to spot without the proper device. I have one, you know," Phineas pulled a small curved device from his pocket. It was roughly the width of a wristwatch and housed a small screen with a tiny array of buttons. He displayed it proudly, holding it up for Jack to see. "It's a BEV device. BEV stands for Birds-Eye-View. It spots out and detects the flight patterns of any non-consumer class machines that fly in the sky. Banned in every country, just looking at one can get you ten years."

Jack pushed it away from his face, forcing it out of view, "Put that thing away!" Jack was well aware of what the device was capable of, and knew that all forms of law enforcement had counter equipment to trace BEV devices. Jack continued, "Where have you been all these years?"

"They locked me up, y'know. I was in Bellevue for three years before being transferred to Carson Mental Research Facilities in Philadelphia. I was there for nearly seven years before I escaped."

"Escaped? I had heard you checked yourself out."

"Where'd you hear that?"

"Never mind," Jack waved him off.

Phineas paced over next to Jack and his bed. He began shaking the blankets on Jack's foldout bed, "Is that what they told you."

"They who," Jack tested him.

"Oh, c'mon, like you don't know," Phineas moved across the room to Jack's desk where he began turning over any loose item.

Jack cocked an eyebrow curiously, "What are you doing?"

Phineas didn't look at Jack as he continued around the room, flipping over framed pictures that were hung on the wall. "Looking for a bug, you never know who could be listening."

"You know the FBI is looking for you, not to mention a US Senator."

"That's why I came as I did, I needed to see you."

Jack didn't have a good feeling about this, any of this. With Phineas, trouble always seemed to follow. It wasn't as if he was looking for trouble, he always just happened upon it, stupidly in most cases. "Phineas, you can't be here."

"Jack, you have to listen to me, I can't trust anyone else."

Jack covered his face in his hands. He didn't know how to take this, what to do. "About what?"

"The truth."

"What truth?"

"I have to warn you, they're not just after me, but you too," Phineas whispered as he began to walk around the room, searching through everything. Jack could only imagine what he was looking for. Phineas stuck his head into a potted plant as he continued, "They want us. They need us."

"Who?" Jack was growing slightly uncomfortable watching Phineas make his way around his office. He was taking books from the shelf and fanning through them before placing them back on the shelf. He even picked up the pot of coffee and dumped it on the floor. "Do you really need to do that?"

"Do you remember when you were recruited by General Dowbromski?"

Jack nodded, "I was out of the military academy for only a couple years. Did SEAL training, Dowbromski said he wanted my skills, told me that he hadn't…"

Phineas interrupted, "He hadn't seen anyone with such amazing potential as you have."

Jack was speechless for a moment before he responded, how did he know EXACTLY what the General said? "Yeah, that's exactly right."

"Do you think it was all just a coincidence that we all ended up in the same unit together, you, me, Huun, and the others? I assure you it was not."

"We all had a killer instinct."

"Of course, we all had the same skills."

"Look, I appreciate your sharing this with me, but I find it hard to believe."

"So did I, at first," Phineas said calmly. "But there was something that didn't add up." Phineas pulled a small COMM device from his pocket and tapped a short series of buttons. He then handed the device to Jack.

Jack took the device and looked at the lighted screen. An image floated less than an inch from the clear panel. It was a series of detailed files, explaining deployment orders, detailed departure times and location arrivals. It was a mission that went deep into the heart of Amazon. Several lines of information were blacked and blurred making it difficult to read.

Jack looked confused, "Their deployment orders, big deal."

Phineas' eyes grew wider, as if awaiting Jack to finally understand, "Look closer."

Jack wrinkled his nose in disapproval. What was he getting at? Why was he so persistent to show him these orders? "I can't read half of the lines here, what am I supposed to see?"

"Read between those lines."

Jack returned to the hovering image. He flicked the image with his finger, sending the paragraphs, both legible and otherwise, scrolling up and around its virtual floating space. The scroll stopped at the end of the document, revealing an image. In the image was a group of men, all from his unit. It was a picture he had seen many times as it hung on his office wall. He quickly identified himself and Phineas. He saw Huun and sneered. He knew all the men in the image, except one. In the background, just behind the top row of soldiers was the shadowy silhouette of a man he didn't remember. He squinted to try to get a better look, but it was still too difficult to identify him.

"Wait a minute," Jack whispered, more to himself, but Phineas heard.

"You see it don't you?" Phineas smirked.

"No, I mean, yeah," Jack was flustered as he tried to think and speak. Jack stood and rushed to the wall where all his framed pictures hung. He plucked the identical image from the wall and held it next to the hovering image that floated above the COMM device in the other hand. It was uncanny, the position of the people, the expressions on their faces, everything the same, except for the man in the back. In his image, there wasn't any indication that there was anyone even there. Normally, a doctored photo left traces of missing data, but it was not easily noticed here. It was odd, they were the exact same image, exact, all except that one person. "I've seen this picture a thousand times; I don't recall this person in the background."

Jack handed the COMM device to Phineas, "Where did you get this?"

"Hacked documents from the Pentagon, I know a guy."

'*Of course you do,*' Jack thought sarcastically.

"He recognized me in the photo and contacted me immediately. Once I saw it, I knew I had to contact someone from the unit," Phineas explained. "You were always the only one I could ever trust."

"Any idea on who he is?"

"A ghost," Phineas said. "If he's even real at all. I ran this image through every photo tracer, image enhancer I could find, legal and illegal. There was not one match identifying the person."

"Maybe the image is just too poor resolution," Jack suggested.

"No way," Phineas countered. "I've scanned worse images than this and they all found enough bits to piece together an identification, but this one…nothing. He doesn't exist at least not in our world."

"Why don't we recognize him or remember him?" Jack stood for a moment. He thought long and hard trying to remember who this phantom stranger might have been. He turned to speak again to Phineas, but he was gone. Jack's heart stopped for a moment, but then he realized Phineas was just being…Phineas. Once he was finished, he always made an unexpected exit. But still, he left Jack wondering, pondering about these new questions that seem to continue arising from a past he always tried to forget, but can never seem to escape. Jack tried to erase the thoughts from his mind. He was felling antsy and uptight. He sat up in bed but felt too wound up to sleep. However, he underestimated the power of fatigue as he finally laid his head down and drifted to sleep.

CHAPTER 10
JACK ZERO'S LAST MISSION

"Zero!" The voice cut through the silence Jack had been relishing. He had been sleeping, something he desired for some time but seemed to elude him. He ignored the call.

"Zero?!" The voice goaded further.

Jack grunted in response. The physical extremities attached to the voice reached out, grabbed Jack's shoulder and began to shake him. Jack reluctantly opened his eyes, slowly at first, but then he quickly snapped them open as he saw he was in a dark room with only a low red light illuminating the face of Phineas Wald kneeling before him. Jack's heart pounded immediately, leaping into his throat. He panicked as he sat up looking around confused.

"Jeez, Zero," Phineas said. "I never thought you'd wake up."

Jack felt the room they were in was moving, the sound of a diesel engine pushing along. He tried to absorb everything at once, but was still groggy from his sleep, "Where are we?"

"Just outside of Nang Shin."

Jack remembered he was in an Aerial Transit Assault Carrier, a massive flying fortress that was equipped with detonation devices and room enough for several battalions of troops. This was a common vehicle for the Skytroopers to take. Anytime they ran a mission, most of which were covert, they took the ATAC. The ATAC harbored several sections devoted to the various divisions that would take the machine as transport. There were several dozen quarters set up for sleeping, a large mess hall, and another half dozen set up for recreational needs, whether one wanted to work out or play games. It was like a flying city, equipped with anything one needed or desired. It gave them the opportunity to stretch out prior to a drop. Jack always thought of it as a luxury hotel in the sky. Service was even better as a Skytrooper; most missions were taken without any other divisions aboard the ATAC, leaving them the run of the place.

Jack liked that; he liked being alone. Not that he was alone. Aside from Phineas and himself, he could see Lt. Crust, his beady eyes and shorn head reflecting the low red glow much more intensely. He was studying a binder that he leafed through on his lap as he was seated on the opposite side of the ATAC. Battle plans no doubt. Next to Crust was a man named Corporal Carol Drent. He was a short man who compensated in other ways for his restrictions, angry and unpredictable; he wasn't someone that you wanted to get on his bad side. Jack personally witnessed Drent take down three men twice his size in a bar room brawl with his bare hands. He was a savage fighter and a brilliant strategist. Drent was the most prolific military strategist in the United States, garnering him his recruitment to the Skytroopers. He took to the role and reveled in every victory he planned.

Jack looked around to see three other Skytroopers, Lt. Commander Vello Gruck, a respected man and third man in succession to their General. Jack liked Gruck; he respected him and often volunteered to follow him on any mission where he was in command. Next to Gruck was CRP FC Gillad Proux, another one that Jack liked. He was an easygoing officer, specializing in science and medicine. The other officer was Lt. Tarin Bealls, the communications officer, a man you wanted nearby when a mission quickly went south.

Jack liked his team. He liked their dynamic, aside from the occasional rift that was usually generated by either Crust or Drent. They all worked well together. They all had their place. Jack was the lead investigator and intelligence gatherer. He was the usually the first person that went in, the point man. He liked what he did and how he fit into the team.

"How much time before we drop?" Jack yawned as he spoke to Phineas.

"Eighteen minutes"

"You couldn't wake me up sooner?" Jack bemoaned. "I'm the first one in and the last one up."

"I tried waking you up a bunch of times, but you kept threatening to punch me," Phineas mused. "Nearly clocked me in the head the last time."

Jack rubbed his eyes with his thumb and forefinger, attempting to shake of the grogginess. "Who has lead?"

Phineas wrinkled his nose, "You won't like it."

Jack rolled his eyes, "Oh, not him."

Commander Caspar Huun entered the ATAC's core room, his

massive presence taking up the doorway as he passed through. "Alright ladies, we're almost over the target drop site, you got ten minutes to get your gear."

Jack threw a disgusted look at Phineas. Caspar Huun, the one man he didn't want in charge. Huun was all business and no nonsense. Huun was not an approachable leader; he didn't like to be bothered. Huun's philosophy was you were given a job, you either did it or you had better be dead. Jack wouldn't admit that he was afraid of Huun, but it was clearly certainly he made him uneasy. Huun came off as unstable, unpredictable, and untrustworthy. Despite Crust and Drent being opposition, Jack could always handle them, but Huun was another matter altogether.

"Zero!" Huun called.

"Yessir," Jack responded.

"You're up first."

"Yessir," Jack repeated himself, almost sarcastically. Huun didn't seem to notice.

"Jack," Phineas reverted Jack's attention. "The drop into Nang Shin isn't easy."

"They hardly ever are."

"I know, but the problem is, they're expecting us," Phineas said cautiously.

Jack hesitated, his stomach suddenly dropping from Phineas' words, "What do you mean they're expecting us?"

Phineas was quick to explain, "Well, it's not like they know we're coming exactly. It's more as if they intercepted intelligence reports and communiques between our troops and Washington. They don't have any details, but they are expecting some sort of infiltration."

Jack was checking his supplies before harnessing his flight pack. It was a large cylinder that ran the length of his back. It was a sleek design with retractable wings on either side. They extended on command and allowed for a smooth, silent glide. Jack fastened the clasps around his midsection and across his chest. He then checked the straps to ensure they were tight enough. He was prepared.

"So what can I do then?" Jack inquired.

"Don't get caught," Crust offered. Drent chuckled.

Phineas and Jack ignored them. Phineas responded, "Keep a low altitude, about 2000 feet, that'll keep you below radar. Avoid the thicker populated areas."

"You recommend a straight and tuck?"

Phineas nodded. He understood what Jack meant. He knew Jack would do a straight nosedive from their height and wait to extend the wings at about 4000 feet, maintaining the nosedive until he can tuck in his legs, performing a midair somersault before he can level off at 2000 feet. "Just be careful."

Jack smiled, appreciating Phineas' concern. Phineas seemed too timid to be a part of this motley crew. Phineas was the last person who wanted a weapon, but he was certainly well trained enough to use one.

"You know, you could come with me, be my point guard again," Jack offered.

Phineas pursed his lips, a wave of emotions crossing his face within seconds. It was almost as if he was preparing to explode at Jack. Instead, he shook his head. "You know I can't."

"Look, Phineas, what happened back then, it wasn't your fault," Jack said reassuringly while he adjusted the last of his straps. "You were doing what you though was right. It could've happened to anyone."

"But it happened to me," Phineas said remorsefully. "God, she was only a kid. Because of me, she'll never be an adult. She'll never grow up and live life. For that, I can't pick up a gun again."

Phineas was recruiting to the Skytroopers for his skills and ability with a long rifle. Phineas was notorious for his skill to pick off anything through the scope of a rifle at incredible distances. Jack had personally witnessed Phineas shoot a soldier in the center of his forehead from over fifty miles away. However, Phineas hadn't picked up a gun in several months. It stemmed from the time he was point guard for Jack, who was gathering intel before being discovered by soldiers. Phineas immediately began shooting each soldier systematically, taking them out in record speed. Before too long, all the soldiers were lying dead at Jack's feet, a total of six. Another person came rushing out, taking Jack by surprise. Phineas didn't hesitate, immediately taking action and opening fire, failing to look through the lens of the scope atop his rifle. He quickly took aim and pulled the trigger, not realizing he had killed an innocent. A young girl of only twelve. She was rushing out to see what happened, concerned that her father was hurt, only to be killed herself. Jack rushed to help the girl, but it was too late. He never blamed Phineas for what happened, but Phineas had a difficult time coping. Phineas vowed never to pick up a rifle again. It was because of this that Huun resented Phineas and Jack for protecting him. He had been lobbying for Phineas' removal from the team for some time, but it was now becoming a deeper concern, one Jack noted. He was now the sharpshooter protecting Phineas. Protecting him from Huun and his supporters. It was why Jack always urged Phineas to come along on every mission. Both he and Phineas knew it was only a matter of time before Huun acted.

"Just be careful," Phineas repeated.

"You too."

Jack made his way to the launch area. It was at the door, surrounded by a transparent tube that sealed the jumper from the rest of the plane. The design was basically to seclude the jumper so that when the launch commenced the jumper would be ejected, uninterrupted and unmolested. Jack approached the tube and stalled a moment before entering. He turned to see the others still putting together their gear.

As he stepped into the tube, General Varcar Zimm entered the launch area. He was dressed in full uniform, as he always was. He believed that any man serving in the military should always be in their best, regardless of rank. There were instances when Jack had unbuttoned one of his shirts by one, causing a mild outrage from Zimm. Zimm was tall, thick and always wore a scowl. He looked down on everyone he spoke with making them feel inferior in every way. His medals and rank insignia were always polished and displayed with honor on his broad chest. They gleamed even in the darkness, always clean and polished.

Huun had jumped from his seat as if he had sat on a tack or been electrocuted in some way. He immediately made his way over to Zimm's side, like a good lackey.

'*Bootlicker*,' Jack thought to himself.

"Sir!" Huun saluted his superior.

"Is everything in order, Commander?"

"Yessir!" Huun replied quickly.

"Excellent." Expressionless, Zimm turned and glared at Jack. "Zero," he hissed in his low, authoritative voice. "You are aware of all mission parameters?"

"Yes," Jack felt his throat dry up making it difficult to swallow. This always happened when he spoke with Zimm. Zimm had a way of striking fear into him. "My part is to go intel on the ground, find any black spots drones may have missed in a scan, then report back to the rendezvous point at 0-500 hours."

Zimm grimaced, "Very good. Proceed."

Zimm stepped away, Leaving Huun the opportunity to speak to Jack privately. "Don't foul this up, Zero, or you may find yourself a casualty on this mission."

Jack threw Huun a disapproving look. Huun didn't frighten him, not as Zimm did. Whatever power Zimm held over him, it wasn't for him alone. Phineas also feared Zimm, even more so than Jack did. What surprised Jack more than anything was the fact that Zimm never even had to lay a hand on his men to keep them in line, a simple glare was more than enough. Jack shook it off, choosing to ignore Huun's comment instead of responding and furthering friction, he already had with him and his men. Jack stood tall and stoic within the tube. He placed his goggles over his eyes and signaled to Phineas with a 'thumbs up.' Phineas nodded before he pressed the large plunger-styled button on the console before him. The door to the tube closed and sealed, squeaking lightly as it sealed itself. A series of red lights flashed as sirens wailed, alerting everyone on board to the upcoming departure. In seconds, the trap door beneath Jack's feet opened up and jack disappeared, swallowed into the night sky.

Once Jack disappeared from view, Huun turned to the team and growled, "Alright ladies, let's get ready to move out!"

The wind pushed against Jack's face with great force as he dove, head first, through the sky, aiming toward the earth below. He kept his body rigid and straight, his legs locked together and his arms firmly at his sides. He plummeted like a stone with less resistance, allowing him to continuously increase his speed. He could feel his skin soften from the intensity of the air pushing his cheeks away from his skull. He kept his mouth closed tightly, his eyes protected with goggles. He could see the ground below, illuminated by the intermittent sparkle of lights that resembled a black backlit drop cloth with several pinholes poked through. Jack closed his eyes allowing the wind to wash over him, the ground rushing up quickly. He had done these types of jumps several times; he felt comfortable enough to 'feel' them through, not needing to see where he was going. He counted in his head, knowing the exact number in which he needed to tuck and release the pack.

Jack let his mind wander while still keeping count, preoccupying his thoughts with his mission, friends, and the life he left behind. It wasn't much as he didn't have many friends. He never cared for them; too many friends meant too many people knew your business. Same went for families as far as he was concerned. It was easy to brush off something one never had. The world he left behind wasn't very impressive. In fact, it was downright depressing. He was better off in the service; that was as close to family and friends as he needed. This way, it was easier to keep them at arm's length with no regrets or guilt.

It was a hollow life, but he knew no better.

He reached the number in his head. His eyes instinctively snapped open and he tucked his legs up to his chest. His body drifted slightly and then twisted before he flattened himself and was parallel to the ground. Jack then reached his hand to a button that rested just above his heart. With a hiss and snap, the wings on his back released. His body jerked back hard, but he was prepared. He held his breath allowing for his body to adjust to the quick changes in speed and pressure. Two small vents raised from the top of his pack above his shoulders. They acted as air brakes, absorbing the wind and slowing his descent. Jack was able to glide smoothly for several miles before he spotted his target location.

A military base, not formal in anyway, but suspected to house many technologies that the US military desired, but that wasn't his orders. Getting data was not his concern. He just needed to see what was safe and where they needed to go in order to infiltrate the base.

Jack soared above the trees of the forest that surrounded the base. He watched the ground beneath him streak past, like lines raked into the sand, there seemed to be no beginning or end to where the trees began or ended. He steadied his slow descent to the ground, looking for an appropriate place to bring himself down. It was at that moment the trees beneath broke apart, revealing a bare spot, to which he estimated was about thirty feet in diameter, a sparse area, but he had landed on smaller platforms. On one particular mission in South America, Jack managed to land on a platform at an elevation of 600 feet from the ground with a diameter of only fifteen feet. It was difficult, but he was comfortable with his glide pack that he was confident in his ability to land safely.

Jack twisted his waste and lifted his right arm. It allowed him to turn 180 degrees to his left. Jack circled back around to the sight he spotted from above and, as he descended above it, tucked his head under which allowed him to bring his body down. The decline was quick, the landing immediate. Jack pressed the button on his chest and retracted the wings of his pack. He rolled as he hit the earth, tucking his head under to help absorb the impact of his landing. Jack ended his roll by stopping himself on one knee. Crouched, he quickly lifted himself up onto both feet and made a beeline for the trees. First instinct is to find shelter, or in this case, cover.

It was dark, quiet, and serene in the forest. A welcomed change of pace, but one that Jack did not have the time to relish. As he ran through the forest in the direction of the base, he ignored the lush wonders of nature that surrounded him. He had a mission to accomplish. After nearly an hours trek through the forest, Jack had nestled a few yards outside the fortified walls of the base. Through his macro-viewer glasses, he could see a typical placement of guards, a total of fifteen, pacing the embankments. They were all armed, and he was sure, well trained.

Jack tossed in his bed. The springs that held his mattress aloft squeaked and groaned loudly as he shifted his weight. His face buried deeper into the pillow, muffling the sound of something stirring outside his office door. A dark spot covered the low light that broke under the door, before it began passing underneath. Several small spheres rolled under the door scraping across the wood, sounding like marbles rolling across the floor. The tiny spheres, several hundred of them, made their way under the door. Once they all passed through, they gathered near the center of the room where they began to pile on top of one another, growing higher and higher. Before long, the pile of spheres began to take on the shape of a man. The silhouette slowly developed features, soon creating eyes that flashed red. The form made its way across the room to where Jack slept, watching him eerily.

Jack didn't notice, he continued sleeping. The form stepped over to Jack's desk and began rifling through the items stacked around, searching. Jack snorted lightly, alerting the stranger. The form hesitated, watching Jack move before finally resting once again. The stranger began to open drawers, sifting through the contents, but not finding what it was looking for; it went to look elsewhere, tearing up the office. All the while, Jack slept.

Jack signaled for the other Skytroopers that recently landed, to join him. His intel had reached the carrier to which the team responded promptly, key members leaping from the plane. Joining him was Huun, Crust, Drent, Gruck, and surprisingly, Zimm. Jack had relayed his intel again to the team, but there was an uncomfortable stir from deep within. Jack knew what it was and he couldn't take his eyes off him: General Zimm.

"Did you assess the internal threat?" Zimm said condescendingly.

Jack was silent for a moment, "No."

"Of course you didn't, why would you?"

Jack grew defensive, "I stayed on the edge out here, but it's hard to determine."

"To an untrained professional."

Jack became more enraged from Zimm's constant jabs. Gruck held up his hand, signaling for Jack to keep his mouth shut. Reluctantly, Jack obliged. He swallowed his pride so often it was beginning to taste bitter. He balled his fists as he turned away. His hatred toward Zimm was growing. He never liked Zimm and knew the feeling was mutual. Ever since he was reassigned to the Skytroopers, Zimm has made it difficult. Zimm picked out the weakest in his unit and would crush their spirit, wanting only to allow the strongest to thrive. Jack saw him as nothing more than a bully.

The team pressed ahead, Huun now in command, taking the lead as they prepared to storm the base.

A loud noise alerted Jack as he groggily opened his eyes. His office was dark, still. Jack rubbed his eyes gently, attempting to ascertain what he was seeing. Nothing seemed to be out of place. Jack shrugged before letting loose a big yawn. His head dropped onto the pillow, instantly drifting back to sleep without missing a beat.

In the corner, a pair of crimson eyes flashed brightly. The silhouette they were attached to was well camouflaged, not just due to its dark form, but also because of the way in which it could change its appearance, taking the form of the wall behind it, replicating the color, texture, and even the framed pictures than hanged there. The creature stared for a long moment at Jack, watching and waiting to see if he stirred in any way again. He remained still. The creature then slowly slid open the filing cabinet and continued searching inside, parting the files, determined to find what it was after.

All the while, Jack slept.

The siege was quick, almost laughably quick. Huun had led the charge, with Crust and Drent, rampaging through the front gates while Jack and Gruck came in from above, swooping in with their glider packs and taking the tower guards by surprise. Jack used the repulsor engine on his pack to lift him into the air. He scooped up two guards and carried them high into the air, before releasing them into the nearby river. Gruck positioned himself on the first tower, using his laser sniper scope, picking off troops on the ground. It was a massacre, only lasting about thirteen minutes before they successfully overtook the base, neutralizing the Nang Shin Military. The smell of burning metal, fuel, and rubber filled the nose of Lieutenant Zero. There was a fourth odor, one much stronger and more pungent that the rest. Jack knew the smell all too well, and it was one he had never grown accustomed to, that of burning flesh. He coughed as the stench enwrapped his head, tightening and squeezing around him like a noose. He heaved as he lurched forward, stifling the urge to vomit. It showed weakness, something he didn't like to show the rest of his company, namely his commanding officer.

"You alright there, Zero?" Phineas asked with concern in his voice. Phineas was a good kid, young and ambitious. He was all of twenty-three, enlisting right out of high school in hopes to find true direction in his life. Most cracked when placed in such a high-tension battle, but Phineas was different, exceptional. He seemed to ignore the carnage. A trait that would frighten any civilian, especially when taken out of the battlefield, but, fortunately, Jack never saw that danger in Phineas. Phineas seemed to have compassion, the trait needed to maintain civility and sanity. Jack recognized it in Phineas, because he knew it was in himself as well.

"Yeah, sorry," Jack said apologetically. "There're just some things you never get used to."

"It's okay. We just gotta keep our heads in the game for the General."

"Of course," Jack smiled at Phineas. Jack handed a pistol to Phineas. Phineas shook his head, waving his hand at Jack, refusing the weapon. "It's not normal for a soldier to not use a weapon. You know that right?"

Phineas shrugged, "War isn't really normal now is it?"

Jack laughed at Phineas' strange philosophy. He simply took back the pistol and slid back the receiver in order to load a bullet into the chamber; however, the receiver stuck when he pulled it back. He tugged it harder until it clicked, cocking the gun. '*Damn gun*,' Jack thought. He stuffed the pistol into his equipment belt. He would worry about it later. Jack Zero had enlisted in the military at twenty-one, once he finished college, Now he was here four years later, in the middle of a full on battle, a moment he had trained for, and he was filled with fear.

Jack and Phineas had been crouching behind an overturned truck, an unfortunate victim to the grisly scene that they were involved. Jack could see the driver of the truck from where he hunched down. The driver dangled lifelessly from the shattered windshield, a steady flow of crimson flowing down his arm and pooling on the ground below. Sorry, pal, Jack closed his eyes in brief memoriam as he prepared to move.

Fire and explosions burst around Phineas and Jack as they ran from barricade to barricade, making their way across the freshly created warzone. As they moved closely along a crumbled wall, a hale fire of bullets rained down around them. Jack pushed Phineas out of the way just missing a trail of bullets that chewed into the brick wall behind them. They quickly scrambled along the ground on their hands and knees, shouting to one another, most of which was inaudible amongst the sound. They had made their way to another overturned vehicle, an armored hovering transport. It was pitched on its side with a gaping hole most likely caused by a rocket assault. Bullets echoed as they tinged against the metallic shell of the hover vehicle. Jack returned fire around the side of the vehicle while Phineas tried to connect with their commanding officer through his communication device.

"Commander Huun, do you copy? General Zimm do you copy, this if Private First Class Phineas Wald. Can anyone read me, over?" Phineas threw down his communicator. "It's dead."

"I'll try mine," Jack slid down as Phineas assumed Jack's station and resumed firing. "Commander Huun, do you read me?"

There was a short response of static, which crackled into a deep, resonating voice, "Lieutenant Jack, I read you. We have your position and we are in route."

Jack sighed, reassured. He set up next to Phineas, "I got them; they're on their way."

"They better hurry, there isn't much ammo left."

"Me neither," Jack said. He gestured in the direction of the gunfire, "They don't seem to be running short." Both men ducked down lower as more gunfire ricocheted across the hover vehicle.

Their assailants continued their barrage of gunfire for another three minutes, not seeming to exhaust their ammunition. About every thirty seconds, the firing would cease for a brief moment as the gunmen took time to reload from their endless supply. Jack peered through a smoldering bullet hole that punctured the metal siding of the hover vehicle mere centimeters from where his head rested. He could see the men snapping clips into their guns and cocking the rifles. He could also see one man that was not reloading. A ploy, he thought, one to flush them out on a false sense of security, feeling there was no gunfire they could make a run for safety, but instead were cut down unexpected gunfire.

"Where the hell are they?" Growled Phineas.

Jack held up his hand reassuringly, "Patience, they'll be here."

The gunfire resumed, bullets pinging and clanging as they showered down on Jack and Phineas' position. More bullets were cutting through the hull of the vehicle. Either the metal integrity was weakening or they were using more advanced hardware. A bullet whizzed through the metal hull past Jack's head. It wouldn't be long now.

'Dammit, Sarge, where the hell are you?' The light on Jack's wrist COMM began to hum, the red light that arced across the top pulsated rhythmically with the hum.

"You boys may want to get down," a deep voice warned, as it crackled over the COMM. Phineas looked at Jack confused. Jack looked up at the building adjacent to them and their assailants. On the roof was a silhouette of two men, one large, which He deduced was Huun, the other a smaller, thicker man shouldering a large cylindrical weapon. A ray cannon. Huun saw Jack and Phineas looking up at him. He gestured heavily, pointing forcefully toward the ground, signaling for the two to get down. Jack realized what was about to happen. He quickly wrapped his arm around Phineas' neck and shoved him, and himself, to the dirt.

"Charge it!" Huun barked to Lieutenant Commander Gruck.

The cannon rested on a padded leather cradle that strapped across his chest whined quickly and then chirped. "Charged!" Gruck confirmed.

"Cut 'em," Huun knocked on Gruck's helmet, confirming his order to fire.

Gruck, flipped the safety case up, pressed, and held the trigger. A bright, white-hot beam erupted from the barrel of the cannon, cut quickly through the darkness of the night and sank deeply into the ground. Gruck swiveled his hips and panned the cannon across the open street where Zero and Phineas had been pinned, tearing through the brick wall behind them, chunks of debris poured onto their bodies. The beam traced down along the ground, ripping the concrete just below their boots, the treads melting slightly from the heat. It skimming over their heads to sever the hull of the hover vehicle, the edges red and molten as the two halves separated, grinding apart, before the top half crashed to the ground with a loud, hollow thud, just missing Jack and Phineas by inches. He could feel the heat emitting from the smoldering edges.

The beam tore through the ground, creating a ditch as it arced toward the assailants who ultimately ceased firing their weapons to curiously stare at the beam quickly ascending on their position. They watched in confusion, looking up at the man on the roof who swiveled his body, directing the white-hot beam toward them. When the realization set in as to what was happening it was too late. The beam tore through their barricade and sliced each of them across their midsections. Their severed torsos flopped to the ground with deadening thuds, their lower limbs toppling after. There were no screams of distress or cries of agony to signal that their aggressors were subdued, except the silence of the extinguished beam and the clatter of rifles dropping against the pavement.

Jack pushed himself from the ground, where he had been shielding Phineas. He grabbed Phineas' hand to help him stand. Both men were slightly wobbly, trying to regain their balance. "You alright?" He asked.

"Yeah," Phineas teetered on his left foot and then caught himself. "Thanks."

"Now we're even," Jack winked.

The two men made their way across the street where overturned cars still burned brightly. They followed the crumbled pavement that had been masticated by the beam. Once across, they found the separated torsos of their assailants.

"Oh, God," Phineas gasped.

"Not likely," Jack retorted. "Let's move."

The two men ran to reach their destination, a rendezvous with their commanding officer, General Zimm.

"Line them up," General Zimm's voice was booming; it was as if he was talking through a microphone. "I want them all to see what is coming."

Zimm's men wasted no time and never asked any questions. Zimm's word was law; it was the final word. There were six men, each with their wrists bound behind their back and rags stuffed in their mouths. His men, Huun, Gruck, Crust, Drent, and Proux each grabbed one; Huun grabbed two of the bound prisoners and lined them up side-by-side. They then pressed down on their shoulders to position them on their knees. Crust's prisoner struggled more intensely, apparently pleading, his eyes becoming wet with tears. Crust pulled back his rifle in his arms and swung it against the pleading man's knees, causing the man to let out a muffled wail as his knees buckled and he fell forward painfully.

The man known as Terped coughed hard as his body doubled over from the intense pain he felt behind his knees. *'Why was this happening?'* He thought, the question rolling around repeatedly in his brain. Why were these people here? The tall one, Terped assumed he was the leader, he appeared older, his hair that peeked out from below his uniformed hat and his moustache peppered with black and white. His chest was decorated with several gold, silver, and colorful pins; they consumed his entire left half of his chest, an honor that must've taken a long time to earn. His skin looked weathered, like well-worn leather, showing its age, along with three symmetrical scars that fell diagonally across his right cheek just below his eye. His eye, the eye that stared deep and hard, almost as if it was looking through him into another dimension. The fact that it was pale blue made Terped think it was blind, but in reality it was fused, normally fusing was a sensible alternative for those that had suffered loss of a limb, brain activity, or even eyesight. Zimm was an exception. Zimm wanted his eye fused even when there was no know ailment affecting it. Zimm simply wanted enhancement for the sake of it, wanting only to trump his enemies.

"You know what makes me a great leader?" Zimm asked the heavily breathing Terped.

Terped shook his head.

"I know how to get my enemies to talk," Zimm paced slowly back and forth. "Do you know how to achieve this?"

Again, Terped shook his head. He was exhausted and in no mood to play games, "Just do as you will with me. Kill me if you must."

Zimm laughed maniacally, "Slow down my good man. You know that's the problem with today's youth, you never take time to enjoy the finer things in life. It's always rush, rush, rush. Haven't you ever heard the adage, 'good things come to those who wait?' Well it's true." Zimm walked slowly up to Terped and knelt down next to him, whispering in his ear, "Besides, I want to enjoy this."

Terped turned away, not wanting to be this close to this American pig. The reaction only made Zimm smile wider.

"Since you want to be so quiet, I'll tell you my secret for making enemies talk. Although, it's not really that much of a secret. The real trick is to learn as much about your enemy as possible, finding their weakness. Once you know it, you exploit it. Just be sure it's the right weakness." Zimm looked over at Gruck and pointed for him to leave, which Gruck immediately did. "In all my experiences, you know what I found to be the right weakness?"

As Zimm turned away from Terped, Jack and Phineas returned. Both men were exhausted, their faces and clothing stained black from the soot that drifted in the air and littered the ground. They each removed their glider packs and set the heavy equipment to the ground near a stack of crates behind them. The packs had slowed them down for quite a ways. They panted heavily, but maintained their composure as they greeted their superior with a proper salute.

"General," Jack acknowledged, lowering his salute.

"Ah, Lieutenant Zero," Zimm looked over at Huun who was

gritting his teeth at the compliment. "You're just in time."

"In time, sir?"

Zimm waved his hands in the air confidently, "For victory."

Jack looked at the pitiful man on his knees, confusion setting in. He looked at Phineas who looked equally confused.

Terped shook his head, pain searing up his spine as he twisted slightly, his bound wrists knotting his muscles. At that moment, almost as if on cue, Gruck returned, but he wasn't alone. He was pushing a woman and child along with the muzzle of his gun. She was sobbing gently as she came into the light.

"Martia!" Terped yelled. The sight of his wife and son made his heart drop into his stomach.

"Terped! Please!" Martia pleaded helplessly. Terped stood and ran toward Martia, but was held back by Huun's vice-like grip of his shoulder. Martia ran toward Terped, but was stopped by the back of Zimm's hand. Zimm held nothing back, drawing his thick arm back and launching it forward with the strength of his entire body. The sting of skin-to-skin contact was tantalizing to Zimm, feeding his sadistic nature. He felt his knuckles split open as they cut across Martia's teeth. She could feel his warm blood flow across her tongue; its distinct metallic taste was overwhelming. The surprise of the sudden impact caused Martia to jerk back hard as her body fell backward, her legs collapsing under her. The unfortunate condition of her bound hands caused her to fall on her side with a solid thud. She could now taste her own blood on her tongue as well. Her jaw ached.

"Mama!" Her son, Frederique, screamed loudly. The sight of his mother's pain both frightened and angered him.

"NO! YOU BASTARD!" Terped yelled at Zimm, trying with all his strength to break free of Huun's grasp. "LET THEM GO!"

Zimm stepped between them. His smile bright, wide, and terrifying. He brought his knuckles to his mouth and licked the blood from them methodically. "Now you see," Zimm said, his voice still upbeat. "The RIGHT weakness."

"Damn you," Terped said, his voice defeated. "What is it you want from me?"

Zimm stood tall. He felt suddenly recharged, invigorated. The RIGHT weakness. Zimm turned to face his prey, a broad grin plastered across his unattractive face. "I want your information."

"What?"

"I want information on the Genesis Hydrogen Missile 12-90."

"I don't know what you are talking about."

Zimm looked up at Gruck and nodded slightly. Gruck slammed the butt of his rifle in the back of Terped's skull. The impact vibrated around his cranium and sank deep into his brain. His ears rang and the throbbing persisted.

"But I think you do," Zimm was sounding more impatient now. Playtime was over. "And unless you give me what I ask for, I am going to have to redirect my attention from you," Zimm walked over between Martia and Frederique. He placed his hands on each of their heads, caressing them sadistically. "To someone more important.

"Please, let them go, I don't know anything."

"So you expect me to believe, the top officer in the research and development of weapons division knows nothing of a highly sophisticated and destructive weapon with the capabilities of wiping its enemies off the face of the earth? How stupid do you think I am? I happen to know that your military has developed a weapon, a projectile missile, codenamed NARF" Zimm approached Terped slowly, grabbed a fistful of his hair and roughly forced his head back, making them stare directly into one another's eyes. "I WANT IT!"

"What's going on here, General?" Jack stepped forward. "I thought this was simply a search and nullify mission. Now it's a search and destroy?"

"Yes," Zimm hissed. "I'm simply seeking the weapon I wish to use to destroy."

"NO!" Jack shouted. "I don't understand what's going on here? The area has been completely evacuated of all civilians, no innocents. We don't do this. We don't hurt innocent people."

"You're so naïve, you always were," Zimm sneered. "There are no innocents. Not this man, nor his wife or child. They live in a home with a man who creates death and destruction. In my experience, they aren't innocent. They're as guilty, guiltier, guilt by association."

Zero balled his hands into fists, clenching them tightly. His stomach turned over, he felt queasy. This was not right. "We only have twenty minutes."

"What?"

Phineas interjected, "The locks are in place, the bombers already contacted. They're on their way."

"We need to wrap this up now," Drent interjected, shouldering his rifle.

"In twenty, this whole area will be one huge crater," Jack assured.

Zimm looked slightly annoyed as he turned his attention back to Terped, "Then we haven't much time." He pressed his pistol against Terped's head. Sweat streaked down Terped's face, his breath erratic. He looked out of the corner of his eye to see his son curled up next to his dead mother; his arms wrapped tightly around his knees, as he tried to act strong and stifled his tears as best he could. Terped knew he could do no less. He had always taught his son to be strong, not to give in to fear. Like when he was afraid to sleep alone in the dark, Terped showed his son there was nothing to be afraid of, or when he fell from his bike, he showed Frederique that he couldn't give up and needed to persevere and try again. This time couldn't be any different. He needed to be strong for his son now. Terped caught his son's eye and winked to Frederique with a small grin. Frederique looked up at his father, terror and love seizing him all at once. What could he do?

Zimm cocked his pistol.

"Dammit Zimm," Jack yelled. "Didn't you hear me, we don't have time! We need to leave now!"

"I am your superior, Lieutenant. I expect you to address me as such," Zimm snarled. He called to Gruck, "Call the Dropper off!"

"You can't," Phineas stepped forward meekly, not knowing what to truly make of the intense situation that was rapidly unraveling around him. He was confused. Whom could he trust? His commanding officer? Or the only person that was descent to him since he was recruited? "According to regulations, once the dropped is called and locked, all communications are frozen in the target area."

"He's right," Gruck said as his COMM device responded with the crackle of static.

Terped was becoming desperate as he watched his wife, tears streaming down her face, trying to hold her composure while his son sobbed next to her, too scared to react. Time was short. "Please, let them go, they have nothing to do with any of this. Let them go, I will tell you anything."

"I know you will," Zimm smiled. "I just want to make sure it's the truth." Zimm drew his pistol and fired at Martia. She fell to the ground, letting out a small yelp. Frederique squealed in terror and rushed to his mother's side. But before he could reach her, Zimm scooped the small boy up with his arm.

"NO! MARTIA!" Terped screamed. "YOU BASTARD! LET HIM GO!" Terped pleaded for his son.

Zimm's expression remained emotionless. He took the pistol that wafted a small stream of smoke from the barrel, and turned it on the boy wrapped in his arm. "You are in a position unsuitable to give orders." Zimm cocked the pistol, pressing the muzzle to the boy's temple. "You now have ten seconds."

"Wait, General, this has to stop, you can't do this," Jack stepped forward angrily. "This isn't how we do things."

"You better watch yourself," Huun lumbered up to Jack.

"Back off," Jack tried to sound threatening against Huun's massive size. By the glare on Huun's face, it wasn't working.

"I can smash you," Huun growled.

Jack rolled his eyes. He knew Huun, all talk. He liked to threaten, but knew he couldn't carry through. That would mean violating his superior, which he could never do; he couldn't bare the humiliation of a dishonorable discharge. Jack didn't feel the same way. He immediately pushed past Huun. "Sir, I can't let you do this."

"Oh please, Zero, what do you think you can do?"

Jack drew his revolver and trained it at Zimm's forehead, "Sir, I'm afraid I'm going to have to insist you drop you weapon and the child and step away. I hereby relieve you of your duties; you are no longer fit to assume command."

Zimm stared at Jack for a long moment. The other men of the regiment looked on in disbelief, not realizing what was happening at first. Phineas had been in service the shortest time. Never did he expect to be privy to such a spectacle. Zimm finally threw his head back and laughed loudly. "Such courage. Too bad you suffer from delusions of grandeur."

"I'm not asking again," Jack pulled the hammer back on his revolver, the click signaling the round being loaded in the chamber.

Whether loyalists or unsure of the protocol shift, Huun, and the others drew their pistols and trained them all on Jack Zero. Jack felt his heart leap into his throat. He tried to maintain his composure, being careful not to reveal any fear. Huun made him the most nervous. He had always shown reserve, but maybe this was his moment to snap. He was very loyal to Zimm. Despite his feelings, Jack kept his focus on Zimm, "Stand down, General."

Unexpectedly, Zimm signaled for his men to lower their weapons. Jack tried not to show he was shaken by this, he simply stole a quick glance around as each soldier lowered their arms. Jack's hands shook as he gripped the butt of his revolver and kept his aim on Zimm. His voice quavered as much of his hands, "General Zimm, I hereby relieve you of your command."

The shrilled sound of Zimm's laughter unnerved Jack. He had to stand his ground and show he was serious. Jack fired a warning shot in the air above Zimm's head, "I'm not going to tell you again, stand down."

Huun's blood boiled as he watched Jack's blasphemous action. He wanted nothing more than to wrap his large hands around Jack's skull and squeeze until it popped like a rotten peach. Zimm threw Huun a quick look that read 'hold back.' Huun sucked in his breath and relaxed his thick muscles, his hands still fists.

"Oh please, Zero, you don't have the guts to pull this off, besides, what do you expect to accomplish."

"To finally put an end to your madness."

"If I recall correctly, you once felt as I did. That this world was not worth saving when it was filled with greed and monsters. Monsters like this man here," Zimm gestured to Terped. "Do you think stopping me will stop them? Don't you remember when I recruited you for my team we had a singular vision."

"You had a vision, the rest of us were blind."

"So this is it, is it Zero," Zimm challenged. "Let's see if you're faster than me."

Jack pulled the trigger of his revolver, the bullet exploded from the barrel. Zimm was prepared, a warrior. Zimm had trained in several countries and knew almost every style of defensive and combative hand-to-hand techniques. Jack knew this. But knowledge was never enough. The bullet sailed toward Zimm, and, as if with lightening reflexes, Zimm dodged the weapon and raised his own firing a shot at Jack. The movements happened so quickly that the second sound of the gunfire was immediate. Zimm's bullet tore into Jack's arm, burrowing deep into the muscle and tissue and shattering the bone. Jack fell backward from the intense pain and shock.

Zimm tossed his pistol to Huun who caught the hot metal with no sensation of pain. He simply smiled as he gripped the weapon.

Crust returned, noisily interrupting the scene at hand. He wore a wide, proud smile, "Got it!" He rushed over and handed a data drive to Zimm. "All their records are on this. Even the Genesis missile project. And some mass-transporter research you may find interesting."

"Excellent!" Zimm voice lifted with glee. "Now, let's get out of here before this place goes up in flames," Zimm snarled. "And take care of him." Zimm gestured to Terped.

With great satisfaction, Huun shot Terped in the head; the bullet rocked his head back as if it was on a swivel. It jerked hard forward as he fell to the ground face first with a wet thud. Frederique wailed loudly as he watched his father chortle out his last breath before blood streamed from his gaping maw, silencing him forever. Huun aimed his pistol at the boy and pulled the trigger, no point in letting the boy suffer what would most likely be a painful and tortured death. Better to end it quick.

However, the bullet never reached the boy. Instead, it punctured through the stomach of PFC Phineas Wald, a young boy on his first real mission. A hopeful soldier looking to make the world a safer place. A boy afraid to die, but not afraid to save an innocent. An innocent himself. The moment was followed by complete silence. Zimm turned to see the crumpled body of Private Phineas lying before the young boy who no longer sobbed or wailed. Instead, he watched at the heroism of the stranger whom now looked up at him with wet eyes.

Zimm scoffed, "Leave him; let's move."

Huun holstered the weapon and turned, following Gruck, Crust, and Proux, not giving a second thought to look back. Leaving behind to dead parents and their frightened child, and two wounded soldiers, colleagues, men he once called brothers. Jack writhed on the ground in pain, his arm shredded, and hanging limply by a small stretch of skin and bone. He looked over at the young boy he wanted to save, and the young man he took under his wing. Both led astray into their own deaths. It was his fault. Soon it would all be erased when the Dropper released the bomb.

"Phineas?" Jack called as loudly as possibly. "Phineas? Can you hear me?" There was no answer. Jack tried to inch himself toward Phineas, he winced at the pain. He was limited in his movement, the pain was overwhelming. Jack needed to move and quickly. He had one good arm. That was a start. As he tried to maneuver himself, he heard the sound of soft weeping. The boy. Frederique was still balled up, his knees to his chin. He had to reach him somehow, "Kid? Hey kid can you hear me?"

The boy was quiet.

"What's your name?"

Still no answer.

"Look, kid, I know this is really hard. I can't even imagine how you are feeling right now. I'm sorry I couldn't do more. I wish I could've helped, done more. I don't know if you can even understand me, but we don't have much time. There is a plane coming our way. On that plane is a bomb that it will drop and when it explodes, it will blow the whole place sky high. We will all be wiped out." It was still quiet. Maybe the boy had given up. Whatever the reason, it was hopeless. "You see that pack over there, the silver one; I need you to get that for me."

Frederique turned his head, looking away from his mother's corpse for the first time. His eyes locked onto Jack's. His eyes, once innocent and unknowing, naïve, now shown as hardened, empty. It sent chills down Jack's spine. Before him, a boy transformed into a man, but in a haunting, tormented way. This boy was forever changed. Forever scarred. Frederique stood and walked over to the pack. He looked it over curiously before hoisting it up. It was heavier than it looked, but he seemed to ignore the difficulty it brought. He dragged it like a mindless robot following its programming. Emotionlessly. The boy dropped the pack in front of Jack.

"Can you get the other one?" Jack implored.

The boy nodded.

Jack rolled himself over, positioning himself onto the pack. He painfully slid his arms into the straps and buckled it together tightly. It took some effort, but Jack managed to get himself upright. His right arm was limp. The bullets had torn his arm up good. It looked as if it had been macerated and then regurgitated. He wrapped it up as best he could with the strips of cloth he tore from his uniform.

Frederique mimicked his motions as he dropped the pack before Jack. With one arm, Jack managed to dress Phineas' wound and then flipped him around. His wound was still bleeding. He slid Phineas' arms into the straps, but before he locked the buckles, he turned to Frederique. The boy still looked around blankly.

Jack called to the boy, "Frederique, c'mere."

The boy obliged silently.

"Sit in front of him," Jack pointed at Phineas.

Frederique sat.

"Look, kid," Jack tried to speak calmly, but knew there was only a matter of minutes remaining. "I need you to help my friend here. You need to steer this pack. Have you ever ridden a bike?"

"Yes," the boy whispered. The question brought up many memories of riding with his family, trips to the market and the first time he rode without his training wheels. His mother was so proud. However, it was all over now, just memories.

"The pack works kind of like that," Jack lied. "You see this?" Jack held up a small square device that clipped to the base of a helmet. All you need to do is move your head slightly, it will steer you in the same direction. Do you understand?"

Frederique was motionless. After a moment, he nodded.

"Good," Jack smiled as best he could.

He quickly strapped the boy in front of Phineas, threading the straps between the two with only his one good arm. Once he was confident it was secured tightly enough he placed his one hand on the boy's shoulder. Looking at him intently, he explained, "I've programmed the pack to take you over thirty miles from here, well past the safe zone. Once you are there, I want you to get help for Mr. Wald here, you got that?"

Frederique nodded.

"Good luck, kid," Jack ignited the pack and Frederique and Phineas lifted softly into the sky before drifting away. He watched them part and drift safely away before preparing himself. In the distance, Jack could hear the low rumble of the Drop Ships engine, purring as it travelled along. It was on its way. He had to flee and quickly. He estimated he had about five minutes to get safely away. He looked up to see Phineas and the boy were out of view, he hoped they were safe. He would have to rendezvous with them later. First, he had a score to settle with General Zimm.

Zimm's rescue lift cruised toward the flying fortress, the same ATAC that brought them. He sat properly in his seat as he watched calmly out the window. Smoke billowed from the carnage below, choking the sky. He smiled to himself before leaning back, the tension released from his body, the base growing smaller as they moved farther away. He felt good. Accomplished. He looked over at Huun who was staring at him vigilantly, although it seemed rather eerie. Huun was an excellent soldier, never questioning orders, obeying always. Whenever Huun was placed in command, his results were flawlessly successful. It was exactly why Huun would never become a commanding officer. Huun was ambitious and hungry for a command of his own, but Huun lacked the ability to think beyond the battle, or look beyond the mission. Had Huun hot been under Zimm, Huun would surely have perished in battle long ago. Zimm wasn't Huun's courage or shrewd ability to make snap decisions, he was more important than that. Zimm was Huun's sensibility. He handled the complication of assessing a situation and determining the appropriate next move.

Zimm thought, *'Jack Zero could do that.'* Zimm knew Jack was a true soldier. In fact, he saw Jack more as a threat than as an equal. Jack would be a great leader, perhaps too great. One better than him. That was why he left Jack behind, and why Zimm was willing to leave him for dead.

Zimm looked over at the other men in his troop. Crust and Proux, and the others, all good men, obedient. None equaled Jack Zero.

"Zero," Drent grunted.

Zimm nearly fell from his seat. How did Drent know what he was thinking? "What did you say?" Zimm asked, confused.

"Zero!" Drent sounded more alarmed as he pointed at Zimm. Or so Zimm thought, until he realized Drent was pointing out the lift's window.

Zimm turned to see a small speck of orange light growing larger against the black sky. "What the Hell is that?"

"ZERO!" Drent yelled just as the once tiny spec had now grown to reveal Jack Zero attached to a glider pack, rocketing through the sky and catching up to the escaping lift.

Zero's body slammed into the door of the lift. His impact was hard enough to dent the side inward. He hit the door hard with his left shoulder. The arm was already numb, so the use of it as a battering ram didn't affect it much. Jack was hellbent on ensuring Zimm didn't escape. Using his one good arm, Jack slid his fingers into the seam of the door, and with the aid of his pack's thrust, tore open the door. He acted and moved fast so as not to allow any of the men inside the time or opportunity to retaliate.

Wind rushed into the compressed compartment, preventing the men onboard to focus quickly even once they had grabbed their sidearm. Jack stepped onto the lift and immediately kicked his boots into Huun's unsuspecting face. Huun fell over like a boulder, dropping to the floor of the lift. Jack quickly turned to face off with his next opponent, Proux. Proux wasn't prepared. Jack made quick work of him, bringing his fist up under Proux's jaw, knocking him off his feet.

Drent pulled a pistol and prepared to aim it, but Jack charged into him. Jack rammed Drent with his left shoulder as hard as he could. His arm holding the pistol slammed hard against the wall of the lift. The gun clattered to the floor, skittering across the rocking airship. Drent's spine also hit the metal wall of the lift hard. The pain shot up his spine, stabbed his skull, resulting in his limbs going taut, and then limp before he fell over, knocked unconscious.

Zimm had hardly moved during the assault. It was after Jack took down Crust that he became more nervous. Jack had taken a fist to his abdomen, buckling over. Before Crust could counter, Jack brought up his head and smashed it under Crust's chin. Crust's jaw clamped shut, his teeth grinding as they smashed together. The noise filled his head, but no matter how deafening the sound was, the pain was more intense. Crust fell over, clutching his chin, his head spinning.

Jack launched himself toward Zimm. Zimm calmly drew his pistol and pushed it into Jack's face. Jack stopped. His eyes locked onto the muzzle of the pistol. This was a position he feared he would find one day, but he hoped only in his nightmares. The pistol was cocked and ready to fire.

"Well, Zero," Zimm sneered. "Who'd have ever thought we'd be in this position?"

Jack did, but he didn't respond.

Zimm continued, "You have gumption, I'll give you that, but you are also stupid. If you used the brain in your head for anything other than impulse, you'd know that you were no match for me."

"I won't let you get away with murder," Jack huffed.

"I already have," Zimm fired, but Jack dropped himself to the floor. The bullet punched through the wall behind Jack. Zimm fired at Jack again, but Jack rolled away, the bullet missing him again. "Stay still you sonuva bitch."

"How about I come to you," Jack ignited his glider and slid across the floor toward Zimm. He lifted his head gently, raising his body off the floor. He flew directly into Zimm's midsection and carried him out the open door. Zimm heaved as he dropped his pistol and clung onto Jack. He had little choice after such an impulsive action.

Huun had come to as he watched his leader fly out the side of the airlift, "NO!"

Jack held onto Zimm with his one good arm, his other hanging loosely. For the first time in a long time, Zimm was afraid. He was in the hands of an adversary who had the upper hand. There was no telling what he had planned.

"What are you going to do, Zero?"

Jack ignored Zimm, pressing across the sky.

"Put me down, Zero!" Zimm yelled, obviously irritated by Jack's silence, "I demand you put me down this instant!"

Jack refused to look Zimm in the eye, "That's just what I had in mind." Jack let slack his left arm. Zimm, his eyes like saucers, slipped from Jack's grip and fell to the ground below.

Huun watched helplessly as his General fell to his death. His throat closed as he gasped. There was nothing he could do. Zimm was dead.

"DAMN YOU ZERO!" Huun screamed into the sky. "YOU WILL DIE FOR THIS! YOU WILL DIE AND I WILL BE THE ONE WHO KILLS YOU!"

Jack snapped awake, sitting up in bed, his body drenched in sweat. He had been dreaming. A recurring nightmare that haunted him all too often. For the first time it was so vivid, so real. Perhaps seeing Phineas again after all the years that have passed dredged up all the details he had so often chosen to repress. He had forgotten some of the faces, he had even forgotten about Huun's threat, but he had never forgotten Frederique or Zimm. Jack shook the thoughts from his dream and looked over at the holo-clock. It was three a.m. He rubbed his eyes and rolled himself over, trying his best to forget the dream and fall asleep peacefully.

The red eyes lit up again from across the room, finding the opportunity to escape finally returning. It had turned over everything in the office. It carried a small file in its appendages, tucking it neatly under its arm. The silhouette walked slowly past Jack's sleeping body, watching his chest rise and fall rhythmically. It slinked slowly to the office door and paused. Jack stirred for a moment, the silhouette froze, waiting and watching. When no more movement occurred, the form dissipated, falling to the floor in several tiny spheres. The file of papers dropped along with the spheres, being carefully held together. The file simply stayed on the top of the wide berth the spheres consumed of the floor. They rolled stealthily along the wooden floor, the file skipping along the tops of the spheres until it all slipped away under the door, disappearing into the night.

CHAPTER 11
THE STRANGE BANK HEIST

The shadows were misleading. What looked like a hulking intruder was only a chair. Another which resembled a spiny skeleton was only a desk lamp. The third time a pack of charging wolves was a fountain pen set. Benji Holdt, or Ben as he preferred, was not going to be spooked by everyday objects, not on his first day as a security guard for New Utica's First National Bank. It was not as if he couldn't handle it, it was simply a fact that the building was old, large in its architecture with lots of open spaces that leant themselves to dark, shadowy areas, perfect places to hide. That in and of itself made him a bit uneasy at times, but he was prepared, ready for anything. Ten weeks of training helped to see he was ready. At least that's what he hoped.

"C'mon, kid, you gonna get around to checkin' the vault downstairs, or what?" Chester barked.

Chester was a seasoned veteran at being a security officer. Thirty-three years in the same bank, he'd often say. It would be charming if he didn't bring it up every other conversation. Chester didn't have much to share, let alone anyone with which he could share. He was well into his sixties and lived a mediocre existence. Since his wife passed away from cancer twelve years ago, he put all his energies and efforts into being the best bank guard there ever was. He tried, not always succeeding. There was an attempted robbery once about twenty years ago, but Chester had the day off. Of course, there were no attempted robberies or terrorist attacks that he needed to quell, but there were several irate customers that needed to be escorted from the premises on several occasions. Despite never being able to win a medal of merit of any kind, Chester certainly liked his job. He especially enjoyed the part of ordering rookies around. They usually allowed Chester to be a bit more, relaxed. How could one not be when the newbie was doing most of the work?

"Well?" Chester urged.

"Yeah, alright, I'm goin'" Ben said with heavy reluctance.

Aw, c'mon, kid, it won't be so bad. Look at me; I've done it plenty of times myself."

"But' it's dark down there."

Don't be such a baby," Chester chided. He reached for his belt, feeling around to his left side, unclipping his flashlight. He tossed it to Ben who nearly dropped it, bouncing it between his hands before he clasped it tight. "Be sure to scream if you see anything."

Ben looked oddly at Chester, not sure if he was being serious or still teasing him. Ben walked away quietly, Chester's laugh echoed across the open chamber. Ben was beginning to hate that guy.

He didn't want the job. Not at first. In fact, the only reason he took the job was that his brother-in-law worked as a finance manager during the day. Ben needed a job, any job, and this one was available. He'd rather continue playing his music, which was a real passion. Not that Greg, his brother-in-law, was happy to help; he'd rather Ben rot in Hell. They never really got along, starting from day one when Ben's sister, Cera, brought him home.

Ben turned the corner, just outside the hallway leading to the main vault when he stopped. There was a strange sensation that crept over him, warm and electric, as if the air were energized by something. He could smell it, like the wind before a thunderstorm. He held his hand out, feeling the charge. It sent heat through his body, energizing and nearly invigorating him. He didn't know what this was from, but it certainly was a welcome change to the dull job. He jumped at the sound of lightening crackling behind him. This time the surge of energy was much more powerful, more electric. He turned to see what could possibly be pushing off such an electrical charge. Perhaps it was a fried circuit, or a loose wire that was sparking behind the wall. Either case, it could result in something serious, like shutting off half the power to the bank, namely the vault. He turned to see if he could determine the location of the charge, expecting to see sparks or smoke, maybe, but hopefully not, even flames. Instead, he saw a man. A naked man. He couldn't believe what he had just seen. He rubbed his eyes vigorously, hoping to wipe away whatever caused him to see such a ridiculously disturbing image. He slowly stepped forward, placing his hand on the butt of his gun. Well...actually, it was a Taser gun, but a gun nonetheless. He walked slowly, heel to toe, trying not to make too much sound and startle whatever it was he saw, and to hear anything that might come his way. His hand shook furiously as it hovered over the gun, poised and ready to act, though maybe not effectively. He made his way toward the vaults, the lower part of the bank, it was very dark and empty, aside from a few large potted plants that lined both sides of the walls leading up to the vault's door. It was a huge, thick metal door that was secured by a giant round handle with spindles surrounding it along the outside, much like the wheel of a sailboat. There were dials for the combination to be input, a code only the bank owners and managers knew. A large cast-iron gate encased the door, the bars close together making it difficult for someone to slink through even if they cracked the locks. Ben had only been down here a couple of times, he didn't feel comfortable being this close during the day. He edged his way into the open, waving the flashlight Chester tossed at him erratically around the room, attempting to wash out any shadow he could. The room was empty, more than usual. Maybe he had been seeing things. He lowered his poised hand and flicked off the flashlight. That was when the first attack came, swiftly and mercilessly.

Chester shoved the liverwurst sandwich deep into his mouth, mustard squirted from the opposite end, falling onto his shirt. "Shit," he fussed as he wiped the stain with his finger and popped it into his mouth. The sound of his lips smacking was disgustingly voluminous. He let out a large belch before finishing the last bite of his snack, a bite that was the equivalent of three for the average human. As soon as the belch reverberated a blast of electricity flashed in front of him knocking him to the floor. Chester quickly rolled from his back on which he landed and stood, drawing his Taser gun from his belt and aiming it in every direction. He could see blue bolts of electricity dancing up the walls and across the ceiling before fizzling out. His eyes were out of sorts, his vision blurred, spots of light floated before him. He rubbed them to regain his vision, but when he removed his hands, the most peculiar sight seemed to appear in front of him. A naked man. He stood motionless, like a Greek statue with a chiseled and defined physique. Chester had never seen the likes of this before, a man appearing from thin air. Could he have been the victim of a blown circuit and now he was seeing things? Or worse, dead? He pinched his hand, the sharp pain registering instantly in his brain. No, not dead or asleep. Could this be a ghost?

"What are you?" Chester said, trying to steady himself. "You a ghost or somethin'?"

"Or something," the naked man replied. He charged Chester who instinctively fired the Taser gun. The electrified tendrils flew rapidly, but did not reach their intended target. The naked man was nimble, superhuman almost, as he leapt into the air above the tendrils, which sailed into the wall behind him. He landed in front of Chester and without hesitation, swung his left foot into the air while pivoting on the heel of his right, landing a kick into Chester's solar plexus. Chester flew back several feet skidding across the ground. He was winded, but not out. He rolled onto his stomach and picked himself up as quickly as his rotund exterior allowed. He tugged his drooping pants up around his waist as he ran. Unfortunately, the man was much faster and more nubile. The man launched himself into the air and cartwheeled over Chester's head, landing in Chester's path of escape. He grabbed Chester by his lapel and raised his hand, preparing to strike.

"Wait!" A voice called from behind. The naked assailant dropped his hand and snapped it to his forehead, saluting another naked man that emerged from around a corner. The blue lightening that Chester saw move along the room snapped across this new man's shoulders. "No fatalities." He was obviously the man in charge, possibly a ranking officer, but to what army?

"Yessir," the saluting man replied.

"Please, don't kill me," Chester pleaded.

The man, who moved more like a hopping toad, never said a word. He simply punched Chester in the face, rendering him unconscious.

"We must find the others," The ranking naked man ordered. "Ensure the remainder of the perimeter is secured and then meet us back at the rendezvous point. And soldier; don't forget to get the clothes."

"Yes, Commander Huun."

Commander Caspar Huun was a tall, muscular man. Much larger and more built than his subordinate. His face was as thick as his neck. His hair, light blonde and tightly cropped. Despite all these marked features, his most noticeable and most striking were his light blue eyes that seemed to bore into the skull of anyone he looked at. He wore a scowl at all times, never allowing himself to express any emotion. Especially since he had just moved miles in a matter of seconds, he was not going to show the queasy feeling he had. He watched as the young soldier trotted off to inspect the remainder of the main lobby. As soon as the boy was out of sight Huun wretched the contents of his stomach all over the nearest potted plant. He stood, his head fuzzy and unbalanced, wiping his mouth, he garnered his composure. He proceeded to disrobe the unconscious guard and dressed in the oversized clothes. He adjusted himself as best he could and made his way to the vault.

Ben was afraid for his life. This was a moment when everything you ever feared about being a bank guard came to fruition. But nowhere in the manual had there ever been anything about a naked man that appeared out of nowhere; especially one that could leap around like some kind of jungle animal. Ben had lost his Taser and was scrambling on all fours trying to find it. It was even harder without the flashlight. He tried to listen for his assailant, keeping as aware to his surroundings as much as possible. It was hard to hear over his erratic breathing, which he did his best to steady. He threw a glance over his shoulder. The room was dark, but also quiet, devoid of any presence other than his self. He panned his head around catching the Taser in his peripheral, just out of his reach. He scurried over on his hands and knees, ensuring he reached it before another onslaught. He clasped his hand around the device and rolled himself over, aiming the Taser into the air at nothing in particular, hoping to hit a target, the right target. He saw a shadow stretch across the wall and ceiling in front of him. He fired. The tendrils flew across the room not quite reaching the wall and dropping to the floor. Not good. The naked hopping man emerged from the shadows, his head lowered, eyes narrowed. He focused on Ben and began to run toward him. Ben needed to act fast. He retracted the tendrils of the Taser and noticed it still had a reasonable charge, nearly three-quarters full. He reset, aimed and fired and the man barreling toward him. The tendrils sank deep into the man's chest; a surge of electricity rippled down the tendrils and ignited the flesh of the man's chest. The man slowed the smolder of light burning under his skin. The smell of cooking flesh filled Ben's nostrils. He gagged, putting his hand up, cupping his nose. He looked up to watch the man fall to his knees. Unfortunately, he stood, unflinching. The man was receiving nearly 950,000 volts of electricity, yet he stood, motionless, his face twisted in rage. The naked hopping man clasped his hand around the tendrils and plucked them from under his flesh. Two narrow streams of blood flowed from the wounds and down his abdomen.

Ben trembled, "Oh shit."

The naked hopping man leapt high, his legs outstretched as he fell from the air and impacted his anterior thigh into Ben's throat. After impact, the man sprung to his feet in defensive preparation. Ben didn't fight back. The attack had been devastating. He rolled over slowly and rattled, reaching up and grasping his throat, trying to relieve the pressure of the blow and regain his breath. The naked hopping man took advantage of the moment. He grabbed the Taser, wrapped the tendrils around both hands positioned himself over Ben, and wrapped the taut cord around Ben's neck. Ben couldn't breathe, the cord grew tighter. He began to see spots before his eyes, a pop filled his ears. Within moments, his vision grew dark. Some first day on the job.

"Enough!" A voice called from behind.

The naked hopping man slackened the cords, releasing Ben who flopped on the floor, wheezing strenuously.

"No deaths yet," Col. Huun explained to another subordinate.

"Sorry, sir," the hopping man said. He looked at his leader who wore a security uniform that drooped ridiculously.

Huun looked down at the guard who breathed erratically, but

appeared unconscious, "Put them on and get the keys, Lt. Crust."

Aye, sir," Crust saluted.

As Crust disrobed the unconscious Ben, he unfastened the keys from Ben's belt and tossed them to Huun. Huun snapped them from out of the air and walked to the vault, unlatching the gate lock with little effort. He pushed aside the gate and turned the vault door several times until it clicked. He then tugged on the release, but the door did not budge. He tried again, but still nothing. The code had been changed from the combination they had obtained. Huun didn't look concerned. It was no matter, he thought. He thought the entire trouble of requisitioning the code was frivolous. Who needed codes when you harbored the strength of nearly a dozen men? Huun gripped the spindles at ten and four, spaced his legs apart, anchoring himself in place as he began to pull.

The sound of metal grinding against metal echoed across the chamber. It drew the remaining two members of this team to find their place, watching their leader intently as he tore the handle from out of a door that was several feet thick, as if it were tin foil. Huun tossed the lock aside. It scraped as it slid heavily, leaving a groove across the concrete floor. Huun made his way into the vault, it was large, spacious, lined with small drawers, each secured with a powerful computerized lock, its security signified by flashing red LED's. Huun scanned the wall of drawers, looking for number 661. His eyes caught the drawer. Within minutes, his fist smashed through the drawer. The charges within the drawer sparked, dancing around Huun's arm. His arm quickly ignited and flared, a bright orange flame lapping up his thick appendage. Without flinching, Huun patted the flame out. There was no mark on his flesh indicating he had even been burned. The only evidence was the charred wall surrounding the drawer the safe deposit box had once been in. Huun reached in and pulled out a black device. He placed it in his pocket and headed out the door.

"Time to go," he ordered.

The four men quickly departed.

CHAPTER 12
ON THE TRAIL OF TROUBLE

Jack's head was still groggy. After his weird encounter with Phineas Wald last night and his awful dreams, he managed to squeak in just over four hours of sleep. It could have been longer had Ceinwen not arrived at 6:45 sharp. As Ceinwen always did, she clattered around the office as she set herself up for the day. Jack thought she had done it intentionally. He had stayed up for some time after Phineas had left, reading over the files he had in his messenger's bag. He was not sure exactly what he was reading in the files, but one name continuously came up in every file he looked through, Dr. Emile Carkleman.

He had requested Ceinwen to forward his messages before he left, hoping that if Phineas or Evelyn attempted to contact him, he would be available. He had taken the public shuttle to the New Utica University campus, which was nestled on the far side of the city. It had been built nearly two centuries ago and the campus still reflected that architecture. There were buildings with elaborate stonework and brick, each with modest modern modifications. It was a lovely campus of only about ten buildings. As he walked onto the campus, he passed under the iron archway that was set across the walkway passing underneath. The lettering on the archway was an elegantly forged title of the college ingrained in the black, thick metal bars that surrounded them.

Jack passed under the arch and made his way into the main quad. The walkway lead to a beautiful three-tiered fountain that flowed freely, the sound was tranquil and seemed to carry over to the students that study quietly, or rested around it. Jack smiled to himself. He had missed out on the college life, his time served in the military made college less available. He had the option to attend once he completed service, but he felt his time had passed once he returned. Instead, he opted to join law enforcement, it was his best option.

He strolled nonchalantly across the campus, looking about curiously at the busy students that passed between buildings, some rushing, no doubt late for class. He pulled out a small piece of paper that he had written on before he left his office. He scribbled the name "Dr. Carkleman" along with his office number "Payne Hall 324." Jack passed by several buildings, The Schaefer Theater, The Jorgensen Center, and Weaver Hall before spotting the large white building that had the name "Payne Hall" carved into the marble plaque that hung above the doors. Jack walked up the series of steps that led to the building and entered.

The inside foyer of Payne Hall was quaint despite its elaborate façade. The modest interior was simply a circular room with doors to stairs and elevators surround the inner walls. An equally circular desk was in the center of the room where an attractive young woman sat. Probably a student, Jack thought. He smiled as he approached her.

"Can I help you?" the young girl smiled coyly, a glimmer of flirtation in her eyes. She looked him up and down finding him to be handsome.

"I'm sure you can," Jack flirted back.

"If the question is 'are you free tonight,' then yes," said the woman, whose nameplate on her desk read; "Lara Gillard" blushed slightly, her cheeks glowing slightly.

Jack couldn't help but smile at the sweet, albeit unconventional and relatively quick, offer, "Well, I'm really here on business, I'm looking for someone."

"Who can I help you find?" She asked embarrassed, which she quickly changed the subject.

"I'm looking for Dr. Carkleman's office," Jack asked, taking a serious tone.

"Oh, Dr. Carkleman," Lara sounded excited at his name. "I took his class on bioengineering last semester. Do you know his number?"

"324."

The young woman took out a slip of paper and began drawing a simple diagram, "Take the elevator right behind my desk to the third floor. Then you want to stay to your left, the numbering is a bit strange and you might get lost going to the right. His door is down the fifth corridor on the right at the very end of the hall."

Jack smiled, "The end of the hall."

The woman scribbled something else on the corner of the sheet before handing it to Jack. He took the sheet and studied it closely. He looked at what was written on the bottom. It was a series of numbers, numbers to a COMM device.

She smiled wider when he looked up to her, "You can always call me on that number at any time."

"I'll keep that in mind," Jack walked to the elevator, Lara kept her eyes on him the entire time as he walked the perimeter of the room to the elevator and stepped in. She waved as the door closed, separating them. He sure regretted missing college before, but maybe there was still time to make it up, at least the fun parts.

The elevator ascended slowly, another throwback piece of architecture that hadn't been updated. This was fine with Jack. He never liked the unnecessarily excessive speed the modern elevators went; they always made his stomach feel queasy. The elevator came to a stop on the third floor with a ding, the number three lit above the door. The doors split apart and Jack stepped out, making sure to stay to his left as he made his way to room 324.

The hallway was relatively quiet. It seemed likely as they were at the end of the current semester. Most of the students were finalizing their work and completing tests. There were a few office doors open on his trek with faculty seated at their desks. He found the correct hallway within moments and walked to the open door at the end. The nameplate was for 'Dr. Emile Carkleman.' Jack peeked his head in as he lightly knocked on the opened door.

"Yes?" Came a deep voice from inside.

"Dr. Carkleman?" Jack asked.

"That's me," Carkleman stood to see the strange man wearing a long coat and fedora entering his office.

Jack offered his hand, "I'm Detective Jack Zero."

"I'm sorry? Detective?" Carkleman repeated as he stood to accept Jack's hand.

"Zero."

"Are you with the New Utica PD?" Carkleman asked. A logical, but strange first question.

"No, I'm a private investigator. I'm working for the Strommel's, you know him?" Jack inquired.

"Ah yes, Heinrich, how is he?"

"He's missing."

Carkleman looked confused, "Missing?"

"Apparently, Dr. Strommel has been missing for a few days now. He was last seen just before he left to work at the lab and no one has seen nor heard from since."

"And?"

Jack found Carkleman's response cold, "And, I was hoping that you might have some idea as to what happened or where he might be?"

Carkleman's expression turned sour, his brow furrowed, "Why would I know?"

"Did you not work with Dr. Strommel? I have records that identify you as a partner on his research," Jack explained.

Carkleman snorted, "Partner? Hardly. The only partner Heinrich ever had was himself. Anytime he reached out to a colleague, it was strictly to steal data and ideas. He burned more bridges in the scientific community than I can name. No one wanted to work with him, not anymore."

"Yet, the files indicate you did," Jack reminded him.

"Against my better judgment and the warnings of others," Carkleman scoffed.

Jack probed, "You don't seem too fond of Dr. Strommel."

"No, and as I've indicated, I'm not alone," Carkleman replied. "I'm sorry, I don't know more. I haven't been to the lab in weeks."

"Why's that?" Jack wanted more information, more details. He felt Carkleman was holding back in some way. Jack let his eyes wander across Carkleman's desk. He saw two tickets resting in the center of the desk, just above Carkleman's elbows. The corners of the tickets were under the suede elbow patches of his coat. Jack squinted to try to read the event labeled on the body of the ticket. He quickly noted it. 'Presidential Arrival Gala: Saturday, November 2. 8:00 pm.'

Jack made sure to commit this information to memory. He quickly turned his attention back to Carkleman and his smug expression.

Carkleman smiled. He admired Jack's moxie. He answered honestly, "Heinrich and I had a…disagreement. About a year ago, I began working closely with Heinrich on a new research project. Cutting edge research."

"What research?"

Carkleman smiled coyly, "That's classified Mr. Zero. Anyway, Heinrich was close to a breakthrough and needed further support, so he knew of my expertise and naturally contacted me."

Jack interrupted, "And what is your expertise?"

Carkleman found pleasure in answering such personal questions, especially those that highlighted his accomplishments, "I am a professor with a doctorate in bioengineering and am the leading researcher in molecular reconfiguration, awarded the Award of Merit in Scientific Research five times and recognized twice by the Nobel Prize committee as a nominee. So you could say, I have a good handle on the type of research that Heinrich was developing."

"Of course," Jack replied. "You were explaining your disagreement with Dr. Strommel."

"Yes," Carkleman continued. "Heinrich was the lead researcher on this project; he made that clear from day one. I accepted this, I had my own research and my duties here at the university to contend with, but I still wanted to help. You see, despite Heinrich's personal shortcomings, he really is a brilliant man. Any scientist posed with the opportunity to work on such a high profile project would accept without question. The accolades alone would warrant participation. Anyway, I eagerly joined and quickly began to reanalyze the initial notes, correcting any oversights or errors they may have made. There were several.

"Naturally, I corrected them and submitted my changes, which in all respect, would have increased the projects output while decreasing its consumption. Heinrich thought my changes were ridiculous and unwarranted. He refused to incorporate them into the final prototype, or so I thought. During a preliminary test phase, I noticed the prototype behaving in a much more efficient manner, and I knew instantly that they were using my input. Naturally, I confronted Heinrich about this and of course, he refused. It was at this time that I realized what all my colleagues warned me about. I threatened to expose him as a fraud and left, but I hadn't spoken to him since."

Jack absorbed everything Carkleman told him. He felt confident that he was telling the truth. "You do understand that if Dr. Strommel is dead, you could be investigated as a suspect."

"He's dead?" Carkleman sounded surprised.

"I said 'if,'" Jack reiterated. "Is there anything else you can tell me, any other enemies he may have had, any other partners working on the project?"

"I don't..." Carkleman began. "Wait, there was another, a quiet man, I can't remember, oh yes, Steinwick, Dr. Janus Steinwick. He was working closely with Heinrich early on. He was there before I started, I'm not sure in what capacity, but he would be a good place to start."

Jack stood and prepared to leave, "Thank you Doctor, I appreciate your time."

"Certainly."

As Jack made his way to the door, he stopped and turned, "Oh, just one more thing, what can you tell me about rational machines?"

Carkleman cocked an eyebrow curiously. Jack couldn't tell if it was out of curiosity or annoyance. "I'm sorry, rational?

"Machines. Machines that develop a sentient personality can, to some degree, think for themselves. What do you know about that?"

"Not much I'm afraid to say."

Jack pursed his lips as he nodded.

"Is that all Mr. Zero?"

"Yes, but..."

"But what?"

"I can't claim to harbor the type of knowledge you or your colleagues share. It's just; I think someone with your expertise in, bioengineering is it? Would want to know something about that."

Carkleman stared intently at Jack. Jack could tell by his expression that he agitated him in some way. This may not be much, but playing a hunch was how you played the game. He now felt confident about following a new direction in his investigation.

"Thanks for your time," Jack tipped his hat as he walked out of Carkleman's office. As Jack walked toward the door, he inconspicuously brushed his index and middle finger across the table near the door leaving behind a small device.

"May I ask you a question, Mr. Zero?"

"Certainly."

"Who exactly hired you for this job, to find Heinrich?"

"Mrs. Strommel."

Carkleman cocked an eyebrow, a look of surprise crossed his face, "Did you say Mrs. Strommel? Heinrich's not married."

"I'm sorry? Did you say not married?"

Carkleman stood instantly and crossed over to the front of his desk. His expression changed from arrogant to fearful, his eyes widening for a moment. "His wife? Oh yes, of course, Mrs. Strommel," Carkleman furrowed his brow. "I nearly forgot for a moment. Have a nice day, Mr. Zero."

Jack hesitated before he finished his full turn to leave out the door he was now holding open with a frozen arm. "Can I ask you another question, Dr. Carkleman?" he finally asked and then stepped through the door.

"I'm sorry, but I really need to prepare for today's lessons," Carkleman ushered Jack out the door before he could speak again and closed it in his face. He then returned to his desk and sat back silently, his hands peaked together at the fingertips. He was happy to see Jack leave.

Jack closed the door to Carkleman's office behind him, happy to be finished with his uneven conversation. He snarled as he watched Jack disappear through the door. Once the door closed, Carkleman immediately grasped his COMM device. He pressed a series of buttons and waited for a response. In a moment, the head and shoulders of a hooded figure appeared, floating just above the transmitter. Carkleman closed his eyes at the sight of the image, "All Hail the High Master."

The hooded man responded, "Forever destiny."

"Forever destiny."

"What news do you bring me?" The image known as the High Master hissed.

"Zero was here," Carkleman informed. "Just as you predicted."

"What does he know?"

"Nothing."

The High Master's image grinned; it was the only part of his face visible from beneath the hood, "Excellent work, Lord Carkleman."

"I am pleased to serve you, High Master."

"Forever destiny," with those words, the High Master's image disappeared. Carkleman smiled to himself, pleased with how the plan was progressing.

He was suspicious of Carkleman. It was obvious he was hiding something, but what he still didn't know. A gentle beeping sound emitted from Jack's wrist. He slid back the sleeve of his long coat and looked at his wrist COMM. It sputtered, the light flashing on and off. He tapped it, hoping to correct the problem. It didn't work.

He spoke in expectation, "Ceinwen? Is that you?" The light on the COMM hissed with static as a beam tried to grow from within. Within moments, and a few more taps, a small blue light flashed and raised from the COMM device. Within the beam a small image of Helix floated.

"Jack?" Helix sounded surprised

"Helix?" Jack said with surprise. "I'm sorry; I thought you were someone else. What's up?"

"Your time if you don't get here on the double," Helix replied snarky. "Get over here."

"I'll be there shortly," Jack replied as he released his squeeze on the wrist COMM. As he walked across the campus amidst the bustling student body that made its way across the campus quad, he watched the students with their lives before them, unknowing what was really out there, oblivious to the dark truths. As he watched, he felt an odd chill creep across the back of his neck. He looked around the quad, but the crowd of traveling students was too thick to see through. Jack shook the feeling and made his trek across campus, but he wasn't alone. In the shadows, a distance behind, he was being followed.

Jack stopped and turned, getting that feeling in his gut that he wasn't alone. It was a sense he had learned to trust. He looked around inconspicuously, trying to look casual. It didn't work. Instead, he looked like a clumsy oaf trying to keep his balance as he twisted his torso. Despite his awkward movement, Jack noticed a short man peering at him from around the corner of a building. He instantly disappeared from view as soon as Jack caught his eye.

'*Who was this man?*' Jack wondered. He knew he had to find out.

Jack took up the chase, breaking into a slight sprint. He wanted to catch up to the mystery man. He rushed across the quad, veering around several students. Jack was able to cut across campus quickly, reaching the building where he caught site of the mystery man. As he turned around the edge of the building, the mystery man slipped around the other side.

'*Oh no you don't*,' Jack modified his sprint into a full run. He rounded the corner quickly, chasing the mystery man between another adjacent building. The man was slow; Jack was able to catch up with him quickly before he was able to reach his arm out and grab the man's shirt collar, stopping him in his tracks. The man's feet slipped out from underneath him as he was yanked from behind. He caught his footing and was able to stand upright. An odor emitted from the man; as his clothes billowed, they wafted the stench directly into Jack's nose. It smelled like scorched rock and burnt flesh. Jack gagged at the mouthful of air combined with the stench entered his lungs. After a series of coughs, Jack regained his composure and began the interrogation progress. He spun the portly man around on his heels and grabbed his shoulders, then roughly shoved him against the nearest brick wall.

"Please," the stocky man pleaded. "Don't hurt me."

Jack had his fist raised, ready to strike, "Who the hell are you?"

"R-Remy," the man stammered. "Remy Oszkowski."

"Why are you following me?"

"Because I was ordered to."

Jack was confused, "By whom?"

The young man smiled coyly. "Someone of deep influence and of great importance," he said cryptically.

"Commissioner Lartanner," Jack bemoaned.

"Oh, man," the man named Remy stammered. "He can't find out. He can't. I can't let him know I screwed up another stake out."

Remy began sobbing uncontrollably. Jack began to feel uncomfortable as he watched the mildly rotund man quake. Jack awkwardly placed his arms around the man's shoulders and patted somewhat reassuringly.

"It's, uh, okay?" Jack tried to sound comforting. "I won't tell."

Remy looked up at Jack with wet eyes and smiled a toothy grin. It made Jack cringe. "Oh thank you Mr. Zero! Thank you!"

"Yeah, sure, just, get yourself together, will ya?"

Remy stood up and straightened himself up, "Sure thing!"

The pat down wafted Remy's odor back to Jack again. Jack gagged, "How, uh, How long have you been following me?"

"Two days."

"I'm guessing with no break?"

"Nope."

"Shower?"

"Nope."

Jack figured. "Well," Jack began to back away slowly. "I'd better get going."

"Wait! You can't go!"

"Oh? And why not?"

Remy swallowed hard, nervous, "I'm not supposed to let you out of my sight."

Jack hid his face in the palm of his hand. This can't be happening. "Listen, Remy is it?"

Remy nodded.

"Remy, you must be new."

"Actually, I've been on the force for three years."

"That's new enough," Jack smirked. "Listen, I'm not one to take kindly to being followed, especially when they're sent on orders by the same man who let me get kicked off the force to begin with."

"I can't let you leave, Mr. Zero."

"Actually, you can," Jack began to walk away. Remy move in to block Jack's path. "What are you doing?"

"I'm not letting you out of my sight."

"Yes you are."

"No, I'm not."

"You don't have a choice, Remy," Jack was getting more annoyed. "And I don't want to hurt you."

"That's alright, Mr. Zero. I can handle myself."

Jack pushed past Remy. Remy quickly reached out and clasped his hand around Jack's bicep. Jack froze and flexed his arm. He felt it tingle slightly. The nanites were active, kicking into gear so to speak. Jack twisted his arm slightly, lifting Remy off his feet. Remy flipped into the air, head over feet, until he landed on his back staring up at the bright blue sky. The wind had been pushed from his lungs.

"Ouch," was all Remy could muster, as he lay prone on his back.

Jack began to walk away, but quickly hesitated. He took in a breath and turned slowly, "Sorry about that. I just can't have you following me. Lartanner doesn't need to know what I'm up to."

"Uh…Mr. Zero…"Remy moaned. "You have…no idea."

"Goodbye Mr. Oszkowski." Jack tipped his hat as he dashed away, not looking back.

Remy picked himself up slowly. He placed his hands on his back as he caught his breath. "Things are not always what they seem, Mr. Zero," he said to himself. Remy dusted himself off and began to leave.

The bell on the door of Helix's store rang its merry song as Jack entered. The shop was quiet, as it often was whenever Jack arrived. He was never quite sure if it was because Helix requested him or that the store was never really that busy. He hoped it was the first, but sure it was the latter. It was a few moments before Helix finally popped his head from the out of the back room.

"Oh, it's you," Helix said, as if he was expecting someone else.

'*Yeah right*,' Jack rolled his eyes.

Helix changed his demeanor. He was suddenly acting live a jovial child opening his gifts at Christmas. "Oh, man Jack, I'm glad you finally got here." He came from the back room and walked around the front counter. "Oh man, do you have any idea what you've found here?"

Helix was holding up the device that Jack left with him the prior day. It was in several pieces as Helix had been dissecting it like an over eager pathologist probing a mysterious corpse. He had examined the device thoroughly; he knew its intricacies and details. Jack could see the elation on his face. It was one of the reasons he always brought these sort of projects to him, not only was he the best set of hands in the business, but he never saw the kid so excited.

"What have you got for me?" Jack asked.

"This is a real divine piece of hardware, Jack," Helix smiled. "Where did you find it?"

"In a Cracker Jack box," Jack smirked.

Helix looked confused for a moment, not understanding the reference Jack had made, "Whatever, this was not easy to get into, let me tell you. This thing was sealed tighter than the Global Reserve Bank. Whoever put this together sure knew what they were doing and that was to keep anyone tampering with it out."

"Anyone except you, eh Helix."

"Well, I have yet to meet any machine that can outsmart me," Helix boasted. Jack withdrew stroking the man's ego too much; he didn't need his head to get any bigger.

"So tell me," Jack prodded.

"This is not standard issue."

"Of course not, it's military."

"No," Helix stressed. "I mean this entire piece of hardware is not standard in any grade."

Helix turned the device over in his hand. He pointed to the innards of the device, a cornucopia of wires and circuitry that looked like everything else to Jack.

"I don't see anything; it looks like any other device to me."

"To the untrained eye," Helix grinned. "But look closer." He held the device up to Jack's face. "You see these small clusters at the base of each receptor."

Jack nodded, pretending he understood.

"This cluster is hand-fused, an unnecessary addition as it adds nothing to enhance the purpose of the device, which is to communicate two-ways. Instead this device is set up to handle a timed task in relation to releasing a times emitter that can activate…something."

"What?" Jack asked.

"That's the thing, I don't quite know. Traditionally, a communicator is simple, and it can typically activate a device easily, but here this is more than just an emitter, it's creating low frequency pulses," Helix's voice grew more excited as he set the device down on the table. He pulled a small laser probe from his pocket and placed it near the cluster. He pressed the button that shot out a narrow blue beam that struck the cluster. Suddenly, the device glowed brightly and pushed out a small glowing orb that floated a few centimeters above the table. It rotated as it hovered, pulsating slightly.

Jack looked at curiously, "What is it?"

"I don't know," Helix was embarrassed to admit. "But it appears to be creating part of something. I'm not sure what."

"How would a simple thug like Thall come across something like this?" Jack asked aloud, but more to himself.

"Whoever had it sure knows how to hardwire something and make it virtually undetectable. What you have here is a real mystery."

The orb glowed brighter, floating softly in the air as it spun gently in a rhythmic circle. Jack leaned forward, getting closer to the orb. The light was bright, but wasn't blinding. He was surprised it didn't burn his pupils. The low blue light was actually quite inviting, soothing. Jack wanted to reach out and grab it, hold it in his hand. He stretched his finger out toward it, his fingertip touching it softly. It wasn't hot, but actually cold. It was quite perplexing. He drew his finger away as the orb began to grow larger and brighter.

"What's it doing?" Jack asked as he withdrew.

"I dunno." Helix sounded nervous.

The orb suddenly flashed, its light flooding the room. Jack dove to the floor, diving under the table. Helix didn't move fast enough. Instead, he lurched backward in a failed attempt to avoid the light that now enveloped and consumed them. As quickly as the light appeared, it suddenly vanished.

Helix was breathing heavily, his nerves tangled and twisted. "Jesus," he heaved.

"What the hell was that?"

Helix looked around the room. All the electronics and technology that was displayed on the backroom stock shelves had suddenly gone black as if they had been turned off. Helix stood and began to inspect the inventory.

"Oh shit, oh shit, oh shit," Helix repeated over and over, as if a chant. His hands were feeling each of the devices, pressing their buttons, and flipping their switches. "They're dead. They're all dead."

"What is it? What happened?"

"Do you know what that thing was?"

"No."

"An electro-magnetic pulse," Helix explained. "An EMP. It generated an EMP."

"What does that mean?" Jack prodded.

"It's a charge that negates all electronic devices," Helix explained. "It renders all devices inert."

"Why would anyone need this?" Jack asked himself more than Helix.

With Helix's last word, the store suddenly erupted with explosions. A hail fire of bullets rained down, shattering the windows along the storefront and sinking into the interior of the store. Jack and Helix both, instinctively ducked behind the counter, diving face first, their chests striking the floor in unison. Both men covered their heads as shards of glass and debris showered them. The bullets didn't stop once the glass was cleared from their frames. The relentless gunfire continued.

"We gotta get outta here!" Jack screamed to Helix.

"No shit!" Helix replied.

"Don't forget the device!" Jack reminded.

"To hell with it!"

"NO!" Jack said. "We need it!"

"Get it yourself!"

Jack scowled as he slowly picked himself up. He peeked over the counter, two bullets skipping viciously around his head. He dipped his head below the counter and then reached only his hand over the counter's lip. His hand searched frantically feeling for the device. It touched his fingertips to which he responded by snatching it into his palm. He slid it quickly over the edge and pulled it close to himself.

He nodded to Helix, "Let's go!"

The two men scuttled along their stomachs toward the rear of the store. Once they passed over the stoop into the back room, they picked themselves off the floor and with their heads still ducked low they ran for the exit. Bullets tore through the wall of the store that separated them from the front of the store. Light filled the stockroom with beams from punched holes that stretched across the width of the room. Both men sprinted as fast as they could. Although, Jack was faster than Helix, who never really exercised all that often, if at all. His slower pace annoyed Jack as he tried to goad Helix forward faster.

They pushed across the backroom until they reached the door. "It's locked!" Helix remembered.

"So open it!" Jack replied.

"I need my keys"

"Where are they?"

Helix motioned his eyes back through the door where they came. Jack rolled his eyes as more plaster filtered through the air onto his head. "Shit," Jack whispered. Jack looked at his arm. The arm that tingled now and again. The arm that had once been damaged and was now reinvigorated with millions of tiny machines that worked as one. Jack closed his eyes and focused intensely on his arm, charging it. He drew his arm back and with a single motion, released it punching the door open in a single blow. The door blew from its hinges as if an explosive charge detonated on the other side, tearing it from its hinges and sending it flying across the alley behind the store until it crashed against the brick wall on the other side. The two men stared out the opening, one with relief, the other in awe. The hinges were twisted and the handle had ripped through the door itself.

"Holy shit," Helix muttered in surprise. "How'd you do that?"

Jack ignored him, "Not now, let's go!"

The two men, squatting, escaped through the back door, the bullets continuing to erupt behind them. As they threw their bodies into the open, the quieting sound of the city streets lifted the harsh noise of gunfire from their ears. It was soon dissolved by the shrill sounds of screams of the crowds avoiding the violence from the front of the building.

Helix smirked, "That was close."

From the opposite end of the alley came angry shouts, "They're escaping out the back!"

Jack looked at the men who were beginning to swarm at the mouth of the alley. They were all dressed well, suits and fedoras, carrying weapons. He recognized the attire as underworld assailants, gangsters. The hitmen always dressed to the nines and were the most resilient assassins he had ever come across. This did not bode well for them. He counted four gathered with more collecting there by the minute. The hitmen opened fire of the two again. The bullets whizzed past them, sinking into the brick wall above their heads.

"Move!" Jack pushed Helix deeper into the alley, "MOVE!"

They managed to make their way behind a large metal dumpster. It was full, helping to stop the bullets from passing through. Unfortunately, Jack knew it was only a matter of time before they cut off their escape route at the other end. Nevertheless, he held out hope, even if it was a small amount. The barrage of gunfire intensified, as they got closer to the end of the alley. The assailants were moving down the alley in pursuit.

"I don't think I can make it," Helix panted.

A bullet sank into the side of his leg. He howled in pain. Another bullet cut into Jack's fused arm. He felt the pain for a moment before the nanites kicked in and began to repair the damage. This was not going well. Helix was limping, dragging himself behind. Jack was trying to pull him along, but he was much heavier than he appeared. Jack wished he could charge his arm up and hoist Helix up onto his shoulder, but he used up what he had when he broke through the door.

"You've got to move!" Jack ordered.

"I can't, my leg," Helix moaned. A small trail of blood followed behind. "We're not gonna make it."

"We will," Jack automatically responded. He wanted to pep up Helix's spirits, or perhaps it was to convince himself. "We have to!"

"Not unless you can pull another miracle out of you," Helix said, all hope lost in his voice.

'*He was right*,' Jack thought. There was no way out of this mess.

"There they are!" Two large, armed men rushing up the alley toward them. Their weapons were raised and at the ready.

Jack, his arms under Helix's shoulders, tried harder at dragging his wounded friend. They were not moving fast enough. Helix tried to kick his good foot to help move faster, but it did nothing but slow they down further.

"What are you doing?" Jack snarled.

"Trying to help," Helix whined.

"Well stop!"

The two men were nearly on top of them; Jack could hear the guns cock. He could even hear the bullets enter the chamber. There was little hope of them surviving this. The guns were trained on each of their heads. Both Jack and Helix closed their eyes tightly. The sound of the bullets exiting their respective chambers sounded unusual. To Jack it sounded as if they were coming from the same gun. How did Jack surmise this? He was in situations like this before. Too often. He was prepared for this, for death. But he felt bad for Helix. He knew Helix was not one for confrontations, and he was certain he never faced down the barrel of a gun. It was his fault Helix was here, and it was his fault they were going to die. '*Wait a minute? Why weren't they dead yet?*' Jack slowly opened his eyes to see two crumpled forms of once menacing gunmen, dead before them. But how? Jack turned to see the smoking gun of a slightly rotund man standing over them, that of Remy Oszkowski.

"Remy?" Jack said.

"Whoa," Remy breathed a sigh of relief. "That was intense."

"But how?"

"I'm not spying on you Mr. Zero," Remy explained. "Lartanner sent me to keep you out of trouble."

"If you explained that to me before, I wouldn't have believed it,"

Jack smiled. "But I can't say I'm not grateful."

"Glad to help."

As if on cue, a half dozen more men began charging up the alley. Remy quickly raised his pistol, but Jack waved him to lower it. "Unless you got more bullets and are a helluva shot, we'd better run."

"My car's back this way."

Jack signaled toward Helix, "Could you help me with him?"

Remy grabbed the opposite shoulder of Jack, and they each hoisted Helix to rest on their own shoulders. They began to run, or at least walk very quickly, as they made their way to the end of the alley. The new threat that rushed at them was catching up quickly. *'Now what?'* They broke to the end of the alley where a large black vehicle blocked their escape. They were cut off. The men with guns chasing them until they trapped them on the other side. Helix could see the look of disdain on Jack's face in the reflection of the clean, polished metal of the vehicles door. He expected it would be the last thing he would ever see.

"This is it then," Helix wheezed.

The door to the vehicle popped open, "GET IN!"

Jack smiled. It was Agent Frisco. For once, he was glad to see her.

"Well, what are you waiting for? MOVE!" Frisco urged.

Jack shoved Helix into the car first. Helix slumped into the empty back seat, laying his body across the entire seat. Remy leapt in beside Helix. Jack climbed into the front seat and closed the door. A bullet sank into it as soon as it was shut. Fortunately, it was reinforced. Jack turned his head and looked over his shoulder. He could see the men were almost on top of them, their guns still ablaze. He immediately hopped into the front seat and shut the door behind him.

Frisco slammed her foot onto the gas and the vehicle squealed as it tore clear of the sidewalk and disappeared into the thick traffic that crowded the streets.

The assailants reached the end in time to see the car flee.

"DAMMIT!" The lead man screamed.

"Well, Dahlmers," the second man with a narrow face stepped forward and said to the first. "Who gets to report this to the big man?"

Dahlmers threw the narrowed face man a dirty look. He wanted to spit in the face of the man he called Plink.

The car disappeared from view.

"You are damn lucky I was nearby," Frisco snarled. She darted her eyes over at Jack quickly, but it was enough for him to feel her stare bore into his skin. "You know, Zero, you have a real knack for finding trouble."

"No, it finds me," Jack smiled.

"Care to explain why in the hell you were being gunned down by those men?"

"Damned if I knew," Jack shrugged. "One minute we were talking, the next we're being invited to do an impression of Swiss cheese."

"Oh God, my store," Helix moaned as he craned his neck to look out the rear window, hoping to see his store, but it was too far behind. "I lost everything."

"Not everything," Jack pulled the COMM device from his pocket and held it out in his palm.

Frisco looked over at the device curiously, "What's that?"

"The cause of most of my troubles of late," He stuffed it back in his pocket.

Helix slumped back in his seat, "I wish I'd never seen that thing."

"C'mon, it's not that bad," Jack said reassuringly. "You're insured."

"Oh, ha-ha, you're a real comfort, Zero," Helix responded snidely. "My life is usually uneventful, just how I like it. I was looking forward to an evening of take-out and jacking into the Duro-net, but no, thanks to my good friend, Jack Zero, now I'm running for my life. This never happens to my Duro-net guild. In fact, everything bad that happens to me always seems connected to you. It's you, you're the reason I've lost my livelihood. I just wanna go home."

"Not likely," Jack smirked. "You left your keys at the shop. That, and the fact that your address is on everything, I wouldn't be surprised if they showed up there already."

Helix slumped down lower, slapping his palm to his forehead, "Oh God!"

"Nice, Zero," Frisco rolled her eyes.

"Relax; he'll get over it in no time."

Frisco drove toward the oncoming intersection at an accelerated speed. Several vehicles were slowing and then racing across the four lanes of road that crossed one another. Frisco furrowed her brow and looked up at the traffic signal, but it was black. No power.

"Traffic lights are out," Frisco called out.

Jack clenched his teeth. He looked about the side of the street as several vehicles were disabled along the sides of the road, "Damn, that EMP stretched more than a block."

"What?" Frisco asked.

"Watch out!" Helix screamed as he pointed ahead of them.

A large hover-trailer was crossing in front of Frisco's vehicle.

"Shit!" She screamed as she yanked the wheel hard to the left. The back end of the vehicle kicked out and the tires skidded violently, kicking up loose asphalt and smoke from the friction of the tires. "Hold tight!" Frisco warned.

She jerked the tire to the right and swung the rear end to the left, to which she quickly adjusted the steering wheel as she regained control of her vehicle and went around the backside of the hover-trailer.

"I'm gonna pass out," Helix wheezed.

"Just put your head between your knees," Jack threw a suggestion over his shoulder not seeing Helix's face turning green. Jack turned to Frisco, "Nice driving."

"Thanks," she half smiled. "So spill it Zero, what's the poop?"

"I'm telling you, I didn't know those guys, but I figure they're a part of this." Jack pulled the device out of his coat and turned it over, revealing the HART symbol.

"The HART?" Frisco sounded surprised. "You were holding out on me!"

"I was waiting."

"For what?"

"To tell whether or not I could trust you."

"I could run you in, again, this time for obstruction of justice."

Jack smiled coyly, "You could but you won't, because you think I'm charming."

Frisco scoffed, "Hardly."

"Aw, c'mon, admit it, you think I'm pretty okay."

Her lip curled up slightly at the corner, "You are...something, Zero." She stole a glance of Jack. As her eyes travelled back, she caught sight of an odd, erratic movement in the rear view mirror. She tensed up, adjusting herself by sitting up and gripping the wheel tightly.

Jack noticed Frisco's change in stature, "What is it?"

"We've got company."

Jack turned to see two vehicle closing in on them, fast. It was obvious they were the same men he had just escaped from at Helix's shop.

Helix perked up and looked behind them, "This day just keeps getting worse and worse."

Remy perked up his head, peeking slightly over the back of the seat.

"Shit," Zero muttered.

"Don't give up just yet," Frisco's brow furrowed in hard concentration. "But you might want to hold onto something."

Frisco jerked the wheel sharply to her right. Remy was not prepared. His entire body shifted with the vehicle. His head violently slammed against the window, his body slumped over into the back seat. Jack saw the man crumple and felt guilt at the temporary fate of his recent savior. Her vehicle weaved between the thickening traffic, nearly scraping the bumper of the car ahead. The pursuing vehicles followed her lead, trying to keep close and not lose their quarry. Frisco kept sight of her pursuers, wanting to ensure they did not cross into her blind spot. She threaded the traffic expertly, sending her passengers' heads bobbing with each weave she took.

Helix slapped his hand over his mouth, "I'm gonna be sick."

"Take the next left onto Bleeker," Jack shouted. "I know these streets pretty well, we can lose them."

Frisco looked at Jack with reservations. Jack offered an unconvincing smile.

"Trust me," he said.

She still wasn't completely convinced, but cranked the wheel sharply as the tires smoked and squealed around the corner, lifting onto two wheels shortly. Jack craned his neck around to see Helix turning green and the first car following shooting past the street.

"I told you," Jack was cocky.

Frisco was about to chastise Jack when the second car made the turn and was closing the gap between them. "You were saying?"

Jack shrugged apologetically. Frisco shook her head as she bared down and prepared to outrun their new threat.

Bleeker Street was narrower than the road they came from, and was filled with more traffic. It was a challenge, but one that Frisco was prepared to accept. She resumed her cool calm demeanor and twisted the wheel as she slickly maneuvered with and against the twin streams of traffic that surrounded them. Jack gripped the handle just above his head as he sucked in his breath and silently prayed to himself. Helix, on the other, was not shy about expressing his emotions.

"Oh shit, oh shit, oh shit," Helix chanted loudly in the back seat.

"Just relax," Frisco tried to sound reassuring. "You just might live through this."

"Might?" Helix gulped.

Frisco swerved between two large transport haulers, nearly scraping her sides between them. It didn't slow the others down. Their pursuers followed her every move with ease. It was starting to irk her.

"Well, genius," Frisco shot at Jack. "Any other ideas?"

"As a matter of fact I do. Left! NOW!"

Frisco obliged, turning the wheel and making the turn onto Jay Street. The pursuer drove past. The driver of the small black car slammed on the brakes. Smoke billowed out from beneath the wheels.

"You missed the turn!" The thug in the passenger's seat yelled in the driver's ear.

"I know goddamit!" The driver screamed back. He tried to turn the wheel, but instead collided head on with an oncoming transport hauler. The car upended and the roof slammed against the nose and windshield of the hauler.

The Hauler driver was terrified, "JESUS!" The hauler stopped quickly, sending the black car forward, the front end crushed under the hauler's folded tires.

Jack could see behind them the remnants of the black car as it was destroyed under the hauler. "That was close."

Frisco sped forward, looking for a means to escape the side street on which they were now travelling in the wrong direction. Horns honked and cars swerved to avoid them.

"Lookout for those people!" Helix pointed frantically.

"SHUT UP!" Frisco yelled.

Frisco guided the vehicle as safely as possible, without hitting a pedestrian. Unfortunately, the same couldn't be said for several garbage cans, a fence, and several iron tables and chairs at a roadside café. A tablecloth and remnants of food speckled the windshield, giving Frisco's nerves a jolt, but they escaped the street relatively unscathed.

"Nice driving," Jack finally released the breath he had been holding.

"Thanks," Frisco tried to calm herself and slow her heart rate.

"You alright, Helix?" Jack turned.

Helix had gone from green to purple. He was speechless, perhaps from fear. Jack watched as he slowly lifted his arm and pointed out the front windshield.

Jack looked at him curiously, "What?"

At the end of the street, the light turned green, but coming from the left was the first car they thought they lost. It was attempting to block their escape.

Helix was now grey in color, "Um...t-that car, YOU'RE GONNA HIT THAT CAR!"

"Maybe we should stop?" Jack interjected nervously.

"Like hell, hold on tight," Frisco slammed her foot on the gas pedal. The vehicle roared forward, barreling down the end of the one-way street. The front of the other car was nearly across the end of the street, but Frisco didn't freeze, she leaned forward and prepared for whatever was about to happen. She veered sharply at the end of the street maneuvering around the front of the car. Jack and Helix stared out their windows with horrified expressions as the saw the hood of the car inch closer. Everything was moving in slow motion. What finally took seconds, felt like hours to Jack. The back of Frisco's vehicle clipped the front grill of the opposition smashing the front end in severely while ripping open the side of her vehicle. The brass at the FBI weren't going to be too happy about this damage. It didn't matter; she would deal with that later.

Frisco's vehicle was much larger and more durable than the opposition, and it made it known. It tore the front end of the other vehicle nearly clean off as the tail end of Frisco's vehicle came into contact. Frisco was expecting it, anticipating it, and took full advantage of it. The moment the cars touched, Frisco pressed her vehicle into the other, knowing it would increase and incur the most damage. The friction also pushed the car out away and spun it out, leaving it to spiral rapidly as she blew past.

"WHOA!" Jack said as the vehicle exited Jay Street and entered Rutger Street. "I stand corrected, THAT was close."

'Helix had finally had enough and passed out in the back seat. It was probably for the best,' Jack thought.

"How did you learn to drive like that?" Jack asked Frisco.

"Motor Pool at Fort Benning, I was the one who drove the vehicles to and from their sites. I took a lot of detours back then."

"Anytime you want to drive for me," Jack said. "You're hired."

"Thanks, but I'll pass. Who were those guys anyway?"

"Whoever they were they knew how to hit us and when," Jack explained. "They must've been tailing me all day."

"And you didn't notice them? You must be slipping."

"Must be," Jack felt somewhat sheepish, ashamed of his lapse in judgment. After marking Remy, he assumed he was in the clear. "Where to now?"

"NULE Headquarters," Frisco guided the car away from the traffic and out of sight.

"Hello?" A sweet and smoky voice asked, following a knock on the office door of Jack Zero.

Ceinwen shot up from her desk, her hands held up before her, each finger extended and separated attempting to keep the fingernails dry, and shuffled to the door, "Oh. Oh my, Mrs. Graves."

She stopped as the door slowly parted further from the frame and Mrs. Graves poked her head through, "I'm sorry dear, am I interrupting?"

Ceinwen looked to her hands that she held up unwittingly, to which she quickly thrust them behind her, careful not to touch her nails on anything. "Of course not," she lied. "Please, come in."

Mrs. Graves sidled through the door that was stuck on the crooked floorboards. She held her clutch in her hands as she made her way in front of Ceinwen's desk. "Oh thank you, dear," she smiled. Her husband, Mr. Graves, shuffled through the half-opened door, pushing it open the fill way as he fell in silently behind his wife. "I got your message," she continued.

"Ah yes," Ceinwen returned behind her desk. She leaned over and attempted to open the drawer with the ball of her hand. She struggled for several attempts, still unable to grip the handle. She let out a low chuckle, "This should only take a second."

Mrs. Graves watched the woman fumble repeatedly with the handle of the long thin center drawer of her desk. "Could I help you with that?" She asked annoyed, despite the sweet smile she wore.

Ceinwen looked embarrassed, "If you wouldn't mind." She smiled as she stepped back.

Mrs. Graves shot a quick look to her silent husband, who raised his lowered head and responded wordlessly. Mr. Graves shuffled behind the desk and slid his fingers around the desk handles pulling it open. It squeaked loudly and shifted unevenly until it was nearly off the track that held it in place. Ceinwen offered a smile, "Thanks."

Mr. Graves returned to stand behind his wife. She reached into the drawer and pinched her fingertips onto the small felt bag that slid to the front. She plucked it up gingerly and reached across the desk, dropping it into the open palms of Mrs. Graves. Her face lit up as she looked into the small bag, a clutch of jewels shimmered back. "Oh my, thank you so much!" She chirped. "Tell Mr. Zero thank you. You have no idea how important this is to me."

"Oh sure, no problem," Ceinwen waved her hand dismissively. "Although, you could thank us by paying the bill." She handed the paper at the top of a pile to Mrs. Graves.

Mrs. Graves, still smiling, snatched the paper from between Ceinwen's fingers and looked it over, "I would be delighted." She tossed the paper to her husband. He immediately reached out his thumb.

Ceinwen held up her credit receiver, a small gray box with a glowing pad at the top and a three buttons evenly spaced beneath, a red button labeled 'cancel,' a yellow button labeled 'enter,' and a green button labeled 'confirm.' Mr. Graves pressed his thumb to the glowing plate. It grew brighter as a beam scanned his thumb. Once completed, the screen displayed the text: 'CONFIRM.' He pressed it and then withdrew his hands and stuffed them back into his pockets. Ceinwen turned the receiver to her face and read the screen that flashed the text: 'PAYMENT RECEIVED.' She spun the device in her hand and set it on the desk casually, "Excellent."

"I just wanted to thank you again," Mrs. Graves chimed, remaining upbeat and cheerful.

"Anytime," Ceinwen replied. "If you ever have another job, don't hesitate to call. And be sure to tell your friends about us."

Mrs. Graves stopped in the doorway and turned. She wore a broad grin that was more sinister than happy as she spoke, "I certainly will." She then disappeared from the office and closed the door.

The sounds of muffled shouts carried through the wall, more clearly than it should have been. Jack sat uncomfortably, less from the yelling that was about him and more about how Helix was resting his head on Jack's shoulder.

"I told you to keep him off the case! Plain and simple, not turning a controlled situation into a complete mess!" Senator Glorm shouted in Commissioner Lartanner's face.

"I understand, but Zero is out of my control, he's not one of my men," Lartanner returned.

"But he WAS! You and he have a connection, I expect you to lean on that when we're talking about the upcoming plans!"

"I know, I will handle it," Lartanner replied meekly.

It was uncomfortable to see Lartanner squirm like that.

"The President is coming in a few days, we expect your men to keep order in your own city without his men having to come in earlier than expected to bail your asses out!" Glorm paced back and forth, he ran his fingers roughly through his own hair, and a technique Jack assumed he use to try to calm himself. "Just get it done."

"It will be."

"It had better be!" Glorm glared threateningly, "Or you will answer for it!"

Glorm stormed from the room, slamming the door behind him. He made his way past Jack, not looking at him. It sent chills down Jack's spine. Fortunately, Jack didn't have time to dwell on that as Lartanner stood in his office doorway. He wagged his finger at Jack, signaling him to come. Jack reluctantly complied.

There was an uncomfortable weight that hung in the air as Jack stepped into the room. The silence was deafening, except for the sound of Lartanner's heavy breathing. He was fuming.

"DAMMIT ZERO!" Lartanner began. "I warned you! I warned you to stay clear of this case, but, like always, Jack Zero does whatever Jack Zero wants."

"Captain, let me explain--" Jack tried to speak, but Lartanner cut him off.

"Shut up!" Lartanner seethed. "Just shut up. I have pulled out my last favor for you, I can't keep the feds off your back if you keep sticking your nose in their business. Last time they threw you in the slammer as a warning, next time, I don't know what they'll do. I've got my men running rampant all over this city preparing for the upcoming Presidential visit; I don't need you fueling anymore fires."

"I'm sorry," Jack said sincerely. "I'm running a case for a woman searching for her husband, I just contacted Helix for some advice and the next thing you know; we were under fire."

"Yeah, right," Lartanner scoffed. "I'm sure you had no idea why someone would want to kill you."

"C'mon Commissioner, you know me."

"Yeah, that's the problem, and that's why, against my better judgment, I have convinced the Senator not to throw the book at you."

"And no one appreciates that more than me," Jack smiled. It didn't impress Lartanner.

"Just promise me, you'll keep your nose clean."

"You got my word."

"That doesn't make me feel any better."

"Trust me," Jack tried to sound more reassuring.

"You're not helping your case," Lartanner's mouth curled up slightly, a tiny smile hidden behind his push broom mustache. "Now get the hell outta here."

Jack angrily reached into the inner pocket of his trench coat and pulled out the small black device he managed to take from what was left of Helix's store. Lartanner looked at the item curiously, then with disdain.

"What's that?" Lartanner huffed.

"I don't know," Jack replied.

"Then why the hell is it on my desk?"

"I got this off Neal Thall, The Caveman," Jack explained calmly. "When we activated it, it released an EMP."

"An electromagnetic pulse?" Lartanner replied. "So?"

"This tiny device was able to generate enough force to knock out power for over a block. Not something you pick up at the local hardware store."

"Zero, you're starting to get under my skin," Lartanner took in a lungful of air and let out a long sigh. He rubbed his brow aggressively.

Jack stood and thrust the device into Lartanner's chest, "Look at the bottom of the device."

Lartanner reluctantly snatched the device from Jack's hand.

"Look on the back," Jack instructed.

Lartanner turned the device over in his palm and studied the back; he quickly noted the symbol, "Is that the symbol for--?"

"Yes," Jack quickly confirmed.

"Remind me where you got this?"

"Caveman, he was carrying it with him."

Lartanner cocked an eyebrow, "But all his effects were confiscated and placed in evidence."

"Yeah, well, I may be borrowed it when Agent Frisco took me down there," Jack confessed.

Lartanner let out the same sigh again. This time it made Jack uneasy. Lartanner's frustration never led to anything good. "Zero, I am placing you in a cell for the night, no bail. I am sick and tired of you stepping on my toes and violating police investigations, obstruction of justice, and tampering with police evidence. You have crossed the line this time. I hope you have the number of a good lawyer."

"Good lawyer? Isn't that an oxymoron?" Jack quipped.

Lartanner was not amused. At that moment, an officer came bursting through the door of Lartanner's office. The officer hesitated as he stepped into the room, sensing the tension that now hung heavily in the air, "Um…sir?"

Lartanner was in no mood, "What is it Lieutenant?"

"Sir, s-sorry to interrupt, but there was a report of a break in at the First National Bank downtown."

"Send the six closest cars," Lartanner quickly spat. He watched, as the officer did not leave, but instead stood and stared. "What else, Lieutenant?"

"Sir, the report was stating that no money or anything of monetary value was taken."

"No?"

"No, only the contents of a single safe deposit box were stolen."

"I don't understand," Lartanner stood motionless, mulling over what was reported. "What are the detes?"

"Well, sir, the guards reported four men, all of which appeared in thin air, then disappeared just as quickly."

"And?"

"Well, they were all…naked."

"Naked?" Lartanner asked.

"Naked?" Jack repeated.

"Shut up, Zero," Lartanner turned his attention to the officer with orders. "Get my car and get your gear, you're coming with me."

"What about me sir?" Jack asked innocently.

Lartanner scowled. He closed his eyes for a moment and then spoke, "Get out."

"Yessir," Jack stood and saluted his once superior. He then turned and scooted from the room as quickly as he could. Lartanner sucked in his breath and kept himself calm. He wanted to trust Jack, he really did. However, with Jack's previous track record on promises, it was going to be difficult.

Jack strode quickly away from Lartanner's office, trying to ahead of the gazes from surrounding law enforcement officials. He walked up to Helix and signaled for him to follow.

"What's up?" Helix asked, feeling the uncomfortable vibe coming from Jack. Helix stood, his leg still wrapped as the portable nanite cast did its work.

"Let's just get outta here."

"Alright," Helix limped.

The two men made their way to the elevator. Standing in their way was Agent Frisco.

"Strike two," Frisco chided.

"Must be my lucky day," Jack smiled, trying to sneak past her.

"Maybe, but I think you're just biding time. It won't be long before I'll be pulling your tail out of the fire and putting you in cuffs."

Jack couldn't help but feel annoyed by her snide comment, "I'll miss you too."

After nearly an hour of groveling and begging, Jack had finally convinced Ceinwen to let him borrow her car. It beat taking shuttles or cabs, not to mention much cheaper. He needed to get to the New Utica First National Bank downtown immediately and without the hang-ups of relying on another transport carrier. At least that what he said to convince her to hand over her keys. She was a good Girl Friday, she trusted Jack completely, even if he had let her down in the past. He couldn't remember how many times he promised her a raise, but was sure it had been nearly three years and he still hadn't given her one. She always came out to assist him whenever he called. He needed to stop taking advantage of her, taking her for granted for so long would ultimately lead to him losing her and, at this time; he needed all the support he could get.

Jack had driven directly to the bank, parking nearly eight blocks back so as not to be noticed by the growing amount of police officers that were now swarming the building. He had to be discreet. Sneaking to the back of the building was not an option; neither was climbing in from the roof. Lartanner had most likely suspected he would attempt to enter via one of those routes. It was times like this that Jack Zero had to become more inventive; use his skills to outsmart the competition. This time Jack was even impressed with his own ingenuity. Jack had almost considered a subterranean entrance, knowing Lartanner wouldn't position men that deep underground, but another opportunity presented itself. Well, maybe it wasn't really that ingenious as much as it was obvious. Jack pulled the police officer's hat lower over his eyes as he shuffled in through the main doors without looking up. He had taken an officers uniform from the back of the officer's transport van. He often wondered why no one ever kept a more rigid vigil when the van was parked at any crime scene, the back agape. He quickly slipped in and plucked a uniform from the rack within. Unfortunately, it was about one size too short. He quickly discovered this as he changed in the back of Ceinwen's car. Not an easy, let alone comfortable, task. However, there was no time to trade in the duds; instead, he hoped walking with a slight hunch might hide the fact that his wrists were too exposed. The procession of a dozen officers, all dressed in their standard blue uniforms, walked in perfect formation. Jack was familiar with this style both from his time in the military and on the force. Lartanner was standing at the door as the officers each walked past, still side by side. Jack peeked out from under his hat as he made his way closer to Lartanner. Lartanner scanned the officers, looking for anything out of place. Lartanner was very particular with his officers being dressed to the nines. Jack wrapped his fingers around until he felt the cuffs of the coat. He then proceeded to pull on them gently, attempting to cover his wrists. Lartanner's eyes caught Jack's hands. He studied the hands that were in fists not flat at his sides. Lartanner squinted, as he looked the officer up and down. He couldn't see the man's eyes and that was another problem.

"You!" Lartanner shouted at Jack. "Officer? What's your operating number?"

Jack didn't respond.

Lartanner was growing annoyed, "Hey, I'm talking to you!"

Lartanner began to charge toward Jack angrily, his nostrils flared. Lartanner wasn't as upset about the uniform issue as much as he gets angry about being disrespected. No officer was going to ignore him and get away with it.

Jack could hear Lartanner coming toward him. He swallowed hard and began to raise his head, preparing to make eye contact with his former chief.

"Sir!" Another voice shouted from behind. "Commissioner Lartanner, Sir!"

Lartanner stopped immediately in his tracks and turned, glowering at the new voice that interrupted his moment, "What?" He snapped.

It was Lartanner's immediate subordinate Lieutenant Samel Barbarosa. Barbarosa was one of the good ones, Jack noted in his mind. He let out a huge sigh once Lartanner turned and walked to the other man. Jack remembered Barbarosa when they were both detectives on the force. During Jack's insubordinate hearings, Barbarosa was the first to come to Jack's defense. They had been partners for a short time. In that time, Jack had saved Barbarosa's life and he returned the favor in kind. Jack smiled as he relaxed. The procession continued into the bank where Jack quickly slipped away from the group in order to conduct his own investigation.

The hallway was dark. Jack had taken the first hallway he had seen in his attempt to escape Lartanner. He hoped Barbarosa was keeping Lartanner busy enough for him to forget the disheveled officer who had supposedly disrespected him. Jack crept slowly, cautiously, so as not to draw any more attention to himself. He walked heel to toe in an attempt to reduce the sound of his footsteps. Jack always wore rubber-soled shoes. They inherently muffled the sound of feet against the floor, something that was extremely beneficial in an empty hallway with vaulted ceilings. Even his breathing was echoing.

Jack slithered along the far wall as he moved as quickly as he could without making any noise. He reached the edge of the hallway, but pressed himself against the wall before he turned the corner. He heard the sound of people talking. He knew it was other NUPD Officers, he could hear their chatter.

"How many were there?" The first officer asked.

"Four," said the second.

"And they were all naked?" The first officer added.

"Yep, as jaybirds."

"Why?"

"Who knows, mebbe they were perverts, looking to get their jollies."

Jack could hear their voices growing louder. They were coming in his direction. The glow of their flashlights began to increase in intensity. They would be in his hallway in moments. Jack sucked in his breath as he searched for a quick escape, some place to duck away and hide from view. Jack stepped backward his hands feeling the wall behind him, for anything, a doorknob…anything.

At that moment, he found one. A doorknob. Unfortunately, it was across the hall from where he stood. Jack swallowed hard as he saw the light glowing brighter. He leaned forward and ran quickly, and quietly, across the hall. The darkness shrouded him, but the concealment would be short lived once the officers turned the corner. Jack gripped the handle and turned it. Locked. Jack brandished his laser-lock picker and immediately activated it, releasing the lock. The door clicked open. Jack sneaked into the dark office and pushed the door closed just as the officers rounded the corner, the beam from their flashlight cutting through the seams of the door that Jack, firmly against, pressed his body. He listened intently as the officer's footsteps stopped before the office door. Jack gripped the doorknob tightly. He wanted it to appear locked. He could feel the weight of another hand on the opposite side of the door grabbing hold. The knob began to turn in Jack's hand. He tightened his grip. The knob attempted to turn again. Jack remained motionless, holding as tightly as he could.

The officer on the other side let loose the knob, "Locked, let's keep going."

The other officer chimed in, "I told you no one is still here, especially if they were naked."

"Whatever," the first officer replied.

Jack released his grip of the doorknob and slump against the door. He was relieved that he wasn't discovered, at least not like this.

"Mark 2.5," a voice rang from behind, startling Jack. He spun quickly on his heel to see where the voice came from.

The room was dark.

"Mark 7," the voice said again.

Jack felt his heart race, fearing who could be in the office. Was it an officer of the NUPD? A bank employee who was left behind?

"Hello?" Jack asked meekly.

No answer.

The voice was silent for a long moment, then it appeared again, repeating what it had said before, "Mark 2.5…Mark 7…"

Jack walked slowly in the direction of the voice, both curious and anxious as to what he might find. The room was small, but housed a magnificent desk, most likely the office of a midgrade executive, he surmised. Jack walked to the desk in the quiet darkness. He waited a moment until he finally hear the repetitive voice again, "Mark 2.5…Mark 7…"

Jack caught the sound of the voice in full earshot this time. It was coming from under the desk. Jack reached for his sidearm as he knelt slowly behind the wooden desk. He cautiously peered underneath.

Nothing.

It was empty. Jack stood again and scratched his head, befuddled by what was happening. "I don't get it," he said to himself in confusion.

Then, as if on cue, the voice returned, "Mark 2.5…Mark 7…"

Jack listened more carefully. This time it was clear where the voice was coming from. Jack gripped the center drawer of the desk and pulled it open. Several pens and pencils rolled from the quick jerk that instigated their perpetual motion. A small black box also dislodged from the back of the drawer and slid partially into view. Jack recognized the device and pulled it from the drawer. He looked it over in his hands and studied its design. It was a COMM device, much like the one he found in the evidence room, the one Thall had in his personal effects. He turned it over to see the back. In the dim moonlight that shone through the window, the emblem on the back of the device glinted. It was an inverted triangle with five small rectangles jutting around it. There was a clear indication that the device belonged to the Dark HART.

Jack silenced the COMM device and stuffed it into his pocket. He then grabbed the nameplate on the front of the desk. The name on the plate read; 'Kurt Fritzche.' Jack imprinted the name into his memory, ensuring he would look it up later. He now had to get himself down to the vault and see what Lartanner and his men had found.

Lartanner paced inside the vault as Barbarsoa and his men investigated the remnants of the heist that occurred earlier that night. Lartanner was floored at the sight of the vault door pitched on its side against a far wall, completely torn from its thick hinges. It had been tossed hard enough to impale the wall where it now leaned, slightly buried into the stone masonry that was hidden behind the once immaculate wall. Lartanner looked frustrated and annoyed, more than he ever looked when scolding Jack in his office. The officers bustled about the vault, gathering evidence from what remained from the heist. An officer scraped the area around the safe deposit box that had been torn from the wall. The officer gently scraped the singed area of blackened metal that surrounded the gaping hole in the wall.

"What do you think could've done this?" Barbarsoa asked.

"A bulldozer?" Lartanner scowled as he scoffed, "I have no idea, but I can be sure I would hate to run into whatever it was."

The officer taking the samples continued his work as he replied, "Sir, see the impressions around the edge of the boxes?"

Lartanner humored the rookie, "Yeah, sure, why?"

"These could only be made by a fist, these impressions are knuckle marks," the rookie explained.

"A fist?" Barbarsoa said shocked.

"Look," the rookie held his fist up the impressions, matching his knuckles with the marks. His fist was much smaller than those of the impressions were. "It's unmistakably made by a fist."

"That's some fist," Lartanner huffed. "Must've been wearing some sort of shielding, a bare fist couldn't have done that."

"Maybe," Barbarsoa agreed, a hint of reluctance in his voice.

"Who did the deposit box belong to?"

Barbarsoa looked at his palm pad and tapped it until he found the answer, "A Dr. Heinrich Strommel."

"The scientist from that lab that blew?"

"I think so."

"Put a tracker on him, I want to ask the good doctor a few questions."

Lartanner stopped for a moment and looked around the vault. He shuddered slightly as he took in everything surrounding them. He had an eerie sense that someone was watching him.

"Samel?"

"Yessir?" Barbarsoa responded.

"Are you sure the building is empty?"

"My men did a full three sweeps, its empty."

Lartanner looked up to the narrow vent that circulated the air throughout the room. He narrowed his eyes as he looked at it intensely. He then shook his head and walked away.

Jack relaxed himself as he watched from behind the ventilation grate. Lartanner had looked at him directly, he was sure of it. He must not have seen him though, but it sure felt close. Jack was taking picture files with his palm camera, a device that folded up into a small, compact cube that he could carry in just about anything. He was sure to keep the flash off so as not to draw any unwanted attention in his direction. As he observed the officer running a detection wand over the scorched marks surrounding the removed security box. The wand emitted a small isotope that detected any radioactive or explosive materials used to open the box. As it passed over the spot identified as knuckle imprints, it let out a low, slow beep.

The officer turned back to look at his superior, Barbarsoa, "Sir, its testing positive for uranium."

"Uranium?" Barbarsoa approached curiously. "As an explosive?"

"No sir, the resin burns were generated by friction, hence the knuckle marks."

"I don't understand," Barbarsoa scratched his forehead.

"The uranium must have been left behind from the object that punched the hole here," the officer offered his theory. "My guess is that it was a fuel used by the thief."

"Fuel for what?"

"Well, if he's fused then it could be a source of power to allow the nanites to generate their power using uranium as the fuel."

"Jesus," Barbarsoa whispered. "What the hell are we up against?"

The officer replaced the want back in his belt and removed another device, this one resembling a Geiger counter. He aimed it at the spot where the radiation was detected and pressed a button. A light electrical charge danced across the opening and then moved around the room.

Barbarsoa ducked as the current passed overhead, "What the hell is that?"

"It adheres to all the uranium within the room, checking for any other spots where radiation may be active."

Barbarsoa looked at the officer and the device in his hand with confusion, "Alright then, um, carry on." Barbarsoa walked away cautiously.

Jack felt his own arm tingle as the electrical current danced across the ceiling and into the vent. It made its way to his arm and wrapped around it painlessly. Jack brushed it off hoping no one saw it enter. When he knew it was clear, he resumed his watch of the room. His eyes followed Barbarsoa as he walked around the room. Barbarsoa stopped at a small scrap of paper that sat at his feet. It was hardly noticeable; the color of the paper matched the tile along the floor. It had also been stepped on several times, disguising it further. Barbarsoa squatted down and snapped the scrap up with his index finger and thumb. He studied it closely, holding it up to his eyes. They weren't what they used to be. He looked around to see if anyone was watching, but all the officers remained preoccupied. Barbarsoa slid his hand into the inner pocket of his coat and pulled out a pair of spectacles. He quickly slid them onto his nose, trying to look inconspicuous. Jack smiled at the sight of Barbarsoa in specs. The two round lenses outlining his eyes and the wisps of gray along the base of his hairline surely illustrated his advancing age. Jack never imagined Barbarsoa ever getting old, but there it was in front of him. As Barbarsoa held the paper closer to his eyes, Jack aimed the palm camera at the paper and zoomed his lens into it. The magnification quickly adjusted and came into focus. Jack snapped a picture just before Barbarsoa lowered his hand and stood to pursue Lartanner with this new piece of evidence.

Jack held the palm camera reader to his face, shielding the blue glow it emitted when activated. He looked over the picture he snapped and read the scribe on the note, '*vault 3, box #67.*' It was in a very familiar handwriting that Jack identified. He reached into his pocket and pulled out a note he was given earlier by Evelyn Strommel. He held it next to the image. It was a perfect match. Apparently, either Evelyn Strommel had given the location of the safe deposit box to the thieves or it was taken. Jack now had several more questions to add to his list for Mrs. Strommel, if that's who she really was. Jack snapped a few more photos with his palm camera. He then made his way back out of the vent and made his way out of the bank.

"Well?" Helix was impatiently pacing back and forth in Jack's office.

"Well what?" Jack snorted as he walked through the door.

"Well, did you find out who the hell shot up my place?"

"Yes," Jack responded mindlessly, then corrected himself. "No. I mean maybe."

"Which is it?"

"I don't know, but I followed a lead to the downtown bank and learned there was an incident involving a crew of naked men who appeared from nowhere and robbed one lone safe deposit box," Jack murmured.

"That's very fascinating," Helix mused sardonically. "The problem is that it has nothing to do with my shop and who shot it up."

"Aren't you listening," Jack flipped his fedora from his head and tossed it across the room like a Frisbee. "This is bigger than me, you, or your shop. That device I found on Caveman, it all stems from there."

"I don't care. This isn't my problem; this is what the police are for. I'm done. I'm out," Helix threw his hands up.

Jack slapped his hands on Helix's shoulders and spun him around, balling his fists under his shirt collar and pulling him forward, "On the contrary, you're in this just as deep as I am. There is definitely something strange happening in this city."

A voice appeared from the shadows, "That's what I've been trying to warn you, Jack."

Jack spun with lightening reflexes, drawing his weapon from its holster as he raised it in the direction of the voice.

"Not the best way to welcome a friend," Phineas Wald emerged from the shadows that made up the corner of the office.

"Dammit, Phineas," Jack let out his breath as he lowered his armed and holstered his weapon. "You really need to start knocking first."

"There isn't time for formalities anymore," Phineas kept solemn. "I just wanted to see what you learned before I leave."

"Don't you mean disappear?"

"Call it what you want, but I can't let them find me. I left that hospital because I had a moment of clarity, Jack. They had me so lousy with medication; I couldn't even remember my own name. When I started to have memory spikes, I knew something was wrong. That's when I stopped letting them medicate me and I started to wake up.

"I came to you because you're the only one I can, and could, ever trust."

Jack turned away and slipped his arms from his coat. He flipped it over his arm and then transferred it to the back of the chair behind his desk.

"Who is this guy?" Helix asked.

"Don't worry about me, kid," Phineas flashed a smile at Helix. "I'm nobody. A ghost."

"He's just leaving."

"I don't care who he is or why he's here. All I care about is my shop," Helix whined. "I'm the real victim here."

"SHUT UP!" Jack snapped.

Helix took a step back. He had never heard Jack react like that and it was a bit of a surprise.

"I'm here to open your eyes too, Jack. I showed you that picture. I know what been happening, it's not too late for you to know too."

"To know what, Phineas? You never told me anything. You just give me cryptic tidbits with no proof. I live my life by finding facts and piecing together what is unknown, but what you talk of is just…"

"What?" Phineas interrupted. "Truth?"

"Speculation."

"Even speculation has merit."

Jack was getting frustrated, "Look, I appreciate seeing you again, Phineas. I hate knowing what happened to you after…after Zimm's death. But look, I can't have you continuing to come here with these speculations. I need proof. I need information from someone who isn't…I mean…someone who…who is…"

"Crazy?" Phineas filled in Jack's missing word that he seemed to have him flummoxed.

"No," Jack tried to back pedal. "You're not crazy. Maybe, you're just, I don't know, scattered."

"Yeah, well, scattered doesn't carry any real diagnosis. According to my doctor's, I was paranoid and delusional."

"I'm sorry," Jack lowered his head, embarrassed for his behavior. "I just, I'm sorry for what happened to you. I just don't know what I can do for you."

"I don't need you to do anything," Phineas walked to the door. "I just need you to be careful. See my visit more as a warning than as a social call."

"I saw Huun," Jack added.

"Here?"

Jack nodded.

"No good will come of this. I'm guessing he wasn't alone."

Jack shook his head, "No, Crust was there, along with the whole gang and a few new ones."

"I guess that's my cue to leave then."

"You don't have to leave," Jack reached out to his once close friend. "I could really use your help."

"I can't help you like that anymore, Jack. I'm not the man I used to be," Phineas stepped over the threshold of Jack's office. "Just promise me you'll watch you back."

"Will I see you again?"

Phineas shrugged, "Who knows what the future will bring." And with that, Phineas turned and slipped from the office quietly.

Jack stood silently for a long moment, forgetting that Helix was still there.

"That's your friend? I'm starting to question the company I'm keeping," Helix quipped.

Jack placed a friendly hand on Helix's shoulder. He then scooped his long coat from the back of the chair and slipped his arms through. He slid open the top drawer of his desk and plucked the HART communicator he stashed there from Helix's store. He stuffed it into his coat pocket.

"You're leaving?" Helix said with both surprise and disdain.

Jack stepped to the door, "Just for a bit, it's something Phineas said. I'll be back soon. You can crash here for now. And let Winnie know if you need anything."

Just as Phineas had minutes before, Jack disappeared from the office. Helix slumped onto the sofa, feeling defeated from the events of the day.

"Just wait here, Helix," Helix spoke to himself sarcastically. "I only had you store shot to hell and your life ruined. See you later. Humph."

CHAPTER 13
TERRIBLE LIES AND BITTER TRUTH

Returning to the scene of the crime was usually a term reserved for criminals, but in Jack's case, it was important to return to the I-ZAN Research facility building near the New Utica University Campus. Even though the fire he started was by accident, it was technically his fault half of the building had been destroyed by fire. What destroyed the other half was still a mystery.

A tasteless lollipop dangled between Jack's lips as he stepped into the blackened hallway. He immediately spat the candy to the floor when he made his way deeper into the charred building. Jack used his small light to see in the darkness. He could see that the walls weren't only burned, but soggy as well, saturated by the water used to extinguish the fire. Jack could smell the stench of wet wood and sheet rock. It wasn't very appetizing. He'd rather eat the tasteless lollipop than smell the odor that hung in the air. He sprinted up the hall, allowing the odor to breeze past him as he held his breath. He just needed to reach the office. The office where the fire started. This room carried a much more pungent stench than the hallway. Jack pulled the collar of his shirt up over his nose. It helped a little.

Jack looked around, panning the light back and forth slowly. The beam shone brightly against the scorched walls, revealing the severity of the damage more vividly. He knew feeling guilty wasn't going to help, and took the path of knowing no one was hurt from the fire as a small victory. He stepped over to the large open window that once made up the wall of the

155

office, until he heaved a desk and HART agent through it to the ground below. He peered over the lip to see the remains of the desk still there. It was a most unusual sight, a man lifting the desk up over his head effortlessly and ripping it apart as if it were paper. He didn't want to think about it anymore. It was rather unnerving to remember. Instead, he kept his focus before him, looking for any further information he might have missed, any clue that wasn't destroyed by the fire. Remains of paper were still scattered about, mostly burned to cinders, save for a few pieces. He knelt down to pick up one such piece. It had the word "Zero" etched across the stark white background.

His old file. Gone. Destroyed, because of him.

He wished he had the good sense to take it with him that night, but amidst the chaos, it was forgotten, now lost forever. The filing cabinet that once housed the file was still there, now lying on its side. The drawers were still shut. Jack approached the cabinet and pulled the top drawer. It didn't budge. He tried harder, still nothing. He closed his eyes, wrapped his fingers more strategically around the handle, and then drew in a deep breath. His body suddenly felt warm and his arm began to tingle. His arm was reacting again, as it had several times before. He pulled at the handle again. The drawer popped open easily, as if it wasn't ever stuck. In fact, the strength of his fused arm was such that the drawer came free of its track and nearly flew across the entire room. Jack was able to slow the momentum of his arm and stop the drawer before it went too far.

More files were loosened and papers were now raining down on him like snowfall. He really needed to figure out his arm and control the strength it possessed. More sheets of paper drifted before him, like leaves falling from their branches during autumn. Jack managed to snatch several of them as they crossed his field of vision. He then began to scoop more from the ground all around him. He scanned each sheet as he reviewed them quickly. None seemed any more important than another, each listing a patient's name and what specific modification they were infused with through nanotechnology. Some were given injections to their legs, giving them the ability to run at great speeds; or their eyes, allowing them to see for miles. Others were given infusions to their organs, like their kidneys, hoping to prevent them from failure. One had infused nanites into a patient's heart, preventing a potential heart attack. Jack nearly fell over when he read of a man, whose brain was fused, increasing nearly every synaptic response ten-fold, not to mention the intelligence level. It was shocking the amount of modifications, some without patient approval, that were administered. It seemed as if Strommel was trying to evolve the human race in some way, as if he were playing God.

'But why? Was it for fame and fortune? Was it really to help people? Or was it just simply because he could? Did it really matter?' Jack thought to himself. As

Jack continued to sweep his arm across the other loose papers, he stopped at the sight of one that was donned with an illustration. The illustration showed an enlarged cross-section of a nanite bead, its intricate circuits and controls were elaborate. Subconsciously, Jack itched at his arm. He flipped to the next page and saw the illustration of a nanite with a cone pointing to the shape of a human. However, the words at the top of the page halted Jack. He felt his muscles tense and his throat close. He held his breath.

'*Autonomous Being: Controlled by Nanites.*'

Jack couldn't believe what he was seeing. '*A being controlled completely by nanites? Was there any trace of a human being in there?*' It appeared to be a humanoid built only of nanotechnology. This violated the accords of the United Nations that strictly forbade any robot construction had to remain separate of looking human. It was the Android Design Machinations and Technology Mandate or something of that nature. Whatever it was, this was illegal. Hopefully, it was just a plan and not actually brought to life.

Something caught Jack's attention. A shadow moving in the distance along with the sound of metal clanging against concrete.

Someone else was there.

Caveman was lying leisurely on his cot, his cell small, and empty, aside from his hulking form. His shoulders and legs hung over the edges of the cot, making it appear more uncomfortable than anything else. He breathes loudly as he lay still, his fingers interlaced across his chest. His eyes were closed, but he wasn't sleeping, simply relaxing.

A prison officer, who paced the hallways regularly, was nearing his cell. It was for something other than the usual check and leave, but instead, it was something important. The steps were faster than usual, the pace steady, but the impact of each foot more confident and determined.

The steps stopped in front of his cell. Caveman didn't move. He didn't even open his eyes to see what was happening. He just continued to lie still.

"Neal Thall," the guard said in a commanding voice.

Caveman didn't move.

"Thall," the guard growled more angrily. "Wake up!"

Caveman let out a low grunt.

"Thall!"

Caveman opened one eye and craned his neck around. He looked as if he was going to fall off the cot. "Can't ya' see I'm restin' here?"

"I don't care what you're doing," the guard shot back. "You have a visitor."

This news perked Caveman interest as he propped himself onto his elbows and looked behind to see the guard unlocking his cell door and a tall, thin man, dressed in a well-pressed, expensive suit stepped in.

The door closed behind him as the guard locked it shut, "You've got five minutes."

The guard walked away, leaving Caveman, now sitting upright, the cot not visible under his mass. Even with his feet on the floor, his knees were raised slightly. He was certainly tall. The man in the suit swallowed hard, intimidated by the massive man standing before him.

"Well?" Caveman's voice boomed loudly, echoing in the small cell. "What the hell do you want?"

The man swallowed hard, "Well, it's less of what I want and more of what I can do for you, well; my client can do that is."

"And who are you?" Caveman growled.

"I'm Dan Grodon, I'm your attorney."

"Get lost," Caveman stood, his head almost touching the ceiling. "I hate lawyers."

"Mr. Thall," Grodon began.

"Don't call me that!" My name is Caveman!"

Grodon cowered back slightly. His gaunt features making him appear more pathetic than usual. "L-listen, I-I'm just here as a courtesy of my client. They have further need of you."

"Who?"

Grodon straightened his coat as he stood tall, trying desperately to look, in anyway, more masculine. In the intimidating presence of the mighty Caveman, he was not. He ran his hand over his narrow, pointed head, his fingers raking his thinning hair.

"Let me just say, these clients still have a special interest in your, shall we say, talents," Grodon smirked.

"So what," Caveman grumbled as he rolled over onto his side, turning his back to Grodon and facing the wall. "I could care less."

"They will increase your current rate."

"Big deal."

"And it will give you revenge on Jack Zero."

Caveman lifted his head at the sound of revenge. Not just revenge, but revenge on his enemy, Jack Zero. The man who put him into this tiny birdcage. Caveman twisted his neck around to see the smarmy face of the rat-faced Grodon. "I'm listening."

"My clients will arrange for your release, on the condition that you will assist them in the elimination of Jack Zero. You will be compensated, of course."

"Hell, the chance to kill Jack Zero. I'd do that for free."

"My clients will be happy to hear…," Grodon was cut short.

"I didn't say I would," Caveman grumbled. "Tell your client there that I'll do it,"

"Excellent," Grodon moved to the cell door. "I'll let my clients know and then we will have you set free within the hour."

Grodon let loose his extended arm salute, "Forever Destiny."

"Yeah, right," Caveman returned the salute half-heartedly. "Take your forever whatsit and shove it. I want to get paid. Oh, and just don't take too long. I'm getting' hungry."

The guard soon returned and let Grodon from within the cell. Caveman returned to his cot, this time placing his interlaced fingers behind his head. *'Kill Jack Zero,'* he thought. "Finally a job I want and know I'll be good at." Caveman smiled to himself as he closed his eyes.

Jet Engines roared above as they lifted from the tarmac all around them. The New Utica International Airport was busier than usual; a plethora of visitors from all over the country seemed to be converging on the area. Perhaps it was for the same reason that Agent Nicolina Frisco stood there for herself. She watched as Air Force One slowly taxied to a stop, away from the main terminal. The area had been vacated and secured, anticipating the arrival of the President of the United States. The stop was rather impromptu, a week ahead of schedule. However, as his campaign advisor continuously warned him, New Utica was an important city, where a swing vote could decide the election. The incumbent needed to focus his energy toward this city in order to clinch his win. Since his main competition, Senator Jensen Glorm was from this state, and the city to be more precise, he would have to work doubly hard to convince this city that he was the better man for the job.

Frisco stared motionless as the hatchway door was unlocked and pushed open from the inside of the plane. To start, several gray and black suited men and woman emerged. Secret Service officers. They assessed the surroundings. Once ascertained to be safe, the members of the campaign team exited before President Adam Michaelson himself emerged.

Glorm stood next to Frisco, both watching steadfast as the President made his way down the stairs.

"Well, wish me luck," Glorm whispered to Frisco.

"For what?" She asked.

"I have to pretend to like this guy," Glorm answered.

"So?" Frisco shrugged," There's no press, who's going to matter?"
"It's not for them," Glorm explained. "It's for me; I don't think I can convince myself."

Frisco stifled a laugh. Glorm threw her a sly wink as he walked forward to meet his competitor. The continuous roars of the engines overhead muffled the sound of the two men greeting one another. Frisco noted the handshake and how each man placed his hand on the other's shoulder, squeezing gently.

It looked convincing to her.

Glorm led the President to an awaiting stretch limousine. The driver, dressed in a well-pressed black suit, held open the door. President Michaelson looked over the vehicles interior. It was fully equipped

"Quite a nice ride," he commented with a suspicious smile.

"I wanted to be sure you arrived in time and on style," Glorm replied.

"Thank you," Michaelson let go his suspicions. "I know we've had our differences in the past. And with the past debates, some…things were said."

Glorm returned a confident, reassuring smile, "All politics aside, sir, this is your night. Now climb in, I've arranged the finest hotel accommodations in the city."

Michaelson's suspicions seemed to fade as he smiled broadly, "That's good to know. I appreciate your assistance. I hope you plan on coming to the gala."

"I wouldn't miss it, sir."

"Good. Then I'll look forward to seeing you there," Michaelson climbed into the limousine, followed by his wife and several service men. Once they were all inside, the driver closed the door. Glorm stepped aside and returned to Frisco's side.

"Seemed genuine, sir," she said.

"Pardon?"

"You're generosity and amicability toward the President." She repeated, "It seemed genuine."

"If I can convince you, then I can convince the voters," Glorm straightened his tie as he climbed into his own waiting car. "See you at the gala."

Before long, Frisco stood alone.

Helix snored loudly as he slept on Jack's Murphy bed. The rattle deep from within his throat kept Jack awake. That and the constant thoughts that plagued his mind. He kept thinking of the bank, about what the officers spoke. He wondered if they were right, about the men appearing from nowhere. *'But how?'* Jack could rack his brain all night thinking about this, but he would never figure out something so complex. If only he could find Strommel. He was certain he could answer all his questions. Maybe Dr. Carkleman could, but he seemed far more guarded and more secretive. He also though about what Phineas had said. Maybe he was right. Jack regretted how he had been short with his friend. It did not matter. He just needed to keep his mind on the case.

Helix tossed himself over with a loud snort.

The sound broke Jack's train of thought. He was used to the quiet his office provided him when the day turned to night. When Ceinwen left for the day, Jack often reveled in the tranquility of his loneliness. However, his guilt allowed him to invite Helix to stay with him. After all, it was kind of his fault his shop had been destroyed.

Helix had taken the circumstances rather well. Jack smiled as he watched Helix flip himself repeatedly under the blankets. He was determined to help Helix get back on his feet. Jack loosed his feet from atop his desk. He spun himself in his chair until he faced the bay windows that were behind his desk. The city of New Utica was dark and peaceful, for once. He wished the city would stay this way, but then he would be out of a job. He could see the street just two floors beneath where he resided. A nondescript black car was one of eight cars that lined the street. He could see the shape of a round man behind the steering wheel. Remy. He was sure of it, without even having to look. He was determined to keep his assignment. You had to respect that kind of determination. He certainly didn't like it, but he respected it.

Jack spun himself back to face his desk. His rolling chair squeaked and creaked under his weight as he leaned back. He threw his feel back up onto the top of the desk, as he got comfortable again. Well, as comfortable as the chair would allow. He folded his hands across his chest and closed his eyes, hoping to catch some sleep. Unfortunately, his mind began to race again.

Phineas Wald threw the remainder of his belongings into his olive drab duffle bag. The same military issued bag he had used when he had been a Skytroopers. It had been one of his only mementos from that time. He preferred to forget. He wanted to forget. Unfortunately, he could not forget. It was not that there were not moments that were not memorable, or times he was proud he had served, it was that he could not remember those times; instead, only focusing on the times that tarnished his memory. He shoved some loose articles of clothing roughly into the opening of the duffle bag. The clothes had been strewn chaotically around the hotel room. He had been staying in the most low-key of the New Utica offerings, the former Hotel Utica, now a sleazy, Heartstar Hotel franchise. A chain notorious for their hourly rates that became so popular for those seeking to commit adultery in an anonymous place.

Phineas wanted to remain anonymous, but could have done without the sleazy part. Oh well, it had only been for a couple of nights and then he was gone. Thankfully, he was ready. He was there for one reason, to warn Jack, which he did. Even though Jack didn't seem receptive to his warnings, he did what he came to do. As he forced the last few articles of clothing into the bag, the lights in his room flickered repeatedly. He stopped, his arm elbow deep in the bag. He looked around, his suspicious nature taking control. His nerves were all on fire, sending a repeated synapses signal to his brain, triggering his fight or flight mechanism.

He had to leave. Now.

Phineas chose to ignore any further items he had, leaving them behind, in order to leave immediately. He zipped his bag closed and slung it over his shoulder. He then stepped over to the door, and cautiously twisted the handle and pulled. The door didn't budge. He pulled it again. Still nothing. He pulled harder, with all his might, but the door didn't give way. It was as if it had been sealed from the outside, but by whom and by what?

The lights in the room flickered again. Phineas counted each flicker. First, it went four times, then seven, and then six, until they went out completely.

The room was dark. Phineas could hear his heart pounding in his ears. He was growing more and more terrified, feeling he was somehow been trapped in the room.

"Wha are you?" Phineas shouted into the darkness, "Who's there?"

There was no verbal response. All Phineas could hear was the sound of something metallic rolling across the concrete floor outside. The sound grew louder as whatever it got closer. Phineas could see a shadow moving outside as the light that shone under the door broke apart. Whatever he feared was now there.

"Who's there?" Phineas called again into the void.

There was still no answer back.

Phineas creeped his hand into his inside pocket until his fingers felt the cool metal of his gun. He wrapped his fingers tightly around the handle and withdrew the weapon. He bared his gun defensively, preparing to fire. The rolling sound continued as the shadow began to spread from behind the door to underneath. A dark, ominous cloud began to consume the light outside as it rolled under the door and into the room. He watched with wide eyes, finally reacting as he raised his firearm and discharged several rounds.

It did no good. Whatever it was, it was still coming.

Soon, all the metal objects had entered the room, the light spilling into the room from under the door once again. Wald used what little light it provided as his eyes searched for where all the tiny objects had gone. Despite the darkness, Phineas could see the rolling metal spheres stacking upon one another in the corner of the room. Once the last of the spheres made their way to the top of the pile, Wald could see he was not looking at objects, but at a person, more specifically, a man.

"My god!" He exclaimed.

The eyes of the newly formed human form that stood before Wald flashed red.

Phineas panicked and began to fire more shots at the thing that stood before him. The bullets sank into the wall behind the creature, but none of them actually seemed to hit them.

Before Phineas could react further, the creature raised its arm and pointed at him. The creature's arm then shot across the room, the finger sinking deep into Phineas' chest.

Phineas collapsed from the strike. Within seconds, he was dead.

The creature watched Phineas' lifeless body fall to the ground with a loud thud. It then stepped closer, circling where he lay. It was obvious he was dead.

Expressionless, the creature turned and then broke apart, each individual sphere released and free. They quickly rolled under the door and out into the night.

Jack awoke with a start, his head snapping upward as he gasped. His feet slipped from the top of his desk and slapped against the hard wood floor. Several sheets of paper were scattered, strewn wildly into the air. Jack watched as the papers drifted listlessly to the floor.

He saw Phineas, but he was dead. *'But how? Why? Why would he have such a dream?'* He just spoke to Phineas a few hours ago. *'Maybe it was the guilt?'* Jack thought.

'Maybe.'

Jack rubbed his eyes, attempting to erase the bizarre image that forced him awake. It seemed so real, yet how could it be? Jack reached his arms over his head, stretching to soften the tense muscles that ran across his shoulders and down his back from sitting in the chair for so long. The chair squeaked as Jack stood. He looked rubbed his lower back. It was stiff from the chair. He looked over at the sleeping form of Helix, comfortable in his bed. Jack cursed him silently, but knew it was the right thing to do, as he had been indirectly responsible for the destruction of his shop. Jack shuffled slowly to the door nearest to the exit. It led to the washroom. He needed to splash some water in his face to clear his mind. He stepped in and closed the door behind him before turning on the light, so as not to disturb Helix. He didn't stir.

A shadow blackened the dim light that shone beneath the door that led to Ceinwen's half of the office. It moved swiftly about, blackening any light that struggled to make its way underneath. Before too long, all the light was gone as the shadow consumed the width of the door. Several tiny spheres began to roll under the door, fanning out in several directions, covering nearly the entire floor. The floor, coated with thousands of tiny spheres, appeared to emit a shine that gave the appearance of glass. Once the last sphere rolled under the door, they began to swirl toward a central location, piling on top of one another as they began to rise higher, taking on a form. Soon the spheres began to take the shape of a human, tall and thick. The blackened form stood nearly seven feet tall. It turned what appeared to be a head, where its eyes flashed a deep crimson red. The creature, or whatever it was, drifted across the room, as if floating above the ground. It glided effortlessly over toward the bed, where it studied the sleeping man that was nestled deeply under several blankets.

The creature's eyes narrowed into tiny slits. It was clear the odd creature had found what it was looking for. It drifted eerily across the floor as it circled the bed. It stopped once it stood behind the snoring Helix. It stretched out its arms before itself, holding them above Helix. It stood motionless. Soon, several tendrils began to grow from its back, reaching higher and further than its own arms. Six newly formed tendrils waved around the motionless creature. Each tendril operated on its own, twisting and spiraling outward until they were all around the bed. Two of the lower tendrils swooped under the bed, wrapping around it from both sides. The tendrils slowly came up from underneath and continued wrapping around Helix as he continued sleeping. They slowly tightened until they began to squeeze around Helix's abdomen. He let out a low groan as his lungs let out his breath under the pressure.

The creature froze its tendrils, not wanting to risk waking its victim before it began. It preferred to kill quickly and undetected. It made it cleaner, easier. If the victim were to awake, then it would have to become messy. The four remaining tendrils rose above the creatures head. It kept its eyes focused on Helix. The out tendrils slid down to either side of Helix's head. The tendrils each flattened until they were able to slide under his pillow. The first came out and then slowly slid across Helix's neck. The second crept across his mouth. The remaining two tendrils, still raised high, began to reform into sharp tips. The creature aimed the tips directly at Helix, one at the heart, and the other at his the temple. It was ready to strike.

The creature began to tighten its tendril around Helix's throat. The bright light from the bathroom door opening instantly washed the room over with illumination. The light, a simple 60-watt bulb, was more than enough to blind the odd creature hovering over the bed. It let loose a shrill screech that shook the walls. Jack cupped his hands over his ears and then dropped to his knees, startled by the peculiar sound.

Helix snapped awake, his vision and mobility were obstructed by the black, snake-like tendrils that surrounded his body. He couldn't scream.

He could feel something covering his mouth.

"HELIX!" Jack called out.

The creature narrowed its crimson eyes at it looked over from Jack to Helix. It was obvious the creature was confused, but that changed as it released its grip of Helix. The tendrils slowly retracted back into the creature's back. It then turned its attention to Jack.

The creature's eyes dimmed, turning a duller, darker red. It recognized Jack in the light. It matched the programming of the target it intended to terminate. The creature floated over Helix and the bed, lunging itself wholly at Jack. He reacted quickly, dodging the oncoming assault by diving to his left. The move was unplanned as it resulted in Jack smashing his head against the edge of his desk. The sound of bone against wood was silenced by the shrill cry the creature made as it quickly reversed itself, pressing its own face through the back of its head, turning itself around without event moving. It raised its arms offensively, reaching out to strike, as it swiftly moved about. It drifted toward Jack, its feet just off the ground.

Helix finally collected himself, regaining his breath, as he sat up in the bed to get a better look at what had nearly ended his life. He rubbed his neck gently, trying to relieve the throbbing pain that persisted. He watched Jack dive from the bizarre assailant. He could tell by the way it moved, and its composition, that it wasn't human. It was some sort of mechanized being. Jack scrambled on his hands and knees to the backside of his desk. He kept his head low, hoping to shield himself enough to buy some time, any time. It worked, for now.

"JACK!" Helix called; his voice hoarse and worn.

"I could use a hand here, Helix," Jack responded wryly.

"It's not organic," Helix explained.

"You mean it's fused?"

The creature outstretched its arms and began to wrap them around the desk. It lifted the desk effortlessly and tossed it aside. The massive oak furniture slammed hard against the wall, cracking the plaster and splintering sections of the desk.

Jack was exposed again. The creature flashed its eyes, focusing on the target.

"No," Helix's mind raced, trying to speak faster than the creature moved. "It's not human at all. It's a machine, some form of artificial intelligence, unlike anything I've ever seen. It's made up of a series of small computers; we just need to figure out a way to shut them off."

"I think it's pretty clear it wants us dead."

"Us?" Helix shot back. "He had the chance to kill me but once it saw you, it went right for you. I think it just wants to kill you."

A tendril lashed out and snapped against Helix's chest. The impact knocked him off his feet and into the air. Fortunately, it was in the direction of the bed, which he bounced off and somersaulted onto the opposite side. He landed on his head, which was against the hardwood floor. It hurt.

Jack watched as the creature began to expand itself, growing larger and taller. It was beginning to become larger than the entire room. Jack needed to think quick and act quicker, before there was no room left to move, let alone breathe. Helix slowly pulled himself up along the side of the bed, rubbing his head gently. He could see Jack pinned against the wall, looking over at the door as a way out. However, there was no way he would make it, not without facing the wrath of the AI creature that could easily block his path. More tendrils emerged from behind its back, waving about wildly as they formed around them in preparation to strike. Jack was trapped and out of options.

Helix stood, still a bit groggy as he stumbled slightly. He looked around the room. It was in shambles from the creatures attack. His glance fell on the overturned desk and then down to loosened drawer, its contents exposed. There, Helix noticed the COMM device. The device that Jack brought to him and dragged him, unwillingly, into this adventure. He then recalled what he told Jack, that the device emitted an electromagnetic pulse.

'Perfect!' He thought as he leapt onto the bed, using it like a trampoline, leapt high toward the other side of the room where the remains of the desk lay.

Jack watched, both surprised and curious as to what Helix was doing. The creature did not take notice, and Jack wanted to make sure he never did. Whatever Helix was doing, even if he was simply saving his own skin, Jack wanted to make sure he got away. He owed it to him for getting him embroiled in this whole affair. The creature turned its head slightly in Helix's direction.

"HEY!" Jack called out in desperation.

The creature returned its focus on Jack. Jack waved his hands over his head, continuing to goad the creature, "Hey ugly! You came for me! Huh? You want me, well, I'm right here!"

The creature accepted Jack's challenge, returning to its enlarged stance, its tendrils poised, again preparing to strike. Jack couldn't help but notice the sharp tips at the end of each of the six tendrils, their purpose was clear. He knew he was going to die.

"What are you waiting for?" Jack preceded to chide. "Do it!" The creature's eyes flashed as he lowered each tendril, its tips aimed at Jack. "NOW!" Jack said forcefully and with finality. Jack held in his breath and closed his eyes, awaiting the inevitable.

There was a loud crack followed by a quick pop. Jack awaited the pain that would follow, but strangely felt the same. He snapped his eyes open to see what was happening. The creature still stood large above him, while just behind he could see Helix, his arm outstretched and holding a bulky COMM device. The device pushed out a wave of violet rings that encircled the creature. The creature let out a shriek as it immediately sank into itself, the tiny nanites that made up its body contracting back into one another. Jack saw the creature was collapsing, writhing about as it was dying.

'The EMP!' Jack realized. He took advantage instantly. Jack charged the creature, ramming his head and shoulders into its midsection. It let out a howl as it stumbled backward from the impact, slamming into the bay window that was behind where Jack's desk once sat. The creature threw its tendrils about wildly, wrapping two of them around Jack's arm and waist. Jack gasped as he was pulled forward toward the creature and the window that awaited behind them.

Helix dove aside as the creature continued to stumble past before smashing through the large window. Shards of glass flew in every direction, wood that framed the glass, cracked and splintered as it was forced from its secured setting.

Jack tried desperately to anchor his feet. He watched fearfully as the creature toppled backward through the gaping window.

"Jack!" Helix called to his friend.

"Help me!" Jack pleaded, struggling to free himself from the creature's grip.

"I don't understand, I hit it with an EMP, it should be deactivated."

"Just get it off of me!" Jack growled.

"How?"

"Try cutting it," Jack choked.

Helix searched around quickly before snatching a large, heavy paperweight. He then held it against the nanite tendril and attempted to skewer it through. It didn't work. Helix brought the glass piece against the metal tendril several times, but nothing happened. Jack was almost to the window. 'Shit,' he thought. The edge of the window was just ahead. He watched as the tendril scraped along the broken glass, flinging small spheres from the deadening arm. Jack was to the wall. He pressed his feet against the baseboard and began to lean back. Helix saw what he was doing and quickly swooped behind him, wrapping his arms around his waist. He began to pull. Jack continued lurching forward. Even with Helix's added weight, it wasn't enough to anchor him in place or break him free.

"Let go!" Jack said to Helix.

"No!"

"Let me go! Dammit!" Jack shouted louder.

"NO! If you go, we both go!"

Jack wrapped his hands tightly around the tendril and clamped his fist, pulling as hard as he could. Nothing moved. He took in a deeper breath and began to pull again. His fused arm began to tingle. A swirl of energy raced up and around his arm, visible beneath his skin. Jack gritted his teeth, clenched his jaw, and began to pull with all his might. The tendril loosened. Jack could feel it. He pulled even harder and within a moment, the tendril tore in half. As it broke free its grip, the spheres broke apart and rolled free across the floor. A surge of energy sparked from Jack's hand and shot down the remaining tendril until it enveloped the entire form of the creature outside the window.

The creature's body exploded, spraying tiny nanite spheres in every direction. Jack, still pulling from the window, shot back suddenly, taking Helix with him. The fell back nearly the length of the room, their backward fall broken by the Murphy bed still laid out across the room.

Helix pushed Jack from off the top of himself, "Get offa me!"

"Sorry," Jack scrambled to roll off and stand away from Helix. "Thanks for the help."

"Hey, you saved me today at the shop, it's the least I could do."

"Looks like my office didn't fare much better than your shop did," Jack mused, surveying the damage that was once his office. "The super always wanted to remodel."

"Yeah, but this time it will be with one less detective," Helix cracked.

"Funny," Jack smirked. He walked back to the opening that was once a window. He peered over the edge to see the street below covered in what appeared to be a black stain. The creature, whatever it was, was gone. "Where do you think it came from?"

"No doubt, the same gang who hit your shop, and who have been ghosting us all along," Jack said.

"The Dark HART," Helix confirmed to himself, remembering the symbol they found inside the COMM device. "But why us? You think this is because we found that COMM device?"

Jack shook his head, "That was just the beginning. We're getting close to finding out why they're here, in the country, in our city, here and now." Jack looked from the window to the mess the creature left behind in his office. '*It was going to take some time to sort through the mess,*' he thought.

Jack noticed a small, flat black object left on the floor. He didn't recognize it as his own. He knelt down and pinched it off the floor. It was blank at first glance. "Is this yours?" Jack asked Helix.

Helix looked at the item between Jack's index and middle finger. He plucked it with his own fingers and studied it for a moment. He then shook his head, "No." He flipped it over several times and then held it still, "Oh hey, you know what this is?"

"If I did, I wouldn't have asked you."

Oh, yeah, I guess so," Helix turned excited as he tapped the corner of the item. Nothing happened.

"What are you doing?"

"Oh, you see, this is a secure invite card," Helix explained. "Only the swankiest parties give out this type of encryption. You see, you press the corner here and it displays the information for the event."

"I don't see anything," Jack stated the obvious.

"Of course not, we weren't invited. Only those who were given the invitation can access its contents. Each invite is encoded with the guests DNA information, and that alone can activate the content," Helix explained.

"So how the hell did a thing like this get one?" Jack wondered. "You think it pinched it off some poor victim?"

"Maybe," Helix wondered aloud. He then went over to the floor and picked up one of the small spheres that had once been attached to the creature, and pressed it against the corner of the invite. The item lit up and flashed a series of images, all explaining the importance of the secrecy of the party attached. Once all the images flashed past, the image of President Michaelson lifted off the invite along with the title 'President's Re-Election Campaign Fundraiser,' a list of dates, times, and locations.

"The President's upcoming gala event," Jack read. "There's nothing secret about that, the whole country knows he's going to be here for the election, trying to win the city's swing voters."

"Yeah, but the event is invite only. Only the elite elitists will be there."

Jack cocked his head and raised an eyebrow, "Then why the hell would a thing like this get an invite to the biggest event of the year?"

"A better question is who would invite it?"

"There's only one place we're going to find those answers," Jack smiled. "Looks like I need to put on my Sunday's best, I've got a party to go to."

"Dammit! You have to listen to me!" Jack pleaded.

Lartanner ran his thick hands through his thinning hair, "No! I am not going to listen to anything you have to say anymore, Zero. Frankly, I've had enough of your nonsense."

"Didn't you hear what I said? The HART are plotting to attack the president. Tonight, at his fundraising gala."

Lartanner waved his hand dismissively, "Yeah, yeah, you told me. Some creature made up of tiny orbs in the shape of a man attacked you."

"Nanites, to be exact," Helix interjected.

"Thank you," Lartanner said to Helix. He then turned to Jack, "Who the hell is this?"

"I'm Helix," he offered his hand warmly with a smile.

"You know, I don't give a damn who you are," Lartanner snarled. "If I'm not mistaken, you were asked, no ordered, to stay away from this case."

"I was," Jack lied. "But the case seems to keep finding me."

"You're full of shit, Zero," Lartanner sneered. "I know you. Once you start a case, you can't let it go."

"Please, sir," Helix tried to reason. "You have to increase security at the President's gala. If you don't, it could mean disaster."

"And you base this on some insane story about a strange creature that attacked you that just happened to have a ticket," Lartanner assessed. "How stupid do you think I am?"

"On a scale of one to ten?" Jack asked playfully. "An eight?"

"Both of you, out of my office! NOW!"

"You're making a mistake, Lartanner," Jack said.

"My only mistake was letting you out of a cell," Lartanner shot back. "NOW GET OUT!"

Jack looked at the heavily breathing Lartanner, his face reddened with rage. Jack was leaning forward, his arms propped against the top of Lartanner's desk. He stared long and hard at his former superior. He hoped to breakthrough by staring him down, but it didn't work. Jack finally pushed off from the desk and slowly began to walk backward toward the door.

"C'mon, Helix," Jack said. "We can't do any more here."

Helix scurried past Jack and rushed out through the door. Lartanner, still red in the face, watched through a furrowed brow until Jack disappeared through the door. He then released a loud, annoyed breath that he had been holding, in an attempt to not erupt loudly any more than he already had. The tension was thick and hanged heavily in the air between them. As soon as Jack and Helix slipped out of the office, Lartanner plopped his backside into his chair and let loose the breath he had been holding deep in his lungs. He then swept his hand over his desk until his fingers found the intercom. He pressed the button and signaled his assistant.

"Could you get me Commander Barbarsoa?" He lifted his finger and leaned back in his chair, contemplating why he took the job of Commissioner in the first place.

Jack stood with Helix just outside Lartanner's door. Waiting for them were four uniformed officers.

"Hiya, fellas," Jack flashed them a quick grin before the four men began herding Helix and him to the awaiting elevator.

Lartanner was deep in thought, his gaze focused on the cityscape outside his office window. Thoughts of regret on becoming Commissioner haunted him. He thought of all the people he had to terminate and those he reprimanded on a regular basis. Jack Zero had always fallen into both those categories. Even now, no longer associated with NULE, he still managed to find new ways to infuriate him. '*Why? Why did he tolerate it?*' Before he could find an answer, a tall, dark, thin man with narrow features and short, cropped hair stood in the doorway.

"Is everything all right?" The man in the doorway asked.

Lartanner smiled, "Barbarsoa, so good of you to FINALLY show up."

"Sorry to disappoint you, Commish," came a deep, familiar voice.

"You're not Barbarsoa."

"Someone still hasn't lost their keen detective skills," the man jibed as he stepped into view. Lartanner recognized the chiseled features of Chief Bendu Aloona.

"What are you doing here?" Lartanner asked as he stood from behind his desk and approached Aloona.

"I'm sorry, was I interrupting something important?" Aloona said scathingly.

"I've had a tough day, I don't need you coming in here and busting my chops."

"Man, you are touchy. Or should I say the opposite. I hardly got a chance to even say "hi" to you this morning."

"You can't seriously be calling me rude and callous. I think that department belongs solely to you," Lartanner shot back.

"Me? I'm not the one who always runs out first chance I get," Aloona shot back. He was a handsome man, his dark complexion enhancing his strong jawline.

"Some of us have important jobs and need to be to work early," Lartanner snapped.

Aloona stepped closer and put his hands on Lartanner's waist, "Someone is in a really bad mood."

Lartanner leaned in and kissed Aloona deeply, "I know, I'm sorry. I'm just having a tough day."

The two men embraced for a moment. Lartanner let himself get lost in the moment, enjoying the strength of the arms that wrapped tightly around him. He felt comfortable, safe. Aloona always made him feel that way. He always did. Even when he first started on the force, Aloona the rookie, Lartanner was assigned as his partner. It was difficult for the two of them to get along and see eye-to-eye, Lartanner was by the book and

Aloona was more about doing what he felt was right. It resulted in many arguments between them. However, over time, Lartanner won over the young and idealistic 'kid,' as he called him often then. Before too long, they were each reassigned, Lartanner taking a promotion and Aloona gaining a new partner, but they kept in touch, and quickly realizing they had feelings for one another. Before long, they forged a relationship, dating for several months, and then moving in together. Lartanner smiled, knowing it was the best decision he made. Aloona was always there for him, supporting every decision. When Lartanner went for the Commissioner position, Aloona was his strongest supporter, always giving him the daily pep talk that 'he could do it,' and 'he was the best choice for the job.' Lartanner was lucky to have someone so supportive and positive in his life, especially with all the problems that had come with the job.

Aloona leaned back, "Maybe you should take out early and when you come home we could order in, maybe Greek? Get a bottle of wine? I could give you a nice back rub."

Lartanner smiled and turned away, "That sounds great, but I have the President's Fundraiser tonight. They're calling for increased security. It's going to be a long night."

"I'd forgotten about that," Aloona replied. He leaned his forearms against Lartanner's shoulders. "How about I wait up for you and draw you a nice hot bath."

"You got a deal," Lartanner turned and kissed Aloona again. A knock at the office door pulled the two lovers apart. Lartanner called out as he returned to sit behind his desk, "Its open!"

A tall, hefty bald man filled up the doorway.

"Hello Barbarsoa," Lartanner greeted the large man.

"Hey Commish," Barbarsoa's deep voice boomed across the room. He was truly a grandiose man, large in every visible way. He wore a genuine smile that countered his oppressive appearance. "Am I interrupting anything?"

"Not at all," Aloona winked. "I was just on my way out."

Aloona walked over to Barbarsoa and held out a flat palm. Barbarsoa slapped his palm against his and they shook hands amicably. Aloona placed a friendly hand on Barbarsoa's shoulder, "Its good seeing you, friend."

"You too," Barbarsoa smiled in return.

Aloona walked from the office and closed the door behind him. The office was quiet, darkening as the low afternoon sun was sinking into the blue sky. Barbarsoa stepped up to Lartanner's desk.

"You called for me?" The man named Barbarsoa stood massive, shadowing the doorway.

"Yeah, thanks for coming so quickly," Lartanner said. "Sit down."

Barbarsoa stepped in, closing the door behind him. He then sat across from his superior. Adrianne Barbarsoa was one of Lartanner's best and loyalist men. He trusted him. In his sixteen years serving with the NULE, he had shown the most impeccable record of any officer before him. For every case, Barbarsoa closed it with an arrest and a conviction. His attention to detail and ensuring he accrued the right evidence each time made him thorough and effective. Lartanner knew he could count on him.

"What's going on?" Barbarsoa asked.

"I need you to assemble a crack squad for me, today."

"What for?"

"I need you on security detail for the President's Campaign Fundraiser at the museum tonight."

Barbarsoa looked at Lartanner curiously. He had never been placed on this type of duty before, "Is everything alright?"

Lartanner shrugged, "I don't know. I just want to be prepared for anything."

Barbarsoa nodded, "You can count on me."

"Remember," Lartanner reminded him. "Best of the best. Got it?"

"Yessir."

Jack straightened the collar of his trench coat. The officers weren't as friendly as the others that have escorted him out in the past. Helix looked a bit shaken up, fearful for the potential consequence of going to jail because of Jack.

Jack saw the stress in his face, "You all right?"

Helix nodded. "I don't know what we're going to do? If the cops aren't willing to help us, then what can we do?"

Jack raised an eyebrow, "Well, for starters we need to get on our Sunday's best, we have a party to get ready for."

"But, that guy told you to stay away," Helix reminded him.

"He says that a lot. In case you haven't noticed, I'm not one to listen."

"But how do you think you're getting into that place? It's going to be fortified."

"That's where you come in," Jack smiled coyly.

Helix's expression sank. He knew this was only going to lead to more trouble, "Oh, I really don't like the sound of this."

CHAPTER 14
THE MUSEUM CAPER

"Good evening, welcome back to the live coverage of the Presidential Gala at the New Utica Museum of Natural History, I'm WTVK anchor Bill Lawler, coming to you live," Bill Lawler, an aging man in his early sixties stood positioned at the base of the steps of the museum. They swooped up dramatically, leading up to the massive opening of the beautiful stone structure that welcomed visitors to the heart of the downtown area. Bill, a seasoned reporter in the city for over thirty years, smiled as he spoke. His cheeks bounced with each movement of his mouth, revealing the aging lines and wrinkles that he tried to mask under layers of make-up.

"For those just tuning in, you can see a plethora of A-list guests showing up to show their support for the incumbent, as President Michealson's numbers continue to sink in the polls. As many of you know, New Utica is the focus of a very dramatic battle for voter support. With the election just a few days from now, this is the opportunity for Michaelson to turn things around in his favor.

"But he is facing stiff competition from local Senator Janus Glorm, whose surprise bid last year, sent shockwaves through the nation. Glorm, who is known to support many humanitarian causes, as well as expressing his support to aggressively challenge terrorist groups, such as the HART, have made him popular among many voters. But the real question is will Michaelson's challenger make an appearance? Stay tuned to find out."

"Now wait just a minute," The security guard held his hands up, imposingly, attempting to prevent any sort of entrance into the museum. "We're closed."

"I don't much care about your operating hours," Agent Frisco flashed her badge that hung by a chain around her neck in the guards scowling face. "This is important official government business!"

"Then come back during our official hours," the guard responded sardonically.

"Ellis, please," came a nasally voice from behind the guard named Ellis. "Go assist in the prehistoric wing."

Ellis frowned as he inaudibly grumbled, walking away into the darkness of the museum. The nasally man smiled cordially at Frisco, his eyes darting from hers to her badge, "My name is Guilderland Drexler, I'm the assistant curator here. How can I be of assistance to you?"

"Welcome back," the smiling face of Bill Lawler mugged for the floating camera-sphere before him. He loved being in front of the camera, he loved addressing viewers, or as he called them, 'his adoring fans.' He did garner the respect of his viewers, keeping a constant high number of viewers every broadcast. What he was unaware was he never had the respect of his peers. Those that worked with him felt he was a pompous, arrogant ass. His colleagues at other media outlets, well, they felt the same way. Regardless, he was the highest paid anchor with the most viewership in the city and surrounding areas. Moreover, he knew it. He continued, "Let's see who is pulling up to the front of the museum."

The front entrance of the New Utica Natural History Museum was alive with activity and an energy that could light the entire city. A bright red carpet lined the front of the museum, leading from the edge of the street, across the extra-wide sidewalk, up the magnificent staircase, and through the impressive brass doors that led into the museum. Spotlights streaked across the night sky as they beamed upward into the endless, vastness of the starry night sky. Like an assembly line, limousine after limousine pulled up to the curb, the passengers' door aligned with the red carpet. As soon as the occupants of one limousine were emptied, the next limo in line was there to take its place. Each impressive vehicle was filled with starlets, celebrities, and politicians, all prepared to celebrate the President of the United States coming to New Utica.

Several media outlets were staked out along the edges of either side of the red carpet. Each angling themselves in an attempt to gain the eye contact with or simple attention of any passing celebrity they could get. Each reporter holding a microphone was preoccupied by whichever passing notable personality was nearby. Several pedestrian fans mobbed behind reporters' row as they snapped pictures of their favorite icon. As each celebrity and politician finished their questions and answers with each reporter they stopped by, they then made their way to the brass doors at the top of the stairs. Aligning the steps and around the door were stationed several guards, dressed in well-pressed suits, that ensured only those permitted into the event entered. Despite their tight convictions, they hardly moved, let alone flinched, as each guest passed. Only in one instance, when a wayward "fan" attempted to sneak into the procession line and sneak their way up the stairs did one guard move. The odd movement the guard made seemed to be quick and blurred. The guard snapped out his arms, clasped his hands around the "fan's" neck, and slammed him face first into the stone steps. The vicious assault was immediately moved away from the steps as the trespasser was moved from the line and away from any eyewitnesses before he was carted off in a van to an awaiting prison cell.

Aside from a single incident, the red carpet procession moved along smoothly. Glorm was pleased. A thin smile crept slowly across his narrow face as he looked across the sea of people that ebbed and flowed along the edge of the carpet, while the elegant, glamorous stream of people moved slowly up the middle. It was truly a glorious sight.

Glorm stepped from his limousine and onto the carpet at the curb. He stopped and turned, hooking out his elbow he offered to his wife as she exited the car right behind him. Clad in his finest black tuxedo, complete with matching black tie and vest, Glorm was joined at his side by his wife, who wore a sheer, flowing pearl-colored dress that adhered to her broad curves and slender waist. Glorm was pleased at the way she looked standing next to him, the perfect complement to his, self-proclaimed, handsome physique.

"You look lovely, my dear," Glorm whispered to his wife, Vennita, "As always."

"Thank you," she purred. "You don't look so bad yourself."

"I clean up nice when I want to," he smiled playfully as they began their walk up the carpet.

Their polite conversation was rudely, if not expectantly, interrupted by the shouts of their names, "Senator Glorm!" or "Senator and Mrs. Glorm!" The reporters, including Bill Lawler, were like ravaged jackals looking to claim their next innocent meal. Nevertheless, this was how it was done, how the game was played. You must put aside your apprehensions and put on your winning smile. Your best personality, whether it truly reflects you or not, must shine through.

Glorm approached the first reporter in the line, flashes from cameras popped in his face, temporarily blinding him, but he pretended it didn't bother him. The reporter's badge read: 'Bill Lawler, WTVK,' the call letter for the local News Network.

"Senator Glorm!" Bill drove the microphone in his hand at Glorm's mouth, just missing his pointed nose. "How do you feel about the President's claim on negotiating with the I-ZAN Corporation's take-over of several American companies?"

Glorm kept his confident smile as he spoke, "As an advocate of American-made products, I have cautioned the talks, even going so far as to halting the bill presented for allowing the monopolization of certain industries by claim of the I-ZAN Corps offer. I want to make 'made in America' mean something again."

Bill asked, "What of the reports of your lead in the polls? Do you think it will affect tonight's fundraiser for the President's campaign?"

"There's hardly a question regarding my chances of winning," Glorm beamed. "But, all competition aside, we are still both politicians working for a better America. Or, well, at least I am."

"The recent Zogby polls show you as the front runner going into next week's election."

"So I've heard," Glorm replied confidently.

"Do you think you have a good shot of winning against the incumbent, whom will be arriving shortly?" Bill probed.

"Isn't that the spirit of our electoral process, the spirit of competition," Glorm gestured grandly, his arms wide, like a peacock fanning its tail. "There are several people who champion my stance and criticism of the current presidency. The people want a true leader, not some figurehead who has little power to sway his fellow legislators. Face it, he's a lame duck."

Another reporter Annelle Jandur, a lovely raven-haired young woman from UNN, the call letters for the Universal News Network stepped over Bill and his camera pod. If there was anything Bill didn't like, it was a pushy colleague, especially one who was stealing his show.

"Senator Glorm, Annelle Jandur from UNN. What of the claims that you have several offshore accounts invested in several of I-ZAN's interest groups," Annelle smirked as she asked her hard question.

"Well," Glorm tried to keep his smile. "I can assure you those claims are false, I can prove them with the public release of my personal holdings."

"We have informants on the inside who claim that you have many of your accounts hidden from record under pseudonyms and fake corporations."

"Ms. Jandur, I appreciate your candor, but I assure you, I am one hundred percent American, all my investments and holdings are American, why even the cars my family drive are made in the fine factories of

Detroit," Glorm glowered, while still maintaining his smile. "I am red-blooded, and blue-collared."

"And white supremacy?" A male voice shouted from the crowd behind.

Glorm lost his smile as the crowd '*oohed*' at the comment. Glorm straitened his coat and ran his hand across his tie as he turned his head to hide his underlying, and boiling, rage. He regained his composure and returned the now awkward-looking smile to his face.

"Many people feel that those with money and privilege look down on those that have none, but that's not true. I worked and clawed my way to global success, and I did it in America, with the help of Americans. I chose to serve in the public trust of politics because I want to give back to the country that gave me everything I earned. I understand the public mistrust of any politician, and in many cases, it's warranted. But I want you all to know, that I would never let the American people down.

"They are my people, they are me. I am here to serve you as your elected official. If there are issues that concern you, then they concern me. We all are in this together. If I were elected to office, my main objective would be to bring those jobs back here, and return America to the once thriving and bolstering economy it once was. I want to make America great again," Glorm held up his hand as he began to move away from the microphone. "God bless America!"

Glorm strode away with his wife on his arm as the reporters up the line past Annelle Jandur screamed to vie for his attention.

The sound of nearly a dozen shoes clicking and clopping against the marble floor of the museum echoed and reverberated across the vaulted ceilings and sparsely decorated walls. Guilderland Drexler walked at a brisk pace, keeping ahead of Frisco with her agents in tow. Drexler was a short, thin man with gaudy, angular features. His small round-framed glasses drooped low on his hooked nose, which he repeatedly adjusted by pressing his finger to the bridge. He breathed heavily as they walked which seemed odd at first, noted Frisco, until he pulled out his inhaler and compressed the medicine into his lungs. An asthmatic, she realized.

"I apologize for our security guard," Drexler said, which seemed like a third time since they entered. "But they're trained to not trust."

"Even a badge," Frisco remarked.

"Especially a badge," Drexler's tone was a bit more serious. "We've been robbed several times in the past, thugs sometimes just like to kick in the door, others get creative, dress as businessmen, policemen. I once had a man come in a fedora and leather coat, claiming to be an archeologist. Turns out he looted our Egyptian prince exhibit, a grave robber indeed."

"I understand your trepidation," Frisco acknowledged. "You don't always know who you can trust."

"Isn't that the truth," Drexler's smile faded almost instantly as he spoke. "Especially with our hosting the Presidential Gala and all. Can't be too careful."

They walked for a moment in silence, no one even sharing a glance at one another. Frisco bounced her gaze around the corridor and then into the large, open room that housed several large exhibits. She craned her neck as she looked up at the massive, complex assembly of bones that made up what was once a tyrannosaurus rex. Its head was posed downward, as if looking at each passerby as prey; its hallow eyes burned into her, could see through her. She shivered. The face of the creature was haunting to her. She darted her glance away, trying to shake the fear she felt, as if feeling the eyes of a killer watching her. It was moments before she realized she was holding her breath. After a moment of heavy, almost smothering silence, Drexler broke the silence. "What brings your authority to my museum at such a late hour?"

"Over the past few weeks there have been a series of mysterious…invasions," Frisco hesitated as she spoke.

"Invasions?" Drexler sounded confused. "What do you mean invasions?"

"Well, we mean unusual men have been spotted inside many locations across the city."

"Unusual, how?" Drexler pressed.

"Unusual, as in, naked," Frisco felt silly stating such an odd claim.

"Naked?" Drexler sounded shocked. "I'm sure any amount of naked men entering the museum would be less than inconspicuous."

"That's the interesting thing, Mr. Drexler," Frisco explained further. "They don't just enter the locations via a traditional method, like through a door or window, instead they are entering mysteriously."

"M-mysterious? How?" Drexler stammered.

"We're not sure. But we're thinking they've developed a method of opening doors without actually using doors."

"I don't understand."

Lartanner sidled up alongside Drexler and Frisco, "We think they are using some sort of teleportation device."

"Interportals," Frisco corrected.

"Interportals?" Drexler questioned. "I thought those were nothing more than a hypothetical theory. A legend worthy of an exhibit in our mythology wing."

"We have reason to believe, good reason, that they are a reality, which means these intruders, if you will, can appear anywhere."

"But why here?"

"We were hoping you could tell us that," Frisco said, her

eyebrow raised.

Drexler turned away from Frisco's stare. He was hiding something, she was sure of it. Drexler seemed to pick up the pace as they made their way across the museum.

"We need cops in here like we need more exhibits," Ellis grumbled. He ran the beam of his flashlight along the marbles walls and columns that alternated between the large, arching windows. The beam shone back blindingly as it glared from the window. Ellis pulled the light away, leaving behind his reflection staring back at him. He looked at his sunken features, haunted by his aged and weathered face. This is not the life he had envisioned for himself. Hell, had he pushed himself like his mother pressured, he could've been a lawyer or physician. *'Who am I kidding,'* he thought to himself, *'I was a terrible student.'* Ellis turned away from his reflection, slight disgust in his eyes. He reached up to the top left side of the window and latched it closed securing the window, a process he did nightly, ensuring the windows were secured before the digital security was activated. If a door or window were not secured, the digital signal that encircles the museums' perimeter, the alarm would sound. Ellis knew the alarm all too well. His first week on the job was his first experience with the alarm. He had been trained to check all entryways by his mentor, Lance he thought his name was. Lance was adamant about reinforcing the drills, a constant check and recheck of all entryways. He took it lightly that first week, but learned quickly that it wasn't to be as he quickly glazed over the latches and didn't realize he missed one completely. Once the digital perimeter was initiated, the signal hit the missed latch and roared to life, wailing through the large, mostly hollowed hallways. The sound pierced his ears causing him to drop to his knees, his hands cupped tightly around the sides of his head. Since then he understood the importance of monitoring the security in the museum, especially his part. Under his watch, no latch was ever left open. Until tonight.

A thin cable pulled taut snapping open the latch that Ellis secured only minutes before. It had been neatly tucked along the edge of the window's seam, a trick Jack Zero learned while on the force. Jack peeked his head just over the window's sill, trying not to be noticed if a security guard happened to be nearby. His eyes darted quickly back and forth. The room was empty. He glanced quickly at his wristwatch, knowing he only had two minutes before the digital security was activated. He didn't have time to waste. Jack shimmied the window open slowly, his fingers wrapped at the base tightly, so as not to make too much noise. He opened it just wide enough to squeeze through to which he kicked his legs up and swung them into the window. He had to keep his hand underneath as a brace or the heavy frame would slam down on top of him. Jack twisted his body, contorting it in order to continue sliding quietly through the opening. He slid through on his back; his head was the last part of his body to pass underneath. He then lowered his hand, closing the window with a quiet thud. He stood for a moment, his knees pitched slightly forward as he poised in a defensive squat. He raised his fists up, prepared to take on anyone that may have seen him, but it was still empty, darkness filling the spaces between the floodlights. He knew it was only a matter of time before the guard returned and just over a minute before the digital security was on. He turned to latch the window, but could only turn part of the way. His heart stopped for a moment as he turned to see what was holding him. He saw the back of his coat was pinned between the windowsill and frame. He tugged it gently at first, but it didn't budge. He then yanked harder, but it only slid a fraction of the way through. The window frame was just too heavy. He looked again at his watch. He had less than thirty seconds to life the window and latch it before the alarm is tripped.

Jack grabbed the indented brass handles at the base of the frame and lifted with all his might, the window shot up from his grasp. Jack pivoted his hips quickly, flaring his coat free from the frame. He tried to catch the frame, but his fingers weren't prepared for the weight and the frame slipped free, slamming against the sill with a resounding bang that echoed loudly across the walls and ceiling. Jack reached up and locked the window just as the hum of the digital security pulsated through the wires that lined the window frame.

That was close, he thought.

"Hey you! Stop!" Ellis called, drawing his low impact energy emitter from its holster. The sound of the window slamming must have lured his back sooner than Jack anticipated.

So much for discretion. "I'm not looking for trouble, pal," Jack said, raising his hands above his head.

"Then you shouldn't have come into my museum," Ellis sneered. He raised the LIEE and fired at Jack. A bright blue ball burst from the prongs of the LIEE and sailed across the room at Jack. Jack dove to his right, avoiding the energy ball as it affected into the wall. A wave of blue lightning reached across the wall, stretching like tendrils that scratched everything it touched. Despite its low emission, it still packed quite a wallop.

"Jeez," Jack bemoaned as he picked himself up. He saw no choice but to charge into Ellis. Jack ran with his head tucked into his chest, his head plowing into the guard's abdomen, knocking him from his feet and onto his back. Ellis coughed loudly as his back cracked against the marble floor, the wind knocked from his lungs. The LIEE fell loose from Ellis' grip and skittered across the floor, disappearing into the darkness. Jack picked himself up and prepared to defend himself, but Ellis wasn't moving.

Jack panicked. This was not what he intended. He pressed his two fingers onto Ellis' neck, feeling his carotid artery. It pulsated. Jack let out a sigh of relief, he didn't want to kill anyone, just undermine Agent Frisco's orders, not to mention Senator Glorm's and Lartanner's. He had far too much invested into this case just to let it go to some pompous Fed. Jack stood and looked around, wondering if anyone had been nearby and heard his scuffle with the guard. It was quiet, but he didn't want to wait around for someone to stumble upon this scene. He grabbed Ellis by his wrists and pulled him into a shadowed alcove, keeping him out of view, at least until he wakes up. Once Ellis was nestled, Jack made his way into the darkness of the hallway.

Glorm and his wife entered Charles Darwin Hall, the main hall of the museum, where the gala was already underway. It was an amazing, breathtaking sight. The room was lit with several gold and crystal chandeliers that hung from the ceiling every few feet across the long room. There were elaborate decorations; silk and crushed velvet tapestries, etched brass candelabras with flickering candles, tables and tables of fine china and silver utensils awaiting the abundant menu that would soon fill each plate. The wait staff ushered guests into the massive hall and to their labeled seats. Others carried trays of hors d'oeuvres, offering their bountiful treats to anyone nearby. Glorm guided his wife through the bustle of guests and hosts darting back and forth in front of them.

A young woman wearing a white shirt and black bow tie approached Glorm, "Are you looking for your table?"

Glorm smiled, "Why yes, thank you."

"This way," the young woman motioned as she lead the two toward their assigned seats.

"Come along, my dear," Glorm smiled to his wife as he held her hand gently and guided her into the room.

He panned his head around to see if he recognized anyone. There were several faces he knew from movies and television, but no one he would consider friends. From outside his peripheral vision came an older, rotund man with white hair that encircled the side of his head, not covering the top. His name was Senator Garand Frimmond.

"Jensen!" Frimmond howled. "Jensen Glorm, m'boy! Good to see you!"

Glorm extended his hand, "Senator Frimmond, good to see you as well."

The shook hands firmly, which Frimmond followed up by placing his fat hands on Glorm's thin shoulders. "You need to come by my office; we need to have ourselves a little chat."

"About what?"

"That industrialization deal that came up, the one with those I fellas," Frimmond patted his hands on his chest, as if feeling for a heartbeat.

"The I-ZAN bill, right, well, I feel I've made my position on that matter very clear," Glorm replied.

"You may want to rethink that position of yours, son," Frimmond took in a deep breath. "The opportunities that follow could be quite…profitable, if you know what I mean?"

"No, I don't know," Glorm scowled. "In fact, if I didn't know better, I would think you were bribing me into changing my position, senator. That's not very diplomatic."

Frimmond grimaced, "Son, you're going to find that a lot of positions, let alone legal, change for a lot of reasons, but never with the wrong intentions. You're new in this game of politics, so I'll give you a pass, but you need to consider what side you want to be on, the side of moral goodness, or the side of surviving. It's up to you."

Glorm hesitated for a moment and then let loose a smile, "I'm a self-made man, Senator Frimmond. I came from a poor family, without being able to rub two nickels together. I started my own business and clawed my way up to be one of the top Fortune 500 companies in the world. Not once did I need advice or direction on what I needed to do to make it. When I was elected to the senate seat, beating out a seven-term incumbent, it was due to my moral stance on doing what's right for the people. I don't need anyone telling me now what I need to do. I think I can make my own decisions, thank you."

Glorm turned and walked away.

Drexler's office was as cluttered as it was large. There were several artifacts from many different eras and cultures around the world that adorned shelves, like knickknacks in an elderly woman's curio cabinet. Crude sketches, detailed maps, and beautiful paintings were scattered on tables, in frames leaning against walls, and rolled up in piles. Drexler's office seemed a projection of his mind, filled with so much details and information, but lacking any form of order. Drexler was comfortable in his chaos as he walked to his desk and slid open a drawer to pull out materials.

"What is it exactly that you are looking for, Agent Fargus?" Drexler inquired.

"Frisco," she corrected him snidely. "We have suspicions that a group of men are looking to assault the museum in an attempt to find," she hesitated, "something."

"Well it would be useful if I knew exactly what 'it' is," Drexler's tone was cold.

"Maybe you could answer a few questions Mr. Drexler." Frisco probed. "It seems you have a bit of a penchant for information."

"And what is that supposed to mean?"

"I did my homework on you before knocking on your door tonight," Frisco stood erect, stretching her spine in an attempt to make herself look taller, more dominant. "It just means that you have a reputation of knowing information."

"That's my job," Drexler curled his lip.

"There were several blights on your personal record," Frisco continued. She pulled a pair of spectacles from the breast pocket of her coat. They resembled a typical pair of safety glasses one would wear in a hazardous area. She placed them onto her face and tapped the side of the right bow. A flash of blue rippled across both lenses. Frisco's eyes focused on the light briefly, blinked twice and then approached Drexler. "Give me your hand."

"What?" Drexler recoiled from Frisco's outstretched hand.

"Your hand, give it to me," she commanded.

"Certainly not," Drexler refused.

"Mr. Drexler, we can either do this easily with you giving me your hand, or hard, where I force you to give me your hand. And I'll warn you, the latter is fun for me, but not for you."

Drexell pursed his lips, his face contorted into a soured expression as he placed his hand in Frisco's. Frisco forcibly, with obvious intention, yanked Drexler's hand up. She curled his fingers under, but left his thumb out. She pressed the thumb against the right corner of the right lens of her spectacles. The lenses flashed red this time, which prompted her to release Drexler's unwilling hand. Drexler winced and stepped back, watching Frisco's eyes dart about rapidly, reading something that scanned across her lenses; something he could not see.

"You have seven priors that leap right up, Mr. Drexler," Frisco quickly stated. "You withheld information from police in not just one, but four investigations. Two priors were hiding evidence."

"I was not hiding evidence," Drexler defended himself. "They were priceless artifact. There was no way I was going to let them into the hands of those, primates."

Frisco cocked an eyebrow as she switched focus to Drexler's squirming expression. She refocused on her lenses. "Well this one in particular is quite interesting; apparently you had two priors regarding sexual harassment. One of which resulted in a sexual assault accusation."

"To which I was acquitted," he was quick to point out.

"You are aware that you are border line in violation of state regs," Frisco explained, a small grin crossing her face. "According to state laws, any citizen in violation of laws with more than eight priors on their record may be subject to criminal prosecution, which can lead to a fine of up to $500,000 and/or up to seven years in federal prison."

Drexler pulled at his collar with his forefinger, trying to release the constriction that seemed to suddenly appear. Frisco was pleased to see Drexler sweat.

"Well...um...I...," Drexler stammered.

"I suggest you cooperate with my investigation, or I add three indictments to your record."

"Th-three?"

"Obstruction of justice, withholding information, again, and being an asshole."

"That's not a law."

"No, it's a character flaw."

Drexler swallowed hard, "All right, what do you want to know?"

Jack sneaked slowly through the open exhibit hall that housed the dinosaur skeletons. The darkness of the room gave him an eerie chill as he moved through. He quickened his pace looking up to the slightly crooked head of the towering tyrannosaurus skeleton. Its eye sockets were directed toward him. It made him uneasy. Jack turned away from the beasts gaze as he hurried past.

In the once quiet darkness, a low moan emerged.

Jack felt his heart stop, as did his legs. '*What the hell was that?*' Jack thought to himself. He slowly turned and looked back to the gaze of the gigantic beast he had nearly passed. It seemed silly to think a long dead beast would make a noise. Jack shook his head and continued on his way.

'*GROAN!*' The noise returned, this time more distinct and much louder. There was no mistake; it was coming from the direction of the Tyrannosaurus Rex skeleton. Jack swallowed hard as he looked back at the tower of bones. The groan came again, this time the beast's head tilted toward Jack as its jaw dropped open, its maw agape looking prepared to devour a human meal. The skeletal body leaned forward, its mouth aimed directly at Jack's position.

Jack screamed at the sight of the oncoming assault. However, before he could leap out of the way, the giant skeletal body lurched forward and exploded into its individual bones that rained all around Jack Zero. Jack watched as behind the once standing giant a small blue light flickered to life and quickly grew into a massive blue wave. The wave encircled itself until it exposed an opening. Jack could see another place within the wave, a different room.

It was a doorway! Jack couldn't believe what he was seeing. It was at that moment the first person appeared through the doorway. A large, hulking, and completely naked man. Jack recognized the man immediately.

It was Huun.

Jack quickly dove for cover, finding a spot to conceal himself before he was seen. He nestled himself securely behind the bones of a long extinct triceratops skeleton. The base was tall enough for him to remain unseen, but gave him enough room to keep watch on the new occupants in the museum. Jack watched as after Huun, who did little to conceal his nakedness, was followed by three other men, Jack recognized them from the research institute. *'But how? How were they able to do this?'*

He was witnessing it, but still couldn't believe it. The men each stood at attention before Huun who sized them up to ensure they had all made it through the portal in one piece.

"Everyone here and accounted for?" Huun queried.

All the men saluted in unison, "Yessir!"

"Good," Huun growled. "Let's get the gear."

Crust, one of the other men in line immediately disappeared into the shadows. In seconds, he came back with a duffle bag. He tossed it down on the floor and zipped it open. He then began tossing clothes to all the others. Each of the men got dressed in full military garb, complete with Kevlar vests and ammunition belts. Once they were all outfitted, Huun knelt down to the bag and dug deeply inside, pulling out weapons, both large and small. He distributed them to each of the men. Each man checked their weapon to ensure they were loaded and armed, ready to use.

Jack classified the large weapons as class eight-eight high impact plasma-pulse rifles. Not the kind of firearms you can buy off the street, let alone through underground channels. The military rarely offered such high-tech weaponry to their soldiers, only specialty outfits, like the Skytroopers. Somehow, Huun still had his connections. But with whom?

"Fan out," Huun ordered the men. "Crust, you take the lower level, I need you to secure the device."

"Yessir," Crust saluted.

"Faust, you take the upper level, Lintz, you come with me," Huun ordered.

The men all departed in their separate directions.

Jack crept out from behind the skeleton in time to see the last man disappear into the darkened bowels of the museum. They each went in their three separate directions. The problem was, which one did he follow?

Drexler was sweating profusely from his brow. He mopped it with his handkerchief before stuffing it back into his lapel. He was nervous. Frisco could tell he was. She turned to the other officers in the room, "Leave us, I want to question him alone."

The other officers hesitated before nodding in compliance. She waited until they left before turning her stern gaze toward Drexler.

"Spill it," she seethed.

"Alright, alright," Drexler swallowed as he spoke, she could almost see his backbone melt away as he slumped forward in his seat to bury his face in his hands. "I was propositioned by a man, to place a bag within one of our exhibits after hours."

"On the night of the presidential gala?"

"Yes," Drexler said timidly. "They offered a large sum of money, I couldn't refuse."

"Sure you could, didn't you ever hear the old saying, 'money isn't everything?'"

Drexler raised one corner of his mouth, "Not when you have more debt than you earn."

"You know, I don't care about your financial problems, Drexler, all I want to know is the who, the what, and the why."

"It was a professor, his name was Carkleman, he's one of our heavy benefactors. He offered me the payout. I don't know what was in the bag; I was just told where to place it."

"Where?"

"The dinosaur exhibit."

"What were they going to do in the dinosaur exhibit?"

"I don't know, I just put the bag there."

"What time is this all happening?"

"I don't know. I swear I don't know!"

Frisco glared at Drexler wickedly. He squirmed more uncomfortably at her stare, tugging his collar as he swallowed. "And that's all I know," he spat out nervously. "I swear!"

"Take me to the bag," Frisco glared.

Drexler lowered his head shamefully, and then reluctantly agreed.

Jack inched along the shadows, following closely behind Huun. He had to be sure he wasn't seen, but he also didn't want to lose his quarry. Huun and Lintz marched through the darkened rooms of the museum, obviously aware of where they were heading. Jack watched as Huun produced a COMM device and tapped it quickly. He brought the device close to his lips and spoke, "Report."

A crackle was followed by Crust's voice, "Secured."

Crust's reply was followed by Faust's, "In position."

"Excellent," Huun grinned. He then tapped the COMM device again.

From the other end came a low, brooding voice that hissed, "Yes?"

Jack didn't recognized the voice. Whoever it was seemed to be running the show. If Jack could get his hands on Huun's COMM device, he could retrace the call and maybe find out where it was coming from.

"Everything thing is set, my master," Huun's voice quavered slightly as he spoke. It was one of the few times Jack had ever heard any fear in Huun's voice. "We will be ready to proceed as planned."

"Well done, colonel," the voice replied.

"Forever destiny," Huun said.

"Forever destiny," the voice returned.

Huun tucked the COMM device away. Huun waved his finger at Lintz. Lintz nodded, understanding the silent, non-verbal command. He made his way apart from Huun and went into a stairwell.

"Shit," Jack whispered to himself. They were all separated now. He knew he needed to stick with Huun. Jack made his way behind Huun at a distance. They had moved into the Egyptian exhibit, appropriately making their way forward through time as they passed between each room. Huun was walking more rapidly, his pace seeming more determined.

Jack followed, but with slight reserve. Something didn't feel right. Jack reached for his weapon. His fingers only felt air. His weapon was gone. It had been taken by the being known as Evelyn. Now that he wasn't armed, what could he do? He felt a cylinder of cold metal press against the back of head.

Shit.

"Don't move, Zero," Lintz's voice growled. Jack heard the gun cock and then begin to hum as the energy pulse cartridge was loaded and charged.

Jack raised his hands into the air.

Huun walked out of the shadows, the smile he wore was sinister and greasy, "So good to see you again, Zero"

"Wish I could say the same," Jack retorted.

"You didn't think I knew you were following me?" Huun leaned in closely to Jack, "I could smell you the moment you came in."

"I'm surprised you smelled me over the shit that fills your head."

"The stench of cowards is always stronger than anything," Huun sneered. "And you wreak of it."

"You know," Jack began. "The last guy who called me a coward I dropped from about 3,000 feet."

Huun drew back his thick arm, prepared to unleash on Jack, but he relaxed his muscles after a moment, deciding to wait to pummel his prey.

Huun turned to Lintz, "Tie him up and get him out of here."

Lintz wrapped his arms around Zero, preparing to slip the rope he had tautly around the motionless Jack Zero. However, Jack was not prepared to be taken. Not yet. Jack snapped his neck sending his head backward into Lintz's unsuspecting nose. Lintz instantly dropped his clasp on Jack and brought his hands up to tend to his now bleeding nose. Jack tossed the rope to the ground as he ran from Lintz. He turned to see Lintz was not about to give chase. His nose was leaking like a burst water pipe, trails of crimson flowed like many rivers between the gaps in his fingers. Lintz's scream alerted Huun who quickly reverted to chasing Zero. He fired his weapon at Zero, the energy charges lighting up the body of the rifle that was aimed at Jack. A hot blue energy ball launched from the mouth of the rifle and flew with record speed at its prey.

Jack dove for cover as the blue energy ball that hummed like a generator primed to activate exploded over his head, just missing him by mere centimeters. The impact of the sphere tore into the wall behind Jack, splintering and shredding it into tiny shards, leaving behind a massive hold that introduced the inside of the museum to its outside.

Jack quickly picked himself off the ground, propping himself up with his hands, he churned his back legs as he ran toward the nearest exit. Huun didn't hesitate to fire off several more energy balls. They sailed toward Jack as he ran.

Frisco roughly shoved Drexler as the entered the hall of the dinosaur exhibit. Drexler stumbled into the hall, the soles of his shoes slapping against the marble floor, echoing at each step.

"There's no need to shove," Drexler moaned.

"Where's the bag?" Frisco demanded.

Drexler paced nervously around the base of the stegosaurus statue. He swept his hands across the base of the display and the floor; it was gone. The only thing left was a slight sense of heat and a strong pungent odor.

"I-it's gone," Drexler stammered.

Frisco frowned as she turned to her men, "They're here."

Jack had nearly been hit by Huun's energy spheres before he dove to the ground, letting them slam into the wall at the height where his head would have been. Jack landed hard against the marble floor, his chin hitting first. His fedora fell loose from his head and skipped across the floor like a stone across placid water. Debris from the spheres' impact rained down on his head, covering him in a fine layer of dust. Jack skated across the floor as he scampered away from the inevitable next series of blasts that would undoubtedly follow.

"Why are you running, Zero?" Huun called confidently in the darkness. "Just hold still and I'll make sure it's over with quickly."

Jack didn't answer. Not because he didn't want to, but because he was too busy trying to escape. Huun reveled in this moment. He knew he had Jack on the ropes. Huun lowered his weapon, not wishing to fry his quarry just yet. Instead, he saw this as an opportunity to have a little bit of fun. Huun lumbered after the scrambling Jack Zero, leaving Lintz behind to nurse his own wounds.

Jack was fully erect now, breaking into a full run. He had a sizable lead on Huun, which was beneficial in that he had always been able to outrun Huun. His bulk always seemed to slow him down, where Jack remain lean, limber, and could keep his pace much more easily. He felt some sense of relief as he broke free of the Egyptian room and was now in the Roman exhibition. The room was equally as filled as the Egyptian exhibit, but seemed to have more armor-clad mannequins in a variety of poses. However, Jack didn't have time to stop and admire the display; instead, he was preoccupied with escape. He could hear Huun's heavy footsteps echoing in the hall behind him. Jack needed to hide and hide quickly. There was a display in front of him of a gladiator astride a chariot. A perfect place to hide.

Jack moved as fast as he could, slipping around the backside of the chariot and stuffing himself behind the legs of the warrior, trying not to knock over the quiver of arrows that leaned precariously on the edge of the vehicle.

Huun made his way slowly through the Roman exhibit. It was dark, quiet, but he knew Jack was hiding in here somewhere.

"Come out, come out," Huun sang playfully. "I know you're in here, Zero."

Huun walked heel to toe, keeping the sound of his heavy boots silent as he listened intently for any sounds. Jack remained motionless, frozen in place. He held his breath, afraid that the sound of his lungs taking in or expelling air would give him away. Huun was not far from where he was hidden, his face adorned with a broad grin, his nose pointed into the air as if smelling for something. '*Odd*,' Jack thought.

However, it may have worked; Huun stopped and turned in the direction of the chariot. Jack swallowed hard. He kept still, not moving. Huun was practically on top of him before he reached over the lip of the chariot and picked up Jack by the collar of his trench coat.

Huun hoisted Jack up high into the air until he was at eye level. Huun flashed a toothy grin as his lips parted from his previous boyish smile. "I told you I could smell you," he sneered.

Huun flung his arm aside, hurtling Jack through the air effortlessly. Jack flew nearly twenty feet before he hit the floor with his shoulder. His momentum was great and his body continued to slide for several more feet until he crashed into a display of Roman soldiers on the opposite side of the room. Spears, swords, shields, and armor spewed everywhere, not to mention the heads and limbs of the mannequins wearing them.

Jack's body hurt. It was a lot of tolerance for a single person to take. The impact was severe, but nothing was broken. Jack picked himself up, pieces of the soldier display rolling off him. His shoulders ached and his head throbbed. Huun had heaved him with incredible strength. Huun was a powerful man, but certainly not strong, enough to throw a solid man Jack's size as if he were a pillow.

Huun strode casually toward Jack, not speeding up, but simply taking his time, continuing to toy with his prey as a cat would a mouse. Jack wobbled to his feet as Huun lumbered insidiously up to him. He towered over Jack, easily by almost two feet. He glowered down as he stood massively above the teetering form of Jack Zero.

"I am so glad you decided to run," Huun seethed. "I was beginning to think this was going to be another boring caper."

Jack wiped the trickle of blood that ran from his nose, "Always happy to oblige."

"I like you, Zero," Huun replenished his toothy grin. "I always liked you. You always had some smart-ass remark no matter when the chips were down. That stupid smirk of yours…it always made me want to kill you more."

"The feelings mutual."

"You know, I am going to really enjoy this," Huun relished.

"Who are you working for?" Jack asked outright.

"Ah, the infamous Zero direct approach," Huun snorted. "Is this where I'm supposed to tell you everything? Am I supposed to spill my guts and explain what we're doing here?"

"It's obvious," Jack said confidently. "You're going to assassinate the president."

Huun threw his head back as he laughed a full guffaw, "Is that what you think? We would do something so petty?"

"Then why attack this gala here for the president?"

"Who said we're attacking?"

Huun drew back his arm and then released it, backhanding Jack across his face. Jack was catapulted off his feet and, once again, sailed through the air several feet. This time he landed on a model of a lion, whose open jaws and raised paw made him a fierce looking adversary to his opposing gladiator. Jack quickly destroyed the ferocity of the beast when he landed square on its back and crumpled the full-scale model into pieces. This time Jack thrashed his arms and legs like a turtle on its back. The lion's mane covered his head, making it difficult for him to see. Jack brushed the mass of hair from his face, anxious to see his aggressor.

Huun hulked over, this time appearing less jovial and more serious, "Alright Zero, fun time is over."

Jack knew he was making his last stand. He had to make the ever-fateful decision to fight or flight. The thing that had always gnawed deeply within Jack's psyche was that he never ran from a fight. Therefore, much to his own disdain, Jack's decision was already made for him.

"You're right about that," Jack retorted. He tucked his head down and charged at Huun, his head sinking deeply into Huun's muscular abdomen. The air escaped from Huun's lungs as he was taken by surprise. He stumbled backward, Jack now in control of where Huun would land.

Frisco shoved Drexall through the hall and into the Egyptian exhibit. He stumbled like an infant taking their first steps.

"Hey watch it," he whined.

"You've got a lot of explaining to do," Frisco snarled. "You knowingly and wittingly allowed a terrorist organization into this museum without alerting authorities."

"Terrorist? Please," Drexall smiled. "Your definition of terrorist is not the same as mine. You'll find that many Americans support what the HART movement represents. The HART wants to free us of the reliance on technology, return us to the days when we relied on ourselves."

"You aren't really that naïve Mr. Drexall?"

"Is it more naïve to depend on a computer to wake you up in the morning? Tell you what to eat? Where to go? We have diminished out role on this planet. Machines are taking over. And now the government wants to ignore this," Drexall lauded. "I think you are the naïve one."

"We'll see," Frisco stared at Drexall intensely through narrowed eyes.

Several sounds of gunfire could be heard, along with the sound of something crashing asunder.

"What's that?" Another agent asked.

"Let's find out," Frisco led the charge toward the commotion. She ordered the nearest agent, "Keep an eye on him." She then drew her pistol as she ran into the adjacent hall.

Glorm had finally found his seat at one of the tables next to his wife. He sat happily; as he watched, the room fill with so many notable guests, all awaiting the arrival of the guest of honor. Glorm looked at the other occupants at his table. He read the nameplates identifying each person and their significant other. Across from him where billionaire shipping magnate, Della Garreth; corporate tycoon Nawson Loomis; and I-ZAN COO Helgor Breithaupt. Glorm squirmed in his seat uncomfortably. There are other places he would prefer to be, other people who he's prefer to be.

Helgor eyed Glorm curiously, as if sizing up the competition. Glorm smiled uneasily.

"You're that Glorm fella ain't ya?" Nawson drawled. He wore a white, sequined tuxedo that stretched across his wide stomach; his outfit was complete being adorned with ten-gallon hat.

"Yes, I am," Glorm responded politely.

"You sit on that committee for corporate control of government spending, right?" Della smiled a lovely grin, her smooth features hiding her sardonic tone.

"I'm the chair of that committee, yes," Glorm replied, still not shaken by any of the harsh looks they threw him. "It's been quite a hot topic of debate."

"It certainly has," Helgor hissed, stroking his white beard as he glared intently at Glorm.

Nawson said, "Must be easy to put through somethin' so obviously un-American when you got the liberal left in your pocket with the president."

"I don't buy my votes; I earn them with the support of the American people."

"Maybe you should think about what you vote for if you value your seat in office," Helgor's tone oozed contempt.

Glorm refused to be shaken, "Well, the law I propose still needs approval from the senate before going to the president."

"You seem to fail to realize how important to our society that our corporations are, senator," Della added.

"My Low-Mart stores alone donated nearly ten million just last year to countless charities," Nawson spat. "Now with your new law, how we gonna fund research for curin' cancer, or feedin' the hungry."

"I'm sure you'll find a way," Glorm said unflinchingly.

"You know who I am, don't you," Helgor growled. "You know who I represent."

"I do, sir," Glorm confirmed. "You work for the sole reason this bill was created. People work hard and need to keep what they earn. The minute we take the power from the people, we lose everything this country was built on."

Helgor stroked his beard more intensely, "If this law passes, you'll lose more than power."

"Is that an official threat from the I-ZAN Corporation?"

"It's a warning," Helgor reaffirmed. "One I would advise you heed. You have a lovely wife, senator. I'd hate for you to lose everything you worked for over some silly law."

Glorm narrowed his eyes as he stared at the man who sat across from him, glaring with equal intensity.

"Well, hell boys," Nawson broke the tension. "Let's not ruin the mood, after all this is a party! Right?"

Jack had managed to shove the hefty Huun against a large stone pillar aligning the mock exterior of the Parthenon. The pillar gave way instantly, the concrete cracking in half as if made of tissue paper. Jack didn't stop there. He responded with a series of punches, balling his fists and connecting with Huun's chiseled face. He landed over a dozen before the pain in his knuckles became unbearable. Huun's expression never changed. The smile was still plastered across his face. The sight gave Jack the chills. Huun was tough. He could take a punch; he could take several punches, but nothing like the beating Jack had just administered. However, Huun stared back at Jack, his face unmarked, his resolve unparsed.

Like a vice, Huun's hand snapped around Jack's face, just beneath his chin, within his hand. The pressure was intense; his grip tightened as he picked Jack off his chest and then held him in the air as he stood on his feet. This was unreal.

"I'm beginning to get bored with you, Zero," Huun licked his lips. "I think I'm done with you now."

Huun flicked Jack, again, effortlessly aside. Jack flew again, crumpling himself against the standing signs that advertised the exhibit's highlights. The sign broke under Jack's weight as he toppled over and around the broken pieces of the sign, adding to the already countless cuts and bruises he had attained. It hurt for him to breathe, but Jack knew Huun had been pulling his punches. There was no time to waste; he had to get away from him. Jack looked for the nearest escape route, but instead all he saw was the debris he had caused earlier, the weapons and mannequin parts.

Huun made his way to Jack, cracking his knuckles as he stormed toward him. Jack had no time to lose. Instead of running, he snatched up a long spear and just as Huun was wrapping his meaty hands around Jack's neck, Jack plunged the spear into Huun's abdomen.

Huun let out a whale as the pain of a spear driven through his body raged across his nerve endings. Huun followed his roar with a solid punch to Jack's stomach, harder than he had ever hit Jack before. He sent Jack flying even farther than before, his arms akimbo as he tried to reach for something, anything to slow himself down. But before he could grab anything, Jack's back hit the large picture window at the end of the hall. He smashed clean through it.

Dinner had just been placed before Glorm and his wife, a fine display of roast pheasant and spinach salad. It looked delectable. Glorm was famished, being preoccupied by so many interruptions throughout the day; he never had time to eat a decent meal. He had been looking forward to this all day.

Glorm smiled lovingly at his wife, knowing she had to tolerate some the discomfort in the conversation that took place. "Looks delicious, doesn't it?"

She nodded.

He picked up his knife and fork and began to cut into the tender meat when from above came a sudden crackle of glass.

The entire room all craned their necks upward to see a man wearing a trench coat and fedora falling backward amongst the rain of glass shards that surrounded him. He was falling and falling fast. The room erupted into panic. Guests ran from their tables, knocking over their chairs, overturning the tables, shattering dinner plates and sending food and drink flying everywhere. The mass exodus of people stampeded toward the entrance, as the shock of a falling man caused the uproar.

Jack could feel the air escape his lungs, but not from the impact of the punch like it had before, but from the freefall, and the fact that he was holding his breath. He was falling and he couldn't see where he was going to land. The tail of his coat furled around him, the brim of his hat flapping erratically. Why hasn't he stopped yet? What was he going to hit when he finally falls?

Fear began to consume him. Jack had been close to death before, but always seemed to get away, to scrape by, and to survive. This time, however, he felt like it would actually happen. He could feel death creeping up on him, wrapping its cold hands around him as it embraced him, welcoming him to the other realm. Before Jack was to leave this world, he felt the wet, cold, and warm sensation of both solids and liquids washing him. Jack had crashed onto several tables, spilling their contents everywhere. Fortunately, he was able to break the fall and once again elude death as he rolled off the mess he had just created.

His back ached. Jack slowly stood, straightening himself. His spine let out a noisy crack that echoed amongst the silent onlookers. Jack wiped whipped frosting from his sleeves as he stood.

Jack noticed all the eyes now watching him in both awe and confusion. He smiled, catching sight of several prominent faces, most notably, Senator Glorm. He nodded casually at the Senator with a wink.

"Sorry for the intrusion, folks," Jack said calmly. "This was just a routine…um…food inspection." Jack scooped a finger full of frosting from his shoulder and popped it into his mouth. "Mmmm," Jack smiled. "Delicious. It's all safe; you can go back to your party now."

Jack plucked his fedora where it had floated onto the large pyramid of champagne glasses. Once he removed his hat, the glasses toppled over and shattered across the floor.

"Well, that, on the other hand, was a safety hazard just waiting to happen," Jack scowled. He turned to a waiter, whose mouth was agape in shock. "I expected better from you."

Through the main door of the hall, Jack saw Agent Frisco and her men enter. He knew now was his time to exit.

"Well, my inspection is done here; you can all go about your business. I thank you for your time," Jack backed off before he finally turned and broke into a full sprint.

Glorm was astonished, he turned to Frisco, "What are you waiting for? GET HIM!"

Frisco followed chase as Jack leapt through the nearest window, smashing the glass as he punched through first with his fused arm.

Huun watched from atop the hall, smiling to himself at the success of his mission, "Crust, lets meet on the roof, we're done here."

With a confirmation on the other end, he departed from the chaos he helped create. Everything was going according to their master's plan.

Jack had managed to slide past several officers, a handful of security guards, and three federal agents. He thought he was in the clear, but still there was one agent he was unable to sneak past.

"Nikki," Jack smiled.

"Don't call me that," Frisco sneered as she raised her pistol and trained it on Jack.

Jack raised his hands modestly. He nodded his head toward the gun in her hand, "There's no need for that."

"Senator Glorm warned you, not once, not twice, but three times not to get involved. And here you are," she glared angrily. "You must be the dumbest man alive."

"I was never known for my smarts," he offered a boyish smile. "Look, why don't we forget I was here and you just let me go."

"I can't do that."

"Sure you can," Jack replied. "You can turn around and I can just slip away." Jack slowly crept toward the exit, but Frisco cocked her pistol, freezing him in his tracks. "Or not."

"Give me a good reason why I shouldn't just shoot you now," she grimaced.

Jack, his hands still raised, palms exposed toward Frisco, he stepped forward slowly, "Because you're not a cold-blooded killer." He inched closer, "Besides, you kind of like me."

"That's a load of crap," Frisco scoffed. "I've never met anyone as ignorant or as arrogant as you in my entire life."

"I find that hard to believe," Jack was right in front of Frisco. Her pistol was noe pressing into his chest. He felt it slowly drop, the hard steel replaced by her soft body as she stepped closer to her him.

"Believe it," she whispered. She stepped forward, pressing her lips against his.

For a very long, silent moment, they shared a long deep kiss. Jack could taste a hint of fruit on her lips. Each movement of pressing and release of their lips intertwined made his heart flutter more and more. She was a woman of great strength and intense passion. She was also one of integrity. She pushed Jack back roughly, releasing her lips from his. She then stepped back and looked into his eyes for a long moment. She then finally spoke, "Get the hell out of here."

Jack stared at her curiously, not sure if she was serious or simply toying with him. But when she turned her back to him, he knew she meant to let him go. Jack began to run, but before he left, he opened his mouth to speak. No words came forth. Instead, Jack closed his mouth, turned, and ran, leaving Frisco behind with the memory of their kiss.

CHAPTER 15
AN UNEXPECTED VISITOR

Ceinwen was sulking. This wasn't uncommon. Actually, this was the norm, what she did every night. And why shouldn't she? Who wouldn't sulk when they lived alone, and came home alone every day to that same empty, lonely home? They'd sulk wouldn't they?

She certainly hoped they would. If not, she was feeling rather pathetic. She was certain she looked that same way also. Here she was on a Friday night, sitting home alone eating yogurt from a single serve container, with a plastic disposable spoon nonetheless. She never bought anything from the grocery store that wasn't portioned out for individual consumption. Why bother, she thought. She was the only one who ever ate with her.

She nearly jumped out of her seat when an unexpected visitor leapt from above and landed on the table. She dropped her container onto the table, the contents spilling slowly from the opened mouth of the small plastic cup. The plastic spoon clattered to the linoleum floor.

"Oh...you...," Ceinwen clutched her chest as she regained her breath. Staring back at her was a thin, gray cat, its whiskers perked up as it purred lovingly toward her. She scratched the animal's head in kind, "Juno, you scared the hell outta me. You're lucky I'm willing to forgive you."

Juno rubbed his head against her hand as she rubbed his back, curling her fingers gently around his curled tail. Juno dropped from the table to the floor. He then tilted his head and began to lap up the sweet yogurt that spread along the table.

"At least I know I can always count on you to join me for dinner," She said wryly. "I wasn't that hungry anyway."

Ceinwen picked up the cup and tossed it into the trash, allowing Juno to have more time to enjoy his impromptu snack. It was getting late, she thought; she had to report to Mr. Zero's office early in the morning. It would probably be a long, uneventful day. They all seemed to be lately, each one blurring into the next.

Ceinwen let out a heavy sigh. It was a pathetic life, but it was hers and it was all she truly had. Love just never seemed to be in cards. She wanted it, more than anything, just a good man to come home to every night, to laugh with, to wake up to every morning. Unfortunately, either all the good men were taken or they didn't exist.

Not that she never dated, she dated plenty of times. In fact, she had just gone on a blind date no more than three weeks ago. She only agreed to go because her mother couldn't resist interfering with her life at every opportunity. It was frustrating every time she meddled. The best part about the date was the free meal, but she did have to pay with her time. It was one time in her life when she wished she could be both blind and deaf. All the man talked about was himself and how wonderful he was. He never even paid her one single compliment. His initial handsome face quickly became twisted and grotesque. Personality did go a long way.

Her last real relationship was almost four years behind her. He was a good man, a handsome professional. He made his living buying and selling stocks and bonds. It paid well; he was always treating her to a nice dinner, showering her in gifts. It wasn't until nearly five years into the relationship that the police cornered her with information about her boyfriend's alleged illegal activities. Turned out he was never a legitimate professional, only a crooked investor, running a pyramid scheme that robbed thousands of people of their retirement. She was glad she was never aware or involved in any way, but she wished she could've been allowed to keep some of the gifts before the IRS confiscated everything. Oh well, just like everything else in her life; easy come, easy go.

She was convinced there really were no good men left. Then she met Jack Zero. He was not like any other men. He was smart, charming, and devilishly handsome. Too bad, she was invisible to him, unless of course he needed something. He always needed something. For instance, she let him borrow fifty dollars on more than one occasion, always with the promise of being reimbursed with something a little extra. He did reimburse, most of the time, but the incentive always seemed to be a day off or an extra-long lunch break. '*How about health insurance as a bonus?*' She thought. '*Or a monetary bonus? Yeah right, like that would ever happen.*' Then there's always the need to use her car. Why did she always allow him to take it? She was a sucker for sure. He could take a bus or cab like anyone else.

She rubbed her eyes as sleep began to overtake her. It was getting late for her, not that it mattered to anyone. Juno was still busy gobbling up the leftovers on the table.

"You coming to bed?" She spoke to Juno. He didn't look up from his treat. "I didn't think so. You men are all alike. What difference does it make anyway? It's not like good men come from thin air, unless it's between their ears."

She flipped off the lights as she made her way to bed. That was when the knock came at her door.

"Who could that be at this hour? As if I didn't know." She said to Juno, as if he'd respond.

"It's me," came the muffled voice of Jack Zero from the other side of the door.

Her heart leapt for a moment that she knew it was actually him standing just outside her door. A gentleman caller, of sorts. She reached for the sliding locks that currently kept Jack from entering. She started pressing the release buttons for the first lock, but stopped. She looked down at herself, seeing the fluffy pink terrycloth robe that wrapped around her body. She pulled apart the overlapped pieces and realized she was wearing a very revealing, somewhat see-through negligée. Embarrassed and gasping to herself, she wrapped the robe around her body more tightly.

"C'mon Winnie, open the door," Jack pleaded.

"J-just a minute!" Ceinwen replied desperately. She tried to think of how she could conceal herself properly without keeping Jack waiting too long.

"Just open up," Jack whined. "What's taking so long?"

"I'm not decent!" She revealed.

"Aw c'mon, it's nothing I've never seen before."

She was appalled, "Not on me!"

Ceinwen looked around to find something, anything that was concealing. There was a large, fluffy throw under her feet. It looked big, and thick, enough.

The series of locks that secured the door clicked and clacked, as they were relieved of their one and only duty. The door slowly creaked open, to which Jack was greeted by a fat, furry beast.

"Jesus!" Jack cursed at the creature that scowled back at him.

Ceinwen was wearing the carpet draped over her shoulders and wrapped around her torso. It looked absolutely ridiculous, Jack did all he could to stifle a laugh.

"Shut up," Ceinwen rolled her eyes, annoyed at Jack's unexpected interruption. "So what are you doing here?"

Jack stepped into the doorway, the light catching his bruised face. "Oh my god!"

"You should see the other guy," Jack quipped. "He looks pretty good in comparison."

"What happened? I thought you were on a routine stake out?" Ceinwen led Jack to the small kitchen table just down the hall. She pulled out one of the two chairs for him to sit. It was the seat always reserved for the guests she never got. "Is my car okay?"

"I'm fine thanks," Jack smirked as her concern switched from him to an inanimate object. He tossed her car keys onto the table. The ring with around a half dozen keys clanked noisily onto the hard surface of the table. "It's still in one piece." He winced as he sat back in the chair. The pain of the evening's events was finally catching up with him. He was definitely sore. The hits he took from Huun's fist hurt bad enough, but the fall through the window really pushed the pain envelope over the edge. He was pretty sure something was broken, if not it was bruised badly.

Ceinwen studied the pained expression on Jack's face, not to mention the reddened flesh that speckled his face, "You look awful."

Jack looked at the odd wrapping Ceinwen wore, "Looks who's talking."

"You know you can leave the way you came in."

"Alright, alright," Jack raised his hands in defeat. "I was at the museum tonight when I came across a small group of HART agents lurking about."

"Seriously?" she replied with a lilt of surprise.

"Yeah," Jack took in a painful breath. "They were up to something. Apparently, they hit a bank the other night too. Didn't take anything, just one thing from a safe deposit box."

"What?"

"That's the thing, I don't know," Jack accepted the glass of water Ceinwen was handing him. "But whatever it is it's important to what they are plotting. At the museum they had a small group and one of them went to the basement."

"For what?"

"Again I don't know. I didn't get the opportunity to follow. Instead I took this beating."

Jack took a sip of the water as Ceinwen made her way to the freezer and pulled out a small package of frozen vegetables. She wrapped them in a dishcloth and pressed it up to Jack's face.

"Ow," he yelped.

"Don't be a baby; this will make it feel better."

"Well, it doesn't now."

"Just relax," Ceinwen gently pressed the frozen bag gently against

Jack's wounds. Jack accepted the help this time with no complaints.

Jack looked up at Ceinwen with sincerity in his eyes, "Winnie, I just wanted to tell you, thanks, for everything."

Ceinwen smiled at Jack fondly, looking into his deep brown eyes. He was handsome. She began to fantasize him kissing her deeply. While lost in thought she neglected to listen to anything Jack was saying.

"Winnie?" Jack snapped her back to reality. "Are you listening to me?"

"What?" She shook the fog from her brain.

"I said...," a knock at the door cut Jack off. "Shit, they followed me here."

Now she wished she had been listening, "Who?"

The muffled voice of Agent Frisco responded from beyond the door, "Miss Sagorsky, this is Agent Frisco of the F.B.I. Please open the door."

Jack shook his head vehemently, his eyes wide as saucers.

"Um..." Ceinwen stammered. "Just a moment."

Jack scowled. He silently mouthed her, '*Why would you say that?*'

She shrugged apologetically.

Ceinwen stood and left Jack's side as she made her way to the door. She reluctantly released the locks on the door and pulled it open.

Filling the doorway was the short stature of Agent Frisco surrounded by the large, hulking forms of her other agents. They quickly pushed past Ceinwen as they made their way into her apartment.

"Please, come in," Ceinwen said sardonically.

Frisco pointed around the room, directing the agents to separate and search separate rooms of the apartment.

Ceinwen was growing nervous, "What are you doing?"

Frisco never looked at Ceinwen as she spoke, "You know why we're here. Where is he?"

"Where is who?"

Frisco stood and turned to Ceinwen, shooting her a dirty look, "You know damn well who."

"You can't come in here without a warrant!"

"I am an agent of the United States government, I can do what I damn well please."

Frisco continued her search, looking to her agents as they returned to her position. They each shook their head; one searched the bedroom, the other the bathroom. Frisco looked at Ceinwen again, "Where's Zero?"

"Did you try his apartment?"

"You know as well as I that he no longer has his apartment," Frisco sneered. "We trailed him here, your car, which he was driving, is currently out front. We're certain he's here."

"Well he isn't."

"Ms. Sagorsky, we can make this extremely easy or viciously difficult, if you're lying to me, to an agent of the U.S. government, I can make your life very unpleasant."

Ceinwen swallowed hard, "H-how unpleasant?"

"I can make it so you wouldn't see the light of day until your ninetieth birthday," Frisco flashed a sinister grin. "I'll ask you one last time, where's Zero?"

Ceinwen shrugged, shaking her head. Her eyes darted to the kitchen where Jack had been. Frisco noticed the nervous reaction and narrowed her eyes into slits, her expression creating a sense of disapproval in Ceinwen's lie.

Ceinwen's mouth turned into an unsure smirk.

Frisco stood tall and confident as she strode into the kitchen at the end of the hall. Ceinwen wanted to call out a warning to Jack, but kept it bottled within. She couldn't let them aware of her knowledge and could only hope Jack was smart enough to hide. She placed her hands to her mouth, not knowing how evident her guilt was.

Frisco made her way into the kitchen area. It was quaint, small. The small table with two chairs consumed most of the room. It was well organized and neat, which gave it the appearance of being larger than it really was. However, instead of exposing the lie and finding Jack seated at the table, all that was there was an empty glass of water and a melting bag of frozen vegetables. The water from the bag ran along the table's surface and dripped over the edge, collecting on the floor.

Jack Zero was nowhere to be seen.

The only evidence that might suggest he had truly been there was the opened window above the table. The curtains were pushed outside the frame and blew precariously in the evening breeze. The scene was clear to Frisco. Jack Zero had escaped.

Frisco backed out of the kitchen. She never looked up, not noticing the anxious expression on Ceinwen's face, or that she had continuously held her breath the entire time. Instead, she stormed past Ceinwen and out of the apartment. Her baffled agents looked confused at one another. Then quickly followed her out.

Ceinwen finally let out her breath as she closed and secured the door. She then ran to the kitchen to find what Frisco had, Jack Zero was indeed gone along with her car keys. She rolled her eyes, not surprised at all.

"Figures," Ceinwen said to herself.

Jack eased into the small car, wedging himself uncomfortably behind the wheel in the driver's seat. The seat was back as far as it could go, but his knees were tightly pressed to the wheel. He really needed to get his own car. He began to slip his arms from his coat before dropping it on the passenger's seat.

"Bad fit?" A voice came from behind Jack. His heart stopped as he forced his neck to turn around and see who was behind him. It was the same portly face he had encountered on the college campus earlier. He remembered the man's name, Remy.

"Shit, you scared me!" Jack exclaimed, clutching his chest as he tried to slow his erratic breathing. "How did you get in my car? Shouldn't you be schlepping behind your commissioner?"

"I told you, I was ordered to follow you," Remy explained with a wide smile, obviously proud of the fact that he had gotten the jump on Jack this time. "I saw the feds coming for you after the museum debacle. I wanted to collar you myself. Besides, you left the door unlocked."

"Right," Jack said sheepishly. "Now that you found me, get out."

"No can do," Remy beamed. "I'm sticking to you like glue."

"Don't make me repeat what happened on our last encounter," Jack attempted to get the verbal upper hand.

"You can't do that this time," Remy's smile remained, unflinching. "I'm ready for you. Where you go, I go."

Jack sneered, "And how do you propose to do that?"

With lighting reflexes, Remy moved. In that moment, Jack felt cool steel against his exposed wrist. He looked down to see a metal cuff attached to his right wrist. He could see the other half attached to Remy's left.

"You son of a...," Jack began.

"Watch your mouth," Remy cut him short. "I told you I was prepared."

"Take this off now," Jack growled.

"Not a chance, where you go, I go. If you want, we could go see Lartanner, I'm sure he's let you out of these."

'*And into a cell,*' Jack thought. Jack rolled his eyes, "Fine, but you do as I say."

"Sure thing, boss," Remy's grin was wider, and to Jack, more annoying.

"Don't call me that," Jack turned, annoyed. The connecting beam between the cuffs allowed him to extend his reach past four feet, where he turned the key, started the car, and drove off.

Jack pulled the compact mini car up the long stretch of paved driveway that lead to Strommel's home. The massive size of the front gates accentuated the small stature of the car. Certainly not a very flattering vision to his masculinity. He accelerated the car until he reached the front, trying to make the length of time spent in the tiny vehicle as minimal as possible.

"Nice digs," Remy commented from the back seat.

"Too nice for you," Jack jibed.

"We going in there?" Remy asked.

"I'm going in," Jack curled his lip. "You're staying out here."

Remy snorted, "I think you failed to remember, you're cuffed to me. The beam that connects us only lets you go…"

"I know, I know, four feet," Jack finished Remy's sentence. Jack then opened the door of the car and stepped out, he held up his wrists, showing the cuff was no longer there. Remy's eyes bulged in shock as he looked to see the other cuff tightly clasped to the steering wheel. "That's why you're staying here," Jack mimicked Remy's annoying grin.

Remy's once jovial expression contorted into a grimace as he realized Jack had deceived him. "Son of a b…"

Jack closed the door before Remy could finish his sentence. He tossed the car key up in his hand, revealing a small skeleton key on his ring, one that can crack any lock. He walked confidently up the steps of Strommel manor as Remy banged on the car windows, his shouts muffled behind the glass. Jack had nearly forgotten how massive the front doors were as he walked up the steps. He reached up for the massive brass doorknocker, but before he could rap it against the carved, finished oak door, it slipped open slightly.

The door was unlocked.

He pushed it open slowly. It creaked loudly, the sound bouncing off the vaulted ceiling in the foyer.

"Hello?" Jack whispered lowly at first. No answer. "Hello," Jack repeated, this time more loudly. Still nothing. Jack stepped inside cautiously. His foot clicked against the marble floor, echoing behind the creaking door as it traveled up to the ceiling. The house was clean, immaculate even. No sign of robbery. Jack flipped back the tail of his trench coat and placed his hand on the butt of his gun. He pulled it from the holster and held it up defensively. He sneaked around the home, searching for any sign of life. He made his way across the foyer, the family room, dining room and then into the kitchen. He heard shuffling coming from behind the kitchen door. He took a deep breath in and then pushed the door open quickly, holding his gun out in front of him, prepared for anything.

Standing before him, slender and beautiful, was whom he knew as Mrs. Evelyn Strommel. She was dressed in a short, form-fitted red dress. It hugged every curve of her sumptuous body. Jack found himself transfixed, hypnotized by her radiance. She moved in slow motion as she stood tall, turning to face him. Her hair flowed like silk across her supple neck as it spilled around shoulders. She was preparing a small meal at the counter, a salad Jack would have noted had he been looking anywhere other than her.

Evelyn's ruby lips curled up into an inviting grin as she smiled slyly at Jack. It made his heart jump. "Detective Zero, what a pleasant surprise," her voice was smooth, sultry.

He lost all ability to speak.

"To what do I owe this unexpected visit?"

Jack swallowed deeply, "Um, the front door was open; I thought maybe something…had happened."

"I'm sorry; the servants must have accidentally left it ajar when they left for the weekend."

"Oh," was all Jack could manage as a reply. He was mentally kicking himself, trying to break himself of his pathetic stupor.

"Well," Evelyn attempted to break the awkward silence that was hanging between them. "Have you made any progress on finding my husband?"

The word 'husband' seemed to be a trigger that snapped Jack back to reality. He shook the intoxicatingly sweet aroma that emanated from every pore of Evelyn's body and brought his focus back. "Actually, I have."

"That's wonderful, what have you found? Is he still alive?"

"Unfortunately, I haven't discovered that as of yet, but I did pay a visit to a colleague of your husband's."

"Who?"

"Dr. Carkleman?"

"Oh?" Evelyn's voice wavered slightly. "And how is he?"

"He seemed fine, I suppose. But he did say something interesting to me."

"And what was it he said?"

"He kind of slipped and mentioned that Dr. Strommel has no wife."

Evelyn was silent.

Jack recognized it, "From your stunned silence, I assume you understand."

Evelyn turned from Jack and returned to the counter.

"Is that it? Silence," Jack prodded. "Don't you have anything to say? An explanation?"

Evelyn stood tall, her slender curves slumping slightly. "I-I'm sorry, Mr. Zero."

"I just want to know why you felt you had to lie to me. And why are you so interested in finding a scientist? Why don't you come clean for me right now?" Evelyn turned around slowly, her eyes red and wet, tears had been streaming down her cheeks. Jack couldn't tell if they were genuine or crocodile tears. She stepped slowly toward him, strutting steadily, one foot in front of the other as she always did. She stopped before him. She smelled delicious. He breathed in her scent, loving its fragrance and its sweet afterglow that lingered like a halo around her head. She moved her head close to his, their lips only centimeters apart.

"Mr. Zero?" Evelyn whispered her voice husky and low. It gave Jack goose bumps up his arms and across the back of his neck.

"Yes?" Jack responded in kind, his voice equally deep, adopting her sultry demeanor but lacking the appeal.

She moved in quickly, pressing her lips to his. He accepted without hesitation, drinking in her kiss like a parched man would swallow his first glass of water. He savored it, her tastes and their softness. She pressed her lips firmly into his; their mouths became intertwined. Jack knew he was supposed to stop, he needed answers from her, but he was compelled to continue kissing her.

He didn't pull away from her, he couldn't. At least not until something shot up from underneath and connected with his chin. The impact was hard and jarred his teeth, clamping his jaw shut. The thud echoed through his head and bounced around inside his skull. The reverberation caused him to lose focus, but not nearly as badly when the impact knocked him off his feet and sent him sailing across the room. His back slammed into the wall cracking the plaster. Jack fell to the floor, consciousness slipping away.

He looked up to see the red dress and Evelyn's face, now twisted into a wicked grin. Her hand was no longer the soft pink flesh he had felt against his cheek. It was now squared-off and metallic.

"Sorry Mr. Zero," her voice echoed in his head. "But lucky for you, I still need you alive."

Then, everything went black.

CRACK! The pain that followed came from his left cheek. CRACK! Same place this time, only the pain was more intense.

Jack slowly opened his eyes. They were hard to pry apart on their own as they had been crusted over from his time being unconscious. He wanted to wipe them clean, but his hands were bound behind his back. His cheek hurt. He flexed his jaw several times to test where the pain was originating. He could feel it just below his eye. He tried to ignore the pain and shook the fog from his brain. His eyes fluttered open; a blinding light greeted his weary pupils. A bombardment of a light was shining directly into his face. He squinted and tried to make out where he was. It was hard to see; outside of the light was darkness and shadows.

"Mr. Zero?" The voice was unfamiliar, disguised through an electronic device. It made the voice sound metallic and deep.

"Who's there? Who is it?"

"That's not important, Mr. Zero," The voice said.

"What happened?"

"You were, shall we say, rendered inert."

"What happened to Mrs. Strommel, or Evelyn, I should say."

The light was immediately pushed aside and standing in full, albeit blurred, view was Evelyn. She looked different to him. She no longer held the sex appeal he saw in her before; instead, she looked wicked and devious. Her smile reflected that. Her eyes were piercing and stared daggers into him. Jack was still unclear as to what she was plotting. "Good to see you again, Detective."

Jack addressed Evelyn, "I wish I could say it was good to see you."

"Aw, you're not still sore at me for what happened."

"I would be if I could remember anything what actually happened."

"I'm sorry things had to come to this, but you just seemed to forget your role in this."

"And what would that be?"

"To follow orders."

Jack cocked his eyebrow. It was a curious thing for her to say. She leaned forward and kissed Jack tenderly on the lips. It lacked the compassion she applied earlier. It could also be his recent detest he developed for her.

"I hired you to do a job. I told you what you were to do and that was all you needed to do," she explained coldly.

"Whose orders?" Jack inquired, not expecting a response.

Evelyn smiled. She silently stepped away and disappeared into the darkness. Oddly, Jack was sad to see her leave; she was at the very least a connection to the known. Now he sat in darkness, alone, tied to a chair.

"What's going on here?" Jack shouted at the darkness.

The electronic voice returned. It was sharp and tinny, reverberating across the small room where he was bound. "You have something of ours Detective."

"I don't know what you're talking about."

"Don't play coy, Detective," the electronic voice responded. "You haven't any position to bargain."

"Apparently I do," Jack smirked, his teeth stained pink. "I have something you need, remember?"

Evelyn stepped forward. She wrapped her fingers around Jack's chin and raised his head to lock her eyes to his. Her expression was wicked. "Enough with your smug arrogance. We want answers and we want them now!"

"I'm surprised in you Mrs. Strommel, you don't seem to be yourself," Jack smirked.

Evelyn squeezed Jack's chin. She tightened the muscles of her arm and then lifted him into the air effortlessly. Jack's feet dangled in the air, swinging between the legs of the chair to which he was tied. Jack swallowed hard; he held his breath as fear began to set. Evelyn was truly not what she seemed to be. Jack looked down to see how far up he was lifted. His dangling feet were just above Evelyn's knees. He saw this as an opportunity. Jack pulled his legs back and kicked them forward into Evelyn's crotch. As his feet made contact, his eyes darted up to hers, in anticipation of her surprised reaction. Evelyn's eyes widened for a moment, but quickly returned to normal. Jack found this to be odd and prepared to kick again, only now his legs were locked into place, they couldn't move. Jack looked down again, but instead of seeing perhaps an arm holding his legs back he saw they were buried in Evelyn's torso up to his knees. Somehow, her body had swallowed his legs on impact, wrapping them with no sign of entry.

"Holy sh--" Jack blurted, but was cut short. Evelyn threw Jack backward. His legs exited her mid-section, a ripple of waves in place of where they were. Jack, still attached to his chair, sailed several feet across the desolate room until he slammed against the farthest wall. The concrete wall stopped his travel and shattered the chair into tiny splinters. Jack rolled across the floor, pain searing his spine. He rolled onto his stomach and slowly picked himself up. He watched as Evelyn strutted toward him, her expression blank. '*What the hell was she?*'

Evelyn was prepared to grab Jack, but was stopped by an order from the electronic voice; "Stop!"

Evelyn did.

"Step away from Detective Zero."

Evelyn complied again.

Jack slumped onto his backside as he sat up catching his breath. "Who are you?"

"You will know in due time," the voice replied. "But first things first, the device Detective, where is it?"

"I don't know about any device."

"Your friends store was just destroyed over it by my men; I think you know what I mean."

"I don't have it."

"Then you will get it."

"Or?"

"I don't think I need to explain the 'or,'" the electronic voice hissed.

Jack knew these people meant business, "I told you, I don't have it."

"But you know where it is?"

Jack hesitated before answering, "Yes."

"Excellent," the electronic voice sounded as if it was smiling. "We want that device, and we want it now."

"Look," Jack tried to sound reassuring. "It's gonna take some time to get it."

Evelyn stood and lumbered forward, "We're done waiting. No

more wasting time." She grabbed a fistful of Jack's trench coat and heaved him effortlessly into the air. Jack's muscles tensed again as he once again felt his feet leave the ground. Evelyn's eyes narrowed into tiny slits as she sneered like a wild animal into Jack's bulging eyes. She pulled him closer to her face, their lips nearly touching, her breath hot on his face. It wasn't the same sweet wind he felt before; this was the breath of someone who was fueled by rage and hate. She was preparing to kill him. There was a slight tremor that disrupted the air surrounding them. Small waves of energy rippled past their bodies and flowed around their heads, caressing their skin. It felt like small crests of water lapping their bodies while lying on the shore, except it was dry. Evelyn didn't seem phased by the sensation. Instead, she reeled her arm out as she threw Jack, once again, across the room. This time Jack felt his body fall limp. He was not going to stop his accelerated speed in time before he hit the concrete wall. He was prepared for the worst. He closed his eyes moments before striking the wall. However, the impact wasn't what anyone expected. Instead of cracking the wall and, hopefully, his bones, he was swallowed into wall that vibrated ringlets from where Jack's body disappeared, like a stone disrupting a placid pond. Head first, Jack Zero disappeared through the wall. Evelyn gnashed her teeth, further enraged. Before she could follow, a large sphere grew from the wall and began to consume the rest of the room. It chewed the contents of the room and scooped a large bowl deep into the floor before vanishing and leaving only a smoldering mess in its wake.

"DAMN!" Evelyn roared. The once confident voice that filled the room was silent. *'That was never good,'* thought Evelyn.

Jack awoke suddenly. His heart raced as panic sank, *'Where was I? What exactly happened?'* Jacks eyes snapped open as he struggled to sit up. The room surrounding him was spinning uncontrollably, or so it seemed. Jack was disoriented; his head felt as if it had been split open by an axe. He blinked his eyes rapidly, trying to push out the pain.

It didn't work.

"Drink this," a low, soft voice said as it thrust a foul smelling hot liquid under Jack's nose. "It will take the lag away."

"Thanks," Jack managed.

"I know how difficult the transition can be," the man's voice was comforting, soothing, like a loving grandparent.

"Wh-what...what is that?" Jack spit out the warm liquid.

"It's a blend of herbs and crushed insects," the man explained nonchalantly.

Jack nearly spat up as he choked down the foul concoction. "Insects?"

"Ants to be precise, red fire ants. I find their venom actually lowers the increased activity in your brain and helps counters the effects of temporal displacement."

Jack's head did hurt, but he wasn't sure if it was what this man said, or the explanation itself. "I'm sorry; I don't understand what you just said."

"It's quite alright, not many do," the man offered a gentle smile. "I'm Doctor Heinrich Strommel." He offered his hand to Jack.

"Dr. Strommel?" Jack mused. "Well ain't you a sight for sore eyes. You know I've been looking for you?"

"Yes I'm well aware," Strommel replied matter-of-factly.

"How did you know where to find me, let alone time that rescue just right," Jack hesitated, trying to surmise how exactly the rescue happened. "What exactly did you do to me anyway?"

"I opened a wormhole."

"A what?" Jack asked, legitimately confused by the strange response.

"A wormhole," Strommel explained. "I basically opened a doorway in space, by bypassing the physical hindrance of distance."

"I'm sorry, maybe it's the bug juice talking, but I have no idea what you just said."

"It's quite all right detective," Strommel smiled genuinely. "The concept is a bit esoteric and does elude the common mind."

"No need to get insulting, doc."

"I'm not insulting, only commenting."

"Oh you are? So where have you been all this time? Why'd you keep hiding?" Jack pressed.

"Well, when one's life is in the balance, one tends to remain hidden."

"That's not very jake." Jack smirked as he tried to stand.

"Jake?" Strommel asked curiously. "Who is Jake? I thought you were Jack Zero."

Jack stumbled a bit, his balance off. He tipped to his left and fell against a small table, spilling the contents all along the floor, the table legs snapping out from underneath.

"Please, Mr. Zero," Strommel rushed to Jack's side and helped to steady the taller man. "The teleportation has adverse effects on one's equilibrium, just sit, and try not to stand."

Jack obliged and sat back down slowly. He shook his head, "Never mind." He took another sip of the liquid and this time forced it down his throat. It was beginning to work. His head felt clear and the throbbing had begun to subside. However, the pain in his jaw still remained, "So you do know who I am?"

"I never forget a patient," Strommel smiled slightly. "Especially the successful ones."

Jack looked to his arm, remembering, "Yeah, I've been meaning to ask you about that. But first, things first, you mind explaining to me what's going on, Doc?"

"Isn't it clear? I've been marked for death."

"But why?"

"Because, I hold the secrets."

Jack rubbed his forehead, trying to alleviate the continued throbbing that plagued him, "You know, I'm tired of this cryptic nonsense. Can't anyone deliver a straight answer?"

"That depends, are you prepared to handle the truth?"

Jack felt a chill run up his spine. He felt Strommel had something to say, that perhaps he was hiding something. "That's all I want to hear," Jack replied cautiously.

"I'm certain, with your background, that you are familiar with the HART?"

"Who isn't?"

"And you're aware of their attempts to overthrow countries in an attempt to control all human activity on the planet?"

"Yes," Jack said, growing annoyed.

"They are evil, detective, that of the purest kind."

"This is all well and good Doc, but you're just regurgitating facts. I want answers to things I don't already know."

Strommel cocked his head slightly, like a dog responding to a high-pitched sound, "I'm sorry?"

"Just tell me what the hell is going on?"

"You see Mr. Zero, I hold the key to world domination in my brain," Strommel placed his index finger to his temple. "And the Dark HART want to obtain it."

"Seem pretty sure of yourself, don't you, Doc?"

"Well, you just experienced its power; don't you think that's reason enough to be sure?" Strommel smirked cockily.

"This whole wormhole thing you mean?"

"Yes, with its power, any force could make their way to any other part of the world in just a matter of minutes," Strommel picked up a small device and rolled it in between his hands. "Just imagine, an entire army marching from their base in Russia onto the White House lawn in Washington, D.C."

"Any army would kill for that."

"I know; that is why I have been hiding."

"But why were you developing such a sophisticated device? You must've known this would have attracted the vilest of interest. Something of this power could certainly be perverted into a weapon of evil."

Strommel lowered his head. "Of course there are always

consequences to anything you create, but I assure you the intent was not malice. I prefer to work in secret, not involving anyone from the outside community, let alone governments."

Jack rubbed his chin, "Then how did the HART find out?"

"One of our benefactors was in the pocket of the HART; he sold us to them instantly."

"Who is this benefactor?" Jack asked.

"He's a professor; he requested our expertise on the project. I wanted to trust him, but it was soon obvious that he had already convinced my partner to join with his underhanded contacts," Strommel explained.

"Lemme guess," Jack interrupted. "Dr. Carckleman?"

"Yes," Strommel smiled broadly, impressed by Jack's deduction. "You truly are a good detective."

"That and the fact that he's a slime ball," Jack smirked. "Or at least he gave me that impression when I spoke with him. I knew there was something about him I didn't trust."

"Carkleman sent a set of heavies to take the device, and I am assuming, kill me in the process, fortunately, he failed," Strommel held up the palm-sized device proudly.

Jack stood finally, maintaining his balance as he wobbled over toward Strommel. Strommel passed the device into Jack's hand. Jack rolled it around and examined it from all sides. It was an odd device, so small and simple looking, yet it caused so much trouble.

"How does it work?" Jack finally asked.

Strommel smiled, he then spoke proudly, "It's able to penetrate the very atomic structure of the atmosphere, restructure them on that very atomic level, allowing a wormhole to generate at just the command of a button."

Jack was still confused, "A wormhole? Like a portal?"

Strommel nodded, "Yes. What actual happens is that space is essentially folded in half, allowing for two places to be in a way, pushed together. What this permits is for a sort of doorway, or portal as you say, to be opened allowing for objects to pass directly through."

"According to police reports, the lab was destroyed and nothing was left," Jack interjected. "I assumed the device you are talking about was among the things taken."

Strommel nodded, "It was, but the device they took was only the prototype, it was still missing the attachment."

"What's this?" Jack held up the device he had taken from Strommel.

Strommel nodded again. "The device they have will still generate the wormhole," Strommel took the device back from Jack. "It creates your portal, but it only allows a carbon-based life form to pass through."

"Meaning?"

"Meaning," Strommel continued. "That the army of the HART could pass through, but only if they are not carrying any non-appendages."

Jack stared blankly, cueing Strommel that he was still confused.

"If they are carrying weapons or wearing clothing, those articles will fuse with their skin. This can also wreak havoc with someone of your persuasion."

"What's that supposed to mean?" Jack asked.

"Your infused with nanites, a non-carbon element, were you to pass through the wormhole, your body would seize and in essence shut down," Strommel was serious, his tone grim. "The machines designed to keep you functional would turn on their host and kill you."

"I see," Jack understood. "And since the HART has agents completely made of this tech, then without that attachment, they couldn't invade."

"Precisely."

"But the portal is small," Jack scratched his chin. "It would take them hours to get all their troops through if they wanted to invade."

Strommel nodded, but was quick to retort, "Yes, but with door markers you could increase the size of your portal."

"Markers?"

"Yes, transceivers that relay the signal from the device and allow the signal to increase in size which in turn allows the portal to be modified in any size."

"Good thing you didn't make those, right?" Jack smiled, looking for Strommel to reciprocate the confidence.

Strommel was silent. This did not bolster Jack's confidence.

"You didn't right?"

"Well, we may have been experimenting with the possibility."

"You may have?" Jack cocked an eyebrow, "Doc, you either did or didn't."

"We did," Strommel admitted.

"But they weren't at the research facility, right?"

Strommel let go a half smile.

Jack rolled his eyes, "Lemme guess, they were and now they're gone."

"That's a good possibility."

"And in the hands of the bad guys? Great," Jack let out an annoyed sigh.

Strommel pulled at his collar nervously, "So what can we do?"

Jack paused for a moment, "Hey doc, you think you can fire up that gizmo of yours again?"

"Of course, but why?"

"I need to pay Carkleman a visit."

CHAPTER 16
COLLEGE RAIDERS

The campus was dark at night aside from the street lamps that outlined the quad, sidewalks, and the surrounding buildings. They left a warm orange glow that hung low against the haze and fog that carpeted the ground. The stone buildings were grayed with age and covered with ivy that scaled the walls like outstretched tendrils grasping for an unexpected prey. At night, they gave an uneasy and eerie sensation to student's passing by. Several claimed it made them feel uncomfortable, almost as if an ominous presence were lying beneath. Tina walked alone and thought those same thoughts as she traipsed across the courtyard. Tina was quiet and normally kept to herself, resulting in her walking alone across campus. Why had she agreed to meet with Dr. Carkleman this late at night escaped her. He told her he needed to meet with her to discuss her grade. At nearly ten o'clock at night seemed a bit late. Although this wasn't the first time, they had met to discuss grades, or for extra help. The only one getting any help was Dr. Carkleman. If only his wife knew what he was really meeting her about. In the beginning, their affair seemed exciting and dangerous. Now it was more tedious than anything. The only reason Tina continued to see him was that Carkleman always gave her direct access to the labs and files outside of school hours, a pathetic reason at best, and also she had no other prospects. The boys on campus hardly noticed her timid demeanor and mousy appearance. Not that she gave them any reason to find anything interesting in her. She wore her hair down, which at its length, covered her face completely. She always hated her face so she like to keep it hidden. Dr. Carkleman was the first boy, actually man, who took notice of her. He was a strikingly handsome man, his jaw line well defined, and adorned with a light salt and pepper shaded beard. More strands of white lined the rim of his hair just above his ears. His eyes were a powerful blue that she swore looked into her whenever they spoke. She always managed to stay late after lecture, sometime she would ask a question, which was often nonsensical, and others she would say nothing at all. In any case, she was last to leave, hoping to be noticed. Within weeks their affair began, intense and passionate, a whirlwind romance that she had never experienced in her life. He made her feel like a woman, not like an outcast. Unfortunately, within the first three months the relationship grew stale. Tina wasn't entirely certain if it was because she never really grew any true feelings for him outside of her initial infatuation or that she now viewed him as a creepy old pervert. So why did she feel compelled to go see him now? He did treat her better than any other man had before, and he was a pretty decent lover.

Tina thought about all her friends and what they were doing tonight. Her roommate was headed to a party at the sorority house. They invited her, a first, but she opted out. Instead, here she was, falling into the seemingly eternal trap that was a torrid affair, one that would go nowhere. She stopped as she stood outside Payne Hall, where Carkleman's office was. She looked up the several floors that lead to the third floor window where his window faced the quad. The light from the window was dim, warm. She was hesitating. She knew she was. This was wrong. Not only was she his student, but he had a wife, kids. This was wrong. She felt the guilt well up inside her and build to near explosive levels in her throat. She wanted to scream at herself, not understanding her own motivation. Tears streamed down her cheeks like a shallow creek, flowing steadily. She watched a form move across the window, blackened by the angle of the lamp. It looked like Carkleman; his shape was built and fit. She did admire him. He was a brilliant man, always sharp and knowledgeable, rambling facts and data that seemed frivolous to the common person. It was what truly made him handsome to her. She reached her hand up to the charm that dangled between her breasts and held it between her fingers, rolling it around as she remembered when Dr. Carkleman gave it to her. It was a large charm, just over an inch square. It resembled scrap steel or a broken piece of a circuit board. It wasn't necessarily romantic. She stuffed it into the collar of her sweater. She mostly kept it tucked in her clothing to keep it hidden, not because it was from her professor, but because it was ugly. Tina clutched her books tightly to her chest, looking for comfort as she struggled with her internal demon. A bright, blue flash burned through the dim light and darkness, lighting up the quad for a quick second. Tina looked up from her self-deprecating moment and returned her gaze back to the window where another set of forms moved past the window. Who else was there? Had he invited another female student to his office with hopes that she would be gone before Tina arrived? That son of a bitch, she thought. Now her feeling of guilt transformed into anger and jealousy. She huffed and stomped her feet, storming angrily into Payne Hall. She headed for the stairs and ran rapidly up them, skipping every other step as she went. Before long, she had reached the third floor. She headed down the darkened hallway, in the direction of Carkleman's office. All the while, she roiled the scenario around in her mind as to how she would tell that two-faced bastard what she really thought of him. Her determination almost prevented her from hearing the sound of thuds coming from Carkleman's office. Did Carkleman drop the stack of books that lined his walls? Had he fallen over, knocked himself unconscious? Suddenly the rage she carried had faded. She now had concern only for Carkleman's safety.

Tina came to the door and heard a muffle of voices from behind the thick, carved oak door. Her heart pounded as she turned the handle, as she had many times before. She pulled the door open and was greeted by Carkleman, whose face squeezed between the open door and its frame.

"Dr. Carkleman?" Tina asked in hesitation, her voice laden with concern and fear, "Are you alright? I heard a noise."

Carkleman coughed slightly, his face ashen and caked in sweat that ran down his neck and soaked the front of his shirt.

"Hello Ms. Goerner," Carkleman breathed heavily, laboriously. "I need to cancel our meeting tonight."

Ms. Goerner? He never called her that unless it was during class so as not to make people think there was anything between them. Carkleman stepped back and began to close the door. Tina wasn't sure what prompted her to do so, but she quickly wedged her foot between the door and the frame, preventing it from closing. Carkleman's expression changed to sheer panic, "Ms. Goerner, I'm sorry if I wasn't clear before, but I need to cancel our meeting."

Something was wrong. He was acting strange. Suddenly, the idea of another woman inside Carkleman's office once again crossed her mind. Jealousy returned. Tina pushed the door with all her might, nearly knocking Carkleman off his feet. Tina stormed angrily into the room, her fist clenched tightly by her side.

"Is this what you do? Huh?" Tina growled through gnashed teeth. "You sleep with me and then throw me aside once you've found someone new?"

Tina tried to keep her focus on Carkleman, when a loud pop startled her. She flinched, closing her eyes for a brief moment. When they snapped open, she watched the frozen expression on Carkleman's face became marred by a faint crimson trickle that started at the hairline and traced a path down the center of his face. Carkleman slumped over dead.

Tina let go a piercing scream as she watched Carkleman's body fall over and slam into the hardwood floor. Blood pooled along the floor, filling the seams of the wood as it slowly flowed around his corpse. From the darkness entered three men. All were tall with tightly cropped haircuts, muscular, and naked. Tina turned immediately at the sight of the first man. She ran out the door and back down the hall as fast as she could. Two of the men stopped to turn to their superior, Colonel Huun. Huun's face became enraged at his subordinate's inability to act, "What are you waiting for? Get her!"

"Condition of the target?" Lt. Crust inquired.

"No witnesses," Huun replied coldly.

Lt. Crust and Lt. Cmdr. Clasp took chase, sprinting quickly out the door. Huun turned his attention away from the door and looked down at the lifeless corpse of Dr. Carkleman. He knelt down next to the body and wrapped his hand around the hilt of the letter opened he had thrown with such force that it penetrated the man's skull and buried the fairly dull blade deep into Carkleman's brain. Huun jerked his wrist back and pulled the opener free from Carkleman's head, which thumped back onto the hard floor. Thick, dark blood covered the steel blade, which slowly began to ooze down the hilt and across Huun's knuckles. He watched it flow for a moment, mesmerized by the wet, glistening blood. He thought for a moment and then looked to the bare, white wall across from him. He moved slowly, raising his hand, he began to wipe the blood across the wall.

Tina pumped her legs as fast as she could, extended them out far enough in order to maintain a large stride, keeping the distance between herself and her pursuers. The vaulted ceilings in the corridor carried the sound of her shoes clacking against the hard floor, echoing everywhere. She was wearing high heels. She never wore high heels, except for Carkleman. She struggled to maintain her stride, her shoes not giving her much opportunity to hold a sprint. Her lungs burned. She had never been so scared in all her life. Seeing Carkleman dead made her stomach lurch, she wanted to heave but couldn't muster the courage to stop. She could hear the men behind her, gaining in speed; her footsteps become louder, closer together. She could hear their breathing, controlled and heavy. They were almost on top of her now. She almost wanted to stop, lie down, and accept her fate, but something inside her pushed her further, faster. She saw the door to the stairs, just within reach. She extended her arm. As she did, the door seemed to drift farther away. The footsteps behind her echoed even louder, closer, her fingers were outstretched, nearly reaching the bar. She was so close; her pursuer was closer. Before her hand could press the bar for the door, it began to move away from her hand. The door began to open for her. A smile crossed her face, what a stroke of luck, the door was opening. But how? Who? As she ran toward the opening door, the silhouette of a man was on the other side. Was it help? Another one of those men? Amidst all these thoughts, Tina soon realized she was running too fast to stop. She crashed into the chest of a man, a rather solid man.

"Please! Help me!" Tina screeched at the mystery man.

The man brushed aside his long coat and brandished a polished silver revolver that caught the dim light of the stairwell. Tina's jaw dropped as she wrapped her hands around her head, tucking her chin to her chest, expecting the worst. The sound of gunfire exploded across the corridor, ricocheting across the hollowed floors and vaulted ceilings. Tina expected the bulleted would hit her almost instantly, but it never did.

Tina slowly lowered her arms, terrified as to what she might see. She opened her eyes to see the man in the trench coat still in front of her, the gun he drew was now lowered at his side, a thin plume of smoke drifting from the opening. She got a good look at his face now, young, unshaven, and handsome. He wore a fedora low on his brow that he tipped back as he looked down at the floor behind Tina. Tina turned slightly to see her pursuer up close. She saw the man sprawled on his back, his pink flesh tarnished by the hole that pierced his chest around his heart. Blood pumped from the wound rhythmically, flowing past the blackened powder burns that lined the outside of the wound. This time Tina wretched, emptying the contents of her stomach. She felt a hand rest lightly on her shoulder.

"It's okay," the stranger said. "You're safe now. I'm Jack, Jack Zero, what's your name?"

"T-Tina," she managed. "Ohmigod! Dr. Carkleman, they—they killed him."

"Alright Tina, I need you to find a safe place, preferably out of this hallway. Find a COMM and call the authorities."

"You're not the authorities?!" Tina was shocked. "I thought you were the authorities."

"I'm the next best thing," Jack offered a reassuring smile.

She watched as Jack ran toward Carkleman's office. She did her best not to pass out.

Jack slowed his pace as he neared Carkleman's office. He stopped mostly to listen for any unusual noises and to not be surprised by any unexpected assailant. Jack brought his revolver up to his shoulder, poised and ready for action. He slinked forward along the wall, his other hand in front, leading his charge, keeping himself steady and alert. Jack's heart was racing, no matter how many times he had been in a similar situation during his career; you could never be fully prepared mentally. He did his best to steady his breathing. It was quiet. Perhaps the attackers had left. Jack made his move. He stepped cautiously into the open doorway of Carkleman's office. It was dark. He darted his eyes about the room systematically checking for any sign of movement, carefully scanning the dark recesses of the office for any presence. Nothing. He saw Carkleman's body lying motionless in the center of the room. Jack let out the breath he had held in his lungs when he entered. He rushed to Carkleman's side. He pressed his fingers to the artery on Carkleman's neck. There was no pulse. He was dead. Jack turned Carkleman's head to see the puncture wound that penetrated the back of his skull. The remaining blood that emptied from the wound was thick and black.

Jack curled his lip up slightly. You never get used to seeing this kind of thing. He pressed his fingers against Carkleman's eyelids, forcing them closed. Before he could reflect on the grisly scene, an attack from behind sent him reeling across the floor. Jack saw flashes of light and dark from the initial impact he took to the head. Fortunately, it didn't knock him unconscious, only rendered him dizzy. He wasn't sure what, or who, hit him, but he knew he needed to move, and fast, to ensure surprise didn't take him again. Jack immediately rolled across the floor, away from the sound of hard slapping that struck the hardwood floor where he had fallen. Jack found his footing and pulled himself upright. His head throbbed, pounding deep inside, between his temples. He tried to steady himself; the blow had rewired his equilibrium, almost as if the strike was intentional. Jack wobbled on his feet, trying to see his attacker in the dark room. The room was spinning. Jack couldn't make anything out. He thought he saw something move from the corner of his eye. He squinted, pressing his eyes closed tightly and shaking his head to free his disorientation. Fortunately, he had been in this room before and had memorized the basic layout.

Jack opened his ears, despite the mild ringing that was a low-level annoyance; he listened intently. He heard the sound of footsteps move lightly across the floor, then silence. He turned in the direction of the sound. The room was still moving; his vision doubled. He kept his senses spiked as he wobbled toward the wall behind Carkleman's desk. He remembered the medieval swords hanging crisscrossed above Carkleman's head when he had been there before. He wished Carkleman had been straighter with him when he had questioned him; he might still be alive. It was too late for Carkleman, but not for him. Whoever killed Carkleman was still in here. They intentionally crippled his vision and balance, knowing when and where to strike. The assailant was a professional and he was toying with Jack now. Batting him like a cat would a mouse. He was good. Jack listened closely; he heard the footsteps again. They were close, behind him to his left and running at him quickly. Jack sidled to the right and loosened his right knee, dropping his body. He placed his hands, palms out, behind himself, catching himself and arching his back. He felt the next potential blow sweep over him, missing his chest by centimeters. The draft from the movement caused his necktie to dance wildly in the air before dropping back in place. Jack pushed off his haunches, tumbling backward, somersaulting head over feet. He planted his feet firmly on the ground. Huun stood upright and launched himself over the large oak desk in front of him.

Unexpectedly, Huun's foot had missed its intended target. His body's momentum was already moving quickly, he couldn't stop as his body continued, flailing over Jack and into a bookcase nearly fifteen feet away. Huun's body slammed hard against the large, thick oak bookcase. His girth was enough to crack the wood frame and knock loose the shelves, sending the volumes of books to the floor, covering his body. Huun winced briefly as he picked himself off the floor, the books sliding from his back. Huun was more than annoyed, borderline enraged. No one had ever deflected his attack, especially after being incapacitated. Huun stood fully extending his limbs to his full six-foot-four, muscularly sculpted body. He rotated his neck slowly, cracking his spine. He cocked his head toward Jack, his face contorting into a viscous scowl. He was no longer toying with the detective; he was now determined to kill him.

"I should've killed you years ago, Zero," Huun growled. "I've watched you for years, my master made sure you never quite became anything important, a threat."

"I've tracked you this far, Huun. What makes you think I'm no longer a threat?"

"Because I'm going to kill you."

A long silence hung between them. This was a recurring challenge, one that had never truly been met. But this was the time for the opportunity to take hold. Time for the two long-time adversaries to end their rivalry.

A chill filled the air of the room.

One of them would die.

Jack had begun to gain his balance and vision back. It wasn't perfect, he still struggled to keep himself upright, but he was no longer seeing double. He needed to rely, not only on his feet, but trust in his body. Jack could see the swords still hanging on the wall a few feet away. A quick movement for a non-disoriented individual would take seconds, but a stretch for him. Jack could see Huun standing, hear his breath quickening, knowing his muscles were tightening. He was preparing to attack and this time he was playing for keeps. Jack didn't hesitate; he was able to propel himself forward by kicking off the floor and twisting his body like a corkscrew toward Carkleman's desk.

Huun could see what Jack's intentions were. He was not wasting time. He broke into a sprint, racing toward Jack. He needed to stop him before he reached the swords on the wall. Jack timed the distance just right, allowing his back to land on the desk and slide across to the other side. He kicked his legs to the front, spinning himself on his backside and turning his feet to the wall. The spin across the desk was smooth as was his slide off the desk wherein he wrapped his hand around the hilt of the closest sword and grabbed it off the wall.

The sword hissed as the metal of the blade scraped against the stone enclave of which it was encased. The blade captured the moonlight that poured in the window, glinting angrily as Jack swung it around toward his attacker. Blinding rage seemed to slow Huun's reactions. He raised his arm to counter Jack's downward slice, but caught the blade on his forearm. The blade sank into his flesh, it sounded wet and thick, until it reached the bone, where it clanked as if striking metal. Jack quickly recoiled his arm, pulling the sword from Huun's flesh. Jack expected blood to erupt from the gash, but it was dry.

Jack stared in amazement, "You're not Huun...What the hell are you?"

"I've been upgraded," Huun grabbed the wound, pressing his fingers into the gaping slash. He ran his fingers up his arm, separating the skin until it hung loose. He tore the hanging flesh and flung it aside, revealing a metallic arm. It was an intricately designed piece of hardware complete with hydraulics that controlled the pressure of the elbow inflections and shoulder movements. At the shoulder was a ball joint that was fused into the flesh, jagged skin was growing over the shiny metal. The gears inside the arm whirred and clicked as Huun raised his arm and the fingers wrapped around the hilt of the other sword on the wall. The sound of the two metal tinged as Huun tore the sword from its mount. Huun drew it up in front defensively. The advantage was no longer clearly Jack's; he now had a true advisory.

"But how could you? You can't be...you're supposed to be carbon based," Jack said.

Huun grinned widely, "But I am. I'm the latest model. It's amazing what science can do."

Huun had handled this type of weaponry before. His training reached back to many archaic battle styles, several Roman-Greco moves, oriental fighting styles both hand-to-hand and weaponry, even medieval combat. He was no stranger to a sword, although he preferred a thinner, sleek style like a katana to this clunky piece. He swung the sword across himself, twisting the hilt around his wrist, slashing the air in a figure eight. The blade hissed as it cut the air, creating a fluid wall. Huun halted his wrist and allowed the centrifugal force of the blade to twist around his hand and wrist before snapping his grasp around the hilt. His attack was fast, hard, and strong.

Jack expected aggressive, but Huun's brute strength was immeasurable. Each blow was full of excessive force that knocked Jack backward. The blades flashed in the dim light of the office. The darkened recesses of the room were illuminated by the clash of steel. Jack did his best to keep up with Huun's speed and stamina. It was as if Jack was fighting something more than just a man, but a superman.

Each blow from Huun's swing was harder and more crushing than the last. Jack grimaced and grunted with each lunge and parry, groaning with exhaustion. He grew winded more quickly, trying to ward off all of Huun's unrelenting advances. Huun wasn't slowing. He pressed forward, moving Jack back. Huun wanted to weaken Jack, position him where he wanted before he finally delivered the lethal blow that would do him in.

Jack was not one to give in or give up easily. He wanted to best Huun, beat him at his own game, and show Huun that he was not superior.

"You're weak, Zero" Huun goaded. "You know you can't beat me."

"Tell that to Zimm!" Jack swung his sword high, aiming for Huun's throat. Huun parried and deflected Jack's attack. Huun countered with a mighty underhand thrust, attempting to slice up Jack's abdomen. Jack dropped his blade horizontally, blocking the upward slice. He pressed hard onto Huun's blade, but Huun was flexing his biceps and shoulders, creating a vicious momentum that Jack was struggling to keep at bay. Huun was strong. Very strong. Jack was worn from the past conflicts he faced, the struggle with the Evelyn creature, and his previous encounter with Huun at the museum. He had never completely recovered from either and was really feeling the exhaustion in his arms, his body, even his legs. Nevertheless, he couldn't give into fatigue, he had to keep his strength, he had to beat Huun, he had to persevere.

Jack mustered as much strength as he could in his entire body. He gnashed his teeth and bared down on the blade. He positioned his hand over the blade, balancing his hold over Huun. He pressed down hard with both hands, the sharp edge of the double-edged blade cutting into his palm, splitting apart his calloused skin. The pain seared through him, up his arms and across his shoulders. Jack ignored it, bared through it. Huun let loose a wicked grin as he began to increase his stance, spreading apart his feet. Jack could see his muscles expand before his eyes. It was as if he was able to increase his mass at will, on command.

"You're getting weaker," Huun laughed with a low grunt.

Jack pushed harder, the blade sinking deeper into his hand, nearly reaching his bones. The pain was intense, firing up his nerves. His mind was screaming for him to let go, but his resolve was keeping him firm. Jack felt his arm heat up. He could feel the individual nanites swarming along his muscles and strengthening his arm. His arm jolted, pressing with every ounce of strength he had. A look of confusion crossed Huun's face as the sword in his hand began to slip from his grasp. Jack let out a deep roar as he freed Huun's grasp from his sword, pushing the blade into the floor at his feet. The blade sank nearly two inches into the floor, splintering the wooden planks that were so neatly polished.

Jack recoiled his wounded hand, balling his fingers into a fist to apply pressure to the gash. His other hand instinctively came up as he sent another fist into Huun's unsuspecting face. The sound of knuckles against cartilage sent a loud snap across the room. The impact of the strike sent Huun stumbling backward, tripping over the refuse he and his men left behind when they were torturing Carkleman. Huun fell onto his back, his spine hitting the hardwood directly. He let out a grunt as the air was pushed from his lungs.

Jack took advantage of the moment. He brought the sword over his head and prepared to strike by swinging it downward onto Huun. Huun was prepared. He rolled out of the way, as Jack's blade cut into the floor just inches from Huun's head. Huun rolled with precision onto his feet. He immediately gripped his sword, pulling it from the floor and raising it in defense to a prepared attack. Jack had bested Huun, weakened him. The advantage was his for the moment.

"Now look who's weak," Jack sneered.

"Savor the victory, Zero, it won't happen again," Huun charged at Zero with his sword raised. Jack raised his own sword in defense.

The battle raged harder. Huun's strikes were becoming much stronger, as if he was gaining strength from the duration of the fight. Perhaps it was Jack who was simply growing weaker. Jack was forced to take a more defensive stance. He swung the sword around to catch a slice aimed at his side. Huun's blade was only mere centimeters from actually sinking into the skin. Jack's brow began to glisten, sweat beading rapidly. Huun could see this; he knew Jack was growing tired, weak. Huun's bleached white teeth flashed as his lips thinned into a sinister grimace. He puffed out his chest and swung the sword around quickly.

Huun drew the sword in his hand over his shoulder, hoisting it high like a baseball player at bat and quickly swung it towards Jack's exposed neck in an attempt to sever the head from the body. Jack moved sluggishly at first, partially taken aback by the stance and quick movement, but pushed himself backward on his heels, rocking precariously, before falling backward onto the ground. The sword broke free of Jack's grasp and clattered across the floor, spinning wildly as it slid out of reach into the dark corner of the room. Jack snapped his neck around from where the sword disappeared to see Huun standing triumphantly over him, a sinister grin decorating his face. Jack had fallen, he was beaten, there was no escape. Huun raised his sword high over his head, preparing to administer the final deathblow. Jack was afraid. His heart pounded hard in his chest. He felt this was the end. Jack wanted desperately to close his eyes, to not watch the flash of silver. But before everything went black, thoughts raced through his head as he panicked slightly, fearing his own demise. He thought it odd that it wasn't his life that flashed before him, but instead he thought of Frisco, the kissed they shared, all the things he wished he had said. He longed for her now, now when it was too late. Jack kept his eyes open, waiting for Huun's final blow. It must have come quickly, because the bright light consumed his vision. It was warm, welcoming. It called to him.

The light was blinding. Not only to him, but apparently to Huun as well. Huun released his grip from Jack's throat and stood, shielding his eyes from the light that tore through the large window and slammed into his face. Huun staggered backwards and tripped over the sword that lay in the middle of the room. He tried to catch himself, but fell over Carkleman's desk and crashed heavily onto the floor.

Jack grappled to regain his breath as he stood. The light burning his retinas. He held his hand out, shading his eyes, trying to make out the source of the light. The source, just out the window that ran from floor to ceiling and consumed the majority of the office wall, turned slightly, its engine emitting its high-pitched whine. A LEHV. What a stroke of luck, Jack thought. The LEHV drifted closely, edging up to the window, he could see Frisco in the passenger's seat. Jack smiled through his blood stained teeth and blurred vision at her. She was truly a vision, it warmed his skin to see her. Frisco smiled meekly back, her expression mimicked more concern than relief. He watched as her lips mouthed something that he couldn't hear. He tried to read her lips, but was not able to make it out as she moved them too quickly. Jack squinted his eyes trying to focus on Frisco's mouth. Her full, crimson lips parted and sealed, looking as if she was saying 'Look out!'

Frisco continued mouthing her words and then extended her arm sharply, pointing just over his shoulder where he stood. He turned slowly, his eyes bulged as he saw Huun leap over the desk and charge toward him, his head lowered, much like an enraged bull charging a matador. Jack was sore, his reactions slowed. He couldn't counter the oncoming beast, so instead sidestepped, dropping onto his shoulder, in order to avoid Huun's ever increasing speed. However, despite his effort to avoid his locomotive-like charge, Huun ran past Jack, missing him by several feet. He didn't even stop to turn around and reinstate a new assault; instead, he continued forward heading straight for the large window where the LEHV hovered. Huun raised his arms to cover his face as he pushed off the floor and dove head first for the glass, smashing through with excessive force. The glass shattered completely, shards scattered everywhere even tearing into Huun's flash as he sailed through the air. Huun never intended to attack Jack again;

instead, he wanted the LEHV.

"Frisco!" Jack cried out.

Huun had sailed across the air, reaching forward toward the LEHV. Frisco recoiled, backing into the vehicle's cockpit. The driver had tried to veer away from the building, jerking the wheel quickly to begin a rapid ascent, but it was too late. Huun had wrapped his massive hands around the rail that lined the side of the vehicle above the door that Frisco had been seated. He perched his feet at the base of the door and quickly worked the handle and tore the door open. Frisco had been prepared. She threw her foot out and connected it with Huun's jaw. Huun barely flinched. His face contorted into a grimace as he hoisted himself up and immediately went after Frisco. She threw another kick, this time into Huun's chest, knocking him backward a bit. Nevertheless, he was relentless and quickly regained his stance. He made another advancement toward Frisco, not hesitating to gain the upper hand as he moved on top of her. She struck Huun again, this time her knee connected to his genitals. Huun froze for a moment and, without flinching, punched her hard across the cheek. She fell into the back of the vehicle hard. Huun made his move on the driver, wrapping his thick hand around the man's throat. The driver struggled to breathe, gasping and choking. He slid his arm down to his hip, unsnapping the holster that held his pistol. He clutched the gun, wrapping his finger securely around the trigger. In one swift motion, he withdrew the pistol, turned, and swung it in the direction of Huun. Huun was ready. With one thrust of his fist, he punched the barrel of the gun and drove it straight into the driver's face, pushing the man's nose deep into his skull. The incident happened so quickly the driver didn't even have a chance to scream. The driver's body simply slumped forward, the gun embedded deeply in his face, and slammed into the steering column. The vehicle lurched forward and began to plummet slowly.

Jack ran to the window, he watched as the vehicle began to fall from the sky. His heart sank. "No!" He screamed, his thoughts about Frisco.

The vehicle pitched as it spiraled slowly toward the ground. Huun remained stoic as he made his way into the driver's seat; he simultaneously popped the door open and shoved the driver's corpse out of the vehicle. The body dropped like a stone, falling fast. It crunched with a wet thud once it hit the ground. Huun slammed the door shut and immediately focused his attention on piloting the craft. He pulled back on the steering column and broke the vehicle from its downward spiral. The vehicle rose up to where it was even with the top floor of the building. Huun looked over to see Jack watching in awe, his jaw open. Huun smiled viscously before he increased the throttle and soared away into the darkness of the night.

CHAPTER 17
THE AIR CHASE

Jack ran from the academic building into the open courtyard. There he saw a squad of law enforcement officials as they finally arrived, late of course. Two LEHVs descended from the dark sky, their lower lights beaming brightly onto the ground showering around Jack who shielded his eyes from the blinding glow. The circumference of the beam narrowed as the LEHVs lowered closer to the ground.

Jack moved out of the center of the beam's ray, allowing the LEHV to complete the near decent to the ground. The first LEHV stopped just a few inches above the ground, the grass beneath blowing erratically in several different directions from the pressure of the engines. Jack watched idly as two fully armed officers rushed from the vehicle. The second LEHV tethered up beside the first Jack watched as several anchors shot from its underbelly. When it stopped at exactly the same height as the first. This time only the passenger's door opened and one officer leapt from the vehicle. It bounced casually from the loss of the man's weight. Jack looked at the first LEHV to see it had been locked, secured from any passenger without the correct palm imprint. The second LEHV still sat, the passenger door agape, awaiting the return of the man who had just left. Jack watched the door longingly, waiting. He then checked to see if he still had his piece. It was securely buttoned in his shoulder holster. He patted it before he pulled his coat close around himself. He looked around to make sure no one was watching, and then made his way for the LEHV door.

Jack drew open his coat and slipped his pistol from its holster as he hopped into the passenger's seat of the hovering LEHV. It bobbed slightly from his added weight. Jack pointed the pistol at the driver, "I hate to do this to you, pal, but I--"

Jack was taken aback at the sight of the driver. "Hello, Jack," Remy's plump face was smiling broadly at him. "You aren't really going to use that thing are you?"

"Dammit, Remy," Jack rolled his eyes and lowered his pistol. "Of course it would be you."

"I'm glad to see you too."

"Look, I don't have time to explain," Jack said, a lilt of panic in his voice. His thoughts returned to Frisco and Huun. Who knows how far they had gone. "I need to commandeer this vehicle."

Remy replied nonchalantly, "No can do. You aren't authorized to drive one of these."

Jack raised his pistol and trained it on Remy, "This states otherwise."

"C'mon, you're not going to actually shoot me," Remy's jovial grin began to wane. "Are you?"

Jack let out an annoyed sigh, "No." He tucked the pistol away in the holster. "Remy, I need to use this vehicle. I have to follow that LEHV that just took off out of here!"

"Oh yeah, I saw that, flew off like a bat outta hell."

"It was a HART agent, one of the top ones," Jack explained. "They have Agent Frisco."

Remy looked at Jack, studying the lines of concern that creased his forehead. The playful smile Remy always wore slowly, gently returned, "Why didn't you say so, strap in."

Jack returned Remy's grin as he sat down and began to pull the straps across his chest. Remy punched the controls before Jack had even latched a buckle and the LEHV roared up into the air. Neither of the men noticed the officer returning to the LEHV falling over from the blast from the underside engines that lit their brilliant blue.

Huun was pushing the vehicle to its limits. It was whining and groaning as he raced across the cityscape at night. The buildings were stark silhouettes against the faint glow that they emitted as they continued to thrive in the ever-darkening sky. The twinkling lights danced like stars hanging high in the deepness of space. None of it mattered to Huun, not the quietness of the night, the tranquility of the sky. Only the mission mattered, it's all that ever mattered. Huun looked slightly comical as his hulking form was hunched in the front seat of the undersized vehicle. Frisco would find it amusing, if she weren't scared for her life. Frisco awoke with her body floating in the center of the vehicle's hold. She let out a high-pitched squeal as fear consumed her completely.

Huun recklessly piloted the car across the rooftops of skyscrapers, pushing the altitude of the LEHV beyond its maximum recommended speed. The bottom of the LEHV scraped the edge of several buildings as it raced more and more rapidly.

"You're driving too fast," Frisco instructed meekly.

"Shut up and hold on," Huun sneered.

Huun steered the LEHV downward slightly, lurching both he and his passenger forward. Frisco felt her stomach spiral from her abdomen to her throat and back again.

"Can't you move this heap any faster?" Jack commented, his voice filled with anxiety.

"I'm full throttle," Remy said calmly, knowing that Jack was understandably upset. "I'm doing the best I can."

"Do better!" Jack snapped. His heart sank as he watched Huun's LEHV increasing its distance between them. The bright red taillights now resembled small rubies. Jack was losing hope.

"I'll catch 'em, don't worry," Remy reassured.

Jack forced a smile, he knew Remy was trying, doing everything he could, but it didn't help him feel any better. Frisco was in trouble. Huun was dangerous, there was no telling what he could do, or had done, to her. Jack didn't want to think about that. "I know," Jack managed. "Thanks."

"Don't mention it."

Remy was a much better pilot of the LEHV than Jack had expected. He traversed the tops of buildings easily, skimming the surfaces in order to propel the vehicle forward. The contact with some form of surface allowed the LEHV to increase its speed. Jack was certain Huun was not aware of this trick. The car skipped like a flat stone across the surface of a pond. The constant bobbing made Jack feel queasy at first, but remembering his days as a Skytrooper evened his nerves. All those months of training he endured to untangle his nerves and make him a better soldier was an effective deterrent those years ago, but some of that fades when a soldier returns to civilian life.

"Now we're gaining momentum," Remy hunkered forward, his large form smothering the steering column as adjusted himself. "If we keep this up, we'll be on him in no time!"

Jack leaned forward as well. He wanted to catch Huun and face him one last time, this time not holding back and letting loose everything he had. Huun was about to incur his wrath and pay for everything he had ever done, not just to him or Frisco, but to everyone he ever crossed. Jack regretted every opportunity he had to kill Huun, but never followed through. His conscience may have given him reason to refrain, but his resolve and his anger would change that.

The LEHV skimmed several more skyscrapers that towered over New Utica, Remy finessed the vehicle expertly around antennas and heating and air conditioning units that speckled the concrete landscape. He veered the ship upward and around the higher buildings. He jostled his thick arms as he repositioned the sky vehicle in line with its quarry.

Jack was growing more and more anxious, hoping they could catch Huun's LEHV in time. It was much larger before them now, its back end filling up nearly the entire windshield.

"We'll be on them in seconds," Remy said. "Get ready."

Jack nodded.

Jack wasn't exactly sure for what he was getting ready. He hadn't really completely come up with a plan. Or at least a plan that wasn't completely insane. There really wasn't much of an option. Huun wouldn't stop to allow them to board his vehicle. Instead, Jack would have to leap from his vehicle onto Huun's in order to overtake him. It wasn't the ideal option, but, again, there wasn't much of one. Jack wrapped the canvas waist and shoulder straps around himself, tightening them snugly. He then reached above his head and grasped a clip that was attached to a thick cable rolled onto a tightly wound winch. He pulled it out with enough slack to clip to the back of the canvas straps he now wore across his torso. He tugged on it twice to ensure its security. He was ready. Jack stood at the side door of the LEHV, the red light bathing the interior of the vehicle. It colored Jack's face a deep pink, making him look sickly, which was exactly how he was feeling. He propped his hands on the doorframe over his head as he squatted slightly before it. He lowered his head and took in a deep breath, closing his eyes and clearing his thoughts. He wanted to be prepared for anything. There was only one chance to make this work. If he miscalculated or hesitated, he could miss the target and drop below the flying vehicles. The speed at which they travelled was already dangerous, and the low flying would ensure his eminent collision with a building. The impact would be deadly. He shook his head, removing the negative thoughts from his mind. He wanted to focus on the outcome he desired, the outcome he needed, to leap from his LEHV onto Huun's.

No matter how much courage he mustered, or how much of his previous Skytrooper training he remembered, he was still nervous. The shrill of Remy's voice cut through his thoughts, "We're about two clicks from the other LEHV. Are you ready?"

Jack held out his hand for Remy to see, his thumb raised, indicating his readiness, no matter how much he was still unsure of himself.

Remy nodded in compliance, he pressed a series of buttons on his console, "Get set!"

The door in front of Jack slid open. A blast of wind exploded into Jack's face, initially pushing his hair back and then blowing it in every direction. The wind filled the cabin, snapping the slack part of the cable like a repeatedly plucked guitar string. Jack let the crisp evening wind cool his sweaty skin. It was comforting, it felt good, but it didn't make it easier to do what needed to be done. He opened his eyes. The goggles shielding them made it easier to see. He saw Huun's LEHV just ahead, only a few feet away. He looked over his shoulder to see Remy jostling the controls as he guided the LEHV up behind Huun. Remy drifted the LEHV to the left, aiming it parallel to Huun's vehicle. Jack watched as the opposing LEHV was revealed from back to front. Remy eased the LEHV up next to Huun's LEHV, their speeds equaled.

Jack looked into the driver's window across from him. Huun stared back at him, his expression of shock and surprise. No doubt confused as to how exactly Jack was able to catch up to him. Jack offered a salute, his two fingers flicking casually from his forehead while his lips curled up into a sly grin. Huun's face twisted into a terrifying scowl.

'*Yep, he was angry*,' Jack thought. All the better to make his move. Jack stood on the balls of his feet, leaning out the side of the vehicle.

"Go!" Remy called out to Jack, his voice barely audible over the roaring wind.

It was enough for Jack to hear. He pushed off his feet and dove out into the open sky.

The darkness surrounded him, embraced him like death welcoming its next victim. Jack spread his arms out to his side, like wings, in an attempt to keep himself steady. Huun's LEHV grew larger as he leapt toward it, a five-foot gap between the vehicles. Remy had lifted their LEHV up slightly higher to give Jack more leverage to compensate the gap.

What seemed like a sure thing, a simple leap, quickly changed. Something unexpected happened. Instead of veering away, Huun veered the vehicle closer, in the direction from where Jack leapt. The sudden shift gave Jack pause; unfortunately, what he could do mentally he couldn't do physically. His body continued to sail through the air precariously. Jack brought his arms back into himself, spinning them wildly as if their resistance would slow his momentum. It didn't.

Remy looked over to see Jack's progress only to see the other LEHV coming toward them, preparing to side swipe them. This would undoubtedly pin Jack between the vehicles, squishing him. Remy did what he felt he had to do. He jerked the wheel to his left and pulled back on the yoke increasing the vehicles pitch. The LEHV lurched upward, the winch detecting the sudden movement, froze.

Jack felt his chest tighten as the canvas straps around him closed in tightly. He was no longer flying toward Huun's LEHV. Instead, he was being pulled back, like a fish on a hook. Jack's arms went akimbo as he suddenly lost control of himself. It was as if gravity decided to reverse itself and his world had suddenly been pulled out from underneath. The sudden change in momentum sent him flying back toward his LEHV. Unfortunately, Remy was now pulling the vehicle upward. Instead of returning through the door he once came through, Jack was swinging like a pendulum beneath. The first swing was a massive arc. The retro rockets underneath emitted an intense heat that Jack felt as he inched closer to the undercarriage of the LEHV. He twisted his body and straightened himself so that his body slid between the boosters. His body slammed hard against the metal, his head jerking backward and knocking hard against the hard steel. Jack then dropped and swung back out from under the LEHV. He was less in control now than before as his body spun erratically as he swung down. He couldn't regain control. He just had to go in the direction it was heading.

Jack watched the skyline rock before him, growing and shrinking with each pass, spiraling around him. It was sickening him to keep his eyes open, but closing them made it harder to regain control. Jack held in his breath as his twisting form was coming back up under his LEHV where he was still tethered. He let his body spin, timing his movement just right. He brought up his knees as he headed toward the undercarriage. His feet connected to the bottom of the vehicle. Jack couldn't hold himself there, but he could stop his spinning. He planted both feet firmly to the bottom of the carriage and then pushed off using them in tandem. It worked as his body no longer spun, but he continued his pendulum-like swing.

Huun watched the body of Jack Zero struggle as he dangled from the LEHV that hovered above. He instantly pulled back on the yoke and brought his LEHV up underneath. Huun's LEHV came up quickly and unexpectedly. Jack was now swinging steadily, but he wasn't prepared to connect with the roof of another vehicle. His side slammed into the solid metal structure of the LEHV hard. Remy must not have been aware of Huun's ascent. He knew Remy could have guided the vehicle off enough to avoid any contact with Huun. It was extremely painful as Jack's ribs were forced inward from the contact. The air was pushed from his lungs and he immediately let out a series of painful coughs. Fortunately, he was no longer swinging. Unfortunately, Huun had a much easier target to hit. Jack watched as Huun withdrew, steering his vehicle downward and then behind. Jack knew Huun was preparing for another assault, one that could be fatal. Jack had to get off the tether and into his LEHV.

Huun had turned his own LEHV quickly less than a mile behind him. Jack felt his heart leap into his throat. He gripped the tether with his hands and began to pull himself up, hand over hand. Huun was closing in at an incredible speed, the front of his LEHV aimed directly at Jack.

"Remy!" Jack called up into the LEHV. "Remy!"

No response. It was a longshot to call up, it was nearly impossible for Remy to hear with the oppressive sound of the wind in combination with the turbines. Jack was on his own.

Remy wasn't ignoring Jack, despite the fact that he couldn't hear his calls. The recall button for the winch was inactive. He couldn't wind the tether back up.

"Jack! I hope you're all right," Remy tried to think of something to do, his eyes scanning the sky in search of the other LEHV. "Now where the hell did that other LEHV get off to?"

Jack had only hoisted himself halfway up the tether. Huun was almost on top of him. There was no way he could make it up to the door before Huun reached him. Jack had only one option. He could see Huun's sinister grin as it grew larger, his speed seeming to increase faster and faster. Jack heart stopped beating as his hand slid down his chest to just above his stomach. His fingers caressed the latch that secured his harness in place. His finger pressed the button that released the straps that wrapped around his shoulders. The harness spat Jack free; he was no longer tethered to his LEHV. He was now falling freely in space.

The look of shock on Huun's face would have been priceless had Jack the time to see it. Unfortunately, he was too busy absorbing the impact of hitting the windshield of the LEHV with his shoulder. The windshield housed two thick layers of protective glass shielding. Jack's body easily cracked and spider-webbed the outer layer of glass instantly on impact. His body bounced high, launching him over the roof of the car.

That was not part of this insane plan.

Jack reached his arms out as he bounced against the top of the roof. He couldn't afford to bounce again. He clamped his hands around anything that he could wrap his hands around that he was sure wouldn't fall off. His fingers wrapped around the bar that stretched between the set of warning lights that lined the center of the roof. His body swung down like a hinged door, slamming hard against the sheer roof. His body had been taking quite a beating. His shoulders felt the strain of his body being pulled away while his hands kept hold. The wind pressure was intense and the frigid air was unbearable, but Jack had to endure. For himself. For Frisco.

Jack channeled all his strength into his arms and hauled himself up onto the roof completely, allowing his feet to find a place to hold. Jack firmly secured himself on the roof of Huun's LEHV, positioning himself sharply and poised for an attack. He reached into his coat, the tail flapping in the wind, snapping like a whip that was continuously released and recoiled, and withdrew his pistol. He knew the LEHV had a tremendous hide, but he had to try. Jack pulled himself up further on the roof. He managed to scrimp himself up to the lip of the roof, just above the windshield. He could see where his body had made its mark. Jack trained his pistol to the windshield in front of Huun and fired a shot.

Just as he suspected, it didn't penetrate the glass, but it definitely made a mark. The bullet ricocheted into the endless void surrounding them, but the sound and sight startled Huun. Huun ducked his head instinctively, seeing the mark from the bullet lined up between his eyes. Huun's expression drifted from shock to utter rage. He never liked to have Jack best him in any way. Huun had the advantage; he had the LEHV. Jack was vulnerable out there. Huun would be a fool not to take that advantage. He pushed forward on the yoke and sent the LEHV in a steep nosedive.

Jack's foot placement was not set for a nosedive. His stomach stayed behind as the car dropped in an almost ninety-degree angle. His feet flipped over his head, his hands still gripping the warning light bar. His backside slammed into the windshield, his billowing coat blocking Huun's view. Huun responded by jerking the wheel at a hard left and then hard right, trying to loosen Jack's grip from the vehicle.

It was working.

Being the nosedive wasn't enough, the condensation that collected on the bar beneath Jack's hands did not make for a solid grip. Jack could feel his fingers slipping from their clasp around the slippery metal bar. He kicked his feet trying to find another place to anchor himself, but the hood offered no recess.

Frisco watched as Jack scrambled for his life along the hood of the LEHV. She wanted to turn away, for fear of watching the grisly conclusion, but instead opted on action. Frisco looked over at her captor, his face in a wicked sneer as he relished in the moment he created, the death of Jack Zero. Frisco felt the fear she once felt subside in favor of the rage that now brewed within. She instantly lashed out at Huun, throwing several punches at his face. She hit him numerous times in the jaw and twice in the nose. The shots to the nose caused Huun to flinch. He let his hands off the wheel. Frisco grabbed it from underneath and pulled back on the yoke, steadying the car.

The sharp movement of the LEHV cause Jack to slide precariously to the front of the hood. He twisted his body, turning himself onto his stomach, in order to grab the lip of the LEHV's front end. He grabbed the bumper of the vehicle with his fingertips, stopping his slide. Jack's body had slid, feet first, over the edge of the hood of the LEHV. His hands gripped the bumper but his legs swung deep beneath him until they kicked the underside chassis of the vehicle. His steel-tipped boots clunked loudly against the rigid metal. The condensation from the atmosphere was beginning to saturate his coat, weighing him down. He had to pull himself back up.

Remy circled his vehicle back around as best he could, without compromising the speed and altitude he had already achieved. The LEHV was a tricky vehicle to maneuver. It wasn't like driving a standard car, but not as clumsy as flying a plane. It didn't have rudders to assist in the turning; instead, it utilized a series of intake and outtake vents that allowed air to pass through while propulsion kept it aloft. If any movement or sudden turn interrupted the airflow in any way, the engine would seize and the LEHV would fall. The ability to restart the engine often took upwards of five minutes, not enough time to prevent a collision with the ground in most instances. Remy was always cautious when he guided his LEHV around. He was conscious of its inner workings and limitations. Remy prided himself of his skills. He wasn't about to cause any problems when going to rescue Jack.

The sky was dark and the cloud cover was growing more and denser as Remy guided his LEHV around. He could see the LEHV Huun was piloting just ahead. He noticed a strange aberration hanging from the front of the vehicle.

"What the hell is that?" He squinted to get a better look. He could see a pair of legs at the base of the object, kicking frantically about. "Holy shit!"

Remy adjusted himself in his seat, repositioning his shoulders and legs. He needed to straighten the nose of his vehicle and punch up the speed in order to catch up. He wrapped his hands tighter around the steering column and reached down for the thrust control. He pressed it sharply and leaned forward to keep his eyes trained on the vehicle and Jack.

Jack slowly brought his elbows up along the hood of the vehicle, they sank slightly into the thinner metal that shielded the engine and power thrusts beneath. The small metal bars that lined the outer edges of the hood provided a proper handrail for Jack to use in order to better stabilize himself and prevent him from slipping or falling. Jack grunted and huffed as he began to life himself back up onto the hood of the LEHV.

Huun was not about to allow Jack the opportunity to live. He growled low and then worked it up to a loud roar as he pulled back on the steering yoke. The LEHV took an immediate upturn as it began to shoot up into the sky. Jack's body flipped over the hood, his hands not losing their grip, until his back crunched loudly into the metal hood shield. He lost his breath for a moment in the thin air, but remembered his Skytrooper training and was quick to control it. He let his breathing become shallow, allowing his lungs the ability to accept the thin air. The moisture collecting along the hood was making it difficult for Jack to maintain his grip and hold himself in place. His fingers slid as he tried to hold on, elongating, extending, as they tried to keep their grip.

Jack closed his eyes as the LEHV shook to the right, just hard enough to loosen his grip. His hands opened and he let go.

Jack felt the wind intensify as his body fell into a free fall through the open, thin atmosphere. The tails of his coat enveloped his body like gift wrap around a present. His head was light and his eyes were heavy. He was slipping from consciousness. At least he would be out before he hit the ground.

With that Jack's body went limp.

Remy pulled the LEHV underneath Jack, moving quickly but trying to keep it steady and even. He looked up to see the freefalling form of Jack Zero heading toward him. His arms and legs were still, not a good indication that Jack would be able to pull himself up and grab onto Remy's vehicle. Instead, Remy had to catch Jack. He looked around his cab desperately, trying to think of something to save him, anything. He pounded his head with fist in a primitive attempt to shake out the fuzz and come up with something.

It suddenly hit him. He scanned the controls before him looking for the button to release the rear door of the LEHV. He spotted it just to the left of the steering column. He slammed it hard with his open palm. The rear door that allowed officers to drop from the vehicle and to load in prisoners, slid open slowly. The wind rushed in like a tidal wave, crashing all around the cabin and jarring loose anything that wasn't fastened down.

Remy then wrenched the steering wheel and allowed the LEHV to twist onto its side facing the open door upward. He was going to catch Jack. He jostled the wheel gentle forward and backward, trying to line it with Jack, who was about to come into range. Remy could feel the air stealing breath from his lungs. Jack was in view, it was now or never.

Jack's body fell into the gaping maw in the back of the LEHV. His body fell sharply to the other side, slamming hard against the door on the other side. Fortunately, it was lined with plush and broke some of the impact.

Remy immediately slammed the button again to close the door and then righted the LEHV into its correct position. It wobbled precariously as it found its balance. Remy wiped the sweat that had begun collecting on his brow now that the wind had been cut off. He heard Jack groan slightly in the back of the vehicle.

Jack sat up and rubbed his head. A big welt was beginning to form at the base of his hairline. He shook his head in hopes to clear his blurred vision. He took in several deep breaths to regain himself. Remy began to push forward slowly on the yoke, bringing the LEHV into a slow decent.

"What the hell are you doing?" Jack wheezed.

"I'm takin us back down," Remy said firmly.

"Like hell you are!" Jack gritted his teeth as he looked into the displays along the control panel. The images of Huun's LEHV soaring away consumed the screen and began to shrink as it went away. "Take us back up!"

"No!" Remy shouted back.

"Take us up!" Jack roared as he reached forward, grabbing the wheel from Remy.

The LEHV lurched backward, pressing Remy against the back of the seat. Jack felt his feel lift off the ground.

"You can't," Remy warned. "The LEHV can't handle this kind of a climb!"

"Shut up!" Jack held tight to the wheel, keeping the vehicle at its rate of speed.

The LEHV's engine hesitated, pausing and seizing as it was pushed to the limit. Remy was shouting over Jack's shoulder as Jack overtook the pilot's seat. Jack let the whine of the engine drown out Remy's voice. He kept his focus on the LEHV before him. The red taillights now much brighter, larger and within reach. Within seconds, they were right behind Huun. Jack swerved the LEHV.

"Damn sheer winds," Jack snarled. "Can't get past him."

Remy was clutching his chest, a fistful of his shirt balled into his hand, "G-good, I think you can take me back down now."

Jack narrowed his eyes and pulled back on the yoke. The front end of the LEHV pointed up and the vehicle continued in an almost ninety-degree angle. Remy howled as he was pressed back hard against the seat. He began to pull the harness across his chest and fastened himself tightly before he could slip out of his seat.

Jack expertly took the stuttering LEHV above the clouds and then thrust the yoke forward. The car dipped in an equal downward angle, straight down. The LEHV's engines sputtered until it ultimately gave out. The engines cut in midair, leaving a deafening silence surrounding Jack and Remy in their seats. Jack held his breath, gripping the wheel tightly, his knuckles bone white.

"We're gonna die!" Remy clasped his hands over his eyes as his stomach leapt into his throat and then out of his mouth. He moved his hands over his mouth to quell the desire to vomit, but quickly replaced them over his eyes when he saw the lights of the city below rushing toward him.

"Just hang on," Jack said between breaths.

Jack held the LEHV as steady as he could. The sheer winds that lashed out at the falling vehicle like a whip, trying to force it in any direction but that which Jack tried to steer. Jack could see Huun's LEHV appearing through the cloud cover just below. He lined the front of the LEHV against the vehicle.

Remy peeked through his fingers to see what Jack was planning, "No! No, no, no! What do you think you're doing? You are not going to ram him!"

"Watch me," Jack said coldly.

"You're gonna kill us!"

"I know what I'm doing."

"Like hell you do!"

Remy reached over Jack's arms for the wheel. Jack let go with one hand and pushed Remy back. The LEHV jerked violently until he returned his hand. Remy's eyes, no longer covered, were as large as dinner plates, his breathing short and panicked.

"I can't let you do this!" Remy managed between breaths.

"Trust me," Jack said defiantly.

Remy gripped the armrests on the sides of his chair, his fingernails digging into the soft leather upholstery. The other LEHV was growing larger and larger. It was a matter of seconds before they would collide. Remy couldn't take anymore; he made another attempt at stopping Jack. This time, instead of grabbing for the wheel, he pressed the emergency engine start button. The engine coughed and then started back up with a whine followed by a loud roar. The thrust pushed the LEHV forward. Jack's muscles locked up as the vehicle lurched. Remy took advantage of Jack's surprise and wrestled the wheel from his hands. He pulled it back just before they would have smashed into the other LEHV. The nose lifted, missing the other vehicle by mere inches, but the bottom of the vehicle hit the roof of the vehicle hard.

Huun heard the crash on his roof, surprised by anything hitting his LEHV. What could it be? Maybe a bird. Huun twisted his neck to look upward, surprised to see a LEHV changing its course above him and pulling away.

With a look of surprise, Huun turned to his passenger. Frisco returned a smirk.

"Dammit Remy!" Jack shouted as he righted his vehicle. He turned to his side mirror to see Huun's vehicle shrinking behind them. Jack wrenched the wheel to its hard right. The rear engines cut in and out to compensate for the change in direction as the LEHV turned sharply. Remy's body slammed around under his restraints, the belts cutting into his skin. He winced from the brief pain.

"If they get away, Remy, I'm killing you instead."

"You should be thanking me that you're still alive," Remy adjusted the straps across his chest.

"I told you I know what I'm doing."

"Yeah, committing suicide."

Jack shot Remy a nasty look, "I've flown this type of vehicle more times than you can count, I know how they handle."

"Like where? Military?" Remy asked.

Jack nodded.

Remy closed his eyes and shook his head, "Military Hover Vehicles are nowhere near as sophisticated as Law Enforcement models. Those things are like flying tanks. These are much thinner, designed more for speed and maneuverability. You smash into another LEHV and we're both done for. Your girlfriend and you get to spend your last days as a street pancake."

Jack scowled. He knew Remy was more experienced since the LEHV's he drove were nearly a decade ago. "Yeah, well…she…she's not my girlfriend."

"Whatever," Remy replied, obviously annoyed.

Jack piloted the LEHV back toward Huun. Huun had not deviated course, now cruising toward Jack. Remy swallowed hard. He knew what was happening and he didn't like it. It was an inflight game of chicken. One from which he knew Jack was not going to back down. It seemed he was going to kill them all instead of letting them get away. And there was so much he had left to do in life. Oh well.

The two LEHVs raced toward one another, neither of their pilots looking to lax on their path or veer out of the way. Jack held a look of determination. A look matched by his adversary as Huun pushed his throttle until it was fully opened. His LEHV had more momentum, more speed than Jack's. He had the advantage and he was determined to take it. Jack held his course. Remy breathing erratically, not able to calm himself down. Jack ignored him, concentrating, focusing on Huun. He had to stop him from escaping no matter the cost.

"M-maybe there's a better way than this," Remy stammered, attempting one last time to reason with Jack.

It did no good. Jack didn't even break his stare out the window. He was lost. Lost and determined to destroy himself, Remy too. Remy closed his eyes, accepting the inevitable. The LEHVs were going to collide any second. The sound of engines whirring and the wedge-shaped vehicles slicing through the air seemed deafening. Jack was close enough to see Frisco in the passenger's seat of the other vehicle. He saw smile meekly. He offered his own apologetic grin in response. Deep inside, he knew she understood. This was the only way.

Everyone prepared for impact. Remy closed his eyes tightly, waiting for the sound of the explosion. The sound that never came.

Instead, Jack had jerked the wheel sharply, not merely in an attempt to avoid collision, but instead, he allowed the back end of his LEHV to kick in, hitting the hood on its left side just right. The move splintered a small black device along the hood. The once blinking red light was no longer illuminated. Instead, it was sparking and coughing out fragments.

"We're alive?" Remy asked with great surprise.

"You didn't think I was crazy enough to hit him head on did you?" Jack smirked.

"Yes, as a matter of fact, I did," Remy replied, still holding his expression. "What did you do?"

Remy looked back to see the now damaged device, "You hit their lift response?"

"Yep."

"That was pretty smart, now they can't fly, but it also allows them to land safely."

Jack smiled and nodded, "I told you I know what I'm doing."

Remy's expression of surprise changed from shock to being impressed. He couldn't believe it, but Jack had intentionally destroyed the lift response mechanism.

Huun's LEHV was dropping slowly, descending through the clouds as it lost its ability to fly.

"Now we follow them down and catch him," Jack said confidently. "Just remember, he's mine."

Huun swore loudly as he tried to regain control of his falling LEHV. Frisco watched him struggle fruitlessly, knowing there was no way he would get it back. Jack had saved her. He knew just how to cripple the vehicle without putting her in harm's way. She smiled to herself, relief washing over her. Jack was coming. Jack was going to save her.
Huun punched the wheel with his boulder-like fist. The wheel bent slightly from his brute strength. His anger mad Frisco happier. She stifled a laugh, not wanting to provoke him further. But Huun was past that; he wasn't concerned with her feelings. Instead, he was concerned with self-preservation. He could see Jack's LEHV in the rear display. It was only a

matter of time now. Huun looked over at Frisco as she held back her smile. Nevertheless, it was irrelevant to him. He needed to get Jack away from him and the solution was sitting beside him.

Jack kept his LEHV at a slow speed, not wanting to pass the other vehicle yet. As he kept his watch on the vehicle, he noticed Huun opened the side hatch. He threw a look over to Remy, "What the hell is he doing now?"

Remy shrugged.

At that moment, a shape flew from the side hatch of Huun's LEHV. Jack narrowed his eyes, straining to see through the cloud cover.

Remy shared the view with Jack curiously, "What is that?"

It was then that Jack realized, it wasn't a 'what,' but 'who.' The form was flailing. It was a body. It was Frisco. Huun had thrown her from the LEHV and she was falling. Jack's heart sank. Every other though flushed from his mind. All he could see was Frisco, falling, screaming, alone. He had to save her. Jack punched the throttle. He roared past Huun who was laughing maniacally and pointing at Jack. Jack wasn't about to let him go. He grabbed Remy by his collar and pulled him closer. "Get on the tow cable, get that LEHV," Jack ordered.

Remy understood and immediately grabbed the control. Within seconds he had aimed and trained the tow cable onto Huun's vehicle and fired. The grapple launched fast above them, quickly gripping onto the first loose piece it could grab and secure itself.

Huun lurched in his seat as he felt his LEHV suddenly increase its decent. He looked over to see what had obviously snagged him. He saw the thick line that ran from beneath his vehicle and traced all the way to Jack's LEHV far below.

"Son of a bitch!" Huun cursed.

"What are you doing now?" Remy groaned.

Jack had opened the side hatch. He fastened a cable to his belt and leaned out the door, "I'm going to get her!" He shouted loudly over the screaming wind that cut fiercely through the cabin.

"You're insane!"

"I'm trusting you to keep this bucket in control," Jack returned. "Can you do that?"

Remy looked worried, "Oh sure, with you falling ahead and that juggernaut dragging behind, should be a cinch."

Jack ignored Remy's sarcasm, "Good!"

Jack flashed a small salute and then leapt from the cabin. Jack spread his arms and legs when he hit the air as his body went into freefall.

He attempted to steady his fall as best he could. He looked around the sky for any sign of Frisco. He spotted her several feet below. He then brought in his arms and legs and pointed his head downward. He quickly increased his rate of drop, racing closer to Frisco.

Huun had climbed from his seat and out to the side of the LEHV. He shimmied himself slowly along the hood, inching himself slowly, closer to the grapple hook that was latched firmly to the underbelly of his vehicle. The wind cleaved the air around him, slicing hard against his face. The whipping wind forced his eyes to tear up making it more difficult to see. As he looked over the grapple hook embedded into his vehicle. He could see that it had punctured the fuel line.

"Damn," Huun growled. He knew if he removed the hook, it would cause the fuel to leak more quickly resulting in his inability to fly any more than it already had. He hanged there for a moment, contemplating what he could do. He looked down the long cable to see the functioning LEHV far below. He caught the sight of someone leaping from the side of the vehicle.

It was Jack; he knew it was. '*He was attempting to rescue the girl. Perfect,*' he thought. Huun wrapped his thick hands around the cable and slid down.

Jack let the wind slide over his body as he dropped like an aerodynamic weight through the sky, closing the gap between Frisco's flailing body and himself. He needed to catch her soon; he could see the lights of the city below becoming brighter.

Frisco felt the air in her lungs get pushed out, the thinned atmosphere making it hard to breath. She took small, shallow breaths between the screams of help that went unanswered. She broke through the clouds and saw the buildings beneath them emerge into view. It was only a matter of time before she was crushed by the impact gravity forced upon her.

She didn't want to die. A little late for that now.

She wanted to let out another series of ear-splitting scream, but couldn't muster up enough energy, or breath, to let it go. Instead, she closed her eyes and waited for the inevitable.

Within a minute, she had passed out. She never felt Jack's arms wrap around her slender waist. She never felt the warm touch of his hand as he pulled her closer and touched her face, trying to warm her frigid skin. She never felt the snap and jerk of their bodies as the cable connected to the above floating LEHV ran out of slack. She didn't feel them swinging softly together for a moment.

She never felt anything. She just slept.

Remy was overjoyed as he watched Jack and Frisco swaying peacefully several feet below. He did it. That son of a bitch pulled it off, Remy thought to himself. He certainly was a man of conviction, one of his word. The spool of cable behind him had ground to a harsh stop. The smell of burning metal filled the vehicle. Its rank odor filled his nostrils, making his stomach flip and flop. He wanted to vomit, but withheld the urge. Instead, he flipped the recoil switch several times, but it didn't respond. The winch had stopped but wouldn't reverse and bring Jack back up to the vehicle.

"Shit," Remy cursed. This wasn't the first time the motor had given out, but now was not a time for this to happen. Remy unlatched himself from his belts. He rushed to the back of the vehicle and checked the motor. It wasn't responding to any of his tests. It could be the extra weight that Frisco added to the line that was causing it to malfunction. He pulled a long lever from the supply case just to the left of the motor. It was a manual crank he attached to the side of the winch. He began to crank the spool with every ounce of his strength. It moved, but it moved slowly.

Jack held Frisco closer; he brushed her windswept hair from her eyes as he checked her breathing. He felt the short, hot bursts of her breath that made its way from her lungs. '*She was beautiful,*' he thought to himself. He needed to get her into the shelter of the LEHV; she needed the warmth before she froze to death. He held her tightly with one arm as he tugged on the cable with the other. '*Remy had to be working on getting them back up there, wasn't he?*'

Suddenly, the cable moved. It was a small, slow movement, but it moved. Then there was nothing for a few moments. Then it moved again.

Remy was coming through. He thought of Remy and his less than fit form. He knew this ascent was going to take some time. Jack took Frisco's arms and draped them over his shoulders and around his neck.

He spoke to Frisco softly. "Nikki?" Jack whispered at first. "Nikki?" He repeated more loudly. "C'mon sweetheart, I need you to wake up."

She didn't respond.

"C'mon," Jack shook her with his free hand. "Nikki wake up!" He finally shouted.

A soft moan came from her dried lips.

Jack smiled, "That-a-girl."

"Oh," Frisco let out another low moan. "Don't call me Nikki."

Jack's smile stretched across his face as Frisco looked wearily into his eyes. "Listen, I know you're weak and tired, but I need you to hold onto me as tight as you can. Can you do that for me?"

Frisco nodded. She tightened her arms around his neck. Jack freed both hands and began to pull himself and Frisco up the cable.

Remy huffed as he pushed and pulled the crank. He wasn't a man in the best of shape, but he did the best he could. The cable slowly wound back up around the spool, bringing the low hanging occupants back to the LEHV. Sweat poured from his brow as he wrestled with the crank. "Damn...motor," Remy sputtered, more cursing slithering from his lips. "Had to...give out...now."

He tried catching his breath, but he couldn't rest long. He had to get them back up before too long. "I...should really...start...working out," Remy told himself.

A loud thump rocked the LEHV in place, causing it to sink slightly. The sound came from the roof; Remy could distinguish the sound of crimping metal bending under heavy weight.

"What is that?" Remy swallowed hard. "J-Jack? Is that you?" Remy hoped, but knew it was probably unlikely. "P-please, be you Jack."

Remy locked the crank in place as he cautiously stood and made his way to the open door of the LEHV. He picked up an energy baton from its sheath along the wall, a precautionary weapon placed in all police vehicles both on and off the ground. He held it in his hands like a baseball bat as he crept slowly to the open door. At the edge of the door, Remy peered out slowly, the wind slapping his face like an opened hand. The sky outside was darker; it was more difficult to see what was outside. The cloud cover blanketed the vehicle, enveloping it like a shroud. Only when the clouds separated was he able to see the city lights below. He could just make out the end of the line. He was sure he could see Jack several dozen feet down. At least he thought so.

What Remy didn't see were the pair of massive boots that swung in from the roof and kicked him square in the jaw. The impact knocked him backward into the other side of the LEHV. The back of his head slammed hard against the window with a hollow thud.

Huun dropped himself through the open maw of the doorway as he firmly landed into the belly of the LEHV. He looked about the cabin, seeing Remy's unconscious form crumpled along the floor. He smiled to himself. He stretched his thick arms and brought his hands together to crack his knuckles. He then wrapped his hands around the cable still wrapped tightly around the winch. He pulled his hands apart and tore the cable as if it were tissue paper. He then let go of the steel line and watched as one-half slid from the vehicle and disappeared into the darkening sky.

"Good riddance, Zero," Huun said lowly to himself, reveling in the death of his adversary. He snickered at the irony of the death, killing Jack in the same way Jack had killed Zimm all those years ago. "The great detective won't have any trouble finding the ground."

Huun made his way to the pilot's seat and stuffed his large frame into the small seat. Huun was comfortable and familiar with the controls; he began flipping switches and prepared the vehicle for his escape.

The steel-wound cable flapped in the harsh wind like a whip flaring out to crack against an angry bull. However, it snapped harshly instead at the dangling legs of Jack Zero. Jack hung from the underside of the LEHV, his arms stretched to their limits. The added weight of Nicolina Frisco hanging from his back, her arms drawn tightly around his neck, certainly made holding on more difficult.

Jack saw Huun enter the LEHV. He was fortunate enough to pull himself up and hang on to the bottom of the LEHV before Huun had seen him. Knowing how Huun thinks and how he works paid off. Jack prepared himself by grabbing the underbelly before he could cut the cable. Now he only had to get himself and Frisco back inside. He could feel Frisco's breath on his neck. She was still alive, he was not too sure if she was still awake, though.

"You still with me, Nikki?" Jack asked, hoping that by calling her Nikki she would be annoyed enough to answer.

She didn't respond.

"It's okay," Jack answered anyway. "I'll get you inside, just keep hanging on." Jack let one hand free to check that Frisco still had a secure grip around his neck. When he was certain she did, Jack began to move, hand-over-hand, toward the door of the LEHV.

Huun reached across the console before him and selected the option to release the rear winch, setting free the other LEHV being towed above. Huun could care less what happened to the machine. He only care that nothing promoted drag and allowed him to escape faster.

The rear winch began to whine and grind as it activated and turned, drawing in the long cable that lagged behind. The sound alerted Jack as he turned to see what was happening. The winch was winding faster than expected, spooling in the cable quickly. Jack could see the other LEHV, still connected to the cable, being pulled in rapidly and heading straight toward them.

"What is that moron doing?" Jack asked rhetorically, aloud. Frisco's head lolled sleepily as he swung himself faster. The other vehicle was almost upon them. Jack was almost to the edge, almost able to reach the door.

It was too late.

The other LEHV crashed into the back of their vehicle with an alarming force. The impact slammed their vehicle forward, jolting Huun forward, his forehead hitting the windshield. A small fissure spider-webbed the glass where he hit. Huun pulled himself upright in his seat and wiped the blood away from his newly formed cut. He watched the rear screen to see the other LEHV tip down, it's back end first before swinging underneath his vehicle. Soon enough it disappeared from view as the hook detached from the grill.

Jack lost his grip with one hand slipping as he tried to grasp forward. The LEHV had come in so hard it nearly knocked him from his perch. As his arm fell loose, Frisco slipped from her hold around his neck. He felt his body turn hot and then cold at once. He felt her hands fall away slowly from around his shoulders. He was losing her.

Sleeplessly she fell. Her body falling limply into the void. Jack quickly shot forth his free arm, clamping his hand tightly around Frisco's supple wrist. Her body stopped, her shoulder jerked as it tightened, allowing Jack to catch her and stop her fall. She stirred as she dangled hundreds of feet above the city. Her eyes flittered open slowly; a haze surrounded her as wind swept harshly across her face. She tried to focus, letting her eyelids naturally clear the heavy sleep that consumed her. Her shoulder hurt and she could feel her arm stretched to its limit. Her eyes adjusted as she looked around to see only darkness. She looked around to see nothing more, and then looked down to see the tops of buildings cutting from clouds underneath.

'Clouds?' She thought. 'Underneath?!'

Frisco looked down again. She saw the twinkling lights drifting past her below. She was above the city. High above the city. She let out a shrilled scream.

Jack pulled her up to him, guiding her arm around his neck again. Frisco didn't hesitate to accept Jack's assistance as she clamored to wrap her arms around him.

From behind them the sound of metal grinding was growing louder as the LEHV that had collided with the back of their vehicle was now twisting loose of its restraint. The LEHV was hinging toward them, the tail section swinging first. The front end was still attached to the winch, preventing it to fall freely. Jack could see what was happening; they were going to be sandwiched between to LEHV's when the other kept its pendulum-like swing as it continued toward them.

"Move! NOW! HURRY!" Jack shouted as he pushed with all his might sending Frisco off to the side. She caught herself on the edge of the LEHV, and found a formidable grip that she could get a solid hold. She noticed she was just beneath the open side door to the vehicle. She just needed to hoist herself in and not be noticed. Jack kept moving toward the front of the LEHV. He scaled the underside like a child on the monkey bars in a schoolyard. The opposing LEHV's momentum increased as it created a scissor like set-up, catching Jack in between. He made his way to the front of the LEHV and gripped the bumper, kicking his legs out from under himself so they swung out, just as the other vehicle crashed into the underbelly of the their LEHV.

Frisco was trying to climb in as the LEHV smashed into the bottom. The jolt pushed her forward, forcing her into the back of the LEHV ahead of her scheduled plan. She landed hard into the hold of the vehicle. Her sore shoulder hit the floor hardest. She held her breath and stifled her scream of pain. Frisco tucked her head down and rolled out her crash landing, preventing herself from colliding with any equipment or with Remy's unconscious body. She kept low and made sure Huun didn't notice her. Fortunately, he threw a short look back, half expecting the impact and ignoring it.

The LEHV underneath swung back, the metal grinding loudly as it slipped free, its bumper tearing clean off. The LEHV plunged into the darkened sky, disappearing into the low-hanging cloud cover below. Huun swung his head back around to look out at the sky ahead, feeling confident he was going to make a clean getaway. At least he thought he would until an object smashed the windshield of his LEHV before his eyes. Huun flinched as he jumped back in surprise, pushing back the seat with his weight.

"What the hell!?" Huun called out, startled. Through the growing darkness, Huun could make out the silhouetted form of Jack Zero. "That son of a bitch lives!" Huun roared as Jack threw two more shots with his right fist.

A small glow emanated from beneath the sleeve of his coat as he drew back his arm. On the second strike, Jack was able to penetrate the thick glass that separated himself from Huun. As his fist punched through the glass, his knuckles were shredded by the jagged glass that formed an odd circle in the center of the windshield, his arm swallowed into the car to his shoulder. As his fist entered the cabin, it just missed Huun's head by centimeters. His reflexes were sharp and acute. He quickly countered Jack's efforts by wrapping his thick arm around Jack's. He thrust his shoulders back and yanked Jack by his arm through the windshield. The glass exploded and showered all over them. Shards spewed throughout the cabin and rained over Frisco as she covered her head in her hands. Remy rocked slowly with the vehicle, not realizing the small particles of glass cut into his flesh as he continued to sleep.

Jack twisted his body around Huun's pillar-like arm and pushed his feet off the floor, bringing them up into Huun's jaw. Huun reeled back and fell from the pilot's seat onto the floor of the LEHV. Huun arched his back and quickly sat up, his assault directed at Jack. They collided in between the front seats, both men snarling and grunting as they pushed one another, each challenged physically. Huun was proving to be the better, his mass overcoming Jack's smaller stature. But Jack was not giving up. Jack pressed on, pushing at Huun with all his might, sweat collecting along his brow.

Unfortunately, he was losing.

Huun pushed harder, taking a step and moving his beefy arms into Jack's throat, Huun's elbow pushing directly on Jack's Adam's apple. Jack could feel his throat constricting, closing in and cutting off his air supply. He coughed as he struggled to let air in, his hands squeezing Huun's arms as he tried to push him away.

Huun was winning.

Bright colored spots began to dance before Jack's eyes as his throat constricted and he gasped desperately to get any taste of oxygen. He could feel the wind sweep around him and caress his body as it made its way around the cabin after coming in through the side hatch. It did him no good if he couldn't use it.

"Time to die Zero," Huun grinned in Jack's blue-colored face. Huun leaned in more, pressing harder on Jack's throat.

Jack's eyes rolled into the back of his head as his arms went limp, their grip lost around Huun's arms. Jack had one last chance. He let his feet fall out from beneath him. With Huun's weight pushing into him, he was able to let his body drop back. The movement took Huun by surprise as he lost his balance and fell past Jack, his body stumbling. He tried to stop himself but couldn't grasp anything. Before he could regain his footing, Frisco shot out her leg. Huun stumbled and tripped as he tumbled from the vehicle and fell through the door. Jack dropped to his knees, then his onto his arms as he coughed and hacked, fighting to regain his breath. He brought a hand up to his throat, rubbing it gently. He couldn't see the redness that had overcome it, but he certainly could feel it.

Frisco rushed to Jack's side, "Are you all right?"

Jack nodded in between hacks. "Yeah…sure…fine," he wheezed.

The LEHV lurched and pitched violently. Jack stood on his feet. He nearly again lost his balance as he struggled to find his footing. Jack could feel the vehicle pitch forward hard. He tried to look out the front, but the wind was rushing through the cabin like a hurricane making it difficult to keep his eyes open. Jack planted himself in the pilot's seat and began to look over the controls, pressing buttons and flipping switched feverishly.

"We're losing altitude!" Jack shouted over the wind. "Controls aren't responding."

Frisco made her way to the co-pilot's seat; it made it easier to hear him, "What are we going to do?"

Jack threw her an apologetic look, "Crash."

The LEHV plummeted like a stone, falling from the sky as its engines cut out. The view of the city below became clear as they fell through the once thick cloud cover. The headlights dimmed, flickered on and off several times before they finally went out. The displays inside the vehicle were behaving the same way, cutting on and off, the power fluctuating as it surged throughout the cabin. A slight electrical charged passed through Remy's unconscious body, the jolt reviving him as he sprang up, alert and surprised.

"Wha?...where?" Remy tried to find his bearings. He slapped his open palms to the sides of his head, shaking it quickly to remove the fog that prevented him from thinking straight. He began to pick himself up slowly, the LEHV pitching forward and then leveling off. Remy stumbled before catching his footing. He fell forward a few steps, catching himself on the frame of the opened door at the side of the vehicle. Remy looked out to see the twinkling lights of New Utica beaming up to him in full view.

"HOLY SHIT!" Remy shouted; his eyes bulging as he held his breath in panic. Remy leapt back, fearing he might fall from the maw of the vehicle and immediately wrapped his arms around the nearest object that was bolted down. It just happened to be the pilot's seat as his arms coiled tightly around Jack's throat. The pain that had been present a few moments ago suddenly returned to Jack's throat. He gasped and choked loudly, hardly heard over the rushing wind. Frisco turned to see why Jack made such an awful noise. She yelped at the sight of Jack being choked again. Fortunately, this time it was only Remy.

Frisco leapt from her seat and pried Remy's arms from Jack's neck, "Remy! REMY! Calm down and back off!"

"Are you kidding?" Remy replied, still panicked. "We're falling!"

"Get the hell off me!" Jack wrestled himself free and pushed Remy aside.

Remy stumbled back into the wall where he was once lying unconscious. He held himself still against the wall, closed his eyes and held his breath.

Jack pulled and pushed the yoke as the vehicle pitched and yawed roughly, tossing the occupants of the cabin about. Frisco returned to her seat and Remy found the nearest seat with a restraint. They both strapped themselves in tightly.

The LEHV was right above the buildings, just a few dozen feet away. It was dropping rapidly. Jack pulled back to keep the nose up, trying to stabilize it.

"Watch out!" Frisco pointed through the shattered windshield.

Jack could just see the dark outline of the antennae spire that rose out of the center of the roof. The LEHV scraped the tip of the array, knocking the blinking red light off the top and bending the thick metal over slightly, tearing the bolts up from the roof. The LEHV kicked out slightly as it regained itself with Jack's aid. They continued their downward angle. The next building was slightly shorter than the previous. It didn't matter much, the LEHV had dipped lower; the back end of the vehicle scraped the edge of the roof. Pieces broke free and spewed everywhere as the vehicle sputtered, its engines firing roughly and dislodging even more parts.

Jack pushed and pulled the yoke in his hands, but it didn't respond, it didn't even move.

"Shit," Jack huffed.

"What now?" Frisco could tell something was wrong just by hearing the tone in Jack's voice.

"The controls are stuck."

"What do you mean stuck?"

"I mean not responding." Jack gritted his teeth and shook the wheel hard, but nothing happened. "I can't get it to move. It must be when we hit something, it froze the rudder."

Remy slapped his open palm to his face, "We're done for!"

"Not yet we aren't," Jack replied.

"How?" Frisco felt hope drain from her. She didn't know what Jack was planning, but he hasn't let her down yet.

"We jump," Jack flashed her a half smile.

It wasn't reassuring. Remy felt sick and he slapped his hand over his mouth, "Oh god!"

"No listen," Jack explained. "We're drifting close to the tops of buildings; we just need to jump when we're close enough."

"If we don't smash into the side of a bigger building first!" Remy knew how to bring things into perspective.

"Well, there is that," Jack agreed.

"We don't have time to waste then," Frisco unfastened her belts and made her way to the door.

Jack and Remy followed. The wind was less harsh than it was before. They were level with the city rooftops, some several feet beneath them, others fairly in reach. Several large skyscrapers went past them, too high to be reached as the LEHV continued its downward arc. They all stood at the edge of the door, looking out at the cityscape as it listlessly drifted past. Besides the wind, the whine of the dying engine underneath them was the only sound that filled their ears. Jack leaned forward, craning his neck to see what was ahead. He smiled and pointed, calling Frisco and Remy's attention.

"Just up ahead! That roof's only about a six foot drop, we can make it!"

"Are you nuts?" Remy's eyes bulged. "No way!"

"Dammit Remy!" Frisco snapped. "You are going to jump not because Jack asked you to, but because if you don't..." She stopped as he forced Remy's head out the door and guided it to look at the massive structure on the other side of the roof upon which they planned to jump. "We won't make it past that!"

Remy swallowed hard, "I see your point."

"We haven't a moment to lose!" Jack instructed. "I'll go first, then Frisco, then Remy."

"Why am I last?"

"Remy!" Jack and Frisco both snapped in unison.

"All right, all right," Remy raised his hands in defeat. "Sorry."

"Be sure to tuck and roll when you land or you could break a leg," Frisco added.

"You make it sound so easy," Remy said sarcastically.

"Shut up everyone and get ready!" Jack commanded.

The LEHV lolled to one side as it drifted lower and lower. The large skyscraper was just mere meters away. It wasn't luck that would get them through this; it was going to be skill. Whether or not they could each use their physical gifts to make their way to the top of that roof safely. Jack leaned out the side of the LEHV; he didn't hesitate once the roof was underfoot. Jack leapt from the side of the vehicle, his body outstretched as he sailed through the air. As he flew, he brought his knees up and lowered his head into his chest, rolling from his feet to his shoulder as he hit the gravelly roof. Jack stood immediately, turning to see his friends just as Frisco ran and leapt from the LEHV. She followed Jack's lead, rolling across the roof. Her landing was a bit rougher. Her feet slipped on the loose tar rocks that were scattered across the roof. She landed on her shoulder, but slid further, her side scraping along the surface.

Jack rushed to her side, "Are you alright?"

Frisco nodded. Jack put his arm around her shoulder and helped her stand. The looked up to Remy who was hesitant, standing still like a statue.

"C'mon!" Jack yelled to him. "Jump!"

Remy closed his eyes and shook his head, "I can't."

"You have to!" Jack yelled louder.

"Remy! C'mon!" Frisco added. "You don't have any more time!" She pointed ahead of Remy. He looked to see the skyscraper only seconds away from impact. Remy closed his eyes and held his breath. He jumped from the vehicle feet first, his arms akimbo. He hit the roof hard, his knees buckling from the impact. He fell forward and landed squarely on his chest. The air pushed from his lungs as he gasped for breath. His ears were ringing and his vision blurred. He looked up to see the smeared forms of

Jack and Frisco rushing toward him, their arms flailing over their heads wildly. As they came more into focus, he could see their mouths moving, as if they were saying something.

Their voices slowly came into his ears as the ringing subsided, 'Look out!' was what he heard, along with 'Move!' He craned his neck to see the LEHV above him, colliding into the side of the massive skyscraper next door.

The fireball was spectacular as it engulfed the entire LEHV, swallowing it within the flame and smoke. The heat from the explosion emitted in a wide berth across the roof, baking Remy's once cool skin where he lie. He now understood why Jack and Frisco were yelling. The sound of creaking metal now replaced the roar of the flames. Remy saw the remnants of the vehicle beginning to tip down, just behind the debris that was now raining down on him. Remy shielded his head with his hands and picked himself up from the roof.

Jack and Frisco were reaching out to Remy, helping to get him out of the way destroyed vehicle. Jack reached Remy first, wrapping his arm under Remy's. Jack pulled him hard, lifting him more quickly and yanking him away. What remained of the LEHV was simply a shell, fire shooting out of the opened doors and shattered glass. It fell like a lead weight. Remy and Jack ran quickly, just missing the metal frame as it slammed hard into the roof, hot metal shards, sparks and fire spraying everywhere.

The vehicle exploded again, fire raging higher. The shockwave pushed Remy and Jack to the roof. Frisco fell backward onto her spine. The vehicle popped and belched flames several more times before it finally slowed and turned into just a small fire that was confined to the vehicle itself.

Jack and Remy lifted themselves from the roof and looked at one another, smiles etching slowly across each of their soot-covered faces. "That wasn't as hard as I thought it would be," Remy smiled.

Jack stared blankly at Remy for a moment before he broke into uncontrollable laughter. He put his arm around Remy's shoulder in a friendly gesture, dust billowing into small clouds as he patted him roughly. "Yeah, right," Jack finally said. He turned to see Frisco sitting up behind them, her knees to her chest as she coughed violently. Jack walked up to her, "You all right, Nikki?"

She wiped her mouth as she stood. She approached Jack and crooked her neck curiously. She then pulled back her arm and threw a punch into Jack's jaw. The connection forced Jack to stumble back into Remy. The two lost their footing and fell back onto the roof.

Remy was knocked unconscious again when Jack landed on him and his head slammed against the hard rooftop. Jack felt his head spin as he looked up to see Frisco standing over him, "Frisco?" He pleaded. "What the hell are you doing?"

She raised her foot and aimed it at Jack's face. The sole of her boot was the last thing he saw.

After that, everything for him went black.

CHAPTER 18
THE BEHEMOTH

Dr. Strommel was finally easing himself into a relaxing position, one he had not been in for quite some time, not that he had permitted himself to feel relaxed in any way. He tugged at the strap that held the Carbon Mover Device around his wrist, loosening it until it was free. He set it gently on the crate that acted as a makeshift table next to his bed. He missed his home, his mansion with its many servants and places for him to seclude himself from reality. He remembered many a night when he would escape from the constant bustle of his busy home in order to dream, tinker with his hands, find a true purpose for his thoughts. He was tired of always having to invent and create for the sole purpose of the benefit of the company, the benefit of profit. Every scientist becomes one in order to benefit humanity, it's a common thought soon bereft by greed. 'The benefit of mankind? Ha! More like the benefit of investor's wallets, bank accounts.' Sure, he made his share and lived well for it. But at what cost? He struggled to make the world better but he was a pawn in greed. Greed was what killed his partner, his friend.

His throat tightened. It hurt to remember Steinwick. How could he have turned on him the way he did. He and Steinwick went to school together; they discovered their passion for science together. Steinwick was the best man at his wedding. He was even there to console him when his beloved Evelyn died. It was during that hallowed loneliness that Strommel discovered what he could do with nanotechnology, how he could manipulate a computer no larger than an atom into doing whatever he commanded. It was there he discovered a way to bring back his wife, just as he remembered her. The nanotechnology that created autonomous sentient beings. It was then that he learned the darkness of man's desires and that ever-present factor of greed reared its ugly head. The first man who approached him when he learned about this technology was viable. He wooed Strommel and before he knew it, stole his research. Now it was nearly a decade later and Steinwick had betrayed him. The one creation he had grown to regret. When his wife began to think and reason, Strommel quickly ascertained she was calculating his death. He had begun to disappear into his own research, leading to the discovery of the portal. Steinwick, his oldest and most trusted friend was the only person he wanted to bring in to help him develop it. Unfortunately, he made another mistake, trusting another. Trust was fleeting. What did it matter anymore? Steinwick was dead. His wife was gone. Now, he was truly alone.

Or was he?

There was a low scratching sound on the other side of the open room. The loft was dark and quiet, as it had always been, as he liked it. This sound was more than noticeable. It was a sound unlike that of a rat or other vermin. It sounded more like…

"Oh no," Strommel whispered to himself, realizing the noise he heard was not good. The scratching began to grow louder, more invasive as it began to echo across the vaulted ceilings. It wasn't something that was simply a minor irritant to the room, but something that was trying to punch its way through.

Someone had activated the machine. They were coming through. "They found me," he said to himself, the shock rolling from his tongue. "I don't know how but they found me!"

Strommel began to scramble, snatching up everything he could. He pulled an empty duffel bag from under his cot and began to stuff in everything he could. He had to escape and fast.

They were coming for him. He shoved the last handful of items he grabbed and thrust them as deep into the bag as he could before zipping it closed. Strommel then ran for the door. He stopped midstride, turned on his heel and ran back to collect the wrist device. He clamped his hands around it and then returned to his sprint. The door was just ahead, only a few feet before him. He maintained his speed and held out his hand. He was going to get out the door before the air could split apart.

Too late.

The crackle of electricity jolted behind him as a small sphere appeared, floating in the center of the loft. It grew as the bolts pushed aside the reality it surrounded and revealed a dark swirling beneath the doorway. A blue liquid-like substance swirled along with the rotating energy bolts, their speed quickening as the doorway widened. Strommel froze. He wasn't quick enough to escape through the door before the first of the naked soldiers passed through the now gaping corridor. Strommel recognized the man as Lt. Crust. He stood tall, muscular, statuesque, and naked as he towered over Strommel.

"Hello, Doctor," Crust smiled wickedly. "Nice to see you again."

"No!" Strommel yelled. He began to turn and run, pulling the wrist device from his arms. He flipped open the cover and began to fumble with the controls.

Crust recognized what Strommel was doing and acted instantly. Crust leapt like an insect, springing from his back legs, at an exceptional distance, across the room over Strommel's head. He landed heavily, his feet flat as they struck the wooden floor. It shook the walls nearby, knocking a hanging picture of Strommel's wife to the floor, the glass cracking as it landed sideways. Strommel remained frozen. He knew what he was facing, what he was up against and he was afraid. Not so much for his life than for the fate of humanity. He was facing the future, quantum leaps into the future of evolution. Humanity was doomed.

"Going somewhere, doc?" Crust grinned, cocking his head like a curious bird.

Strommel didn't answer. He simple turned and headed toward the large windows on the other side of the room. It was a futile attempt, he knew it, but he had to try. Crust moved unlike any human could, running along the wall and onto the ceiling before dropping between Strommel and the window.

"I'm beginning to think you don't like me very much," Crust laughed maniacally. "But that's all right. You don't have to. I'm just here for what's rightfully ours. We want the device."

"I...I d-don't have it," Strommel lied poorly. He wrapped his arms tightly around his duffle bag, making it evident what was inside.

"Oh come on, Doctor. We're all friends here. Just give me the device and we can move on," Crust taunted.

The device. The device that cost him the death of his laboratory animal, the death of his partner, Steinwick. The device that could allow for intra-dimensional mass transport for multiple composition elements. Transportation for anything. Strommel regretted inventing these devices, this technology. He only wanted to advance humanity, and help it grow. Instead, it had been bastardized into something vulgar. If he could take it all back, he would.

"Please…just leave me alone," Strommel acted irrationally, throwing his duffle bag at Crust's face. Crust, his smile never leaving his face, brushed the bag aside before it even came close enough to hit him. As Crust deflected the bag, Strommel had already started running in the other direction.

Crust knelt and opened the bag, seeing the device he desired was no longer inside. He watched Strommel run away, the device in his hand. His smile stretched wider, he always loved a good chase. "There's no point in resisting, doc," Crust called out after him as he strode insidiously after Strommel. "We want the device and will do anything to get it."

The vortex that brought Crust into the room still sparked and swirled as it groaned loudly. The low groan soon turned into a violent cough. The lights from the edge of the opening began to surge, the lights pulsating. Someone else was coming through. There wasn't much time. Strommel had to escape and fast. Two more naked men emerged from the swirling vortex. They landed roughly on the smooth floor, their balance compromised by the teleportation.

"Get up you dolts!" Crust ordered as the two soldiers watched Strommel slink rapidly past.
They hardly moved. The first soldier slowly stood, he stumbled, and nearly toppling over before spreading his feet to keep what was left of his balance. The other soldier began to pick himself up. His thick, muscular arms shook under the weight of his own torso. A thin string of crimson flowed from his nose before his eyes rolled into the back of his head and he flopped onto his side. Dead. An aneurysm.

'*Typical*,' thought Crust. Pure carbon-based travelers always have the hardest time moving through. Crust rushed past the still stumbling soldier and bounced over the dead one as he raced after Strommel.

Strommel had a considerable head start, since Crust entrusted the new soldiers to snag him as he passed them. However, being that he eluded them, he was almost to the door. Crust was going to have to ramp up his pursuit. He began to churn his legs fast as he picked up speed to close the gap between them. Strommel fumbled with his coat pocket, his fingers stretching deeply inside, like tendrils, until they wrapped up around the thick object packed within. He slid it gently out as he strapped it around his wrist. He began to tap at it feverishly. Crust was now on top of him as he reached for the door. Crust's wide hand wrapped roughly around Strommel's shoulder. He was yanked off his feet as Crust pulled him back toward himself. Strommel's fingertips slipped from the cool metal of the door handle as he was lifted off his feet and turned around to face Crust.

"There's nowhere left to run," Crust said.

"Yes there is," Strommel brought up his hand; he aimed the device wrapped around his wrist at Crust's throat. A small needle protruding from the device sank into Crust's neck. A small, purple hued energy wave pulsed into Crust's body and travelled throughout. Crust, whose expression of triumph slowly began to melt away, soon to be replaced with that of lifelessness. His fist, gripping Strommel's shoulder fell limp. Strommel dropped the few inches he was raised to the ground, falling on his posterior. He watch as Crust's eyes rolled into the back of his head and he fell to the floor with a thud. He was dead. Strommel looked at the lifeless body and at the needle strapped to his wrist. A low-level EMP injected into Crust's body ceased his life force. The nanites were no longer able to function and maintain his life. Strommel let out a sigh of relief as he stood and went for the door. He pulled it open and prepared to flee. Instead, he ran out the door and straight into a brick wall. Or at least he thought it was a wall. Again, he found himself on his posterior. He craned his neck upward to see the massive form of Huun towering over him.

"Hello Dr. Strommel," Huun's voice boomed. "Your presence is requested."

Huun reached out with his meaty hand and hoisted Strommel off the floor. He leisurely tossed the feeble man across the room. Strommel skidded across the floor, skipping like a flat stone across the placid surface of a pond, before he disappeared into the gaping hole of the vortex.

Huun smiled. He looked at the lifeless body of Crust, "Never send a glimp to do a true soldiers job."

Huun strode across the room, stripping the clothing from his body as he moved. He then stepped into the vortex followed by the staggering soldier. The hole closed behind them, leaving the room empty and dark, a large part of the floor and wall now gone.

Like a lead weight, that's how Jack equated his head felt. It was buzzing, filled with static and confusion. He couldn't lift his head from the hard ground that rested beneath him. He found it even more difficult to open his eyelids. It was as if they were anchored by fishing lures. He forced his lids open, tearing them apart like sheets of paper, the mucus build up nearly sealing them shut. The fluttered open like a shade snapping up, rolling repeatedly until it was closed. He shifted his eyes about, assessing his situation, deciphering where he was. He hardly remembered anything from before. In fact, he didn't even know how long he had been unconscious. He looked around, his eyes alternating from clear to blurred, soaking in the surroundings. He saw girders crisscrossing above his head. They were several feet above him, marking seams and anchors in whatever structure they supported. He wanted to reach up and rub his forehead in an attempt to alleviate the pain, but he was unable to move his arm. It didn't take him long to surmise why, always the detective. He could feel the cold metal that rubbed against his flesh as he shifted slightly. He was cuffed.

Jack sat up quickly at the realization. He remembered the chase in the air with the LEHV and Huun. He remembered jumping to safety. He remembered rescuing Frisco. And he remembered her turning on him and kicking him in the face. That's all he remembered. Now here he was. But where exactly he was, he was unclear. He had been captured at some point after his becoming unconscious. He writhed and wriggled, trying to break himself free, but to no avail. He was truly trapped.

"Wh-where am I?" Jack whispered to anyone that could hear. There was no answer, although he could still only hear a buzzing in his ears. He assumed it was part of the vibration he could feel under his feet. It was a low rumble that reverberated up his legs, through his spine and up to the base of his skull where it traveled to his jaw and chattered his teeth.

The room was moving. He was on a moving vehicle. But where? And with whom?

"Jack?" A familiar voice reached out.

"Who?" Jack was startled to hear his name. "Who's there?"

"Jeez, you think you know a guy," the voice said sarcastically.

Jack twisted his neck attempting to find the source of the voice. He knew its sound, hesitant and cautious. "Remy? Remy is that you?"

"Who the hell is Remy?" The voice replied, a tinge of offense in the tone.

Jack was more confused now. He was having a hell of a time trying to find his own bearings, let alone play an infernal guessing game. "I don't have time for games!"

"No, but you always have time to intrude in my life, and destroy it," the voice sounded more familiar now.

Jack hesitated, trying to surmise why he was hearing that voice and where exactly he was, "Helix? Is that you?"

"Yes, Jack, I'm here."

"How the hell did you get here?"

"Long story. You?"

"Longer story," Jack quipped. "Tell me yours first,"

"Well, after I left you, I went back to my shop to see what was salvageable. There wasn't much left. There was a couple of goons waiting there for me, staking the place out. Before I knew it, they were after me. So I ran."

Jack felt guilty, "Sorry about that."

"Well, not much can be done now. At least I have insurance," Helix softened the news. "Hopefully I'll live long enough to file it. Anyways, I was there only a few minutes before some more goons showed up and muscled me around. I tried to get to the NULE. I tried to warn

Commissioner Lartanner, and you, but they had their meat hooks into me pretty quick-like, and I'm not one known for my speed and prowess."

Jack let out a small chuckle.

"Anyway, they roughed me up good; hit me with a brain neutralizing relaxer, which rendered me unconscious. Then next thing I know I woke up here with a roommate."

"Are you alright? Are you hurt?"

"No, I'm fine."

Jack couldn't see him, "Do you know where we are?"

"Yes, no, I'm-I'm not sure," Helix replied, confusion lacing his voice.

"Can you make anything out?"

"I see a lot of steel and I can feel the vibrations," Helix responded breathily. He sounded nervous, anxious, and afraid.

"Look," Jack said reassuringly. "Everything is gonna be alright, we're gonna get out of this, wherever we are." He lied. Or at least it felt like a lie. He didn't know if they would be all right or if they would actually get out of there. Jack tensed his muscles and stiffened his arms. He hoped he could either loosen his shackles or, at the very least, slip his hands free. No such luck.

"I made sure they were extra tight," a low voice chided from out of Jack's view.

Jack turned his head hard, straining his neck. He heard the voice, its low familiar tone. He knew it, but had to see the face just to be sure.

"What's the matter, Jack?" The voice said, sounding louder, followed by footsteps. Whoever it is was coming closer. "Don't you remember me?"

Jack adjusted his focus to look at the man circling him. The man turned his head to make himself visible.

"Zimm?!" Jack gasped. "General Varcar Zimm?!"

Zimm smiled, "I'm so glad you remember me, Jack. To think after all this time that's passed, but how could you forget, after all we've been through."

"This can't be…you're dead!"

"WAS," Zimm corrected.

"I watched you," Jack still couldn't believe what he was seeing. "I watched you fall. I saw you die."

"Yeah, funny thing about that."

"But how? How can this be?"

"I look rather dashing, don't I?" Zimm posed in parody. "Especially after having my brains smashed all over the ground."

"You're not real, you can't be." Jack's head was spinning now. His mind couldn't wrap around the atrocity he was witnessing before him. The bastardization of a man, or something else. "You were fused? Teched?"

"Teched?" Zimm snorted. "You're still so naïve Zero. I wasn't teched." He leaned into Jack's face and smiled a broad, toothy grin. "I AM tech!"

"What did you do with her?" Jack snapped angrily.

"So crass, but you always were," Zimm curled his lip nastily.

"Where's Frisco," Jack snarled back. "The woman that came in with me."

Zimm was silent. With a smile, he snapped his fingers and stepped aside. Two soldiers fell in behind Zimm. They were escorting a prisoner, who was hunched over slightly, their hands bound in front of them and a nylon hood placed loosely over their head.

"Who's that?" Jack asked.

"Does it matter?" Zimm responded coldly.

Jack pursed his lips as he looked hard at Zimm, "Is that her?"

"Whom?"

"Agent Frisco," Jack gnashed his teeth. "The woman who was with me on the roof."

"What woman?" Zimm smirked.

"What did you do to her?"

"What I did to her?" Zimm chuckled. "Shouldn't I ask what she did to you?"

Jack fell silent.

Zimm relished in Jack's discomfort, "You remember don't you? The woman you cared about. The one you fought so valiantly to save. The one who turned around and rendered you unconscious?"

Jack stewed, "Where is she?"

Zimm motioned with a short flick of his head to one of the soldier behind him. The soldier nodded silently, and walked from the room.

"What's going on?" Helix asked.

No one answered. Instead, the soldier returned followed by Frisco, who was clad in a dark blue jumpsuit that fell loosely over her body, obviously too large for her. She wore a vacant stare, emotionless and cold.

"Nikki!" Jack shouted her name, both in relief and confusion. Why had she done to him what she did? Why did it appear as if she was allying herself with the enemy, his enemy? "Nikki! It's me! It's Jack!"

Frisco didn't answer. She just continued staring at him.

"Agent Frisco's here?" Helix tried to look over his shoulder, but couldn't twist his neck far enough around to see anything. "Thank God," he added blindly.

"Nikki, c'mon, talk to me, please!" Jack pleaded.

Still nothing.

Zimm wore his smarmy grin, one Jack would have loved to have wiped from his face were he not bound. Zimm leaned up to Frisco's ear and whispered softly. Zimm moved back as Frisco seemed to become alert, her eyes still blank. She stepped up to Jack and leaned in closely. Jack could smell her breath; it had a faint hint of peppermint and coffee. Her lips were close to his, nearly touching them. Jack wanted to kiss her, find out why she was here, why she was acting as she had. He urged his neck out further in an attempt to meet her lips. But before they touched, she recoiled her arm and let loose a punch that caught Jack under his chin. His head jerked backward and slammed into the back of Remy's head. Helix yelped as he was unexpectedly forced forward, the weight of his body nearly pulling him forward to the floor, but the legs of his chair fell back to the floor as he tipped backward again.

"Ouch!" Helix sneered as he tried to shoot Jack an annoyed look. His head throbbed.

Jack shook his head and rotated his jaw in an attempt to relieve the pain. It didn't help.

"Temper, temper, Mister Zero," Zimm taunted. "You perplex me. Why would you be so obsessed with someone who obviously turned against you? Of course, you do still obsess about someone you tried to kill."

Jack felt the chills race up his spine as he stared into Zimm's cold, soulless eyes. Zimm was reveling in his apparent superiority. "It's good to see you, Jack. Zimm and Zero, together again."

"Yeah, why don't you untie me so I can give you a hug?"

Zimm threw a look to his two soldiers. They nodded and stepped away from the prisoner. Zimm approached the hunched form and wrapped his thick fingers around the hood, yanking it free. Jack held his breath, anticipating seeing Frisco's apologetic face, but instead was looking into the tear soaked eyes of Ceinwen Sagorsky.

"Winnie?!" Jack tried to free himself, pushing against his bonds with all his might. "Let her go!"

"There's that temper again," Zimm paced around Jack's chair. "You really should learn to govern your emotions. They will be your undoing."

"You know something you're absolutely right," Jack said calmly. "Maybe you should untie me so I can thank you for the advice."

"J-Jack," Ceinwen's voice trembled with fear. She did her best to hold back her tears. "I'm sorry. They were dressed as police officers. They said you were in trouble and told me you needed my help. I...I had to go with them."

"Did they hurt you?"

She shook her head as she held back her sobs despite the tears that flowed regardless.

Zimm snickered. He walked up to Ceinwen, his face nearly pressed against hers as he circled her, like a predator toying with its prey. She was afraid, Jack could see her bulging eyes and crinkled brow, hear her heavy breathing. Tears began to flow down her cheeks. Zimm, his eyes locked on Jack, brought up his hand and traced her cheek.

"Get your hands off her!"

"She's lovely, Zero," Zimm threw a look back at the frozen Frisco. "They both are. You have good taste. Although I would say, they're both out of your league. Ladies as dignified as these two would want something that wasn't so…repugnant."

"You would know what scum is," Jack retorted.

Zimm cocked his head playfully as he stepped from Ceinwen. He held up his hand and his skin rippled slightly. It continued up his arm and along his body, repeating as it traveled along his torso. His fingers slowly shrank as they disappeared into his hand before changing. Jack couldn't believe what he was seeing. Zimm's hand was transforming into something else. His hand began to break apart, turning into thousands of tiny spheres that rolled with sentience around a central point. Before long, they began to spiral into a small cyclonic funnel. The spheres reformed into a claw-like shape. Zimm held them up to his face wickedly, and then reached out toward Jack.

"Shit," Jack let slip. He felt fear; unlike he had felt for a long time.

Zimm clamped the newly formed claw-hand shut, the sound of snapping metal made Jack flinch. Zimm laughed hard and then walked behind Jack. "Don't be such a ninny, Jack. I'm not going to kill you, not yet anyway. You're still very important to us." Zimm brought his hand down to Jack's wrists and his claw snipped the restraints holding Jack. They clattered to the floor. Jack quickly shot up from his chair and turned to face Zimm. Zimm raised his hands innocently; his palms outward, the claw-hand reforming back into its original shape. "Easy Zero, no need to try and be a hero again."

Jack looked over at Ceinwen. But she was gone. Frisco was gone too. He tried to shake his sympathy for Frisco. She had turned on him; after all, he had done for her. After what they shared. It didn't matter. She didn't matter. Not now. Ceinwen was all that he needed to concern himself. "Where is Ceinwen?" Jack asked desperately. "Where did you take her?"

"In due time," Zimm offered a snake-like reply. "Like I said, I still need you. Better to have a little insurance to make sure you cooperate."

"I want to see her. NOW!"

"You are in a position unsuitable to give orders," Zimm hissed.

Jack had heard that before. Zimm was serious and Jack needed to listen. "To hell with it," Jack ignored his intuition and lunged at Zimm. He quickly threw a left hook, a certain swing that would clock Zimm right across his cheek. However, Jack never felt the connection he made. Instead,

Zimm's face broke apart, much in the same way his hand did previously. Jack's fist passed through Zimm's face as if it were made of smoke. The tiny spheres that made up Zimm's appearance disassembled and reassembled almost instantly behind Jack's fist. Jack nearly spun around and fell over from the momentum of the swing. He rubbed his tender wrists gently. They had been reddened from the shackles. Although his pride was stinging far more deeply. He was staring in what was once the face of his superior, now a different man, if he were even a man. "What the hell are you?"

"I'm the next evolution," Zimm replied.

'He wasn't real. He couldn't be,' Jack thought. 'But his fist sure was.' Solid, hard. It hurt as it connected with Jack's face, cutting across his cheek and knocking Jack to the ground unconscious.

Jack awoke with a metallic taste in his mouth. He smacked his lips; they were dried and chapped. He licked them with his tongue in an attempt to moisten them. He tasted the dried blood that collected along the bottom edge of his lower lip. He felt groggy as he slowly began to wake, his eyes too heavy to open right away. Images flashed in his mind. Images of faces from his past, especially the face of General Varcar Zimm. He remembered having a conversation with him; it felt like only moments ago. 'But Zimm was dead. Wasn't he?' It was a dream; it had to have been. He dreamt his fist passed through Zimm's face. How could that have been real?

His head hurt. He brought his hand up to rub the pain and felt a large goose egg on the side of his head. It was tender and felt sore to the touch. He then remembered the punch from his dream. It was just a dream right? The pain in his head that lingered from Zimm's fist. Still just a dream?

"Welcome back," came that harsh, low voice. "I was hoping I didn't hit you too hard. I wouldn't want you to miss the show again."

"This can't be real."

Zimm smiled, "Oh its real. As real as I am standing before you."

The floor that they stood on suddenly became uneven, leaning slightly to the right. Jack lost his footing and stumbled. Others in the room fell almost completely, except for Zimm. Zimm stood stoic, unmoving and unflinching as the room around him shifted. The floor just as quickly evened out. While others picked themselves up and rediscovered their footing, Zimm only smiled, still unmoving.

He wasn't real. At least not in the way Jack remembered him. "Where are we?" Jack asked.

"You're aboard the mother ship of the HART," Zimm beamed. "We call it the Behemoth."

He raised his arms in triumph, reveling in the size of the machine. Jack craned his neck to look around the room. It was incredible in its girth and mammoth stature. The room was hundreds of feet in both width and height. There were another two levels above them, not enclosed, but open, a grated balcony encircling the walls above him. Railings traced along each of the balconies. It was speckled by several armed soldiers, all dressed in black and carrying large weapons. At the ceiling were crisscrossed girders of iron that reinforced the massive structure.

Jack was impressed, but he didn't want to show it. This was not just some airship. This was a floating citadel. An amazing construct of both practicality and monstrosity. It was all of the fears he had perceived come true. A gigantic beast designed for one purpose: to destroy. A vehicle like this in the hands of a man like Zimm made it all the more dangerous. Encircling the room were large panes of glass that stretched from just above floor to the first set of rafters and surrounded the structure on opposite sides. Jack could see the clear night sky as the stars twinkled in the rich black canvas. The moon was full as it crept into view. He could see the lights of the city below them, glowing brightly, like the embers of a fire. They were coming from offshore, drifting slowly into the city limits. He imagined how he had gotten to where he was. His head was still ringing. He twisted his neck uncomfortably around, trying to see more of what surrounded him.

"Where's Winnie?" Jack asked.

"Are you still harping on about that?" Zimm said. "You always had a one-track mind."

"Where is she Zimm?"

Zimm cocked an eyebrow, "I don't care for your tone, Lieutenant."

Jack was growing annoyed at Zimm's indifference. He wanted badly to hurt Zimm. Jack grimaced and gnashed his teeth, the anger in his stomach boiling. He wanted to throttle Zimm, worse than he had been before, this time he wanted to savor in his pain. Jack drew back his fist and launched it at Zimm. Zimm stood motionless as he watched Jack lunge at him. As Jack's fist came flying forward it was stopped. Not by Zimm, but instead by a wall; or at least it felt like a wall. In reality, it was a massive chest, one that belonged to an even more massive foil, that of Huun.

Huun growled.

"Hi," Jack said wryly while discreetly shaking the pain from his fist.

Zimm laughed, "He still hasn't forgiven you, you know."

"I can give him a few new reasons to hate me if he steps aside, Zimm."

"That's General Zimm to you Lieutenant," Zimm snarled. "Until you can begin showing a bit of respect, I have no time for your clout in making demands."

"Oh come now, General," rang a voice from above, its tone echoing across the high ceiling, "Must you continue to tease our guest? He's not a toy to play with, you know."

Jack turned, knowing who he was about to see, "Senator Glorm."

"Jack my boy, I wish I could say it's good to see you again," Glorm smiled, his arms opened wide. Glorm was dressed in a full tuxedo, looking dapper and neat. He was straightening his cuffs as he walked down a spiraled staircase, his sleek shoes clicking as he skipped down. "But I am glad we at least get to see one another again, I wish it were under more comfortable circumstances."

"Like your funeral?" Jack shot back.

Glorm smiled wide, amused by Jack's flippant remark. Zimm was less than amused. "Or yours?" Zimm shot back.

"General, play nice," Glorm continued to smile at Jack. "No need to continue making it blatantly obvious, but he just doesn't seem to like you. Can't say I blame him. You did kill him once, quite barbarically I might add. Besides, you aren't a very likeable person. Even you must admit that."

"I knew it. Somehow I knew you were involved in all this," Jack claimed. "It's typical, predictable really. All politicians are underhanded and slimy in some way. But you I always hoped were different. You talked a good game, made people believe again. Hope again. I just never thought you'd sell yourself and your soul to a bunch of second hand crooks."

"HA!" Zimm snorted. "You of all people should know I am far more than just an average hood."

"Not much can be said of your associates, Zimm," Jack thumbed toward Huun.

Huun grunted.

"Down boy," Glorm warned Huun. "In good time." He turned his attention back to Jack, "Politician or not, everyone's for sale. Just not to everyone. Why would I ally myself with such abysmal company? Me?"

Jack scoffed, "Why that's easy, you're for sale to the highest bidder."

Glorm chortled, "Of course the money is important. I'm corrupt, not stupid. But what you fail to realize what we represent, what we are trying to do, and how important it is."

"I know what you are, you're all nuts."

"So closed minded, blinded by the lies they feed you," Glorm said disdainfully. "It's that lack of vision that prevents the real saviors to rise up and seize power. Instead, we're forced to hide like vermin and strike from the shadows, painted into horrible monsters by the popular media. Fortunately, that's all about to change."

"You're deluded, just like Zimm had always has been," Jack retorted.

"Delusions are created by those with weak minds," Glorm said smoothly. "We are building a reality. A future that will reestablish this country back to the glory it once was."

"All we need is a way in," Zimm walked to the window that surrounded the front of the zeppelins controls. He looked over the dark sky that enveloped them; a thin layer of clouds scraped the edges of the window as they passed. He drew in a deep breath. "Glorm is our way. With a nation in turmoil, faith shaken in their current president, this country is hungry for new leadership. Glorm was approached years ago, groomed to be the ultimate people's politician. He scoffs at the big conglomerates while they unknowingly line his pockets. The populace trust him, he's perfect, a shoe in for the election."

"When he wins, we're in," Huun growled.

"And we win," Glorm rubbed his hands together hungrily.

It all made Jack ill, his stomach queasy. He couldn't believe this was happening under the nose of the public. The trust they threw to their elected officials who, in the public eye, ensured they did what their constituents asked and desired, but behind closed doors, they become involved in underhanded, seedy, and even villainous undertakings. Trust, it meant nothing to them. He fought to protect that very fragile component of human freedom, only to realize it was all for nothing. They destroyed whatever faith he once had in this country.

"What exactly do you hope to accomplish?" Jack finally managed to ask.

"Accomplish?" Glorm was confused by the query.

"With the HART? What do you hope they will give you?"

"Me?" Glorm thought for a moment. "They've given me all I need. Fame. Fortune. It smiles on those most fortunate. Who care what happens to the rest of the world. I get what I want; they get what they want. What does it matter what happens to the little people. They just need to be coddled into believing I'm looking out for their best interest. I tell them that I'll preserve their rights, abide by the constitution; they can have their guns and whatever else, but in reality, I lull them in and then snare them without them even knowing it."

Jack wanted to wretch, "A perfect plan."

"Almost."

Huun stood tall, "And then along came you, Zero, again."

"You have an unsettling way of always getting in the way, even when I repeatedly told you not to," Glorm shook his head unapprovingly. "It's no wonder you aren't able to keep a job."

"I'm not a liar like you!"

"We're all liars," Glorm said smoothly. "Some of us are just much better at it. It's those of us who succeed more than others like you."

"Succeed?" Jack scoffed. "More like cheated."

"Always the boy scout," Zimm snickered. "Grow up, Zero."

"So I can be more like you?"

Zimm shot back, "So you can survive!" Zimm stepped up to Jack and pushed his face into Jack's. Jack could smell the stale, rotted meat that still hung on his breath. Zimm seethed, "I always had high hopes for you, Zero, but you always let me down."

"Good," Jack spat.

"You were the one I wanted by my side, the one I wanted to be there when I helped take over the world, but instead you wanted to do what was right. Look where it got you."

"Look where your way got you," Jack retorted. "Smeared all over the concrete."

"NO!" Zimm shouted in rage. "It made me this! Stronger, smarter, and better than any mere mortal man. I am invincible, I am forever!" He took a step back, "Do you think you can stop me?"

"I did once."

"General," Glorm interrupted. "This is all very fascinating, but I don't care to see you both continue in this pissing match. We have work to continue." Glorm shouted an order into a large curved funnel-like brass tube, "Pilot?"

"Yessir," came a metallic response.

"Adjust heading to approved coordinates," Glorm continued.

"Aye, sir," the pilot replied.

Jack could feel the floor vibrate more rapidly. His equilibrium also adjusted. He had to space his feet apart wider to keep himself from falling over. "What is this?"

Glorm beamed, "This amazing behemoth is a one of kind air vessel. This dirigible is the flagship of the HART."

Jack recalled overhearing the conversation Glorm and Frisco had within Lartanner's office. He wondered if all that was an act, that Glorm had supplied the information to the FBI in order to control them and their information. It wouldn't surprise him. Glorm was slippery, underhanded.

"What are you planning?" Jack asked; probing for answers, he knew Glorm couldn't resist.

Glorm accepted the bait, "Planning? Oh, nothing more than just a little reorganization, that's all."

"Reorganization?"

"Oh come now, you don't expect me to believe you, a man who once served his country, at one time nobly I might add, of course before your dishonorable discharge," Glorm threw a look at Zimm who glared menacingly. "That you are not disenfranchised at the state of our world. Poverty has become the hot button of this now global economy. Crime is on the rise, you know that the average middle-class family is engaged in nearly twenty acts of felony within a six month period?"

Jack shook his head, half listening to Glorm prattle on and half looking for a way out.

Glorm continued, "The statistics are staggering. Our world's morality is unraveling at an astonishing rate. With the current climate, it's believed that crime will consume the Earth in a matter of years. Before the end of this decade, eight out of ten households will be engaged in some form of illegal activity."

"That's, um, interesting," Jack answered aloofly, his eyes snapping back to look at Glorm.

Glorm narrowed his gaze before he began again. "Interesting?" Glorm sounded annoyed. "This is the fear that wakes me up in the middle of the night. Our world is crumbling. We are at the threshold of another Saddam and Gomorrah. Anarchy. The world as we know it is over. It's time for a new regime to step in."

Jack's eyes traced the rafters that stretched across the cabin, wide enough to walk across and the struts and supports ample enough to shield them from the inevitable onslaught of gunfire that will rain down on them. His eyes followed to a radio room and a ladder that led up the side. It was concealed to give him enough time to climb it before they started shooting. He just had to get Helix to join him. He's not much of team player, especially when death is a factor. It didn't matter. "And let me guess, you're just the man to do it."

"You have someone else in mind?" Glorm flashed his famous toothy grin. "You perhaps?"

Jack threw his head back and laughed loudly. He used the thrust generated from the movement to pull at his bindings around his wrists. The plastic fastener slipped slightly.

"Something amusing, Mister Zero?"

"Just funny, the idea of you being in control," Jack looked around the room his eyes falling on Huun and the Zimm. "Something tells me you won't be in control. I'm willing to bet you won't have any control once they sink their claws in."

"You truly lack vision, Jack," Glorm licked his lips as he spoke. "This isn't about one man in control; it's about all men in control. We are the salvation of this broken world."

"Well, I know from experience, you don't want to lay your trust into the hands of these two here, they're more apt to leave you behind than to help better mankind."

"Shut up!" Huun roared.

"We'll see," Glorm stepped away.

Jack continued to wriggle his wrists, sliding the fastener lower on his hands. It wedged when it reached his thumb. '*Damn*,' he thought. He tucked his thumb in toward his palm. He then, subtly pulled again at the fastener; he began to slowly, and painfully, move his hand further through.

"What are you doing leaving him up here?" Huun growled at Glorm, shoving his face at Glorm until they were nose to nose.

Glorm pushed Huun back with a single finger, "I'd step back if I were you. You'll wrinkle my suit."

Huun sneered and roughly wrapped his thick fingers around Glorm's neatly pressed lapel. He yanked him forward, lifting him off his feet, "Watch what you say, fancy man!"

"Huun!" Zimm snapped. "Let him go."

Huun hesitated, his anger stewing deep in the pit of his stomach. He finally opened his meaty hand and let Glorm loose. Glorm stepped back, his expression unchanged. He smoothed out his jacket and stepped back. He stopped when he reached Zimm, "You'd better keep your pet under control. I'd hate to have to reprogram him."

"You can't leave him up here, Zero's too dangerous!" Huun interjected angrily, still demanding to be heard.

"He's right," Zimm said to Glorm. "We can't trust leaving him up here, if you're all finished talking with him, we should return him to his cell."

Glorm looked at Zimm and then at Jack. He nodded, "Very well, take him back."

"I'll do it!" Huun glared viciously at Jack.

"No!" Glorm snapped. He turned to Frisco who continued her blank stare. "Let her do it."

Zimm nodded in compliance. Jack pulled his wrists up into his sleeves and balled his hands into fists, attempting to conceal the fastener he loosened. "Get him out of here," Zimm ordered Frisco as he waved his hand in Jack's direction.

Frisco nodded hypnotically. She drew up her rifle and aimed it at Jack's midsection.

"Nikki," Jack spoke to her, using the name she had openly despised. "Nikki, listen to me, you don't have to do this."

"Let it go, Zero," Zimm smiled. "She doesn't hear you."

"What the hell did you do to her?"

"Do?" Glorm chimed in. "We didn't do anything to her. She's just been...activated."

"Activated?"

"Agent Frisco is one of many sleeper drones."

"Sleeper?"

"Agent Frisco has been an agent of the HART for many years, since we created her."

Jack looked at Frisco, puzzled; her blank expression chilled him. "What do you mean created? She's a nan-droid?"

"Not at all. She's flesh and blood. Frisco is one of many beings generated in a lab," Zimm explained proudly. "When the HART began nearly a century ago, after failed attempts at world domination, it was conceived that in order to achieve their goal, they needed to plant men, and women, in positions of influence. Several children born of influential family lineage were sent to live as regular people. Each of their children were selected and fused, making them accessible to the HART whenever called upon. Each of them placed with a predetermined destiny, ensuring they would be able to be implanted into prominent placements throughout society. Lawmen, government officials," he smiled at Frisco. "Frisco is one of many, just like Huun here, and your dear senator. They were created to help save this world."

"From what?" Jack probed as he tried to hide his shock.

"From itself."

"And you?" Jack snapped at Glorm.

Glorm cracked a small grin, "Me? What of me?"

"Are you a drone?"

"Don't be ridiculous, Zero," Glorm snickered. "To be in true power, one must be conscious of that power. Besides, I didn't need convincing to join. My family was a part of the HART since the beginning. We're what you would call, royalty."

"I can think of something else to call you," Jack growled.

"Make him gone," Glorm waved his hand.

Frisco pressed the muzzle of her rifle into Jack's back. The hard metal dug deeply into his flesh as she shoved him roughly until he started walking. The large, cavernous hallway they passed through echoed the clanking and clicking of their footsteps against the metal grating loudly.

"This is a bit awkward, isn't it?" Jack asked.

Frisco continued pushing Jack forward. The jabs were beginning to hurt as she pushed harder against his ribs each time.

"Fine," Jack tried to ignore the biting pain. "Don't speak. I'll just talk for both of us. How was your day? Mine? Fine. Yours? Well, I raced in a flying car to save a friend; at least I think she is my friend, which almost crashed by the way. Then I was leaping between two flying cars, hundreds of miles above the city, mind you, only to save this friend who then turned around and kicked me in the face." Jack turned to look at Frisco's face, hoping to see a reaction of some kind. Nothing. "I thought maybe this would give us an opportunity to talk, maybe you can explain yourself," Jack tried again.

Still no response.

"Dammit Nikki! Talk to me! What the hell has happened to you?

Why are you doing this? Speak!"

Frisco stopped. For a moment, Jack though maybe he had gotten through to her, reached her. He was wrong. She reacted. She lowered her rifle and wrapped her free hand tightly around Jack's throat. She lifted him off the grating and pressed him against the wall about four inches off the ground. Jack gasped and choked for air as he kicked his feet, trying to find his footing.

"The Master is all powerful and all knowing. He is my savior. He is my champion. I will give my life for him," Frisco spoke in a low, monotone pace.

"Who...who's the m-master?" Jack spat out through his constricted esophagus.

Frisco opened her hand and dropped Jack to the floor. He coughed and gagged as he rubbed his throat to try to ease the pain. It worked on his throat, but not his heart. He risked everything to save her from Huun, only to have it all come crashing down. Why had she done this? Why had she turned on them? On him? What had Glorm meant when he explained about sleeper drones? Could it be true? Could she really be something else?

"I know you're still in there, Nikki," Jack rasped. "No matter what they did to you, I know it's you in there."

Frisco grabbed his shoulder and shoved him forward, her newfound strength evident. "You know not what is coming," she lazed.

"What is coming?"

"The Great Equinox," was all she said before returning to her blank stare.

'*The Equinox?*' Jack thought. "So we have to be prepared for equal day and night?"

She didn't respond. She stopped in front of his cell door. She opened it and waited for him to enter.

Jack started to walk in, stopping as he crossed the threshold, "What about Remy? Did you kill him?" She pushed him inside. Jack stumbled over his own feet from the force of her thrust. She sure had become strong. She looked down unflinchingly at Jack, her hands balled into fists. She was through with him. Jack turned and prepared to face off with a woman to whom he had grown attracted. They were becoming closer, just like the time they shared a kiss. That time seemed so far away. Now he was backing away from her, she was ready to attack. All this in a matter on a few hours. Jack stood to face her. He placed is hands behind his back.

"I'm not going to fight you," Jack said calmly.

She didn't flinch.

"You can do what you want to me, I won't fight you," Jack continued.

He stepped back from Frisco slowly. She didn't hesitate as she lunged toward Jack. Jack closed his eyes, preparing to allow Frisco to do what she felt she must. Instead of feeling her fists throttling his face, he only heard a loud thud. Jack waited for a moment. Nothing seemed to be stirring. He slowly opened his eyes. Before him, Frisco was lying sprawled out across the floor. Standing over her was Helix, panting, holding a metal rod loosely, but wearing an expression Jack had never seen on him before; rage.

"Helix?" Jack asked. "What did you do?"

"Put her to sleep for a little while."

"Will she be alright?"

"Oh yeah, she'll be fine," Helix dropped the metal rod in his hand. It clattered on the floor. "I rigged this metal leg from the chair to emit a low level charge," Helix explained through each heavy breath. "I took a little wiring from the binding they had around my wrists and was able to charge it magnetically. When I applied it to the chair I was able to enhance the charge and whammo!"

"Whammo?"

"She's programmed, dude," Helix said. "Look, I could hear them talking."

Jack looked at Helix oddly.

"Hey, I've been here for over a day, and these walls are like paper," Helix said. "They program all these people, like when they are kids, you know. Once they are set, they begin the programming. It's the best way to explain it, like an infection. They pump you full of nan-droids and fzzzt, instant soldier."

"Can they come out of it?" Jack asked, looking down at Frisco's lovely face.

"I guess, I dunno, I guess they can be reprogrammed. Maybe."

"Or deprogrammed?"

Helix shrugged.

"You think you can do it?"

Helix raised an eyebrow playfully, "If it runs on ones and zeros I can do it."

Jack put his hand on Helix's shoulder, "No time like the present to get started then."

Helix's expression twisted, now unsure of himself, "With her?"

"I think you can handle her," Jack grinned.

"What are you gonna do?"

"First I'm gonna find Winnie, then I'm gonna crash this ship," Jack slipped out the door.

Helix watched him leave, his heart sinking. This didn't sound promising. He looked down at the unconscious body of Agent Frisco. He swallowed hard as he knelt down next to her, "Here goes nothing."

Jack crept softly across the metal floor, walking heel to toe to muffle the sound of his hard-soled shoes. There were soldiers and guards lining every hallway. The walkways and hallways were lined with series of doors, each leading to either an office, technical room, or sleeping quarters. Jack sneaked his way along each corridor, trying to find the control room. As Jack slinked slowly along an adjacent hallway, he saw a small platoon of soldiers, armed and in formation, marching militantly along the metal walkway, their boots clinking noisily as they tapped in unison. Jack dove into the open door nearest to him. He scrambled to duck into the shadows and keep himself out of view. The sound of their clicking heels and the rattle of their rifles was a sound he remembered all too well from his military service.

"Commander Huun wants us to take prisoner Zero to the lower decks," the lead soldier stated.

"Is it another private execution?" Asked another soldier.

"Possibly," the lead soldier replied. "As long as I get to instill the punishment."

The laughed as they marched past the room where Jack kept hidden. He watched their boots from under the gap in the door, waiting until they went completely by, and then made his way out. Execution? He thought. Looks like Zimm was finally finished with him. The soldier did say the order came from Huun. Perhaps Huun was overstepping his bounds and defying his superior's orders? That would not go over well with Zimm. Jack knew how Zimm reacted when anyone went over his head to defy his orders. He smiled to himself. He would love to see Huun get his, no matter who it was delivering the punishment.

Jack emerged slowly from the shadows. He looked about the room. It was a small munitions locker, housing small firearms laid out neatly on several racks. Jack grinned like a schoolchild getting an A on his paper. He quickly collected a handgun and released the chamber to inspect the clip. He was quite skilled at doing this, having plenty of experience. His stomach dropped when the cartridge slid into his waiting hand. Empty. Well almost, there were three bullets still inside. He searched the room quickly, looking for any available rounds. Nothing. They must keep them in a different room. Typical play by Zimm. 'Never keep your munition with your weapons,' he often reminded his troops. That way no one can get the upper hand if they uncover one of those rooms. Jack didn't have much choice. He tucked the gun into his waistband. It would have to do. He needed to put down Zimm, Huun, and whoever was calling the shots, this so-called Master. Three bullets would have to do.

Suddenly, another round of clacking boot heels echoed across the high ceiling and along the metal rafters. Another patrol was coming through, or worse, a regiment sent to find him. Jack was holding out hope that no one knew that he was missing.

Helix scratched at his thick beard that hugged the sides of his face. His skin was beginning to hurt. He had been scratching for so long he thought his beard was going to start falling out. He was still staring at the unconscious form of Agent Frisco, except he had moved her onto the other chair that still had all its legs. She sat loosely, her limbs sagging low at her sides as he torso slumped forward, her chin pressed into her chest. Helix knelt down beside her. He lifted her head with his finger under her chin and looked over her face. He then propped her head back and then pried one of her eyes open. Amidst her vapid stare, he could see hints of copper coloring aligning the blue color of her iris. The particles shone in the sunlight that bore in through the high, barred window way above their heads. When the light hit her eyes, the colors swirled and danced about wildly.

Helix raised an eyebrow curiously. He was beginning to get an idea of how these machines worked. But how could he reprogram her? The door to the cell clicked loudly. A key being slid into the lock and released. Someone was coming in, and he was sure it wasn't Jack. What was he going to do? It was only him, and of course the all but conscious Frisco. He wasn't prepared to handle a guard. He had to think fast. In that flash of a moment, he turned Frisco's chair around.

The door to the room holding the prisoners creaked as it was pushed open. The guard removed the key from the lock and clicked the large ring, with several keys jingling about, onto his belt. He carried in his one hand a tray of food, consisting of two small bowls of a gray stew, the steam leaving wispy trails into the air, along with small slices of bread.

"What's going on in here?" The guard looked down at Helix who was seated in his chair, his arms bound behind his back. The back of his chair was pressed to the back of the chair behind him. In that chair was another prisoner, that prisoner looked unconscious. "What's wrong with him?"

Helix threw his glance over his shoulder, "Who? Him?"

"Yeah," The guard nodded suspiciously. "What's wrong with Zero?"

"Oh, he just fell asleep," Helix smiled.

"So wake him," The guard eyed Helix with deeper reservations.

"Well, perhaps I should give him some time, he only fell asleep a few minutes ago, I'm sure he's tired."

"He doesn't look asleep to me," the guard looked closer at the body behind Helix; it didn't move or appear to be breathing. He began to walk toward it cautiously.

Helix stuttered nervously, "Um, no, I'm sure he's alright. He's just sleeping, is all."

"We'll see about that," the guard set down the tray of food and walked toward the lolled body. As he walked around the two bound prisoner's he kept his gaze on the unconscious prisoner behind Helix. As soon as he rounded to see the prisoner's face, it became evident, "That's not the prisoner!"

The guard turned around as Helix stood up from his chair, which immediately toppled over from the missing leg. Helix held the chair leg high and brought it down in a crushing blow onto the guards head. The loud, deadened clunk echoed across the room and out into the hallway. The guard fell to the floor in a crumpled mass. Helix looked down at the guard's body and then at the chair leg he held, once again, in his hand. "This thing is getting pretty damn useful."

He closed the door, picked up a wedge of bread from the food tray, and took a big bite. He then returned to his work of attempting to fix Frisco. He sure hoped Jack appreciated all this.

The regiment of guards patrolling the walkways and gantries surrounding the behemoth's interior continued. Jack pressed up against the wall behind the door that was pushed open by the two curious guards that were sent to inspect the weapon's room.

Jack kept still; quiet.

The two guards stepped slowly over the threshold, looking about the small room quickly.

Jack could see their backs as they entered deeper into the room. The tips of their guns stretched out before them as they poked them through first. Jack turned his head to his left; he could see a small gap between the wall and one of the tall gun cabinets. He slinked slowly toward it, trying to maintain his undetectable presence.

However, sometimes, that wasn't enough.

The sound of the pistol tucked into the back of his pants scraped against the metal wall behind him. Jack closed his eyes in disappointment, knowing he had given himself away. "Shit," he whispered to himself.

The two guards leapt forward and prepared to train their weapons onto the noise. Jack was prepared, or at the very least, ready to strike. Jack immediately lunged at the men, his hands wrapping around the barrels of both men's rifles. Jack felt the warmth in his arm intensify as he lifted up and pushed the guns into each of the guard's faces. The hard metal slammed violently against their flesh and bone. The first guard was hit square in the nose and across his mouth. His nose made a sickening crack as it split, followed by the crunch of his teeth shattering against the steel. The other guard managed to turn his head, but took the brunt of the impact against the side of his face. His cheek broke open and his neck jerked back hard before he dropped to the floor on top of his partner.

Jack stood over their bodies, holding a rifle in each hand. He looked at them and then slung one across his back. He then pushed both bodies aside before adorning one of their uniforms, which happened to be a bit large, a small price to pay since the other was too small. He then walked to the door and made his way out, walking prominently in order to blend in as best he could. He made his way to the nearest set of stairs and ascended, keeping his mission for finding the control room foremost in his mind.

CHAPTER 17
AT THE MERCY OF EVIL

Dr. Strommel was forced to his knees, Huun's weight pressing down on his shoulders. He groaned and moaned under the pain that shot from his shoulders and down into his knees. Strommel's pain pleased him, as Huun grinned to himself.

Strommel looked around as he tried to ignore the pain that chewed into his limbs and around his back to the thick fingers that squeezed his tender shoulders. He saw the massive computer screens and boards that traced the walls of the room. The lights on the switchboards blinked on and off in a devout syncopation that appeared like a choreographed dance. When the lights were all bunched together, it reminded Strommel of looking at a city at night from the sky. The thrum of the machines filled the room with a soft din that soothed and eased his tormented soul.

The control room, he deduced. Not the place he thought would be the last he would ever see. Huun leaned forward harder against Strommel's frame, crimping his spine. He winced again, sucking air in through his bloodstained teeth.

Zimm paced before Strommel in his weakened posture, his arms behind his back, fingers laced. "Now you will tell me what I want to know, or you will be forced to."

Strommel scoffed defiantly, "There's nothing you can do to me that will make me talk. You forced me to do your work once! You destroyed my home! My wife! What more do you think you can do to me? So who's going to make me talk? You?"

Zimm smiled, "Of course not." He walked to the door at the far side of the room. He pressed the pressure plate at the edge of the door and it slid open. Strommel's jaw dropped as he saw his Evelyn Strommel enter the room. She wore a tight fitting white dress that showed each muscle in her body flex and pop as she took one-step after slinky step. Her ebony hair bounced along her shoulders as her eyes, transfixed on that of her husband's, bore deeply, burning and filled with a hidden desire.

She was gorgeous.

It was difficult for Strommel to ignore her, as much as he wanted to avert his eyes.

This was not his wife and he knew that.

"Hello darling," her voice was like satin, smooth and silky. "I missed you."

Strommel swallowed hard.

Evelyn placed her finger under Strommel's chin and lifted his head up to look at her. "What's wrong, dear?"

"You're not my wife," he shot back defiantly.

She drew her finger back toward herself, her long nail scratching Strommel's skin lightly. She pouted her lips, "Ouch, that hurts, my love. Besides, you created me."

"Not like this I didn't."

"Oh but you did," Evelyn challenged. "In fact, it was you who allowed my own neural sensors to allow my programming to be altered by my own observations. You allowed me to see this world as it truly is, through that I found my true calling."

"Calling? Destroying the human race? You're monsters."

She threw back her head and laughed, "Monsters? We're nothing more than shadows of your own conscious. You created us and we're the monsters?"

"I never meant for you to become like this, you were supposed to...to...," Strommel couldn't finish his words.

"To be what? You're wife? Your slave? At your disposal? To please you when you so desired? I am not mere flesh and blood. I am more than that now!"

Strommel turned his head away. It angered her, "But I am more human that you want to admit. You yourself were compelled to include the actual DNA of your wife to...complete me. Each of us still harbors our hosts DNA. That was your idea; you said you wanted us to be more human, didn't you?" She grew more enraged, "Look at me!"

Strommel refused, keeping his gaze at the floor. Evelyn stomped up to him, rage consuming her. She drew back her hand and let it loose. It connected against Strommel's cheek with a crack. Strommel fell backward, landing awkwardly as his bound hands kept him from catching himself. He rolled onto his side as he tried to straighten out his legs. They bent in ways he was certain they shouldn't. Two guards behind him stepped forward and helped him back up to his knees.

"You shouldn't defy me," Evelyn hissed. "I could kill you."

"That's why I left."

"You're a coward."

"No, I'm a survivalist, like any human. I would do anything I could to keep you from getting what you wanted."

Evelyn's once twisted expression fell and was replaced by a sweet, gentle smile, "You will give us what we want."

"Not while my heart still beats in my chest," Strommel sneered.

She leaned in closely, "Then maybe I'll tear it out and show it to you."

Zimm stepped between her and Strommel, "Alright, all this foreplay is getting rather annoying. We get it, Strommel, you created us, we owe you that."

"They made me create you," Strommel shot at Zimm. "I never wanted anything to do with someone like you."

"But you did. Like all humans, your weakness is greed. You missed your wife when she died from cancer. You wanted her back, so you did the only thing you knew how to do. You built her anew. When my master learned about your bastard invention, of course he contacted you. And you agreed for a hefty sum. "

"I never did it for the money," Strommel snapped. "I'm a scientist, I wanted to prove we could improve on mankind, make us better. Instead you took my invention and twisted it, creating these hollow, dark, mirrored images of mankind."

"You created Gods!" Zimm roared.

"And I can destroy you!" Strommel threatened.

The room broke into laughter. Zimm's was the loudest. "You have courage, Dr. Strommel, albeit a bit misguided, but you do have it. But courage doesn't do you much good if it gets you killed."

"I'd rather die than give you the device!"

Huun interjected, "Don't worry, you will."

"Now, now Commander," Zimm stepped up to Huun. "Let's not be too hasty. The good doctor is going to share with us everything we need to know."

"And why would I do that?"

"If you don't, the death of millions of innocent humans will be on your hands."

Zimm's expression was haunting, filled with wicked sincerity and malice. He was serious.

"You can't make me," Strommel swallowed hard. "Their deaths will be on your hands, not mine."

"You think so?" Zimm snapped his fingers. Almost immediately two guards entered ushering in a soldier, his feet dragging like weights behind him. The soldier, still clad in his dark fatigues, screamed defiantly, pleading to be let free. The two guards dragged him forcefully, their arms yoked under the frightened man's shoulders. Zimm approached the man slowly, his poise stoic. He reached out with his hand and ran it across the top of the whimpering man's hair. The hair collected in wads between his fingers as they moved through. As Zimm's hand crested at the top of the pathetic soldier's head, he balled his hand into a fist, grabbing the hair and yanking the man's head back. The soldier yelped timidly, trying to repress his anguish as best he could. The young soldier, his name badge read: 'FORWING,' wore an expression of sheer terror. He was afraid, as well he should be. Forwing was caught the night before attempting to go AWOL. When he enlisted in the military, it was to serve his country and help his fellow man. His parents encouraged him to enlist. He wasn't ready for college or to start a career, he wanted to see the world and this was the best option available. Forwing visited the recruitment center for the United Global Front, a worldwide peacekeeping organization. However, before he could even walk in, another recruiter intercepted him and talked him into enlisting in what he called "the future." The man told him the world was in need of assistance and the HART movement was just the place to begin. It was supposed to be in favor on humans, but he learned it was just the opposite. Instead, he had become part of a nihilistic cult that was looking to overthrow humanity and become the new dominant species on the planet. When he learned the truth, he wanted out. All he wanted to do was to return home. Now it was too late.

Zimm looked deeply into Forwing's eyes. He raised his other hands and pointed it at Forwing's face. Slowly, and almost unnoticeably at first, Zimm's finger began to dissolve. A long trail of particles, looking like dust, began to cloud around Forwing's face. The particle cloud encircled the man's head before it formed a sharpened point and stabbed into Forwing's ear. A large amount of particles entered the young man's skull, leaving Zimm without a hand.

Strommel watched as Forwing's once defiant and fearful expression became void and empty. Zimm stood before the boy and barked a command, "Stand."

Forwing stood.

Zimm dropped a pistol on the floor. The metal against metal clanked loudly. "Now pick up the weapon."

Forwing obeyed. He scooped up the pistol in his hand, his eyes vacant, as he appeared to look blankly ahead.

"Put the gun to your head."

Forwing did just that, pressing the tip of the pistol roughly into his own temple, his skin rumpling under the pressure.

"Pull the trigger."

"NO!" Strommel screamed. "DON'T DO THIS!"

"PULL THE TRIGGER!" Zimm screamed.

Strommel closed his eyes. Forwing squeezed the trigger and fired a round into his brain. The gunshot's echo silenced Strommel's pleas. A cloud of crimson exploded from the other side of Forwing's skull. The young man's body dropped to the ground like a bag of concrete.

He was dead, by his own hand, but not his own will. Strommel opened his eyes slowly, tears flowing behind. He felt responsible. Everything he had done, the research, the development of the nanites and tech, all led to this young man's death. It was his fault. The small particles of nanites slowly seeped from the young man's ear canal and flew into the air, spiraling about playfully before reassembling along Zimm's wrist, recreating the hand that had once been there.

Zimm snapped his fingers again and the obedient guards collected the remains of Forwing and carried his corpse from the room. Zimm turned his attention to Strommel, "You see, my good doctor, I can make you do anything. In fact, you WILL be responsible for the deaths of millions. Do you understand?"

Strommel was silent. He understood. His choices were limited and his time was running out.

Jack breezed up another set of spiral stairs. As his boot clomped onto the landing he quickly looked around to be sure, no one noticed he was not one of them. Soldiers moved about, back and forth, along the walkways, all focused on whatever their orders were. It was strange, he thought. Despite the infiltration he had taken, there didn't seem to be much alertness to tracking him down and catching him. Soldiers were climbing into various elevated platforms and securing themselves in, strapping several belts around there torsos. Others would disappear into small openings in the floor, sliding deeply into long tubes. Jack slinked behind a clopping troop of six soldiers. He kept close proximity to them as they made their way to a set of six hatches in the floor. They each opened them and crawled inside. Jack peered into the tube to see where they led. At the end of the tube, he saw a cockpit situated in a small aircraft. They were docked alongside the airship. From his position, he could see nearly fifty aligned along the edge.

It didn't take a detective to deduce what they were for: an Invasion. A fleet of small one to two man fighters could easily infiltrate any nation and their cities, bring it to its knees. Jack shook the abysmal thought from his head. He didn't want to think any further of what could happen, or what will happen if he didn't find that control room.

"What are you doing?" A voice questioned from behind.

Jack froze. He felt his body stiffen and his muscles tighten.

"I asked you a question," the voice asked again, this time more forcefully.

Jack stood slowly and turned. He was face-to-face with a Lieutenant Commander, decked out in full dress uniform, his insignias and medals polished and shined. He was pressed and proper, from his polished calf-high boots to his black leather gloves that stretched tightly across his hands. He folded them one in front of the other as he stood, his chest puffed out and shoulders broad.

"Well?"

Jack ran his hands along his uniform, it was loose; he tried to smooth it flat. "Well, sir, I was just...um...inspecting the...fleet."

"From up here?"

"Well, um. Yes, of course, sir."

The Lieutenant Commander traced his eyes along the rumpled man before him. He was lying. It was simple to see. He was certain and was prepared to eliminate this trespasser, "You don't belong here."

"How do you mean, sir? I am only following orders," Jack replied.

"On whose order?"

"Commander Huun, sir."

The Lieutenant Commander drew his sidearm and brought it forth to aim at Jack. Jack lunged at the officer's arm and forced the gun downward. He then brought his elbow against the inside of the officer's arm, loosening the man's grip to which he dropped the pistol. Jack then brought up his elbow and connected with the man's chin, knocking him backward off his feet. The man toppled over and slammed his head against the metal railing. It vibrated loudly as he slumped over onto his side and went unconscious.

Jack worked on catching his breath, not so much from the effort but more from the anxiety. He thought he had been caught for sure. His instinct kicked in, not to mention his nanotech arm, and he reacted. He had to get out of there and quickly. He began down the steps and then hesitated. He looked back at the officer lying still. Then he realized an officer's uniform might get him more access than this oversized mess he was currently wearing. Jack began to remove the Lieutenant Commander's uniform.

CHAPTER 19
JACK ZERO'S LAST MISSION

Frisco was stretched out along the floor on her back as Helix rushed about her, attaching several different wires he had managed to cull together from the wall socket he pulled apart. Some of the wires had been used to bind the guard's ankles together and arms behind his back. He was still unconscious. Helix didn't want to take any chances with him coming to and attacking him. It was easy for him to take out an assailant when they weren't looking, but a whole other matter when they come after him directly. Besides, he needed a ground. Helix had set several of the wires against the guard, knowing he would be able to take the brunt of the charge once it was activated. It wasn't easy mustering up a mild electromagnetic pulse from assimilated material around the concealed room, but it was the only way he could reprogram Frisco, or at the very least, reset her.

Helix had a lot of experience with computers and machines in general. He knew them, felt comfortable with them. He understood them. But most importantly, machines understood him. At least it felt that way to him. Machines have always been there for him when he needed them; filling in the empty, lonely days and nights, he endured as a child. He didn't have many friends growing up, so working with computers was the answer. He enjoyed their company and their language, ones and zeros. He enjoyed the binary tongue; he became fluent in it. He could easily speak to any device and make it understand and do whatever he requested. Moreover, they listened. They always listened. Isn't that what one asked for in a friend?

He secured the remaining strands of wires along the guard's body and then tugged one last time on his restraints. He was paranoid; he wanted to be sure that it was safe. He always felt paranoia wasn't a psychological condition, but more a precautionary tactic. Besides, it was better to be safe than sorry. Once satisfied with the restraints he applied, he returned his attention to Frisco. To his surprise, she was no longer on the floor where he left her. His heart stopped for a moment as he looked around the small room. His eyes caught Frisco, as she stood, emotionless, behind him. Helix swung his fist striking Frisco in the shoulder and once across the cheek. She remained expressionless as she grabbed him by the throat and lifted him into the air. With the strength of what felt like a grizzly bear, she threw Helix across the room. His feet never touched the floor before his back struck the wall a few feet behind him.

Helix hit the floor hard, but didn't let it stop him. He scrambled to his feet and looked for a way to escape her as she strode toward him. Frisco was on top of him before he could get halfway across the floor. She gripped the back of his shirt and lifted him like luggage, tossing him aside. This time Helix struck the wall hard, denting the metal. The air had been forced from his lungs as he rolled onto his stomach and propped himself up on his arms and legs. He coughed as he tried to regain his breath. Frisco didn't hesitate for the next assault. She bounded hastily, pushing her foot against Helix's back. She pushed down onto his spine until he gave way and collapsed to the floor on his chest. Another expulsion of air followed.

Frisco knelt down, her knee deep into his back as she wrapped her arms around his neck. He was still struggling to regain the last breath of air he lost as she squeezed his windpipe tighter, cutting off his oxygen. Things began to blur. He failed Jack. Most importantly, he failed Frisco. He slumped forward, trying to wrangle himself free by loosening her grip. It only allowed him to get closer to the floor. Another failure.

Or was it?

In front of Helix were the wires he had pulled from the wall. He quickly shot his arms forward and scooped up the bundle of wires. He twisted his arm behind his back and connected to Frisco's neck. She howled in pain as she let loose Helix and flew from his back. The energy blast struck her directly. Helix yelped as the remaining jolts passed through him and along the floor. Within moments, Frisco lay unconscious on the floor. Helix rolled onto his back and sucked in a huge lungful of air. It felt good to breathe again.

A spark flared again across Frisco and a bright light instantly filled the room.

Jack moved quickly, now clad in a more appropriate uniform to suit his status, or a status he felt he deserved. Maybe deep down, he regretted never continuing his military career. He certainly had the drive and skills to make higher ranks, but after his confrontation with Zimm and his discharge, he never looked back. He tugged the brim of the officer's hat lower on his brow. He didn't want to be spotted. He strode past several regiments of troops as they rushed to the hangar. They were gathering into position for something. Jack didn't need to be told that they were getting ready for battle, or more precisely, an invasion.

Strommel tripped over his own feet as he was shoved roughly from behind. He was being led along the walkway across an open hanger, following behind General Zimm and his lackey Huun. Strommel was hunched over as he walked, slumped in defeat. Strommel saw his life's work, his passion, his creation used against him. He had suffered through trials and turmoil before, impoverish at first, struggling to patent his inventions and find a way to make money in order to survive. The loss of his wife to cancer. He had been defeated before. He had felt the weight of loss in his heart, and each time he had persevered. Now, he was at the mercy of his own ideas, his own self. All he ever wanted was to better humanity, but now his benefit was a blight.

"Where are you taking me?" Strommel asked.

"To the observation level," Huun strode, not looking at Strommel when he spoke.

"The observation level? Why there?"

"So you can see exactly what your genius has wrought," Zimm smiled.

They marched further along the hangar as several pilots positioned themselves in their aircraft. Strommel swallowed hard.

Jack walked along the open hangar, watching the men prepare their crafts for flight. He enjoyed his inconspicuous disguise. It made him blend in; feel a part of the revelry that was growing. He watched as young pilots checked over the craft, inspecting it in every minute detail. Some crawled excitedly into their cockpit, awaiting the moment when the order was given to take flight, to siege and destroy.

He had to stop this.

Jack made his way along the long walkway that stretched over the hangar. It seemed to run the length of the airship. It was only a small portion of the nearly three-mile long airship. Jack kept his disguise intact as he strode across the bustling platforms. He needed to make his way to the front of the ship. He wanted to get a location and see exactly where they were. Maybe, just maybe, if they were far enough out, he could safely bring the ship down, only injuring those inside. That wasn't an issue with him, he felt that everyone inside certainly deserved to die. Even himself. He didn't want to sacrifice the life of Frisco or Helix, even Dr. Strommel, but if it meant saving all of New Utica and the millions of people who lived there then they would understand the importance of their sacrifice.

Jack walked through a large iron archway, onto an open platform that ended at the front of a large, open window. The window ran from floor to ceiling and lined the entire wall of the semi-circular room. There were a few console spotted sporadically around the edge of the platform where a thick railing separated the edge of the platform from the glass. It was an observation deck. Jack looked around in awe. It was an amazing view to take in, so many sights. Jack was a bit taken aback, expecting to see the lights of New Utica twinkling in the darkness; he looked out over a vast ocean, darkness surrounding them.

'*Where exactly were they?*'

A commotion of footsteps broke Jack's concentration. He froze and turned to see several shadows stretching along the floor as they were entering the room. Jack began to look around for a place to hide, then realized he was still wearing his stolen uniform. Why was he worried? He could simply blend in, right?

"No dawdling Doctor," a familiar voice cut through the air.

Jack immediately recognized it as Zimm.

'*Shit,*' he thought. There was no way he could hide now. He looked around in desperation. He needed a hiding place now. Unfortunately, he was in a room with no furnishings aside from the thin consoles that encircled the room. Nothing that would conceal his presence. He gripped the railing that was behind him tightly. It was cold against his hot, sweating palms. There were at least a dozen people with Zimm, hardly the best odds for fighting his way out. It was then that he realized what he must do. Jack turned and leapt over the railing. The small gap between the window and the platform was narrow, but wide enough for him to fit. He slid quickly and quietly through just before Zimm and his crew, ushering Strommel ahead of themselves, entered into the room.

Jack hadn't thought much before he leapt. Not where the gap

would lead or if there was a landing beneath him to break his fall. Things one would think of when leaping into the unknown. However, he did think enough to leap forward facing the railing. At the very least, he could grip an awaiting railing in his decent. His fingers instinctively wrapped around the railing nearest to the platform on the observation deck. There was a low clang from the impulsive movement that fortunately went unnoticed.

"I don't understand what you want me here for?" Strommel asked; fear thick on his tongue. He noticed they were flying high above an open body of water, nowhere near the city.

"Oh come now, Doctor," Zimm chided. "Certainly you want to see exactly how your device works don't you?"

"My device?"

Zimm enjoyed moments like this. Moments when you reveal to the prey exactly how you torture them prior to pouncing, "Of course, your prize invention. How else do you think we're going to get this airship all the way to New Utica?"

"You're going to pass this ship through a portal?" Strommel was confused. "That's impossible, you can't open a gateway that size. Even if you could, the destructive ramifications that would render on the city would be catastrophic."

Zimm only responded with a smile. Strommel didn't believe it; he shook his head in disbelief, "No. You can't possibly do this. The gateway isn't capable of accepting anything this massive without the proper amplitude."

"You mean like planting devices throughout the city in order to generate the power and berth for a gate of such magnitude?" Zimm confirmed Strommel's fears. "What do you think my men have been doing around the city? They've been planting the appropriate devices strategically in preparation for our entrance."

"But why?" Strommel asked. "Why not just fly in and take them by surprise? Why go through such theatrics with my device?"

"It's rather difficult to fly a three-mile long airship unnoticed into the city on the eve of the election for President of the United States," Glorm interjected.

"We would be torn down in minutes," Huun added.

Zimm continued, "With your transporter, we can slip into the city undetected and be upon them before they realize what has happened."

"You're insane," Strommel gasped.

"No, I am genius," Zimm corrected.

Strommel felt his blood begin to boil. He was getting angry. For years, he had been used for his creations and his ideas. It was one thing when it was for business, corporations using his concepts to make a buck without paying him a cent. However, this was different. His inventions were being used to destroy his city and the people who lived there.

Strommel gnashed his teeth, "You're drunk on your own power, suffering from delusions of grandeur."

Zimm sensed Strommel's underlying anger. Strommel didn't threaten him in any way, but he wasn't going to stand for anyone disrespecting him, especially in front of his men. Zimm strode slowly up to Strommel and leaned down until their noses nearly touched. He smiled a broad, toothy smile. It sent chills down Strommel's spine.

"My dear, Doctor," Zimm hissed. "Delusions are for those with a lack of drive to achieve their aspirations. I'm am a realist, a man who has convictions."

"The convictions of a madman!"

"You truly are blind. Even your partner could see the truth. This world has a cancer and that cancer is in the rulers of every country in this world. None of them fight for your rights and your freedoms. All they do is selfishly motivate and line their own pockets while fattening their bank accounts. Not any longer. What the HART wants is to crush their tyranny and regain control of this world in the hands of the people," Zimm paced around the open floor of the platform as he spoke.

"All you've done is taken out one tyrannical power and put in another, your own," Strommel snapped.

"Now who suffers from delusions?" Zimm retorted.

"So you're just going to...appear in the city and attack the President and his cavalcade? You don't think there will be repercussions from the people? You think this is what they want?" Strommel drilled into Zimm deeper.

"Like all other countries we have helped, they'll welcome us with open arms."

"So you can enslave them?"

"So we can liberate them."

"But who will liberate them from you?" Strommel said coldly.

Zimm cocked his head to one side and offered a half grin, both playful and annoyed. He was through playing around with Strommel, entertaining his silly jibes. Despite his intelligence, Strommel didn't understand. He would never understand. It didn't matter anyway. In fact, nothing Strommel thought was going to matter. Soon his usefulness would be outlived.

"Prepare for transfer," Zimm ordered.

Jack had wrapped both hands around the railing tightly, they were beginning to burn from the intensity. He needed to let go, but he couldn't see below to know where he would land. Going back up was not an option either as he would be face-to-face with Zimm and his cronies. But he had to do something soon. His arms were feeling like rubber, he couldn't hold on much longer. He felt his right arm warming up. It was the nanites, they were charging up, as his muscles grew weak. He looked down again. It was dark, but he could make out another railing at least twenty feet below. It was a long drop, but he could fall with minimal injury. He hoped.

Jack closed his eyes and prepared to let go, but a shrill order broke the silence beneath him, "Hey! You! What are you doing there?"

Zimm strode proudly out of the observation deck as his men secured everything in place. Huun and Glorm followed their leader like baby ducks following their mother. There incessant need to please him grew tiresome to him at times. There were times he wanted to execute them, well at least Glorm. Had he not become so important to infiltrating the United States, he would execute Glorm himself. At least he could revel in one execution, Strommel's.

Strommel struggled against the grip of his enemies. He wanted to break free and lash out at Zimm. Even if he could just spit in his face, that would be enough to satisfy his thirst for vengeance. It was at that moment that Strommel was prepared to succumb to defeat. He watched as the form of his wife, now a reprogrammed nest of nanites, slinked onto the observation level. Evelyn Strommel wore a tight leather body suit. It hugged every one of her curves. The zipper along the front that ran down her chest to her abdomen was unzipped hallway down her chest, revealing the tops of her ample breasts. They bobbed with each step she took. All the men's eyes on the deck were locked on her as she moved and she was well aware of this. It made her smile knowing this form gave her control over men. The sight of her made Strommel regret what he created, an emotionless sentient android. Despite her beauty, he feared her.

She approached Strommel. He looked away, not wanting to make eye contact. She enjoyed the game he was playing with her. She gripped his chin and forced his head in her direction.

"Hello dear," she cooed.

He pulled his chin from her hand and looked away again.

She tsked, "Oh, it hurts that you don't want to look at me."

He remained silent.

"You loved me once," she reminded him.

"Yes," he finally replied. "When you were alive. When you were truly my wife."

"You made this, me, in her image."

"I made you to fill the void of her death, not to create a monster."

"I am only what you wanted, what I became was you're doing," her ruby lips parted as she moved in and kissed him tenderly.

He pulled away.

Zimm acknowledged the anger that grew on her face, "What shall we do with him, my dear?"

"After the transfer," Evelyn spoke simply as she walked away, "kill him."

Strommel swallowed hard.

Zimm just wanted Strommel to see what they had done with his inventions before they killed him. As Zimm walked out of the room, the sound of shouting forced him to stop and drew him back into the room.

Jack saw that a soldier had looked up and spotted him while on patrol. That ruled out going down. The soldier drew up his weapon, "Hey! I'm talking to you!" He shouted up to Jack.

"Great," Jack said to himself. His hands were slipping as they became saturated with sweat. Despite his arm enhancing in energy, his hands still accumulated perspiration. And they were losing their grip.

"Come down from there!" The soldier ordered again, this time taking aim with his rifle.

Jack could feel his fingers giving way. The only way out was up. Jack felt his arm surge as he launched himself upward, over the railing and onto the platform of the observation deck, just before a round of bullets clattered against the railing he gripped to only moments before. Jack looked up slowly from his crouched position. Standing before him were the surprised expressions of several armed soldiers and one Heinrich Strommel.

"Hiya, fellas," Jack smirked uncomfortably. They all gawked at Jack, their mouths agape in surprise. "Weren't you men trained to salute your superior?" Jack shot as he stood and flattened his uniform with the palms of his hand.

Zimm pushed his way through the slack-jawed soldiers to look upon the uniformed Jack Zero. His face contorted into rage, as he looked upon Jack desecrating the very uniform he wore. "ZERO!" Zimm shouted.

"Hey there, Zimm, long time, no see."

Zimm roared as he thrust his arm toward Jack, pointing as he commanded, "GET HIM!"

Jack reacted by charging into the soldiers head-on, like a football linebacker tackling the opposition. The soldiers all toppled over like a chain of dominos. Strommel was wise enough to step back slightly in order to avoid being taken down along with them. Jack wrapped his hand around Strommel's arm and pulled him along as he made his way for the exit.

Zimm was furious to see Jack, once again, besting his men and making an escape. Zimm no longer wasted his time on waiting for his troops to move. Instead, he drew his pistol and aimed it at Jack. Zimm fired several rounds, narrowly missing Jack as he crouched into his run. Zimm continued to fire, his eyes narrowed as he made a clearer aim. This time Zimm was able to hit Jack in his shoulder. Blood misted from his shoulder where the bullet dug deep into his tissue. Jack stumbled from the pain and crumpled to the floor. Zimm cocked his arm back grinning victoriously as his prey lie before him, bleeding.

"Mr. Zero, are you all right?" Strommel asked, kneeling next to Jack.

"I'm fine," Jack said sucking in air through his teeth as he tried to move. The pain shot through his body, across his receptors and ignited his desperation to escape. He turned to Strommel, "Get out of here, Strommel!"

"Not without you."

"Run you old fool!"

"I wouldn't move if I were you," Zimm's rage had left him. He returned to his calm, arrogant self. "Unless you want to die much sooner than planned."

Strommel threw up his hands in surrender.

"That's more like it," Zimm smiled triumphantly. He stood over Jack, a glimmer shone in his eye as he watched the puddle of blood grow around Jack's shoulder. "There's no escape for you this time, Zero."

Zimm turned to Huun, "Get him up and secure him, do it right this time!"

Huun nodded. He leaned down and gripped Jack around his wounded shoulder. He intentionally squeezed hard as he lifted Jack to his feet. Jack winced, but tried not to scream. He didn't want to give them the satisfaction of his pain. Huun wanted to hear Jack squeal. He lifted him up to his feet and then pressed Jack against the nearest wall as hard as he could. Jack yelped slightly. Huun smiled a broad grin that looked more like he was in excruciating pain than expressing pleasure.

"You've always been a real pain in the ass, you know that Zero," Huun said low enough for only Jack to hear. He ran his thumb around the opening of Jack's wound, streaking the blood into a swirled pattern.

"You know, I'm surprised you even know the difference between your ass and your own head," Jack managed to spit out.

Huun sneered as he pushed his thumb deeply into the bullet hole in Jack's shoulder. Jack let out another painful cry. "I'd watch my mouth if I were you, Zero."

Jack winced and groaned, trying to keep his composure as he spoke, "The only thing...ungh...you're going to...ungh...watch...hugnh...is your precious airship going up in smoke!"

Huun drew back his arm; the thumb bloodied and stained, and

threw his fist into Jack's chin. Jack sank like a rock sinking to the ocean floor. The sound of his body striking the flat surface was deafening in the silent room. The roar of Zimm's voice only shadowed the sound of the body's impact.

"DAMN YOU HUUN!" Zimm's nostrils flared. "I said Zero was not to be harmed!"

Huun huffed, keeping himself silent as he pouted internally.

Zimm snarled, "Pick him up and bring him along." He turned to Strommel, "Well, doctor, it looks like you get to live a little longer after all."

Helix gripped the weapon tightly in his hand as he watched Frisco slowly open her eyes and pick herself off the ground. He watched her eyes closely, looking for any spark of humanity that seemed to disappear when she went all robotic. He was able to administer her with nearly three-thousand volts of electricity. He was fairly certain he was able to restore her to her original settings. Fairly. Still, he didn't want to take any chances. He held up the leg from the chair like a batter ready to swing at the next pitch, ready to strike if needed. She pushed herself up with her arms into a seated position. She looked around, rubbing her head gently. Her fingers ran through her hair. It felt stiff and crispy, the brittle tips breaking off in her hand. She felt an energy surge through her, like a current of electricity was somehow giving her the energy to move. She brought her hands up to her face and turned them around. She swore she could see lightening crackle under her fingernails.

"Wh-what happened to me?" Frisco managed.

Helix slowly lowered his weapon. He looked at her suspiciously, "Agent? Agent Frisco? Is that you?"

Frisco slowly stood on her feet, "Yeah, who the hell else would it be?"

Helix dropped the chair leg. It clattered loudly to the floor. He swiftly rushed to embrace her. His arms wrapped around her shoulders, locking her arms at her side. She let out a small grunt from the unexpected move.

"It's so good to see you again!" Helix exclaimed as he overstepped his duration of physical connectivity with Frisco.

She timidly pushed him away, partially from wanting her distance from him, but also due to her still feeling weakened. "Alright already!" She said under another grunt. "Where exactly have I been?"

"It's a long story," Helix smirked as he realized he had been too close for too long.

"Do we have time?"

"Not really?"

"Where are we?" She asked.

"We're on board the HART flag airship," Helix explained. "I'm not sure where we're going."

Frisco furrowed her brow, she was thinking hard for a moment. "New Utica," she finally said.

"What about it?"

"That's where we're going."

"How do you know?" Helix was confused.

"I don't know," Frisco rubbed her head with her palm. "I just, somehow, know."

Helix was still confused, "But why New Utica?"

"The president!" Frisco felt her heart stop for a moment. "They're going to attack the President when he arrives in New Utica! We have to go! Where's Jack?"

"I-I'm not sure. He was here, but when we got loose, we split up."

"We need to find him. Now!" Frisco grabbed Helix by the arm and dragged him behind her as she ran from the room.

"Wait!" Helix pulled away from Frisco's grip. "We need to get to the radio room. We need to alert NUPD about the invasion!"

"We don't have time!"

"Then we need to make time! Without warning them, the city will be taken by surprise. They could destroy this city and all this will be for nothing."

"Fine," Frisco thought for a moment, trying to think as to where the radio room might be. She then reached down to her belt. She withdrew a large black COMM device and handed it to Helix. "What about this? Can we contact them with this?"

Helix smiled, "I can make sure we can."

Jack felt woozy as blood continued to flow from his shoulder. He was dizzy; the loss of blood was taking its toll. He stumbled a bit, catching himself on Strommel's shoulder. Strommel wrapped his arm around Jack's shoulder blades, yoking him over his own shoulder. Jack let out a low groan, hoping to keep it unheard. He was struggling with his pain, but he didn't want Zimm or Huun to see.

"How are you holding up?"

"I've been better," Jack managed to speak without wincing. "I've had less holes in me too."

"Just keep moving; you may not be able to move much soon."

Jack was confused, "Why's that?"

Strommel explained, "Once the transfer begins...we may experience some disorientation."

"Like?"

"I don't know," was all Strommel offered,

"Great," Jack said sarcastically.

CHAPTER 20
TRAVERSING THE VOID

Benji Holdt lifted his flashlight slowly, his hand shaking. He had remained skittish ever since that night not too long ago. After being jumped by the odd lot of naked men, he had been met with internal trepidation. But after avoiding work, his girlfriend, Brandee, finally convinced him to return to work. She was always smart, a fiery redhead with a single pension for keeping him in line. She never let him rest too long on his laurels. It was her suggestion for him to return to school years ago, where he struggled before landing a career in law enforcement. However, when he failed to pass the exam to gain a spot on the New Utica police force, it was her idea to get into security. It seemed like a perfect fit. He enjoyed the work and the quiet night hours he had to spend in the huge bank at night. It gave him time in between his patrols to catch up on reading or watch television. He had been able to watch several shows he always seemed to miss because he was either working or sleeping. The only unfortunate aspect of his return was that Chester was no longer here. Chester decided to quit after the attack. In the interim, they had hired a replacement for Chester, a young rookie named Peyt. The kid was ambitious and seemed to mean well. He was always on guard, not allowing himself the down time that Benji held so dear. It didn't bother him; he simply let him loose to do what he felt was 'making a difference.'

He did miss Chester. Chester always packed the best lunches. Chester's wife would always put together an elaborate meal that she sent with her husband. However, it was always food he didn't like, such as meatball tunnels. Chester always complained it gave him heartburn. So instead, he would trade his meal with the humdrum offering that Benji had, which was usually some bland leftover. Brandee was a smart girlfriend, but not a great cook. He took another big bite and choked it down. He slugged down a mouthful of coffee to aid the tasteless swallow down his throat. It was hard to take and it nearly made him choke. Liverwurst on rye with mustard. He hated mustard. And rye. And liverwurst. Oh well. He was hungry and needed to eat or he wouldn't last through his shift.

"Watcha got tonight?" Peyt smiled as he sat next to Benji and flipped open his metal lunch pail.

Benji held out the half-eaten sandwich, globs of mustard excess plopped to the floor with an echoing splat, "Liverwurst."

Peyt recoiled a bit, curling his lip, "Eww."

Benji shrugged as he took in another big mouthful.

Peyt took out a well-crafted sandwich that looked as if it had leapt from the pages of a recipe book. It was piled high with delicious meats and vegetables. Only an ample amount of condiment could be glimpsed between the top slice of artisan bread and the leaves of lettuce that poked out of the edges. The sandwich was a sight of beauty and it made Benji salivate with jealousy. He stared with envy as Peyt took a huge bite, his expression that of ecstasy.

He really missed Chester.

A sudden surge of electricity erupted in the darkened hallway outside the dimly lit break room where the two men sat.

"What was that?" Peyt asked as he spit out his mouthful of food.

Benji gladly set down his food as he reached for his weapon, "I don't know, but we're getting paid to check things like that out."

Peyt swallowed hard, "Lead the way."

Benji crept slowly from the break room, more hesitant and alert than he had been in the past. He remembered what happened last time he didn't take precautions. A naked man nearly killed him. Not this time. No one was going to get the jump on him.

"Wh-what is it?" Peyt asked nervously.

"I don't know yet," Benji replied, annoyed. He sneaked slowly into the darkened hallway where the sound of electricity crackled lightly. Benji drew his weapon, a Taser that only stuns its victims mildly, up to his chest, poised and ready for anything. As he inched slowly down the hallway, he looked around with caution. He remembered his attacker appearing from out of nowhere, but he wouldn't let that happen again. As he approached a curve up ahead, he held out his hand to halt Peyt. He then crooked his knees before springing forward and landing around the corner, his weapon out before him. Benji fired his weapon. It released a bright purple and white beam that zigged angrily across the spacious hallway. It flew unobstructed until it crackled against the wall on the opposite side. The beam chewed into the marble wall, cracking it slightly.

Benji dropped his arms as he realized there was no one, nothing, there. "Damn," Benji's voice bounced along the vaulted ceiling and smooth walls. He realized his mistake.

"What is it?" Peyt asked impatiently.

"Nothing," Benji said, a slight lift to his voice as he felt relief. Benji approached the wall where his beam had punctured the rock. He ran his finger along the crack. Loose debris fell to the clean floor. Benji looked to the damage only to notice an unusual object embedded in the wall behind the damage.

"What the hell?" Benji began to chip at the wall to expose the object. It was a large, black device. It was in the shape of a crescent, beginning from a thick base to a narrow tip. The tip adorned a small blue light that blinked intermittently. He stared at it curiously, but still cautiously. Peyt crept from behind the wall, "Is it safe?"

"I think so," Benji rubbed the light with his finger. It began to blink faster, followed by a high-pitched beeping sound.

"What's that?"

Benji's heart sank, "Get down!" He dove to the floor, landing hard on his chest. A thick blue beam of electricity ripped from the device and tore across the air. The intense heat it produced scorched the back of Benji's uniform as it soared overhead. He covered his head with his hands as the sound of electricity crackled through the air loudly. Despite his cry of warning to Peyt, it failed to reach the rookie in time. The bolt instantly curved and contoured with the room until it connected with Peyt. The energy surged through him violently. He screamed to no avail as the current continued through him and past him. Benji watched in horror as the smoldering body of Peyt fell to the ground, the bolt bouncing away.

Benji stood and raced to his new partner. He immediately checked for any vital signs. He found a pulse by pressing his fingers to the young man's neck. He then pressed his hear to Peyt's lips. He could feel a faint warmth emitting from within. The kid was alive!

"Oh man!" Benji grabbed his communicator and began to tap the buttons, "Hang in there, pal. Help is coming!" As he listened for a response, the device began to pulsate again. Benji watched in awe as this time several tendrils of electricity reached out from the center of the device, clawing into the surrounding walls, dancing until it found a release. The windows. The bolts tore into the glass and shattered it to pieces. It was as if they were looking for a way out. Benji stood and watched in shocked amazement as the beams shot into the night sky and connected with another set of similar beams. When the beams closed a circle, a vortex began to swirl and form in the center of the beams. "My god," Benji's jaw dropped. "This is not good."

The captain of the airship stood stoic on the bridge, watching his men hustle. He looked over them with his hands behind his back. "What's the position now ensign?"

The ensign, a young man of nineteen, still green and untested, his expression of nervousness was prevalent, "We're approximately six-thousand feet below our expected altitude, sir."

"Adjust the altitude then," the captain said calmly, his beard cloaking his pursed lips.

"Aye, captain," replied the lieutenant at the helm. He tapped several buttons and twisted knobs.

The captain felt his knees buckle slightly as the behemoth began to change its position in the air.

"Keep calling out the altitude, ensign," the captain said.

"Aye, sir," the ensign replied.

"Lieutenant," the captain directed his orders to the helm, "Keep the speed at a steady three-thousand knots."

"At your command," he responded.

The captain smiled, his beard keeping it hidden, but noticeable to those nearby. He always ran a tight ship. His men were like a well-oiled machine, their responses lightening quick, their timing flawless. He was proud of his crew and what they were setting out to do, reclaim their homeland.

The massive airship drifted above the waters at a steady speed. Its sleek outer shell glinted in the moonlight as it crested over a cluster of clouds that began to move past. The water beneath it sparkled like crystal, the reflecting light of the moon danced along the water's ripples like playful children. The ship moved soundlessly, edging its way along through the night sky.

The sky before it began to spark and come to life. It was as if an electrical storm began to manifest from nothing. The sky became alive, sparking and growling as the clouds began to swirl toward a central point.

298

The clouds became more and more active, spiraling more intensely until they formed a vortex. Despite the intensity of the brewing storm, there was no wind and no damaging lightening. It simply churned and crackled around a single area, spinning faster and faster as the vortex formed directly in front of the airship. The vortex grew larger as the winds continued to spin more violently developing a long tail that stretched behind the opening in the center of the spiral. The opening began to grow wider, like the maw of a whale looking to feed.

Jack, still feeling unsteady and woozy from his wound, stumbled from the sudden vibration that shook the airship, like a more rugged and violent turbulence. Strommel maintained at Jack's side, studying his stance. He helped Jack keep his balance by leaning him against him more readily. The lights on the airship flickered and then went black as a chain of pink lightening danced along the hull of the ship. The lights shone brightly through the windows of the ship, laminating the dim walkways. Jack and Strommel shielded their eyes while Zimm, Huun, and Glorm watched with relish as the lightening signaled for the beginning of the transition.

The beak of the behemoth slowly drifted toward the swirling vortex. The captain steered the vessel with precision, keeping it on task, never wavering from its intended position. The swirl of clouds awaited the airships arrival into its opening, an opening that began to reveal a series of twinkling lights that blurred and streaked with the ripples and waves that covered the opening like a film. Within the opening was what appeared to be a liquid-like center, rippling like a placid pond that had been disrupted by a stone; the ripples quickly smoothed out and revealed a cityscape. The city of New Utica was clearly visible.

Jack quickly broke away from Strommel and made his way to the window. He looked out to see the vortex ahead of them. He could see New Utica on the other side. It looked peaceful, serene. Its tranquility would soon be disrupted and Jack stood helpless against it. He lowered his head in defeat, forgetting the pain that throbbed in his arm. Strommel took Jack's arm gently, hoping not to inflict further pain. Jack reluctantly followed Strommel's lead as they walked away.

"Let's keep moving," Zimm growled. "Time is of the essence."

"MOVE!" Huun shoved Strommel from behind.

He stumbled and nearly fell, almost taking Jack with him. Huun snickered; he was hoping for the dismay. Strommel was growing tired of being pushed around, by everyone. Strommel leaned closely to Jack's ear, "How's your strength."

"Been better," Jack replied.

"I need you to focus," Strommel explained lowly. "I need you to focus on your enhancements. They can repair you; they just need you to instruct them what to do."

"How?" Jack shot back.

"Just will it."

Jack rolled his eyes. Strommel was a genius, but he was nuts. How could his will help repair his arm?

"KEEP GOING!" Huun roared.

The floor shifted beneath them again. The ship was moving at an increased speed.

The airship slowly moved into the awaited and opening of the vortex. Soon it disappeared as the vortex stopped swirling and quickly dissipated, vanishing as quickly as it had appeared. When it was gone, the sea beneath them calmed and the stars, once again, dominated the clear night sky.

The airship was gone.

New Utica was a thriving metropolis that embraced its nightlife culture. It began sometime after nine-o'clock and stretched until the early morning hours. At this very moment, the evening was just getting underway. The nightlife always attracted the young, the young-at-heart, and the lonely. Not just lonely in the sense that they had no friends or significant other; instead, it referred to their place in life, a hollow existence that they forged through a day-to-day existence. At least that is how Velina Trace felt. All too often. It wasn't that Velina wasn't an attractive woman. She was twenty-seven, petite, with long, flowing auburn hair. Her porcelain skin, set with her bright green eyes, gave her hair a luster and glow that set her apart from other woman that frequented the rooftop bar called Altitudes. It was a trendy, hip club that welcomed her ilk, a collection of jet-setting, self-determined, driven young professionals from all parts of the sprawling city. Here Velina stood, among her kind, young people looking to set the beginning of the weekend on fire as they danced, drank and behaved as they did years before, carefree, like a college freshman. Unfortunately, Velina didn't feel much like partying tonight. She felt alone. Not that she WAS alone. She came with her two best friends, Cetsy and Jun. She knew them since college. Cetsy was her roommate and Jun was in her first psych class she took at the local college. They managed to stay close over the years, even after graduation. They stayed in the city, graduating from Utica College; Velina became a practicing psychotherapist for the recently reopened Marcy Psychiatric Center. She worked with the patients, helping them get better through talk and medicine. It was a good job, a rewarding job. She was happy there. At least, she thought she was. Both Cetsy and Jun worked for the New Utica City School District. Cetsy a teacher and Jun a school psychologist. They always made time to meet out at the end of the week, whether at one of their apartments for cheesecake and wine, or at a nearby restaurant. She liked Symeon's for their Thracian chicken dish; or O'Scugnizzo's for their New Utica-styled pizza, the kind where the crunchy crust was topped with a thick layer of cheese and then sauce slathered along the top. Tonight, however, they agreed to meet out at the new hot spot in the city, Altitudes. Unfortunately, for Velina, she would rather be somewhere else. She recently broke up with her boyfriend, Haddam, who she had been dating for nearly six years, five years, ten months, and eighteen days to be exact, but who's counting? She thought he was the one, the one that she was going to spend her life. She was waiting for him to finally pop the question. She had been waiting for years for that question, but it never came. Instead, she received a break-up letter taped to the television in her apartment when she got home from work after an exceptionally trying and exhausting day. That was three weeks ago. She was supposed to be over him by now, at least that's what Cetsy and Jun kept telling her.

'*Forget about him,*' they said. '*He's a jerk,*' and '*You can do better.*'

She didn't think they were right. There wasn't better. Not out here, not for her. She often felt as if her own existence was for nothing, that she had nothing to offer, nothing to give. Now here she was, sitting on a rooftop bar, surrounded by other bright, young Uticans who seemed to be happy and celebrating by dancing and drinking to their hearts content.

She wanted to go home.

Unfortunately, Cetsy and Jun wouldn't let her. Not until she was either drunk or in a deep conversation with a guy. Why? She didn't need that. She didn't need anyone. She was a strong, independent woman who could do just fine on her own. She looked around to see both Cetsy and Jun talking to men. It always came easy to them, or to be more precise, they always came easy. No matter where they went, her friends seemed to be able to assimilate and socialize with no problem. She resented that about them, but they were her friends nonetheless. She just wished they left her alone, at least until she felt ready to go.

She turned to her drink that sat in front of her at the small table. A margarita. She told the bartender she was hoping it would make her feel more exotic. He didn't seem to think it was that amusing. She took a small sip and tried to look busy. She pulled out her phone and began tapping at it mindlessly, not really searching for anything in particular, but not wanting to look pathetic.

It was then that a handsome stranger approached her table and asked, "Anyone else sitting here?"

She looked up and was immediately captivated by his chiseled form and manly good looks. He was tall, dark, and handsome. His dark hair was messy atop his taut features. His deep blue eyes were hypnotic. His face wore a small amount of stubble and his dress shirt was buttoned to just below his well-formed chest.

Velina looked around to see if perhaps this man was mistakenly talking to the wrong person. "Are-are you talking to me?" She asked in return.

"Well, yes, who else would I be talking to?" His voice was smooth, inviting and warm. "Well? Is anyone sitting here?"

Velina shook her head, "No. No. Please have a seat."

He smiled, "Thanks." He swung his leg over the back of the chair across from her. She eyed his worn jeans as they tightened around his muscular leg, which bulged as it lifted over the seat.

'Wow,' she thought, 'This is too good to be true.'

"I'm Percival," he said.

She melted as his eyes bore into her. "That's nice," was all she said.

He laughed, "And your name?"

"Oh, yeah, right, I'm Velina."

"Velina, that's a beautiful name," his smile was as intense as his eyes. "I couldn't help but notice you don't seem to be having a good time."

"Me? Sure, I'm having a swell time," she smiled a faux smile. Did she just use the word swell? 'Way to look like a bumpkin,' she thought.

"You don't have to convince me," he replied. "I'm bored out of my mind."

"You?"

"Yeah. This whole social-setting thing isn't really my scene," he said as he scanned the room. "I'm more of a stay-at-home, pajamas and t-shirt kind of guy. I prefer watching a good movie or reading a book than trying to have to make nice with people who won't even remember me in the morning."

Velina smiled. It was a smile that stretched across her face, squinted her eyes and filled out her cheeks. It was a genuine smile. One she hadn't made in a long time. Long before she and Haddam started fighting. Long before, he finally left her.

"Really?" She replied. "That's my idea of the perfect evening."

"That's cool. I was dragged here by a few friends; I didn't even want to come."

Velina couldn't believe this; it had to be too good to be true. This guy was saying all the right things and he was handsome to boot.

Percival smiled at her, "You want to get out of here? Go somewhere and maybe talk?"

She found herself nodding by reflex, before she finally formed the words, "Yeah, sure. That'd be great."

She looped her arm into his and they began to walk toward the exit. Velina's friends watched her, Cetsy winking at Jun.

Velina breathed in his cologne; it was intoxicating. He smelled like a blend of fruits and spices. She looked into his eyes and felt herself get lost. They were like two shimmering pools that sparked and sizzled with an unusual purple tint. She gazed curiously, as the purple began to dance in his eyes and slowly begin to swirl within the center of his pupil.

"What is it?" Percival asked, finding her stare a tad unnerving.

"Y-your eyes," Velina stuttered. "What's wrong with your eyes?"

Before Percival could answer what or why, the sky suddenly charged to life, the clouds in the darkness swirled with great energy and rage. "Oh. My. God," Percival's jaw dropped open.

Velina turned to see the sky crackling, shards of lightening slicing across the sky. She screamed.

The rooftop bar of Altitudes, a place where young twenty-somethings came to forget their cares and wash away the stress of the week, meet others like them, now were devolving into a chaotic mess of mass hysteria. People ran in every direction, screaming and crying, looking for an escape or help as the sky above their heads tore open. Velina rushed in Percival's arms, looking for his protection. Instead, he pushed her aside and leapt over the lip of the roof onto the awaiting fire escape.

'Typical,' she thought. She scanned the crumbling crowd for her friends. She instantly caught sight of Cetsy. She raced to her friend, but before she could reach her, a streak of lightening shot from the mouth of the vortex and wrapped itself around Velina. Her body felt like it was on fire, her hair standing on end before bursting into flames. Velina was picked up off her feet and thrown across the room. Her body slammed into the bar and onto the floor. Her body felt numb and then went limp.

Everything for her went black.

The vortex was forming, slowly. It grew, swallowing the lights of the city and the glow of the moon as it widened. Lartanner stood at the window of his office. He watched, awestruck and dumbfounded, as the sky and the rooftops several miles from him were consumed by a giant gaping hole that formed from out of nowhere.

"Commissioner!" Desk Sergeant Flur Delacourt, a young woman with long blonde hair that was pulled back into a tight ponytail that came from the back of her head. She wore a blue uniform traditional for officers in the NUPD, along with an expression of concern and worry. "Reports of power failures are coming in from all over the city."

"I know, get as many men together as we have on hand," Lartanner ordered. "Whoever isn't on duty call them in, we're going to need all the help we can get."

The behemoth inched slowly across the rift. The ship was still, as if it was stuck in a lake of honey. Within the massive airship were all the passengers; soldiers, officers, and prisoners alike, including Jack and Strommel. They were frozen, floating in midair. A side effect of the rift, a state of catatonic sleep, no movement or change will alter anything while travelling through the rift. Everything and everyone contained within the rift was frozen where it last stood. As everything within floated unknowingly, the tip of the behemoth airship crowned through the opening of the vortex over New Utica.

Police cars tore from underneath the NULE headquarters. The tall, slender tower stretched above the city like a statuesque protector, watching over the helpless and innocent. It was what the NULE stood for; it's what they did every day, Lartanner thought as he saw the building shrink in his rearview mirror. He then looked to his lap where his pistol rested in his hand. He drew it up and slid the clip into its handle. It clicked in place and he tucked it under his jacket. He looked over at his driver, Chief Bendu Aloona. Aloona wore a serious expression that didn't change as he drove forward, leading the fleet of cars that trailed behind. His ebony skin was bathed in the red and blue lights that alternated along the front hood and top of the LEHV he drove.

"You ready for this partner?" Aloona grimaced.

"No," Lartanner replied. "But let's go."

Aloona pressed several buttons on his console and the vehicle lurched upward, a blast emitting beneath. The LEHV lifted into the air, lights ablaze, as Aloona steered it toward the incoming threat. The several dozen vehicles that followed each took flight in sequence behind them.

The behemoth crossed through the rift, the front half of the vehicle clearing the spiraling vortex. As each section passed over the threshold of the vortex, the once frozen interior was released. A glass of water set on a nearby desk that jostled and spilled from the initial transference was frozen in half-spill, the water splaying out in several directions, like the tentacles of an octopus. Now the water was free as gravity returned. The water instantly dropped to the floor spreading along the surface until it was thin and could no longer pool. The glass toppled over the edge of the desk and shattered against the solid floor.

Everyone began to awaken as the ship passed the barrier and crossed the vortex. Jack felt his stiff arm loosen and fall free. He could feel his body return to its normal rhythms. His heart began beating again. The pain returned to his arm as he doubled over from the initial sudden shock of it pulsating through his body.

Jack tumbled onto the floor. Strommel soon began to move as well. He broke free of the frozen spell he had been under and immediately rushed to Jack's side.

"I can't go on," Jack whimpered.

"You can and you must!" Strommel ordered. "Remember what I told you, concentrate!"

"I can't, I just can't."

"Jack, when you were my first patient, the great experiment, I incorporated a program that allows your nanites to communicate with your thoughts," Strommel explained. "You have the ability to make your nanites do whatever you command."

"H-how?"

"Just think! Think that you want them to repair your arm and they will!"

"I'll try," Jack closed his eyes.

Strommel looked behind them to see those pursuing them were beginning to slowly move, their fingertips wriggling slowly. "We don't have much time! It's time to do it!"

Jack closed his eyes tightly and began to think of his arm healing. Strommel watched as Jack's arm began to glow with a deep red. The light quickly congregated into a line along his arm, tracing the route of his arteries. The light then began to follow the flow of blood through his system, making its way to the wound on his arm. It swirled like a swarm of insects around the area of the gunshot and began to heat his body. Jack screamed in agony as the nanites began to bore into his muscle and through his skin. Slowly his skin began to close, the wound growing smaller as it sealed. Within moments, the wound was gone and Jack's flesh was repaired, smooth, as if there had never been any mark or blemish there before.

Jack, his forehead and chest soaked in sweat, stood, panting, gasping for air. He looked to his arm and studied it dumbfounded. The healed flesh that had once been an open and angry wound took him aback. The only trace or indication of any trauma was the streak of blood that stained his arm. Jack felt the area and there was no longer any pain. He felt better. He felt like he had been refreshed.

"I don't believe it," Jack said looking to Strommel.

Strommel smiled, "That is only the beginning of what you can do."

Jack moved his arm around in amazement and disbelief.

Strommel took another look back. The guards were breaking free. Time was up, "We have to go! NOW!"

"STOP THEM!" Huun could be heard over the emerging sounds that began to return to the ship, the regular din that went all this time unnoticed.

Jack grabbed Strommel's arm and broke into a sprint, pulling Strommel behind him. Gunshot erupted around them, pinging off the metal girders and ricocheting around the metal gantry. Sparks ignited with the impact of each bullet.

"NO!" Huun roared as he swung his boulder-like fist into the head of the guard firing his rifle. "NOT INSIDE HERE YOU DOLT!"

The unsuspecting guard crumpled to the floor, his consciousness gone.

"Use your stun beams!" Huun corrected the guard's mistake. "Don't let them get away!"

The sound of gunfire made Frisco perk her ears. She held up an open hand that Helix walked right into. He stopped and looked down at her manicured fingers and supple hand. He soaked in her touch, not realizing the ridiculous look it left on his face. Frisco caught Helix's unusual expression, realizing why he was making it, and instantly drew her hand away from his chest.

"Ewwww," she twisted her face into a look of disgust.

Helix wore a side smirk, "Oh, c'mon, it can't be that bad."

"Just shut up and follow me, closely and quietly," she sneered.

"Whatever," Helix replied, his eyes rolling.

Jack could feel the nanites surge through his arm, generating a slow heat and a low glow as they began to unite beneath his skin.

"It's working!" Strommel exclaimed.

"I-I can feel it, unlike before," Jack reached over to touch his arm with his other hand. It didn't feel like his own arm. It felt foreign to his body. He closed his eyes as the sensation traveled across his body and took over his consciousness.

Strommel watched with anticipation, awaiting for Jack to release his potential. Unfortunately, nothing happened.

"I can't," Jack slumped forward. "I can't do it."

Strommel tried to disguise his disappointment, "It's all right. Give it more time."

"We can't stall any longer, we need to keep moving."

"Too bad there's no way to go!" Huun raced around the corner as he saw Strommel and an exhausted Jack. "STOP THEM!"

Huun's men began to open fire on Jack and Strommel. Bolts of electricity shot from the barrels of their weapons and arced through the air as it sought out its intended targets. Both men found their speed and began to run once again. This time, however, they weren't alone. From just ahead an oddly shaped object, one that resembled a metal pipe wrapped in a series of wire with knobs and fasteners protruding from the various parts around its cylindrical shape.

"GET DOWN!" Came a familiar voice from behind the flying object.

Jack didn't stop to see who shouted the order, he knew. The familiar sound of Nicolina Frisco's voice was unmistakable. The explosion was brief but loud, absconding the air as it erupted into a black cloud. The floor beneath Jack's feet shook. It wasn't enough to move him from where he lie, but it did singe the walls and crack the nearest glass panes. Jack felt debris, mainly from the explosive device than the surrounding ship, rain down upon him. He picked himself up and aided Strommel in standing. Strommel was coughing from the smoke and dust. Jack pulled him behind himself as he ran in the direction of the frantically waving Helix.

"That was some trick," Strommel remarked.

"No trick, just simple ingenuity," Helix smiled.

"It was my idea," Frisco glared at Helix, robbing him of all his undeserved glory. "My cocktail."

"Well, it was my design," Helix recovered.

"Save it, at least we're getting away from them," Jack kept his pace up as the others followed.

He was grateful for the intervention. It wasn't an explosion intended to destroy, but more to cloak.

"We'd better hurry then before they catch up," Frisco kept up with Jack.

Bolts of energy arced around them, appearing through the smoke. They kept themselves clear of any strike, but had to be cautious with each step they took. Huun waved his hand in front of his face, trying to clear the smoke that clouded his vision. His soldiers stood around looking dumbfounded. Huun could see their confused expressions. This enraged him, "What are you all standing around like idiot for? AFTER THEM!"

The soldiers snapped out of their trances and followed their superior's orders.

Jack, Frisco, Helix and Strommel had followed the path along the outer edge of the behemoth down two levels. Jack was determined now more than ever to reach the hangar. He wanted to commandeer a small airship, get to the ground, and warn the city of the impending doom. Hopefully it wasn't too late. However, he feared it was.

"Where are we going?" Helix asked, a small bit of whine in his voice.

"The hangar," Jack replied. "We need to get to an air vehicle quickly."

"What for?"

"We need to get to Lartanner and tell him everything," Jack explained.

"What if it's too late?" Frisco asked.

"We have to try," Jack reaffirmed, his own faith shaken as they rounded the final corner to see the hangar was emptying before them. The last of the one-man aircrafts were dropping from the hangar and falling into the night sky below.

"It's too late," Helix pointed to the falling ships. "The invasion has begun."

The last of the New Utica Law Enforcement LEHVs rose into the air, in pursuit of the incoming vehicles poised to attack the city. Lartanner's LEHV led the charge, swooping high into the air as their adversaries raced toward them. Lartanner gripped the handle just above the doorframe. He clasped his fingers around it tightly. His stomach dropped into his feet as the LEHV twisted higher into the air. Aloona had the steering column pulled back into his lap. Lartanner could feel his cheeks peeling back from his skull, the sensation of zero gravity taking control. The decisive moment was upon them. They were engaging an enemy. THE enemy.

The city was under siege. There was little that could be done aside from a full-scale assault. Lartanner felt his throat close up as he watched the first airship from the behemoth open fire. Strips of red bolts sliced through the night air. It traveled in a long, straight stream, penetrating the side of the LEHV. The sound of the laser connecting with the metal sounded like bacon sizzling in a hot pan. The putrid stench of burning rubber filled the cabin.

"Damn!" Aloona coughed.

"They must've hit the tires," Lartanner held a cloth over his nose, trying to mask the odor that forcibly filled his nostrils.

"So much for a safe landing," Aloona said darkly.

"Doesn't matter," Lartanner lowered the cloth, accepting the odor. "Walking away from this isn't part of the plan."

The lead LEHV, its driver side tires belching smoke violently behind itself, flipped and spiraled as Aloona piloted it with precision into the thick of the advancing blitzkrieg. The sky lit up with laser fire from the incoming onslaught that raced out from within the belly of the floating beast. The LEHVs returned with gunfire of their own, tearing apart several airships that broke past the upward blockade the NUPD offered. Several airships threaded between LEHVs that performed a serpentine maneuver. The conflicting air fighters proceeded to open fire on one another, several ships transforming into red and orange blossoms of fire as they erupted into flames.

Lartanner gripped the overhead handlebar tightly, his knuckles turning white. He could feel his stomach drop into his ankles as his LEHV climbed higher. Fortunately, his stomach didn't stay there for long. Unfortunately, his stomach shifted several times thereafter, moving from his ankles to his throat, up into his head, and then back into his feet. The LEHV had twisted and spiraled in the sky as it dodged and maneuvered around energy blasts and exploding crafts. Not only did his stomach shift, but so did his entire body. His backside raised from the seat and his shoulder pressed against the window.

"Can you hold this thing any steadier?" Lartanner grunted as he tries to pull himself back down.

"Not unless you want to die," Aloona snapped.

He didn't. He put his faith into Aloona, a man he trusted and felt safe placing his life into his former partner's hands. The sky outside the window was lighting up like the Fourth of July. He shielded his eyes with his hand, blocking out the blinding light. He hoped Aloona was not easily distracted by the incessant glare that seemed to violate their vision repeatedly. Fire in the sky burned as aircraft and vehicles alike burned and fell to the earth below.

"We need to keep this firefight away from the city," Lartanner spoke. "There's too much falling debris. We need to keep the citizens down there safe."

"I don't think they much care," Aloona spat as he gestured toward the massive airship before them.

Lartanner scooped up the COMM device off the control panel and relayed his orders, "Attention everyone. Lead them out away from the city. We need to ensure that the citizens of New Utica are safe. Engage the Elevation Shield."

The Elevation Shield, a protective covering that was enabled above the exposed streets and sidewalks. Approximately ten feet above the streets an electrified shielding protected the streets, allowing for anything that may fall to the streets below to disintegrate, protecting those below. It was a sure-fire method to keep the citizens of New Utica safe.

Aloona, despite his protest, began to engage a cluster of aircraft bearing down on the closest buildings. "For your sake, I hope this works."

Lartanner let loose a rare, but small, grin. He had good officers; even when they disagreed, they followed orders. Within moments, they were in the thick of battle.

CHAPTER 21
THE THICK OF BATTLE

Jack led the small group along the walkway over the remaining aircraft that were still being readied to be let loose into the sky. He held up a hand that Helix walked into, not paying attention to Jack's lead, only to the scrambling soldiers below. They clustered about like a swarm of bees working busily within their hive, each knowing their role and working in perfect synchronization.

"Wait here," Jack whispered.

"No," Frisco sneered. "You're not going down there without us."

"We only need one pod," Jack explained. "There's only one pilot. Do the math."

Jack began to lower himself down to the loading zone where the aircraft was prepped for launch.

"Pig headed jerk," Frisco whispered to herself.

He slid behind the craft, out of view of the crewmember that removed the hose from the craft's tank. He quickly pressed himself against the side of the craft, keeping himself as invisible as possible. He sneaked around the opposite end. The craft's pilot was busy going through the preflight checklist, ensuring the craft was ready for flight and fully loaded for attack. Jack took this to his advantage as he crept up behind the pilot. He gripped the pilot's neck and thrust their body forward, slamming it hard into the console. The pilot fell limp in his grasp, knocked unconscious. Jack twisted his neck around to see if anyone had noticed his assault. Fortunately, they were all too busy to see anything out of the ordinary, almost as if they were all under the same trance Frisco had been under at one time. This made things much easier. Jack still kept himself low and out of view. He turned to signal the others to come down.

Helix acknowledged Jack's signal and moved aside for Frisco to pass him, "After you."

She snorted as she walked by, not appreciating his subtle jab at her disdain for Jack's machismo. The three of them, including Strommel, dropped down next to Jack. Jack had been stuffing the unconscious pilot into the far corner of the launch bay behind the aircraft. Frisco looked at the pilot to see it was a woman. "Good thing you went ahead," she said glibly. "Otherwise I may not have been able to handle her."

"I didn't realize he was a she."

"Maybe you need to go back to anatomy class, Zero," she smirked.

"Well, looks like you're the one who needs to put on her uniform, since it will fit you," Jack directed. "The rest of you climb into the back."

"This thing is pretty tight in here," Helix commented. "How're we all going to fit in here?"

"We're not," Jack replied.

"What's that supposed to mean?" Helix asked.

"It means you three go ahead, do what you can to slow them down," Jack said. "I'm staying behind."

Frisco finished zipping the front of the flight suit, her face twisting with anger at what Jack was saying, "What?! No way, not again, not this time, we're in this together, we're not leaving anyone behind."

"I know," Jack smiled. "No one is left behind. Winnie, she's still here somewhere."

"Winnie?" Frisco said confused. Jack realized she was under the trance when Winnie was brought to the bridge.

"They captured her and brought her here. I can't leave her."

"Then we'll stay with you," Frisco said.

"No, you know you can't. You have to go down there, warn Lartanner before it's too late."

"We already took care of that, right Helix?" Frisco turned to Helix who was nodding in agreement.

"Then get out there and help them," Jack said. "You'll do more out there than up here."

Helix stepped up to Jack and threw his arms around Jack's neck, "Good luck, pal."

"Th-thanks," Jack choked, Helix's arms constricted tightly around his throat. Helix finally released Jack and walked away. Jack rubbed his tender throat as he gasped for air to return to his lungs.

Strommel approached Jack next. He held out his hand to Jack. Jack smiled as he accepted it firmly. Strommel leaned over and whispered into Jack's ear. Jack smiled again in return. He patted Strommel on his shoulder as he walked to the airship and climbed in behind Helix.

"Jack," Frisco felt her chest tighten, her breath stop. "I-I don't want to lose you."

He touched her face gently, his thumb caressing her cheek, "You won't, whatever it takes, I've gotta get Winnie outta here."

"Be sure to get yourself out too," Frisco threw aside her tough side and let her vulnerability show, a rarity Jack knew, as she threw her arms around his neck, pulling him in tightly, "Be careful."

"I will."

They shared a kiss, their lips initially pressed tightly together and then loosened as they kissed more deeply, passionately. Frisco closed her eyes as she let him take control, his lips guiding hers. She held her breath before he finally pulled away. He didn't look back once he turned away and slipped into the shadows.

Frisco stood motionless for a moment, as she watched him fade into the darkness of the behemoth. She felt as if she was watching him leave her for the last time. Then, he was gone. She closed her eyes tightly, holding back any tears that tried to escape. She wouldn't let her vulnerability show through more than once. Both Strommel and Helix stood silently, looking away from her sheepishly, ignoring her slight emotional moment. "What the hell are you all standing around for?" She asked, a slight choke in her voice. "Let's get aboard and get off this damned thing."

Jack didn't look back as he made his way deeper into the belly of the behemoth. He never liked goodbyes, especially those that may be forever. He shook the thought from his mind. It wasn't what was important now; saving Winnie was. He knew time was short. If he wanted to find Ceinwen, get her out of here; and maybe himself too. He had to find her fast.

Jack retraced his steps as he returned deeper into the behemoth. The walkways that were once bustling with soldiers were now empty. '*This was good*,' Jack thought. He figured the soldiers were now all congregating in the main hangar, awaiting orders to deploy when they reach their destination. He would make sure that wouldn't happen, just as soon as he got Ceinwen off the ship safely. He slipped along the narrow grated planks swiftly, peeking in every room he passed.

Nothing. No sign of Ceinwen.

"Help!" A familiar voice cried out, echoing across the large ceiling above. It was Ceinwen. He heard her cry out again. It sounded much closer this time.

Another voice polluted his ears, "Shut up or I'll kill you myself!"

'*Glorm*,' Jack confirmed in his mind. He followed the direction of the shouts. He picked up his pace, starting with a slow trot and then breaking into a full sprint. He had to save Ceinwen before it was too late.

The aircraft drifted aimlessly through the clouds, darkness enveloping the city beneath. Frisco steered the vehicle the best she could.

"Can't this thing go any faster?" Strommel asked.

"I don't know," Frisco responded.

"Can't you keep this thing straight," Helix added as he clapped his hand over his mouth, stifling the unsettling feeling that was churning in his stomach.

"I'm trying!" Frisco snarled. The last thing she needed was back seat drivers. "The steering column is stiff."

"Figures we'd take the one that was broken," Helix felt queasy. He slid forward as the aircraft dipped sharply.

Helix fell across the back of Frisco's seat, his arms draping over her face. She roughly grabbed a fistful of his shirt and shoved him backward, "Dammit! Strap yourself in will you!"

"I can't, there are only two seats," Helix snapped back.

"Just stay out of my way!" Frisco barked.

She guided the vehicle with difficulty, wrenching the steering column with every muscle in her body. The airship responded in kind, violently twisting in the air. They were drifting toward the aerial battle that was below. The sky ahead lit up with blossoms of fire and streams of beams that streaked from ship to ship.

"This thing isn't broken," Strommel realized. "It's programmed to take you to the battle."
"Great," Frisco frowned.

Helix hid his face in his hands, wanting to escape from this madness, but the one word that struck his ears made him perk up, "What did you say?"

Strommel repeated, "This ship is programmed to take us into battle, there's no avoiding it."

"Programmed?" Helix whispered to himself.

He lunged forward, his body overtaking Frisco's view.

"Get out of the way!" She commanded.

"Shut up!" Helix began to claw at the instruments panel, found a

314

small control panel door and tore it open.

"What the hell are you doing?" Frisco tried to keep her focus out the front window.

Helix was gripping handfuls of cable and wire and wresting them loose, "I'm gonna hotwire this thing and get us off this crazy autopilot!"

"You can do that?"

Helix turned to her with an unsure smile, "We're about to find out."

Her heart sank into her stomach. "Great," she replied wryly.

CHAPTER 22
THE FANTASTIC AIR BATTLE

The sky lit up, flashing light and dark intermittently, like a light switch being flipped on an off repeatedly. Several LEHV's grouped together and engaged several fighters in a v-shaped formation. Their weapons screamed as they tore open the night sky slicing through the darkness and connecting with their intended targets. Six more Dark HART airships exploded.

Leading the charge of LEHV's was Lieutenant Remy Oszkowski. His expression was filled with experience, engagement, and determination. He had been Lartanner's direct subordinate, right-hand man and extension of himself since he came out of the academy. In many ways, Remy was superior to Lartanner in almost every way, even being asked to assume the post of Chief above Lartanner's partner, Aloona. However, Remy never pursued that path. Instead, he reached the rank of Lieutenant and then refused any other offer of advancement. According to Remy, it was because he never wanted to be in charge, a leader. He fancied himself one to take orders, not give them. But he knew Lartanner was aware of his insipid disdain for paperwork and administration. In fact, he knew deep down he did it so that Lartanner could succeed. He respected and admired Lartanner. Remy knew Lartanner was an exceptional leader and was truly the better of them. He led the newly formed LEHV squadron for another pass, flanking the enemy on an open side to the west of the streaking fighters.

Remy had been in the hospital after the crash. The pursuit they had to rescue Frisco had ended badly for him. He had been hurt, unconscious. When the other NULE officers arrived, they immediately transported Remy to St. Elizabeth's Medical Center where he was in intensive care for nearly eight hours. The doctor's had even determined him unable for released, but Remy was a fighter. Sure, he was overweight, and often kept to himself, but he wasn't going to allow his meager personality to hold him back. Remy held onto his memories while in the hospital, thinking about Jack and Agent Frisco. They were there for him, showed him what he was capable of, and he wanted to be there for them. When he heard the officers that visited him talk about the disappearance of Jack and Frisco, he made sure he was well enough to leave the hospital, against the advice of the doctors. He wasn't going to lie there while his friends were in danger. Remy checked himself out and assumed his LEHV. Even Aloona and Lartanner protested his desire to return to active duty, but Remy insisted. They knew he was the best pilot they had, and in the impending assault, they needed him.

"Take them!" Barbasoa shouted into his headset, the order ringing into Remy's ears breaking his memories and bringing him back to reality.

The firefight was fierce and abrupt as Remy's LEHVs became engaged. He personally took out two of their airships. They each combusted, popping loudly as they became engrossed in flame and began to drop from the sky.

Aloona guided his LEHV nearby Remy. They both drifted behind Barbasoa's lead LEHV. Lartanner was anxious as he leaned forward in his seat, "Watch where you're dropping those ships, Barbasoa!"

"Lartanner?" Barbasoa responded, "Shouldn't you be behind your desk?"

"Dammit Barbasoa! I want you to lead those fighters away from the hub of the city, get them closer to the water or over the forest."

"Let me ask them if they'd be okay with taking the fight somewhere else," Barbasoa quipped. "Sorry, I don't think they care."

"There are people down there!" Lartanner spat into his COMM. "We need to protect them!"

Barbasoa grimaced, his leathery skin cracked and folded. He knew Lartanner was right. He let out a long sigh, "Fine."

Barbasoa pumped his controls and encircled a legion of enemy crafts. Remy was quick to follow, mirroring Barbasoa's moves. The airships took the bait and opened into full pursuit of them.

"Get your hands off me!" Ceinwen's voice echoed across the high ceiling of the behemoth. "I said don't touch me!"

The shrill of her screams and struggles sent shivers up Jack's spine.

He found her, but she was obviously not alone. He needed to get close to her without being seen. Jack sneaked along the wall until he was close to the room where Ceinwen was being held. It was the control room.

'*Of course,*' he thought to himself. '*They couldn't pick a less guarded room?*' Jack swiveled his neck as he took in his surroundings. The majority of the guards had been sent out into the airships and the remaining squads were stationed in and around the control room. Seems logical since all the leaders were in there. Now he just needed to find a way to get himself in there, unnoticed and still be able to handle a small regiment of troops along with Glorm, Huun, and Zimm.

'*Sounds easy, right?*' Jack mused to himself. There was only one-way he could get in, and that was up. Jack craned his neck and pivoted it around in order to see how. An exhaust vent stared down at him. Its grid looked like a tooth-filled mouth growling at him, eagerly anticipating his entry into the open maw and to quell its insatiable appetite. Jack began to hoist himself up to the awaiting vent.

An explosion rocked the ship forcing the steering column to slip from Frisco's hands. Helix smashed his head against the console, his hands slipping away from the wires he had gripped. Sparks flew from underneath the console. Helix recoiled, covering his eyes.

"We're gonna die!" Helix cried.

"Shut up!" Frisco snapped. She wrapped her hands around the column and locked the muscles in her arm in order to hold the vehicle steady. It didn't respond to her at first, but soon began to level off. Frisco let out a long sigh and then turned to see if anyone noticed that she was nervous. Fortunately, both Helix and Strommel were too busy looking at the mayhem outside the window to notice.

Frisco began to weave through the oncoming barrage of LEHV's. Their beams blazed through the darkened sky. Frisco kept her calm and eased the steering column as she guided the vehicle around each fire, threading it like the eye of a needle. She was beginning to feel the hang of the vehicle. She had to get through without harming them.

"They're going to annihilate us!" Helix groaned again.

"Helix!" Frisco snapped. "Would you quit whining and get over here and help me with this radio!"

Frisco was flipping switches and pressing any button near the radio. Helix seemed to forget about the peril outside as he watched Frisco display her reckless technical abusive behavior, "Are you some kind of barbarian?" He asked. "You keep banging away at that like you are and we'll be making a nose dive for the concrete below."

"Well, how else am I supposed to find the right frequency to contact those NULE officers so they stop firing on us?"

"You ask me, that's how."

"So quit talking and start doing!" Frisco smirked out of Helix's view, satisfied that she was able to take his mind off the incessant danger just outside.

Helix began tapping the controls. He seemed confident, but it soon faded from his face as he realized he was getting nowhere. "That's odd," he said.

"What?" Frisco asked.

"These controls aren't responsive, at least not in a normal way; they seem to not react to any logical actions."

"So do something illogical!"

"It doesn't work that way," Helix sounded annoyed. "This relay set up is all backwards. I need to reroute the communications so that it understands our frequencies."

"So do it!"

"It's not that easy," Helix snapped. You can't just order it that way. This is delicate work and requires a certain amount of finesse." He squeezed himself next to Frisco, the area cramped for two, especially when one is Helix's size, "I need to open up the panel gently." He clawed at the panel unsuccessfully, "I need a tool or something to get this open."

Frisco let out her breath under a growl as he pulled back her arm and threw a punch into the panel. The steel buckled from the impact. Frisco smiled, shaking her hand to relieve the small pain she felt in her knuckles.

"Thanks, I think?"

"Just get to work," she said.

Aloona cranked the steering column hard to port as Lartanner screamed into his ear, pointing erratically, "That way, follow them! Go!"

Lartanner watched as the enemy airship flew effortlessly around the opposing LEHV's that continuously opened fire upon it. He could feel his blood boil. The ship in particular was trying to evade the battle. It appeared to be making its way into the heart of the city. Some sort of suicidal mission, like a kamikaze of old, Lartanner thought. But it wasn't going to happen, not on his watch.

"All right, all right!" Aloona huffed. "This thing isn't that smooth when it banks you know."

"That ship is getting away, don't lose it!"

"I'm on it, dammit!" Aloona growled. He was tired of Lartanner's constant barking. "You want to drive?"

"Just fly!"

"I will if you let me!" Aloona twisted the column and sent the LEHV spinning into the thick of battle. He weaved around several enemy aircraft as he pursued the one that seemed to want to break past the defenses on both sides and venture deep into the city. He opened fire, trying to cripple the craft. The cannon fire he let loose missed the pursued, striking either other enemy aircraft or surrounding structures. Lartanner cringed at the thought of concrete and metal debris raining down onto the unsuspected city below. He hoped the rest of the NULE officers had evacuated the inflicted parts of the city.

"Take down that son of a bitch!" Lartanner snarled.

"That's the general idea."

The aircraft was wedging between buildings, searching for a narrow enough channel to escape through.

"They're heading down Bleeker, the street narrows when you get closer to Grimaldi's," Lartanner shot. "Don't let them get in there!"

"You sound like a skipping audio file!" Aloona pushed down on the triggers, opening another round of laser fire.

"The wiring on this thing is a mess!" Helix growled. "I can't figure out how to rewire this without pulling out the whole panel."

"I thought you were some kind of electrical genius or something," Frisco shot back.

"When I know what I'm doing!"

"Just great!" She groaned.

A flash of a laser beam sizzled past the windshield, burning the plexi-steel that held it in place. Helix ducked down in fear, not realizing it was nowhere near hitting him. "They're still on us!" Helix gulped.

"You don't think I know that!" Frisco kept her focus straight ahead. The buildings ahead were closer together, making the area between narrower. This smaller, lighter aircraft she was flying was more nimble, smaller, and lighter than a LEHV. If she could get their without being hit, she could get away. "Sit back and strap in!"

Strommel inched over slightly as Helix, a man with more girth than him, squeezed down next to him. They each grabbed half of the harness straps that reached across the seat. Unfortunately, the strap couldn't meet in the middle. Helix let loose an apologetic smile. Strommel reluctantly threw back a sympathetic gaze, hoping this snag wouldn't result in either of their unfortunate deaths. The aircraft twisted as it slipped into the narrowing channel. Gunfire erupted around them, tearing at both sides of the buildings as they bobbed the aircraft up and down out of each blasts range. The smell of scorched air seeped into the cockpit. Frisco held her breath as she maintained her focus on her flying, but the acrid odor made Helix gag harshly.

"You better keep that down!" Frisco ordered, "Or I'm ejecting you as countermeasures."

Helix swallowed hard, keeping his sick inside, and out of fear that he knew she would actually do it. Frisco guided her LEHV carefully, pitching it to the side as it entered the confining space. He felt the vehicle jolt roughly as the bottom scraped against the stone of the building on one side. Sparks spewed from the belly of the LEHV, bouncing off the hull and raining on the ground below. She instinctively pulled back in order to raise the vehicle out of channel and above the building. Frisco smiled to herself as she watched in her rear display the pursuing LEHV lifting into the sky behind them. They were in the clear. She felt her body relax as she let out the air she held for so long in her lungs. As Frisco reveled in her ability to maneuver between the buildings without a scratch, her forward screen was suddenly filled with the sight of two more LEHV's cutting off her path.

"Aw shit!" She moaned.

Helix shouted, "What are you waiting for? SHOOT!"

"I can't! They're not our enemies!"

"They're gonna kill us!"

Frisco knew Helix was right. There was little they could do save smashing into the buildings they were sandwiched between. The LEHV's had their weapons aimed and charged. It was only a matter of minutes before they were cooked.

Helix continued his pessimistic stance, "We're dead."

Strommel couldn't take the back seat any longer. He sprang to action lurching forward in his seat, the strap holding him back slightly, but his arms could still reach the panel in front. He reached around Frisco and flipped three switches before pressing a button. The front cannon of the aircraft retreated within while a panel opened between the weapons. A large round opening pushed forward and a pulsating light grew. Within seconds, a ball of energy blasted out of the front of the aircraft and quickly, silently sailed across the channel until it enveloped the two opposing LEHVs. Lightening and energy wrapped around the two vehicles as they each slowly spun and drifted slowly down.

"What the hell was that?" Frisco asked.

"All these ships are equipped with an EMP device, at low settings it can cripple an opponent without harming them," Strommel explained.

"How did you know about that?" Helix added.

"I designed it," Strommel smiled sheepishly. "My colleague sold all my tech designs to the HART without my knowledge, but fortunately, I learned it all while I was their prisoner."

"And you waited until now to tell us?" Sneered Frisco.

"We weren't facing off against friends before."

'*He had a point*,' Frisco thought. She pushed down on the throttle, opened up the engine as it roared loudly, and propelled them out of the narrow channel and into the open sky around the city.

It wasn't long, however, before Aloona and Lartanner's LEHV had regained control and returned to the pursuit.

"Hang on tight, it's time for round two," Frisco pressed forward on the throttle and continued into the sky above the city.

Jack slinked his body through the ventilation duct. It was a tight squeeze making it difficult to move quicker than the snail's pace he currently moved.

"I want the weapons charged and ready," he heard Glorm's voice echo around his ears. "Once the local law enforcement is taken care of, the big guns should arrive. Let's be prepared to wipe them out quickly."

"We're taking an awful risk, Glorm," Jack recognized Zimm's voice. "This full scale assault of yours had better work."

"Of course it will work."

Huun growled, his voice still boomed from the distance they shared, "Why are we listening to this simpering fool?"

He could hear the sickening glee in Glorm's caterwaul, "Because, my dear Huun, I know how the government functions, their tactics and tech. Every move they make reads like a high school playbook. We will destroy them in one fell swoop."

"I hope you're right, Glorm," Zimm hissed. "The Master will be displeased if we fail. He's invested a lot in you, your campaigns and rise to political success. He doesn't take too kindly to failure."

"Don't worry yourself, General Zimm," Glorm cooed. "We have an unstoppable force, far outnumbering the pathetic New Utica police force. With the President in town, under a small protective guard, and the majority of the military fighting the dark threat overseas, we can't lose. The President will be in our control, and the United States will be brought to its knees with me as its savior, nothing could be more perfect."

Jack had inched himself over the grated opening that overlooked the massive control room below. He could see the tops of Zimm and Huun's heads. Not far from them, he could see Glorm, his thinning hair visible from the more than fifteen foot height. How was he going to get down quickly and quietly? A task that seemed daunting, if not impossible.

"What are you going to do with me?" Ceinwen's voice now rang out sweetly from the foul din of the other gravelly voices.

"Patience my dear," he could see Glorm reach out and touch her face. She recoiled in disgust. "The Master has special plans for one such as lovely as you."

"Don't touch me!"

"Such fire," Glorm said amusingly. "You will make an ideal sacrifice."

Ceinwen swallowed, "S-sacrifice?"

Glorm only showed her his charming, yet sinister smile. It made her ill.

"Jack Zero will save me!"

Zimm laughed maniacally, a full guffaw, "Zero? Zero's dead!"

Ceinwen felt her stomach tie in knots. She couldn't believe it. She wouldn't believe it. Jack was careful, brave, and strong. He wouldn't let himself be taken so easily. "You lie!"

"I saw to it myself," Huun walked into the room, his form brooding and wicked. He knew what Zimm was playing and joined in, "Dead."

Tears began to stream down Ceinwen's soft cheeks, leaving trails of damp, jagged streaks behind them, "I-I can't believe it!"

"Believe it my dear," Glorm continued to smile, now much more broadly than before. He reveled in this.

Jack could feel his blood boil. He watched helplessly from above. He needed to drop in on them unexpectedly, gain the upper hand and rescue Ceinwen. But how exactly would he do that?

Jack scanned the room through the grating, trying to find a quick and quiet way he could sneak out and down in order to spring his surprise. He should probably come up with whatever he planned to do once he got down there as well.

Ceinwen let out a high-pitched shriek. Jack saw Huun was clasping his massive hands around her arms. She struggled to break free, but Huun's hold was too strong. There was no time to waste. Jack began to sidle his body again, slinking through the vent further. As his stomach crossed over the great, it bowed under his weight. Without warning, the grate gave way. Jack screamed as he fell from the ceiling above and into the snake pit of the command center below. He certainly had the element of surprise now.

Had Jack known the bolts holding the ventilation system up where what had weakened from the transfer across the void, not from his own weight, perhaps he would have been more careful when he moved. Now it was too late. Jack lay on his back, his spine registering large amounts of pain as he struggled to regain his breath and movement all at once. Instead, he only remained prone.

Ceinwen shouted at the sight of her would-be savior, "JACK!"

Glorm wrapped his arms around Ceinwen, clamping his hand across her mouth to muffle any further outbursts. He then directed a nasty look at Huun and Zimm, "Dead, huh?"

"He is now," Huun growled.

Huun stepped over the debris that cluttered the floor. He stood over the crumpled and motionless form of Jack Zero. Jack didn't stir, but that didn't prevent Huun from picking him up by his neck and lifting him high into the air. Jack's hands instinctively gripped Huun's thick wrists. His hands couldn't event touch the others fingers. "You never know when to quit, do you Zero?" Huun sneered.

"No," Jack squeaked.

"Let him go!" Ceinwen leapt at Huun and began beating his back with her fists. It didn't do any good. Huun let loose one hand from around Jack's neck and gripped his palm over Ceinwen's face. He shoved her away with hardly a nudge. Ceinwen stumbled back several feet and collapsed to the floor.

Jack bared his teeth and mustered up as much strength as he could, swinging his fists wildly at Huun's face. Several blows connected with little avail. One throw finally struck Huun square in his Adam's apple. The impact took Huun off guard and resulted in the release of his grip around Jack's neck. Jack fell freely to the floor. His knees gave out at the moment his feet hit the ground. Jack rolled just before Zimm could pull out his sidearm and fire a shot. The bullet chewed into the floor where Jack had once been.

Glorm reached out and threw his weight onto Zimm's arms. "What the Hell are you doing?" Zimm shouted.

"No guns idiot!" Glorm ordered. "If you hit the envelope we'll explode!"

Zimm wanted to shoot Glorm for bringing light to the truth. However, he knew Glorm was right.

He huffed and scoffed before holstering his pistol, "He dies, NOW!"

Glorm smiled, "In due time."

Jack was brought to his feet by armed guards, each armed with their electricity wands.

"Welcome, Detective Zero!" Glorm greeted the swooning Jack. "I wish I could say it's a pleasure to see you, but like every other time before, your presence is a nuisance."

"I'm always happy to help," Jack grumbled.

"Always with the quips, doesn't it ever get boring?"

"I'll let you know."

"Unfortunately, you won't have the opportunity," Glorm walked circles around Jack as he wiped the blood trickling from the corner of his mouth. "You see, Detective, you'll soon be dead."

"Funny, you keep saying that and yet here I am."

Huun gnashed his teeth angrily and stepped forward. Zimm held his hand out to stop his assault, "I'll kill him now!"

"Easy big fella," Jack smirked. "I'll get to you soon enough."

Huun let out a low grunt, his eyes darting to Zimm who still kept him back with his glare. Zimm could feel the same rage boiling up inside him that Huun was openly ready to release. Zimm could visualize himself tearing Jack's limbs from his body. It didn't matter, as long as he could inflict pain. But he would have to wait. For now.

"I assume your cohorts escaped on one of our vehicles," Glorm sneered, Ceinwen struggling to break his grip from under his arms. It was of little use. He was strong. Stronger than he looked. She used her eyes to communicate her fear to Jack. She caught his gaze and she could see he understood.

Glorm continued, "I assume you stayed behind to save this one." He gestured his head toward the top of Ceinwen's.

"Let her go," Jack responded, his arms still locked in the grips of two surrounding soldiers. "This is between us, not her."

"Ah, but you actually care about her, so why would I release my leverage over you?"

"To be nice?" Jack interjected.

It was an off-putting remark, one that even Ceinwen stopped struggling and contorted her expression into a confused look. Even Huun curled his lip in disbelief of what Jack said.

"Nice try, Detective," Glorm laughed. "But nice is reserved for children on the playground. Here, we can be real, and real means we can put aside niceties in favor of self-motivation. You are driven by self-motivation aren't you?"

"Go to Hell."

"Come now, Detective," Glorm scoffed. "I know you better than this; you aren't petty and simple when it comes to insults. You want to know."

"Know what?"

"Why everything, of course."

Jack was silent. He looked over to Ceinwen. She was terrified, her eyes wet and cheeks stained with tears. He wasn't sure what Glorm was getting at, but he had to continue baiting him in order to keep her safe.

"You silence speaks volumes," Glorm felt the satisfaction of putting Jack in his place. "Why would a man in a prominent and influential position ally himself with an organization revered the world over as villains? But the truth is the villains are those in power right in your own backyard."

"Heh," Jack snorted. "You mean like you?"

"Hardly." Glorm retorted, "The Grand One is this world's savior, I am merely the vessel that will deliver his message and him to the people.

You can't deny that this world is falling apart. Just look at the division in this country alone. Republican and Democrats at one another's throats, neither accepting their own blame. Each feeds the populace with what they want to hear and they eat it up, like a child in a candy store. It's sickening. You know as well as I that this is true."

"You're blinded by your own crusade, cloaked in fearmongering and the same two-sided play that you're opposing. Sounds more like hypocrisy."

"Hypocrisy? You just aren't enlightened. But don't worry, you soon will be," Glorm paced the floor between him and Ceinwen. "You see, you're predestined to become a part of us, you were always from the beginning. When the Grand One saw how you took action into your own hands when you, unsuccessfully albeit, opposed your superior and tried to overthrow our dear General Zimm, you were earmarked as a candidate."

"What do you mean candidate?" Jack felt uneasy.

"You see, when you went into surgery for your accident with your arm, you were implanted, with special tech that would prepare your inclusion into the Army of Light."

"You mean like you tried with Agent Frisco?"

"Tried?" Glorm chuckled. "She's still under our control."

Jack felt his heart sink. "What do you mean?"

"We knew you would do anything to protect her, save her, if you will, so we programmed her to react to your devices, make her appear as if she was her 'old' self. She's still very much in our control, under out influence."

Jack felt all the anger and rage boil inside him. He lunged forward, reaching for Glorm's neck, but being held back by the arms of the soldiers who kept him back. His weakness from the fall didn't help either.

"You bastard!" Jack snapped.

"Now, now, Detective. You didn't think we would make this too easy for you. Did you? You really thought you were clever enough to outsmart us? You truly are gullible, and easily manipulated. Just like a good soldier."

Glorm's laugh was more irritating than malevolent. Although Glorm had him and he was now at their mercy.

"Keep it steady! I can't get the EMP online if you don't hold it still!" Helix yelled into Frisco's ear. "Look! There's the NULE Headquarters!" Helix pointed to the tall building not too far in the distant, the spire towering high into the stark night sky in the center of the city. "We can make it!"

"You need to get that EMP operational and now!" Frisco shouted back.

"It's almost there, just watch where you're flying!"

"Stop backseat driving!" Frisco growled through gnashed teeth. "Just forget it! Sit back and shut up!"

"But I've almost got it."

Frisco pulled back on the yoke. Helix fell back into his crowded seat, his hand still reaching for the electromagnetic pulse. The aircraft had veered sharply still working to outmaneuver their pursuant. He was nervous that their inability to speak to them and identify themselves was going to result in their being shot down violently. He felt his inside flip-flop as they rocked back and forth, dodging several blasts from their opposition. Overall, he at least felt safe with Agent Frisco at the controls.

The light of a blue screen illuminated his face in the darkness. He looked to see Strommel tapping feverishly at a palm device.

Helix questioned, "What are you doing?"

"I'm checking something," he said in a low voice.

"What?"

"Never mind!" He snapped at Helix.

Helix recoiled slightly, taken aback by the aggression. He never had seen Strommel react like that. It was out of character and off putting. Helix slumped back and folded his arms like a scorned child responding to a parent that told him 'no.'

The radio on the console began to crackle, allowing for garbled pieces of misunderstood language to come through, "zzzzt...craft seven-seven....zzzzt...heading four-four-one....zzzt...are you armed?"

Helix ignored Strommel and leaned forward to see Frisco responding to the radio.

"Armed and ready, my master," she replied.

"Forever destiny," came the garbled voice again.

"Forever destiny," she replied.

CHAPTER 23
REAWAKENING

Aloona kept a tight tail on the airship that continuously attempted to outmaneuver and dodge every attempt he made at bringing it down. The ship was elusive, an experienced pilot at the control no doubt.

Lartanner leaned forward, "Look ahead." He pointed out the front shield. In the distance, the New Utica Headquarters loomed in the sky, towering over the city. "They're headed toward NULE Headquarters."

"Why would they go there?" Aloona asked.

"I don't know, unless," Lartanner thought for a moment. The hum of the engine was the only sound heard. "Unless they're heading towards the communications array at the top of the tower."

"And why would that matter?"

"The communications array keeps all LEHV units in sync; it prevents them from firing on one another and allows the ships to maintain the same course trajectory while in combat or pursuit. It also permits the LEHVs to maintain their weapons. If that array were knocked out, the ships would be out of control, unarmed and unprotected. It would be chaos for our men."

Aloona hunched forward, "Then they'd better not get to that tower."

"Who was that on the radio?" Helix asked. "I thought it wasn't working."

"It was nothing," Frisco replied. "Probably just a rouge transmission we picked up from one of the nearby housing units."

"But I heard you respond."

Frisco gripped the steering column tighter in her hands. She grit her teeth as she hesitated for a moment. She couldn't constitute a convenient lie quickly enough. She had to act fast in order to complete her mission and return to her place in the HART. Helix's incessant whining continued from behind her. She wished she could have left them on the behemoth. It was too late now. Instead, she had them with her. She had to convince Jack of her loyalty in order to secure the last transport. Fortunately, he stayed behind. Now she just had to deal with these two, but they should present no problem.

Helix continued to pester her with a barrage of concerns, "Maybe it was a transmission from the main ship," "Maybe they have a relay bomb in this ship that set to go off in case it was stolen," "What are we going to do?"

The NULE Headquarters tower was just ahead. She could see the communications array lining the flat roof of the tall building. She couldn't waste time; she had to make the first assault count.

"You're going in awfully fast," Helix commented. "How are you planning to land?"

With one quick motion, Frisco threw her elbow back and cracked Helix in the chin, "I'm not," she said.

Helix reeled backward and slumped into the seat, this time unconscious. He fell across Strommel, pushing down on his arms resulting in his dropping the device he had in his hands.

Strommel let out a small groan as he took on the weight of Helix, but he refrained from making any louder noise to keep Frisco's focus off him. The palm device he was using now lay between his knees, just out of reach of his hands that were pinned by Helix's body. He stretched his fingers as far as they could extend in an attempt to place it back in his hands. Unfortunately, he had to move Helix to do so. If he leaned forward in any capacity, the device might drop and get lost somewhere further out of reach.

Frisco switched on her targeting, the weapons on the airship charged up, emitting a high-pitched squeal that indicated their readiness. She switched her hand placement on the controls to the triggers for the weapons. She grasped them tightly and prepared to fire. Strommel continued his struggle as Helix rocked slowly with the pitch and yaw the ship took. Each movement made it more difficult for Strommel to grasp his device. Frisco pulled back on the controls and lifted the aircraft up at a sharp incline. The abrupt motion caused the device to roll directly into Strommel's hand. He gripped the device tightly this time, his thumb, although somewhat hindered, he began tapping feverishly. He looked up every few seconds to ensure the beeping didn't attract Frisco's attention. She kept her focus straight ahead.

Jack charged at Glorm, but the heavy hand of Huun smacked hard against his face. He fell onto his back, his breath pushed from his lungs as he hit the floor. Huun stood over Jack's body. He slammed his fist into his other palm as he watched Jack struggle to stand.

"You've always been so driven by your emotions," Glorm said to Jack. "It's your greatest weakness."

"Some say..." Jack stood clutching his jaw. "Some say it's a strength."

"Emotions, bah!" Glorm walked to the great observation window at the front of the large airship. "Emotions just hold you back, drag one down. Why do you think I invested in technologies? Because they don't need emotions. Thinking, no reasoning, just programming. Tell it what you want and it responds exactly as expected."

"They're soulless."

"Soulless?" Glorm smiled, "What is a soul anyway? Nothing more than a moral roadblock if one puts too much reservation in it. It's a hindrance, an anchor. No one believes in a soul, unless they're lost and looking for guidance, then you can convince them that you have a soul and are directing them to follow. People are sheep, easily lead, easily manipulated. How else could a man with ties like mine get elected to such a prestigious position?"

"You mean it wasn't just your charm?" Jack quipped.

Glorm continued grinning. He wasn't going to let Jack's cynical attitude take away from his moment, "But this is just the beginning. The city will fall and the world will look to the failed government and demand a new leader."

"And let me guess, you answer that call."

"It's inevitable."

"It's insane," Jack said seriously.

Glorm's grin melted as he turned to face Jack, "Tomato, to-*mah*-to." Glorm stepped up to the control panel and studied it for a moment. He then turned his attention to the captain of the airship who stood with great stoicism, statuesque, as he remained motionless, awaiting commands.

"Captain?"

"Yessir!" The man machine known as the captain snapped to attention.

"Are we in position?"

The captain responded in the same way, "Yessir!"

"Then prepare for separation," Glorm ordered.

The Captain snapped his arms straight along his side. He reached forward his right arm, his hand flattened in front of him, raised high in salute. "Forever destiny!"

Glorm looked to Jack as he gestured to the Captain-man/machine and raised his eyebrow, "You see? Flawless."

"Inhuman," Jack retorted.

"Now do you see why you won't win this?" Glorm smirked more viciously than before. "You lack any kind of vision."

Jack watched as the Captain commanded his underlings across the bridge. They moved mechanically, as if they were simply designed to perform the task they were completing. It was haunting, unnerving. It made Jack feel as if he were watching something from out of a dream, where nothing was as it seemed and you moved as if mired in mud. He stole a quick glance at Huun. He seemed preoccupied with the activity that was now in full swing across the bridge. Switches were thrown and levers pulled as the Captain called out a final command, "Prepare for separation!"

Aloona pitched and swerved his LEHV as he weaved through the city streets. The commotion of the battle in the sky brought out several spectators who looked out their windows in order to see what was happening. To the surprise of one unsuspecting onlooker was the underside of Aloona's LEHV. The heat from the exhaust engines threw the portly man back even before he could see what nearly hit him. He clutched his cat tightly as he was swept off his feet and sent travelling several feet from the living room to the kitchenette, slamming hard into the counter that separated the two room. Even in spite of the impact, he never let go of the cat. Aloona kept the vehicle in line with the target ahead of him, the fleeing HART airship that broke off from the fleet and decided to take off on its own. Aloona knew better than to let such a sneaky adversary escape. Lartanner gripped tightly to the armrests after checking the harness that strapped him in place, to ensure it was secured. He looked over at Aloona, whose face was wrought with determination.

"Are you sure about this?" Lartanner questioned his friend.

"You're questioning me?" Aloona responded caustically.

"I'm questioning your skills."

"You know me, we were partners for over 14 years, you never questioned my skills then," Aloona said.

"That was before I thought you were trying to get me killed."

"We've been in tougher scraped before."

"All of which were on the ground, solid ground," Lartanner said, a slight quiver in his voice.

"You still afraid of flying?"

"I'm afraid of crashing."

Aloona smiled, "That explains why you took the desk job."

"A desk job with a promotion," Lartanner scowled. "A promotion that could send your ass straight to meter maid duty!"

"You'd miss me too much," Aloona winked.

"You, maybe, but not the sidewalk," Lartanner swallowed hard as he felt his body get pushed against the seat.

Aloona pulled back on the yoke and sent the LEHV up and over the crest of a tower that popped up before them. Aloona confidently maneuvered the vehicle while Lartanner closed his eyes tightly.

Ahead of them, Frisco continued to outmaneuver her pursuer. She darted her eyes to her rear display screen, seeing that the LEHV was still close with no sign of lagging. She was an exceptional pilot; leave it to her misfortune to come up against a pilot that nearly equaled her own skills. Nearly.

Frisco pulled the vehicle high above the city, over the tops of the tallest buildings. The city ahead looked peaceful, unaware of the carnage that lie ahead. Behind them, the stark sky sparked with pocks of lights that flashed and dimmed as explosions erupted and then just as instantly went out. It was a glorious sight. Nothing better than the sights and sounds of victory, especially when on the winning team.

Helix still lay unconscious, sprawled out across Strommel's lap. Strommel continued tapping at the device in his hands. He continued to look up at Agent Frisco to ensure she was not paying any attention to him. She was still hyper-focused on her objective, whatever it was, but it remained before her. Helix let out a low moan as he began to regain his consciousness. He was attempting to open his eyes, but they flapped several times, as if too heavy for his body to handle.

"W-what's going on?" Helix managed.

"Shhh," Strommel said lowly. "Just don't move and keep quiet."

Strommel looked up again to see if Frisco had heard anything. As he looked up, he saw she had craned her neck around and was looking directly at him.

"What are you doing?" She asked, her eyes looking at his hands.

Strommel made sure the device was tucked inconspicuously beneath them. "N-nothing, Agent," Strommel spat out.

"I want that EMP weapon functional immediately!" She demanded.

"But...I...," Strommel began, but was instantly cut off.

"But nothing!" Frisco snapped. "I want it online. NOW!"

"Y-yes, of course," Strommel obeyed. He slid the palm device into his pocket unnoticed. He hoisted Helix up as much as he could, which was only his upper half, and slid him to the left side of the seat. He pushed off Helix's thick torso as he rose from under the harness he unhitched. He then made his way to the console in front of Frisco and began to punch several commands. Within moments, the console lit up.

Frisco sneered as she grabbed the back of Strommel's neck, "You'd better be doing what I asked. If you try anything else, I will snap your neck like a toothpick! Understand?"

Strommel nodded. He finished typing and the computer spoke in a sweet tone, "Electromagnetic Pulse Device online."

Frisco smiled, her lips thin, her smile sinister, "Good, now sit back!"

Strommel meekly returned to his seat and slipped the palm device from within his pocket. Helix held to the side of the seat, freeing Strommel's arms to work more freely. He had only seconds to complete his work.

The HART Aircraft flew across the top of the city as the LEHV poked out from underneath, just catching up to its prey. Aloona took hold of the steering column and with a quick gesture from his thumbs, snapped open the tips on both sides of the yoke in his hands. Under each tip was a firing button, allowing the LEHV to engage its weapons.

Lartanner opened his eyes long enough to see what Aloona was attempting. "Are you sure you don't want me to man the weapons?" Lartanner asked.

"Just sit back and let me handle this," Aloona said assuredly. It didn't reassure Lartanner.

Aloona leveled off the vehicle in line with the aircraft. Just ahead, he could see NULE Headquarters in view. They would be there in minutes. He had to stop that vehicle before it could get there. Aloona pressed the buttons under each thumb. From underneath the LEHV, a barrage of laser light fire erupted, popping as it sailed across the night sky in an attempt to strike their target.

Frisco was swift as she veered the vehicle out of the line of fire. Bolts of light zipped past her as it continued into the night sky until it was no longer visible. Aloona continued his constant firing, each bolt missing the target as the aircraft dodged each beam. It was like a well-choreographed event, like to objects dancing in sequence against the night sky.

Aloona was growing agitated, "Stay still, damn you!"

"Do you think she's heading for the array?" Lartanner questioned.

"Why else would they send a rogue operative into the city?" Aloona answered. "They're heading straight for NULE tower."

"If they knock out the COMM array, our fleet's LEHVs have no chance, their weapons will be disarmed."

Aloona wore an expression of pure determination, "Not if I can stop him!"

Frisco watched her monitors intently, watching the LEHV sway behind her as it kept firing. It was her opportunity as the LEHV slipped into her range of fire. She immediately pressed the button. From beneath the LEHV, a purple glow throbbed and then burst forth. It spread like rings from under the vehicle, like the ripples of water after a stone disrupts the placid surface. The purple beam reached out as Aloona noticed what was happening. He attempted to avoid the oncoming wave, but unfortunately was unable to miss. The wave struck the side of the LEHV. Once it connected, it converted into electricity as it covered the exterior of the vehicle. The bolts of electricity crept across the hull like a predator's tendrils wrapping around a frozen prey. The lights on the LEHV began to dim and flicker as the ship dipped from its position in the sky.

"What's happening?" Lartanner nearly screamed in fear.

"We're losing power!" Aloona tried to hold the wheel stead as it pulled from his hands.

"How?"

"They hit us with some electromagnetic pulse wave, we're going down!" Aloona desperately fought to keep the vehicle in the sky. It pitched and yawed as it slowly descended.

Frisco grinned triumphantly. She had won. Now, nothing could stop her from reaching the NULE building and completing her mission. She switched her weapon control. The screen before her switched from the rear view of the LEHV falling to the NULE Headquarter building before her. She could see the building gleaming before her. She pressed the targeting button and zeroed in on the communications array that stood tall in the center of the building's rooftop.

"We're falling!" Lartanner screamed.

"No kidding!" Aloona retorted.

He tugged at the steering column, but it wouldn't budge. They were losing altitude, and the enemy aircraft that was now drifting away.

"Do something!" Lartanner was desperate.

"I'm trying!" Aloona flipped every switch and pressed every button across the control panel before him, but only small surges of energy seemed to be pushing through.

Lartanner took note, "Look! There's some energy coming through, can't we use that?"

"It's not that simple," Aloona explained. "An EMP wreaks havoc on electronic components."

"The circuits seem like they're trying to come back on, doesn't that mean something?"

"Maybe," Aloona looked across the board as the lights flickered again. The ship continued to dip and rise with the power fluxes. Aloona paused for a moment before he unstrapped his harness. The constant rise and fall of the ship caused him to stumble as he stood.

"Where are you going?" Lartanner gulped.

Aloona silently slid to the rear of the vehicle. In the main hold, he rummaged through the chest that lined the floor. He tossed out several tools before picking up a small, hand-held pair of pliers. He rushed back up to the front and into his seat.

"What are you doing?" Lartanner asked as the vehicle dipped again. Aloona slid under the panel and pulled out a shield that covered several wires and circuitry. He began to pull out thin strands of wire and clipped them with the pliers, "I'm rerouting the power. You take the controls."

"What?"

The controls, I need you to take them," Aloona instructed.

"I don't fly," Lartanner reminded him.

"Today you do."

Lartanner closed his eyes and took in a deep breath. He switched the controls from the pilot to co-pilot. The wheel in front of him activated after dimming, pushing out forward into Lartanner's hands. "Now what?"

Aloona kept his focus on the wires, "Steer."

Strommel tapped the last key on his palm device. It was set. He smiled to himself as he looked up to see that Frisco was directing their airship toward the roof of the NULE Headquarters. She was different. She wasn't the same woman he met a few hours ago. She certainly wasn't the same girl that kissed Jack Zero before they left the hangar. Whatever has been happening to her was not good. Strommel raised the device and aimed it at the back of Frisco's head. He poised his finger over the activation switch, but before he could press it, the airship shifted. The result was Helix rolling his massive form onto Strommel, over his arms. Strommel dropped the device again.

Lartanner struggled at the controls of the LEHV. He wasn't comfortable guiding such a large vehicle, especially the flying part. Nevertheless, he had no choice now, he had to do his part and ensure the vehicle stayed in the air until Aloona finished doing…whatever he was doing.

Aloona's head was buried under the console, his back the only part visible.

"How much longer?" Lartanner asked; trying to keep his concern undetected in his voice.

"Almost got it!" Aloona said; his voice muffled.

"Well whatever you're doing do it faster, I don't know how much longer I can keep her in the air."

"Got it!" Aloona shouted. The console sparkled to life as the components that lined it across lit up.

"Great!" Lartanner said. Confusion soon crossed his face. "Now what do I do?"

Aloona emerged from within the panel. He looked at the visual that aligned the targeting. He could see that the enemy aircraft was within view. "This!" Aloona slammed his open palm against the weapons button. The vehicle shook as two missiles ignited and launched from underneath.

The missiles flew straight across the sky toward the HART aircraft piloted by Agent Nicolina Frisco. She looked into her rear display to see the oncoming threat. "Damn!" She shouted to herself.

Helix rolled again as the vehicle pitched. This time his eyes opened slowly to look up at Strommel and then out the window. He saw the outline of a long cylinder with flames thrusting from the rear.

"MISSILE!" Helix snapped awake. He jerked his body as he pushed up from the seat. He didn't realize that he pushed himself too hard. His heavy form pushed against the pilot's seat. His arm also slipped from his control, his elbow slamming into the back of Frisco's head. Frisco grunted as he was forced forward, her forehead smacking the switches along the console. The weight of her body pushed against the yoke. The vehicle fell forward, nose-diving down toward the roof of the NULE Headquarters.

The first missile connected with the tail end of the aircraft, exploding just far enough away from the back of the vehicle. The explosion forced the aircraft toward the roof faster, causing them to crash hard. The impact was rough as the aircraft skipped against the rooftop until it skidded to a stop in the middle, a large air conditioning unit that consumed a major portion of the area stopping its slide. A small fire burned along the tail section as it rocked slowly.

Strommel and Helix lurched forward as the vehicle came to its stop. "Are you all right?" Strommel asked Helix.

"Y-yeah," Helix replied. "I think so."

"Good, let's get the Hell out of here!" Strommel clawed quickly at his harness in his attempt to escape.

Lartanner threw his hands up in triumph, "We got 'em!"

"Great," Aloona said with little enthusiasm.

"What? Aren't you happy?"

"Oh sure," Aloona confirmed.

Lartanner tried to pull on the controls, but they didn't budge, "The controls aren't working."

"And they won't," Aloona added.

"But you just…"

"All I did was keep us in the air for a few minutes so I could get the weapons online and fired, the thrusters and flight controls were beyond repair," Aloona explained, his voice not quavering.

"So we're going to…?" Lartanner began.

"Crash?" Aloona finished. "Yes." Aloona sat in the co-pilots seat next to Lartanner and began to strap himself in with the harness. Lartanner stared at him in disbelief. "You may want to buckle up," Aloona instructed.

Lartanner began to feverishly strap himself in.

Jack watched, as the front of the massive airship broke free of its moorings. It drifted slowly as it cleared its range from the larger section. It moved slowly, elegantly, as a whale moves through the ocean, letting the current take it to wherever it was heading.

"An astonishing piece of technology, eh?" Glorm beamed.

Jack nodded. It was an amazing feat of engineering. However, the purpose of its use was something else altogether. Jack stared out the front to watch the city listlessly coast by beneath them. It felt as if they weren't moving at all.

"It's the gravity floor," Glorm explained. Jack looked at Glorm with confusion. "Why, it feels like we aren't moving. The floor activated when we released from the chassis, it moves as the vehicle moves. No movement to render you unbalanced."

Jack hid his emotions, "That's swell. Now how about we drift on over to the police station and turn yourselves in?"

Glorm returned Jack's smirk. "Don't worry, Detective. We'll return you in due time, but we need to make a stop first."

"Where's that?"

Glorm simply smiled.

Strommel and Helix emerged from the crashed vehicle, his palm device gripped tightly in Strommel's fist, a slight limp in Helix's steps. "Hurry," Strommel waved for Helix to follow.

"I'm moving as fast as I can, my leg hurts," Helix complained.

"I don't think that aircraft is stable, it might blow."

Helix hesitated and turned to see the fire on the tail section was growing larger and spreading. His eyes bulged as he began to run faster. Inside the wreckage, Frisco began to stir. The stench of burning metal and Sulphur filled her nostrils. The acrid aroma woke her into a coughing frenzy. She looked around to see her vehicle was no longer moving. Crashed, in fact. The smell she took in was the vehicle she sat in was on fire. She immediately loosened her harness and leapt from the cockpit. She fell to her hands and knees as soon as she hit the roof. Her head throbbed as she massaged it slowly. Her vision was blurred slightly and the rubbing helped to clear it. She looked around to see both Strommel and Helix running away. She slowly stood on her wobbly legs and pulled her pistol from her holster. She fired it into the air, Strommel and Helix stopped in their tracks and turned around.

"Hold it right there!" Frisco commanded. She leveled the gun at the two men who raised their hands high into the air. "Don't move."

Strommel positioned his thumb over the activation button of his palm device. Helix took notice, "What is that?"

"You'll see."

Frisco approached the two men, her gun slowly moving in the direction of Helix, "You, fat one, I need your help."

Helix frowned, "No need to be rude."

"Shut up!" She roared. "I want you to deactivate the array."

"I don't think…"

Frisco cut Helix off, "NOW!" She cocked the pistol to show she was serious.

Helix swallowed hard, "Okay, alright. Sure."

He mouthed a "Help me" to Strommel.

"What about him?" Helix asked gesturing his head toward Strommel.

Frisco curled her lip, "Him? I no longer need him."

She took aim with her pistol, ready to fire. Strommel pressed the palm device. A high-pitched frequency emitted from the device. The waves penetrated Frisco's head immediately, the waved wrenching and pinching her brain like a clenching fist around a grape.

"ARGH!" She screamed as she brought her hands to her head, trying to shut out the pain. She clenched her eyes tightly as she fell to her knees, the pain searing through her brain.

Helix looked at Strommel with surprise, a small smile curled up his lips.

"It's a jamming device," Strommel explained. "The signal disrupts the chip controlling her."

Frisco lowered the gun and fired at the men, "Damn you!"

Both men dove for cover, bullets ricocheted around them. Frisco let her hand loose from her head as it reached deeply into her pockets and produced a small explosive charge.

"She's got a bomb!" Helix exclaimed. "We can't let her use it!"

More bullets danced around them as they each ducked lower.

"I'm too far to get enough signal to scramble her chip," Strommel replied, looking at the device in his hand. "You got a plan to stop her?"

Helix shrugged meekly.

Lartanner pulled at the controls of the vehicle, but it no longer budged. Aloona shrugged as he reached across the dashboard, his fingers stopping above the switch that that was labeled 'eject release.' He let loose a smile just as his fingers had flipped the switch. Suddenly, the doors on either side of the LEHV in the back section slid and popped off. A blast of steam puffed from the air compressor that held the doors in tightly. Their seats then dipped them each backward before sliding them rapidly along an unseen rail. The seat aligned to the opened doorway. Each seat turned outward, the passenger facing out into the sky, wind whipping past violently. Lartanner shut his eyes tightly, fearing what was next. As the LEHV began to sink lower, nearing the roof of the NULE building below, each seat was launched from the sides of the vehicle. It was moments before the front end of the LEHV caught the lip of the NULE building roof.

Helix and Strommel turned to see the commotion, as did Frisco, but the sight of the interlopers returning made her rush toward the communications array more quickly. It wasn't until several stories below that it exploded before the remaining debris crashed to the ground below.

The chairs holding Lartanner and Aloona launched them over the roof of the headquarters, each seat falling fast. The parachute in the back of Lartanner's seat released almost instantly. The wind caught the chute and billowed it open to its full girth, but because he was too low in the sky, it didn't slow his decent. Lartanner's seat landed hard on the roof, but the harness held him securely in his seat. Lartanner quickly unlatched his harness and pushed himself free of the seat. He was instantly greeted with open fire from Frisco's weapon.

He dove for the nearest cover.

"Welcome to the party," Helix smirked.

The LEHV crashed into the roof, sliding roughly as the bottom of it grinded loudly against the concrete. Sparks showered from underneath, wearing down the metal and tearing off pieces of it as it slowed down. It skidded to the edge of the building; the momentum was still strong enough for it to crash through the stone lip that raised up about four feet from the rooftop. Concrete exploded the car ultimately stopped. Half of the vehicle was over the edge, teetering slightly forward until it balanced itself out, the back half slamming hard against the roof.

It rested calmly, for the moment.

High above Aloona saw the crash and the sight of Lartanner's chute unfurled, catching the air as it descended, assured him his friend made it safely. He breathed a sigh of relief knowing Lartanner's seat carried him to safety. Aloona's chute didn't fare so well. The thrust from the LEHV caused the chute to malfunction; it wasn't able to release.

Frisco held the explosive device in her hand and activated. She turned to the COMM array, "Forever destiny!"

Aloona's sense of self-preservation kicked in as he leaned back in his seat and directed the back half of the seat to hit the ground. This maneuver also allowed him to loosen his harness. The chair his the roof hard and began to skip, rising into the air still maintaining its speed. Aloona released himself from the harness and rolled from the seat as it began to somersault across the roof.

Before she could toss the bomb, Aloona's seat tumbled out of the darkness, still gathering momentum, until it connected with Frisco. Her screams echoed as she disappeared over the edge of the building.

Aloona skidded across the roof, rolling and sliding, before he hit the edge of the building. He slid fast, the back of his seat kicking up dust and dirt from underneath. The cloud that enshrouded him made it difficult to see as he flipped over the lip of the building and fell from view.

Lartanner stood as he watched his partner vanish over the side of the building, "NO!"

CHAPTER 24
OVER THE EDGE

The bomb was knocked from Frisco's hand and skipped toward the array. It ricocheted against the side of the array tower. It then bounced against the side of the LEHV, pinging several times until it rested between the vehicle and the tower. The bomb exploded; the explosion was large enough and powerful enough to damage the array, crippling the nearest tower and dish, bending the metal and forcing it to topple. The LEHV lurched forward from the blast and flipped over the edge of the building, toppling head over heels, as it fell to the ground below, engulfed in a fireball on impact.

Lartanner quickly rushed to the edge of the building, his thoughts on Aloona and what could have happened. None of them were good. He immediately reached the edge and leaned over. The building was high, and his anxiety began to take form inside him. He felt dizzy. He did not see any sign of Aloona or Frisco. Instead, he heard a low whimper that cried, "Help."

Jack tried to maintain his balance as the entire bridge began to shake. He looked around to see if he could tell exactly what was happening. He thought maybe one of the NULE vehicles had targeted and affected the Behemoth, but soon learned it was not damage that was causing the shake. What was happening was a transformation. Jack looked out the windows of the massive airship to see the front section of the undercarriage was pulling away, separating from the rest of the ship.

Outside, several LEHV's veered around the hysteria of the air battle that plagued the skies above the city. Before them, the front of the giant zeppelin drifted from within the giant ship and began to sail away from the heart of the battle. The ship was four times the size of one of the enemy aircrafts. It was in the shape of a crescent, the edges thinning out toward the edges, creating the wings of the newly formed ship. It was sleek and appeared to be nimble as it was able to twist itself away from the battle, swirling around the edge of the firefight. In the rear center of the new ship were engines that propelled the vehicle through the air swiftly and quietly. Jack stood in awe as he watched the world drift past.

"Incredible, isn't it?" Glorm said proudly.

"It's...," Jack hesitated, refraining from speaking with too much excitement or admiration. "It certainly is something."

Glorm could see the admiration in Jack's eyes. He felt triumphant, his expression filled with gloat. It made Jack ill. Jack recoiled, holding back from looking too eager and excited.

"What are you planning, Glorm?" Jack asked.

"We're fixing this country," Zimm finally broke his silence.

Glorm interjected, "What my over-zealous friend is so eloquently attempting to say is that this country is going to receive the cleansing it has needed for far too long."

Jack was growing annoyed, "Yeah, I get it, the country is flawed and you're the only one that can save it."

"More so than that, Mr. Zero," Glorm's tone was thick. "In fact, we are going to change everything."

Glorm stood silently for a moment, "Do you remember when you were removed from your service in the military?"

Jack felt himself clench. He was suddenly overcome with anger as his body heated up.

"You know I do," Jack replied. "And I know you do, too. We talked about this not long ago. Remember? In Lartanner's office?"

"I don't forget."

"Why are you bringing this up now?"

Glorm's expression grew solemn. He seemed lost in thought for a moment before he broke his brief silence, "Your report said you saved a boy that day."

"Yeah, I know what I did," Jack said. "I'd do it again if the choice came up."

"Of course you would, just like any of us, we take in the deeds we do; we project them as an extension of ourselves. Our choices are not mere coincidence; they are preordained fabrications of our inner beings. Our destiny, if you will. Like me, my destiny is now, right before me. This was all laid out ahead of time, prepared for me. Now, I'm here to claim it. The future, your future, is mine."

"You are nuts," Jack sneered sardonically.

Zimm stood tall and looked to the captain of the bridge, "Get us to the designated location, Flortsim, we have no time to lose."

Flortsim, a tall, thin man with a thick mustache, nodded, "Yes sir!"

Jack slowly backed away. He needed to fade back, blend into the background. He watched as the men continued their busy activities, like ants, drones following the orders of their queen. He looked over toward Glorm where Ceinwen was standing. She caught Jack's glance and let loose a meek smile. She was scared and he could tell. He gave her a stoic glance, hoping to make her feel more at ease. He was hoping she would remain calm enough until he could come up with a plan.

He looked around and tried to surmise what was left of the room now that they pulled free from the rest of the ship. The options were now limited. He looked again to Ceinwen who was gesturing with her eyes. She would make them larger and then roll them to the right. Jack was confused, but followed her gaze. Her eyes travelled across the ceiling and down the back wall of the newly formed ship. At the end of the path formed by her eyes, Jack could see a lever. But what reason would she want to make sure he saw a lever? He ran his eyes along the perimeter of the lever to see the label that read, "Pressure Release Valve."

Jack looked to see where the release hatch was placed. It was labeled as "Pressure Hatch" and was located in the rear section of the bridge, just a few feet from where they currently stood. It was so close. All he had to do was reach out and he could grab the lever and pull it down. The pressure of the air outside could rush in and throw them all off balance, giving him the opportunity to take control of the ship.

Jack stood and watched as the bridge crew continued to work, hustling about busily to ensure the craft kept in the sky. Jack took a step to his left. The crew was too preoccupied to notice what he was doing, what he was planning. Jack looked to see the lever was now in his reach. He slowly, calmly, extended his arm. His opened hand immediately clasped around the lever as soon as his skin felt the cool vinyl that surrounded it.

He subtly tensed his muscles and began to pull the lever before something stopped him. It wasn't just something stopping him, but a thick, heavy item that seemed to wrap itself around his arm.

It was a hand. Not just any hand, but a large, meaty fist. Jack looked to see whom it was attached only to come face-to-face with Caspar Huun. Huun's face twisted as he glowered with rage, "Naughty." Huun threw a hard punch with his free hand. The powerful blow picked Jack up off his feet. He flew backward, unable to stop himself or slow himself down. Fortunately, Huun still held tightly onto Jack's arm. Before Jack could travel any further back, Huun pulled him back, his fist still balled and ready to strike.

Strike he did. Huun had drawn back and thrown another full force punch into Jack's stomach. This time Jack doubled over, falling forward onto his hands and knees. He coughed and hacked as he fell to the ground, Huun releasing his arm.

"You never learn do you, Zero," Zimm scoffed.

Glorm placed his arm around Ceinwen and began to turn her away from Huun and Jack, "I really hate to break up this wonderful reunion, but I have a city to save."

"JACK!" Ceinwen called out.

"No need to worry about him, my dear," Glorm smiled. "He's in good hands."

She turned away from Jack just as Huun threw his fist into Jack's unsuspecting jaw. Jack's vision blurred as he watched Glorm swiftly exit the room. He looked over to Ceinwen to see her eyes, filled with tears, as she reached her hand helplessly out toward him. He wanted to reach out and wrapped his hand around hers, but the massive hands that wrapped around his collar and violently hoist him in the air. Jack had hardly enough time to collect himself, his head spinning from the punch he just took. His feet dangled above the floor, his legs hardly moving to find any footing. He expected Huun to sneer in his face, gloating. He felt his hot breath, which wreaked of rotted meat. Jack squinted his eyes, attempting to see who was before him. He shook his head quickly, which oddly worked, clearing his vision.

"Hiya, Jackie Boy," was the smiling face of Neal Andrew Thall.

"Thall?" Jack spurted out in surprise.

Without warning, Jack was hurled sideways, flying uncontrollably across the room. His body fell sharply, skipped roughly across the floor, before stopping hard against the opposite wall. His spine hit the solid metal wall with an echoed thud. Thall had drawn his EMP baton from the belt he wore around his bulbous waste and threw it upward until it connected with the underside of Jack's chin. Ceinwen screamed.

"I HATE BEING CALLED THALL!" Thall roared as he dropped

the baton to the floor and pressed his right fist into his palm, cracking his knuckles loudly. "I hate that goddamn subname!"

Zimm was smiling gleefully, "We really must be going now, Lieutenant. I'd say I see you again soon, but..." Zimm gestured to the hulking form of Thall, who was heaving with rage, preparing to attack. "You two have fun, and Thall, don't be gentle." Zimm snapped his fingers for Huun to follow, which he obliged like an eager puppy. The left, giving Thall freedom to do with Jack as he pleased.

Jack felt any ounce of hope escape his body. The only thing he needed to be aware of was how he and Ceinwen could escape. But first...the pain was intense as it coursed instantly through his nervous system, lighting up every nerve ending in his body. He rolled onto his stomach, groaning as he attempted to move himself. Caveman lumbered across the room toward the writhing form of Jack Zero.

"You know somethin', Zero," Thall growled as he stalked Jack. He twisted his neck as he strode angrily, rage consuming his expression, his spine cracking loudly, "You never learned."

"Yeah, it's an annoying habit of mine," Jack managed to quip weakly.

"You really need to just shut up," Thall rushed up to Jack, drew back his foot, and kicked Jack square in his ribs. The impact lifted him off the ground several inches. He flew the short distance between the foot and the wall, hitting the metal that had previously been dented by him moments before. It hurt worse this time. His spine sank deeper into the wall, caving the dent in even deeper. It was harder to move, harder to stand as Jack tried to get to his feet.

"That was for taking my jewels. And this is for puttin' me in the slammer!" Caveman kicked him again in the ribs, not letting up. Jack felt his ribs cracking, caving in with each kick. "And this is for trying to mess up this gig for me too," Thall drew back his leg again. However, instead of kicking, he lurched forward roughly, as his upper body weight shifted. He felt the small frame of a young woman leap onto his back. "What the hell?" He growled.

Ceinwen began throwing her hands about, thrashing at Thall's face, neck, and chest, "GET AWAY FROM HIM!"

The slaps and punches were miniscule to his thick skin and large form, but the annoyance was enough to prevent him from finishing off his nemesis. Thall threw his own hands over his head in an attempt to swat the small woman from his shoulders. Unfortunately, his own larger frame and thick arms made it difficult to reach even the top of his own head. This gave Ceinwen the advantage. She used her long nails and thin fingers to cause as much damage as she could. She scratched his skin across his forehead and cheeks, and pressed her fingers into his eyes.

Caveman screamed; a deep, resonate bellow that echoed across the open room.

Jack finally managed to pick himself up and get on his feet. He watched the bizarre sight that played like a strange sideshow attraction: four arms flailing akimbo around a large mass with four legs. He cocked his head curiously, as he watched it spin and flail erratically about, accompanied by both a deep, low howl and high, shrill screaming. Jack shook his head as he looked down. His eyes immediately fell on the baton that Thall conveniently discarded. It was an opportune moment as he scooped up the weapon and raced up to the giant.

"Hey! Thall!" Jack called. The shrilling, howling form stopped instantly as both Thall and Ceinwen turned to look. "Winnie! Down!"

Ceinwen pushed off Thall's back and tumbled to the floor. Jack swung the baton until it connected with Thall's face. The electric current sparked to like as it touched flesh. The explosion was swift as it emanated from the top of the baton and surged between both Jack's arm and Thall's head. Jack flew back a third time, this time falling short of the wall. He slowly stood; it was hard to stand as his arm was limp, not functioning. He lifted his arm with his other hand, examining it as closely as he could, but it seemed to be unable to move. He realized the nanites were no longer active; his arm was heavy and difficult to move. He looked to see Thall still standing, but motionless. As Jack stood, still clutching his limp arm, he watched Thall, who wore a blank expression where he stood. Jack was unsure as what he should do. The pulse took away his arm and he was left defenseless. If Thall were still at full strength, then he would make easy work of Jack.

There was a small, arid cloud of smoke surrounding Thall's head, emanating from his clothing that appeared to be smoldering.

Ceinwen rushed up to Jack, but he kept his eyes on Thall, "Jack! Are you all right?"

Jack nodded, "Yeah, I think so."

They both watched Caveman as he shifted his eyes about, looking at them and then around the empty room. He then let out a grin, revealing his blackened teeth, a pillow of smoke floating from between his parted lips. His mouth then twisted into a bizarre grin as his arms went limp. Caveman then fell forward, his face slamming against the floor.

He was out cold. Jack turned to Ceinwen in bewilderment, meeting the same expression on her face. Jack then grabbed her with his working hand and pulled her to the door, "We need to get off this ship!"

The massive airship travelled through the city, menacing and ominous. There was mass hysteria on the New Utica streets below. Several vehicles swerved and crashed, striking other vehicles. People scattered in every direction, fearful of what was coming.

Jensen Glorm watched delightfully from his perch on the edge at the front of the ship. The open door allowed him to look down and see everything first hand. The chaos that was erupting on the streets below, the eve before the most important election of his career was exactly as he had imagined, as he had hoped. He felt his heart race, pounding like a drum in his chest. The rush of the cool evening air washed over his body, eased his nerves and calmed him. After all, he was about to become President of the United States.

He watched as the tops of the buildings sped past beneath him. He took in a deep breath; the fresh air filled his lungs. He looked ahead to see what he searched from where he stood. Ahead of the ship, jutting up high into the night sky was the top of the nearest building. "Gentlemen," Glorm turned and spoke to the men that surrounded him. "Tonight we make history. We finally turn the tides that will set in motion a new regime that will change the course of ourselves, our beliefs, our country, and our future."

The men all snapped to attention, bringing together their heels and raising their hands in salute, "Forever destiny!"

"Forever destiny!" Glorm echoed.

Glorm turned and stepped from the edge of the open door. The lip of the platform that jutted from underneath the massive airship nearly scraped the edge of the building. It floated mere centimeters from the concrete lip that prevent anyone, or anything, from simply stepping over the edge. It was approximately three feet high, not something anyone could simply walk over. However, stepping in was another matter. Glorm stepped from within the ship and walked down the slight decline of the platform. As he reached the edge of the platform, he stepped off, over the concrete lip, and onto the rooftop below.

Without flinching, Glorm pressed his coat with his hands, straightening the collar, and without missing a beat, walked to the door at the center of the roof. It opened as he approached. A smiling, burly, bald man in a suit, a communication receiver visible in his ear, greeted him. "Greetings, sir," the man said evenly.

"Good evening, Hindo," Glorm was upbeat. He placed his hand on the man's shoulder as he passed. "Spirits up, tonight's going to be a big night!"

"Yes sir," Hindo responded his tone still even. As soon as Glorm passed, he closed the door behind them.

Jack rushed along the open corridors of the behemoth, dragging Ceinwen behind him with one hand, his other arm swaying lifelessly with each step. "Where are we?" Ceinwen asked.

"I don't know," Jack replied. "This place is huge."

"How are we going to get out of here?"

"I'm working on it," Jack stopped short. Ceinwen nearly collided into him, but caught herself before her nose his shoulder.

"What are you doing?" She asked. Jack let loose her hand and slowly stepped forward. Ceinwen could hear the distant chatter of people speaking. She leaned forward, trying to listen as carefully as possible, "What is it?"

"Shhh!" Jack silenced her. He stepped closer to the edge of the raised platform they had been running across, trying not to lean too far over the railing. He pressed his chest against the railing to peek over the side.

Ceinwen threw Jack a sneer as she silently stepped back. She stayed close enough to him to still hear what was being said. To her it sounded like a jumble of nonsense.

Jack, however, listened as closely as he could and he was able to make out the garble.

"...We only need to last another hour or so, then we jump again," said one voice.

"Then what?" Asked another.

"Then we return to let the Great Master take over."

"But what about all this?" asked the second voice.

"This?" The first voice scoffed. "This is all for show, a ruse. It's all for the benefit of our savior, the one who will bring us to glory. We just have to keep the police at bay while the others do what they need to prepare for the Equinox."

"Yes, the Holy Equinox. The world shall repent that day."

Ceinwen couldn't hear, but she noticed the intense look on Jack's face that he was hearing what was being said. She tried to get even closer. Instead of hearing more, she stepped on Jack's foot.

"OW!" Jack yelped.

"What was that?" Asked the first voice.

"It came from this way," said the second.

Jack watched as two shadows turned and drew weapons from their waists. Jack threw a disgruntled look at Ceinwen. She offered an apologetic smirk.

"HEY!" The two men came into view below them. "Hold it!"

The two men fired several shots at Jack and Ceinwen; Sparks flowered as lasers ricocheted against the metal girders and railings that surrounded them.

"C'mon!" Jack clasped his hand on her wrist and pulled her behind him. Being on a higher level gave Jack and Ceinwen the advantage, but not necessarily the ability to escape their pursuers. Jack took long strides as he raced along the upper catwalk, being careful to keep his steps quiet by walking heel-to-toe. Years of military training ingrained the practice of stealth and preparation for the impossible. Unfortunately, Ceinwen didn't receive that same training. Jack winced at the sound of her flats slapping against the surface beneath their feet. He stopped short again, this time wanting Ceinwen to collide with him. He was sure to turn and catch her arms as she ran face first into his chest.

"What are you doing?" She asked angrily, due both to her fear and desire to escape.

"I need you to keep quiet," he whispered.

"I'm doing the best I can!" She whispered back angrily.

"Do better!" He snapped back.

From down below came a series of angry orders directed at Jack, *"Hey you up there!"*, *"Hold it!"*, and *"Stop right there!"*

"Now who's making too much noise?" Ceinwen goaded.

"Shut up!" Jack pulled her along behind him.

Gunfire erupted all around them; Sparks danced along the metal railing that secured them along the walkway. Both Ceinwen and Jack ducked their heads, hoping to protect themselves from a stray bullet that could potentially hit them. Jack pulled her along the exposed walkway toward the doorway at the other end.

"BRING THEM DOWN!" Shouted a sentry as he aimed more carefully. He pulled a bullet from his belt and slid it into the chamber. Under normal circumstances, bullets were forbidden within the airship, except in the case of snipers.

Jack saw the sentry looking through his scope, taking aim toward them. He felt his flesh grow hot and his heart pound harder in his chest. Within moments, the crack of the rifle echoed in the open room. Jack immediately took action, swinging his body around Ceinwen, shielding her from danger. His limp arm swung freely with his movements, pendulously swinging upward. The bullet reached them, just as Jack's arm came up. The bullet hit it directly, sparking brilliantly, and then ricocheted toward the ceiling.

The sentry watched, breathlessly, as his bullet tore through the ceiling. Jack knew the disappearance of the bullet was not a good sign. Up until now, laser fire was all they needed to deal with, but now he has a sinking feeling things were about to get worse.

"We need to hurry!" Jack peeled himself from around Ceinwen. He pushed her ahead of himself and ran for the door.

The bullet flew with great speed and force that it was capable of ripping through several layers before it reached the envelope at the top of the airship. The envelope was enclosed around a large energy generator that hummed a low song, rising and falling rhythmically as a floating swirl of tachyon energy rotated in sync. Despite the amazing power within the envelope that powered the engine of the massive airship, it seemed like a tranquil and sober environment.

The bullet that entered immediately disrupted that as it bounced between several metal rafters before sinking into the large node that protruded from one of several four-foot spires that surrounded the energy swirl. Each spire emitted a thick beam that surrounded the energy source with a field in order to protect the ship from the unstable fuel. However, if the field is disabled, there is no other protection. The spire groaned as it began to tip, the crackle of electricity snapped and danced around the tip of the spire until it fizzled out. The spire faded as its part of the beam flickered and faded. As soon as it disappeared, its link to the other spires each slowly vanished. Within seconds, the field was gone.

The tachyon energy suddenly began to hum faster and louder, the energy swirl beginning to expand in size rapidly. The girders that held the shell of the behemoth in place began to quiver slightly. The swirling energy was increasing, causing the curved metal beams to groan as they slowly began to pull inward, toward the swirling mass. It wasn't long before several rivets were pulled free and zipped quickly across the open space until they were swallowed by the energy swirl.

The battle above New Utica raged intensely. Several NULE vehicles soared across the night sky, either in pursuit of or being chased by the Dark HART's smaller, one-pilot crafts. Their vehicles were less bulky, maneuvering better and more nimbly that the chunky NULE crafts.
Remy looked out his display view at the layer of lights that moved erratically across the dark sky. Their contrast to the motionless stars made the firefight more distinguishable. He could see what started with nearly one hundred fighters was down to only a few dozen. LEHV's were falling at an alarming rate, their exploding vehicles flashing momentarily, and lighting up the night sky.

Nearby, Captain Barbasoa watched in silent disdain as another of his officers dies in a fiery explosion from the thin laser bolt that tore through the LEHV, resulting in the ignition of its fuel, and ending in a bright red and orange fireball. His men were outnumbered, outmanned, and outgunned. With each passing moment, with each subsequent destruction of a LEHV, their own numbers dwindled. These pilots they were fighting were much more prepared for aerial combat. The NULE force was never trained in air combat maneuvers, save for a few days devoted to piloting through the narrow alleys and streets from above. But it was handled on a simulator with only a few flight hours logged in before finishing the course.

Barbasoa silently counted the Dark HART's ships. He stopped counting after he reached fifty. There was still at least another fifty or even one hundred more. They were seriously outnumbered. He watched as several more LEHV's exploded, their flaming remains falling toward the earth. The debris bounced off the protective field that rested about twenty feet from the ground, allowing it to disintegrate before it could harm anyone below. Barbasoa grabbed the dashboard COMM device and brought it to his mouth, "Attention, this is Captain Barbasoa; I need all available LEHVs in the southwest sector   to follow my lead, and let's hustle!"

Barbasoa looked to his partner seated next to him and lowered his gaze soberly. He shook his head slowly, "May God have mercy on our souls."

Several enemy aircraft sliced through the defensive line the NULE attempted to create with its thinning numbers. Several LEHVs hovered next to one another as they created a wall with their vehicles. Remy's vehicle hovered in the center of the line, he watched on either side as several vehicles filled in, creating a long wall that was now three lines, two hovering below Barbasoa's own vehicle. Some LEHVs disengaged from the aerial battle as they joined the vehicle wall.

"Alright men," Barbasoa growled into the COMM. "We need to hold this line and keep those slimy bastards from getting to the NULE tower. Some of us may not make it, but we joined the force to protect this city and I'll be damned if that's not what I'm going to do!"

Remy smiled at the round of appreciation from the other men at his side. It made him smile, knowing he could count on them. They were a team. Now more than ever.

"Let's give 'em Hell!" Remy roared, as several enemy aircraft began to circle for an attack. He held his breath as he prepared to engage.

"Help," the meager cry came again.

Lartanner rushed to the edge of the room and looked over the side. There he saw Aloona. He was still buckled in his seat, dangling precariously over the edge of the roof. One of the restraining straps had snagged a piece of metal that had been exposed from underneath the concrete wall. Lartanner realized that it must have been from the crash of the vehicles earlier. "You lucky son of a bitch!" Lartanner tried to contain his smile, but couldn't.

Aloona tried to keep himself calm, despite the fear of falling that currently gripped him, "Yeah, I'll be sure to buy a lottery ticket, but let's get me out of this first!"

Lartanner began to crawl over the lip of the roof and onto the narrow ledge that was only about a foot wide. Lartanner stepped cautiously, his feet barely fitting across.

"What are you doing?" Shouted Helix from behind. Both he and Strommel raced to Lartanner's side. Helix was breathing heavy after the brief sprint. He tugged up the waistband of his pants as he leaned over the edge of the roof. A sense of vertigo overtook him for a moment. He felt dizzy as he looked down the long distance to the ground below. At the very bottom, he could see what looked like the prone body of Agent Frisco. She seemed such a miniscule speck from where he stood. It was hard to believe she had helped them not long ago, only to turn on them.

"Holy smog!" Helix groaned as he clamped his hand over his mouth and stumbled backward. He quickly came back to the edge, this time his hands gripping the lip tightly, his knuckles turning white. He was overcome with both vertigo and nausea of seeing Frisco's corpse below.

"Be careful," Strommel warned. "Don't fall."

"I'll try to keep that in mind," Lartanner quipped. He crouched slightly as he reached his arm out to grab for the straps that secured Aloona in place. He wrapped his fist around the strap that teetered on the metal rod that jutted out from the concrete. He gave it a slight yank.

The entire chair jerked forward as the strap Lartanner yanked slid forward a bit, closer to the edge of the rod.

"WHAT ARE YOU DOING!?" Aloona screamed.

"I just wanted to test how secure it was," Lartanner, said assuredly.

"Well don't!" Aloona replied.

Lartanner stood, his lower half pressing against the edge of the roof behind him. Strommel looked to Lartanner with a slight smile, "How secure is it?"

"Actually, it's pretty tight," Lartanner began. "It should hold, so long as he doesn't move. Or breathe."

Strommel lost his grin and his face went white, "So what do we do?"

"I'm open to ideas," Lartanner said softly.

Still afraid to look over the edge, Helix kept his gaze inward, staring across the roof. His eyes traced over the wreckage of the vehicle and the remains of Lartanner's ejected seat strewn about. The chute that slowed his decent, and kept him from hitting the roof to hard, or falling over the edge like Aloona happened to do, puffed in and out with the breeze, like a pair of lungs taking in oxygen. Helix wanted to turn to help Lartanner, but instead offered all he could, "I have an idea."

The first wave of enemy aircraft began to assault the wall of cars that Barbasoa orchestrated. Their blasts were direct, bolts of laser energy tearing into vehicles. A LEHV, about six vehicles to Remy's left exploded as a beam sliced across its fuel tank and ignited the engine. The blast sent a shockwave that pushed the cars surrounding it. Another vehicle below exploded, rocking the LEHVs above.

"HOLD YOUR GROUND!" Barbasoa shouted.

The LEHVs moved in accord, keeping the wall above and below, left and right, no matter the direction of each attack. The Dark HART continued to take different angles and actions in their continued onslaught. But the NULE officers kept their positions. With each new attack, the NULE officers met the movements made by the enemy aircraft with the appropriate defense.

"On your right," cried an officer into his COMM.

A set of three aircraft were locked in a pyramid formation as they twisted around and maneuvered toward the LEHV wall. The trio of ships glided smoothly across the night sky as they kept their ships evenly apart from one another, maintaining a delicate balance. They swooped quickly, the lead ship striking first. Its laser fire sliced through the darkness and quickly found a target, burning through the hull of the lowest craft at the left side of the LEHV formation.

The ship exploded.

The two craft following the leader broke out from wither side of their leader and immediately opened fire on the other ships on that same end, destroying them as quickly. The shockwave from the blasts rocked each vehicle in line, forcing them to loosen their positions as the reeled slightly, some even colliding into others. The push from each vehicle resulted in a chain reaction that caused the entire bottom row of the wall to lose their positions.

Remy struggled to hold the yoke steady, attempting to prevent his own vehicle from careening out of control. He was able to hold his own position while others around him seemed to lose their ability to keep in place.

"Steady, men!" Barbasoa shouted into the COMM. "Steady!"

"Sir, we're losing our thrusters," shouted an officer in reply.

"Their coming around again!" Cried Remy.

The trio of enemy aircraft were circling around, still locked in their distances from each other. Like a predator hunting, stalking its prey, the crafts glided effortlessly, their sleek bodies slicing through the air with no resistance. Their chrome exteriors reflected the light from the city below as well as the darkness from above, making them appear as if they were waves of heat being emitted into the atmosphere. The refraction of lights danced across their hulls, distorted by the imperfections that decorated them.

The ships struck again, this time to the right of the wall. They mirrored their own actions, taking out three more ships and sending the rest into disarray. The screams of his officers dying in a fiery explosion echoed through Barbasoa's cockpit. He closed his eyes tight, regretting the actions that led to this moment. But this is the duty of a NULE officer. This is for what they enlisted and trained. This is what being a dedicated officer and protector of the citizens of New Utica can result.

They all knew this.

Barbasoa knew this.

Remy knew this.

It is expected. Not desired, but it is their job, their duty. Moreover, they were not going to stop.

The next set of attacks came immediately after, now to the left, taking out two more LEHVs. "Alright men," Barbasoa finally addressed his men. "We cannot tolerate this any longer. We need to be on the defensive. I need you to be ready. Wait for my signal."

Helix had begun to enact his plan. He had rushed to the abandoned ejector seat that delivered Commissioner Lartanner to the rooftop relatively safely. He had sat within the seat in order to test the controls. He toyed around with various buttons and levers, as if he were a child being permitted to sit within his father's vehicle. Helix had always been fascinated with technology and cars, especially those that were designed to fly. He had studied the blueprints and conceptual renderings of the LEHVs since he was a young boy. The very idea that a vehicle, normally permitted to drive along the ground, could defy gravity and fly into the sky. The thought of them being used exclusively by military and law enforcement was exceptionally attractive about them as well, exciting that the normal layperson couldn't use the technology, unless they enlisted. Or, were arrested.

"You come up with that plan yet?" Lartanner shouted from the other side of the roof.

"Working on it," Helix answered habitually. He always answered with 'working on it' as it was the equivalent of, 'I'd rather be playing virtual games.'

"Work faster!" Lartanner prodded.

"Hey! If this were a computer, or digital device, I'd be able to give you a solid answer if when I expect to be finished, but since I don't, I'd ask if you'd kindly leave me the hell alone to let me work."

Lartanner turned from the edge of the roof to look back at the portly man known as Helix. Despite the fact that his back was facing him, it didn't stop Lartanner from shooting him a dirty look. He looked back down at Aloona who still gripped himself tightly within his chair as he held onto his life.

"Don't worry," Lartanner called down to him. "Help is on the way."

"I'll try to stick around long enough," Aloona, quipped.

Strommel tried to look busy and useful, even though he did not have much to do. Lartanner had told him to help Helix, and Helix said to leave him alone. He simply stood near the lip where Aloona hanged precariously and Lartanner stayed within sight of him. He looked back to Helix, who was still fidgeting with the ejector seat, although he was not sure why. He looked around the city; off into the distance he could see the aerial battle still raging. He could see the giant airship floating toward them steadily. He looked down at the ground far beneath him and his heart sank. He suddenly felt as if he was no longer going to survive this. This wasn't a typical way for Aloona to think. Normally, he kept his doubts hidden, bottled up deep within. Instead, he always kept an outer appearance of confidence and fortitude. It was important for him to keep up the appearance of looking confident, for his officers, certainly, but most importantly, his partner.

Unfortunately, Lartanner could sense Aloona's fears. Call it a sixth sense, but it was always this way, since they started as partners on the force and even more so when they began their relationship outside of work. It was Lartanner who realized he had feelings for Aloona, and Aloona wasn't willing to pursue anything further than their professional partnership. Lartanner was persistent, showing up at his apartment late, showing up at the restaurant where he was ordering take out, even one time ending up at the library when Aloona was just looking for a quiet night to read. Every time he showed up, Aloona would get more annoyed, but yet there was a charm in Lartanner's arrogance. His incessant badgering, even begging until Aloona said 'yes' was part of the appeal. Aloona had never been pursued, let alone desired, by anyone. Certainly he was an attractive man, but being an African-American growing up in Mississippi shortly after the state legislature proposed it was legal to discriminate against individuals of religion, sexual orientation, and color, he fell into all three categories as a gay African-American Muslim.

It was hard. Hard to let anyone get too close to him, but Lartanner wanted to get to know him. Never before had he been the object of another's affection. But Lartanner did, despite what he saw as his own flaws. It was him who wanted to keep their relationship a secret at first, not wanting the force to know they were living together. Lartanner didn't agree. He wanted to tell everyone, but Aloona convinced him to slow down and wait to see how things progressed. Before too long, the word was out. To Aloona's surprise, no one seemed to mind. In fact, most already assumed they were a couple long before. They had been together for over ten years now, and Aloona reflected on those years fondly now as he dangled several hundred feet above the ground.

"How're you holding up?" Lartanner called down, his voice thick with concern.

"By a strap," Aloona forced out a laugh.

Lartanner snorted a chuckle, more to ease his partner's nerves than finding the comment amusing. "Just relax; we are working on getting you out of there."

"Just do me one favor," Aloona asked.

"What's that?"

"Hurry."

Lartanner heard the urgency in Aloona's voice. He turned to Helix and Strommel, "What's taking so long?" He watched as Helix and Strommel scurried around one another, they had been braiding the ropes that led from the seat to the chute.

"We're about set," Helix replied.

Lartanner called down to Aloona, "We're coming now!"

Aloona nodded. His seat moved slightly, the belt loosening from where it had been secured. He sucked in his breath, holding it, "P-please...hurry!"

Lartanner spun on his heel to see Helix and Strommel carrying the newly fashioned rope. They quickly began to feed it over the lip of the roof.

"The rope is coming down to you, hold tight!" Lartanner called down.

They fed it down fist over fist. It slithered along the side of the building like a snake. The end of the rope lapped at the night air, whipping left and right, wagging like an excited dog's tail.

Aloona saw the tip of the rope come into his line of sight. It hanged just a bit to his left.

Lartanner shouted orders, "Just try to reach out and grab the end, we'll pull you up."

Aloona reached over cautiously, his fingers outstretched, his arm locked at the elbow. His fingertips brushed the frayed end of the wadded strands of rope. Each time they connected with the rope it snapped away from him, swinging farther away.

"I...c-can't reach it!" Aloona cried.

"Hold on!" Lartanner called back. He leaned over the edge of the roof and grabbed a fistful of braided rope. He began to swing it like a pendulum, aiming it toward Aloona. Aloona watched the end of the rope as it reached him, the tip snapping against his chest. "Can you get it?" Lartanner called again.

Aloona slowly raised his arm. Once his hand was raised, he

snapped his fingers around the rope. However, the quick movement wasn't in accordance to the balance of the chair. The strap holding him in place jerked hard. It slid forward, edging to the tip of the metal rod that held it in place. Aloona fearfully released his hand from around the rope and dropped his arms to his side. His heart was pounding harder than before, nearly smashing through his rib cage and jumping from his chest.

He felt it. He was going to die.

"Shit!" Lartanner cursed. "Don't move!"

He began to scale the lip of the roof, gripping the braided rope as he began to dangle his own legs over the side.

"What the hell are you doing?" Helix asked. He began to release his grip on the rope, but Lartanner held up his hand, stopping him in his tracks.

"Don't let go!" Lartanner commanded.

"You can't!" Helix argued. "You can't go down there!"

"Look! If he moves, he's going to fall. I have to go down there and get him!" Lartanner calmly instructed both Helix and Strommel, "Just hold on as tight as you can. I need you both to anchor me while I go down to get him."

"But…what if…" Helix began.

"You can do this!" Lartanner looked directly into Helix's eyes. "I know you can."

Helix reluctantly nodded, not masking the expression of doubt that took over his face. His attempt to remain hopeful was shattered by a scream from below.

"NO!" Aloona shouted, his voice forceful. "Do not come down here!"

"I'm not leaving you!"

"You can't risk yourself for me," Aloona sounded calm. "Let me go. Get Strommel to the Feds, he needs to help them stop them all."

"Goddammit! I am not losing you!" Lartanner pushed away from the building and began to climb down, hand over hand, trying hard not to lose his grip. "When I get down to you, I need you to release the safety belt."

"I-I can't. I-I'll fall."

"I'll catch you! Trust me!"

Aloona watched as Lartanner's feet came into view. His legs, then the rest followed soon after. Aloona smiled at the sight of the man he loved.

"Hey," Lartanner smiled.

"Hey," Aloona replied.

The aloof greeting they often shared when they each arrived home from a long day seemed comforting now. Lartanner steadied himself, the soles of his feet planted firmly against the side of the building. His right arm was wrapped several times with the braided ropes. "Hey partner," Lartanner said with a smile. "You been waiting long?"

"Don't make me laugh," Aloona cautioned. "Any movement and I could…" He didn't finish his sentence, but Lartanner knew what he was saying.

"Don't think like that," Lartanner was stoic. "You can…we can do this." Lartanner held his left hand out to Aloona, "Give me your hand."

Aloona slowly reached his hand out until Lartanner was able to clasp his around it. He felt his seat shimmy slightly. He held his breath. Lartanner sensed his fear, his grip tight. He could see both hands turn pink, then white from the intensity of the grip. "I'm ready when you are, just unlatch the restraints," Lartanner instructed.

Aloona didn't respond. He slowly raised his hand until he felt the cold steel of the latch. He looked into Lartanner's eyes. Without a word or an expression, he pressed the button. The click of the latch releasing was the only sound either man heard at that moment. Aloona felt gravity take control. His body began to fall. The seat also slipped loose of its hold, the strap sliding free of the metal rod. It spiraled to the ground below.

Helix watched in amazement as Aloona swung away from the seat, his feet kicking outward. Lartanner held his grip, holding Aloona tight, his arm swinging in tandem with his partner.

"I gotcha!" Lartanner said reassuringly.

"I h-hope so," Aloona swallowed hard.

Helix watched the seat hit the ground below, wondering if it landed onto poor Agent Frisco's lifeless body. Instead, he saw the seat smash into pieces as it ripped into the concrete surface. But there was no sight of Frisco's body.

"Hoist us up!" Lartanner shouted up, breaking Helix's concentration.

"Y-yes!" Helix turned to Strommel, "Let's pull them up!"

Both men, not known for their strength and prowess, pulled with all their might. Strommel had come up with the idea of wrapping the chute-rope around the antennae, giving them more leverage. It was working; they could feel the two men lifting as they struggled to pull them to the roof. Within minutes, they had successfully pulled both Lartanner and Aloona to the apex, their bodies spilling over the lip as they rolled onto the rooftop.

"We did it!" Strommel exclaimed with excitement.

"Yeah we did!" Helix offered his hand in congratulations. Strommel shook it willingly.

Lartanner began to pick himself up off the roof, resting his arm on his partner's back, "Thanks, both of you."

Strommel smiled, but it disappeared as quickly as it appeared. The once lifeless body of Agent Frisco lifted Strommel into the air.

"Holy shit!" Helix screamed as he dove for the roof.

Frisco turned and snarled, her eyes flashing red. Without a word, she leapt against the antenna and climbed it, still clutching Strommel in her arm.

Remy shouted into the COMM device, "Stay close!" He twisted his craft through the sky, the remaining LEHVs following his lead. The line of airships moved like an ocean wave, rippling across the midnight blue sky. The set of aircraft twisted in rhythm, following the ship before it as they spiraled their formation toward their set of attackers. Remy, still maintaining the lead of the charge, was the first craft to open fire. The bright green streaks of light emitted from the underside of his LEHV, slicing through the air, unhindered by any obstruction. The first set of beams sailed past the attackers, missing them completely.

The attacking airships each spun in a counter clockwise direction, the beams gliding effortlessly past. They immediately spun back into their attack formation, preparing to attack. As they began to bear down on the defensive LEHVs. But before they could fire, Remy dropped his vehicle downward. As the ship dipped, he could feel his stomach drop. He had done these types of maneuvers in training many times, but only on simulators. Nothing could ever prepare a pilot for a real moment. The move worked. Lined up behind Remy's ship were three LEHVs. The spread out of their tandem formation and immediately struck. Several beams emitted from the underside of the LEHVs.

The opposing aircraft quickly responded, each twisting their ships in different directions in their attempts to avoid being hit. The lead vehicle was able to maneuver his aircraft past the approaching beams, but the craft to their left wasn't so fortunate. A beam sliced through the craft, breaking the seal that secured the cockpit, maintaining the pilot's air pressure. The front shield of the vehicle imploded as the heavier air pressure immediately rushed inward. The beam continued its path through the remainder of the craft, making contacting with the fuel reserves. The ship exploded instantly.

"YES!" Barbosa cheered over the COMM. "Good work men!"

"We're not out of danger yet!" Remy replied over the COMM.

The leader of the HART aircraft increased its speed and barreled forward, increasing its front shields. The craft was preparing to ram its way through their defenses. Its sister ship quickly flew up and over the bulleting craft and began to open fire. Their strategy worked as it took out three LEHVs immediately. The explosions acted as a shield, allowing the lead craft to push through unmolested.

"Those slimy bastards!" Barbasoa roared. "We can't let that ship reach NULE tower!" Barbasoa pulled back on his yoke and sent his vehicle into a barrel role. His ship spiraled upward and around, leveling off as it aligned its sights on the lead aircraft.

"I need support!" Remy shouted. "All available LEHVs, I need your assistance in pursuit of the vehicle."

Several laser blasts sizzled past his craft. He expertly maneuvered around each beam carefully, "And someone take out the other guy!"

Jack pulled Ceinwen behind him as they made their way through the sinking airship. His limp arm that had taken a bullet was beginning to tingle. He could feel life slowly returning as energy began to rush throughout the nanites that were imbedded under his skin. It felt good. He was beginning to feel complete once more.

"Where are we going?" She asked, her concern evident in her tone.

Jack raised his limp arm slowly. He looked over as they ran past a series of windows exposing the inside of the ship to the outside world. He saw his reflection beaming back as he watched himself move his arm. Looks like those little buggers installed in there weren't completely knocked out by the impact. Maybe Strommel wasn't kidding when he said he was a special case. Patient Zero. Jack shook the thoughts from his mind and returned to the task at hand: escaping. He looked out the windows into the night and across the cityscape. He could see the buildings of New Utica growing slowly. The ship was still sinking, slowly. The ship's hull was compromised somewhere. "I don't know," he said to her. "But we need to get off this ship and fast."

"What's happening?" Ceinwen felt vibrations rattle beneath her feet.

"The ship's going down. We don't have a hell of a lot of time before it crashes."

"Oh my gosh," she let loose her hand from Jack's and covered her face as she stopped running. "We're going to die, aren't we?"

Jack stopped and walked over to the now sobbing woman. He placed his hands on her shoulders and said, "No."

"But how?" She asked. "How do you know?"

"Because," he replied with a smile. "I said we aren't, and when have I ever let you down?"

Ceinwen cocked her head and smirked. Jack didn't need to read her mind to know what she was thinking. He was sure every time he promised to pay her, or every time he assured her, the rent was paid for the office when it wasn't. How many times had the electricity been turned off? Or the water?

"Don't answer that," he said. "But at least trust me now. We are going to be fine."

Ceinwen pursed her lips, trying to dig deeply into her own mind, hoping to convince herself that Jack was telling the truth and not only his version of it. She finally nodded in acceptance.

Jack smiled again, "Alright then, we can't stop." He looked back out the glass walls to see the tops of the taller buildings were no longer in view. "We really need to move."

But before he began to run, he noticed the necklace that dangled around Ceinwen's neck began to slowly move. The charm that once hung above her cleavage was now beginning to rise into the air. He watched it curiously, wondering why such a thing was occurring. Could they be capsizing? No. If they were, they both would be falling to the ceiling. It was something else. Jack began to look about the room to deduce what was happening. He looked to the walls, the floor, and the ceiling, but nothing seemed out of place. He placed his hand on the railing nearby and felt an odd sense of vibration. He ran his hand along the steel bar, noticing the vibration was increasing the closer he came to the center bar that secured the rails to the floor. He saw the crews that held it in place were also lifting, as if being yanked from their secure placement in the metal flooring. It didn't seem possible. What could have been causing such a peculiar phenomenon?

"What the hell is going on?" Jack mused. Several screws suddenly pulled from the floor and whizzed through the air wickedly, like bullets fired from a gun. Jack shielded Ceinwen with his body, pushing her to the floor. "Take cover!" He ordered.

The screws ricocheted against the walls and ceiling, tinging and clacking as they rattled throughout the room. Jack looked up, his body still covering Ceinwen. He saw the door they had just entered begin to shake, the creaking of metal echoing across the room. He watched for a moment, fearful thoughts that raced through his head were suddenly realized as the door pulled inward, the center indenting, the metal spiraling as it drew it in harder, the pressure behind it increasing.

"Run," Jack said lowly.

"What?" Ceinwen asked.

"RUN!" Jack exclaimed.

She turned to see the door torn from its hinges, the screeching and scraping metal piercing their ears. It disappeared into a vast whirling slight that seemed to be back toward the center of the ship, deep within the bowels of the behemoth. Something was happening to the ship and it was happening fast. Jack picked himself off the floor, helping Ceinwen to her feet as well. Without hesitation, he pulled her behind him. He made his way to the door, which flung open wildly from the increasing pull that was sweeping farther and farther across the ship. He pushed Ceinwen through and then turned to grab the door handle. He used all his strength, but could barely get the door to move. He closed his eyes as he moved his fused arm. It felt more a part of him at each passing second. He wrapped both hands around the bar that served as a handle and pulled again. It still hardly swung. Looks like the strength in my arm isn't back yet fully, he thought. He then placed his feet along the steel molding and used his legs to assist. The door moved, slowly but more accepting of his force. He struggled for several seconds until he had almost closed the door. With less than an inch of space between the door and the latch, Ceinwen rushed behind Jack, hooked her arms under his shoulders and then fell backward. The extra force and weight was just enough to seal the door shut.

Jack fell to the floor as Ceinwen stumbled backward until she landed in her bottom. She felt the pain sear across her spine.

"Ow!" She howled.

Jack leaned up in his elbows, "You all right?"

Ceinwen nodded, "Yeah."

"Can you run?"

"Yeah."

"Good, because I think we only have a couple of minutes before this door's gone too." The door clunked loudly as it sank into its hinges and deeper into the molding.

Ceinwen let out a small shriek at the sound of the door. She quickly scrambled to her feet and began to run for the other side of the room. Jack was surprised at how quickly she moved. He immediately leapt to his feet and sprinted off behind her.

"Hey!" He called from behind. "Wait for me!"

The central engine core was no longer visible. It was now a large spiraling light, a large vortex of energy that was growing larger and humming louder. The rumble it produced could easily be confused as the low growl of a large creature awakening from its slumber. The growling grew louder and louder as the vortex swirled more intensely. It seemed to groan with satisfaction as several small screws flew into the room and disappeared into the blinding white light. It was soon even happier when a large, metal door whipped across the air and disappeared into its awaiting maw.

CHAPTER 25
TOP OF THE WORLD

"Welcome back, Senator Glorm," said the eager young man who opened the door for his leader.

"Thank you…," Glorm stopped and looked at the nametag that adorned the young man's lapel. "Kohpe Gentry," he finished.

"Just Kohpe, sir," the young man interjected. "And might I say you are an inspiration. We all see what you're trying to do."

"And what might that be?" Glorm looked at him curiously, wondering what he might say.

"You're looking out for the little people, you know," Kohpe added. "You're looking out for our best interest. All this talk of war, it's what this world needs. The United States needs to show that terrorist group who's really in charge and reclaim this planet for liberty and justice for all!"

Glorm stopped and smiled, "I like your moxie, kid. What is it that you said you do for me?"

"I didn't sir, but I handle all the interoffice communications, you know, all the important stuff that your constituents need to know. I get it to the right people."

Glorm straightened his bow time confidently, "I like you, kid. Give my office a call in the morning, there just might be a promotion in there for you."

Kohpe's eyes lit up as he beamed a broad smile, "Really? Thanks, sir!"

"Now, if you'll excuse me, I have a public to address and an election to win," Glorm spun on his polished heel and stepped through the curtain that led to the stage and podium just beyond.

The lead aircraft spun his ship as he broke past the LEHV blockade that had been keeping them at bay. However, their ability to slip past Barbasoa and his men was an indication that the defensive was only successful for a short time. They had to pursue the escaping craft before it reached the NULE tower antennae.

"I need my backup, now!" Remy shouted into his COMM. "We need to stop this guy before he gets to that antenna!"

"I'm with you," came support from his left.

Another two on his right immediately followed it. It was a thin offering, but the rest of the ships needed to stay behind and fend off the remaining HART aircraft that were still attacking.

"I need you men to put your speed down hard, we can't let them escape!" Barbasoa ordered.

"*You got it,*" "*On it,*" and "*Yessir,*" came as a series of responses.

The streets of New Utica were a chaotic series of mass hysteria and panic. Cars were speeding around slower vehicles, others crashed into those they followed too closely, and others swerved to avoid people that were running aimlessly into the streets. The sound of screams, honking horns and screeching tires was much louder than the normal din that filled the cityscape daily. It was peppered with the shrill screeches and curses of people trying desperately to escape the dangers and turmoil that invaded their once relatively peaceful lives. The flashes of light that were now known to be exploding aircraft lit up the dark sky high above. Most citizens were ordered to evacuate buildings that were higher than eight stories out of fear that they could be struck or collapse, since they stand outside the NNET security shield.

Deputy Officer Rowleigh Dawson was thrust into the thick of the escalating scene as soon as he punched in for his shift. He had been on the evening shift for the past two years and usually enjoyed it. Aside from the occasional drunk quarrel, or fistfight, he was normally just telling vagrants to go home or sleep it off somewhere else. The most interesting incident was when he had to ticket a man for public nudity. This was the first time he ever dealt with a situation of this magnitude. He watched as people ran amuck. He did his best to try to organize them and calm them down.

It wasn't working. No one was listening. Self-preservation had kicked in and each person was thinking only of themselves. *'It was going to be hard to find order in all this,'* he thought to himself.

"Help!" Came a shrill cry from behind.

Rawleigh turned around to see a woman being pushed to the ground by a large group of men. He reacted immediately, drawing his pistol as he raced to the woman's aide.

"HEY!" He shouted. "HOLD IT RIGHT THERE!" He aimed his pistol in front of him and trained it on the group of men. "Step away from the woman!" He ordered.

The men obliged, raising their hands over their head.

The woman stood and rushed to the officer's side. "Thank you," she sobbed.

"I just want to be sure you're safe," he said, not taking his eyes off the group of men. He didn't feel the EMP baton sliding from his belt. Nor did he feel its impact as it smashed against the base of his skull. Rawleigh dropped his pistol and fell to the ground unconscious.

"Stupid pig!" The once victimized woman spat at the unconscious officer. "I got his energy thingy."

"Good work, baby," the largest of the group of men stepped up to his lover and greeted her with an open-mouthed kiss. "Now that we got one of their sparklers, we can start taking over this cesspool."

"What about all them ships up there?" Asked another of the men.

The large man smirked, "Who gives a shit. Let them kill all the cops, then there won't be nothin' to stop the Equinox!"

"I'm going up after him!" Lartanner growled as he looked up at the tall, thin antennae array that made up the communications hub of the New Utica Police Department. It scratched the night sky, high above the rest of the cityscape. A red light blinked rhythmically at the tip of the array. He looked out across the night sky as he scaled the ladder that ran alongside the large aluminum structure.

Lartanner hated heights. Aloona knew this as he watched his partner slowly, cautiously climbing the structure. "Be careful!" He called up, more for to himself than to Lartanner.

Lartanner looked up to see Frisco had scaled to nearly the top of the array. She lumbered more slowly than she could with her nimble frame being that she carried an extra 180 pounds of weight across her shoulders. Fortunately, her embedded nanotech allowed her to increase both her strength and stamina. She grunted as she scaled further up the ladder.

"A-Agent Frisco, please, if you would, please set me down and you can go on your way," Strommel asked timidly.

Frisco didn't respond; she just kept her focus on the top of the antennae. As she took another climb, she turned her neck slightly out into the cityscape behind her. She could see two small lights, ones she recognized as the front of a HART aircraft. They were growing larger, coming closer. She smiled triumphantly to herself. She was almost to the top of the antenna; she had Strommel, and a means to escape.

Her master will be pleased, she thought.

Lartanner tried to move faster, wrapping his arms tightly around each rung as he made his way higher and higher. He could feel his heart pounding; the sound was filling his ears. He was terrified, trying his best to not look down.

It didn't work. He instinctively twisted his neck to look down. He was up high, much higher than he thought. He could see Aloona on the roof below. He was small. Not as small as the cluster of vehicles and people scattering several hundred feet along the street below. The sight of it all made him dizzy. He closed his eyes tightly and turned his head away, resisting the temptation to look again. He turned his attention to what was ahead, or more to the fact, above. He could see Strommel, dangling from the edge of the tower by his color, frozen and unflinching. Most likely terrified. He saw Frisco; she had turned around on the ladder and was waving a free hand wildly in the air, signaling for someone. He turned to see a foreign aircraft coming closer. '*The HART, no doubt,*' he thought.

The HART aircraft was getting farther and farther ahead of Barbasoa and his men. He pushed harder on his throttle, opening up his engine, but he was not speeding up any faster.

"You men still with me?" He called over the COMM.

"Yes," came three tandem replies.

"He's getting away, his ship is too fast for us," Remy explained. "I'm going to take a shot."

"Remy?" Came a concerned voice.

"Is that even possible?" Asked another.

Remy continued, "I don't know, the laser range is only within proximity when you lock onto the target, but we're running out of options here. Unless you all have a better idea."

Silence was the only response he received.

"I guess that settles it," he replied. "This is going to require all my resources along with my attention; I'll need you guys to keep any enemy craft off me while I set up and take the shot."

There was a short moment of static before a meek reply crackled across the COMM, "Whatever you need Remy, we're with you."

"Good, I'll need you."

Remy set his autopilot switch. The steering column collapsed into itself and was pulled into the console. The ship maintained a steady course, only dipping slightly from the currents of air that coursed across its metal chassis. Despite their solid and strong design, they were still heavier and more obtrusive than their enemy's ships. What he needed was for it to remain stable and with no distraction. The choppy night air didn't help. Remy reached over his head and pressed a release button. A panel slid open and lowered a set of retinal devices. He slid himself behind the thick goggles and pressed his face against the padded edges. A series of lights danced around the external edges of the goggles while within a display faded up, filling his vision with a three-dimensional layout of the entire city. It surrounded every part of his peripheral vision as well, even as he turned his head.

"Real-time display," Remy said.

The screen in his vision sent a beam that swept across the landscape before his eyes. As it moved, various changes occurred, ships appeared that weren't there before, damage and devastation that had incurred was now visible. It was disheartening to him, to see his city being destroyed before his eyes, with little he and his force have been able to do. He shook the thoughts from his head and forced his attention on the two ships that appeared directly in front of him, just beyond he could see the NULE communications array, still intact.

"Target display," he added. The moving imagery that filled up his vision became more alive as lines of light stretched across the field of view. A crosshair appeared within the direct center of the display.

"Aligning targeting display," chirped a computerized voice. The crosshair moved slightly until it stopped directly in front of Remy's eyes.

"Ocular recognition achieved," the computerized voice acknowledged.

Remy shifted his eyes slightly to the left. The crosshair moved in tandem. He then shifted to the right. It followed. He smiled to himself. Now he was ready to engage.

Helix watched fearfully as Strommel dangled dangerously out from the side of the antennae where Frisco kept him. Strommel's feet swung precariously from the heavy breeze that swept over the rooftop and swirled around the array. He felt his shirt jostle and slide further down the pole.

'After all Frisco had endured to capture me, would she allow him to drop so easily to his death?' Strommel thought to himself. *'Although, she did say she was done with me. Perhaps this is revenge.'* The wind licked his feet and pushed them out again. His shirt slid another millimeter. He didn't want to die. Not now. Not like this. In the distance, a glimmer of light flashed brightly. He squinted his eyes. Even with his glasses, he wasn't sure what he was seeing. More to the fact that he was hoping it was one of theirs, maybe even Jack, coming to his rescue.

Frisco flashed a broad grin, "At last!"

Any hope Strommel once held was suddenly gone.

"We have to help him!" Helix shouted.

"There's not much we can do from down here," Aloona replied.

"There has to be!" Helix looked around the roof for anything that he could use. Nothing caught his attention.

"Hey what's that?" Aloona pointed up into the sky at the fast approaching aircraft.

Helix turned, "Is that one of ours?"

"Not sure," Aloona said, moving about to find a better vantage point.

"It's coming in awfully fast," Helix observed.

"My guess is it's not one of ours," Aloona surmised. He immediately turned and looked up to his partner still scaling the array. "Lartanner!"

Lartanner didn't respond.

Aloona cupped his hands around his mouth and yelled louder, "Lartanner! Get down from there!"

Lartanner shook his head and waved his hand behind him, signaling he wasn't turning back. Aloona suddenly grew even more concerned. The thought of Lartanner so openly exposed terrified him. "You stupid, brave, son of a bitch," Aloona cursed to himself. He turned to Helix, "You see that ship up there? It's heading this way to get your friend, kill my partner, and take out this array. We need to make sure that none of that happens! Do you understand me?"

Helix nodded.

"Good, now help me find a way to stop that thing!"

Helix continued nodding.

"Well don't just stand there!"

"Right!" Helix snapped to and began to scramble about. He found the access panel at the base of the antennae. It was covered with a metal plate. He tried to pry it open, but it was locked. He struggled several times at attempting to force the metal plating from the panel. Aloona was growing annoyed with the grunts and groans that Helix continued emitting. He pulled the baton from his belt and swung it down until it hit the lock. He activated the baton just at it struck the lock, sending a vibration charge that immediately deactivated the security and allowed the lock to fall free.

"Pretty nice trick," Helix mused.

"Never mind that, what's your plan?"

"Well, I can reverse the signal of the array to stop sending the COMM signal and created a pulse that could mess with their navigational equipment."

"But if you turn off the signal, won't that crash our ships?"

"Not if I slide the signal into every third pulse. The signal will keep your ships flying and then send out an erratic signal that will catch ships in a close proximity."

Aloona looked somewhat confused, but nodded anyway, "Do it! I'm going to help my partner!"

Helix nodded and dove into his work. He pulled out a small black box from his coat. He pulled two thin cords from the side of the box and plugged them into the panel. Within seconds, he was typing feverishly onto the mini keyboard that slid from the other side of the small box.

The evading enemy aircraft sidled left and right as it tore across the sky to its intended target, now only a few mere miles away. It loomed ahead like a giant monument. The pilot slid his hands across the board to his left and then moved to the one over his head.

"Target is in sights," the pilot informed.

"Roger," crackled a reply.

"Weapons are ready. Prepping to destroy target," the pilot continued.

"WAIT!" cried the crackled voice. "Look at the tower."

The pilot averted his attention from the display and took a close look at the figure waving their arms wildly atop the array. He touched a series of switches as the display lit up with beams of yellow and blue tracing around the form of the figure. Text on the screen began to blink wildly, reading: '**IDENTITY CONFIRMED** *Agent Frisco.*'

"Positive identification on the figure," explained the pilot. "It's one of ours."

Another text string flashed over the first, this time alerting. '**IDENTIFIED**: *Dr. Strommel.*'

"And she has Strommel," the pilot added.

"Abort targeting," interjected the crackling voice. "We need Strommel alive."

"Roger, aborting weapons and converting to rescue," the pilot confirmed. The weapons on the outside of the craft tucked in underneath the sleek ship as it slowed its speed. The pilot called to his companion flying nearby, "I need to slow my speed, so you need to keep any threats off my tail."

"Roger," the crackle replied. He watched out his side as his wingman pitched away, disappearing behind him.

"That's it you son of a bitch," Remy growled. "Slow down so I can get a clear shot at you."
He watched as the targeting crosshair stayed within the center of his windshield, his eyes locked on the craft. The ship to his target's left drifted out of his line of sight, making him nervous. He knew he couldn't turn his head in fear he would lose his lock. "Uh, guys, one of the ships just flew out of view, I need your eyes on him while I complete my shot," he requested.

"I'm on him," came a confident reply over the COMM.

I hope so," Remy whispered to himself.

The accompanying HART aircraft twisted away from his companion as he swooped behind, turning around to face the pursuing vehicles. The craft didn't hesitate to open fire on Remy's LEHV first. The shifts in air currents jolted the craft, causing the laser bolts to miss his vehicle. It wasn't long before reinforcements were swooping in to protect Barbasoa. Remy tried to keep his eyes locked straight ahead, not allowing the target to move from view. He maintained his visual position.

Remy's wingman barreled around his ship, each roof nearly touching. The LEHV effortlessly flew circles around its companion and instantly engaged the HART craft. The firefight was intense as each ship countered the attack and aggressive movements of the other. Several beams were fired, slicing through the air and cluttering Barbasoa's view screen. He kept his focus on the fleeing craft.

"Alright, you've gone as far as you're going," Remy talked to himself softly, keeping his tone soothing and mellow in an attempt to remain calm despite his nerves. He placed his thumb over the trigger of his weapons. His eyes were beginning to water from being open so long. He knew it was happening and he didn't want to blink and lose his aim.

His target was aligned. It was now or never.

"Here goes everything," Remy sucked in his breath and held it. He pressed the trigger. As the guns began to fire, the air battle-taking place around his LEHV was ending. His companion fired at the HART fighter and hit the target directly in the center of its view shield. The beam sliced through the center of the ship, piercing the pilot as it made its way through the entire craft. Before the man had time to scream, his ship exploded.

The shockwave emitted from the explosion of the craft rippled outward, pushing everything in its path, including Remy's LEHV. He jerked from the impact of the blast as his finger pressed the trigger. His head jerked violently right and then left, throwing the crosshair on the screen in every direction. Barbasoa swayed from the bounce of the ship as he tried to regain his equilibrium.

"DAMN IT!" He screamed in frustration. He knew his accuracy was compromised, but by how much?

The weapons from beneath his LEHV discharged their beams. The sailed in a straight line, despite the jolt the ship took at the time of their release. They hit their target. About twenty degrees lower than he hoped. Remy watched as his beam scorched the underside of the fleeing craft, just beneath the right engine. The engine exploded from the laser blast, sparks eschewed in every direction. The ship bobbed slightly from the damage and then lagged on the right side, like an injured animal limping after a fight. He smiled to himself. He hit it, not where or exactly how he wanted to, but he hit it. Chalk it up to a small victory, he thought.

"Great shot, Oszkowski," came Barbasoa's approval over the COMM.

"Thanks Chief, but let's not break out the champagne yet, he's still moving and he's almost to the tower," Remy stated.

"You want us to take him out?"

"No," Barbasoa gritted his teeth. "You all form around Oszkowski, get back out there. I'll make sure no one gets closer to you."

The accompanying NULE LEHVs disbanded Remy to follow their leader back into the battle. Remy pushed down on his throttle and opened his engines. He could feel the speed pick up, as the fleeing craft grew larger, closer. He contemplated his next move, knowing he couldn't close the gap completely before the other ship reached the array. His mind raced as his eyes darted about the cabin, landing on the controls for the winch.

A small grin stretched across his face.

Frisco saw the small explosion that crippled her rescuer. She grew angry as she watched the injured craft slow as it still moved toward her. Fortunately, the blast didn't complete render the craft useless, but the escape was going to be more challenging as now she and her prisoner were going to add extra weight. Unfortunately, at this point it was her only option.

Frisco looked below to see Lartanner still making his slow ascent. 'He looked like no threat,' she thought to herself.

There was a low eruption from the back of the HART aircraft, as it pushed itself forward with a bit more thrust. The pilot was obviously trying to hurry, somehow using whatever energy reserves he had left to speed up his ship. Frisco knew it was time. She leaned over and grabbed Strommel's collar, lifting him up as if he were made of paper.

Lartanner looked up at that moment. '*Damn!*' He thought. Time was running out. Lartanner lowered one hand to his hip and slowly withdrew his pistol from its holster. He wasn't going to look down, out of fear his vertigo would kick in and he would drop his weapon. He slowly brought his hand up to the rung of the ladder and looked up. Strommel was dangling over the edge of the antennae. Frisco scooped him from where he hung and wrapped one arm around his waist and secured her other arm around the rung behind her. She remained facing out, the wind sweeping her hair from her eyes. Lartanner trained his pistol on her lower half, in fear that he might hit Strommel if he aimed too high. His hand was shaking as he took aim. He fired a shot.

The bullet missed Frisco by mere centimeters, sparking against the metal near her feet. The sound of the ricochet sounded hollow as it reverberated through the thin atmosphere.

Frisco sneered as she looked down at her enemy. Another annoying, insignificant subspecies. She shuffled her feet to her right as she stepped from the ladder rung. Lartanner watched as she moved. He had to readjust his position to get a clearer shot. Lartanner took in a deep breath as he prepared to move.

Suddenly, the ladder he gripped onto tightly shook violently.

'*What was happening?*' He thought. '*Were the ships finally here, attacking the array?*'

No. He looked up to see Frisco slamming her foot against the ladder. Her strength and where she was striking the ladder was loosening the bolts from where they were secured. The ladder creaked and groaned as it broke free from its once secured foundation. She was going to kick it free until it fell. Or he fell, whichever came first.

Another kick shook the ladder again. This time Lartanner slipped, his hand falling free as his pistol dropped. It clinked as it hit varying girders on its journey down. Aloona hugged himself to the side of the array, hoping to avoid the falling weapon. Once the weapon passed, he continued scaling the side of the array, away from the ladder.

"Hold on!" He called up to his partner.

Lartanner didn't hear Aloona calling up to him. He was consumed with the fear of falling. The ladder had shifted, falling back slightly. He had his arms wrapped around one rung, while his legs were wrapped around another. Aloona watched from below. He couldn't hesitate; he had to help Lartanner.

Helix continued typing feverishly, despite the chaos that was happening overhead. He needed to complete what he was starting before it was too late. Anyway he could help was crucial, especially if he could stop a flanking enemy ship. "Almost there," he said quietly to himself. He typed a few more commands into the interface. Once he typed 'end,' the program responded.

'*Program Accepted.*' It displayed on the screen.

Helix smiled. He did it. Now he had to see if it did what he promised.

Slamming the door behind them was easier as the door was being pulled by the mysterious force from deep within the bowels of the Behemoth. Jack twisted the lock on the door, hoping it would brace it a while longer.

What Jack didn't expect to see, was hiding behind the door, unnoticed. He heard the click of a gun cocking as a bullet loaded into the chamber. He turned to see Evelyn Strommel, or the creature that looked like her, aiming it at him. Ceinwen let out a loud scream, one that echoed even more loudly across the empty room.

"Evelyn," Jack was startled. He instinctively raised his hands at the sight of the gun.

"You do realize that you're heading in the wrong direction. The bay with the aircraft is the back of the ship," she spoke in a sultry tone.

'*Damn, she was sexy,*' Jack thought. He had to remind himself that she wasn't real, but an abomination of humankind. "Evelyn, you don't understand what's happening here."

"What? You, attempting to escape?" She mused.

"This whole ship is about to come down around us," Jack explained. He gestured toward the window, "Look out there. See the buildings? We're sinking."

"Sinking? Surely, you're overreacting. I'm sure it's just part of the Great Master's plan."

Jack was growing annoyed at the sound of the so-called Master. Who the hell was he? Who did he think he was?

"We just came from the back half of the ship," Ceinwen, too, was getting frustrated with the constant interruptions with guns and bad guys. "It was sucking itself in."

"Shut up!" Evelyn snapped, turning the gun toward Ceinwen.

Jack stepped between Evelyn and Ceinwen, keeping the attention on himself, "It's true."

"Do you expect me to believe that?" Evelyn said accusingly. "I'm sure you'd say anything to escape."

"Have you ever known me to lie?" Jack offered his best smile. She didn't look convinced.

Evelyn looked at Jack for a long, silent moment. She was studying him, as if analyzing him. Calculating her interactions with him to determine if he was lying. Jack smiled a bit more widely as he took a step toward her. She straightened her arm, aiming the pistol as she tightened her finger on the trigger. "Don't," was all she said.

"Okay, alright," Jack stepped back quickly. "But I can tell you, I saw it with my own eyes, this ship is pulling itself apart."

"See for yourself," Ceinwen gestured her head toward the locked door beside her.

Evelyn didn't take her eyes off wither of them. In fact, she didn't even blink. It was eerie, but unsurprising, since she was, after all, a machine. She circled sideways as she made her way to the door, the gun still trained on both of them. Jack pushed against Ceinwen as they mirrored Evelyn's steps in the opposite direction. They stopped when they reached the railing that separated the walkway from the window on one side of the room. Jack, not breaking his eye contact with Evelyn, took Ceinwen's hand and pressed it against the cool steel of the railing, pushing his hands over her fingers until they were wrapped around the bar.

"Get ready," Jack whispered from the side of his mouth. "Grab hold tight."

"Remember, I am superior," Evelyn spoke. "If you make any move at me, I will stop you, and this time it will be permanent."

Jack nodded, "Understood." Jack stepped in front of Ceinwen and grabbed the rail with his good hand, shielding her with his body.

Evelyn switched the pistol from her right hand to her left, still keeping it pointed steadily at Jack and Ceinwen. She reached behind her and wrapped her hand around the lock. She effortlessly flicked her shoulder and twisted loose the latch to the door.

"Jack," Ceinwen whispered fearfully into Jack's ear. He felt her body tightly against his. She was soft, warm, and trembling. "I'm frightened."

"Trust me," Jack whispered back reassuringly.

Evelyn pulled the handle, freeing the door from its latches. It pushed open wickedly as the impressive force that had followed Jack and Ceinwen all this way had once again caught up with them. The room filled with what sounded like a screaming vehicle plunging over the edge of a cliff. It ripped through the room as it lashed in every direction until every space was filled with its rage. Without blinking, or even flinching, the force ripped Evelyn off her feet and pulled her within. Her body slammed against the edges of the door, folding her body violently as it swallowed her.

She was gone.

Jack felt his legs lift from the floor. He took advantage of the opportunity, swinging his legs and kicking the door. It swung hard and slammed shut with a loud clang. At that moment, the screeching force stopped. The room quieted as both Jack and Ceinwen released their grips and dropped breathlessly to the floor.

"Are you alright?" Jack panted.

Ceinwen nodded, trying to catch her breath. "Now what?" Ceinwen asked, panting wildly in an attempt to catch her breath.

"We keep going," Jack said somberly, knowing it was not what she wanted to hear. "I know you're exhausted, I am too. But we have to be only a few more rooms from the hangar. We make it there, and then we can get the hell off this damn thing."

Ceinwen nodded, knowing there was no other choice; "I hope you're right."

"Me too."

They trotted to the other side of the room, one that was much smaller in length than the previous rooms they ran through. An indication they were getting to the end of the ship. He hoped. He grasped the door and flung it open, relieved they were there before the door behind them was sucked away. He pushed it open hard, with the anticipation there would be a force preventing him from doing it easily.

The door whipped open, to which Jack instinctively pushed Ceinwen through. She stumbled ahead of his arm and fell into something firm, yet with both a hardness and softness. Whatever it happened to be was large and smelled odd. She stepped back and looked up into the face of General Varcar Zimm.

"We meet again," he hissed.

Jack stopped short at the sound of Ceinwen's scream. '*Now what?*' He thought. A fist to his jaw was the only answer he received.

CHAPTER 26
END OF THE LINE

The control panel of Remy's LEHV suddenly began to blip wildly. He flipped a switch and changed the view screen before him. A series of numbers began to scroll across his screen, one alerting him to the distance between his craft and the HART aircraft in front of him.

'*1100 meters.*'

He watched the numbers flicker down rapidly.

'*900 meters.*'

He was closing in quickly.

'*700 meters.*'

Almost there.

'*500 meters.*'

Perfect. He pressed his control panel marked winch. The winch at the front of the vehicle fired its tow cable at the back of the HART aircraft. The metal hood hit the rear of the vehicle hard enough to penetrate the outer metal shell, securing itself tightly within the craft.

"Gotcha!" Remy cheered. "Now to reel you in." He flipped the recoil switch. The winch ground to life as it began to reel in the steel cable attached to the imbedded hook.

The HART pilot jerked forward in his seat. Despite his thick, canvas flight suit, the nylon straps that secured him into his seat dug deeply into his shoulder and thighs.

"What the hell?" He searched around his display to see what could possibly be causing such an abrupt change in his speed and maneuverability. All engines, beside the one, were online. Even the reserve thrusters were operating. They suddenly alerted him by flashing a red '*OVERHEAT*' icon. The reserve thrusters were beginning to smoke. He quickly shut them off. He immediately checked his rear display. He could see what was behind his craft. There he saw the NULE LEHV he had been outrunning only a few meters behind and growing larger. He noted the steel cable that ran from the front of that vehicle and seemed to be impaled into his.

"Bastard!" He cursed angrily. He flipped his reserve thrusters back on, turning them to maximum.

"Dammit!" Remy cursed, something he seemed to do more frequently as of late. The yoke in his hands shook and pulled until it wrenched free of his grip. He felt his vehicle lose control as it pitched about wildly. He grasped the steering column firmly and held it in place as best he could. He watched as the pilot that he was now tethered to whip his craft about wildly. The erratic movements were getting more and more violent. Remy's LEHV was thrashing in complete disorder, as was his own body in his seat. Alarms and sirens began to wail loudly, alerting him to the dangers his vehicle was undergoing.

'**DANGER**: *Stabilization Failure.*'
'**DANGER**: *Thrusters Overheating.*'
'**WARNING**: *Crash Imminent.*'

It was evident this tether approach was not the best idea. He reached forward and pressed the switch that controlled the winch. It stopped retracting the line and kept the vehicles about twenty feet apart. The HART aircraft did not let up its desire to be split from its lagging anchor. Now that Remy had regained some control, he began to ease back on his own thrusters to slow the advancing fighter.

It worked. For the moment, at least.

Remy knew he needed to separate his attachment, but he couldn't let the ship escape. He prepared to charge his weapons. Since he had been channeled into the long-range weapon, he needed to reconfigure the short-range weapons. As soon as they were set, there was a low beep accompanied by a green light.

The weapons were ready. It was now or never.

Lartanner was frozen with fear. The ladder in his grasp was now free of the tower and falling backward. He closed his eyes tightly as he hugged him limbs around the rungs.

"Hold on!" Called up Aloona.

He did not intend to let go. The ladder dangled over the edge of the NULE tower, Lartanner now hanging over one-hundred stories above the ground. He was petrified with fear.

"I'm coming to get you," Aloona tried to offer his support.

"NO!" Lartanner shot back, still clinging desperately to the ladder. "I won't have you fall too!"

"You're not going to fall!"

Helix watched from below as his friends continued their fight for survival. He saw Lartanner holding tight and Aloona reaching the bend in the ladder, contemplating the safest way to save his partner. Higher above them was Strommel, clinging fearfully to Frisco's back. He stood below them all. Helpless.

The thunderous applause were light a glorious concerto, composed just for him. Glorm smiled at the packed auditorium, filled with his constituents. He felt proud, achieved.

"Thank you," his voice boomed through the microphone at the podium where he stood. "Thank you all for you tireless and wonderful support."

The applause continued.

"Tonight is a very important night," he continued. "Tonight this country will elect the leader that will take this country where it deserves to go. A leader who is here to serve the people. A leader who will fight for each and every one of you!

"Our previous leader, he turned this country against itself. He led us down a path of darkness and despair. Now look at us, on the brink of war, with a weak leader. You can't win this fight against our global enemies with ideals of talk and promises of treaties. That only leads to opening the gates to those that wish to destroy our way of life. No. We need to destroy our enemies with power, with force. I will be a leader that shows this world that we will no longer be pushed around. That we are not the weak country that President Michaelson has made us. We will take back our country and make it the great nation it once was!"

The crowd leapt to their feet and applauded even louder, now cheering and whistling for their candidate.

"In a few hours the polls will close, and a new President will be elected. I have faith that we will take the glory and find out destiny! Forever!"

He raised his hands high over his head triumphantly.

"Destiny forever!" Shouted the crowd in unison. They chanted the words repeatedly, bringing an even bigger smile to Glorm's face.

Zimm ushered his two reacquired prisoners to the bow of the great Behemoth. Jack looked to Ceinwen apologetically, but she was too overwhelmed with fear to notice. They had returned to the control center where they had been only a couple of hours before. It was quiet. The view of the city seemed less active than what Jack expected. He wondered if the NULE had taken care of the impending HART pilots. He then remembered

"Dammit Zimm, you have to listen to me!" Jack pleaded angrily. "This ship is falling apart. We have to get off now!"

"Yes, you said the great force that was pulling everything to the center of the ship, but yet here we are. Not being pulled into any mysterious force," Zimm sneered.

"He's telling the truth!" Ceinwen added.

"Be careful, my dear, but our Mr. Zero here is never been one to tell the truth."

"If we don't leave now we are going to die!"

"Not before the cavalry arrive!" Zimm shot back.

Jack looked at him confused, "But the police are here already."

"You dolt," Zimm snickered. "The police are like mosquitoes, you swat them and they go splat. We're waiting for the real threat. And they should be here any moment." Zimm looked to a man in a white jump suit seated near a series of screen, a set of headphones affixed tightly to his head. "Kelper?"

The man named Kelper slid the earphones from his head and rested them on his shoulders, "Yessir, I'm getting a new ping now."

"Excellent, is it native to the hardware?"

"No sir, it appears to be coming from a secondary device, it's duplicating the original signal and then rearranging the digits to send out a scrambled signal. I think they intend to destroy our ships."

"And, can they?"

"Not at all, sir. Our shielding with prevent any penetration from their signal."

"I am pleased to hear this," Zimm smiled.

At that moment a soldier came running into the bridge, "Sir, our spotters have detected an incoming fleet."

Zimm smiled, "Ah, just in time." Zimm strode to the controls at the front of the room, facing the large window that extended the view of the world before them. Zimm stared at the large radar screen that displayed a series of semicircles with a long arm that swept around the screen. As it swept around the eleven o'clock position to reveal a large mass of green blips. "Finally," he sneered. "The military is here."

"Good! Just in time to kick your ass!" Ceinwen shot back.

Zimm spun on his heel and then marched up to the young woman, "So feisty." He ran his hand through her loose strands of hair that hung in her face. She jerked back hard as he tucked the hair behind her ear. "Fortunately, I won't be the one who is…kicked, you say? In fact, it will be my own fleet that will be distributing the kicks, meaning we will be the ones that shall be victorious."

"Your fleet has been thinned and your ship is crippled," Jack pointed out. "How in the hell do you intend to win?"

"By shutting down their ships," Zimm explained. "Via your city's tallest communication tower."

Jack threw his head back and laughed, "You fool, Zimm. There no way you'll take over that tower. The NULE Police Department will stop you."

"Of course they will, in the most effective way possible, by using their own communications tower. You see, with their tower down, their puny police force is dismantled, but active and sending out a signal, then we can use their own COMM signal to destroy the United States military."

Jack's heart sank. He was out of time.

Strommel felt his heart beating rapidly, echoing through his ears like a drum in a concert hall. He could see everything around him and beneath him. Everything seemed to be spinning around him, as if the world was spinning faster on its axis yet he somehow managed to stay still. The woman that was holding him high above the city was strong and one he once called friend. Now he was at her mercy, hanging hundreds of feet above the ground. He was her prisoner. A prisoner of the evil organization that once employed him, until his escape. He tried to keep his composure, squirm, or fall from her grasp. He didn't want to die. Not now. Not like this.

The screams of a man in danger echoed loudly around him. He craned his neck around to see Lartanner, clutching for dear life as the ladder he was once climbing was now bent precariously backward.

He had to stop Frisco. But how? She was stronger than him. He was relatively inert at the moment, not only being hoisted on Frisco's back, but he was also terrified at the prospect of falling. All he could do was stay frozen and not move. Right? Wrong. He had to act, stop the nanite threat that stole his life, killed his wife and replaced her with a replicated version. He created the technology, so he could stop it. He knew how to stop it. He just had to act at just the right time.

The ladder groaned as it leaned deeper and deeper into the black night sky, dangling closer to the edge and a certain death for Lartanner. He could hear Frisco laughing triumphantly. He inched his outer arm along his side until it reached his hip pocket. He slid his hand inconspicuously into his pocket and slid out an EMP baton that he placed their on the zeppelin.

Without thinking and without hesitation, he activated the baton. It shot out to its fullest length and crackled to life. Frisco was too preoccupied with her adversaries and the incoming aircraft that she didn't notice his shifting weight. He quickly drew back his arm, but this time his weight shifted more than before. In fact, it pulled Frisco backward, forcing her to readjust her feet in order to keep her balance. She knew her prisoner was struggling. Wearing a vicious sneer, she cranked her head around to see the baton swinging at her, hitting her right between the eyes.

The explosion was harsh, erupting loudly and sparking in every direction. Sparks showered across Lartanner and Aloona, raining down to the rooftop below where Helix covered his head with his arms to avoid any extreme amount of debris landing in his long hair.

Frisco stared blankly out into the open sky. Her grip upon Strommel loosened as her muscles began to lax and her body began to sag. Strommel felt himself beginning to slip. Soon, his body was free of Frisco's grasp. He could feel the open air as it began to surround him like a blanket, wrapping around his body with its cool breeze.

He was falling.

Pressing his thumbs hard against the trigger, Remy's LEHV spat out a rapid series of green bursts of energy erupted from his short-range weapons. It looked like a fireworks display as it crackled and sparkled from the front of his vehicle. The beams shot toward the vehicle that fought to break free of the umbilical-like bond that tethered the two airships together. The beams arced across the sky, scratching the darkened night sky like the sharp talons of a raptor tearing the flesh of its prey.

The HART vehicle twisted and turned itself in its violent attempts to break free of the steel cable that had punctured its tail. The thrashing about, akin to a fish trapped in shallow water, continued to jerk and pull Remy's vehicle roughly through the air. Had he not been such an accomplished pilot, he would most certainly crash. But he kept his cool and followed the movements of the vehicle to his front.

Remy continuously fired his lasers, hoping, eventually, that one of the bolts would hit the enemy craft. It took his determination to finally strike the craft. One of the green bolts struck the rear engine underneath. The contact resulted in a sudden burst of acceleration. Fire burst from the engine as it exploded and then coughed out an increase in speed. This unexpected change in speed pushed Remy backward in his seat, slamming the back of his head against his seat.

The two vehicles were suddenly thrown out of control, each twisting and turning in their own directions, still connected by the tether. As the HART aircraft spun around, it pulled at Remy's LEHV, forcing him to fly in front of the smaller craft. With the momentum it created and the weight of the vehicle, it pulled the smaller craft around, slinging it like a bola weapon.

Helix nearly fell backward as his head craned upward to follow the incredible battle happening above. Once he noticed the tether between the two vehicles, his eyes traced their trajectory. His heart stopped as he noted that the wire was going to snag along the array, unquestionably. He immediately slammed his portable computer shut and stuffed it under his arm, turned, and ran.

Remy tried desperately to maintain stability, but it was no use. The vehicle was out of control. The two vehicles slung and twisted around one another spinning like a large top, flying toward the array. The speed was intense, but as it passed over the roof of the NULE headquarters, each vehicle was far enough apart from the other that the tether between them wrapped around the array. The array quickly slowed each vehicle, pulling them back, but not to a stop, instead they wrapped around the array again. The thick cable twanged as it tightened and pulled at the array structure. The two airships crossed each other several times before the tether that held them together no longer had any more length. The steel cable wrapped around the upper portion of the array, where Agent Frisco had been standing. After being smacked by Strommel's stick, she began to lose her balance, but the cable caught her before she could fall. More than just catching her, it wrapped around her torso. When the cable became taut, it squeezed her flesh, tearing deeply into it until it sliced her bones. As the two airships collided, causing a large explosion, two halves of Agent Frisco were freed from the cable and dropped limply from the roof and fell to the ground below.

Strommel could sense the weightlessness that took him over, as he fell toward the roof below. He shut his eyes, not wanting to see where he was or when he would reach impact. How could anyone subject themselves to the horror of the macabre moment?

Suddenly, he felt his entire body lurch backward, as if being pulled by some force. Whatever the force was, it slowed him, by snagging his shirt. Unfortunately, the shirt did not have the same tenacity to hold him in place. The buttons and seams of his shirt instantly began to split.

"HOLD ON!" Shouted Aloona from above.

Strommel forced open his eyes and looked to see Aloona gripping a fistful of his shirt intensely.

"I can't hold you much longer! GRAB ONTO SOMETHING!" He called out again.

Strommel immediately wriggled his arms free in order to grab a part of protruding metal. He wrapped his arms around what was the rung of the ladder that Frisco had knocked free. Once he had a hold, Aloona released his grip on the shirt. The sudden change of weight and pull caused Strommel to slip. He lost his own grip on the ladder rung and fell to the ground below. Fortunately, the fall was short, only a few feet, that the impact was hardly noticeable.

"Strommel!" Helix shouted from halfway across the roof. "Get out of the way!"

Strommel looked up to see the two airships twisting around one another. He watched as the steel cable between them wrapped tightly around the array. He also saw the two halves of Agent Frisco's body toppled from high above.

He turned away in horror, the macabre scene forever etched in his mind. Frisco was dead. This time for sure, he thought. It was too late to think more of her, of her death. Strommel had two large aircrafts preparing to fall upon him in seconds. He quickly picked himself up and ran toward Helix.

The LEHV spiraled along the side of the array as it rolled at its widened base. Remy tried his best to remain calm, despite his intermittent screams that he let loose. His harness held tight, keeping him from flying all around the cabin. But now, he wanted to break free, to escape this metallic deathtrap before it was too late. The only option was the ejection seat, if it wasn't damaged from the crash. He slid his hand along his side until he felt the lever that resided near the base of his seat. He wrapped his fingers around the handle and pulled.

The ladder broke free of its bolts. The added, albeit temporary, weight of Strommel along with the catastrophe happening above, certainly factored into the destruction. Aloona scramble rapidly from the former front of the ladder to the back, which was now the top. He clung tightly as it slumped further forward. Aloona kept his gaze solely on Lartanner, who was now hanging upside down. He still maintained his tight grip around the rungs, in his attempt to ensure himself that he will not fall.

It didn't help. His confidence was shattered as the ladder pulled itself apart from the array. Aloona anticipated the shift and quickly grabbed the nearest part of the array. Aloona slammed his chest against the jutting metal bar. He felt his breath get pushed from his lungs. He wanted to catch his breath but knew there wasn't time. He climbed up onto the bar and turned toward the falling ladder. Above him, the two vehicles were becoming intertwined as they wrapped themselves together around the array.

Aloona acted quickly. He looked around for any chance to get himself and Lartanner down to the roof. He noted the long cable that ran up the center of the array was the perfect opportunity. The aircraft above were beginning to tighten around the array. Aloona freed the cable from within and tugged it roughly to ensure it would hold. He pulled enough slack free and wrapped it around his waist.

"Lartanner!" Aloona shouted. Lartanner didn't respond. "Lartanner, I need you to listen to me!"

Lartanner let out a meek response, "Y-yeah?"

"I'm swinging over to you. When I signal you, I need you to let go of the ladder!" Again, Lartanner didn't respond. "Did you hear me?" Aloona yelled.

"I...I don't think I can do that."

"Just trust me."

Lartanner nodded rapidly.

"Hold tight!" He called to Lartanner. "I'm on my way!" Aloona then leapt from the bar where he stood and swung gracefully around the structure, wrapping the cable neatly around the array. He circled the tower. As he came to the front, he called out to his partner, "Alright, let go, NOW!"

As he passed under Lartanner, Lartanner released his grip from around the rungs. Aloona opened his arms and caught his partner in an awkward manner. The impact of the catch resulted in the loss of his grip, causing the two men to slide rapidly down the cable as they crashed hard against the surface of the roof. They each rolled out of the way, as the two vehicles above them collided in a massive fireball. The heat from the explosion was intense. Debris rained down onto them in massive chunks of fire and metal.

"Move! Move!" Aloona shoved his partner ahead of himself.

They ran as fast as they could, not looking behind them. The sound of the array creaking as it bent filled their ears like a roaring beast charging. The sound of it tearing through the air haunted their escape. Aloona didn't hesitate to put Lartanner first. He could feel the ominous presence of the large tower edging closer as it slowly continued to fall. The shadow it cast from the moonlight above creeped across the roof slowly, growing like a massive weed that seemed to have no end.

Lartanner watched as his own shadow that stretched several feet before him was quickly swallowed by that of the towers. He picked up his pace, widening his gait as he hastened to outrun the falling structure. It seemed fruitless. They were never going to outrun it. Suddenly, Lartanner felt something push him from behind. He immediately lifted off his feet from the force of the shove, which he knew was from Aloona. He flew a few feet before landing hard against the roof, his chin scraping against the rough concrete. He slid several feet before rolling to a stop. Lartanner lifted himself up to see where he had landed. As he watched the tower topple over, he saw the last sight of his partner, his friend, his lover, Aloona disappear under the collapsed metal array.

"NO!" Lartanner screamed.

But it was too late. Aloona was gone.

CHAPTER 27
THE VORTEX RETURNS

"Alright men," General Hogarth Portnoy chomped down on his moistened cigar as he shouted his orders. He stood stoic at the top of the Roamer Tank, a hovering armored vehicle with a forward-facing turret. He was an older man, his face worn, wrinkled, and weathered. He wore a thick mustache that covered his upper lip. The whiskers were parted each time the cigar swiveled around his mouth, resting between gnashed teeth. He looked up above the tops of the surrounding skyscrapers, watching as lights streaked past, some bursting into a ball of flames. He was the first to answer the call, when they scrambled to get their regiments organized and sent to New Utica from Griffiss Air Force Base from the nearby city of Rome-Delta. General Portnoy stepped up, wanting to take such a terrorist organization on first-hand.

He may have been old, but he was eager, filled with moxie. Old, never. Seasoned was what those that didn't want to be called old would prefer. He certainly was seasoned, but he was also experienced. General Portnoy squinted his eyes in determination, "We are looking at the enemy. We need to be prepared and one-step ahead. These bastards are trespassing on American soil. My soil. My country. Our country."

A crackle of static was the reply that came across the COMM that Portnoy held in his hand. A voice cut through the static, "Just give the word, General Portnoy."

Portnoy smiled, despite it being hidden under his mustache, "Attack!"

Behind Portnoy, several crafts lifted into the air, more heavily armored that the NULE LEHVs. To Portnoy, the battle was just beginning.

"Dammit Zimm! Listen to me!" Jack was still trying to connect with Zimm's rational side. Fat chance.

"I'm through listening to you, Zero," Zimm snapped. He was keeping his eyes locked to the screen in front of him, watching a series of ships lifting into the air. The military had arrived, and they were engaging into battle. Zimm turned to Kelper, "It's showtime."

Kelper flipped a series of switched and then typed a command that Jack couldn't read, onto his screen. When he tapped the "return" button, there was a low rumble. The COMM dish below the Behemoth was moving.

"Well?" Zimm said impatiently.

"The signal is sent," Kelper replied confidently.

Zimm didn't show any reaction, which made Kelper uneasy. Zimm spoke coolly, "And?"

"And?" Kelper replied nervously, his confidence shaken.

"And how will we know it works?" Zimm asked.

Kelper pointed to the screen. Zimm leaned forward and squinted his eyes as he looked intently at the screen. Zimm watched as several military armored vessels were flying into the air, above the city.

Jack stood and watched over Zimm's shoulder. He knew Zimm was aware of him there, but he didn't react. He was certain Zimm wanted him to see. However, Jack was suddenly distracted by an incessant tapping at his shoulder. He swiveled his head quickly to see Ceinwen digging her finger repeatedly into his shoulder. He wanted to shout at her, annoyed by her distraction, but her expression was of pure horrification. He followed her eye line to the door at the back of the cabin. There was a low clang as the door began to pull inward.

'*Shit*,' Jack thought. '*The force was here.*'

There was another odd sound, a lower more rhythmic sound coming from the other direction that Jack had previously been looking. He pivoted his head again. He saw several military vehicles sputter in midair before they slowly dropped, falling from the sky. They never reached the battle.

"Excellent," Zimm laughed. "Excellent work."

Kelper's confidence returned. He sat up in his seat with a large smile.

Jack's jaw went slack. The battle was over before it even began. A different sound returned, catching Jack's attention. The returning sound of metal twisting was louder. Loud enough that it caused Zimm to take notice. "What was that?"

"It's what I told you," Jack retorted. "It's that force. It's here."

Zimm turned to a soldier at his left, "Go check it out."

The soldier nodded and trotted up to the door. He looked around, as if expecting to run into something invisible. It was actually comical to watch as the soldier stepped over nothing. He looked around excessively, as if his neck was on a continuously rotating ball joint.

Ceinwen was clawing at Jack's shoulder, trying to pull him away. Jack brushed her away, waiting for the right opportunity to make his move.

"Well?" Zimm asked impatiently. "Anything?"

The soldier shook his head, "Nothing, sir."

It all happened so quickly. No one, not even Jack, or Ceinwen, were expecting it. The thick metal door that the soldier inspected intently creaked once and then flew from the frame, torn from its hinges as if being pulled by a massive, enraged beast. The soldier was sucked through as well, his head slamming against the metal frame, snapping his neck instantly. Chaos consumed the bridge of the dirigible in seconds, a spiral of turbulent wind screeching in every direction. It was as if someone released a hurricane from a bottle and let it run rampant.

The vortex tore through the bridge, not looking to be merciful or to single anyone person out. It was angry and it wanted everyone aboard to know. It whipped and pulled anything and everything in its path. Ceinwen screamed as two-crew member were ripped from their posts and were swallowed through the door. Even equipment, seats that were bolted down, came free and disappeared into the vortex. The doorframe was chewed apart and crumbled free after several objects, humans included, kept colliding with it. The opening was bigger, the maw of the vortex wider.

"What the hell is happening?" Zimm shouted over the wind.

"I don't know!" Kelper matched Zimm's tone.

Zimm looked for Jack, but saw he was already gone.

Jack had recharged his arm and was using it to pull him and Ceinwen toward the nearest exit. Ceinwen's body was sideways, her legs off the ground as the force pulled her toward it. Jack held her tightly with one arm and pulled them by gripping the nearest railing. He shot Ceinwen a reassuring look, hoping to alleviate any fear she harbored. Her eyes were filled with tears as she tried her best to look calm.

"ZERO!" Zimm called behind him.

Jack and Ceinwen both turned, surprised there was a noise louder than the sound of the impressive force that wrapped its wind-tendrils around all of them. Jack let loose a sly smile and coy nod, signaling to Zimm that he was escaping and leaving him, once again, to die. Jack pulled them to the door, quickly flung it open. It was instantly torn from its hinges, spiraling wildly across the bridge as it disappeared through the increasing hold in the wall they passed through moments earlier. The ship was collapsing into itself. It wouldn't be long until it was completely destroyed. Jack wanted to leap through the door, but the force was stronger, pulling harder. He needed both hands free.

"Winnie," Jack called to Ceinwen. "I need to grab around my neck."

Ceinwen didn't ask, she just nodded, understanding. She climbed up his arm until she was able to wrap one arm around Jack's shoulder. Jack then lifted his arm helping her to slide across his back easily. She wrapped her hands around his neck, locking one hand around the other wrist. Jack then hooked one hand on the doorframe. He felt his arm tingle as he pulled himself forward. He hooked his other hand to the other side of the doorframe and then, mustering up all his energy, leapt through the open door.

General Portnoy watched as another dozen military air vehicles dropped to the street below, exploding on impact. He lost more men than he ever had in his distinguished career and he was not happy. He clenched his jaw, his teeth tearing through the remains of the cigar blunt that still rested between his lips. His teeth tore through the blunt as the smoldering tip fell from his lips and bounced off the sides of the tank armor, disappearing into the darkness beneath.

"General?" Came the voice of Sargent Yungher, a man Portnoy respected having worked with him on several missions. He was a man

Portnoy trusted and requested when he volunteered to take this assignment. "What do we do?"

Portnoy lowered his head in defeat, "We put out faith in those police cruisers up there. We hope. And then we pray."

The force was still strong on the other side of the bridge, where Jack had flung both he and Ceinwen as far through as his fused arm allowed. They were alive, but Jack knew there wasn't much time left. They had to get off the airship. There was no more time to waste. Jack could feel a light rush of air pulling around them. The force was there, but its power was still focused on the bridge. He could see they had entered a locker room. It was filled with flight suits and helmets along one wall. It was the pilot's area.

Ceinwen slid from Jacks shoulders, "What are we going to do now?"

Jack didn't answer. He simply rushed about, pulling open the doors to each locker that aligned another wall. Each locker was filled with nothing personal, simply bare-bones uniform accoutrements. It wasn't until Jack reached the last three lockers that he found what he hoped he was looking for.

"What is it?" Ceinwen asked as she was curious why Jack stood motionless at the one locker before him.

"It's our way off this boat," Jack turned holding out his arms. Dangling from the straps that Jack held was some sort of engine.

It didn't take long for Ceinwen to surmise what Jack was holding. "Is that what I think it is?"

Jack nodded.

She shook her head, "Are you nuts? There is no way I am letting you use that thing."

"Winnie, I've been using these for years," Jack winked. He threaded one arm through a strap, his eyes tracing the gauges on the side of the engine. He noticed the fuel was nearly empty. He ignored it, reassuring himself that it would be enough. At least he hoped. He slid his other arm through and strapped the engine securely across his chest and abdomen. He guided Ceinwen forward, leading her through the next doorway and into the docking bay. He quickly led them to the nearest bay doors and slammed his fist against the plunger that opened the gate. The doorway rolled upward as the wind, complete with the sights and smells of the city slapped their faces.

"Are you ready?" Jack asked Ceinwen. She didn't answer as she looked out at the sinking landscape before them. "We have to go."

Ceinwen wrapped her arms around herself, trying to warm herself from the chilling night air, "I'm afraid."

"Do you trust me?" Jack asked.

She nodded. Jack didn't hesitate. He spun Ceinwen around and kissed her deeply. She responded in kind, accepting this moment of passion and pulled her toward him until her back was pressed to his chest. Her hair bounced playfully across his face. He could smell her hair. It smelled sweet. He inhaled her fragrance deeply. He wrapped his arms around her slender waist and held her tightly. He could hear her gasp and then let her breath out in a longing gasp. She pursed her lips and closed her eyes. Jack stepped from the lip of the opening. With Ceinwen wrapped in his arms. He pressed the activation switch that ran up his sleeve and into his palm.

Ceinwen's scream echoed across the rooftops surrounding them as the leapt from the side of the Behemoth. The sounds of destruction from the force that burst past the bridge, through the locker room and into the launch bay behind them overpowered Ceinwen's cries. But to Jack's surprise, they did not seem to be escaping as fast as they should have. Jack pressed the activation switch, but nothing happened. Was their less fuel than he read? He pressed the switch again. They still didn't move. It didn't make sense. He pressed the switch, fuel should be sent to the engine and flame should be erupting from the exhaust ports on either side, but it wasn't. But any propulsion that had sent them any distance from the ship had stopped. Jack and Ceinwen were not moving. They were simply stuck, hanging in midair, defying gravity around them. He looked down below them to see the city streets, still alive and bustling. Why had they stopped? What could have kept them from plunging to their deaths?

Ceinwen had stopped her screaming when she realized the intense freefall had ended and they were now hanging in midair. She looked about curiously, wondering what was happening. Even Jack was confused. He looked around Ceinwen's body that was clinging tightly around him. The city was far below, the lights and vehicles shining brightly.

It was a long way down.

Jack wriggled one hand free from around Ceinwen, who unsurprisingly wrapped her arms around Jack tighter. He smashed his thumb against the activation switch, but as expected, nothing happened. The rocket pack was still inactive. Jack was able to deduce what was happening. He twisted his head around to get another look at the behemoth just above them. The airship was unrecognizable. The center of the ship was nearly non-existent, having been turned inward. The bow and aft had each been pulled inward, resembling sunken holes on both ends of the ship, leaving two protruding bulged, overly expanded halves surrounding each inverted hole. Jack watched as the control deck and quarters beneath begin being pulled upward into the ever-growing vortex that was swallowing everything in its path. The gravitational field that emanated from the vortex was holding them in place; they weren't close enough to be dragged in yet. But Jack knew as the vortex swelled, it would certainly pull them inward. He had to do something, so he began to kick.

Jack kicked his legs and moved his arms, while Ceinwen wrapped her legs around his waist. His kicking and thrashing, which resembled a, sort of, warped form of swimming, managed to move him slightly forward. The wind of the thin air blew across his body, flapping the tails of his long coat behind him. Despite the wind, Jack was managing to move across the open sky. He couldn't help to wonder how far in front of him the gravitational field stretched. Hopefully it extended as far as the rooftop that was about fifty feet ahead, and maybe eight to ten feet down. If he could push them that much farther, then they could drop. The distance wouldn't be too high to injure them.

"What are you doing?" Ceinwen asked.

"I'm moving us to that building just ahead," he explained. "We're out of rocket power, so I'm going to try to push us there."

"If we're out of fuel, how are we still floating then?"

"That vortex in the HART ship if putting out a gravitational field that's holding us in place, kind of like the moon and the Earth. We're far enough away so that we can't get pulled toward it."

"That's good," Ceinwen let out a low sigh.

"However, if the gravitational ring expands," Jack began.

"Then what?"

"We're going straight on through to the other side."

Ceinwen swallowed in the remainder of her sigh.

Jack continued, "I want you to climb up onto my back."

"Why?"

"Because when we reach that roof, we may drop and I don't want to fall with you underneath me. Besides, you can help me by kicking out your legs. Maybe we can get there faster."

Ceinwen nodded as she shimmied her body around Jack's torso. The shifting in weight caused Jack to drift both left and right haphazardly. He could feel her sharp nails dig into his back through his clothing and across the back of his neck. Her knee connected to his abdomen before sinking into his side as Ceinwen finally pulled herself onto his back, wrapping her arms around the two exhaust ports that jutted out of either side of the pack behind the wings. Jack rubbed his side tenderly, "You all set back there?"

Ceinwen replied, "Y-yes." She found it more difficult looking down at the city far beneath them than looking up into the sky with the city at her back.

"Alright, let's kick our legs together, okay?" Jack instructed.

Ceinwen nodded as she replied, "Okay."

Both Jack and Ceinwen began to kick their legs, slowly at first, as Ceinwen was nervous of slipping off Jack's back. They continued their efforts, slowly matching the others rhythm until they managed to get in sync.

Jack could feel them inching forward slowly. The rooftop was getting closer.

"Hey!" Jack shouted over the thin atmosphere. "I think we're going to make it."

For the first time in a while, Ceinwen felt a tinge of hope within her body. They were going to make it. They were actually going to make it. Unfortunately, he spoke too soon. Jack and Ceinwen immediately stopped moving forward and suddenly were jerked backward.
The gravity ring was expanding and they were being pulled into it.

The vortex was growing, swirling more erratically, a large funnel growing from the center of the once massive airship. There wasn't much of the ship left, just parts of each end and the quarters below, which was twisting as it lifted upward. He wondered who was left inside. Most of the soldiers were being sucked into the vacuous opening when they leapt from the edge. He even wondered if Zimm was still alive.

"Why aren't we moving anymore?" Ceinwen asked.

"We're stuck in the gravity field," Jack said calmly. "I can't break free of it."

"What are we going to do?"

Jack was frustrated. Frustrated at her question. Frustrated at his inability to save them, and he answered with frustration on his tongue, "Unless you can add some extra weight to us, there's nothing I can do!"

Ceinwen recoiled from Jack's unexpected and unwarranted snap. She couldn't help to feel a little insulted. What had she done to deserve his disrespect? She couldn't help but respond in kind, "Extra weight? Where the hell am I going to get extra weight? Like I can pull it from out of the sky?" As if on cue, something heavy pushed against them, landing hard against their legs. Both Ceinwen and Jack turned to see what had hit them. It was Zimm.

"Hello Zero! Did you miss me?" Zimm cackled loudly.

The impact and the increased weight of Zimm now pushing against them, they were able to break free of the gravity ring that held them in place. They were falling. Fast. Jack could feel himself losing control as they were suddenly plummeting. Ceinwen was screaming loudly, as it split Jack's skull with the shrill sound. Jack threw his hands out in front of himself, hoping to catch something, anything to stop their fall. The roof they had so desperately tried to reach was about to sail past their line of sight. Jack acted quickly reaching around his back and clamping his hands around Ceinwen's forearms. Jack could feel Zimm's arms gripping his legs, which made it difficult to turn, but Jack managed. He was able to loosen Ceinwen's grip of his neck and pulled her around to his front. She lost her breath, her scream silenced for the moment, as she loosely fell forward. Jack was able to swing her like a pendulum back and forth twice. Just before they passed the roof, he let go of her arms and she began to fly through the air, heading toward the roof.

Ceinwen hit the roof hard, rolling on her side as she slammed hard against the concrete surface. Fortunately, she didn't fall far enough to be injured, but the fall sure did hurt. Her side slid against the rough surface, tearing into the fabric of her clothing. Her exposed legs that stretched from under her skirt took the most damage, generating a deep rash from the contact. When her body stopped sliding, she lay there for a moment before mustering up the strength to stand. As she stood, just several feet before her, there was a loud boom. The roof shook under her feet causing her to fall back to the roof.

A cloud of smoke billowed around the area where the crash took place. When the smoke settled, Ceinwen watched Jack and Zimm lunging for one another as they fought hard. Jack had unfastened the straps of the rocket pack from his shoulders. It dropped to the floor with a resounding clunk. It didn't slow Jack down. As soon as the straps slid free of his arms, he raised them defensively against Zimm's oncoming attack. Zimm threw three punches. Jack dodged the first two by ducking low and stepping backward. The third he caught with his forearm. He instantly threw his own punch and connected with Zimm's jaw. Zimm stumbled from the blow, but quickly shook it off and continued his onslaught.

Ceinwen stood back as she watched the two men clash, their fists flying, each strike connecting against the others face or torso. Zimm landed several strong blows. Jack stumbled from each hit, but never hesitated to throw his own punches.

"What's the matter Zero?" Zimm chided. "You've gotten soft."

"It's over Zimm, you've lost," Jack snarled.

"You think so?"

"Look!" Jack pointed to the gaping hole that was forming in the sky as the remaining parts of the massive airship were being pulled. "Your ship is gone, your invasion is over."

Zimm threw his head back and laughed. Behind him the vortex began to swirl more ferociously, the returning aircraft piloted by their own men were being dragged into it unwillingly. "You think this," Zimm pointed to the sky. "All this, was for an invasion?"

Jack was silent. Zimm's words were odd, strange to him. What did he mean? Was he wrong in thinking the invasion was the center of all this?

"You still haven't figured it out have you?" Zimm continued.

Jack continued staring at Zimm blankly.

"Not such a great detective after all," Zimm added wickedly.

"If the invasion wasn't the purpose, then what was?"

Zimm simply grinned in response. Jack took a step forward, angrily, wanting to beat an answer out of Zimm, but before he could react in any way, he was hit hard from behind and knocked to the ground. Jack felt his energy pushed out of him as he hit the firm roof.

"It took you long enough," Zimm growled.

Ceinwen screamed loudly. It echoed across the top of the city. Jack looked up to see what had hit him. Standing over him was Caspar Huun. Huun released the rocket pack from his shoulders, allowing it to drop to the roof with a thud. Huun was huge, hulking, as he lumbered forward, pushing his sleeves up past his elbows. Jack looked over his thick arms as he stalked closer and closer toward him. Jack quickly scrambled to his feet and raised his own fists in defense.

It wasn't enough. Huun wasted no time in his assault. He immediately drew back his muscular arm and launched his ham-sized fists at Jack. The first punch knocked Jack off his feet, lifting him up into the air and sending him across the roof several feet.

Ceinwen was in shock at the sight of the massive man's return, but even more so, at the way he hurtled Jack across the roof. "NO! JACK!" She shouted to him.

Jack was sore. His ribs hurt from where Huun's fist had sank in deeply. He clutched his side as he stood, catching his breath.

"I should repeat my question," Zimm's voice echoed. "What's the matter, Zero?"

Jack ignored Zimm's prodding. Instead, he charged. He charged straight at Huun. His charge was quickly thwarted by another fist that crushed the side of his face. Jack's body spun from the force of the blow, twisting him awkwardly as he lost his balance and, once again, crashed to the floor.

"Perhaps too much pain?" Zimm smiled triumphantly. "Or perhaps it's the realization of losing everything."

Jack sucked in his breath as he slowly got back on his feet.

"I just want you to understand one thing, Zero," Zimm sneered. "Despite all your best efforts and what you think is right, you will not win." Zimm placed his foot on Jack's back and pressed hard, forcing Jack to fall back to the roof, striking his chin hard and forcing his jaw to clamp shut. The sound of his teeth slamming together echoed through his head.

"Leave him alone!" Ceinwen called out, the sight of Jack weakened in front of her was frightening. Ceinwen came to his defense, rushing up behind Huun, who was preparing to pounce once again at Jack. She leapt at him and began to pummel his thick shoulders with her small hands. Huun stopped for a moment, and quietly reached behind himself. He plucked

Ceinwen from his back and tossed her wildly aside. She fell to the roof hard. Jack watched her drop and quickly reacted. He threw his fists in a maniacal moment of rage, striking Huun in his abdomen, across his cheeks, and under his jaw. Huun recoiled for a brief moment before drawing back his massive arm and planting his fist to the side of Jack's head. Jack instantly dropped to the roof, his head ringing as the reverberation of the impact ricocheted throughout the inside of his skull. It hurt.

"You can't stop us, Zero," Huun growled. "It's over."

Jack squinted hard, his attention to Huun despite facing the floor as he answered, "So long as I'm alive, you or your bastard leader are not getting away."

The sound of Zimm's laughter pierced his ears, "Always the hero."

With his eyes still closed, Jack felt the hook of a foot kick into his ribs. He rolled onto his back in pain as Zimm circled around his writhing body. Before Jack could pick himself up, Zimm drew back his leg and kicked again. This time, the kick was harder, stronger. It picked Jack up from the roof and landed him several feet away. Ceinwen cried out in anguish, hoping her screams would stop Jack's assailants. It didn't. They came still, stronger, harder, and more furious.

Huun picked up Jack by his collar, lifting him high into the air. He buried his fist into Jack's stomach twice before tossing him to the other side of the roof. Jack flew like a rag doll, his limbs limp and ability to react slowed. He couldn't fight back.

"Why can't you just die?" Huun sneered, lumbering toward Jack's body.

Jack slowly picked himself up; the pain that surged through his body ignited each and every one of his nerve endings and made him want to scream out in agony. Instead, he bottled it up as he stood, "What can I say; I was never good at following orders." Jack staggered as he stood, his legs obviously weak. He was quickly knocked onto his back by another resounding punch from Huun's club-like fist.

"Alright, Huun," Zimm called out, holding back a chortle as he spoke. "I think our dear, Mr. Zero has had enough."

Jack let out a series of violent coughs. His ribs hurt with each release, making him stifle each cough as they came. He still managed to make it to his feet. "Are you kidding?" Jack spoke, his words slurred from a mixture of exhaustion and pain. "I was just getting warmed up."

"You always were a loud mouth braggart," Zimm smiled at Zero, his grin masking his impotent compassion. He wanted to hit Zero. Hard. Beat him to a pulp. Kill him even. But he would refrain, as he had so many times up to this point.

As much as it displeased him, Jack still had a purpose, and the Equinox was coming. Instead, they would have to find another way to shut him up. Unfortunately, Huun didn't share the same sentiment as Zimm. Instead, he only saw rage, and the only way to quell his rage was to kill its source. Huun skulked forward, his eyes glazed over and empty. Jack felt his heart sink at the sight of the lumbering giant. He could see within his glare that he wanted nothing more than to throttle him. Zimm snatched Ceinwen by the arm and pressed her tightly to his chest, allowing her to still face Jack and see him defeated. Jack was prepared, or at least thought he was. Despite Zimm's protests, Huun seemed an unstoppable force that was no longer willing to listen to reason of any kind. His first punch was atomic, the crushing blow seemed to shake the foundations of what was under Jack, as well as the joints within his bones as well. His jaw clenched and his teeth cracked as he was lifted through the air, high, until he crashed hard to the floor.

"I have had it with you, Zero," Huun roared. "For far too long you have haunted my shadows, held me from greatness. You took my General from me. Even now, you've taken my army from me. NO MORE!"

Jack was picking himself up when Huun's fists swung down onto his back like a sledgehammer. His limbs buckled underneath him and he collapsed back to the roof.

"LEAVE HIM ALONE!" Ceinwen cried from Zimm's tight grip. Zimm wanted to repeat her sentiment, but he knew Huun was in his state. His focus was on one thing and he was like a locomotive, nothing could stop him.

Jack rolled out of the way, as Huun slammed his massive foot into the floor, the concrete cracking under his feet. Huun didn't let it slow him, instead, he stomped after Jack's rolling body. He was rolling toward the edge of the roof. Huun knew either he would have to stop, and the he could crush him under foot, or he could fall over the edge to his death. Either way, Huun was going to kill Jack Zero. The stomping of thick rubber soled against concrete reverberated loudly, sounding like an incoming thunderstorm preparing to unleash a maelstrom of mayhem. Jack could see he was running out of roof, Huun's foot stomps gaining in volume and impact, shaking everything around him.

"JACK!" Ceinwen called out.

Jack's shoulder hit the lip of the roof. He stopped rolling. The first of Huun's foot swung over Jack and kicked the wall that Jack hit, shattering the bricks as if it were made of paper. Debris rained down on Jack as he felt half of his body hanging over the exposed edge. Far below was the street, at least twenty stories down.

"Your choice Zero," Huun growled. "You can jump, messy but quick, or I can be the one who kills you, slow and painful."

Jack looked over his shoulder, seeing the lights from emergency vehicles flashing like twinkling stars. It was a long way down. He turned to see the enraged face of Caspar Huun, his fists balled and poised to attack. His eyes pierced straight through Jack, as if they were staring past him, maybe it was his way of choosing Jack's fate for him.

"What will it be then, Zero?" Huun's voice was deep, empty, and haunting. "It's your time to die." Huun raised his arms high above his head, ready to deliver a crushing blow. Jack closed his eyes, waiting for the moment to come. But it didn't. Everything seemed to stop at that moment. It was as if the world turned itself off for him to take and find inner peace before he met his end. But that peace was quickly interrupted by Ceinwen's scream.

Jack snapped his eyes open. Standing before him was a frozen Huun, his arms still raised over his head. But oddly, Huun's face was twisted; his expression resembled one of great focus amidst frustration. Sweat was beading along his broad forehead as the muscles in his jaw clenched as tightly as possible causing his cheeks to shake. He was trying, with all his might, to bring down his fists against Jack's skull, his hopes in crushing him. But he couldn't move. Ceinwen screamed again. Jack looked past the frozen Huun to see Ceinwen floating high above the rooftop. She was obviously as surprised to be in the air as Jack was to see her there. But how? How was she able to float in the air like that? Just beyond Ceinwen, floating like he were swimming in water was Zimm.

The gravity was changing as the event horizon of the vortex where the massive zeppelin once flew. Jack gasped at the sight of the vortex that swirled around a black hole that was pulling everything toward it.

"Ceinwen!" Jack called out to her. "NO!"

"JACK!" She called back. "HELP!"

Ceinwen floated higher as the building beneath her began to disassemble brick-by-brick, the chunks zipping past her until they flew into the aping maw of the vortex. The roof was tearing apart around them as chunks shot up through the air. The pieces ripped around Ceinwen fiercely, whistling as they passed her, just missing her floating body. Zimm wasn't so fortunate. Roof chunks pelted his body, sending him twisting and twirling through the sky awkwardly and out of control. The chunks continued until they were swallowed by the vortex. Zimm grunted as each piece hit his flailing form, despite his best efforts to churn his arms and push away from the hail of debris.

"Oh shit!" Jack could feel his body beginning to lift from the roof just as Huun began to float as well. Jack didn't know if he should feel relief that his assailant was no longer a threat to him. Huun was floating higher and higher, but so was Zimm. And so was Ceinwen. Jack felt himself becoming lighter as he lifted into the air slowly. He could feel the pain in his body becoming more intense as his limbs no longer had a firm surface to press against. He couldn't let it make him stop and quit. He had to keep fighting and figure out a way to save both him and Ceinwen, who was now several feet into the air. Jack's toes scraped the surface of the roof as he drifted in the direction of the vortex. He needed to think quickly. Jack began paddling his arms, trying to steady himself. Unfortunately, it only caused him to spin around at varying speeds. He was still low enough to the roof to grab any object that was still fastened down. Several HVAC systems jutted out from the central sections of the roof. However, they were far too large for him to grasp, but it wasn't long before he was able to clutch one of several pipes that were attached to the systems. The first set he was unable to grab, underestimated the force of the vortex's pull. He was soon able to wrap his arms around a particularly thick pipe, which was able to stop his ascent.

He could see that the roof was continuing to erode, being broken apart as it was pulled up into the sky. It wouldn't be long before the part of the roof he was currently securing himself to would begin to crumble.

There wasn't any more time to plan or mull over a solution. He needed to act. It was then that the pipe in his arm began to creak and groan. The metal was starting to bend and twist. Jack could feel his stomach pull, as if he was dropping down a steep hill at a rapid speed. He remembered feeling this same way the last time he rode the Comet roller coaster at the Sylvan Beach Amusement Park, about a half-hour outside the city, when he was just a boy. The sensation was exhilarating, filling him with a charge of excitement and danger. Now he was feeling the danger, which took the fun out of what was happening all around him. The pipe broke. Jack released his grip, keeping his arms low to the roof as his feet were still pointing upward. His fingertips were now scraping against the course surface of the roof. The pull in his stomach was getting stronger. He was getting closer to the vortex, which meant he was going to be pulled into the sky where he would have no options and no control.

Suddenly the rough texture of the roof changed to a cool, smooth surface. Jack immediately looked down to see his hands were touching a rocket engine, just like the one he had strapped to his back when he and Ceinwen escaped the Behemoth. However, this engine wasn't his. It was the one Huun wore, which meant it still had fuel. It was still functional. Jack immediately grabbed for the engine, feeling for anything he could hook his fingers around. His left arm found one of the leather straps. Jack quickly looped it around his wrist while his other hand clasped around one of the exhaust ports.

As if on cue, Jack was pulled away from the roof, which continued to break apart and whiz past him, finding its way to the vortex much more rapidly. As Jack floated higher, he slipped his arms through the rocket pack's straps. His body spun and flipped around as he wrestled with the buckles, trying desperately to affix them before he was too dizzy. He aligned the center strap that ran across his chest, pushing the clasp tight with the balls of each hand. As soon as it was secure, Jack steadied himself and activated the engines. Fire erupted from the exhaust ports that jutted out on either side of the pack behind each shoulder. He quickly sped across the sky, the new sudden boost pushing him faster toward the gaping vortex. He weaved his way through the stream of debris that also whipped around him. He set his trajectory to Ceinwen.

CHAPTER 28
TO SAVE CEINWEN

"ALOONA! ALOONA!" Lartanner shouted to his partner amidst the twisted metal structure that surrounded them. Lartanner ran up a metal beam that now acted as a ramp, searching for any sign of Aloona within the debris. Sparks sprayed through the night air, crackling and hissing from the severed and frayed electrical wires that slithered about. He stepped cautiously, but still saw no sign of his beloved.

Helix circled the end of the one tall array. The red light that would blink at its tip had faded. Pinned underneath it was Agent Nicole Frisco. She was motionless, blood stained the corner of her mouth. A larger, darker pool of blood collected under her waist. She was only half, the upper half. On further examination, Helix saw the small metal rod that had pierced her abdomen. He felt sympathetic to her plight, after having known her, despite her turn. How could she still be alive?

Her breathing was laborious as she opened her mouth to speak, "He-Helix…"

Helix cocked an eyebrow at the sound of his name; her tone had seemed to change. She no longer sounded vicious and evil, but instead sounded like the compassionate woman he first met.

"Frisco?" Helix asked with caution in his voice. "Is…is that you? I mean really you?"

She masked the pain in her face as her expression changed to a look of confusion, "What...the hell...are you talking...about?"

Helix smiled as tears began to well in his eyes. Could it be? Was it really her? The real, real her? Helix knelt at her side, scooping up her hand in his, "Hey, Agent, it's good to have you back."

"What...ha...happened?" She asked, wincing from the intense pain that gripped her. "How did I...get here?"

"Oh, that? Well, that's a long story," Helix replied with a reassuring smile. "What we should be asking, is how we can get you out of this."

"Where...are we?"

"On the roof of the NU Police Headquarters," he answered, looking around now for any sign of help. In the distance, there were many sets of flashing red and blue lights heading toward them. The LEHVs were returning to port. "Help is on the way," He added.

"I don't...remember anything," Frisco coughed. "We...were in the LEHV...then...then...I can't remember."

"It's okay," Helix continued to try to reassure her. "Whatever happened is over now. It looks like we won. Whatever Jack did, if he's even still alive."

"Jack? I forgot...Jack."

"I'm sure he's still out there. If I know Jack, he's never been one to give up, and he always told me, 'death was the quitters' way out.'"

She smiled weakly for a moment, and then returned to her pain.

Helix stood and circled Frisco, surmising what he could do to free her from the rod that pinned her to the roof. The array was narrower at the top, and the metal surrounding it had broken clean from the rest of the antenna tower. It seemed a viable option to attempt to lift the wreckage off from her. He ran his hand along the beam that was atop the rod and gave it a small tug upward. It seemed light enough to move.

"Hey Frisco?" He asked with precaution.

"Yeah?" She responded in a graveled voice, her throat still thick with blood.

"I think I can lift up this metal and get you out from under there," he explained hopefully. "I just need to know you'd be okay with me doing that."

"Yes!" She quickly snapped her reply. "Get this...damn thing...offa me."

"Alright," Helix looked again over the crumpled metal. "I'm gonna...I think I can...I'm gonna lift this."

"Just...do it slow," Frisco requested.

Helix nodded. He spread his legs wide to steady himself. He then turned his hands and cupped them under the lowest metal girder. He pressed his chest to the metal and then began to push upward. The metal creaked as it was raised into the air. Helix grunted as he lifted with all his might, his arms raising over his head. His rotund belly shaking as he lifted it higher. Frisco screamed as loud as she could as the metal rod was pulled out of her body. She lifted slightly into the air as her upper torso was lifted at a forty-five degree angle and then dropped to the roof once she was loose from the rod.

When Helix saw Frisco was free from the array, he pushed the wreckage away from them with all his might. The array creaked as it crashed against the roof a few feet away. Helix dropped to his knees in exhaustion, his forehead and chest caked in sweat. He was breathing heavily as he lowered his forehead to the rooftop.

"I think...I need...an ambulance," came the humble request of Nicolina Frisco. And with those words, her eyes flashed red, flickered several times, and then went blank. Helix slid his hands over her eyelids, closing them gently. He was thankful he saw her, the *real* her for the last time. And with that, she was dead.

Lartanner began to push any loose piece of metal away from the toppled tower.
"Aloona!" He called out.

There was no response.

He called out again, "ALOONA!"

A small groan was the only reply Lartanner heard.

Lartanner felt his heart stop for a moment. He felt himself lock up, turning off the noises that surrounded the, frozen, listening.

"I...I'm...I'm here...," a garbled voice tried to call out, but was too weak to cry out any louder.

'It didn't matter,' Lartanner thought. He heard and he immediately reacted. He leapt from above the toppled metal structure and crawled his way through the twisted metal debris until he found the source of the voice. Aloona lay there, his body frail, his face and chest covered with blood. Lartanner held back his tears, the torment of seeing a loved one in such a dire position made him feel helpless. He wanted to pull Aloona up and hold him tight, but he couldn't. He didn't want to move him until he was certain that he wasn't critically injured, and that he knew emergency help had arrived.

"Hey, baby," Lartanner cooed. He slipped his hand around Aloona's and pulled it gently to his chest. Aloona let out a small cough, a small trickle of blood flowed from the corner of his mouth.

"I must look...terrible," Aloona forced a smile as he quipped. It hurt.

"Are you kidding? You look amazing, I'll bet you'll be doing push-ups in no time," Lartanner said reassuringly.

Aloona shook his head, "I'll be lucky if I can walk again."

Lartanner looked down at his partner's legs. They looked pinched under a particularly thick and heavy metal girder.

"Hey, don't worry," Lartanner gripped Aloona's hand tightly. "I'm gonna get you out of this, help is on the way."

Lartanner looked back in hoped of seeing an emergency vehicle heading there way. But there was nothing. The sky was lit up miles away; a bright blue swirling light seemed to be tearing open the sky. It didn't look any more hopeful than he felt. He looked back at Aloona's eyes. They seemed sullen and defeated. Lartanner's heart sank in despair. He didn't want to think about losing the man he loved. He didn't want to think about his life without the most important person in it. He couldn't. "Dammit, don't you leave me," Lartanner pleaded.

Aloona let out a smile as he looked back into Lartanner's eyes. He brought up his other hand and touched his partner's face tenderly. Tears began to streak down Lartanner's cheeks. His heart was breaking. "It's gonna be okay," Aloona smiled. "You're gonna be okay."

"No," Lartanner shook his head. "No I won't. Not without you. I can't. I can't do it."

"You did it before you met me," Aloona reminded him. "You'll do it again."

"Stop talking like that," Lartanner snapped, masking his pain with anger.

"Just promise me," Aloona spoke. "Promise me you won't let them win."

Lartanner shook his head, the tears flowing harder as he began to sob loudly, "I will…I mean we will. Like we always do. We will take them down."

Aloona smiled as his hands dropped to his side and he closed his eyes.

Lartanner dropped his head and cried.

Jack soared higher, twisting his body as he dodged the chunks of debris that tore past him. The jet pack pushed him higher and faster, he could see the floating body of Ceinwen just ahead. He furrowed his brow as he stretched his body out long, letting the wind flow over his body. He aerodynamically cut through the air, closing the gap between him and Ceinwen. Her own body was spiraling and twisting through the sky as she was pulled faster and closer to the gaping vortex. She was afraid, terrified. She was going to be swallowed by the incredible swirling mass of light along with anything else in its path. But where did it lead? Where would she end up? Her heart was beating rapidly. She was more afraid that she was going to die.

Several pieces of stone that once made up the roof of the buildings below, struck from every side. When she felt all was hopeless, she hear her name called out in the distance. "Winnie!" she heard faintly in her ears. She tried to look around, her eyes scanning for the source of the voice. In the far distance, she could see a flash of light. It appeared to be attached to the back someone that was gaining in speed and getting closer. She knew it was Jack.

"JACK!" She screamed in response. Ceinwen outstretched her arms as long as she could, her body still tumbling head over heels, as she tried to steady herself. "JACK! Help me!"
"I'm coming!" Jack called back, hoping to give her hope and reassurance. Jack pressed the trigger in his hand, sliding the lever upward, increasing his speed. Fire roared from the exhaust ports as he flew faster, Ceinwen growing larger as he got closer. "Hold on!"

The sky was wide above the city, the bright blue light that emitted from the vortex was blinding the closer he got. The city seemed to be dulled in comparison. Jack squinted in an attempt to shield his eyes from the blinding light. Jack found it strange that despite its glaring aura, there was no heat. It was as if the light wasn't real, maybe artificial. It didn't matter. All that mattered was saving Ceinwen before she disappeared into the vortex, or before he could no longer see her in the light.

Jack couldn't bear to lose her. Not now. Not when he realized how important she was to him, and he knew it wasn't just for her work ethic. He loved her. Why it took him so long to figure that out? Well, he wasn't that smart. He may have been a good detective, but he was stubborn and blind when it came to matters of the heart. He could see her, make out the features of her face. She looked terrified. Her mouth agape as she screamed. She was no longer spiraling, spinning, or twisting. She was flat, her arms reaching out toward him. Jack reached out as well, opening his hands as the trigger for the engine slipped into his sleeve. He could see her in full detail; he was so close. He could even smell her perfume amidst the wreckage that surrounded them.

"Jack!" She smiled for the first time in a while.

"I'm here, don't worry," Jack stretched his fingers to meet hers.

"You came for me!" Her voice lifted.

"I would never leave you! You know that!" He gave her a sly grin.

Their fingertips touched. He just needed to grab her hands and the thrust of the engine would pull them away freely. Suddenly, Jack felt himself be yanked backward. Ceinwen screamed as Jack suddenly was pulled away from her, "NO!"

Jack turned to see he was not flying alone. General Zimm had grabbed him; his own rocket engine had carried him there. For a moment, everything seemed to stop, except himself. He felt himself continue to tumble where everything surrounding him just hung there in midair. He could see the fearful expression that Ceinwen wore, her face filled with surprise and terror, as she was pulled into the vortex, her lips mouthing his name before she vanished.

"WINNIE!" Jack called out. "NO!" It was too late. She was gone.

Zimm was all he could hear, laughing manically, his vengeance was more complete than he had expected. All he hoped to do was take down Jack, but instead he was able to take down the woman as well. Sometimes the impromptu vengeance is the sweetest.

"What's the matter, Jack?" Zimm cackled. "Did you miss me?"

"You son of a--" Jack ignited his rocket and charged straight at Zimm. As he crashed head on into Zimm, they were pushed through the sky, toward the vortex.

"That's it, Zero! Let your anger loose!" Zimm goaded.

Jack couldn't hear him, he couldn't even see straight. All he could do was quell the fire that was erupting inside of him, and the only way to do that was to kill Zimm.

"Good evening," smiled the older, male news anchor into the camera. "Thank you for watching the WTVK's Action News, evening edition. I'm Bill Lawler."

"And I'm Dina Worden," smiled his co-anchor seated next to him. "Tonight, citizens of New Utica have, no doubt, seen the eerie blue light that has blanketed the city over the past hour. But what is it and where is it coming from?"

Bill continued, still smiling, the wrinkles in his face looked like cracks through his thick makeup, "We go now to our own Joseph Ferris, who is downtown live."

A flash of static separated the newscasters seated safely behind their desks to the chaos that surrounded Joseph Ferris. The younger reporter looked frazzled, his thick dark hair mussed and his once neat and clean suit was dirtied and rumpled. He continuously ducked and dodged the dashing people running past and the falling debris that showered around them. The cameraperson tried desperately to keep Ferris in focus and in frame. The bright blue light that washed the landscape didn't help much. If he had his choice he's drop the camera and run, but he needed the paycheck.

"Thanks Bill," Ferris shouted over the raging commotion of shouts and crashed that filled the air. "As you can see the chaos that has filled the once peaceful streets of downtown New Utica on the eve of one of the most important presidential elections in the history of our country. When a mysterious airship appeared from out of nowhere, announcing the presence of the once secretive HART organization many have dubbed the 'Dark HART.'

"Now it seems that the very airship that seemed to offer a threatening message has now, once again, mysteriously disappeared; swallowed by the very vortex that brought it to our city in the first place. But why? This is the question on everyone's mind as citizens flee in terror." Ferris turned to the building behind him and pointed the effigy that was painted across the wall in large, bold letters. "Citizens have even left warning messages, but are they to our citizens or to the 'Dark HART?' A cryptic message that has been tagged throughout the city; 'Beware the Equinox,'" he read aloud.

From the studio, Bill Lawler commented, "That's an unusual message. Does anyone know the source or meaning behind the message?"

"Not at this time," Ferris replied. "But the large airship that mysteriously appeared over the city has since vanished. Is there a connection between the two? No one is certain."

"Vanished?" Dina asked inquisitively. "You mean the same way it arrived?"

"Not exactly," Ferris added. "It appears to have been pulled into itself, as if turned inside out, but instead it simply disappeared, as if it swallowed itself."

"That is strange," Lawler smiled as he turned to the camera. "That's our own Joseph Ferris. We'll come back to him in a moment, but first, today is Election Day and the polls are still open for another three hours, but it appears the results are rolling in steadily with several counties reporting, all of which seem to be in favor of the challenger, Senator Janus Glorm."

"That's right, Bill," Dina replicated his smile. "And it's not just here in New York, but in fact, some states are already declaring Glorm the winner by a landslide."

"What does this mean to our country?" Bill added. "We'll examine that after this commercial break."

Zimm pulled Jack down hard. Jack's engine was still roaring as he pushed back at Zimm. He couldn't shake the image of Ceinwen's face, flushed with terror as she was pulled into that vortex. He couldn't save her. He tried. But he failed. He failed her. He couldn't forgive himself for that. He channeled the anger and rage that surged through his body and threw his fist at Zimm. The blow connected with Zimm's cheek. It had little effect. Zimm could see the anger fill in Jack's eyes. It pleased him, fed his insatiable hunger to destroy him.

"Revenge is sweet Jack," Zimm roared. "I am going to take everything from you, just like you did to me."

"You killed her!" Jack snapped back.

They spiraled across the sky, their packs hurtling them in every direction.

"Haven't we been here before, Jack? Haven't we been in this same situation, except this time, I'm the one in control!"

"I'll kill you!"

"You did once, and look what it made me," Zimm sneered. "I'm a god!"

Jack threw another punch, another null effect against Zimm's face. Their bodies dipped lower, Jack was beneath Zimm as they skimmed the top of a skyscraper, Jack's engine scraping against the stone the encircled the rooftop. The stone split and sprayed debris everywhere. Zimm pressed his palm against Jack's chin, attempting to push him even lower. Jack could feel the coarse texture of the roof brush against the back of his head. He pressed back into Zimm's hand, keeping him away from hitting anything. Zimm was strong, powerful, but Jack was not going to give up easily. He was going to fight. He managed to wrap his arms around to Zimm's back. He pulled with his left and pushed hard with his right, flipping Zimm and himself around. Now Zimm was beneath Jack. Jack took advantage of the move and pressed his knees against Zimm's thighs, angling his back toward the roof. The thrust of the engine pushed them lower until Zimm's head smacked against the surface.

The impact pushed the two men apart from one another. Zimm rolled across the roof, but Jack was able to push himself upward. Jack streaked high and quickly somersaulted in midair, before heading in a nosedive toward where Zimm landed on the roof. Jack was like a bullet heading toward Zimm, but Zimm wasn't slow. He immediately reacted by wrapping his fingers together and swinging both arms like a hammer. He hit Jack on the side of his head, throwing him off course. Jack hit the roof, tumbling head over heels, but his momentum forced him over the lip on the far side.

Zimm watched silently, hoping he had finally silenced Jack Zero. He touched his toes, then feet to the rooftop, switching his engine off. He couldn't help the grin that stretched across his face. He felt good. Vindicated. The death of Jack Zero, it had a certain, pleasant ring to it, he thought. The irony alone weighed thick on his tongue as he licked his lips with eager anticipation of seeing the fallen body against the ground below. He strode to the edge of the roof, placed his hands along the ledge and peered over.

The victory Zimm hoped for, longed for, and desired was short lived. Instead of a dead Jack Zero he was greeted with the roar of an engine as Jack fired up his rocket and pushed himself from the unseen ledge just a few feet below. The propulsion was immense and took Zimm by complete surprise. Without a hesitation or pause, Jack grabbed the exposed straps of Zimm's engine and pulled him into the air.

It was surreal to experience the sensation of déjà vu, but Jack was all too familiar with the way this moment raced through his mind. He played a scene repeatedly from his memory. He held tightly to Zimm, while he guided his rocket pack higher into the thinning atmosphere. He remembered the anger he harbored toward Zimm. He felt it now, even more intensely. He hated Zimm. He despised him, loathed him even. He wanted Zimm dead. This time for real. They soared high into the air, reaching the apex of the event horizon that was slowly beginning to diminish. The gravitational pull was still strong; Jack could feel it still attempting to drag him into its opening. Jack cut the engine of his rocket. The gravitational field kept them floating in the air. Zimm began to laugh loudly.

"What the hell is so funny?" Jack sneered.

"You," Zimm quickly replied. "And me, this whole situation. It all feels so familiar, doesn't it Jack?"

"And as I recall, it didn't end in your favor," Jack reminded him.

"And look what became of me. I became so much more than you or anyone else before me. I am power, Zero," Zimm snorted. "Try and kill me again. I'm beyond death."

"Not if I make sure they can't ever put you back together again."

"Do it then!" Zimm goaded him through gritted teeth. "Drop me. See what happens then!"

Jack pressed the trigger that ignited his engine. Zimm's eyes widened at the unusual turn in Jack's typically predictable behavior. What was he doing? What was he thinking? The fire burst from the exhaust ports as the engine roared loudly, overtaking the cacophony of flying debris and the continuously shrinking vortex noises that surrounded them. They soared through the air, threading around and through the remaining pieces of buildings still being pulled into the forceful gravity of the vortex. Their speed was increasing. Jack used the gravity of the event horizon to drift faster toward the vortex.

Caspar Huun watched with a mixture of rage and terror, at the sight of his leader, his mentor, his master, the greatest man he knew, General Varcar Zimm, was being dragged across the sky. He balled his giant hands into fists, looking for any way he could to crush the man carrying him. Jack Zero had to die.

"What are you waiting for, Zero?" Zimm cried out. "Just do it! Drop me!"

Jack remained silent for a moment, letting the moment hang heavy. Then he spoke, letting go of his anger, but instead allowing his tone to be cold and hard. "I'm not going to drop you this time," Jack said coldly. "I'm not letting go of you at all."

"What will you do, Zero?" Zimm didn't try to struggle. He simply allowed Jack to carry him. He harbored no fear and he showed it with great zeal. "Go through? Do you even know what's on the other side?"

"It doesn't matter."

"Doesn't it?" Zimm smirked. "Are you prepared to take the chance that it's nothing? Are you prepared to die?"

Jack didn't reply. He kept his focus straight ahead, staring deep into the vortex. Zimm convinced himself Zero would cave, stop this boorish behavior and drop him, or something of that ilk, allowing Zimm to remerge with his nanites and destroy the world for the Dark HART. But Zero was not diverging from his path toward the vortex. He was determined. He was serious. This was not the Jack Zero he knew. The predictable Zero.

'*Damn*,' thought Zimm. He was serious. He had broken many men, but they all bend eventually. Zimm could play chicken; he never backed down. Even in his youth, when racing cars, he would always veer his vehicle towards the other, panicking that driver, and allowing him the win. Throughout his military career, he never once backed down from an adversary, or a superior. It's what helped him achieve his rank of General. Until they stripped it away, posthumously. And when Jack killed him, he didn't succumb to death, instead he was reinvented as a new, a better, man. But, perhaps this time he pushed Jack Zero too far.

"Where will it go?" Jack asked. "This thing. This portal. Where does it go?"

"I don't know."

"TELL ME!"

"I DON'T KNOW!" Zimm shouted back. "I'm a military leader not a scientist. Just take us through and find out, Zero. But I can assure you; those waiting on the other side won't be so welcoming."

"Not if I take them by surprise," Jack gestured his head toward his waist.

Zimm looked up to see several grenades attached to his belt. Jack was planning a suicide mission. Zimm scowled at the audacity of Jack's bold move. Zimm had to make a move of his own. They were closer to the opening of the vortex. They felt as if they were drifting more on the gravity than on the waning thrust of the rocket pack. The opening only a few meters ahead of them had grown much smaller, now only about the size of a small window. Not much space for two to fit.

Zimm shifted his body, "But not if I warn them first."

To Jack's surprise Zimm pressed his heels into his knees, Zimm pushed his heels. The sudden shift of weight and the pain that overtook his body, starting from his knees, spun him around in aerial somersaults. Jack released his grip on him. Zimm, understanding the nature of aerodynamics and the pull of gravity, twisted his body around until he was lying flat and facing the portal before him. He wore a broad, winning grin as he let gravity take control and pull him toward the opening.

"Forever destiny," he whispered to himself as he reached his hands for the opening.

Jack steadied himself, stopping his out of control spinning. His head was dizzy. He was seeing two Zimm's before him, floating in midair, which was an unusual vision. He shook his head quickly to regain his equilibrium. It was then that he realized Zimm was using the portal to escape. Jack bore down on his engine, his fuel reserves running low. He aimed himself for Zimm.

"ZIMM!" Jack screamed.

Zimm turned around, his smile still broad, "You're too late, Zero! It's over! You lose!" His fingers entered the portal that was about the circumference of a beach ball now. It felt like water, but it wasn't wet. The light rippling gently as he slowly crossed over. The light was cool, almost refreshing. The gravity not only pulled him in, but it made him feel welcome as if inviting him to enter. At least it felt that way to him, but it could also be the victory of defeat as he escaped.

Jack watched as Zimm began to slowly disappear. A rage brewed deep inside, like a fire in the pit of his stomach. Zimm had disappeared up to his waist; he was almost gone. The opening was almost the size of Zimm's shoulders at this point and getting smaller. "You're not getting away this time!" Jack was closing in on Zimm. He thrust his arms in front of himself and grasped at Zimm's ankles. He wrapped his fingers around tightly and kicked his legs underneath himself to turn his position.

Zimm's body jerked. He felt his stomach drop as if he were falling down a steep slope. Something was pulling at his ankles. He turned to see, but the portal distorted his vision. He didn't need to see to know it was Jack. He could feel the change in temperature and sensation as his body left the portal. The roar he bellowed started muffled but suddenly echoed across the sky as his head emerged.

"DAMN YOU ZERO!" Zimm shouted as he freed one ankle from Jack's hand. He drew it back and then launched it into Jack's face.

The kick was solid, and unexpected. It connected against the top of Jack's head. His neck collapsed from the impact, forcing him to let go of Zimm's legs. Zimm felt the pull of gravity from the portal as he watched

Jack drift farther away from him. He did it. He escaped. He turned to await the crossover once again, but the portal looked even smaller, about the size of his head, which started to go through. Zimm suddenly realized the hole was collapsing, and quickly. Zimm began to flail his arms, trying to swim in midair in order to push himself faster through the opening.

Jack was almost out of fuel. He had drifted too far from Zimm to catch him now. He was going to get away. He looked back to see Zimm circling his arms crazily about, a curious and unusual sight.

'Damn him,' Jack thought. But before he let defeat sink in, the portal snapped closed, disappearing as if being turned out like a light. But Zimm hadn't escaped, Jack saw his body suddenly freeze and then it began to fall limply toward the earth, but he no longer had his head. Jack watched in awe, realizing only Zimm's head had crossed over as his decapitated body plummeted to the city below.

Zimm was dead. Finally.

Jack let out the breath he had held in for the past few minutes. He felt relieved for the moment. Until he thought about Ceinwen.

Huun watched from afar, as the portal closed around the throat of his leader, separating his head from body. "NO!" He called out, enraged.

He turned his head from the sight of the body falling. He slumped over in defeat. It was over. Zimm was dead. And if Zimm was dead then...

"Jack Zero must die," he growled.

"NO! DAMN IT! NO!" Jack screamed into the empty sky. His voice echoed across the now quieted night as he floated alone. The debris that had been pulled from so many buildings and even from the streets below had been released from the gravitational field. The fall was cacophonous and deafening as it all hit the ground almost simultaneously far below. Even the screams of panic could be heard several hundred feet in the air. But it all didn't register with Jack as he stared blankly into the darkness before him. Zimm was gone. So was Ceinwen. What could he do? Without Zimm, how could he find her?

"Oh Ceinwen...I'm sorry...," Jack whispered to himself, secretly hoping, wherever she was, she could hear him. He could feel his position sag as the engine on his back began to sputter. He was running low on fuel. He almost wanted to let himself fall. He felt guilt. It was his fault she was involved. Now he had to find her. Whatever it took. Jack turned and pressed his engines to ignite, taking him away from the epicenter of the destruction and into the night.

The blood red lights of the rescue vehicles strobed across the roof of the NULE Headquarters building. When the light struck the collapsed array, the reflection shone brighter. Lartanner stood motionless, his gaze low, as he watched Aloona being lifted into the back of the vehicle. Helix stood somberly beside him, placing his hand warmly on Lartanner's shoulder.

"He'll be okay," Helix said hopefully.

Lartanner dropped his head in sorrow, hiding the tears that were flowing freely from his eyes. Helix pretended to ignore his tears. He looked away to see Frisco's gurney. He couldn't help but feel it was her doing, her fault that the events happened as they did. She wasn't herself, he tried to convince himself. Lartanner lifted his head as she was pushed past. The rage that crossed his face was undeniable. He was angry, hate filled. Helix watched as Lartanner clenched his fists and raised his arms, the look on intensity stretched across his face. Helix squeezed Lartanner's shoulder, acknowledging his anger, in an attempt to quell any intention he had to unleash. Lartanner lowered his arms and released his fists. Despite the rage he wanted so desperately to satiate, he had to resist. Not just for his job, but for Aloona, and all those that respected and looked up to him. Instead, he had to live with the hurt. For now.

"Hey," a voice called to Lartanner. He looked up to see the paramedic signaling to him.

"Are you riding with us?" The paramedic asked.

Lartanner was silent, his heart heavy.

"Go," Helix said to him.

Lartanner gave him a meager smile. Helix nodded silently in acknowledgement. Lartanner leapt onto the ambulance just before the rear doors closed. Helix gave a wave as the vehicles soared away into the night.

CHAPTER 29
AFTERMATH

The mouth of the portal opened up wide and quickly spewed from its maw the form of Lt. Crust. Crust tucked his head into his chest and rolled in proper military fashion, a trait of his training. He wasn't sure what to expect when his head encountered the surface of wherever it was he was emerging. He was pleasantly surprised at the softness of the surface, especially since he half expected it to be solid, like concrete. He rolled several times along the soft carpet before he finally snapped himself into a prone position. He needed to be prepared for anything; after all, he was unarmed and naked. He soon realized he wasn't in any immediate danger. He was greeted by several shocked and surprised expressions. He himself was surprised at the maroon and black robes that adorned the staring me. They looked vaguely familiar to his bleary eyes. He squinted his eyes into narrow slits to try to make them out more clearly. As he looked at the men up and down, his eyes happened upon the black insignia of an outstretched hand, its fingers spread open, inside a pyramid that had a sun peaked over the pyramids spire. Crust pulled up his forearm and looked at the tattoo that decorated it in dark black ink. It was the same as those on the robes. It was the symbol of the HART. Crust let his tensed muscles relax and he stood erect and looked around to gather his bearings. He was standing in a long hallway with vaulted ceilings, at least twenty to thirty feet high. The ceiling came to a point from rounded edges and were lined on two sides by massive stone pillars that stretched from floor to ceiling. The carpet he landed on was the same maroon and black colors as the men's robes, and in the center of the carpet, in the center of the hallway, was a large embroidered replica of the HART symbol, woven in black and the crest of the pyramid pointed the way to a large staircase that seemed to go on forever.

"Is he alright?" One of the robed men asked.

"I'm not sure," the other, shorter robed man answered.

"Who is he?" The taller one asked.

"Is it not clear," The elder robed man said, his voice filled with hope. "He is one of thy brethren, one of our warriors." The elder robed man approached. "Brother Crust, is that you?" He asked in a gentle, soothing voice. It reminded Crust of his grandfather.

"Yes," Crust responded. "I believe so."

The elder dropped his shoulders back and let his robe slip. He then brought it around and threw it over Crusts bare form.

"Thank you," Crust managed. He pushed his arms into the sleeves of the robe and then pulled it tight across his chest. The robe was much smaller on him than it was on the old man. The elder man smiled, his eyes lost in the wrinkles that lined his face. As Crust stepped back and walked toward the steps, he realized the robes he wore were of the Advisors, a lofty position in the ranks of the HART. The advisors were just below counselors, the true voice of the HART. The Lord of the HART spoke only with counselors, who in turn, got their advice only from advisors. Crust found it to be a strange sequence, but respected the chain of command in any structure. Whatever the course of action, his place was clear in the regime; he was a warrior, a soldier. He only followed the orders of his commanding officer, Huun. He felt he did his best at his role. He liked the feel of the Advisor's robe, it felt soft and warm, very different to the weeks of running around in a variety of different costumes, because that is what clothes were if they weren't a uniform, and being naked. Crust made his way up the steps, walking slowly, his steps shallow and weak. For the first time in a long time, Crust felt defeated. He had failed on his mission to infiltrate, to conquer. At least his commanding officer was still there. The inexplicable randomness of the teleportation device must have saved Huun and the others, but unfortunately, it sent him here, here to the Great Hall of the HART, the hall that housed their all-powerful, all knowing leader. The stairs led to the chambers of the Lord of the HART, and it was Crust's duty to report to him.

The torches that lined the enormous stairway were ominous and brooding. They were golden conical shafts that rested in bright; shiny sconces in the carved stone wall at about ten paces in between the next. Each emitted a low, orange glow that gave the impression of a culture that embraced its past, its heritage. Unfortunately, it also gave the impression of a forthcoming doom. For who, Crust was not sure. Crust reached the top of the staircase to a pair of large, hand carved wood and steel doors. They were towering, nearly twenty feet high, although they never quite touched the ceiling. The doors were laden with several depictions of man, namely as a conqueror of beings. The image that was directly before Crust's eyes was that of a warrior leading a grand army. He was carrying a shield in one hand and had his other arm raised over his head. He held a sword tightly in his grip, and by the gnashed teeth and determined expression, he was preparing to use it. Crust's eyes followed the direction of the sword strike, which would be right across the neck of an oppressive foe. 'Total annihilation brings total domination,' a mantra he said many times as a servant of the HART. He didn't feel so much a champion at this time.

The large handle in the center of the two doors spun rapidly and the gears of a large mechanism groaned and echoes in the vast hallway. The handle spun in a clockwise motion, the spiral shape made it appear to be endlessly spinning outward. It was almost hypnotic. The handle stopped spinning with a loud 'clang.' It snapped Crust from the trance he had nearly fallen into. The massive doors weight caused the hinges to whine painfully as they swung open. Behind the door was another elderly, meek-looking monk, his head clean-shaven. He kept his gaze down at Crust's feet as he pulled the door open. The monk quickly transferred himself to the other side of the door as Crust stepped into the room. The monk quickly closed the door and sealed it shut behind him. Crust expected the sound of the doors striking together to be as extreme, filling the inner chamber with its echoing sound. But it didn't. Instead, it closed with a deafening thud, the sound deadened by the enclosed chamber. The sound was foreboding, ominous. Crust swallowed hard as he looked around the inner sanctum of the Lord of the HART. The room was sparsely decorated, filled only with wall hangings, a narrow strip of carpet that led into the room and a small oval-shaped rug in the center of the room, and a small altar that allowed for kneeling surrounded by several candles on varying stands. The symbol for the HART was etched deeply into the wall above the altar. Kneeling quietly in front of the altar was a cloaked figure. Crust couldn't make out the size or gender of the person, only that it was human. Crust stepped toward the center of the room slowly, hesitantly. He had hoped his movements would signal the cloaked figure to rise and greet him, but he was nearly in the center of the sanctum before the man so much as twitched. Crust froze once he saw the cloaked figure move. He watched as the form raised its head slowly, it then extended its arm, reaching with outstretched fingers toward the symbol above the altar. The figure stood, tall and lean, despite the loose fitting robes and the fact that it never removed its hood, Crust could tell that underneath was a man. This was him, the Lord of the HART. Crust had only been in the Lord's presence only once before, during his graduation ceremony from military training. Even then, he was no closer than thirty or forty meters. He had never been this close. He never wanted to be. But here he stood, in the presence of the all-powerful Lord. It was inspiring and terrifying all at once.

"You are ahead of schedule," The Lord's voice hissed, but also harbored a metallic tinge. It vibrated soothingly.

"The teleporter malfunctioned," Crust's voice trembled. "It split apart our ship and our men."

"Did you succeed at your mission?" The voice vibrated soothingly as the Lord extinguished the cluster of candles surrounding the altar.

"Aye, my Lord."

"I sense fear in your voice, my son."

"No fear, only humility before you, my Lord," Crust knelt to the ground; he lowered his head.

"You are sharing with me an untruth," The Lord's tone became that of disappointment.

Crust held his breath for a long moment. He felt his heart race and his entire body shake. The Lord of the HART knows all. "Aye, my Lord, we had not completed the mission. But I am quite confident that our remaining squad can finish with success, excelsior."

Through the hood, Crust could see the Lord's thin mouth twist into a scowl. He was not pleased.

"I am not concerned with your theories and speculations. I am only concerned with success, to which you have proven none."

Crust interrupted, "But, my Lord, we had managed to obtain—"

The Lord held up his thin hand, instantly silencing Crust. "How dare you interrupt your overlord!"

Crust's head immediately fell forward, as if his spine was removed.

"I will determine what qualifies as success and what is vagrant disregard to loyalty, honor, and the duty you possess for your Lord. You were given a simple task to complete and your return has thrown a shadow of doubt on your ability to succeed. I will not tolerate disobedience, nor will I allow failure. You are HART until your death. Your devotion is to the HART and all we stand for. Never forget that."

Crust felt his heart sink like a stone and then shoot immediately into his throat, "Please forgive me, my Lord. I am a devout follower. I serve the HART and vow to carry our message to all countries of the world and their people."

The Lord's thin mouth turned to a wicked grin, his teeth flashing brightly, "Good, my son. You may stand."

Crust raised himself from his knees. He still hung his head low in shame. He felt like a child disappointing their father.

"If there is one thing I am is forgiving. What kind of ruler would I be if I weren't?"

"You are truly merciful, my Lord," Crust reassured.

"You are forgiven, my son," The Lord extended his hand and ran his spiny knuckles across Crust's cheek. It was damp with sweat, sweat brought on by fear. The Lord liked this tremendously. "However, I do expect my consequences for failure."

The Lord then withdrew his hand and reached into his robe. In a flash, he brandished a small shiv and buried it deeply into Crust's unsuspecting neck. Blood sprayed from the wound. Crust's expression turned from fearful to horrified, his eyes wide and mouth agape. He instinctively clutched his neck, feeling the warm liquid spray his hand and deprive him of life. Crust chortled and gagged as he fell to his knees. Within seconds, he dropped lifelessly to the floor. The Lord dropped the shiv next to Crust's corpse, discarding it much like a tissue.

The door groaned as it quickly opened and several robed advisors entered the sanctum. One scooped up the shiv in a cloth while the others rolled the body in the narrow carpet that led into the room. Within moments, Crusts body was gone and the Lord returned to his altar.

Lartanner held his head in his hands, exhaustion overwhelmed him. He sat next to Aloona, who was resting in a hospital bed, several tubes connected to vital parts of his body. Lartanner felt his stomach knot every time he looked at his partner. It pained him to see his loved one in silent agony. He wished he knew what was happening, that a doctor would tell him what to expect. But it had been hours since they arrived and the only notification he heard was that Aloona was in 'critical condition.'

'*What did that even mean?*' He thought. The din of the hospital outside there room was distracting. Lartanner stood. He looked out the window, seeing all the way to NULE tower. There were several emergency vehicle lights flashing, illuminating the early morning sky with red and blue, highlighting the purple hue in the clouds. '*What a mess,*' his thoughts continued. It would take several months for the city to recover. Lartanner walked around Aloona's bed, touching his face as he passed. He closed the door to the room and let the silence sink in, but it was too much. He needed something to take his mind of Aloona, and the destruction of his city. He turned on the HoloCOMM unit, tuning in to the local news report.

"The events of this evening have left the city devastated and torn," reported Bill Lawler. "The mystery of what exactly occurred is still being investigated. What we have been told is that the arrival of the giant airship that plagued the citizens of New Utica was the result of a Dark HART assault. Thanks to the efforts of the New Utica Law Enforcement, the invasion was short lived. What their plan was and what their ultimate goal was is still unknown, but we will keep you current on this developing story."

Dina Worden nods as the camera cuts to her, "Well, Bill, in lighter news, it seems the populace has spoken and we have a new leader for the nation. Last night, in a landslide victory, Senator Jansen Glorm has become our new President Elect.

"In what many predicted an easy victory for outgoing incumbent President Michaelson, has become the upset of the century. Only minutes ago, Michaelson conceded to Glorm in one of the most active elections in history with a record turnout of voters. It looks like the people have spoken and their voices were heard. We now go live to Glorm Presidential Headquarters downtown where he's prepared to give his acceptance speech."

'The roar of this crowd is intoxicating,' thought Glorm. He threw his head back in satisfaction, his eyes closed as he absorbed the chanting accolades directed toward him. He won.

The taste of victory was sweet. He savored it as he sat backstage, waiting for his cue to step up onto the stage and assume his position of power behind the podium. He won, he reminded himself, just as his master predicted he would. They were another step closer now.

"Ladies and gentlemen," came a booming voice that echoed loudly. "Please welcome, your new President of the United States: Jensen Glorm!"

The sound of his name rumbled the ground beneath his feet. But not as much as the thunderous applause that followed. Cheers and even foot stomping erupted from the entire three-thousand seat auditorium that Glorm rented out, months before believing in his victory. Glorm stepped out from behind the blue curtain and walked across the large stage. The applause seemed to increase in volume, creating a cacophony of happiness that filled Glorm with warmth. His victory was historic and he had the people right where he wanted them, on his side.

As he stood before them, his hands raised high in the air; he soaked in the energy they provided through their enthusiasm and excitement. He loved it.

"Thank you!" He shouted over their cheers, but it was hardly audible. "Thank you so much," he continued as the crowd's cheers began to ebb. As soon as they were silenced, preparing to listen, Glorm spoke. "I couldn't have made it to this moment without all your endless support. We did it! We did what so many said couldn't be done. We were able to defeat a president that everyone said couldn't be beaten. And how? With the support of all of you! You believed in me! So I won't let you down."

The crowd exploded into applause once more. Glorm smiled, '*Right where I want them.*'

"The time has come to return this country to the greatness it once held, and to stand against the tyranny that threatens us every day. Michaelson was weak. I'm not! I won't allow some terrorist group, like the HART, to push us around and take over the rest of the world while we sit idly by. No! We will take the fight to them. We will fight them until they are no more. We will go toward if we have to!"

The crowd cheered, just as he wanted them.

Jack's office was dark, quiet, and for once, it actually felt lonely. He hated being there. He hated what it was now that Ceinwen was gone. Gone? More like taken. And it was his entire fault. He had lost her; let her be pulled into the vortex. The events of the night weighed heavily on him. It had been only several hours since, but it haunted him every second. Jack could feel the anger inside him rising, bubbling up in the pit of his stomach. He swept his arm across his desk, pushing everything from it to the floor and across the room. This reaction didn't make him feel any better. The pain he felt was not like any he had before. He felt this pain deep in his chest, tearing at his heart. He hated how it felt, how it made him feel. He felt ill, as if he wanted to vomit but couldn't. He missed Ceinwen. He wanted her, no, he needed her back.

But she was gone. And it hurt.

Jack stared for a long minute at the door in front of him, the one that led to Ceinwen's desk. He stood and grabbed his nearest canvas sack. He opened the top and began to stuff it with whatever clothing was within his reach.

The door opened, creaking loudly and drawing Jack's attention. His heart skipped a beat. He was half hoping to see Ceinwen enter, as she did often, making him aware of her arrival. Perhaps she was able to escape the vortex and find her way back to him. Perhaps it was all a bad dream and this was just her coming to work like any other day. Wishful thinking was never one of his strongest abilities.

The door opened. Jack held his breath until he saw Helix peek in his head.

"Oh, it's you," Jack said disheartened.

"Glad to see you too," Helix said with disdain.

"Just get lost, would you?" Jack groaned.

"I was going to ask how you were doing, but I guess that's obvious."

"Great. You got your answer so get lost."

"Hey," Helix grew somber. "I'm really sorry about Frisco."

Jack turned away; not wanting to reveal any emotion to Helix. He kept silent.

"In the end, you know, right before she…," Helix stopped himself from saying the word 'dead.' "You know, she came back, like she was. I thought you would want to know that."

Jack nodded, still not looking at his friend.

Helix immediately changed the subject, "Did you hear the news?"

"No," Jack snapped. "And I don't care."

"Glorm won," Helix continued, ignoring Jack's cynicism. "He's the new president."

"I told you, I don't care."

"That's a load of bunk and you know it," Helix shot back. "If anyone of us cares more, it's you."

"Yeah, well, that was before," Jack continued stuffing his bag. "Now I don't care."

"It's just the remorse talking," Strommel stepped from around the door. Jack was surprised to see him. "Believe me I know."

"Not you too," Jack sighed in annoyance.

"I thought you could use the insight," Helix added.

"Insight?"

"If you recall, I lost someone close to me," Strommel interjected. "My wife."

Jack was silent. He remembered the version of Strommel's wife he met. The one that he saw pulled through the vortex earlier. Despite the monster she became, he was sure the real Evelyn was actually sweet and caring, like Ceinwen. He could surmise that if Evelyn were still alive, Strommel would do whatever he could to find her. That was what Jack needed to do. He needed to find Ceinwen.

"I understand what you went through," Jack said to Strommel. "I really do. But Ceinwen's not dead."

"How do you know?" Helix asked; surprised at what Jack said. He wondered if Jack was not suffering from trauma and thinking straight.

"I saw her pulled into the vortex. All I need to do is find out where the other side opened. I find the other doorway, and I find Ceinwen."

"Jack," Strommel responded compassionately. "The probability of finding that doorway is a million-to-one shot. It's virtually impossible."

"But not completely impossible," Jack snarled, frustrated with Strommel's negativity. "And if there is just the slightest, remote chance that I can find Ceinwen, then I am not giving up." Jack zipped his bag closed and slung it over his shoulder. "Now if you'll both excuse me. I have to follow a trail while it's still hot."

"Where?" Strommel scoffed. "Where exactly will you begin? Where will you end up? You don't really know do you?" Jack didn't respond. Strommel continued, "There is no way you could. That vortex could have led to anywhere."

"I can't just give up. I've got to at least try."

Helix stepped up, "But how can you when you have no idea where to begin?"

Helix was right, and Jack knew it. He hated that Helix was right.

"I may have a solution," Strommel interrupted. Jack turned to face Strommel. He said nothing, but his glare spoke volumes. Strommel didn't flinch. After all, he had dealt with all types of assailants; hulking beasts, nandroid generals, and vicious politicians, just to name a few. "If you're interested, that is."

Jack walked over to Strommel, "What? What is it?"

Strommel shrugged, "Perhaps if you asked nicely."

Jack grabbed Strommel roughly under the collar and lifted him from where he sat, annoyed by his chiding, "Tell me!"

"Take it easy, Mr. Zero," Strommel raised his hands, pleading, "Roughing me up won't help you. Not only that, but I can't show you how I can help. Yet."

"What do you mean, yet?"

"What I mean is; I can use the trace amounts of tachyon particles that remain in the air from the vortex to help triangulate where Ceinwen may have ended up. Give or take."

"Give or take?" Jack cocked an eyebrow. "Give or take what?"

"Well, there's no precise method to determine exactly where a portal goes without coordinates, but I can approximate within a hundred miles."

"That's close enough," Jack dropped Strommel. "So get started."

"I can't."

"What do you mean you can't?"

"Well, there's currently no device that can actually do that."

"But you just said…"

"I know what I said, but I would need to actually build the device."

Helix smiled as he slipped in between Jack and Strommel, "And he would need someone with advanced technical knowledge to assist him," he turned to Strommel. "Am I right?"

Strommel nodded, "Of course."

"Let me guess, I can't go unless I take both of you with me?" Jack rolled his eyes.

"Precisely," Strommel smiled.

"Fine, but you had better be right about this," Jack narrowed his eyes as he threw Strommel and Helix a piercing glance.

"Hey, have I ever let you down before?" Helix offered with his arms open.

Jack didn't answer. He plucked his fedora from the coat tree and slapped it onto his head. He then scooped up his bag and stepped out the door, "Let's get going. And Doc, you need to tell me about Experiment One."

Strommel stopped, his face grew ashen in color and his jaw dropped open. Helix rushed past, and Strommel slinked through before Jack could prod any further. It was going to be a long journey. There adventure was just beginning, but Jack knew time was running out. Despite what was happening in the country, Jack had to keep his focus on his first priority: finding Ceinwen.

Mrs. Graves shuffled into the dim office, the soles of her shoes scuffing against the stone floor echoed loudly across the vaulted ceilings of the large chamber. She made her way to the small curtain at the far side and knelt at the small bench that decorated the wall on the opposite side. She leaned against the wooden wall, where a window framed around the curtain.

"Good morning, my friend," came a soft, inviting voice from the other side of the curtain. "How may I help you on this fine day?"

"Fine?" Mrs. Graves twisted her face in a confused look. "Don't you watch the news? The city is in shambles. Some crazy battle in the air last night."

"Yes, I heard," said the voice, still soft. "But we like to focus on the positive aspects of life."

"Of course," Mrs. Graves complied.

"Now how can I help you?"

"Well, it's not that you can help me," said Mrs. Graves. "It's how I came to help you."

"I'm sorry?" The choice responded, the softness replaced by confusion.

"Well, I recently came across something that was lost," she explained. "It's something of an embarrassment, from my family's history."

"I'm sure it's all forgivable," replied the voice, its softness returned. "Please, continue."

"Well, you see, this…lost item…was a symbol of a past I want to forget. It represents the blood of the innocent and I don't want to hold onto it any longer."

"I understand."

"Well, what I want to do is give it to you," Mrs. Graves admitted.

"To…me?"

"Well, to your organization," Mrs. Graves explained. "I'm sure you can do something with it that will make it feel more useful, to help with your…cause." Mrs. Graves pulled the small velvet bag that contained her reclaimed jewels. She slid it through the curtain to where the voice was on the other side. There was silence, a long pause, and then a response.

"Well, I must say," said the voice, a lilt of excitement and surprise replacing the softness. "This is a most generous gift."

"The jewels are worth quite a bit, I'm sure they will go far."

"Yes, most definitely," replied the voice, still filled with excitement. "Thank you. This gift will provide us closer to reaching our mission."

"You are most welcome, I want nothing more than to help and find ways to remove the taint of my family memory," Mrs. Graves smiled. She stood and turned to leave. Before she walked away, she replied with a wicked smile, "Forever Destiny."

"Forever Destiny," the soft voice answered in kind.

Kyle A. Lince

JACK ZERO WILL RETURN
with book 2:

JACK ZERO
in the
Time of Darkness

ABOUT THE AUTHOR

Kyle A. Lince is a Professor of Computer and Information Science at Mohawk Valley Community College in upstate New York. He lives with his fiancé, Chelsea Hopkins, and his three sons. He enjoys reading everything from comics to novels and the backs of cereal boxes. He is an avid collector of all things kitsch. He is currently busy writing his fourth novel: "The Gemini Act" and planning the novel to "Jack Zero in the Time of Darkness."

www.ingramcontent.com/pod-product-compliance
Lightning Source LLC
Chambersburg PA
CBHW060808030726
47503CB00002B/392